BRIAR VALLEY

THE COMPLETE DUET

J ROSE

WILTED ROSE PUBLISHING LTD

Published by Wilted Rose Publishing Limited
Edited & Proofread by Nice Girl Naughty Edits and Kim BookJunkie
Cover Design by Designs by Danielle

ISBN (eBook): 978-1-915987-28-0
ISBN (Paperback): 978-1-915987-29-7

www.jroseauthor.com

J ROSE SHARED UNIVERSE

All of J Rose's contemporary, dark romance books are set in the same shared universe. From the walls of Blackwood Institute and Harrowdean Manor, to Sabre Security's HQ and the small town of Briar Valley, all of the characters inhabit the same world and feature in Easter egg cameos in each other's books.

You can read these books in any order, dipping in and out of different series and stories, but here is the recommended order for the full effect of the shared universe and the ties between the books.

For more information:
www.jroseauthor.com/readingorder

WHERE BROKEN WINGS FLY

BRIAR VALLEY #1

DEDICATION

For all the women just waiting to be rescued by a shirtless mountain man.
Here, have three instead.

TRIGGER WARNING

Where Broken Wings Fly is a small town, reverse harem romance, so the main character will have multiple love interests that she will not have to choose between.

This book is dark in places and contains scenes that may be triggering for some readers. This includes human trafficking, forced marriage, domestic abuse, sexual assault, PTSD, bereavement, self-harm, unplanned pregnancy and a miscarriage.

If you are triggered by any of this content, please do not read this book.

"You know that to love is both to swim and to drown. You know that to love is to be whole, partial, a joint, a fracture, a heart, a bone. It is to bleed and heal. It is to be in the world, honest. It is to place someone next to your beating heart, in the absolute darkness of your inner, and trust they will hold you close."

- Caleb Azumah Nelson

Willow,

I know that you don't know me, and right now, you probably think that you're all alone in the world. It shouldn't have taken your father's death to bring us together, but I need you to know that you have a family. I am your grandmother, and I love you very much.

Please let me help you.

Come home, Willow.
Your family is waiting for you in Briar Valley.

Yours,
Lola x

PROLOGUE

OUTRUN MYSELF - JACK KAYS & TRAVIS BARKER

WILLOW

SMILE.

Pretend you like it.

Pretend you love it.

Bag the cheque.

The day I set foot in my first strip joint, driven by starvation and desperation, I was taught one invaluable lesson.

Life is nothing without suffering.

I'm not talking about the kind of pain that you discuss over fancy coffee and a box of tissues. Nor the kind that wins expensive book deals or documentaries on prime-time television.

I'm talking about the quiet kind of suffering, reserved for the empty space between existing and living. Not pretty. Not sellable. Not inspirational. It's more of a deafening *ache* that never abates.

I learned to occupy that space from a young age. Doing homework amongst the discarded needles and breathing in secondhand fumes while my father shot up instead of, you know, being a fucking parent.

I'm still here, years later.

Even though he's dead, life never got better.

Staring into the depths of my bright, hazel eyes, I blink tears aside. The outfit I've been assigned to wear tonight is unbearable. A string bikini top and matching thong, with towering high heels that I haven't quite mastered walking in. This is only my third shift.

"Five minutes!" Mario yells. "Move it, sluts!"

Shaking myself out of it, I swipe bright-red lipstick across my generous pout. My coal-black hair lies in natural ringlets, cascading down my near-skeletal frame. I haven't got the curves of the other girls, who are all older than me.

I had to beg Mario for a job and kiss his slimy ass to convince him to overlook my age. While everyone I used to know finishes school and begins to plan for their bright, promising futures, I'm getting ready to take my clothes off and give perverts lap dances.

Damn, Willow.

This is a low point.

Working here is a last resort, despite the handwritten letter screaming at me from my discarded coat pocket. The words have played on repeat in my head ever since.

I'd rather sell my soul than go searching for some long-lost relative of my father who is trying to lure me in. I have enough problems to deal with because of him.

"You ready, Willow?" Lia throws an arm around my waist. "Come on, you don't want to piss off Mario tonight. He's on the warpath and will only dock your wages for it."

"Sure," I mutter.

"What's up?"

"Nothing. Just didn't sleep well."

With a wink, she flourishes a clear baggie, full of white powder. "Have a bump. It'll take the edge off. Trade secret."

She tips some onto the back of her hand before snorting it up. Shaking my head, I inch backwards, nearly falling straight on my ass in these stupid heels.

"I'm fine, thanks. I'll grab a shot or something."

"You sure?" She frowns.

"Yeah. See you out there."

"Suit yourself, newbie."

Turning on my heel, I stumble away before she can force the drugs up my nose. All of the girls here do it. Some even take it from the customers, uncaring of the risk.

It makes it easier to do this job every day, I suppose. The sultry smiles come far more naturally, and your hips sway that little bit extra when you're too high to be disgusted.

Heading out onto the main floor of the club, the oppressive heat hits me first. Heady smoke and expensive aftershave come next. The smells are eye-wateringly strong.

I follow the click of high heels on sparkling marble floors, my head already pounding from the thud of bass music. The DJ is spinning tracks in the corner of the huge room.

Some of the women here enjoy this job. They find some sense of liberation in it. I already hate this place and everything it represents, even after two shifts.

I'm only here to pay off my deadbeat father's significant drug debts and clear my name so I can finally get off the streets. I am sick of being scared and hungry. This is my ticket out of this life.

By halfway through my shift, I've found my not-so-happy place. Numb is safe. My ass hurts from being slapped so hard, but I've learned to tune the throbbing out.

Retreating to a quiet corner of the club, away from prying eyes, I take a breather and wipe sweat from my forehead. Every inch of me is exhausted and hurting from the night.

"Willow! There you are, my beautiful girl."

"Mario," I greet, dropping my eyes.

The nightclub owner is a slimeball, but he's also my boss. Even though he spends half the night staring at my ass rather than making sure the other women aren't swindling him.

He's a stone-cold asshole, no two ways about it. I've met bad men like him before; my father used to get his backside beaten by them for owing too much money.

"Having a good shift, darling?"

"I suppose," I whisper back. "Keeping busy."

"So obedient. You're a quick learner. Fancy earning yourself an extra cheque?"

Perked up by his offer, I nod and stare at his designer trainers. There's another pair of shoes standing directly behind him, as if waiting for something. We have company.

"I've got someone special here for you, Willow. A dear friend. I want you to show him a good time. Do you understand?"

"Yes, sir. I understand."

Mario hums his approval, turning away from me. "She'll take good care of you, Mr Sanchez. Willow is brand new, like you requested. She's yours for the price we discussed."

The other man advances, marked by his Italian-leather dress shoes that scream wealth and high standards. The scent of cigar smoke burns my lungs while unease trickles down my spine.

I don't dare to lift my eyes from the floor. I'm surrounded by sharks, and a single wrong move might just end my life. These people aren't to be trusted—even I know that.

"She's a virgin?" a deep voice rumbles.

"Of course. Nothing but the best for you."

"How can you be sure?"

Mario runs a hand over my lowered head. "Feel free to take her out back and inspect for yourself. Willow will be a good girl, won't you?"

Frozen by terror, I can't respond. *Check? Virgin?* This isn't right. I'm supposed to be giving lap dances and taking drinks orders, nothing more like the others sometimes do.

A large, rough hand grabs my chin, forcing me to look up. I meet a pair of ice-cold blue eyes, framed by thick lashes that accentuate the frosty depths of his irises.

"Hello there, *chica*. You'll do nicely, hmm?"

This man is middle-aged and, admittedly, very handsome. His appearance screams of foreign charm and confidence. But that doesn't stop dread from pooling in my gut.

Something's wrong here. There's a look in his eyes—a sick, lascivious gleam that sets off mental alarm bells. He's staring at me like I'm his dinner.

"I'll take that inspection, Mario."

My heart somersaults.

"You know I like to be thorough," he adds. "Especially given the price."

"Of course," Mario blusters, shooting me a stern look. "Go with Mr Sanchez, Willow. Best behaviour. Don't let me down now."

"But—"

"No buts or I'll be keeping tonight's pay cheque."

Fuck. I really need that money. It's been almost a week since I ate a real meal, and my stomach feels like it's eating itself. I've been sleeping on the park bench every night.

I had to use last week's cheque to pay off one of my father's old friends who tracked me down, threatening unspeakable violence if I didn't cough up the money he wanted.

Dragged away before I can protest further, we leave Mario's boastful grin behind. I'm guided through the curling smoke and writhing bodies towards the dreaded unknown.

I have no choice but to follow the overbearing, muscled frame of my captor into a private room out back, drenched in black leather and the sensual shadows of darkness.

The door clicks shut, and the snick of the lock sends terror spiking through my veins. I'm locked in here with no escape route, and the stranger prowls towards me.

"On the bed," Mr Sanchez orders. "Clothes off."

"My... clothes? The b-bed?" I repeat.

"Yes, child. Are you deaf?"

Trembling all over, I inch towards the metal bed frame placed in the exact centre of the room. It's covered in blood-red satin sheets, accompanied by built-in leather restraints.

I haven't been in this room before, but I've heard the screams that echo through the locked door. The other girls have warned me to never come here. This is really bad.

Run, Willow.

No amount of money is worth this.

Before I can flee, two firm hands grab my hips from behind. I'm shoved forwards onto the bed, my face smacking into the slippery sheets. Pressure explodes across my scalp as he yanks on my long ringlets.

Roughly flipped over by my hair, Mr Sanchez splays me out across the mattress. In this position, I'm completely vulnerable, and my legs are forced wide open for him to step between.

He stares down at me with visible lust. "You're such a beautiful girl, Willow. So beautiful. Perfect."

"Thank y-you," I stutter.

His vivid blue gaze hardens, filling with rage. "You will address me as Mr Sanchez. Nothing else. Is that clear?"

Staring deep into his eyes, gleaming with intelligence and framed by neatly combed salt-and-pepper hair, I nearly swallow my tongue from fright.

"Thank you, Mr Sanchez."

"Better. How old are you, *chica*?"

"Eighteen," I lie easily.

Mr Sanchez's glare grows even colder, and he rolls up the sleeves of his expensive dress shirt, discarding twinkling diamond cufflinks that would clear my name in one payment.

"That's a lie," he spits. "You want to try that again?"

"It's the truth."

The backhand comes so fast, I cry out in shock. His slap splits my lip open, and stars burst behind my eyes from the sheer strength of it.

"Another lie."

Licking the hot flow of blood from my lip to buy some time, I try to clear the haze fogging my brain. He isn't my first monster. I won't survive this if I don't play along.

"Sixteen, Mr Sanchez."

"That's the truth?"

"Y-Yes."

"Good. I'll have no lies, Willow."

"Sorry, Mr Sanchez."

"If you're to be mine, then you will learn some discipline and respect. I won't have some careless slut walking around my home, understand?"

"Your home?" I dare to whisper.

Lips spreading into a satisfied grin, Mr Sanchez pops a few of his shirt buttons, exposing the dark hair smattering across his chest that covers swirling tattoos.

I can see the bulge of his growing erection through his grey suit trousers. It's so obvious, near bursting out with anticipation. He cups it and squeezes, his lips parted on a sigh.

"I haven't purchased you for the night, my love. I just want a trial run before I commit, you see. Then you'll be coming with me and leaving this filth behind."

"I don't understand."

With a snarl, he rips my flimsy bikini top in one cruel move. It hits the floor, leaving my small, growing breasts on full display. When I try to cover them, he hits me again.

Mr Sanchez licks his lips and stares at my slumped form with hunger. Dizzy from pain, I've collapsed back on the bed in a lifeless, compliant heap.

He laughs, unzipping his fly to free his dick. "I want to hear how good your screams are. I'll want to hear them every day when we're married."

Married?

Every day?

Too petrified to move a muscle, I silently beg for someone to come and rescue me. He climbs on top of me and pins my wrists above my head, preventing my escape.

"P-Please, let m-me go!"

"That's it," he praises. "Beg me louder."

"Please... you c-can't do this."

Two fingers wrap around my nipple, and he twists so hard that agony races across my chest. His disgustingly hard length is rocking against me, inching ever closer.

"Keep it coming now."

He hits me again, and the hard punch to my jaw steals any remaining defiance inside me. Limp and sobbing freely, I realise my mistake. I trusted Mario, against my own instincts.

I thought that I was adult enough to navigate this place, and I was wrong. I've waded into the danger zone and been snapped up by a ravenous predator.

Leaning closer, his tongue scrapes up the side of my cheek, lapping up my fast-flowing tears. His mouth travels lower, over my shuddering chest, so he can rip the rest of my clothes off.

"Legs open, Willow. Let me see you."

Unable to escape, I shut down instead. The tiny voice in my head is begging for relief, but no one comes to stop his assault. The door remains locked as Mr Sanchez breaks me.

That night was the beginning of the end. I didn't know it at the time, but my life would never be the same. I thought I knew suffering, but the lessons were only just beginning.

Sometimes, existing in empty spaces can be fatal. But sometimes… it's the only way to survive.

CHAPTER 1
WILLOW

MARS - YUNGBLUD

TEN YEARS LATER

STARING into the woman's empty eyes, I feel absolutely nothing. Not even a scrap of sadness for her death in all its brutal cruelty as blood gushes from between her thighs.

I should be screaming.

I should be running.

I've learned that neither works.

My husband, the notorious Mr Sanchez, thrives on two things—fear and control. He demands compliance in all aspects of his life, from his successful real estate business to his disgusting depravity in the bedroom.

Laying here, immobile and utterly silent, is the only power I have left in this world. Depriving him of my terror starves the beast. He loves the nights I sob and beg him.

I'm not always the one getting hurt. Like tonight, he sometimes enjoys an audience and brings a plaything along to bear witness to his sick desires. We suffer together.

"Stupid whore. I thought you'd last longer," Mr Sanchez sneers, wiping blood on a handkerchief. "Must be a new record. What do you think, Willow?"

Fighting the urge to flinch, I stare up at the panelled ceiling, lit by a black chandelier that casts an oppressive light into his playroom. He keeps it dark in here, full of shadows and curling cigar smoke.

"I can't hear you!" he shouts viciously.

"Yes, Mr Sanchez."

"Don't disobey me, wife. You know what happened last time."

I battle the urge to throw up. My body is still healing from the last time I defied him and was beaten within an inch of my life. That's why silence is safer.

"I have a new whip. Perhaps we can play with it later."

Casting a final disgusted look at the woman's still-warm corpse lying broken at his feet, Mr Sanchez tosses his bloodstained handkerchief aside. She's just one in a long line of faceless sacks of flesh to him.

I'm handcuffed in my usual position on the bed, restrained and deliberately placed to have the perfect view of the room. He likes me to watch as he abuses these women to teach me a lesson when the beatings fail to inspire my obedience.

This wing of his vast mansion is my least favourite. Through endless, echoing halls pathed in polished marble, velvet and gold, my husband's playroom awaits in the quietest corner.

None of his staff come into the playroom—only Pedro, one of Mr Sanchez's personal bodyguards. He is actually a good man, trapped in the devil's lair.

Pedro hates seeing me like this and tries to avoid entering this room now. He usually unlocks the door for the cleaner and keeps his eyes averted to ignore the blood stains.

"She was weak, breakable. Unlike you, *chica*."

Mr Sanchez saunters over to the bed, trailing a finger along the silky sheets to reach my restrained legs. His nails bite deeply into my skin, leaving bloodied welts.

"You'll have to finish off what she started, won't you?"

"N-No, please. I'm still r-recovering—"

"Did I say you could fucking speak?"

Slapping me hard enough to burst my crooked nose with his solid-gold wedding ring, I sob through a river of blood running down my face. Not again.

It's barely healed after he broke it last month. I've lost count of the times he's done this to me, leaving the bone permanently crooked. Every time I look in the mirror, I relive each blow.

"How dare you defy me," Mr Sanchez spits.

"I'm s-sorry, please…"

"You're sorry?" he utters. "That means jack shit to me, darling."

Punching me in the stomach, I scream through the sickness battling to expel from my throat. My black and blue ribs howl in pain with each blow, loosening my tongue.

"Good, because I didn't mean it!" I yell at him.

"Is that so? I see how it is."

Striking me in the face, the cut on my eyebrow reopens. Hot, copper-scented blood streams down my face, painting the room in violent shades of red.

The beating continues. On and on. Blow after blow. Punch after punch. When Mr Sanchez halts, he's panting and sweating hard, watching me sob with wild eyes.

"You continue to defy me, even after all these years."

My emotions flare, desperate and ugly.

"Because you're a monster!"

Kneeling on the mattress, he reaches beneath the bed. "Time to teach you another lesson, darling wife. I thought you'd have learned after all this time."

My left arm burns at the thought. The bones never quite set properly after he shattered two of them a few years back. They ache and grind together, especially in the winter.

Injuries sometimes buy me a brief reprieve, until he grows impatient with letting me heal and drags me in here by my hair. The prostitutes only keep him sated for so long.

He likes to save his sickest games for me. Mr Sanchez flourishes a long, metal pole from beneath the bed, setting my teeth on edge. He twirls it in his hands, smirking to himself.

"N-No, not the s-spreader… p-please."

Punching me again in the face, I howl in pain, unable to hold it in. After a few too many brutal beatings as of late, my strength has waned into insignificance. I can't take this for much longer.

"As much as I love to hear you beg, I'm in no mood to play games with you tonight." He attaches the spreader to the restraints pinning my legs open. "Open wide. Let me see your cunt."

With the click of a button, he extends the bar to its maximum length. My legs are spread so far open, it makes my joints sear in pain. I hate this thing so much.

With no panties on, he can see every inch of my bruised and aching core. There's no hiding from his stare as he removes his shirt, still drenched in another woman's blood.

"Scream, Willow."

"Fuck you," I shout instead.

Striking my heavily bruised ribs, I let loose a blood-curdling scream that rips apart my sore throat. Mr Sanchez leers, practically drooling as he drinks in my visible terror.

"More, *chica*. Don't make me bring Arianna in here too."

I lose all sense of self-preservation. He can do whatever the fuck he'd like to me. Beat me. Rape me. Bruise my skin and break my bones. But no one threatens my daughter.

"Leave her out of this, you bastard!"

"She's my daughter," he insists. "And you are my wife. That means you will both do as I say or face the consequences."

With no choice but to accept the torture, his twisted games last hours. My mind returns to its safe place. Empty nothingness. I let that deep pool of water suck me into its depths.

When he's too exhausted to continue, Mr Sanchez grows tired of toying with me and settles for another brutal violation. This time, when he tells me to scream, I oblige.

Not for my own sake.

For hers.

Once his men arrive to smuggle the prostitute's corpse to a watery grave, Mr Sanchez drinks himself into a stupor and staggers back to his private quarters to pass out.

For a long time, I lie motionless on the bed, trickles of blood staining my inner thighs. The tears silently fall as I ease my stiff joints from the unfastened restraints and pull on my robe.

It takes a long time to put myself back together into a fragile persona after washing the blood from my skin. I have to pretend, even to myself. Arianna needs me. I can't be weak.

Limping down the dark, marble-lined hallway on trembling legs, I hug my midsection. I shouldn't be up or even attempting to walk in my state.

The entire world is spinning and threatening to disappear on me. But I have to see her. I have to know that she's safe from the monster beneath the bed.

Once inside her generous suite that's lit by glow-in-the-dark stars and the ever-present nightlight on her bedside table, I pad over to my daughter's sleeping form beneath the covers.

Neither of us cares for the opulence around us that barely conceals the reality of life inside this mansion. Mr Sanchez has hit her enough times when he grew bored of hearing my cries.

I've always thrown myself between them, sacrificing myself first, but I'm ashamed to admit that he's still managed to get to Arianna on occasion. She's taken those blows too.

"Mummy?" Sitting upright in bed, Arianna's ringlets stick up in all directions. "Why are you standing there?"

Crawling between the pale-pink, flower-spotted sheets, I snuggle against her tiny body. She's very small for a six-year-old, but so beautiful it makes my heart ache.

All angelic blonde hair and doe-like blue eyes, Arianna looks just like her father. She inherited his stunning good looks, but thankfully, not the impenetrable darkness within him.

"Are you crying?" she asks sleepily.

"I'm fine, my sweet girl. Go back to sleep. I've got you."

Her face nuzzles into my neck, breathing in my scent for comfort.

"I'm s-scared. I had a bad dream again."

"There's nothing to be afraid of, Ari."

"It's the dark," she whines. "I don't like it."

"That's why we put the stars up, remember?" I breathe in her sweet scent. "No matter where you are or what sky you're looking up at, you're never alone."

"Really?" Arianna whispers.

"Of course, baby. Even if Mummy isn't there."

"No! No!" she shouts, thrashing in my arms. "I don't want the stars. I want you. Please don't leave me on my own."

Hushing her cries, I stroke her face and murmur reassurances. Arianna clings to me with surprising strength, her little fingers bruising my skin with the ferocity of her love.

"I'll never leave you, Ari."

"Do you promise?" she demands.

"I promise. We're going to go on a little trip when everything is ready. I need you to be brave for me. Can you do that? Be a big, brave girl?"

"Where are we going? What about Daddy?"

She's such an inquisitive child. I have no idea how this damned place hasn't scared that curiosity out of her, but on many levels, I'm grateful that it hasn't broken her too.

I make myself speak calmly. "Daddy isn't coming. I can't tell you where we're going because it's a surprise. But soon, okay? We'll go somewhere fun, somewhere nice."

"Will there be ice cream?"

"Yes, baby. You can have all the ice cream in the world."

Chewing her lip, Arianna's striking blue eyes lift to meet mine. It's like staring back at a living embodiment of the demon that's controlled the last ten years of my life.

But instead of the revulsion my husband inspires within me, I feel nothing but love for my daughter. She isn't his. Arianna is my girl, my baby.

I'll give her the entire world, even if I have to burn it to the ground to make it perfect just for her. She's seen and suffered through far too much for such a short life.

I want to give her everything I never had. No one loved me or protected me as a child, and I promised myself the day she was born that I'd never allow her to feel the loneliness I did growing up.

"Deal, but I want sprinkles and fudge sauce too," she declares.

I press my lips to her temple. "Me too. Mint chocolate chip and strawberry ice cream, I think. What flavour do you want?"

"I don't want that toothpaste ice cream. Yucky!"

"Mint is not yucky."

"It is too. I want bubble gum."

"Deal. Go back to sleep, Ari. We'll have ice cream soon enough."

It takes a while for her to drop off, but she eventually goes limp in my arms, snoring lightly. I hold her against my chest, stroking every inch of golden-blonde hair falling down her back.

Every part of my body is pounding with agony, and I can still feel the warmth of slick blood running between my thighs. He was brutal tonight, borderline murderous.

This isn't living, not really. I've spent a decade pretending that I could survive here, but I can't do it anymore. I'd rather die trying to escape than remain here for another second.

It's taken years of careful planning and stolen whispers, preparing our grand escape. Pedro sourced the British passports that should get us both home, far from this mansion.

We'll have new names, new lives. A fresh start. One free from this hell. I never had a parent to save me, but Arianna is my everything. I won't let her die here with me.

Repositioning her sleeping body, I tuck the covers up to her chin and force myself to return to my nearby bedroom to take some painkillers and continue preparing.

Next to my open fireplace, the loose ceramic tile in the wall prises away easily. Inside the secret spot, two fake passports reside, along with a wedge of stolen cash.

Months of stealing and sneaking around have allowed me to collect enough to buy aeroplane tickets for me and Arianna to get across the ocean, to a life I left behind when Mr Sanchez stole me.

Pedro has promised to get us out, no matter what it takes. He's the only friend I've ever had, but his family is here. He can't come with us. We'll have to find our own home.

I can't remember what England even looks like; it's been so long since I was there as a struggling sixteen-year-old girl. But I have one thing—a breadcrumb trail.

The faded, dog-eared letter has somehow survived the last ten years. It's the one possession that I've taken care to hide from Mr Sanchez and his destructive rage.

Please come home, Willow.

Briar Valley is waiting for you.

Written and delivered a decade earlier and discarded in my youthful arrogance, it tells the tale of a long-lost family that I had no intention of meeting back then.

If I had taken that leap and gone to these relatives when I had the chance, it might have turned the tide on the worst ten years of my life. Instead, I ran straight to the Devil.

Well, no more. I won't watch Arianna cry herself to sleep in fear for a moment longer than I have to. It's time to take a stand. It's time to run.

Into the arms of who, I don't know.

CHAPTER 2
WILLOW

BROKEN - ISAK DANIELSON

GRABBING THE SMALL, black duffel bag we boarded the aeroplane with, I take an unsteady breath and check our passports for the fifth time. Still there. Still safe.

This final flight back to England is fraying my almost non-existent nerves. The hustle and bustle of the tight space has anxiety tightening my chest, which is already constricted by the wrap of bandages around my ribs.

My first aid is rudimentary at best, but I have no other options right now. I can't afford to go to a hospital and run the risk of Mr Sanchez tracking us down. We've come too far.

Burying the pain at the back of my mind, I focus instead on the look of wonderment on Arianna's sweetheart-shaped face. I've dreamed about this day for so many years.

"Mummy! Look, I can see land."

Pointing frantically out of the window, she watches the approaching greenery as we begin to descend. I buckle both of our belts in preparation.

"Hold on tight, baby. Nearly there."

"The sea is so pretty," she coos, her nose pressed up against the glass window. "I want to go swimming in it. What would happen if I jumped out now?"

"That's not a good plan, Ari. But when we get to our new home, I'll teach you how to swim. We can go whenever you want."

"Really? Daddy won't be mad?"

"Daddy isn't in charge anymore," I murmur, tucking blonde hair behind her ear. "We can do whatever we want. No more rules, no more hiding."

Arianna frowns with childlike confusion. "Isn't Daddy coming to meet us? What about Pedro? He said he was right behind us."

Dragging in an agonised breath, I crush the dark memories that her questions bring. Blood. Bullets. Shouting. Terror. It's almost too much to hold in. I can't breathe.

When Arianna repeats her questions, I press her head to my chest in an attempt to silence the conversation. I don't want to remember. It's taken everything to get this far.

The ultimate sacrifice.

I've had enough worried looks in the past few days of hurried travel to last a lifetime. An airport security guard even asked me if I needed help and didn't buy my excuses when I declined.

I've been severely beaten and forced to flee across the continent with a young child with nothing but a single bag and a sizable stack of cash between us. It's not a good look.

"Mummy?" she repeats.

"Daddy has some business, and Pedro has to help him," I answer in a whisper. "It's just us, Ari. Like we talked about. We're going to be on our own from now on."

She offers me a gut-wrenching smile. "Daddy doesn't let me eat ice cream or go swimming, and he makes you cry. Can we stay on our own forever? Just me and you?"

I link our pinkie fingers, squeezing tight. "Just me and you."

"Okay. Does your face hurt?"

I try to muster a smile and fail. "I'm fine, Ari."

She reaches out, stroking her little fingers over the deep-purple bruises that are swelling my face to almost twice its usual size. Even that tiny touch pains me.

I have two black eyes, a broken nose that I've clumsily strapped into place and a fat lip split right down the middle. I must look like Frankenstein's monster on a bad day.

Mr Sanchez spent every night of the past month beating me, spiralling further and further out of control. His rage has grown to disproportionate levels of unholiness.

The final straw was when he threatened to kill Arianna, drunk on his own violence and power. I knew then that it was time to make a run for it, planning be damned.

Even more mottled bruises sneak beneath my plain, white blouse and faded-blue jeans, carefully hidden with a well-placed scarf. There isn't an unmarked part of me.

He trampled me like a bug beneath his shoe, laughing his head off for the entire time. In that soulless moment, I thought I was finally going to die.

I had no choice but to take action and ask Pedro to steal us away under the protective cover of night. It was either that or risk leaving Arianna alone in the world when Mr Sanchez finally managed to kill me.

Arianna presses her lips to my cheek, swiping away tears that I didn't realise had escaped my eyes. "There. All better now."

"Thank you, baby."

"No more crying. We're going on an adventure!"

"We are. I'm so proud of you, Ari. You've been such a brave girl."

"My fingers don't hurt anymore," she boasts proudly.

Staring down at the burned tips of her tiny fingers, I nearly lose my final remaining shred of self-control. Guilt is corroding my insides and making me dizzy with sickness.

"I'm so sorry. Mummy didn't want to hurt you."

"I know. It's okay."

She's so matter of fact, despite the fact I seared off her fingerprints in an airport bathroom with a cigarette lighter, my hand clamped over her mouth to silence her screams.

Nobody can know who we really are, or who her father is. It would be a one-way ticket back to the demon's lair, where we'll both be punished for running.

Pedro already took his punishment. If it weren't for him, we would still be trapped there. I'll never get the chance to thank him. All I have left is the never-ending guilt.

Cuddling each other tight, we don't let go until the aeroplane touches tarmac, announcing our arrival in England. Arianna claps the moment we're on the ground.

"He didn't crash it," she declares, causing a nearby couple to frown at her sassiness. "We're here!"

I quickly hush her. "Shhh."

"No, Mummy." Her glower is defiant. "I'm excited! We're home."

It was a long flight from Mexico, with two changes and a stopover on the way to throw my husband's men off the scent if they managed to follow us. She's been cooped up for days.

I release the breath I've been holding since we snuck out of the Sanchez Mansion last week, stealing across the sun-baked country with nothing but desperation and the good will of strangers to keep us going.

I didn't think we'd make it.

Somehow, we're here. *Home.*

"Hold on tight to my hand, Ari."

Inching our way into the aisle, we cling on to each other, sandwiched between the press of impatient bodies. I forget how to breathe, searching the crowd for any familiar faces.

I don't allow myself the luxury of a single ounce of relief until our feet hit the tarmac and the tickle of cool February sunshine dances across my skin in greeting.

Ignoring the frazzled travellers around us, I crouch down and graze my blistered fingertips across the cold ground, savouring the bite of gravel. While I'll miss the rugged beauty of Mexico, this country is a welcome sight.

"We did it," I mutter to myself. "It's over."

Part of me never believed I'd live to see this day come. After years of hopeless dreaming, we're finally home. This is what freedom feels like—this feeling, right here.

"Mummy!" Arianna bellows impatiently. "What are you doing? I'm hungry."

I grin at her, despite the curious looks sent our way by onlookers. "We did it, baby."

"Did what?"

Staring deep into her frost-bitten eyes lit with the innocence of childhood, I feel tears soak into my cheeks. "We made it."

"On our adventure?"

"Yes. This is the first day of the rest of our lives."

With a squeal, she throws herself into my arms for a hug. If I could, I'd spin her around me and celebrate loud enough for the whole country to hear.

"Excuse me, ma'am?" someone calls out.

Fuck!

Freezing on the spot, I shove Arianna behind me and square my shoulders. It's just an airport attendant, holding my dropped duffel bag in her hands.

"You dropped your bag," she explains with a smile.

"Thank y-you," I stammer.

Breathe. Act normal.

"You need to go inside and head through security. Are you okay? Do you need a hand with anything?"

"No, we're fine. Come on, munchkin."

Snatching my bag back, I grip Arianna's hand tight and we race across the airstrip as fast as my numerous injuries will allow. Her small legs can hardly keep up.

Panic is riding me hard. All I can hear are the faceless staff that have called me *ma'am* for the past decade, averting their eyes and ignoring the abuse.

Running on autopilot through the passport checks, bags searches and a terrifying wait at customs, we make it to the arrivals lounge with no hiccups.

I nearly fainted when security frowned at our fake identification, before it was green-lighted by the system. I paid a small fortune for those fraudulent passports.

It took nearly two years of stealing petty cash here and there, poking into Mr Sanchez's affairs to secretly gather the money without him realising. There were several close calls.

Assessing the numerous CCTV cameras and police officers milling about the busy airport, I struggle to lift Arianna up, holding her on my hip for my own peace of mind.

She barely weighs a thing. My first priority is getting some meat on her bones, since neither of us has to suffer the consequences of disobedience anymore.

"Mummy." Her head slumps onto my shoulder. "I'm so tired."

I stroke her tangled hair, ignoring the flare of pain her weight causes. "Go to sleep. I'm going to find a taxi. I'll wake you up when we get there."

"Where are we going?"

Running through my mental checklist, I nod to myself. "We'll find a cheap hotel, somewhere to sleep for the night."

"One with ice cream?"

"We'll find some. I know I promised."

"I thought we were going home?" she mumbles.

"Soon," I lie easily.

I've had to figure this parenting thing out alone. Rule number one? Don't scare your damn kids with the truth. She doesn't need to know that we don't have a home.

Locating an available taxi is surprisingly easy, but my anxiety doesn't abate. There are too many people. Too many faces. I can't keep us safe out here in the open.

Mr Sanchez could have his well-paid thugs looking for us at this very moment, even if he's thousands of miles away on the other side of the world. He's still in my head.

Bundled in the back of a sleek, red taxi, I fasten Arianna's seatbelt and catch the lingering, concerned look the driver gives us both. I'm barely standing on my own feet.

My head pounds steadily with pain as the adrenaline that's kept us going finally begins wearing off. My skin burns with a growing fever, but I can't rest yet. Not until we're safe.

"Where will it be to?" he asks.

"You know any cheap hotels around here?"

The driver studies me with soft eyes, radiating sympathy. "How cheap are we talking?"

"Nothing fancy. I just need somewhere to rest my head for a few hours. We're heading northwest in the morning."

"Got far to go?"

"A few hundred miles, I think. I'm looking for somewhere called Briar Valley."

He throws the car into gear and pulls away from the bustling airport. "You're far from home. Are you sure that's where you want to go?"

"Why? You've heard of it?" I ask in a rush of panic.

"Nah. But no offence, you look like you're in need of a good hospital. Or maybe the police station? I'll take you right there, no questions asked."

Staring at him, I catch sight of my battered, hideous face in the rearview mirror. It's so swollen and discoloured, I look more like a lifeless hunk of meat than a person.

No wonder people were staring at me. I'm visibly dead on my feet, unrecognisable beneath bruises and violent swelling. My nose is still crooked from where I failed to set it straight with flimsy strips.

"That won't be necessary," I say in a low whisper.

"You sure?"

"Please take us to a hotel. I'll figure the rest out from there."

He shrugs, indicating to join the flow of traffic. "As you wish. Don't die in my taxi, though."

"I'll try my best not to."

Slumping in the seat with a sleeping Arianna slung across my lap, I let my gritty eyes slide shut. Just for a second. I need to gather my energy again. I'm in so much pain.

Something's wrong with me, but I don't have time to worry about my injuries. All that matters is getting off the radar, and far from where my husband can track us down.

Then, we can breathe again.

Perhaps even live a little.

CHAPTER 3
KILLIAN

LONELY - MACHINE GUN KELLY

LIFTING the axe above my head, I bring it down on the log, splitting it perfectly down the middle. After tossing it on the growing pile, I line up my next victim, cracking it in two.

The sun beats down on my weathered, heavily tanned skin beneath a layer of blonde fuzz that covers my torso. It's pretty warm, despite being February.

"Kill!" Zach bellows from our cabin's wraparound porch. "Finish up. We're heading out in ten."

I glower up at him as I prop the axe against the lawn. "Alright, kid. No need to fucking yell."

"I didn't know if you could hear me over your brooding lumberjack routine."

"Hilarious."

"I suppose splitting logs is cheaper than therapy. One session with you and the shrink would run away screaming."

"Wanna come here and say that to my face?" I snarl at him.

"I'll pass on the beating for today. Thanks, though. You're always so thoughtful."

Shooting me an innocent smirk, he traipses back inside, his caramel-coloured hair shining in the sunshine. Smug asshole. He won't be grinning when I break his short legs.

We need to drive down the mountain and into the nearest town this afternoon to collect more propane for the tanks before Lola chews me out again. It's a long, treacherous drive that I've been putting off all week.

I don't like venturing back into civilisation often. After spending all thirty years of my life in Briar Valley, the outside world beyond our property lines holds little appeal.

Grabbing the final log on my pile, I brutally rip it apart by hand. There's nobody around to stare at me. Everyone is preparing for this evening's party in the town square.

Tonight is a special night. Lola insists we celebrate the town's anniversary every year. It's been four decades since Briar Valley was first established in the rugged Welsh countryside.

In that time, the town has grown exponentially from a single cabin to almost forty eccentric residents spread throughout the thick forest of pine and birch trees, spanning across five miles of private land.

Lola has been here from the beginning and built the very first, hand-carved cabin with her late husband. Then another desperate family sought refuge in the woodland, and another, until an entire town was built from nothing.

This is a place for lost things.

A family of choice, rather than blood.

With all my wood pile chopped and ready to be taken to Lola's cabin for the bonfire, I load it up in the bed of my peeling, russet-red truck and begin the winding drive back down into the depths of the valley.

A cabin is a poor choice of word for Lola's ten-thousand-square-foot monstrosity built in a clearing off to the side of the town square, surrounded by carefully pruned orchards and allotments.

Three stories of gleaming, hewed timber and tinted, clear-cut glass, the cabin spans the entire length of the clearing with enough space for the whole town to socialise in, though everyone has their own cabin and patch of land.

Parking the truck, I begin to unload the bed, piling up wood at the edge of the square to add to the bonfire for tonight's celebrations.

"Killian?" a voice shouts.

"Yeah, it's me, Grams."

The carved oak door slams open, and Lola emerges from her cabin while smoothing her paisley dress.

"Ryder is bringing down the fuel and kindling."

"I'm heading into town to collect the propane delivery with Zach. You need anything else while we're there?"

Thumping down the wide, wooden steps, she meets me in the clearing. Lola is barely five feet tall, wizened and twinkle-eyed with a cloud of floss-like, silvery hair.

Despite her tiny size and wholesome appearance, she's tough as nails. Her skin is calloused from a life of hard labour, and her limbs are tough and wiry without an ounce of fat.

She isn't my real grandma, but everyone around here calls her Grams. She's the closest thing to a family that I have left, along with Zach and Micah. Everyone else is gone.

"No, we're all set," she declines.

"Alright. We're gonna head out now."

"Hurry back. You don't want to be late. It's a long drive."

"We'll be fine. Right on time."

Wiping flour-spotted hands off on her apron, she glances back up the dirt track that leads through the woods to where our cabin lies. We're set above the town, isolated even further from people.

"Take Micah with you," Lola suggests, her voice stern. "That boy needs to see the light of day for once."

"You know he won't leave his studio, Grams."

"Then make him."

"You want me to handcuff the poor bastard and throw him in the back of my truck?" I snort, chucking the final log onto the pile. "I'm not saying no."

"I doubt he would appreciate that." She sighs with a head shake. "At least tell him that he has to attend tonight. For me."

Not even emotional blackmail works on Micah. He won't come out of his art studio for anyone, including Lola. If I set it on fire, I have no doubt he'd happily burn inside of it.

Pressing a kiss to her wrinkled cheek, I muster a smile. "I'll try my best."

"Good lad. Have a safe trip."

Hopping into my filthy truck, I drive back up to the cabin that I share with Zach and Micah. The former is waiting out front, throwing on a denim jacket over his black jeans and tight, white t-shirt. His brother is nowhere in sight, as usual.

"Get in, brat," I shout out of the window.

"Aww. Don't flirt with me, cuz."

"Then don't fucking call me that."

He cocks an eyebrow. "You're still my cousin, right?"

"Wouldn't be if I had a choice in it."

"Charming as always." Zach climbs into the passenger seat. "You know, it's lucky we're related. No one else would put up with your miserable backside in this town."

"Trust me, I'd be okay with living alone."

"You'd miss me too much. Don't deny it."

Turning up the blare of heavy rock music to silence his incessant chattering, I follow the bumpy track that bisects the entire town, peppered with jagged rocks and tides of mud.

Beyond Briar Valley, a snaking track is cut into Mount Helena, a two-thousand-foot peak capped with snow and spruce trees that touch the clouds. It's a long, uncomfortable hour navigating the route back to civilisation.

At the base of the mountain, Zach turns down the music, grumbling about a headache. His eyes are glued to his phone, scrolling through one of his usual dating apps.

Life in Briar Valley doesn't equate to much female interaction, so on his regular trips into town, I know he takes full advantage. He has a much higher tolerance for people than me.

"You see Micah today?"

With his boot-covered feet propped up on the dashboard, Zach shrugs. "Nope. He's been in there for three days now. This is the longest episode he's had in a while."

"We've tried to coax him out."

"Yeah, and a fat lot of good that did. He's more withdrawn than ever."

"He'll come back, kid. He always does."

"I'm tired of waiting for his episodes to pass," he admits angrily. "I used to know what he was thinking before he did, and now it's like we're not even brothers."

Unsure of what shallow comfort I can offer, I focus on the road flattening out. Micah's condition is hard on everyone, but it's hardest on Zach. He lost his brother too, along with everything else.

"Zach—"

"Forget it," he interrupts.

Resting his head against the door, he shuts his eyes and angles himself away from me, effectively ending the conversation. My grip on the steering wheel tightens in frustration.

Another tense hour later, we pull into the narrow, cobbled streets of Highbridge. Nestled amidst the picturesque countryside, it's a medium-sized town and our closest source of supplies.

It takes both of us to load up the truck with enough propane for the fifteen cabins that occupy Briar Valley, three of which are still being built. Lola is an absolute stickler for being prepared for all eventualities.

While we're heading out of the winter months now, the weather can still be unpredictable. We were snowed in for weeks in December, though we have enough allotments and greenhouses to be self-sufficient for food.

Regardless, I'm glad to see the first whispers of spring. Zach and I spend our days working for Lola, performing town maintenance and building cabins. It's a lot easier when we're not being pelted with snow or rain.

"Let's stop and get some booze," Zach suggests, locking the truck bed. "We still have time to get back for the party."

"You really think that's a good idea?"

He's a notorious lightweight when it comes to alcohol and often makes a complete fool of himself, even after only a few beers. And I'm the idiot that has to deal with it.

"Lighten up. It's a party, isn't it?"

"Not if I have anything to do with it," I grumble. "Go on then. I'll wait here."

He punches me in the shoulder before heading for the nearby liquor store. Propped against the back of the truck, I study my surroundings, my skin tight with discomfort.

A few of the locals give me a wave of greeting or the odd smile, but none dare approach. Briar Valley has a reputation for being notoriously private, and I've had my fair share of run-ins with people spouting bullshit.

We simply prefer to keep to ourselves up on the mountain, but most locals think we're fucking satanists or some shit like that. In reality, we just like to be left alone.

"Killian!"

My head perks up.

"You're just the man I wanted to see."

Jogging over to me, Trevor offers me a hand to shake, his face shielded by a well-worn baseball cap. He runs the local bar and has bailed Zach out of trouble several times.

"What's up, Trev?"

"We had some woman asking for information yesterday," he answers. "Wanted to know all about Briar Valley."

"What? Who was she?"

"Never seen her before. She was beat up pretty bad, barely able to walk. Got a scrawny little kid with her too. Friend of yours?"

"Do I look like I have friends?" I drawl.

Trevor shrugs. "Ain't my business to presume, but she wasn't asking for you. Claimed she was new in town."

"Who did she ask for, then?"

"Your Grams. By name."

Unease prickling across my scalp, I glance around to ensure no one is close by or listening to us. Not many people know Lola's full name. She's even more private than me.

We don't socialise with outsiders beyond the odd business transaction and our monthly supply runs into town. That's exactly how we like it.

"You know where she went?" I ask neutrally.

"Sorry, pal. Not a clue."

Shrugging, I decide to play it cool.

"If she ever makes it to Briar Valley, I'll deal with her. Don't breathe a word of this to anyone, alright? You know Lola doesn't like people snooping into her business."

"Gotcha. Take it easy, Kill."

Watching Trevor head back into his bar, I can't shake the sense that something isn't right. The thought of some woman and her kid wandering through the woods has a bad feeling pooling in my gut.

"Are you trying to burn a hole in the road?" Zach laughs as he returns, armed with overflowing plastic bags. "Stop glaring. You'll give yourself an ulcer. Let's go."

"I don't glare."

"Correction. You don't smile."

Piling back into the truck after checking the propane tanks are secure, I wipe Trevor's warning from my mind. No one gets all the way up the mountain and into town without knowing the way.

If trouble's coming, it won't ever make it to our doorstep. Even if I have to search the surrounding woods with my hunting rifle to protect everyone from some dumb fucking stranger looking to start shit with us.

"You get beer?" I ask Zach.

Eyes glued back on his phone screen, he unwraps a lollipop and sticks it in his mouth. "Thought you didn't want any booze?"

"You're a little shit, kid."

He turns up the rock music, startling several nearby locals. "Of course, I got your fucking beer. I know you, asshole. Now hurry up, I'm hungry."

CHAPTER 4
WILLOW
EUTHANASIA - POST MALONE

THUMP. *Thump. Thump.*

Still alive. Still hope.

Thump. Thump. Thump.

Keep walking. Don't stop.

Focusing on every footstep that echoes in the endless woodland surrounding us, I ignore the beat of my erratic, struggling heart. Arianna is stumbling beside me, more asleep than awake at this point.

We've been lost for hours, fumbling through darkness and driven by survival instinct alone. I tried to follow the vague instructions we got from a shop owner, but without a map, we soon got lost as the sun disappeared.

I can't stop. I won't stop. Not until we're safe and I have the answers I've been looking for. That damned letter is a decade old, but I'm too desperate to allow that to stop me from taking this risk.

"Keeping going, baby."

"Tired," Arianna moans groggily.

"I know, me too. Just a little further."

We push on through the overbearing pine trees and thick underbrush, guided by the moonlight. I have no clue if we're heading in the right direction or, at this point, if Briar Valley even exists.

It feels like a myth to me, the stuff of folklore that parents entertain their children with over late-night fairy tales. We've been walking for hours and have found absolutely nothing but more trees and the odd startled deer.

All I have are the handwritten words of an unknown woman, claiming to be my grandmother and beckoning me in with open arms when Dad died ten years ago. This is the most reckless decision I've ever made.

What if she left?

What if it's all a hoax?

Fire licks at my insides, the stabbing pain in my chest forcing me to stop for a second. I'm gasping hard and struggling for breath. The taste of blood is thick on my tongue, flooding my mouth with a constant coppery flow.

Hunched over with my hands gripping my trembling knees, I hack up several mouthfuls of blood as black spots interfere with my vision. Everything is blurry.

I'm running out of time. I know that I can't keep up this pace for much longer. The mad scramble over rocks and moss-covered banks to get this far almost killed me off.

"Faster, Ari," I beg her. "We have to keep going."

"Too tired," she complains.

"Please, baby. For me."

Hand bunched in my sweat-drenched shirt, Arianna clings to me as we hike onwards through the darkness. Our feet crunch over twigs and rocks, adding to the strange symphony of sounds deep in the forest.

I've never seen anywhere like this place. It feels like the trees are alive, their powerful branches stretching so high above us, it's a wonder they don't kiss the clouds.

"I wish Pedro were here," Arianna whispers. "He could carry us both."

Stumbling on numb feet, the vision of his final moments comes back to me. Collapsing in a puddle of blood, his usually warm, compassionate eyes were empty of all life.

I can't waste his sacrifice. We have to make it. There's no other option, and I'll die trying if that's what it takes to get my little girl to the safety of Briar Valley. Arianna has to live.

Time trickles by in a blur of darkness, pain and exhaustion. My strength is fading fast, sapped by the constriction of my lungs, which are burning so fiercely it feels like I've swallowed a lit match.

With my eyes barely open, I spot the huge tree root in the path far too late. Losing my footing, a scream locks my throat up as I fall backwards over a deep ridge.

"Ari!"

Her tiny hand is ripped from mine, and she shrieks so loud, the terrified sound slashes through my ribcage and spears my heart. It hurts far worse than the thorns shredding my exposed skin as I fall with nothing to grab hold of.

Falling. Falling. Falling.

This is it.

My death.

Gelatinous mud fills my hands in my frenzied search to stop myself from sliding further down the steep bank. My hand catches on another exposed root, but it breaks off with a loud snap, and I scream again.

Warmth trickles down my face. All I feel is blinding pain as I tumble on and on through the mud, eventually hitting the bottom of the ravine and splashing into a current of freezing-cold water.

"Mummy!" Arianna's cries pierce the night.

Clawing my eyes open, frigid water batters my body, blurring into the beat of fists on flesh. He's here. Mr Sanchez is going to break every last bone inside of me this time.

"Mummy! What should I do?"

I can't even open my mouth without choking. Pain assaults me from every direction. Pounding. Piercing. Slashing my flesh into ribbons. Taking the last vestiges of hope that led me into these woods.

The welcome numbness of darkness approaches with open arms, punctuated by her sobbing from above. Clinging to consciousness, I beg the world on my knees to keep her safe. My little girl. My angel. My one light at the end of this very long tunnel.

If I must die, I want her to live for us both. Arianna is the best part of me, the only proof I have that my life has been worth living. I need to know that she will be okay.

"I can see lights! I'll get help!"

Hit by another crashing wave of nausea, I succumb to the warmth of unconsciousness. My only company is the bitter, hateful voice that has tattooed itself into my mind over many years of relentless torture.

My husband. My abuser. The monster who fathered my sweet girl. If the devil were a person, he'd wear calculating blue eyes and the perfume of sweet cigar smoke. That's who Mr Sanchez is. That's who he'll always be.

I won, darling wife.

You're nothing without me.

My blanket of numbness is stripped away all at once, exposing me to the harsh bite of water once more. Something is touching me. No, *someone*. I can feel their rough hands.

The world filters back in with each ragged breath I take, illuminated in vivid snapshots. Shouting. Panic. Probing fingers. A flashlight in my eyes. It hurts so bad.

"P-Please, help her! Mummy!"

Crying. Begging. The sharp bite of wind and frosty water. I try to reach for Arianna and fail, caught in a dark mental prison with no windows and no doors. All I can hear is her increasingly frantic crying.

"Move out of the way, squirt," someone orders in a firm rasp. "We've got your mum."

"No! Mummy!"

"Ari," I moan in pain.

"Zach, go find reinforcements. We need more muscle."

Two huge hands engulf my cheeks, their thumbs pinching my skin as they gently shake. My eyes are still too heavy to lift. I can't drag them open, no matter how loud my internal voice wails.

"Mummy! Mummy!"

"Someone get rid of the kid. I need more space."

"No! Let me go!"

I can sense a strong pair of arms around me, then another explosion of pain as I'm lifted. Everything hurts. Life hurts. Breathing hurts. If it weren't for Arianna, I'd surrender.

"Call Doc. Tell him to set up at Lola's cabin."

"What should I say?" a lighter voice responds.

"She's in a bad way. Prepare them for the worst."

I feel the last scraps of life drain out of me with that whispered name. *Lola*. She's alive. She's real. We've made it to our destination. After all this time, I can finally let go.

"You got a name, kid?"

"You're a stranger," Arianna argues defiantly. "I can't tell you."

"Get in the truck then. You're safe now."

On the count of four, I'm lifted from the ravine with a series of colourful curses and huffed breaths. I think I black out a little while being carried, because next thing I know, a car engine is rumbling.

"Ari," I groan.

"Mummy!"

Tiny hands cradle my face and help to peel my eyelids open at last. Two stunning, azure eyes filled with fresh tears stare down at me. She looks so afraid. I hate it.

"I got help," Arianna sobs. "These big men are going to make us safe. Please, Mummy. Don't go to sleep again."

The pair of burly arms wrapped around me tighten into a vice. Arianna's face is replaced by a pair of burnished-brown irises that resemble smouldering ashes. The man stares at me, his thick lips pursed tight.

"Why are you here?" he demands.

"L-Lola."

"Where did you learn that name?"

"We're looking for home," Arianna whimpers.

"Home?" the man echoes.

The car jolts as it hits a bump in the track, causing me to let out a shrill scream. Suddenly, breathing becomes even more difficult. Air slips through my fingertips as I try to suck it in and fail. I'm drowning on dry land.

He studies my breathing, his pale eyebrows drawing together. "Something's wrong."

"What is it?" another voice replies.

The blonde-haired beast lowers his ear to my chest, listening to the wet, pained gasps slipping past my parted lips. He pushes Arianna away so she can't watch me struggle.

"She has fluid in her lungs, I think. Hurry the fuck up."

"We're nearly there. Doc's ready and waiting."

A rough, calloused hand cups my jaw as the big guy leans in close, a single breath separating our lips. He watches me with frantic eyes, unable to help as I slowly choke.

"You're clearly a fighter, so don't give up on me now," he implores. "You've got a beautiful girl here who needs her mother."

"Look… after… h-her," I choke out.

"That's your goddamn job. Keep your eyes open. She's not my kid or my problem."

The last thing I see is him staring down at me with the hellfire of an avenging angel, his steely, intimidating facade cracked by a hint of fear.

I lose grip of the world and let my eyes slide shut, safe in the knowledge that if this is my deathbed, I got Arianna out of the hellhole of her childhood.

CHAPTER 5
ZACH

FOREST FIRE - BRIGHTON

PACING the length of Lola's warm, fire-lit living room, I fist my cropped caramel hair and curse the cruelness of the world. It never ceases to fucking amaze me.

The little girl, Arianna, is finally asleep. She whimpers with her eyes glued shut, the odd tear still pouring down her cheeks. Without her mum here, she's struggling to settle.

Killian holds her tiny, slim frame against his chest, glaring at the tears like it will stop them from falling. No amount of glowering is gonna make this situation any better.

"Why is she still crying?" he murmurs. "I fucking hate seeing it."

"You shouldn't have given her the sleeping pill. They're not for kids, for fuck's sake."

"She was hysterical, Zach. It was for her own good. I halved it to be safe."

Poking the flames crackling inside of Lola's wide, open fireplace, the mantelpiece lined with family photographs, I fight the urge to smack him around the face. When it comes to other human beings, he can be so fucking dumb.

"She watched her mother nearly die. No shit she was hysterical."

"I didn't want to let her scream and suffer," he points out.

"Drugging kids isn't good parenting."

Killian's eyes narrow. "Good thing I'm not her father then, isn't it?"

Lapsing back into tense silence, I pour myself another measure of whiskey from the mahogany liquor cabinet set beneath a hand-painted map of Briar Valley that Lola's late husband, Pops, crafted years ago.

We were deep into celebrations when all hell broke loose, and I'm not done drinking for the night. Every year, the entire town gathers around the bonfire to eat, drink, trade stories and celebrate the town.

Everyone was getting tipsy, and Albie had just begun one of his usual convoluted stories when all of a sudden, this kid appeared out of nowhere, screaming her damn head off. We were all stunned, to say the least.

Picking through the mountainous forest that encapsulates the five miles of private land that carves out the town was treacherous, but we eventually found the kid's mother.

Fuck. Me.

Someone so badly injured shouldn't be hot, but I'm not fucking dead. Even beneath the blood and bruises, her otherworldly beauty took my breath away for a second.

The angelic wisp of a woman with hair the shade of midnight had slipped into a ravine and was getting beaten to shit by cold water. It's a miracle she survived the fall.

Even though she looks like one strong wind would kill her off, this bruised and battered woman somehow made it miles uphill through impenetrable woodland with a kid in tow. She had to be desperate to brave that trek with no guidance.

"Where did she come from?" I ask aloud.

Killian shoots me an apprehensive look. "She was looking for us."

"What do you mean? For Lola?"

"She's been asking around in Highbridge for information, apparently."

"What?" I snap at him. "Since when?"

Killian shrugs, stroking the kid's blonde ringlets that tumble over her shoulders in a pearlescent waterfall. I've never seen him within three feet of a child, let alone having one asleep on his chest like a sloth.

"I hate it when you keep secrets."

"Lay off, Zach." He sighs heavily. "I just chose not to tell you."

"Isn't that the same thing?"

"Why are you getting so bent out of shape?" Killian accuses, deflecting as usual. "I didn't think it was important at the time."

"I'm not a child anymore, Kill."

"You act like one, so who can blame me for treating you as such?"

Anger burns in my gut. "Fuck you."

The front door slams so loud, it rattles the photographs on the mantelpiece. Lola strides into the room with an authoritative boom of greeting that halts our argument.

"Enough!"

She's followed close behind by Ryder and Albie, both of them covered in streaks of fresh blood from where they helped us get the woman into Killian's awaiting truck.

"What on earth happened?" she shouts at us.

"Grams. We can explain."

Arms folded, she challenges us both with a stare. "Better be a hell of an explanation."

"We found the woman on the edge of the property. This one led the way." I gesture to the kid, still moaning under her breath. "It's her mum."

Killian's grip on the sleeping girl tightens ever so noticeably. No one here is buying his *I hate children* act, that's for sure. He's so full of shit.

"Where is the woman?' Lola demands.

"She's in the other room with Doc, Rachel and Miranda."

"Who is she? This place isn't on the map for a reason."

"Ask Killian." I jab a finger at the asshole himself. "He has all the damn answers."

With a muttered curse, Killian repositions the kid on the sofa beneath a hand-knitted, multicoloured blanket and stands. Facing Lola, he runs a hand over his tired face.

"Trevor approached me in town earlier. He said some woman and her kid were asking for you. By name. I figured it was nothing, so I didn't mention it."

"By name?" Lola utters.

"First and last name. She knows exactly who you are."

Processing this new information, Lola rests a weathered hand on the mantelpiece above the roaring fire. She looks deeply troubled, staring into the flames for a brief pause.

"What is it, Grams?" I dare to ask.

While Lola rules over Briar Valley with an iron fist, ensuring the survival of such a remote town, she has the biggest heart of everyone here. Worry and anxiety are written all over her face right now.

She turns to face us again. "Nothing. I need to see the woman for myself."

"She's unconscious," Killian rumbles.

Marching over to the sofa, Lola crouches down to study the sleeping girl. She doesn't look much like her supposed mother—a tiny dot, all blonde hair and bright-blue eyes, compared to her mother's coal-black hair and sparkling hazel irises.

They do share the same slim, bird-like features. But more so, there's a sense of palpable desperation that clings to them, silent but deadly. They look indisputably lost in the world. Lola seizes the girl's small hand, freezing when she uncurls her little fingers.

"Look at this."

Killian leans over to look, his face paling. "What the actual fuck?"

"That can't be accidental, can it?"

"What is it?" I ask, straining for a peek.

Flattening the child's hand in her own wrinkled palm, Lola lifts it to show us all the bloodied, scabbed-over mess that's on display. Each of her fingertips have been carefully burned to remove all traces of her prints.

Albie curses up a storm, moving closer to check each fingertip in turn. "Hell of a job."

Looking away with his golden-brown face turning white as a sheet, Ryder refuses to look. Out of us all, he has the weakest stomach. Killian mocked him for months when he decided to go vegetarian, unable to stand the thought of an animal suffering.

"You good, Ry?" I pat his shoulder.

He nods, taking a deep breath.

"Whoever these two are, they clearly don't want to be found," Albie surmises. "Someone did a damn good job of burning these off to avoid being identified."

Lola places the kid's hand down again, watching as she sucks her thumb into her mouth for comfort. She's a cute little thing, even I'll admit.

"Then we keep them safe until we can get answers," Lola decides, still studying the girl.

"Why?" Killian cuts her off, hands raised in the air. "What if they bring trouble into town? We cannot take that risk."

"We're equipped to handle any bloody trouble," she returns hotly. "I'm not casting them out without more information. You know that's not how we work better than most."

Killian's face falls. "That isn't fair."

"If you don't like my decision, you can leave. But it's final."

Without another word, he purses his lips and stalks from the room. The front door slams again so hard, it rattles the glass in the room's huge bay window.

Lola sighs. "That temper of his will get the better of him someday."

"It usually does."

We're all too familiar with Killian's intolerance for the human race. That man's an erupting volcano with very brief periods of calm. Even those are few and far between.

His family is usually on the receiving end of his infamous temper and sharp tongue, although he's very for beating the shit out of any intruders with his bare hands too.

"Let's go see Doc," Lola says tiredly. "I've sent everyone else home for the night."

Placing my empty glass down, I gesture for her to go ahead. They set up in the massive family kitchen out back, giving them space to attend to our newest arrival.

The minute we walk into the brightly lit room, the scent of fresh blood hits me. I nearly gag. It's so thick in the air, you can taste the copper droplets of death on your tongue.

"Needle," Doc orders his wife.

He's crouched over a semi-naked, spread out body on Lola's dining table. Taking the needle in hand, he begins to sew the oozing gash on the woman's forehead where she hit a rock. Rachel and Miranda watch with terrified expressions.

"Gauze and antiseptic, Rach."

Setting myself up in the corner with an increasingly queasy Ryder, Lola and Albie step closer to the table to watch. They command the room with wordless authority as the two elders present.

Rachel and Miranda pass the remaining equipment and slink backwards to make way for Lola to move closer to our guest. She's sweeping her eyes over every inch on display, but her expression doesn't betray a thing.

With a final stitch, Doc snips off the suture and smooths gauze across the woman's forehead, turning his attention back to her bare torso. They sliced the blouse from her body, revealing her mottled midsection.

Letting my gaze trail over her, my mouth goes bone dry. She's covered in dark bruises, the purple and green splotches reigning chaos across her flesh. Lola stares down at her with a blank expression.

"How bad is it? Will she live?"

Doc sighs, pushing blood-smeared spectacles up his nose. "We're out of the woods. She had fluid in her lungs, so it was touch and go. The other injuries are treatable."

He gestures down at the hollow needle protruding from the woman's chest, with blood and fluid sprayed around the entry sight. Ryder makes a quiet heaving sound as he looks away, his tolerance finally failing.

"These bruises look pretty bad," Lola observes.

"She's been severely beaten." Doc gently probes the woman's ribs while frowning. "She was bandaged up when we undressed her. Must've been nursing the wounds for a while."

"How the heck did she get here then?"

Albie shakes his head. "It's a hard trek up the mountain and down into the valley by foot. We found her a couple miles from here."

"Talk about determination."

"That one word for it."

Albie has been Lola's right-hand man since her husband died a few years back. He's the closest confidante and aide to our formidable leader. Any problem in the town, him and Killian are the first ones on the case.

But while Albie provides a level-headed perspective that keeps things running smoothly, Lola thinks with her heart over her brain. She's actually an incredibly kind woman beneath the bravado. Her home belongs to everyone.

"You see the prints?" Doc lifts a limp, bloodied hand.

Identical to her daughter, this woman has had her fingerprints brutally burned off too. No identification would be possible if the police caught up to her. Whoever did it to her knew what they were doing.

"She's here for a reason. I don't know what," Lola muses aloud. "I know we don't like outsiders, but this poor creature has been through something horrific."

Deferring to her authority, we all wait for her decision. If she wants these two gone, we'll dump the woman back in the woods where we found her, even in this state.

"We'll patch her up and take it from there. Understood?"

Relief overcomes me, even if I don't know why I care about a total stranger. Everyone else echoes their compliance, each meeting Lola's widened eyes in turn to confirm it.

"Finish up," she orders Doc. "I'll stay. Everyone else out."

Doc resumes working, leaving the rest of us to file out without protest. I grab Ryder's shoulder and steer him outside to light up cigarettes beneath the shining moon that casts light across Lola's vast back garden.

"You should check on Killian," Ryder suggests, blowing out a ring of smoke. "He seemed pretty upset earlier. I haven't seen him look that worried before."

"Killian can take care of himself."

"This would've stirred shit up for him, Zach. He needs you."

"What he needs is to lighten up and get laid."

He snorts. "Don't we all."

"Your sex life is a hell of a lot more interesting than mine."

"I doubt that." Ryder crushes his cigarette beneath his laced-up boot. "Long-distance relationships don't exactly equate to many wild, passionate nights. Especially out here."

"You mean Ethan won't tickle your pickle over the phone?"

He playfully shoves my shoulder. "That is none of your business."

"You're right. I really don't wanna know what disgusting shit you two get up to. I'll never be able to look him in the eye over dinner again."

Eyes straying over to the window, we both watch as Lola pulls up a chair next to the kitchen table. Her eyes look haunted from here. She's intent on staying while Doc continues his work on the unconscious woman.

"What's with Lola?" Ryder wonders.

I shrug, baffled. "Fuck knows."

"You recognise her? Or the kid?"

"Nope. She's a total stranger."

"That isn't the concern Lola has for total strangers," he replies pointedly.

I'm sure that exact point is what has riled Killian up so badly. He's right— Lola doesn't give a fuck about strangers, until they're accepted into town and become family instead.

She's keeping secrets from us.

This woman means something to her.

CHAPTER 6
WILLOW

NEVER FEEL ALONE - THE DANGEROUS SUMMER

"WAKE UP, MRS SANCHEZ."

The covers are ripped from my body, exposing violent purple bruises and whip marks. Light streams through my bedroom window, a fiery ball of raw heat breaking the solitude of my sleep.

Mr Sanchez's harsh voice is interrupted by the wail of Arianna crying nearby. It cuts through my grogginess, forcing my heavy eyelids open.

"Shut that whining kid up before I do it for you," he threatens.

No. No.

He won't lay another finger on her.

I'll take the beating myself.

Casting his arctic-blue gaze around my bedroom, devoid of any personal effects, a sneer overtakes his handsome features. The world doesn't see him as I do. His picture-perfect exterior hides a devilish truth.

When his eyes stray over to the marble fireplace, my heart erupts in my chest. I've been sneaking into his bedroom in the dead of night to search through his belongings for cash. We're so close to being ready.

"We have a very important gala to attend tonight." He glances back over me, his lips curled in a sneer. "You need to cover yourself up and put a damn smile on. Don't let me down."

Laying still until he gets bored of trying to intimidate me, I breathe out a sigh of relief when he disappears. The moment he's gone, Arianna comes bounding into the room, her face soaked with tears.

There's a bright-red handprint on her cheek, and the sight of it drags me from the bed to capture her in a tight hug. She throws her arms around my neck, her shoulders shaking with each sob.

"It's okay, baby girl," I murmur into her hair. "I'll make it better, I promise."

No matter how long it takes.

No matter what I have to do.

We're getting out of here.

———

Startling awake, I force my eyes open and blink until my vision settles. Wooden beams are stretched across the ceiling above me, hand stripped and rustic. It takes a moment for the ringing in my ears to die down.

When I try and fail to sit upright, blinding pain rips through me, crackling its way down my spine. I can barely lift a finger, and my eyes flit around the room in search of answers.

I'm in a sprawling family-sized kitchen, laying across a huge table with a pillow propped beneath my head. A multicoloured, knitted blanket is pulled up to my chin, and when I peek beneath it, my blood freezes.

My clothes have vanished, leaving my entire body on display beneath my bloodstained bra and panties. Someone has re-wrapped my ribs and tended to the new cuts and bruises that have appeared.

"Ari!" I shout hoarsely.

Nothing.

I'm alone.

Attempting to work some feeling back into my stiff limbs, I wiggle my toes and try to sit up again. An adhesive dressing has been smoothed over my sternum. My chest still aches, but it isn't the awful pressure that I experienced before.

That's when it hits me. Before. The woods. Rocky outcrops and steep banks. Trees. Moonlight. Falling. Screaming. Blood. Water. Voices and hands lifting me.

"Arianna!"

Battling for every breath, I stifle a terrified wail when loud footsteps approach and the door to the kitchen slams open. A very familiar looking stranger arrives like a bat out of hell, following the sound of my yelling.

Filling the entire wide door frame, the wild beast wearing human skin stalks into the room with the ease of a trained killer. His eyes land on me, and I recognise the fiery, burnished-brown depths from my memories of the car ride here.

I've seen my fair share of burly, over-muscled thugs who were paid a small fortune to protect my husband, but this mountain of a man is in a whole league of his own. The muscles that carve his frame look like beams of polished steel under his skin.

"Who are you?" I scream at him.

"Stop moving," he rasps in a smoky voice, reminiscent of aged whiskey. "You're going to hurt yourself if you're not careful."

"Where is my daughter?"

Scraping a hand through his shoulder-length, dirty-blonde hair that looks permanently bleached by sunshine, he sighs. "She's safe."

His barrel chest is cloaked in a dirty, red flannel shirt, paired with well-worn blue jeans that boast holes through the kneecaps and a pair of mud-caked outdoor boots. I can see the size of his rippling biceps through the shirt's material.

With a tangled beard that's long past fashionably styled and more of an untamed bush, he looks like a rugged outlander with zero regard for society's standards. Even his wide, strong jaw and straight nose are tanned a bronze shade of brown.

"Where?" I repeat anxiously.

"Take a breath. She's eating breakfast."

His chest seems to vibrate with every word he rumbles in that deep, toe-curling voice. It's almost a drawl, each syllable laden with exasperation, like he views me as nothing but a distraction from his solitude.

"I want to see her right now."

"You really want her to see you like this?" he counters, lifting a pale brow that pulls at the crinkles framing his eyes. "You should clean up first."

"I'm fine."

The giant heads for the kitchen sink built into a row of dark-brown cabinets, and he fills a glass with water. His stroll is so casual, so assured, that the sense of dangerous ease clinging to his oversized frame causes my pulse to skitter.

I couldn't escape him if I needed to. Someone of his stature could squash my pitiful strength with a single blow. I'm still not sure if he's a threat or not, even though I know he was part of the group that rescued me.

Returning to my side, he slides a huge palm underneath my head and lifts to bring the glass to my lips. I hate having to be assisted, especially by this abrasive asshole.

"You don't look fine to me," he murmurs. "In fact, I'd argue that everything about this situation is pretty damn *not* fine."

Draining the glass in several frantic gulps, I could cry from relief. The water feels so good sliding down my raw throat. He gives me a nod of approval and retreats, allowing me to relax a fraction.

"Like I said, I'm fine."

He snorts, shaking his head. "Whatever you say, lady."

"Where is my daughter? Is she okay?"

"She's outside with my cousin, annoying the fuck out of him. Little thing has a hell of a smart mouth on her."

I slump, releasing my held breath. "Thank God."

"You've been out of it for a while. Doc had to sedate you while he patched you up."

"How long?"

"Twelve hours or so."

"Shit!" I try to wrench myself up again and fail. "I need to see her."

Grabbing hold of my hand, he slides his under my left shoulder and slowly helps me sit up. I cling to him tight, my teeth gritted against the searing pain. It takes several seconds of manoeuvring to move me into an upright position.

"Easy," he murmurs.

"I'm good."

"Yeah, like you keep saying."

Once my foggy head clears, I blink as the kitchen settles around me again. It's neat but well lived in with rows of packed spice racks, clean dishes drying next to the sink and flower-printed tea towels hanging from the oven.

The blanket has slipped down and pools at my waist, revealing my stained underwear. Gooseflesh spikes across my skin as the stranger studies me with interest. He isn't even pretending not to look at my naked skin.

"Do you mind?" I snap at him.

"Not in the slightest." He smirks and starts unbuttoning his flannel shirt. "Here, take this."

Now it's my turn to drop my gaze with each button that pops open, unveiling his bare chest that's smattered with a carpet of light-blonde hair. Jesus. This guy has no shame.

Face schooled into a blank expression, he drags the shirt over his wide-set shoulders and wraps it around me instead. The woodsy scent of musk and fresh bonfires envelops me. Gripping the warm material, I slide my arms inside.

My cheeks flush hot as he buttons it up for me. His eyes are downturned to focus on his task, which gives me the perfect opportunity to check him out. I'm only human, and he looks like he was sculpted by the gods.

"Thank you," I mutter, cheeks flaming.

"Don't mention it. Give me your hand."

Daring to place it in his awaiting palm, I grit my teeth again and manage to swivel to the side, setting my feet on the kitchen floor. It's made from more planks of raw wood, polished to perfection with the odd blood splatter.

"On three," he directs.

Counting down, he pulls my arms and helps me to stand at last. His shirt swamps my body, falling to mid-thigh and thankfully covering my panties. I clutch his hand tight as dizziness washes over me again, taking a few seconds to breathe.

"Still with me?"

"Yeah," I force out. "Just dizzy. Where am I?"

"The kitchen."

Apparently, he does have a sense of humour.

"I'm serious."

"Briar Valley," he says reluctantly.

"B-Briar Valley? Really? I made it?"

"You were looking for us then. Wanna tell me why? You're actually trespassing on private land."

Releasing my death grip on his hand, I take a tentative step alone. The pain has abated to a dull ache. I'm a pro at plastering on a fake smile and pretending to be alright. This is nothing in comparison to previous states I've woken up in.

"Take me to my daughter please."

"She's fine," he growls with a little more fire. "Tell me why you're here."

"With all due respect, I don't know you. I want to see her first, and then we can talk."

When he tries to grab hold of me, I shudder and immediately back away. My tailbone collides with the kitchen counter. Freezing on the spot, he lets his hands fall.

"I'm not going to hurt you."

"I'd prefer it if you kept your hands to yourself."

Ignoring his quizzical expression, I drag my battered body from the kitchen and limp away from him as fast as my injuries will allow. Through the door, there's a long hallway with ceilings that stretch up into the heavens leading deeper into the house.

It looks to be some kind of cabin, but it's oozing with luxury. The walls and ceiling are made from more carved wood, supported by huge beams built into the ceiling and adjoining panels of tinted glass.

I've seen cabins on television, but they didn't have any of these back home. This place doesn't look like the off-grid, bare-bones structures depicted in movies. Light is pouring in from every direction, warming the comfortable space.

Limping onwards, I inch towards the front door at the end of the hallway. Other rooms branch off on both sides, but they're empty and don't hold my attention. All I can think about is setting sights on Arianna.

"Hey! Wait up!"

Footsteps follow hot on my heels.

"At least tell me your name."

"And what exactly is your name?" I say over my shoulder. "Why should I trust you?"

Overtaking me to block the door, he pins me with a fearsome scowl. "It's Killian. Trust works both ways, you know."

Gulping, I duck my gaze. "I'm Melody."

"Melody," he tests, like it doesn't sit right.

"Uh-huh, that's my name. Please move out of my way."

Killian steps aside and motions for me to go ahead. I seize the bronze doorknob and step outside into blazing sunshine that burns my retinas. Darkness has abated, giving way to a crisp, blossom-scented morning.

An expansive wraparound porch hugs the entrance to the cabin, stained a dark shade of cherry red. Wicker furniture sits atop, offering a perfect, undisturbed view of the mountain range surrounding the valley on all sides.

Squinting in the daylight, I stumble a few more steps before dread nearly runs me over. From the grassy clearing in front of the cabin, dozens of eyes are locked on me—including my bare legs on display and the huge shirt barely covering my modesty.

"Asshole," I curse under my breath.

Killian chuckles behind me. "You wanted to come outside."

"Could've warned me."

"Welcome to breakfast time. You might want to cover yourself up."

Tugging his shirt even lower to make sure it's covering as much of my body as possible, I stare at the huge clearing stretching out in front me. Two long tables have been built into the ground, carved from slabs of roughened wood.

At each table, a small group of people has gathered, chatting as they share steaming mugs of coffee and trays of breakfast sandwiches. Every single one of them is staring at me with varying degrees of shock.

"After you," Killian invites with a grin.

I remain frozen on the spot. "Uh."

"Problem?" he taunts.

Interrupting his little game, someone rises from the table on the left. He has a headful of luscious, light-brown hair the hue of rich, molten caramel, and a rough scruff of stubble covering his jawline. His curious green eyes burn a path over me.

He's a little shorter than Killian but built with the same stockiness afforded by their rural home. Ropey lines of muscle threaten to burst through his V-neck white t-shirt and jeans, all the way down to his generous, rounded butt.

"Mummy! Mummy!"

A blonde angel shoots up next to him, dressed in another child's clothes. Her hair has been neatly braided in two, and the streaks of tears and dirt are gone from her sweet face.

"Arianna!" I shout back.

She races across the grass, flying up the wooden steps with a squeal. Before she can collide with me at high speed, Killian steps in and grabs hold of her to block the collision.

He swings Arianna around in a circle, causing her to happily bellow his name at the top of her lungs. She's never been one to let other people touch her—especially not men.

"Careful, peanut." Killian places her back on her feet. "You don't want to hurt your mama now, do you?"

"No, Killian," she recites obediently.

He casts me a smug look before releasing her. "She's all yours."

Arianna throws her arms around my waist and buries her face in my stomach. I cuddle her close, letting the exhausted tears roll down my cheeks.

"It's okay, beautiful girl. I'm here now."

"You s-scared me," Arianna cries.

"You've been so brave, baby."

Fisting handfuls of my borrowed flannel shirt, her gaze trains on me, full of fierce defiance. Sometimes, she looks a little too much like her father. Arianna has his fire and determination, but unlike that monster, hers is borne of innocence.

"We made it," she says with an excited smile. "I saw the lights down the mountain and found this giant to help. We're here, Mummy. Home."

I shush her, but it's too late.

"Home?" Killian echoes.

He fixes me with a stare, and I nudge Arianna behind me. There's an air of danger that suffuses his entire frame. I know men like him. They use the threat of violence to bend others to their will.

I've spent half of my life living in that state of abject fear. Never again. Inching away from him, most of the people wander off, leaving a small group to approach the porch. I recognise a couple of the men next to the shorter guy that held Arianna.

Everyone wears wary smiles, studying us closely.

A short, elderly woman walks up the wide steps. She must be in her seventies at least, but she's fit and wiry beneath her floral blouse and skirt. Like everyone else, her skin is a golden bronze, seeming to shine with the gleam of the sunlight above us.

"This lady owns the town," Arianna whispers shyly. "She said she'll help us."

I keep her trapped behind me, a fine quiver racing over my skin. She may be an old lady, but everyone is forming around her with obvious respect and deference. I can recognise power when I see it. She's in charge of this place.

"Please, I mean you no harm," she placates, stopping beside Killian. "My name is Lola. You're safe, and no one will harm you here."

"You're Lola?" I ask hopefully.

She watches me closely. "Yes."

Clutching Arianna's tiny body even tighter, I need her strength to ground me before I collapse into a relieved puddle. I've thought of this moment for so long, and for many of those years it felt like a childish fantasy.

"What's your name?" she asks gently.

Staring into her kind eyes, framed by deep smile lines and papery wrinkles, I feel no threat. For the first time in so long, I want to throw myself into someone's arms. No one has ever caught me before.

"This is Arianna." I try to steady my voice. "My daughter."

Sneaking out from hiding behind me, Arianna gives her a wave, even though they've already been acquainted. Lola beams, and there are tears staining her cheeks. She knows who we are. I can see it in her eyes.

I glance at Killian. "My name isn't Melody."

His scowl deepens, burning with mistrust.

"So much for trust," he deadpans. "Who the hell are you then?"

Twisting the thick, golden wedding band I still wear on my ring finger, I clear my throat. "I'm Willow Sanchez."

"Sanchez?" Lola notices the ring.

"Formerly Willow Castlemore. I'm your granddaughter."

CHAPTER 7
WILLOW
HOME - GABRIELLE APLIN

EASING myself onto the butter-soft sofa, I pat the space next to me. Arianna curls up against my side and stares at all the other adults in the room. She's a smart cookie, but she's also well trained at knowing when *not* to speak.

These people might be our real, long-lost family, but in my experience, blood isn't thicker than water. Not really. Family means nothing to me, not after the hellish mess my father left me in when he died.

Killian props himself up in the corner of the room after locating a new shirt to wear, maintaining his steely, pissed-off silence. Two other guys have joined us, and one is the caramel-haired man who was looking after Arianna.

He slowly approaches me, wearing another easy smile that reveals dimples in his cheeks. Sticking his hand out for me to shake, he laughs under his breath when I decline.

"I just wanted to introduce myself. I'm Zach."

I take in his tight t-shirt and jeans. "Willow. Thanks for looking after my little girl."

"Don't mention it, babe. You need anything else, I'm around."

"Alright, kid," Killian hisses. "Back off the poor woman."

"Just being a good host," he snarks back.

Killian full-body shoves him into an armchair. Zach must be the cousin that he mentioned. I can see a vague resemblance in the rounded shapes of their eyes and strong, straight noses, though Killian looks a lot older than him.

The other guy gives me a friendly wave. With a headful of dark ringlets, warm blue eyes and a smile that lights up his whole innocent face, his presence is immediately welcoming. I tentatively return his smile.

"I'm Ryder," he explains. "Welcome to town."

"Um, thanks."

Arianna tugs on the sleeve of my flannel shirt, dropping her voice to a hushed, conspiratorial whisper.

"Zach has ice cream in his cabin, and he said that if I'm a good girl, I can have some later."

"Is that so?"

I watch Zach grin at my little girl. "What can I say, I'm a people pleaser."

We're interrupted by an older, grey-haired man entering the room, draining a thermos of coffee. He's maybe a few years younger than Lola, his long hair tied back in a ponytail that shows off his weathered face.

"I'm Albie." His voice twangs with a thick British accent. "Ryder's my nephew. We already met briefly last night, but it's nice to meet ya properly."

"Thanks for, you know... rescuing me."

Albie shrugs it off. "It's what we do."

Two middle-aged women, Rachel' and Miranda, appear to hand out drinks after introducing themselves. Their matching silvery eyes and thick, red curls make it hard to tell them apart from each other. Sisters, for sure.

They disappear back into the kitchen to give us some privacy, leaving Lola to stride inside with a plate of chocolate chip cookies in hand. They smell fresh and homemade.

My stomach growls so loud, Killian shoots me another scowl before stealing the plate and dumping it in front of us.

"Eat," he thunders.

I clear my throat. "I'm fine."

"I'm getting really sick of you saying that. It wasn't an invitation. *Eat.*"

"That's enough, Killian. Willow is our guest," Lola scolds.

He returns to brooding silence, but still stares at me with determination. I can't decide if he wants to murder me or pin me to the floor until I agree to eat. Both scenarios are equally worrying.

Arianna begins to stuff her mouth with chocolate chip goodness. Lola smiles at her enthusiasm, taking the seat closest to us. She can barely keep her eyes off me, and wonderment is softening her aged features.

"Willow," she whispers my name in awe. "I don't know where to start. I can't believe you're here. It's been so long."

"I've been abroad for the last decade."

"I see. Well, that would make this little one my great-granddaughter, correct?"

Arianna sucks her thumb into her chocolate-stained mouth. I squeeze my arm around her, wincing as she rests her head on a particularly nasty bruise across my chest.

"Yeah, this is Arianna."

"How old are you, poppet?" Lola enquires softly.

She automatically looks up at me for permission before answering. I nod, squirming under the collective attention of the entire room.

"I'm six, but I'll be seven in forty-nine days," Arianna replies.

"Forty-nine days! Such a big girl, aren't you? And so brave, looking after your mum like that."

She accepts the extra cookie that Lola offers her and demolishes it without complaint. Lola smiles again, loving every moment, before she glances back at me.

"You seem young to have her."

"I'm twenty-six," I answer evenly.

"And your husband? Is he coming?"

Anxiously twisting the strangling weight of my wedding band, I ignore Zach's and Killian's cold facial expressions. Somehow, they both seem to sense my change in emotion, their hackles rising in response.

Arianna shivers beside me and tugs on my shirt sleeve. Even her smile has vanished, and she abandons the rest of the cookie that she was about to inhale.

"Yeah, baby?"

"You said Daddy wasn't coming," she whispers.

Gulping hard, I feel the weight of several interested stares watching our exchange. I really don't want them to know too much about us at this stage. It isn't safe for them or us.

"He isn't coming, munchkin. I told you, it's just us now."

"So, I don't need to be scared?"

Unshed tears sparkle in her big, blue eyes, unhinging the box containing my weary nerves. Lola's gaze is burning a hole in the side of my head, silently demanding answers. When Killian cracks his knuckles, I fight the urge to flinch.

"Let's talk about this later, Ari."

"No," she demands, her bottom lip jutting out. "You promised! I like it here. They have ice cream, and a lake for swimming in. I want to stay."

"Ari, shush."

"I don't want to go home." Her pout increases as a tiny, sparkling tear rolls down her cheek. "It's bad there and Daddy makes you really sad. We need to stay here!"

"Nobody said anything about going home," I murmur back, my own tears spilling over. "Please, Ari. Be quiet."

"No! This is supposed to be our adventure!"

Burying my face in my hands, I scrub away the traitorous moisture leaking down my face. It's been days of non-stop travel and running for our damn lives. Arianna's entitled to a meltdown. I think I might join her at this rate.

"Come on, Ari." Zach approaches us and sticks out a hand. "Let's go and get some hot chocolate, okay?"

She looks up at me again, still mad but seeking permission like she's been trained to do. I gently push her towards him, mustering a thankful smile. Zach winks in response, leading her out of the room.

We all remain silent until the door closes behind them. Despite my audience, more tears fall, escaping the constraints of my fading control.

"I'm sorry, she's been through a lot."

"She's a good kid," Killian speaks up from his brooding.

I take a moment to wipe my face again. "We've travelled thousands of miles to get here. She's exhausted, that's all."

"Where did you come from?" Lola asks.

"Mexico."

"Willow, I'm sorry but I need you to answer me something right now. Is someone looking for you? We couldn't help but notice your fingerprints."

"Ah… it was an accident, that's all."

"An accident?" Killian repeats in disbelief. "Bullshit."

Panic wraps around my throat. I had no intention of letting anyone see the mess I made of our prints. None of this was supposed to happen.

"A car accident, uh, last week. There was a fire."

His eyes bore into me. I know he can sense my lying, even from across the room. I drop his intense gaze, playing with my wedding ring again. I wanted so badly to leave it behind or toss it to the bottom of the ocean, but this is our safety net if it all goes wrong.

"We had to leave our home in Mexico," I add with a sigh.

"Why?" Killian questions.

"I'm getting divorced. We wanted a fresh start."

"Does this divorce have something to do with the state you arrived in?"

"Of course not. How is this any of your business?"

"When you trespass on our land, it becomes our business," Killian retorts. "Tell us the truth, Willow."

"There's nothing else to tell!"

Before he can launch another attack, Lola silences him with a raised palm.

"Willow isn't here to be interrogated by you. She's our guest."

"I'm concerned for the town's safety," Killian argues. "That's my job."

"And I'm telling you, that's enough! Out."

"Grams—"

"Get out! Everyone."

Killian's mouth snaps shut. Eyes burning with anger, he stalks out of the room, leaving Ryder to trail after him with an apologetic smile. Lola motions for Albie to go too.

"I need to speak to Willow alone."

He vanishes after the others without complaint. Once we're alone, Lola takes the empty spot on the sofa next to me. She pulls my hands in hers, squeezing them so tightly, my bones creak together.

"I know you have no reason to trust me. I sent you that letter for a reason when I heard of your father's death."

"Why?" I can't help but ask.

"Because we're family," she explains simply. "Please let me help you. It's the least I can do. I didn't even know that you were still alive."

"I wouldn't exactly call it living."

Her fingers ghost over my gold wedding band. "Who is he? Should I be worried?"

"It doesn't matter. He's in the past now."

"Can I ask why you had to leave?"

I take a breath for courage. "We couldn't stay in Mexico. The divorce got... uh, complicated. We decided to fly home to England instead. I knew that I had to find you."

Eyes sparkling with tears, Lola draws me in close. My face is buried in the crook of her wrinkled neck. She smells like freshly baked cookies with a floral burst of wildflowers. I've never even met her before, but she still smells like home.

Sobs tear at my chest, clawing up my throat in clinging tendrils, until I'm falling apart in her arms. I've always been strong for Arianna's sake, but with her strength propping me up, I can finally let go.

The cries pour from my mouth with such frenzied desperation, I don't know how I'll ever stop. I've never done this before, but it feels oddly cathartic to let myself be weak.

I cry for all that we've lost. The suffering and pain inflicted on my precious daughter. The terror that drove us thousands of miles from the only home we've ever known, even an evil one, searching for a better life.

We have nothing left.

Nothing but our lives.

"Whatever you're running from won't find you here," Lola comforts as she strokes my long, black hair. "You have my word."

"I'm so sorry," I hiccup through sobs. "I shouldn't have brought this to your door. I didn't know where else to go."

"Nonsense. I'm your grandmother, and this is your home now."

Her easy acceptance only adds to my uncontrollable tears. I've never been embraced with such motiveless, unconditional love before. Not even from my father. I have no idea how to handle it.

"I want you to tell me the truth," she implores, holding me at arm's length. "Were you really in a car accident? Is something else going on here?"

Feeling like the worst person in the world, I manage a stiff nod. "Nothing else is going on."

Lola grasps my cheeks and makes me look her right in the eye. She stares at me with such determination, I get myself under control and straighten, needing to prove to her that I'm stronger than I look.

"I don't know what's happened to make you so afraid, but you can tell me when you're ready." Her thumbs wipe my tears aside. "Until then, let me take care of you."

"I don't know…"

"Please, Willow. All I want is to look after my family."

"Maybe we should go."

"You're not going anywhere but the hospital."

"No!" I shout, startling her with the fire in my voice. "Please, no hospitals. I can't risk it. He could be searching for us. It isn't safe."

"Searching for you?" she repeats.

I bite my lip. "He's… very powerful."

Lola contemplates my words. When she sighs in defeat, I know I've won the battle. For now. Something tells me this isn't the last time we'll have this fight. I hate lying to her, but I have no choice.

"No hospitals," she reluctantly agrees. "You're going to stay here and rest. Let yourself get better. That's the deal."

I submit with a nod. "We'll stay."

"Good. Come on, I'll show you to the guest room. I've asked Rachel and Miranda to sort some more clothes out. Their children are around Arianna's age."

Letting her help me stand back up, I hold her hand as we leave the living room. The others have all made themselves scarce.

Wrapping an arm around my waist, Lola helps me climb the staircase, dodging discarded shoes, woollen hats and the odd Wellington boot. Despite the pristine design of the cabin, it's littered with enough clutter for a whole family.

"How many people live here?" I ask, breathing hard.

"Just me in this cabin, but we have dozens of families spread throughout Briar Valley. Most of them treat this place as their home too. That's how I like it."

"Do you have any other children?"

Helping me hobble down a hallway painted a calming shade of light blue that contrasts the dark, wooden floorboards, Lola casts me an uncertain look.

"No. Didn't your father talk about me?"

"Not so much. We didn't have a great relationship," I admit. "When he died, I thought I had no family left."

"Christ," she curses, opening the last door on the left. "Things are a little complicated where your father is concerned, Willow. We have a lot to talk about."

I limp into the guest bedroom, breathing in the scent of fresh, crisp linens and waxed wood from the floorboards. It's painted a comfortable shade of light cream, and the furniture matches the rest of the cabin—basic but comfortable.

Lola walks past me and fusses over the bed, smoothing non-existent creases. I spot the duffel bag that's been placed next to the wardrobe. It survived my tumble in the woods. Panicked, I grit my teeth and bend down to search inside.

Our fake passports and meagre supply of cash are where I left them. We have a few personal items, but no clothes or toiletries. I couldn't afford to spook Mr Sanchez by packing anything that might've given our plan away.

Arianna's baby box rests at the bottom of the bag, safe and sound. It's light enough to lift out, and I inspect the carved box for any signs of damage. It looks a little dented from the fall, but nothing irreparable.

"What's that?" Lola eyes the box.

I pass it over to her to look inside. "Arianna's baby box."

Both sitting down on the edge of the bed, we look over the collection of random items. A blonde curl, tied with a silky, blue ribbon. Her first pair of shoes—tiny baby sandals, perfect for the Mexican heat. I even have a single cotton sock.

Mr Sanchez fired his housekeeper after he spotted her helping me put the box together. He didn't like his staff getting close to us. I wasn't to be seen or acknowledged by any of them, and they all knew the rules.

Pedro was the only one who treated me like a normal human being, but he was careful with his affection. I'll never forget the first time he spoke to me, daring to ask if I was okay while I nursed a badly sprained wrist.

He should be here.

This is his victory.

"How much did she weigh?" Lola breaks my thoughts.

"Uh, a little over seven pounds. She was a home birth. I delivered her myself."

"You did?" She gapes at me.

Shit!

"I mean, things happened so quickly," I rush to alleviate her concern. "We didn't have time to find a hospital before she arrived."

Lola returns to inspecting the items. My breath hisses from between my teeth. I need to think before I speak. The cruelness of my life is normal to me after so long, but not to the rest of the world. I can't let the truth slip out like that.

"We've had many home births here." Lola closes the box. "Miranda and Doc's third baby was actually born downstairs. He delivered it himself. It was such a beautiful day."

I stash the box back in my bag. "It's nice that you're all so close. I've always wanted a big family."

Lola chuckles with mirth. "Careful what you wish for, Willow. Things get very rowdy around here, but that's how we like it. You'll see."

"I guess so."

"Do you need anything else?" she fusses, looking around the room. "I'll find some clothes for you to wear. The bathroom is next door, and towels are in the wardrobe."

"I'm okay, thank you. Just tired."

Lola pulls me into another hug before I can protest. She holds me for several loaded seconds before releasing me and standing up, taking a moment to swipe a finger underneath her reddened eyes.

"Get some rest. We can talk more when you're feeling better. I'll find you some pain relievers too. Doc should have some stashed away."

"Thank you, Lola."

Dragging down the bedsheets to unveil the marshmallow softness of the mattress, I feel the adrenaline drain out of my body in an instant. I've only been awake for an hour or so, but I feel completely depleted already.

"Can you send Arianna up?"

"Don't worry. I'll keep an eye on her." Lola winks at me. "I need a hand in the greenhouse this afternoon."

"Oh, I guess that'll be okay."

Blowing me a kiss, she halts in the doorway. "I'm so happy that you're here, Willow. I never thought I'd have a chance to be your grandmother. I won't waste it."

Closing the door before I can answer her, I'm left alone in the room, wrapped in silence. Despite knowing that we made it here alive, terror still slinks down my spine.

At any moment, I expect the door to smash open and for Mr Sanchez to stride in with his favourite whip in hand to punish me for daring to leave him. I can't begin to imagine how angry he must be right now.

I'll never be safe, not even here.

Maybe coming to Briar Valley was a mistake.

CHAPTER 8
KILLIAN

TO LOVE SOMEBODY - THE HOWL
& THE HUM

GLARING at the lumpy pancake batter in the mixing bowl, I continue to take out my aggression on it. Once all the specks of flour have disintegrated, I use the ladle to pour four decent-sized puddles into the pan.

I've been in a foul mood since the coal-haired beauty flinched away from me a few days ago, believing that my hand was raised to strike her. That fucking hurt. Even though she's a total stranger and I shouldn't give a shit.

"Jesus Christ." Zach appears in the kitchen, pulling a paint-flecked blue t-shirt over his bare chest. "This is domesticated as hell."

"Good morning to you too."

"Where's your flowery apron, champ?"

"Don't test me, kid," I warn him. "I'll withhold breakfast rights."

"You wouldn't," he challenges.

Grabbing a wooden spoon from the utensil spot, I whip it across the kitchen with perfect aim. It hits him in the back of the head as he fills his coffee cup from the French press. Zach yelps, almost dropping his morning brew.

"Ow! That fucking hurt!"

"No bacon for you," I chastise. "I told you not to test me."

Zach mutters a curse and takes a seat at the breakfast bar connected to our messy, disorganised kitchen. He dumps far too much sugar in his coffee cup, wincing before he takes a sip and adds another huge spoonful.

"Real coffee doesn't need sweetening."

He facepalms. "Don't start this shit again, Kill."

"You eat like an eight-year-old with a sugar addiction."

"It's seven o'clock in the morning. Can you please give it a rest? I'm not awake yet and really don't need you on my ass."

Piling a chipped plate high with pancakes, I take pity on him and add some bacon from the frying pan. He immediately perks up and promptly covers his entire breakfast in golden syrup while offering me his best shit-eating grin.

"Eat up." I pile my own plate high with food. "We need to work on the Jacobsons' cabin this morning and clear the bonfire site from the party."

"Got it, boss," he drones with a mouthful of food.

"Is your brother up yet?"

"I heard him come to bed at three o'clock this morning. That's four days straight, Kill."

"I'm sure he napped in his art studio."

"Don't bullshit me. I'm not Lola," he replies, pointing his syrupy fork at me. "We need to do something about these depressive episodes. That last therapist seemed to help him."

"Until he refused to go anymore."

"Maybe we can talk him into going again?" Zach muses, pausing to lick his plate clean like an animal. "You'll probably have more luck than me."

"What's that supposed to mean?"

He shoots me a pointed look, swigging on his coffee. "Well, last time you threatened to bulldoze his art studio and build a home gym instead. That got him to come out."

"Lola went fucking ballistic when she heard."

"It's not like you were actually gonna do it."

That's what he thinks. I would've taken a wrecking ball to that damn studio if it got Micah to come back to us. None of us can pretend to fathom his complicated mind. As Zach's reclusive, introverted twin brother, we've always known that he's different.

Even when they were kids, Micah didn't smile or laugh like others did. It's like he was born without that part of his brain functioning properly. My parents used to call him a tortured artist, but it's far more than a lazy stereotype.

They adopted both of the twins when I was still a young kid. Their father, my mother's older brother, died of prostate cancer, leaving his two young sons behind as their mother was long gone by that point.

While we're actually first cousins, we grew up together like brothers. Zach and Micah are both twenty-four years old, but the six years between us feel like a lifetime.

I've assumed the role of parent since my folks died too, and all the responsibility that brings fell on my shoulders. Most days, I feel older than Lola.

"I'll talk to him," I concede. "No promises."

"Thanks, Kill. I just want to see him well again, you know? I get that he'll always struggle, but we can't pretend that how things are at the moment is normal."

"Yeah, I know. Come on, finish up."

Dumping our empty dishes by the sink to clean up later, we pull on our mud-splattered work boots and thick denim jackets before heading out into the early morning sunshine. The February air is crisp and refreshing.

I can hear Ryder's headache-inducing eighties music blaring from the garage behind their cabin from here. He's working on my truck, changing the oil and checking the engine. His work always entails him blasting terrible music that should remain in the past.

"Morning, campers," Zach calls out. "Can you kill the shit music, Ry?"

Ringlets appear from beneath the huge engine, and I can see that Ryder's boyish face is already covered in grease.

"Morning! Any breakfast left for me?"

I gesture towards the cabin behind me. "Left some pancakes and bacon for you next to the oven. Coffee's fresh too."

"Score," he replies. "Thanks, Kill."

Albie also appears from the back of the garage, lugging a secondhand tyre in his arms. Even at his advanced age, he's fighting fit and stronger than a fucking horse. He dumps it next to Ryder with a huff.

"You fellas heading out to the Jacobsons' cabin?"

"Yeah, we'll get the roofing fixed today." I grab my battered toolbox and drop it in a wheelbarrow. "Should be ready by next month."

He wipes his hands on a rag. "I'll let Aalia know. She's desperate to get out of temporary accommodation. The government ain't providing shit for her or the kids."

"We know they don't give two craps about refugees, no matter what their half-assed policies say." I check our equipment again, coming to a decision. "We'll work overtime."

"Yeah?" he echoes.

"Tell her it'll be ready by next week."

"You're a good one, Kill."

"Don't tell anyone. They'll think I've gone soft."

"Hardly," Zach comments as he lumbers past me.

Leaving them to their work, we traipse through the overgrown grass and clusters of wildflowers that surround the cobbled path heading down into the centre of Briar Valley. Zach walks ahead, leaving me to push the wheelbarrow.

Our two cabins are alone atop the hill that rises above the valley, aside from the smaller one across the road left abandoned since my folks died. We prefer it up here, away from the constant hum of activity.

Briar Valley used to be quiet.

Now, it's growing by the day.

Snaking back down into the valley, several more cobbled paths wind through the thick woodland. They lead to different corners of the town, with more cabins tucked into the foliage of pine trees, wild mushrooms and overgrown weeds.

It's easy to get lost here amidst the unrestricted chaos of nature. We're constantly expanding the town to accommodate new residents. Lola owns the land for miles around and grows more determined to take the world beneath her wing every day.

Stopping by the rusted metal supply shed where we keep the pre-cut wood, Zach helps me load a second wheelbarrow with the roof supplies, complaining the entire time.

"Morning, boys." Rachel stops behind us, her red curls pulled up into a ponytail. "Just heading to Lola's to do the monthly shopping list. Any requests?"

"Rach. Just the person I wanted to see." Zach beams up at her. "I'll take my usual snack order. Some shaving foam too, if you can get it."

"You put the money in the jar?"

"Sure did."

"Shaving foam?" I ask him. "You looking to impress someone?"

His grin is lopsided. "Maybe I have a hot date. How would you know? Oh, and Rach, Ryder wanted extra of those weird pretzel sticks he likes."

"Weird pretzel sticks," she recites, adding to her list. "Gotcha. Kill?"

"Lola's got my order."

"Cool. See you both later on."

Rachel vanishes with a wave, snaking towards Lola's cabin. The whole town chips in for a bulk order every month. There are some things we simply cannot grow or make ourselves here, and we source them from Highbridge instead.

With all the materials loaded up, we're ready to set off for the unfinished cabin to get to work. An excited squeal lances through the air before we can move, causing us both to freeze. I recognise the little spitfire's voice without looking.

"Look! Real flowers!"

"Arianna, keep it down. You'll disturb people."

"I don't care," she sasses. "Hurry up! Let's go!"

As Arianna barrels through the clearing in front of Lola's cabin, I watch the blur of ethereal blonde hair running fast on little legs. We haven't seen Willow for the past few days as the pair settled in and rested after their traumatic journey.

"And a butterfly!" the enthused voice bellows. "This country is awesome."

Arianna isn't looking where she's going. She traipses through the long grass, inspecting every flower and insect. Lola told us that she was the same when she took her to the vegetable patch the other morning.

Lunging forward to intercept her, I easily pluck Arianna off her feet while she's distracted. Tossing her over my shoulder, she shrieks loudly and laughs so hard, I'm worried she might actually pee on me.

"Gotcha, peanut."

"Killian!"

"You're very loud for this early in the morning."

She stares up at me with big, blue eyes that sucker punch me right in the damn chest. I don't usually like children—too loud and demanding—but there's something about this tiny speck of sass and fire that I find endearing.

"I missed you, giant."

I blink, taken aback. "Me?"

A smile blooms across her pink lips. "Where have you been?"

"Hiding, obviously."

"You're too big and fat to hide from me!"

Zach laughs his stupid ass off, and not even my glare shuts him up. Arianna joins in, and the cackling pair attract the attention of Josie and Stewart, two of our younger residents who are working on their allotment across the road.

"Zach," I grumble.

He fights to take a breath. "The look on your face. Priceless."

"I am not fat."

Arianna reaches out and pinches my waist, her fingers clamping down on a roll of skin. "Then why are you so big?"

"Someone has to do all the work around here, peanut."

Footsteps approach, slowly catching up to us. Willow appears in the clearing, still limping but looking a lot steadier on her feet than the last time we crossed paths. I still feel like a dick for how I treated her.

It wasn't anything personal. I'm not good with people, let alone strangers. Her secrets are practically written across her face, and it killed me to know that I couldn't wrangle them out of her, even by force.

"I'm so sorry," she rushes to apologise.

Zach shoots her a wave. "Hey, Willow."

"Morning, guys. Arianna, leave them alone."

Her voice is a melodic tinkle that licks against my hardened skin. She's a technicolour painting of purple and black bruises, but the swelling on her face has settled down enough to reveal her slightly crooked nose, naturally plump lips and effortless smile.

Fuck me.

She's gorgeous.

No, no. Don't go there.

My hands curl into fists at the stark bruising that still stains her slightly tanned skin. I want nothing more than to beat the shit out of whoever put the fear in her eyes. She takes one look at my face and shudders.

"Come on, Ari. Let's go and get some breakfast."

She really can't stand me. I've seriously fucked this up.

"No, Mummy." Arianna crosses her arms in defiance. "I want to stay out here with the pretty flowers and the giant."

"You can come back after you've eaten."

"I'm not hungry," she whines. "You can't make me eat."

Willow bites her lip as she awkwardly lowers to her knees, fighting hard to conceal her pain from us. Arms outstretched, she beckons Arianna into her welcoming embrace.

"Now, what have I said about mealtimes?"

Arianna's eyes are downcast. "That if I don't eat, I won't grow to be a big girl."

"Exactly. There's plenty of food here, so no excuses."

"But—"

"You want to grow up to be big and strong like Killian, the giant?"

Sparing me a doe-eyed look, Arianna unveils an innocent smile that steals my breath away. I don't know how to react, shuffling my feet like a damned idiot instead. These two are confusing the fuck out of me.

"Yes, I do," she declares.

"Then march yourself inside and eat the food Lola has made for you. No arguments, missus."

"Fine," Arianna drawls. "But then I'm coming back outside."

Willow watches as she races back across the clearing and inside Lola's cabin, already shouting for her great-grandmother's attention. I have no idea how Arianna's smart-mouthed attitude came from someone as reserved as Willow.

When she tries to stand back up, she gasps in pain and nearly falls flat on her perfectly round ass. I move lightning fast, catching Willow in my arms before her legs crumple beneath her. It happens before I know what I'm doing.

Her hazel eyes are blown wide, and she stares up at me, her glistening lips parted on a breath. The swirling depths of her brown and green irises threaten to breach every last shield I've constructed over the years.

"Thank you," she murmurs quietly.

"Don't mention it."

"You can let go of me now."

Clearing my suddenly thick throat, I set her back on her feet and step backwards. "You should take your own advice. Go let Lola feed you."

"Is that another order, Killian?"

There's a playful smirk stretched across her inviting mouth. A weird sense of tension is snapping between us. Jesus Christ. I think I preferred it when she was scared of me and flinching from my touch. That was at least simpler.

Right now, all I can think about is sealing my lips on hers and seeing if she tastes as sweet as she acts. I've already seen what's beneath her clothing, and the sight of her wearing my shirt has haunted my dreams ever since.

"You bet it is."

"Interesting," she quips. "I thought Lola told you off for doing that."

"Lola isn't here, is she?"

The need to drag her into my arms, pin her there for the rest of her goddamn life and feel her gorgeous curves in my hands is riding me hard. I don't know this woman, but I still want to claim her as my own.

What is wrong with me?

Zach stops by my side and flashes her a blazing grin. His presence snaps us both out of it, taking a step back from each other. Somehow, we gravitated closer. My fingers are still twitching with the urge to stroke her black curls.

"You're looking a bit better, babe. Finally got bored of Doc?"

Willow lets out a deep, rasping laugh. "More like I finally convinced him to let me out of bed. I'm perfectly fine."

"Fine?" I repeat incredulously. "Again with this?"

Zach sighs. "That's our cue to leave. Catcha later, Willow."

"Zach, she is not f—"

"Move," he cuts me off.

He drags me back towards our discarded supplies. I'd very much like to punch him in the fucking face. There is nothing fine about the mess that Willow showed up in. If she thinks it's okay to be in pain, we're gonna have a serious problem.

Willow disappears back into Lola's cabin as we set off, lugging the heavy wood towards the eastern stretch of the valley where our newest construction site awaits. As soon as she vanishes from sight, Zach bursts out laughing.

"You don't know how to do this, do you?"

"Do what?" I growl at him.

"Be charming."

"What the fuck are you going on about?"

"I've seen the way you look at her." His smile is oh-so-fucking smug. "You like her."

"What are we, six years old?"

"Just admit it. She's cute, right?"

If he weren't my cousin, his body would be thrown off the mountain and shattered to pieces already. No one would find him out here. My life would be so much more peaceful.

"You better get your scrawny ass up to that cabin before I rearrange your face for that woman to see. You can try and be charming then."

Zach glances at the cabin up ahead. "Reckon I could pull it off."

"You really are a brainless moron. How are we related?"

"Geez, thanks. You're so sweet, cuz."

"Shut the hell up and move or Micah won't have a twin anymore."

CHAPTER 9
WILLOW
PLEASE DON'T BE - HAZLETT

SITTING in one of the wicker armchairs that rest on Lola's wraparound porch, I watch the blazing sun sink on the horizon in a riot of fire-tinged colour. The sunsets here are so beautiful, illuminating the snow-capped mountain peaks and ridges.

It's the most incredible panoramic view, offering untouched beauty in every direction. Sheer rock faces, towering pine trees and the sharp, inclining slopes of Mount Helena surround the valley on all sides.

"Willow? You okay?"

Lola pokes her head out of the front door to catch my attention. She's dressed in her usual floral dress, another ingredient-speckled apron tied into place,

"I'm good. Is Arianna still asleep?"

"Passed out like a light," she confirms. "I must've tuckered her out with all that baking earlier on. Are you hungry?"

"No, I'm fine."

"Nonsense. I'll cook something for you to eat."

She disappears back inside before I can argue. It's taken me a few days to get used to her constant fussing, but in truth, I love being cared for by her. She seems determined to fulfil our every need, no matter how small.

Stretching my legs out, I take a deep breath of fresh forest air. It even tastes different from the raw humidity of Mexico. I didn't mind the heat, but something about this crisp coldness feels like home.

It's been a tiring day of introductions and explanations. Several different families from across the town have come to say hello as news of our arrival spread over the weekend. Briar Valley is more than I ever imagined.

There are so many generous people offering their counsel and support. Miranda let me look through her wardrobe and she organised more clothing for Arianna this morning, no questions asked.

The little devil has already ripped a hole in her borrowed jeans from chasing a butterfly until she tripped over. I chose the comfiest leggings she had and a loose linen shirt for my healing body. Everything is still pretty tender and sore.

Rachel appeared too, finding me buried in her sister's wardrobe, and organised several more outfits for me to take from her own clothing stash. I had to suppress tears as they sent me packing with a stuffed bag.

"Willow!" Lola's voice calls. "Come inside, poppet."

"Be right there."

As I stretch my limbs, the sun ducks behind the mountains and the few remaining people milling about disappear. I can imagine families sitting down, trading stories over platefuls of homemade food and surrounded by their smiling children.

It's so far from the life I've come to know. There's no violence here, no rules or punishments that threaten bitter consequences. Everyone is happy. Not necessarily all of the time, but they've found contentment. Maybe we could too.

"Thank you." I stare up at the stars becoming visible in the rising darkness. "Thank you for getting us here. Thank you for keeping me and my baby alive long enough to escape that hell."

The wedding band around my finger weighs heavily, strangling those first glimmers of hope. No matter how peaceful this slice of heaven is, the person Mr Sanchez made me into remains—a malleable puppet, shaped by his will and fists.

Darkness falls, and storm clouds begin to bubble on the horizon, growing heavy with thunderous intent. The weather is so volatile at this altitude, it can be blazing sunshine in one moment and a torrential downpour in the next.

The first fat raindrops hit the porch, then more follow. Fascinated, I toe off my shoes and walk barefoot down the grass. The rain is falling faster in thick sheets, soaking through my clothes and perfusing the soil to release a sweet, heady fragrance.

Overcome with emotion, I twirl in the wet grass, my head tilted back. Rain is drenching me, and the droplets burst on my tongue. It feels like some almighty force is peering down, granting me this moment of realisation amidst the growing storm.

"I'm free now," I whisper, smiling to myself like a madwoman. "We're safe. We never have to go back."

The screaming wind answers me—howling in its own celebration. Even something as simple as standing fully clothed amidst a rainstorm is proof of the precious freedom I've gained. Never again will I take such a small luxury for granted.

Footsteps slap through the rain, interrupting my peace. I crash back into my body, realising how insane I must look. A figure has emerged from the nearby trees, shivering as he tightens his coat against the rain.

He's heading straight for me, his face concealed by the hood of his black puffer jacket. Short, stocky and built with hard-earned lines of muscle that bulge through his loose, blue jeans, his heavy gait betrays him.

I nearly collapse with relief when he comes close enough for me to recognise his light-brown hair, unshaved stubble and gentle, rounded features softened by two perfect dimples that match his moss-green eyes.

"Zach? What are you doing?"

His eyes dart about furtively. There's something about him that's different. Rather than the flirtatious confidence that usually accompanies his presence, now he seems strangely timid and afraid to even make eye contact.

"I'm not Zach," his treacle-like voice explains, rasping with disuse. "Wrong brother."

We stare at each other in the middle of the rainfall. I realise that his caramel hair is actually a bit longer, curling around the base of his skull and ears. Instead of smiling with open curiosity and warmth, the look on his face is one of apprehension.

Even his clothes are different now that I'm paying attention. His blue jeans are straight cut, and his t-shirt is splattered with paint. There's also a shining silver ring pierced through his strong nose, matching his rougher, edgier persona.

"You're not?"

"I'm Micah," he mutters, rubbing the back of his neck. "We haven't met."

"Micah?"

His green eyes barely meet mine before darting away again. "Twins."

Standing in front of him, it's now completely obvious to me. This person couldn't look less like Zach even if he tried, despite their matching exteriors. I can see the darkness swirling amidst his malachite irises, unlike his brother's motiveless warmth.

"I'm so sorry. I didn't know."

"And you are?" he asks awkwardly.

"Uh, I'm Willow. New around here."

He looks longingly into the distance, like he can't wait to get far away from me. I inch backwards, feeling totally embarrassed.

"I have to get back inside."

Micah nods and turns on his heel without saying goodbye. I watch him stalk away, his short, powerful legs teetering in the rising winds. He cuts a stark figure, alone in the night and shrouded in a cloak of sadness.

Shaking off the weird encounter, I head back inside. Rain falls from my long, raven-coloured hair as I sneak upstairs to dry off and check on Arianna. She's right where I left her, curled up in a tight ball in the middle of our double bed, snoring her little head off.

I stroke her hair back. "Sleep tight."

Swapping out my wet clothes for a comfortable pair of Miranda's sweats and a loose, blue t-shirt that covers my bruises, I leave Arianna to sleep and decide to poke around while Lola cooks. I haven't had much of a chance to explore yet.

On this floor, there are a total of four generous bedrooms. Lola sleeps next door—she insisted on having us close by. There are three bathrooms, one shared and two ensuite, all lined with oak units and slate tiles that contrast the gleaming, clawfoot bathtubs.

Trailing my fingers along the wall, I inspect the rows of framed photographs. Lola is featured in many, gardening or helping paint cabins, surrounded by smiling adopted family and friends. She looks younger in most of them, but her radiant smile hasn't changed over the years.

It's clear her happiness comes from one thing—Briar Valley and its colourful collection of residents seeking refuge in the mountains. Pausing at the final photograph, my heart drops to my stomach. I recognise this person.

Lola is posing with another man, their arms wrapped around each other. They wear loving smiles and between them, a small, slim boy with a shock of black hair refuses to play along. His mouth is pulled down with visible boredom.

It's my dad.

It hurts to see his younger self with a perfect family surrounding him. The man I knew never talked of his parents, let alone their lives here in Briar Valley. He had parents. A loving family. A whole life. I don't need Lola to tell me what happened.

Drugs.

He was an addict.

Instead of telling me about my grandparents and raising me as a father should, he chose to bring me up in a world of pain and disappointment. I grew up around discarded needles and tarnished spoons, our meagre money fettered away on more narcotics.

Where other kids my age had parents who picked them up from school and loved the very bones of them, I had nothing. For my father, I didn't exist. All he wanted was to get high and forget that Mum had left us, destitute and heartbroken.

If it weren't for him and the debts he accumulated over years of drug abuse, I never would've started stripping at sixteen. The mounting bills he left behind fell on my shoulders to pay. His death was mine too, in so many ways.

My future died with him.

Fleeing the bad memories, I head up to the third floor where Lola's home office resides. It's spacious and light, with a gabled roof and warm sconces built into the beams. She has lots of gardening books and a filing system for the town's paperwork, neatly organised into the attic space.

There's a computer too. Heart racing, I sit down and wiggle the mouse. It powers up on a cooking website that she must've been looking at for recipes. Anticipation thrums beneath my skin as I open up a new search tab.

Mr Sanchez's high-profile reputation in the real estate business grants him certain privileges. Most of his work takes place in the States, but he prefers to live in the freedom of Mexico. It's easier to conceal his crimes that way, far from any public scrutiny.

He sells luxurious properties for extortionate fees. Many of his clients are celebrities, looking for a slice of heaven to expend their hideous wealth on. As a result, he's become a pseudo-celebrity himself. The estate agent and property developer for the stars.

With shaking hands, I type his name and hit enter before I can talk myself out of it. His website floods the screen, and I almost swallow my tongue from fright. It's a slick, glossy marketing campaign that matches his spotless image.

Sanchez Real Estate is a flawless brand, covering properties from Los Angeles to New York, San Francisco to Seattle. He caters to some of the most illustrious clients in the world and banks every drop of money, wealth and power that it provides him.

Scanning the rest of the results, my blood chills when I spot a suggested news article. It looks like some stupid gossip site, the kind of thing I used to drool over as a nosy teenager. Clicking on the article, dated a decade ago, I want to be sick.

There were no photographs from our wedding. It was a private affair on the well-guarded grounds of Sanchez Mansion, tucked away in an expensive corner of Mexico City. I heard the whispers that day from his staff as they watched on, silent and culpable.

Another wife.

I hope this one lasts longer.

It was the single worst day of my life, even beating out the late, snow-swept night I found my father dead in a clutter of discarded drug paraphernalia. Mr Sanchez was determined to rival that slice of despair with his own personal brand of pure evil.

I can still taste the tears that soaked my cheeks as he dragged me to his playroom for the very first time. There was no point in running, even when he tore my flimsy white dress and yelled vicious curses that broke my courage before he broke the rest of me.

Sixteen years old.

A child to anyone else.

It didn't stop him. From the conveyor belt of women he shipped in for years after our wedding, it became clear that Mr Sanchez likes them young. Trafficking me across the globe against my will wasn't enough for him.

He grew tired of breaking me, over and over again. No amount of depravity was ever enough for him. Abandoning the computer, I try to stand and end up falling to my knees. My lungs are so tight, so constricted, that I feel like my chest is on fire.

The walls are closing in on me as Lola's office melts away, replaced by the familiar dark-red walls of the playroom. What if he somehow tracked our movements? Or if he uses his fortune to hunt us down? I know how determined he is when it comes to inflicting misery.

As much as I fucking hate myself to admit it, I would rather take Arianna and plunge us both off a cliff before returning there. At least we'd both be safe in death. He can't hurt my little girl if she's dead at my side instead.

"Willow? You up here?"

Creaking footsteps ascend the steep staircase up to Lola's office. I tighten my arms around my trembling legs, making myself small and invisible. It doesn't stop Zach from kneeling down in front of me, his fruity scent and light voice revealing his identity.

"Open your eyes, babe."

"Go away," I squeeze out.

"Not happening."

Gentle fingertips coast along my jawline, encouraging me to look up at him. When I manage to pry my eyes open, I'm looking into the green depths of Zach's orbs. The forest stares back at me in a canopy of olive-tinged vines.

"What are you doing here?" I whisper.

"Arianna woke up," he explains with a faint smile. "She couldn't find you. I was talking to Lola when she came downstairs crying."

"Is she okay? Let me up."

"Lola's got it under control." His hands grip my arms, preventing me from running away. "I'm more concerned about you. What are you doing up here alone?"

Knocked off balance by the soft croon of his voice, I find no desire within me to lie. Something about Zach invites trust; he's non-threatening in every sense of the word. In fact, there's an almost child like lilt to his smile.

"I was making sure we're safe."

"How?" he asks.

"My husband hasn't reported our absence to the authorities. The media would know by now if he had. We'd be splashed all over the news."

"The media? Why?" Zach frowns.

"He's kind of a big deal in the business world."

A tangled strand of light-brown hair falls across his eyes, and I fight the urge to swipe it aside so I can drown in the warmth of his presence again. The realisation is like a cold bucket of water on my head. I can't touch him.

I'm running from a sadistic son of a bitch with enough money and power to bend the will of God if it pleases him to do so. The last thing I need is another person up in my business, making this mess even more complicated.

"Why did you come looking for me?" I ask him instead.

Zach shrugs, flashing a cute dimple. "I wanted to make sure that you're okay."

"But why do you care? Any of you?"

Sitting back on his haunches, his brows furrow. "Because… why wouldn't we? I know you've been relying on yourself for a long time, but here in Briar Valley, we're a family."

"I don't have a family."

"That's not true." His widening smile is simple and honest. "If you think Lola would let you leave now, you've got another thing coming."

I don't know this man. In fact, I don't know any of them, but I've allowed myself to get comfortable already. Nothing is guaranteed in life. I can't let my guard down. It will only hurt more when this temporary peace is ripped away from me.

"Please move out of my way." I struggle to my feet, aiming to dodge past him. "I don't need you to care about me."

Zach's eyes soften with sadness. "I think that you do."

"Stop trying to get in my head."

"Maybe you need some company in there, Willow. Maybe even some help. You should let someone in for once."

I throw my hands up in exasperation. "Are you calling me crazy now?"

"I'm saying that we want to help you."

"And I'm saying that I don't need your help."

He grabs my arm again when I try to squeeze past. His grip is tight enough for me to flinch as the past slams into me. I drop my eyes, making myself small and insignificant. Silent. Breakable. Just like the monster wanted.

If I didn't fight, it would always end quicker. Mr Sanchez would grow bored of the games and crawl on top of me, his breath hot and disgusting. It felt wrong, speeding the whole process up and encouraging the inevitable violation.

Sometimes, I just wanted it all to be over. Enough to let the unthinkable happen. Does that make me at fault, somehow? Did I want it? If anyone else asked me this, I'd never allow a victim to think like that. But the same logic doesn't always apply to ourselves.

Zach quickly releases me. "Willow?"

My body moves on instinct to assume the position that's been ingrained in me through years of training. Kneeling on the floor with my palms facing up on my legs, I keep my head lowered and lips sealed.

The world fades away as my eyes close, preparing for the first blow. I can't hold back a pained gasp as two big hands cup my tear-stained cheeks. It hurts to be touched, even with good intent. Zach's thumbs softly stroke my skin, and his voice filters in.

"Who did this to you?"

All I can do is shake my head.

"Breathe for me, babe. I've got you."

"Zach... I c-can't... do this."

"Just listen to my voice. That's all."

His arms wind around my shivering body, and he sinks to the floor beside me. I'm pulled into his lap, and the solid press of his built frame beneath me offers a welcome distraction from the billowing darkness trying to strangle me.

He smells so good, like the fresh pomegranates and tropical fruit I used to look forward to for breakfast. On him, the fragrance is a tantalising promise. The soothing scent drags me from the depths of my nightmare and allows me to take a deep inhale.

"You're doing good," he praises in a gentle croon. "Keep breathing nice and deep for me. Nobody is going to hurt you. We're safe up here."

"Not s-safe, n-nowhere is safe."

Rubbing circles into my back, he begins to rock me back and forth like I'm a scared child in need of comfort. I clutch his t-shirt even tighter, dragging in ragged breaths. Arianna used to crawl into my lap like this when she was younger.

With the roles reversed, my head is spinning.

I've never been cared for.

It feels… good.

"There we go," he murmurs, his hand moving up to stroke my curly hair instead. "You're doing good. Keep breathing slowly."

Using his words to focus, I block out everything else. The pain. The fear. Endless fears and anxieties, the never-ending line of what-if scenarios threatening to unhinge my fragile sanity. None of it matters when I'm in his arms.

"You're here. You're safe."

He repeats it over and over again, a soothing mantra that combats the screaming voice telling me to pack up, grab Arianna and hightail it out of here to some place where no one knows my name.

I'm not sure how long we sit tangled on the floor for, wrapped up in each other with an unnerving amount of intimacy for people that met not long ago. It's like Zach knows exactly what I need. My eyes grow heavy as the adrenaline rushes out of me.

I'm completely slumped against him, unable to hold my own head up with no energy left inside of me. His heartbeat is a steady roar against my ear, so loud it almost vibrates.

Buddum. Buddum. Buddum.

"Zach."

His hand stills in my hair as he ceases massaging my scalp. "Yeah, babe? You back with me?"

"Kinda. Your heart is beating really fast."

"You scared me for a moment there."

"I scared myself. Sorry, things just got a bit much."

"Don't worry about it."

But still, his arms don't move to release me. He's cuddling me so close, I can feel the rise and fall of his chest with each inhale he takes. I've never held someone close enough to experience their breath before. No one beyond Arianna.

"How did you know?"

"Hmm?" Zach hums.

I manage to lift my head up and meet his eyes. "How did you know how to help me?"

"Oh, that." He unleashes a crooked smile that makes my heart rate triple. "My brother, Micah, has some issues. He suffered from pretty bad panic attacks for a long time."

"That's rough."

"It was. I always knew when he needed help, though. It's a twin thing."

"Twin thing?" I repeat.

"We used to be close. I always knew when he was in trouble."

Helping me to stand up, Zach places me back on my feet. My legs are still trembling, but he doesn't release my hand as he clambers up as well. Our fingers have somehow slid together, interlinked in an unbreakable knot.

"You good?" he double-checks.

"Think so."

"Then let's go find your girl. She'll be missing her mama."

With Zach's presence anchoring me back down, I have the strength to leave the office and my overwhelming terror behind. Who would possibly dare to hurt us with him at my side? Even sweet and sensitive, he still has the raw force of a warrior.

I feel safe with him.

Safer than I've ever felt in my life.

CHAPTER 10
WILLOW
THE ONLY - SASHA ALEX SLOAN

"MUMMY! TIME TO WAKE UP!"

"Go back to sleep," I groan.

"No! We've been in bed all day. I'm bored."

Grabbing the pillow that's covering my head, Arianna exposes my eyes to the harsh glare of sunlight. It's long past lunchtime. The last couple of nights have been riddled with sweat-soaked nightmares. Even Arianna couldn't sleep through my screaming.

"Mummy! Let's go!"

With Arianna tugging on my arm, I nearly fall out of the bed. Rubbing my eyes, I manage to get my feet beneath me with a pained grunt. Arianna peers up at me, and her blue eyes are on the verge of spilling tears.

"Did I hurt you?" she worries.

"No, of course not. I'm getting better, baby."

"And you won't be sick anymore?"

Stroking her sleep-rumpled blonde hair, I run a fingertip down the slope of her tiny nose. "What do you mean?"

"Daddy always said I'm too loud. Am I too loud? Do you want me to be quiet?"

Heart aching, I crush her against my chest. "You can be as loud as you want. No more being quiet. Shout, laugh and sing even more than Princess Elsa, if that's what you want to do."

"Better than Elsa?" Arianna grins.

"And even more beautiful, my princess."

"Well, Princess Elsa was locked inside too," she sasses.

Her snarky, six-year-old attitude is growing with each day. She's never been prone to temper tantrums or talking back, but she's getting more comfortable talking and questioning the world around her. In such a short space of time, the change is huge.

"Then I suppose we should go outside, huh?" I give in.

"Yay! I want to wear my new boots that Grams gave me."

Racing over to our sparse wardrobe in the corner of the bedroom, she digs around inside and reappears with a pair of bright-red boots that I've never seen before.

"Grams?"

"Lola is your grandma," Arianna points out.

"Well, yeah. But not really."

"Why not?"

I locate some clothes to pull on. "We haven't seen each other for a long time, Ari. Sometimes, adults have to figure stuff out."

"Grams loves us," she deadpans. "What's there to figure out?"

There's no arguing with that. Arianna's view on the world's complexities is simplistic, but perhaps it's a good thing that she isn't swayed by the same doubts and fears that adults can't ignore. Her love isn't conditional on any expectations.

After grabbing a cable-knit cardigan to cover the black handprints still visible on my arms, I help Arianna into her new shoes. She races ahead of me, thudding down the staircase and breaking outside without a second glance.

"Ari! Be careful."

"I will!" she yells back.

The smile on her face as she steps out into the sunshine makes it all worth it. Everything I endured for the past ten years. That's what I fought so hard for, that smile right there. It's the most incredible sight, and I'll never grow tired of seeing it.

Outside the cabin, she races through the long grass and chases a stray butterfly that's dancing amidst the blooming wildflowers. I sit down on the bottom step of the wraparound porch, content to watch her play. The town is hard at work around us, as usual.

I'm coming to recognise there's a natural sense of routine around here. No schedules or rules are needed though. Everyone has a part to play and gets on with the work without complaint, all contributing to the smooth running of the town.

Lola is the taskmaster, and Albie acts as her iron fist. They keep Briar Valley spick and span, from ordering in supplies and organising the various greenhouses and allotments that provide food to each household, to maintaining the books that pay for it all.

"Mummy, look!" Arianna's hands are cupped around a butterfly that she's caught. "It's so pretty and colourful. Can I keep it?"

"No, Ari. You have to let it go."

"Why?" she whines.

"It belongs outside, baby."

With a grumble, she opens her hands, and the butterfly takes flight. Her enthused gaze follows it up into the air, escaping to a nearby patch of sunflowers sprouting through the earth. I caught her trying to eat one the other day too.

"I can't take another family right now." Lola's voice floats through the open front door from the phone call she's taking in the living room. "We're at capacity."

There's a brief pause, before she curses.

"Alright, send me the information. I'll take a look."

Lola rehomes people in need, from refugees to displaced families fleeing flooding or debt. With minimal funding and an iron will of determination, she gives them a new life, safety and the warmth of a caring community.

Driving past in his age-spotted truck, Albie waves at me from the driver's seat. He's transporting a huge, ride-on lawn mower in the back. Next to him, Ryder is riding shotgun with a pair of shades shielding his eyes from the sunshine.

"Hey, Willow!" he shouts.

I wave back with a smile. "Hi."

Ryder is the resident gearhead. He's lived in the valley for most of his life after being raised by his uncle. I've heard that his boyfriend is a criminal investigator working hundreds of miles away in London. He rarely makes it out to Briar Valley.

Asking Albie to pull up at the edge of the clearing, Ryder hops out and bounds over to me with long, loping strides. He's ridiculously tall. Stopping to ruffle Arianna's hair on the way past, she's too distracted by the flowers around her, staining her clothes with pollen.

"How's it going?" Ryder stops at the steps.

"We're good." I gesture to his uncle. "Going somewhere?"

"Just finished my latest job. The lawnmower is going back to Highbridge. I'll be glad to see the back of that piece of shit. It was a nightmare to repair."

"Why don't they take it to a mechanic in town?"

"Because I'm the best around and everyone knows it," Ryder answers confidently. "Hell of a job getting it up the mountain though."

"You're so modest."

He shrugs, unfazed. "I've been working with engines and cars for my whole life. Albie taught me everything I know. We're lucky to have decent clients who pay well."

"Can I ask you a couple of things?" I glance around. "In confidence?"

His smile expands into a conspiratorial grin. "Oh, gossip. Fire away."

"Okay, so Rachel and Miranda. Sisters."

"Yep," Ryder confirms.

"But they're both with Doc? Like… *with with* him?"

"Been married nearly fifteen years. Not legally, of course. But they've been together forever as a kind of shared unit. Mia, Henry and Phoebe all belong to them."

I figured as much, having observed their behaviour over the past week or so. Rachel and Miranda both clearly love Doc with everything they have. Their kids are lovely as well, all offering their clothing and toys to Arianna.

"You look a bit mind blown right now." Ryder snorts.

"Not at all. It's just a bit unconventional."

"Sure, but not around here. We don't judge. People can live however they want."

"And it works?"

"So far," he replies with a wink. "What's the other question?"

Feeling myself flush pink, I curse my curiosity. Ever since I ran into Zach's sullen, antisocial twin in the middle of the storm, I've been dying to know more about the three gruff men that have captured my attention.

"I met Micah. He seems interesting."

This time, Ryder howls in amusement.

"That's not the word most would use."

"I was trying to be polite," I retort, biting back laughter. "What's the deal with those three? Are you related to them too?"

"Nah. Just neighbours, though, we've been best friends for as long as I can remember. Killian grew up here and the twins were adopted by his folks when they were kids."

"Where are Killian's parents?"

His smile falters, grief filtering across his face. "They passed away years ago, hiking Mount Helena. There was a freak accident. Killian was eighteen at the time."

"Shit. That's awful."

"Yeah, it was pretty rough on Killian for a long time. He kinda closed himself off after that, but the twins were still underage and ended up being entrusted to him."

That explains so much—Killian's abrasive attitude and obvious sense of mistrust, his clear protective instincts and inability to tolerate other people's pain. Beneath his barked words and prickly exterior, he's simply trying to protect the family he has left.

"Listen, I should get going." Ryder jabs a thumb over his shoulder. "You need anything picked up from town while I'm there?"

"Oh, I don't think so."

"Alright. Take it easy, Willow."

"Be careful on that mountain road."

"Worried about us?" He chuckles.

I wave his antics off. "Whatever."

Still laughing to himself, he shoots me a final wink before jogging back over to the truck and climbing inside. The pair disappear, their taillights swallowed by trees. With the new information, I have an idea of all the residents in Briar Valley.

The other cabins are occupied by various families, all with their own colourful stories. Marilyn and her husband, Harold, moved here twenty years ago after going bankrupt and fleeing loan sharks. Lola gave them a chance to rebuild, beyond their credit histories.

Their neighbours, Andrea and Theodore, lost a daughter to terminal illness in the nineties. They moved to town to escape the reminders of their loss and found a new family here, going on to have two more children.

I've listened to every word and scrap of information that's been given to me in the time we've spent hiding out here. Nothing is without struggle in the valley, but I've come to realise that the residents fight for the family they've chosen in this tree-lined paradise.

"Poppet?" Lola rests a careful hand on my shoulder.

Startled, I plaster on a smile. "Yeah?"

"You're up late. Everything okay?"

"Oh, fine. Just tired. I'm sorry."

"There's no need to apologise," she replies, pocketing her phone in her apron. "I just wanted to make sure you're feeling okay. I can get Doc to look you over?"

"I'm alright, Lola. You don't need to worry."

"Very well," she submits, though her beady eyes still survey me. "I see Arianna is enjoying her new boots. I asked Albie to pick them up in town last week."

"You're spoiling her."

Lola looks hopelessly sad as she looks away from me to watch Arianna dancing through the grass. It hurts me to see her grief. She hides it so well in front of everyone else.

"I didn't get the chance to do any of this for you. All I ever wanted was to be a grandmother. It's the least I can do now."

Splashing into a disappearing rain puddle, Arianna soaks through the floral dress and tights she decided to wear. Lola sinks down on the step next to me, laughing at the mess she's making of herself.

"She's so beautiful. I see so much of your grandfather in her."

"You do?" I glance at her.

"Oh, yes." She presses her lips together, tears welling up in her eyes. "I wish he were here to see you come home. It would have meant the world to him."

My throat thickens with emotion. "What was he like?"

Lola wipes under her eyes. "He was the love of my life. We met in the early sixties at a freedom march, calling for equal rights. I still remember the moment I saw him in his tie-dyed shirt and sunglasses."

Looking down at her wrinkled hand, I note the wedding ring still in place, even after all these years. If there's one thing I've learned about Lola, it's her steadfast devotion to everything she does. Including taking care of those she loves.

"Losing your dad broke his heart," she chokes out.

A chill settles over me at the mention of my useless father. I wring my hands together, biting back the urge to tell her to stop, because a broken part of me wants to know what we missed out on for all these years.

"We loved your dad so much, but it wasn't enough. We could barely make ends meet back in the early days of Briar Valley. He grew up and started mixing with the wrong crowd in the city. The drugs came later, and that was it."

"I used to think he loved me," I admit in a whisper. "Even when he forgot to feed me because he was too high, or when he sold my toys to buy more drugs. When he died and left me alone in the world, I realised I was wrong. He never did."

"What happened, Willow?" Lola seizes hold of my hand. "The police called us, but we were too late. You were already gone. We searched everywhere, and there was nothing."

"I didn't want to end up in foster care, so I took off."

She shakes her head, expression cracked with regret. "Oh, Willow. I sent that letter as a last resort, just in case you ever returned and found it."

Fiddling with a loose thread in my cardigan, I shrug. "I ran as far and as fast as I could. Dad owed people money. I took to the streets instead, begging for scraps of food."

"Christ," she curses.

"When I thought it was safe to return home, I'd been homeless for nearly three months. I found your letter in the ruins of our home. A friend of his had turned it into a drug den."

"Why didn't you come?" Lola urges. "We would have looked after you."

"I'm sorry, but I didn't want to find you. I was too angry with everyone."

She sucks in a breath, wiping away more gleaming tears. I don't want to hurt her, but I owe her the truth, at least. Choosing to ignore that desperate letter was the worst mistake I ever made. I had no idea back then where my life was headed.

"I'm so sorry, Willow." She sniffles loudly. "We failed you. I should've searched harder. You were all alone in the world."

"It isn't your fault."

"He was my son, my responsibility."

I take her hand in mine. "You're being too hard on yourself."

"I shouldn't have accepted him leaving home and cutting all contact with us. We didn't know you existed until the police told us that he left a child behind."

The bright, open space of the valley is a cruel taunt compared to the dark memories festering inside of me. Dad was so young, lost and far from home. He couldn't look after a child. That didn't stop me from being born and suffering right along with him though.

"How did you survive?" Lola asks quietly.

Pulling my hand free from hers, my own wedding ring is revealed. I still can't bring myself to remove it. I'm too scared the dream will lift and in the cold light of day, I'll wake up back in that dreaded mansion again.

"I didn't survive," I answer without emotion. "I was married by the time I was sixteen. I had Arianna four years later. She became my reason for surviving each day."

"Sixteen?" she gasps.

"I didn't have a whole lot of choice in it."

Lola doesn't know quite how to respond, staring at me with a look of pure horror twisting her features. Part of me wants to tell her everything, the whole horrid tale, but I can't face delving into the past again.

Not yet.

I just want to forget.

Unable to continue the conversation, I walk down the steps to approach Arianna. She's sitting amongst the blooming flowers, their petals opening with the first whispers of spring in the air. Laying down next to her in the long grass, I stare up at the sky.

Lola doesn't dare follow. I know she's watching us both from her perch on the steps, too flabbergasted to wrap her head around the truth of our family. All these years, she's saved countless families in need of a lifeline. All but her own.

Arianna weaves together a crown of daisies and drapes it over me. "For you."

"Thanks, baby."

Her beaming smile grows even bigger as someone approaches us, their intimidatingly loud footsteps making the ground shake. A huge, dark shadow falls over us both.

"Damn, peanut. You're picking all my flowers."

Trunk-like legs halt beside me, and I shield my eyes with my hand to stare up at Killian through the beams of sunshine. His long, white-blonde locks are pulled back in a sloppy knot, highlighting his beard and firm jawline.

"You can grow some more," she replies cheekily.

Killian booms a laugh. It sounds so strange emanating from him. I'm used to every other word from his mouth being a threat or order. For a moment, I think I'm dreaming as he flashes bright-white teeth. He's smirking down at me.

"What are you smiling at?" I snark.

"You're covered in daisies."

"Her fault."

I narrow my eyes at Arianna, and she giggles even harder. Crouching beside us, Killian struggles to fold his legs beneath him. His quads bulge against the worn denim of his jeans. They're falling apart, full of holes and in need of a good wash.

To my shock, he stretches out to lie down in the grass next to me. Arianna wastes no time adorning him with his own tiny daisy crown. Killian grumbles a complaint but doesn't stop her from dressing him in flowers.

"Now we match," I whisper to him.

"If anyone sees me in this shit, my reputation is ruined."

"You're the one that laid down. Suck it up."

Still grumbling, his cinnamon-soaked eyes slide over to me. I hold my breath as he seizes a strand of my hair and tucks it behind my ear, looking puzzled by his own reaction. I'm terrified to breathe in case the spell breaks.

"I came to ask you to come for dinner tomorrow. In our cabin."

"Dinner?" I repeat, dumbfounded.

"Both of you."

"In your cabin? Dinner?"

"Am I speaking French or something?" he rasps.

"I'm just surprised that you want to let us girls into your bachelor pad. Does this mean you'll pick up the dirty flannel shirts from your bathroom floor?"

"What?" Killian's mouth falls open in outrage. "Who told you that? I do not leave my shirts on the floor."

"Nobody."

"It was Ryder, wasn't it?"

"I'm saying nothing," I reply lightly.

"That asshole. I'm gonna run him over with my truck. He's the one who leaves dirty socks everywhere. Even in our damn cabin, and he doesn't live there."

"I'm sure Lola would have something to say about you murdering Ryder in broad daylight. Who will run the garage?"

Killian snorts. "Literally anyone else."

Clambering back onto his boot-covered feet, Killian looks down at me, his shadow blotting out the sunlight and submerging me in darkness. The look he trains me with sets a fire in my belly that I don't understand.

"Dinner tomorrow, seven o'clock. No buts." His eyes dart to Arianna, then back to me. "Wear the daisy crown if you want, princess."

"Yay!" Arianna exclaims. "I want to eat in the giant's cabin."

She's far too attached to this overbearing asshole for my liking. He knows it too, her declaration making his eyes crinkle in that satisfied, smug way that accompanies his rare smiles.

"I'll pick up my washing," he adds. "Don't be late."

I'm sure the sound of my laughter follows him all the way home.

CHAPTER 11
ZACH

FLAWS - BASTILLE

"LET ME GET THIS STRAIGHT."

"Again, Zach?" Killian moans.

I take a swig of beer. "I'm just curious how this situation came about. You are infamously the most unsociable person I've ever had the displeasure of meeting, cuz."

Killian's scowl would set whole fields of crops alight. "You know, I'm sure Lola would understand if I murdered you after Ryder and buried your body in the allotment."

"Me and Ryder in one day, huh?"

"Sounds like a fucking dream to me."

"You're really stocking up on good fertiliser for the summer."

"Quality annoying asshole fertiliser, sure." He flicks off the kitchen tap, soaking dirty dishes in water. "I could sell it in town and make a hell of a profit."

"You're a bit sadistic, you know?"

Killian takes a pull from his own beer. We're working together in the kitchen to roast one of the chickens from the town's coop that he shot last night, while the potatoes and vegetables roast in the oven.

"Noted," he submits.

I'm not much of a cook. Killian has always kept us fed, clothed and well looked after, ever since our aunt and uncle passed away. Nobody asked him to, but he took me and Micah under his wing and never turned his back on us, death threats aside.

Killian lost both of his parents that day and gained the responsibility of two young boys who needed someone to look up to. He didn't even stop to grieve before getting to work. That's just who he is. I still remember it clearly.

"Gravy," he realises.

"Make extra. You know it's my favourite."

"Yeah, I know. You and Micah drink it like water."

Returning to his place of power at the overflowing oven top, Killian focuses on mixing gravy granules with boiling water and loading it into a saucepan. This would be so much easier if Grams was cooking. She's much better than us at it.

"You think he'll make an appearance tonight?"

Killian looks up. "Micah?"

I nod back.

"I dunno, kid." He stirs his gravy with a shrug. "He's retreated back into his studio this week. I spoke to Doctor Holmes. She's happy to take him on as a client again."

"We just have to convince him to go there."

"Basically."

Grabbing plates, cutlery and hand-sewn napkins that Lola made for us last Christmas, I lay the table. We rarely sit here to eat dinner, usually preferring the sofa or outside in the summer. Entertaining guests is an even rarer occurrence.

None of us have much luck convincing my brother to do anything, let alone speaking to a therapist he has no interest in working with. He lives on his own plane of existence, far from our reach. Not even I can get through to him.

"Maybe Lola could talk him around?" I suggest hopefully.

"Don't get your hopes up. He won't speak to anyone."

A timid knock at the front door interrupts our conversation. Both of our gazes immediately zip there, and the tension in the room explodes. Killian would never admit it, but I can see that he's nervous. This dinner was his idea.

I have never seen my cousin date or even show a remote interest in women. He's always been content to devote his life to the town and nothing else. That's why the offer of dinner with Willow nearly caused me to fall over when he told me.

"I'll get it, shall I?" I glance around the open-plan living room and kitchen. "This place is a mess, Kill."

"We're guys," he argues. "She'll understand."

"Lola would kill us both if she saw this bomb site."

"I'm not your mother. Clean your own crap up. Don't I do enough around here?"

Rolling my eyes at him, I smooth my unbuttoned, loose blue shirt and jeans, throwing the door open before I can chicken out. A blur of blonde hair rushes straight at me. I stumble back to catch Arianna before she bowls me over.

"Zach!"

"Hey, squirt."

She clings to me like a spider monkey, using her weight to force me to crouch down so she can press her lips to my cheek. "I missed you."

I brush a stubbly kiss against her skin in return. "Missed you too, Ari. Go and attack Killian now. Make sure to smother him in kisses."

Placing her back on her little feet, I watch as she launches herself at the giant in the kitchen next. He barely hesitates before picking her up. I swear, this alien parasite living inside my cousin's body is really starting to freak me out.

"Killian!"

"Peanut," he greets. "What did I tell you about running everywhere?"

"That I should always be ready to throw a punch to go with it?"

"Kill." I gape at him.

"That's my girl." He tucks hair behind her ear, clearly proud of himself. "Go on, make yourself at home. Dinner's almost ready."

Standing in the doorway, Willow is silent. I drink her in, from her slightly curling, midnight black hair that contrasts the olive-toned shine of her skin, to the light yellow dress she's wearing that I recognise from Miranda's wardrobe.

Her body begs to be touched from the rounded curves of her hips and to the sharp angles that carve her breathtakingly beautiful face. She's full-chested and fills her clothing in all the right places. Fuck. I'm staring now.

"Willow! Come in."

Her eyes dart up to mine. "Zach… thanks for the invite."

Disregarding the palpable tension, I engulf her in a hug, only remembering her injuries when she squeaks in pain.

"Sorry," I quickly blurt.

"It's okay. How was your day?"

"Better for seeing you."

I ignore Killian's exasperated scoff.

"Oh." Willow's cheeks blush pink. "Well, I'm happy to see you guys too."

Patting my arm, she walks past me and spares Killian an awkward smile of greeting. He nods back, hiding behind the safety of the oven and various bubbling saucepans. Touchy-feely isn't really his style, though I'm beginning to doubt that too.

"Wow," Willow exclaims.

She's looking around our home in awe. Killian and his father built the cabin with the intention of us all living together when we were older, leaving them to retire in peace. Having three boys in the house was loud and messy, but Aunt Lorelei loved it.

She doted on us like we were her own kids, especially after our dad died of cancer. It's no wonder where Killian got his big heart from, though he has his father's steely exterior and high standards.

Our cabin is smaller than Lola's modern monstrosity, but it's still a monolith of glossy mahogany, exposed steel support beams and huge windows that stretch all the way up to the ceiling, revealing unfettered views of the surrounding forest and mountains.

We added a massive dark leather corner sofa that could fit a whole family, and a flat screen television that takes up an entire wall. Killian loves shooting zombies when he runs out of wooden logs to smash to pieces.

For a while, Micah joined our video game nights. That hasn't happened for a long time. Willow turns in a circle to take it all in, running her fingertips over granite surfaces and plaid cushions that soften the admittedly masculine furniture.

"Your home is beautiful."

"We used to live in the empty cabin across the road." I grab three fresh beers from the fridge. "That was before Killian and his old man built this place for us."

"How long did that take?"

"Four years or so. It was an ongoing project while we grew up."

She accepts the beer. "Thanks. You're very talented, Kill."

Still hiding behind the breakfast bar that separates the two rooms, Killian's nostrils flare as he struggles to accept the compliment. He actually looks a little shy. Fuck me sideways. Willow is bringing out a whole other person inside my cousin.

"My parents were some of Briar Valley's original residents," he explains, still stirring his gravy. "They knew how to build something to last. We designed this place together."

"So that's your aunt and uncle?" she asks me.

"Yeah. Micah and I moved to Briar Valley when we were kids after our dad died." I fill in the gaps. "Years passed, and we never left."

"This must have been a great place to grow up."

"We were home-schooled by Pops and spent most of our time playing on dirt bikes or pissing Lola off when we trashed her flower beds."

"*You* trashed her flower beds," Killian corrects.

"He never went long without getting grounded." I gesture towards the scowling asshole. "Always getting in trouble."

"Only because you were a little rat," he accuses. "And a fucking loudmouth."

I flip him off. "Not my fault you got caught the most."

"Pops?" Willow smothers a laugh.

"Your grandad," I clarify. "He taught all the kids around here and kept us out of trouble. It hasn't been the same around here since he died. The whole town loved him."

She fixes her gaze out of the window at the steadily falling rain. Shooting me a death look, Killian gestures for me to do something about the smile disappearing from her face. I didn't mean to upset her.

"Zach?" Arianna breaks the silence. "Can I watch a movie?"

Her eyes are glued to the huge TV screen as she flops onto the sofa, its huge size dwarfing her sheer tininess. Grateful for the distraction, I grab the remote.

"Sure, squirt. Whatcha fancy?"

"I like animals and princesses."

"Who's your favourite?" I wink at her.

Her mouth falls open. "You can't make me pick!"

Chuckling at the outrage on her face, I grab a blanket and wrap it around her shoulders. Her eyes have turned into giant saucers as the movie begins, dappling bright colours into the room.

Willow fusses over Arianna for a moment, ruffling her hair before joining us back in the kitchen. The tense moment has passed, and she's wearing another carefully constructed smile. I doubt she realises that I can tell the difference.

"Need help with anything?"

"It's all under control," Killian says as his timer goes off. "Well, unless you want to help serve. I can't do fancy presentation or shit like that."

"Sure. Where do you want me?"

I watch them work in comfortable silence as they load up five plates with food, dancing around each other with a weird kind of ease. I've never seen Killian so relaxed around someone else. He can be a moody bastard, even around us.

Something about Willow brings out the calmer part of him that longs to have the warmth of a family again. It's been years since we've had dinner like this. When we were kids, we gathered around the table every single night, without fail.

"Ari," Willow calls. "Go wash your hands."

"But Mummy, the movie!"

"It will still be there afterwards."

Moodily stabbing the pause button, Arianna disappears to wash her hands. When she returns, Willow sets her up in the corner seat and tucks her chair in. She takes the next place, watching us both as we find our own chairs.

Killian naturally finds his way to the head of the table, deliberately ignoring the empty space at the centre of us all. None of us expected Micah to accept the dinner invite I delivered. He was on his way out of the front door at the time.

With everyone settled in, we begin to eat. Killian carves the chicken into neat portions and dishes it out while I pass around the dish of veggies and roast potatoes. There's enough food for a small army, but I'm sure he'll demolish it all.

"Thank you both." Willow looks between us. "This is amazing."

"Nothing beats a home cooked meal." I steal the salt and pepper straight from Killian's hands. "Anyone want gravy?"

Killian flips me off. "You go last, kid."

"What does that mean?" Arianna lifts her middle finger, mirroring Killian's move.

He looks horrified. "Ah, shit."

"Language," I chastise.

Laughing around a mouthful of beer, Willow nudges Arianna to encourage her to drop her middle finger and eat instead. Killian's ears are still burning as he dives into his plate, stuffing down mouthfuls of food to escape his faux pas.

"We never had food like this at home," Arianna says. "I want to stay here forever!"

Killian watches with pride as she drowns her roast potatoes in an unholy amount of gravy. Next time he restricts my consumption, I'm going to put on an Arianna pout for him. The little devil has clearly mastered the Killian code.

"That's enough," Willow scolds. "Eat your food."

"But it's so tasty!"

"That doesn't mean you can eat it all."

"Sorry, Mummy."

We eat in companionable silence, broken by the sound of knives scraping and Arianna loudly chomping on a chicken leg. Willow mostly pushes the food around the plate, even when Killian glares at her in warning.

She disregards his scowling face completely. Fuck me, it's the most hilarious to watch. He's not used to being overruled in this house. As I open my mouth to crack a joke that will piss him off even more, there's a creak from outside the front door.

Killian stands up so fast, his cutlery clatters loudly against his plate. Startled by the loud noise, Willow flinches and immediately grabs hold of her daughter.

"Mummy!" Arianna complains. "I'm eating."

Then the front door cracks open, and everyone relaxes. A thick headful of messy hair held back by a pencil hangs over Micah's paint-splattered face. He's dressed in his usual painting clothes, a pair of ratty grey jeans and oversized t-shirt stained different colours.

"I'm late," Micah says without looking up.

"No problem." Killian quickly recovers, forcing himself to use a patient tone. "This is Willow and Arianna. They're eating with us tonight."

Freezing while washing his hands, Micah casts a nervous look over his shoulder. "We've met. Good to, erm… see you again."

Christ on a cracker, he could win awards for awkwardness. My twin is a social pariah and certified textbook introvert. While he's a hell of an artist, perhaps even more talented than he realises, he won't win any medals for conversation.

"You've met?" Killian looks at them both.

Willow anxiously plays with her hair. "Briefly. I thought he was Zach, to be honest."

"It happens a lot." I wink at her, loving the way she blushes bright pink again just for me. "I'm the better looking twin, obviously, and I'm older than him."

"By three and a half minutes," Micah corrects.

"Still counts, Mi."

Sliding into his empty chair, Micah keeps his head lowered and eyes averted. Arianna is giving him a fierce stare as she tries to figure him out. His jaw ticks, and after several loaded seconds, he finds the courage to look up and meet her eyes.

"You're covered in paint," she points out.

Micah swallows hard. "I was varnishing something."

"Is that why you're late? It's rude, you know."

Killian nearly chokes on his mouthful of food, and he has to take a deep pull of beer. Staring at her daughter like she's an alien from another planet, Willow looks stunned by the little ballbreaker's sharp comment.

"Something like that." Micah clears his throat. "Sorry for being rude."

Arianna doesn't let up. "And what is varnishing?"

I half expect him to jump up and run for the fucking hills. One-on-one conversation is never a good way to approach Micah when he does grant us with his presence. Swallowing hard, he briefly looks at Arianna.

"It's when you seal something with clear paint to preserve it."

Her nose wrinkles. "Preserving?"

"So it lasts longer and can be displayed."

"Enough with the interrogating, Ari," Willow snaps at her. "Let the poor man eat his dinner and worry about your own plate, okay?"

"I was just asking," she defends.

"It's fine, really," Micah replies in a rush. "I make… sculptures. Out of wood and stuff. I paint as well. It's kind of a business, so people buy them from me."

That's one way of explaining his borderline-neurotic art business that earns more money than he'd admit. Micah's intense mood swings and unstable mental health are conducive to one thing, and that's creating stunning pieces of art.

"Can I see?" Arianna smiles broadly.

"Uh."

"Please?" She bats her lashes.

Micah splutters before answering. "Sure, I guess."

Fist pumping the air, Arianna dives back into her dinner with gusto now she's won the argument. Taking a breath, Micah helps himself to some food, but not before I catch sight of something odd happening to his mouth.

I think… it's a smile.

Fucking hell.

Killian stares in shock until I give him a pointed look. He refocuses on his plate, fighting a small smile himself. Neither of us have seen my twin brother do that for a very long time. What Arianna just achieved is a fucking miracle.

CHAPTER 12
WILLOW

WE WERE THE SAME - MATT MAESON

LEAVING Killian and Zach to flip a coin to decide who has to do all of the washing up, I slide my borrowed pair of shoes back on and grab the woollen coat that Miranda located for me to wear when it's cold out.

I really need to go clothes shopping soon. We can't sponge off other people's generosity forever. The prospect of leaving the safe bubble that encapsulates Briar Valley makes me feel physically ill, but I think it might be time.

"Follow me," Micah mumbles.

Arianna breezes past me. "Let's go!"

Sliding her hand straight into his, Micah's nervous eyes blow wide. He studies her tiny stature like she's a venomous snake intent on sinking its fangs into him, rather than an excited six-year-old. I doubt he likes being touched so freely.

Outside the cabin, we walk around the back, ducking beneath an apple tree surrounded by an overgrown vegetable patch. I spot several chilli pepper plants blooming in the intense periods of rain and sunshine high on the mountain.

Micah looks over his shoulder. "Zach likes spicy food, and there aren't exactly many takeaways up here. Killian started a mini chilli farm last year."

"Good solution."

"He thought so until Zach started sneaking chillies into all of his food to prank him."

His voice is rougher than his brother's smooth tenor and raspy in a smoky, fascinating way. Everything about Micah is understated, from the hunch of his broad, muscular shoulders to the slightly overgrown hair that covers his eyes in a protective shield.

He makes himself small and silent, even though he's just as well-trimmed as his twin brother. His presence is so intense, he could never slip under the radar. For some reason, I want to know more about him.

"The studio was a gift from Killian on my eighteenth birthday," he explains, his voice still strained with discomfort. "Think he was sick of me getting paint everywhere inside."

The simple, barn-like structure is built from rough hews of wood. Warm, yellow light spills through the gridded windows, illuminating the circular stone slabs that act as stepping stones across the grass.

With another deep breath, Micah waves for us to go ahead. Arianna barges inside like she owns the place, leaving me and Micah to follow behind at a slower pace.

"Cool! Mummy, come look!"

"After you," Micah invites.

"Thanks."

Squeezing past him, I slip inside the studio and turn around to drink it all in. Rough, unvarnished wooden floors and panelled walls are revealed by candlelight, burning inside old-fashioned style lanterns built into the wood.

It cloaks the studio in a welcoming warmth that makes the lofty, cold space feel more like home. There's a huge, three metre workbench that takes up most of the room. It's cluttered with tools and drying masterpieces that are hand-carved to perfection.

"This is crazy," I whisper in awe.

There are a mixture of clay and wooden sculptures cluttering every surface. Some are dried and ready to be varnished, while others are darker with the tint of wet clay, slowly hardening on drying racks. So many different creatures—wolves, deer, birds, even owls.

Paintings cover almost every wall, haphazardly hammered into place while others are stacked up in the corner to be packaged. I study the closest one, recognising the familiar landscape of Briar Valley depicted in all its lush, undisturbed greenery.

It's like Micah's recreating the world from behind the safety and security of these four walls. Each piece is stunningly realistic, a snapshot of reality caught in the permanent stasis of paint and ink. I've never seen talent like it.

"You have a real gift. These are beautiful works of art, Micah."

He fiddles with his stained t-shirt. "No one sees my art. I sell it online and package it up for Zach to run into town."

"The others haven't seen this? Seriously?"

"I like my privacy."

But he let us see, a traitorous voice whispers.

Arianna's eyeing up a stunning sculpture of a butterfly. Each papery, stained-glass wing has been recreated in so much detail, it's hard to believe that it isn't a real butterfly fossilised in fresh clay.

She strokes the tip of her finger over its hand-hewn spine, her mouth hanging open. Her fascination for animals and insects has grown after our move here. There wasn't much beyond cicadas and locusts in Mexico.

"No touching, Ari."

"It's fine," Micah quickly says.

"I don't want her to ruin your hard work."

"It's so pretty," she coos. "I like it."

Wringing his hands together, Micah walks over to her and picks up the small sculpture. He grabs a pen and scribbles something on the bottom of it before kneeling down next to Arianna.

"Keep her safe for me, will you?"

"Really? For me?" Arianna blusters.

"Butterflies don't belong locked up inside."

Before he can flinch away from her touch, she squeals and throws her arms around his neck. Micah full-body shudders, becoming as still as the hardened clay that fills his workspace. Arianna squeezes him tight before releasing him.

"Thank you. I will look after her, I promise."

Watching them both, I can't help but smile as Micah bravely ruffles her hair. Deciding not to push our luck, I hold out a hand for Arianna to take.

"We should head off. It's getting late."

"S-Sure," Micah stammers.

"Thank you for showing us around."

"You're welcome." He stares down at his shoes. "I'll see you around, I guess."

"Come on, Ari." I take her hand in mine. "Let's leave Picasso here to his work, hmm? I'm sure Micah's got lots of stuff to do tonight."

She gives him a little wave before pulling her hand free from mine and running off, shouting for Killian to come and look at her new toy. I watch her go for a moment, smiling to myself. Her confidence is so good to see.

Micah stops beside me, wearing an unreadable expression. "She's a cute kid."

Drawing my coat tighter against the cold air, I sigh. "She's getting louder with each day we spend here. I think Killian's charming ways are rubbing off on her."

Stepping outside to head back to the cabin, I'm halted by my name rolling off Micah's lips in an almost-audible prayer. He's staring at me with such unspeakable intensity, it feels like he's searching for something buried deep beneath my skin.

"Yeah?"

Panicked, he shakes his head. "Nothing."

The door suddenly slams shut in my face. For several astonished seconds, I stare at the rattled slab of wood, eventually making my feet carry me back up the garden. That went better than it could have gone, I suppose.

Talking to Micah feels a bit like navigating choppy water with nothing but a broken life raft. I get the sense that no matter how hard I battle, there's no opposing the powerful pull of isolation that keeps him locked in the depths of his own private ocean.

Back inside the cabin, Arianna has retaken her spot on the sofa. She's smiling to herself and snuggling the butterfly like it's a teddy bear rather than a solid lump of clay. Her eyes are growing heavy, even as she battles to keep them open.

Zach reappears in the door. "Everything okay?"

"All good. Micah's studio is amazing."

"I wouldn't know. He won't let me in there."

Tugging on my elbow, he steers me over to the breakfast bar where Killian awaits with a bottle of liquor and three glasses. The dishes have vanished, and the kitchen is relatively clean, albeit still cluttered. They seem to have called it quits.

"Drink?" Killian rumbles.

I stare at the amber liquid. "No, thanks."

Whiskey was Mr Sanchez's drink of choice. The scent holds nothing but bad memories. It clung to his skin and acid tongue as he lashed out at me, inebriated and furious. His fists hit extra hard when he was drunk.

"We should get going."

"Arianna is almost asleep." Zach pats an empty bar stool. "Stay, we won't bite. Well, Killian might, but I promise I'll put him down if he does. I know a good vet."

"Screw you," Killian snarls at him.

"Behave, mutt. We have a guest."

"Call me a fucking mutt again and see what happens."

Cursing under his breath, Killian pours two measures of whiskey and knocks his glassful back. I reluctantly take a seat. The way they watch me out of the corner of their eyes is unnerving.

Something sits in the air between us, the weight of everything left unsaid. I feel it with everyone in the town. Their gazes are questioning and curious, but they're too polite to pry into our business.

"Are you staying in Briar Valley?" Killian asks bluntly, forgoing the niceties.

"I… don't know," I answer. "We don't have a whole lot of options. My plan was to make it here. That's about it so far."

"What else do you want?" he urges.

"Well, I want Arianna to have a home."

"You know Lola loves having you stay with her." Zach nurses his own drink. "But if you wanted your own space, there are plenty of cabins going spare."

"There are?"

"Sure, we've got a couple. We're moving a new family in at the weekend. Refugees from overseas. Two young kids as well."

"A home for lost things, huh?" I say with a laugh.

Killian scoffs. "Like I said, Lola's a bit of a collector. That woman would've made a damn good politician in another life."

"She's determined to fix the whole world," Zach agrees.

Sadness invades me. What might my life have looked like if she'd been in it? Or if I'd gotten over myself after my dad's death and ran into her arms? Things could have turned out very differently. I think I'll always regret that.

"Where'd you go?" Zach waves a hand in front of me.

"Sorry. This place is a dream come true and a slap in the face all at once."

Killian meets my eyes. "What do you mean?"

I'm too tired to bite my tongue. "I wish Arianna could've grown up here instead. She was the best thing that ever happened to me, but sometimes I wonder what world I brought her into."

"We're never given more than we can handle." Killian rubs a hand over his blonde beard. "At least, that's what my folks used to say. Like with Micah. They knew how to handle him. I'm doing a shitty job in comparison."

"That's not true," Zach interjects.

"Yeah, it is."

"You picked up the pieces, Kill. You stuck around. That means something to me, and it does to Micah too. You need to get that through your thick skull."

Feeling like I'm intruding on their private moment, I look back over to Arianna. She's now fast asleep with her thumb tucked into her mouth. I realise that both men are also looking in the same direction, smiling at the sight of my baby sleeping on their sofa.

"You need to stay here," Killian decides.

"What?" I stare at him.

"Let us keep you safe. We ain't worth much out there in the real world, but we can throw a mean punch. Whatever's chasing you won't find you here. We won't allow it."

Zach hums in agreement. "I have a decent swing."

The most exquisite sense of warmth spreads through my veins, melting the ice that froze around my heart so long ago. I feel like I'm stepping off a merry-go-round and breathing for the first time in years. It's dizzying and reassuring at the same time.

More than anything, I want Arianna to live freely. She can run, play, laugh and relax here. There's no threat of violence hanging over us. I don't need to sleep with one eye open, using my body as a bruised and beaten shield to keep her safe from harm.

"What do you say?" Zach stares at me.

"We could stay put."

Killian perks up, his head tilted. "Is that a yes?"

"Maybe."

"Not good enough. The word you're looking for is *yes*."

Snickering, I meet his expectant gaze. "You're a pain in the ass, aren't you?"

"You're just figuring that out about me?" he counters.

Shaking my head at his bullshit, I look back at Arianna again. Seeing her asleep and safe, nestled amongst tangled blankets with that bloody sculpture, seals my decision. I can't take this away from her, and I don't want to.

"That's a yes," I submit.

Thumping his glass of liquor down, Zach suddenly pulls me into a hard, fast hug. I let myself melt in his wiry arms, my eyes connecting with Killian's over his shoulder. Even the grumpy lumberjack is wearing a relieved smile.

"You're officially one of us," Zach announces, deepening his voice to a playful growl. "One of us. One of us."

"Alright, get off me."

Killian snags his cousin's t-shirt and yanks him backwards, freeing me. Zach picks up the empty glass and fills it with a small measure of whiskey. I reluctantly accept and knock it back this time, needing some liquid courage.

Fire burns a path down my throat, and the warmth seeping into my bones is comforting in a strange way. Even if it tastes like death. I'd prefer to replace the bad memories I have of this drink with this pure, untainted moment.

"I was wondering if one of you could take me into the nearest town to get some stuff." I place the glass down and hug myself tight. "If you don't mind, that is."

"I'm going on a delivery run for Micah next week," Zach suggests. "You sure you're ready to venture out?"

"I've got to some time."

"Cool. We can make a day of it."

Clinging to the tiniest scrap of courage, I make myself nod. Being cooped up here for another week won't make it any easier to leave. If we're staying in Briar Valley, I need to get myself together and start settling in. Our lives here still feel temporary right now.

"I'll come too," Killian adds.

Zach shoots him a perplexed look. "You will?"

"What?" He glares back at him. "Your scrawny little ass won't do shit if you run into trouble. I'll bring my rifle along and knock any creepers out."

"Creepers?" I exclaim.

"He means men," Zach clarifies with a short laugh. "You belong to the valley now. We protect what's ours. Better get used to this possessive fucker following you around with his gun from now on."

Killian looks thrilled at the prospect, cracking his knuckles in anticipation. "It's been a while since I had a good hunt."

"There are no men in my life to hunt down," I splutter.

He eyes me. "Yet. Give it time."

CHAPTER 13
WILLOW

BURY ME - FRIDAY PILOTS CLUB

ANXIOUSLY BOUNCING ON MY FEET, I wrap a scarf around my neck, glancing in the mirror that hangs in Lola's hallway. The bruising on my face has faded to a mottled green and yellow in the last few days. It hurts less to touch now.

Inky bruises still stain the skin under my hollow eyes, but overall, I'm looking a lot better. Running my fingers over my black hair, I study the long length with a clinging sense of hatred. I always hated it like this.

Mr Sanchez never let me cut it. I'd secretly trim the ends, but he liked a good headful of hair to wrench as he dragged me through shadowed halls. It makes me sick now. He's still in control, no matter the miles between us.

Quickly braiding it to the side, I turn my back on my reflection and startle. Lola is standing at the bottom of the stairs, silently watching me without saying a word.

"Are you sure you don't mind me leaving her behind?" I repeat for the tenth time.

"Willow, I can look after my own great-granddaughter."

"I know, it's just that we've never been separated before."

"It's safer for her here, until we know where we stand," she says firmly. "Go and take my credit card. Get everything you need and use those boys' muscles to your advantage."

"I'm not taking your money. I have cash."

"You will take my card and use it. This isn't up for discussion. No family of mine is going to use blood money to put clothes on their backs."

My stomach bottoms out. "Blood money?"

"I'm a patient woman." She gifts me a loaded look. "You're going to have to trust me sometime and tell me why you're here. I can't help you if I don't know what's going on."

"I… I know that."

"Then sit down and tell me the truth."

She's straying dangerously close to my secrets, and I need to throw her off the scent. Lola isn't the kind of person to let evil exist in the world unchallenged. I'm scared of what she'd do if she knew the truth.

"It isn't safe. I have to think about your safety too."

"What's so dangerous about some real estate agent? What don't I know?"

A loud ringing in my ears drowns everything else out. Head spinning, I bend down to lace my leather boots, turning the cuffs of my jeans up several times to fit better.

"Where did you get that information?" I force an even voice.

"If you're going to use my computer, you should clear the search history. I'm not trying to snoop, but I'm your grandmother."

I bite my lip, holding back a curse. This is exactly what I was worried about when I agreed to stay in Briar Valley. I want to belong here, but I refuse to endanger anyone else.

"Let me in, Willow," she pleads.

Backtracking to put more space between us, a thousand escape routes zip through my mind. Arianna is in the kitchen, preparing for a day of baking. She would never forgive me if I put her in Killian's truck and drove away from the first home she's ever had.

"I'm sorry. I can't."

I watch Lola's face fall.

"One day, I hope that you'll trust me," she begs. "I'm here to listen."

"It isn't a matter of trust, believe me. I've got to go."

Grabbing my coat, I flee the cabin before she pushes any further. A faded red truck is idling outside for me. Inside, two solid lumps of muscle watch me descend the porch steps. I race over and climb inside as Zach finishes puffing on a cigarette.

"Morning, guys."

Zach shoots me a wink, flicking the stub aside. "Good morning, babe. You ready?"

"As I'll ever be."

Killian nods in greeting, his blonde hair loose and tangled as it hangs over his shoulders today. He seems preoccupied, contemplating the thick coverage of pine trees ahead of us that part to reveal the dirt track out of the valley.

Throwing the truck into gear once I've buckled myself in, he takes off in a spray of wet mud and fallen leaves. Zach turns the radio up, chattering in the background. I tune him out, preoccupied by our surroundings.

Seeing the forest in the cold light of day, I realise how insane I was to attempt it on foot, let alone the mountain road that leads down into the valley. We pull onto rocky terrain, lined with heavy boulders marking our route back up into the world.

Once we reach the top of the bumpy path stretching into the heavens, I gasp at the undisturbed view of the surrounding countryside. It's nothing like Mexico, home of the relentless heat and sand as far as the eye can see.

I prefer the luscious grass, countless spindly trees and the scent of fresh rainfall across the mountains. The cold wind on my skin and the mist in the air are my favourite things about our new life. Each morning feels like being reborn, over and over again.

"Where are we headed?"

"I need to drop Micah's deliveries off in Highbridge." Zach rolls down the window to light another cigarette. "If you don't mind small shops, it's a good place to start,"

"If you need anything bigger, we'll have to head into the city," Killian chips in moodily. "It's another hour away on top of that."

"No, I don't want to be that far from Arianna. Maybe another time."

"You'd love it there," Zach replies.

"If she likes stupid people, tons of traffic and jumped-up assholes selling shitty life insurance policies," Killian mutters darkly. "I'll pass, thanks."

"Ignore his complaining." Zach smirks at me. "Killian isn't a city boy. He prefers to live in the dark ages."

"You can walk back up the mountain, kid."

"Try it. I'll tell on you to Lola."

Killian snorts. "We both know I'm her favourite anyway."

"That is so not true! You're full of shit."

"Ask her yourself. She'll tell you as much."

"Maybe I will," Zach threatens.

Letting my eyes slide shut, I tune out their arguing and enjoy the ride. Even on the bumpy path, Killian's huge truck absorbs much of the friction. I've heard it was a custom job that Ryder helped him with to haul lumber and supplies back up the mountain.

We pull into Highbridge a long hour later. The rural, picturesque countryside town looks exactly as I remember. Stone cottages and tiny shops line the quiet street, along with lamp posts and swinging baskets filled with fresh flowers.

When we first arrived here after hours of travelling north, I was dead on my feet. I can hardly recall walking around the town, fishing for information from locals milling about. It's miraculous that we made it at all.

Perhaps fate was on our side.

I find that comforting, somehow.

Locating a tight parking space off the main street, Killian groans as he manoeuvres the truck into it, complaining the whole time about being back in civilisation. Zach finishes his third cigarette and claps his hands together as the engine cuts out.

"Let me drop off Micah's crap and we'll go find some shops."

Lifting a massive plastic crate bursting with wrapped parcels from the bed of the truck, Zach heads for the nearby post office, situated beneath a bright-red overhang and more flower baskets.

Opening my door, I hesitate when Killian walks around the truck and offers me a hand. He's dressed in his usual flannel shirt and jeans, though these ones are cleaner than his usual pair. I eye his hand with doubt, and he stifles a scoff.

"Lola's right, Willow. You have to trust us sometime."

"What? How do you know she said that?"

"We talk. She's family to me too, you know."

"I don't like you all gossiping behind my back."

Reluctantly taking his hand, I let him help me down from the truck. Killian peers around, assessing for danger, before throwing an arm around my shoulders. I freeze for a second, forcing myself to breathe and relax.

His familiar musky scent clings to his shirt. He smells so good, like raw bonfire embers and the freshness of pine trees blended into an intoxicating fragrance. I feel tiny next to his staggering height, and I'm not exactly small.

"We weren't gossiping," he adds.

"What would you call it then?"

He searches my face and frowns like usual. "She cares about you. I'm not going to get all emotional and shit. All I know is that we want you to be safe."

A strand of tangled blonde hair falls across his naturally bronzed face. With the warmth of his body heat pouring into me, I reach up to swipe it aside. Killian inhales sharply, his eyes dropping to my lips for a split second.

"Why?"

"Why not?" he growls back.

"I'm a stranger. You said that yourself."

He's still staring at my mouth, his eyes burning with heat.

"You're not a stranger," he almost purrs.

Highbridge fades around us, disappearing into insignificance. All I can feel is the sensual weight of his eyes on me, demanding something I don't know how to give. Even his touch is electric, causing bolts of excitement to race up my spine.

"I thought I had to protect Briar Valley from you," Killian murmurs, wetting his bottom lip with his tongue. "But I forgot to protect myself."

Warmth unfurls in my lower belly, curling around my nerve endings and magnetising me closer to him. All I want is to be engulfed in his embrace, protected from every last threat the world has to offer.

"Why do you need to protect yourself?" I ask softly.

His hand lifts, the backs of his knuckles stroking over my cheekbone. When his thumb meets my lips and strokes over them, tracing every last inch, I almost melt into a puddle.

"Because I don't trust the way you're making me feel," he admits. "And I can't afford to let anyone else fuck up our family any more than it already is."

"I would never dream of hurting your family."

"You might not intend to. That doesn't mean it won't happen."

Then his touch is gone, leaving me cold and bereft. The bubble of anticipation encapsulating us bursts with each step he takes away from me. By the time Zach returns, Killian has turned his back completely and I'm holding back tears.

"Uh, am I interrupting?" Zach blurts.

Without a word, Killian storms off towards the high street, causing pedestrians to leap out of his way in fright. Zach takes his place and throws an arm around me.

"What was that all about?"

"Beats me," I answer. "Your cousin confuses me so much."

"Honestly, same. I still don't understand him."

Letting Zach steer me after Killian's furious steps, I push my anger aside. It shouldn't hurt to be disregarded by Killian, yet somehow, it does. I wasn't sure what to expect from him, but that little performance wasn't it.

Guiding me into a cute shop, Zach stretches out his hands to gesture around.

"Have at it."

I look around the well-stocked space. It's full of children's clothing in all manner of garish colours, including a great deal of pink. Arianna would love it in here. She's a real unicorns, rainbows and glitter kind of girl.

"Need help picking stuff?" Zach asks.

"You know much about girls' clothing?"

"I'm a fast learner."

Giving him a basic list of clothing and Arianna's sizes, I watch him head for the nearest employee, plastering a charming smile on his face. Those damned adorable dimples are back out. My hands clench into fists by my sides before I realise what I'm doing.

The thump of footsteps betrays Killian's presence before he halts at my side, his carefully blank facial expression back in place. Whoever the man that touched me so reverently outside was, he's long gone back into his hiding place.

"I got a basket." Killian spares me a look. "Why the long face?"

Is he serious right now?

"Nothing. Let's get this over and done with."

"Willow, wait."

A lump gathered in my throat, I peer up at his overwhelming height. An almost indecipherable emotion flits through his eyes before it dissipates, swallowed again by darkness. I can't decide if I want to kiss him or punch his lights out.

"Yeah?" I hum impatiently.

Killian falters. "About what I said."

"What about it?"

Waiting for an apology that doesn't come, I watch him deliberate for several excruciating seconds before I give up and abandon him among the clothing. He's literally incapable of vulnerability. Part of me feels sad for him.

I've lost a lot of people in my life. Family. Friends. Myself, even. But I never want to allow that grief to consume me or take away my ability to connect with others.

Then, I'll be the monster in my own story. What's there left to fight for if that happens?

Throwing myself into the task, within half an hour I have several baskets full of clothing. Long-sleeved t-shirts, leggings, two pairs of jeans, a couple of floaty dresses and skirts in every shade of pink and yellow.

Arianna even has a new coat for the rainy weather, pyjamas covered in tiny little giraffes, and an extra pair of shoes. Zach has excelled himself. It will cost pretty much my whole budget, but I can't wait to see the look on her face.

Finding Killian standing at the checkout counter, I catch him shoving a giant stuffed elephant into a plastic bag. He clears his throat when he sees me, caught red-handed.

"There's a new family coming. They have nothing."

"How is that possible?" I wonder.

"The two kids didn't come to the country with any toys. They were fleeing a warzone." Killian's visible rage could cut down whole armies with a single glance. "Every kid should have a toy."

And that right there is exactly what's so infuriating about this man. He's riddled with contradictions—caring and kind, hateful and possessive. Cold in one instant and fuelled by the fires of passion in the next. His entire presence is dizzying.

Killian packs the rest of my clothing into several bags before flourishing a shiny bank card. I attempt to grab it from his hands, but he's so much taller than me and holds it out of reach, until I'm jumping up and down like a lunatic.

"Stop it! You're not paying for this. I won't let you."

"Lola already gave me the funds." He cuts off my protests. "She knew you wouldn't touch her credit card. This isn't up for discussion."

"I have my own money."

"Well, it's no good here."

"Killian!" I bark at him.

All he can do is offer me a smug grin, far too satisfied with my inability to snatch the card from his hands. He swipes it so fast, the payment is done and dusted before I can mount another attack.

Sneaking up on us, two firm hands land on my hips, tugging me back against a wide-set chest. The possessiveness of the move steals my breath, even though I can smell Zach's familiar tropical scent from behind me.

Fear races down my spine faster than my mind can catch up with. Zach looks startled as I extricate myself from his embrace, needing space between us. My internalised defences can't tell the difference between him and my memories right now.

"Babe? You good?"

"I'll be outside," I croak.

Fleeing the shop before they can ask questions, I escape into the alleyway down the side of the building and collapse against the brick wall. Shouting echoes in my head, growing louder by the second.

You will do as you're told, Mrs Sanchez.

You and that little brat live under my roof.

Break the rules, and there will be punishment.

I still remember the day Mr Sanchez found out I was pregnant. He was always careful to use protection, treating me as more of an impersonal transaction than a human being, even as he defiled and broke the most private parts of me.

After a few too many drinks and an unsuccessful business meeting, he had come home full of rage. I was still weak in those days before I had Arianna and found the strength to fight back for her sake. He didn't even have to restrain me.

I let him shove me into the dining room table as he ripped my dress down the back, grabbing me hard between the legs. I could hardly breathe with his weight pinning me to the table, trapping me in his toxic orbit as he forced himself inside of me.

Let me hear that beautiful screaming, wife.

Beg for mercy.

I can't hear you.

I laid broken on the floor after he stalked off, unable to even attempt to move. His men outside heard everything that happened. I heard them laughing and trading jokes after as I sobbed and begged for death.

One month later, the pregnancy test I convinced one of the housekeepers to purchase for me came back as positive and my entire life changed in an instant. The subsequent beating still makes my bones ache; the memories are so raw.

Distantly, I can hear someone calling my name. Hands slide under my legs as the press of hard muscles wraps around me. Panting between clenched teeth, I force my eyes open, terrified that I'll find one of Mr Sanchez's bodyguards here to take me away.

Killian is crouched in front of me, his choreographed numbness nowhere in sight. In fact, he looks horrified by the sharp, agonised rasps of my lungs attempting to suck in air.

"That's it, baby," Killian coaxes. "Breathe."

Underneath me, Zach holds me tight in his lap. "Take some deep breaths."

I lurch to the side, overcome by a sudden rush of nausea. Throwing up the entire contents of my stomach, I narrowly miss Killian's mud-caked boots. When I'm done heaving, my throat is shredded raw.

I can't hold my tears back any longer. I don't have the strength. It's all too much. We're supposed to be free. Why can't I get him out of my head? It's like my monstrous husband has followed us across the continent by hiding in the depths of my mind.

It takes an age for the grip of anxiety to finally release me. My breathing slowly evens out, and I'm left utterly spent. My mouth still burns with the acidic taste of vomit, while a light sheen of sweat covers my face and neck.

"I'm so sorry," Zach says helplessly.

"Please… don't touch me like that again."

"I didn't mean to scare you."

Struggling to my feet, I leave his lap and brush myself off. I can't look at him, even though it wasn't his fault. Every instinct inside of me is screaming that I should run away from these men and their lack of boundaries.

"Let us take you home." Killian watches me closely. "We can come back another time to do the rest of the shopping."

My mouth is fuzzy and disgusting, but I shake my head. I'm not that person anymore, unable to protect herself or her baby girl. I'm a woman now. A survivor. I'm no longer Mr Sanchez's broken ballerina, forever twirling in her broken music box.

"No. I want to do what we came here for."

"I don't think that's a good idea," Zach worries as he stands.

Cutting them both a fierce look, I straighten my clothes. "I refuse to live in fear. Now, take me to the women's clothes shop and keep your hands to yourselves, okay?"

They hang back after me, keeping their distance as I storm past. Secretly, I don't want them to stay away. Far from it. But that's exactly why I need them to stop breaking down my defences with each gentle smile and tight embrace.

I'm terrified of the way they make my heart race, even when Killian's doing his utmost to piss me off. This fear is far stronger than what I felt when Mr Sanchez prowled towards me, his erection straining against his trousers.

I knew that monster. His evil was familiar and, in many ways, I could handle it for that reason. My mind was prepared for his torture, shoring up its defences and building safe escape routes for me to slip into when the pain became too much.

What I can't handle is their love. Affection. People caring about me and wanting to get close enough to really hurt me. That's what these men are doing, day by day. And even if a traitorous part of me wants to, I absolutely cannot fall for them.

I won't survive it.

And neither will they.

CHAPTER 14
MICAH

THE VIEW BETWEEN VILLAGES - NOAH KAHAN

STUFFING BOTTLED WATER, granola bars and sachets of energy gel into my backpack, I throw a paint-splattered hoodie over my head and take a final glance around my messy studio. It's in even more chaos than usual after my latest bout of depression hit.

I've been waiting on a delivery of art supplies and the disruption to my routine when these episodes hit is proving difficult to handle. Keeping busy with my hands is the only thing that allows me to keep the darkness in my mind at bay.

I'm itching to escape.

I'll drown if I don't run.

With my walking boots laced up, I heave my backpack onto my shoulders and head outside. Killian and Zach are working around the town this afternoon, battening down the hatches in preparation for a big storm that's blowing in tomorrow.

We've dealt with extreme weather for a long time. It's a pitfall of living in the mountains. When the storms come, they hit hard, but usually blow themselves out pretty quickly with minimal damage.

"Hey, Micah," Albie calls out. "Off hiking?"

"Yeah. I'm heading out now."

In the garage behind him, Ryder is working on his newest treasure, an old VW beetle covered in peeling green paint. It looks ready for the trash heap. They have a knack for finding crappy cars and restoring them to their former glory for profit.

"Tell your brother that he still owes me for a tank of fuel." Albie slides back under the car with a spanner in hand. "And those damn cigarettes too."

"Sorry, Al. I'll let him know."

"You better."

Ryder appears from the garage, wiping his hands off on his overalls. "You gonna go through the overpass? There's a storm coming in."

"It's set to make landfall tomorrow. I'll be fine."

He studies me for a moment, seeing far more than I'd like. Ryder is like a brother to me. The four of us grew up here together, running from grief and loss. I'm the only one that didn't make it out the other side of that particular storm.

"Run out of supplies again?" Ryder hazards a guess.

"They're due to come in next week."

"That long, huh?"

"I'll figure something out."

Ryder knows as well as anyone that my art keeps me alive. Without it, functioning is excruciating. I'm forced to interact and remember that the world exists around me.

My old therapist said it does more harm than good to isolate myself, but I told him to go fuck himself and never went back. I don't need anyone attempting to rationalise the madness that runs riot inside my brain.

"I'll speak to Kill and see if there's anything we can get in town."

I cast him a weak smile. "Thanks, man."

"You got it. Go hike, sort your shit out. Just be careful."

"Always am."

Leaving him to continue his repairs, I set off and traipse down the winding path leading back into town. Harold waves at me from his garden when I pass, his hands buried in his vegetable patch. Everyone else is preparing for the storm to arrive.

Reaching the edge of the forest that leads back up into the mountains, a heart-wrenching sound drags my feet to a halt. Crying. It's coming from inside the crop field. The soft sobs and occasional whimper daggers me in the heart.

Cursing myself for giving a shit, I duck through the towering stalks of corn and barley, searching for the source of the noise. It doesn't take me long to find her tumbling black locks and tear-logged hazel eyes hidden in the shrubbery.

Willow is curled up with her knees to her chest. I'm unable to walk away as I usually would at the sight of someone else's pain.

"Willow?" I ask softly.

Her head snaps up. "Micah. What are you doing here?"

I gesture towards the trees. "Hiking."

"Oh."

"Are you okay?"

Wiping her red-stained face, she doesn't bother to nod when it's clear that she's not alright. Dropping my backpack, I sit down next to her, both of us hidden by the coverage of crops. We're alone in this slice of solitude.

"Do you want to talk?" I pause, unsure of myself. "You don't have to though. I don't like talking, but some people do. Like Zach, he's a talker. Ryder too."

She blinks, speechless.

"I'm rambling. Forget I said anything."

"Wait, Micah."

Her hand shoots out to grab mine before I can flee, and her sparkling hazel eyes beg me for relief. She's alone in the world while surrounded by people who don't understand how she feels. I know exactly how awful that invisible prison is.

"Please don't go," she pleads.

"Uh, sure. Okay."

Sitting back down, we lapse into silence, listening to the sound of far-off voices. Nobody can find us here. I pick a stalk of unripe corn, stripping apart the plant to keep my hands busy until there's nothing but husks left.

"No painting today?"

I shake my head. "Waiting on supplies. I was going to hike."

"I didn't know you liked hiking. Do you go often?"

"Only when I have to."

Willow fiddles with her left hand, twisting a golden band around her wedding finger. *Married.* No one mentioned a husband to me. Not that I've been having casual conversations with anyone, including my own family.

"Is your husband here?" I blurt.

"No," she answers in a panic. "He's not here."

"I see. The kid's dad?"

Willow nods nervously. "We came here for a fresh start."

"Well, this is a good place to get lost."

The way she looks at me sets my teeth on edge with anxiety. I'm so used to running and hiding from everyone to avoid the awkwardness of interacting with them. I hate the way she seems to know everything about me with a single innocent look.

"Are you here to get lost, Micah?"

"Some people don't want to be found in the first place."

"I thought I was coming here to get lost," she reveals with a hiccup. "Part of me wonders if we shouldn't have come at all."

"Why?"

Willow shrugs. "It was easier to pretend like I'm fine when I was alone."

"Because you don't have to pretend to be something you're not, right?"

Her eyes flit over to me. "Yeah."

"I understand what that's like. Being alone feels safer somehow."

I have no idea where this burst of raw honesty has come from. I've never opened up like this, not even to a professional. Something inside of her calls out to me—dragging the despair from my soul and offering to dance.

"You don't have to be alone forever," she whispers.

"Trust me, no one out there wants to be around someone like me."

"Why not? You're a good person, Micah."

I glance up at her, my throat constricted. "I'm damaged goods."

Her hand tentatively reaches out to cradle mine. I don't move. It feels weird, letting someone touch me. Her palm is warm and dry. I can almost feel the anguish pumping through her veins.

"You are not damaged goods," she says fiercely.

"I don't need you to comfort me. I'm okay with being alone."

Her dark eyelashes flutter. Intelligence and curiosity writhe in her gaze as her eyes search mine. The bruises on her face are nearly healed after a few weeks, revealing the natural beauty that first ensnared me.

There's something about the way that Willow wraps her pain around herself, forming an almost-visible armour to keep the world at bay. She looks like a fallen angel, all broken dreams and pain, wrapped into a shell of bittersweet beauty.

I tried to paint her last week, but I couldn't do it. Her tentative smiles and glimmers of hopeful optimism can't be reduced to paint on a canvas, no matter how much I want to immortalise my memory of her for when she disappears.

"What about you?" I make myself ask.

"Huh?"

"Are you lonely?"

Willow curls her hand around mine. "Sometimes. I've never really had any friends or people close to me. But that felt normal, even if it wasn't."

"It was your normal. There's nothing wrong with that."

"That doesn't help other people understand though. Everyone wants me to feel safe here like I can somehow forget about the past. My normal isn't feeling safe."

I stare down at our interlinked hands. It doesn't take a genius to know she's feeling something pretty fucking dark. The look in her eyes is something I've seen staring back at me every time I look in the mirror. Existence carved from inescapable pain.

"Maybe that's okay." I absently stroke her knuckles, tracing each vein. "You're allowed to feel the way that you do. No one can rush you into feeling at home here."

Willow tilts her head. "I didn't think of it like that."

"Just a thought."

"Did you feel at home when you came here?"

My throat locks up with a wash of grief. "I've never felt at home. My home died. When Killian's folks took us in, all I saw in their love was the potential for loss."

"Because of your dad's death?"

"Yeah. I couldn't separate the two."

Fuck knows why I'm spilling my soul among unharvested crops to a woman I've known for a matter of weeks. Willow is little more than a stranger to me. Somehow, there's comfort in that. She can't judge me like my family can.

Knowing that the same darkness festers inside of her makes me feel seen. Nobody else has ever made me feel like that. They can empathise, perhaps even care, but they can't understand. Not without living inside my head.

"Killian knows a bunch of therapists." I force myself to release her hand, though I don't want to. "In case you wanted to talk to someone."

"I'm talking to you, aren't I?"

"Someone qualified. I'm just… me."

Willow offers me a sad smile. "Micah, I have a feeling you're far more qualified than any shrink to talk to me about this."

The sound of my choked laugh is foreign. "Killian sent me to a therapist for most of my teens and early twenties. I gave up a year or so ago. I think I'm beyond fixing."

"Maybe you don't need to be fixed. You said it first. Not everything has to be okay."

"Tell that to him. He's determined to make me normal."

An unfamiliar ache sears beneath my skin as I subtly watch her from the corner of my eye. I don't know what I'm feeling. My hike feels pointless now. I'd rather sit here and talk to Willow for another hour, or even longer.

Staying detached has been my saving grace. It's kept me alive as we suffered loss after loss. So much death has a way of changing the way you see the world. Caring for others becomes more potential for loss.

But with her, I'm yearning for something that I can't find in myself. An intimacy. A closeness that my lifeless clay and pallets of oil paint can't provide.

"Anyway," she says hoarsely. "Thanks for the pep talk."

I nod reluctantly. "Anytime."

"You're a good friend."

"Friend?"

Her smile is so pure and innocent. "I could use a friend."

"I've... never had one of those before."

"You don't have to," she rushes out.

"No," I cut her off. "I'd like that."

Willow opens her arms to offer me a hug. Seized by fear, I bury it down deep and let myself be drawn into her embrace. Her hair smells like strawberries, sweet and sugary. Lola's endless supply of homemade cookies has left a homey perfume on her clothes.

Holding my breath for fear of doing something wrong, I feel her arms wind around my neck to draw me closer. With my head buried in her throat, I take a deep inhale, smiling to myself. Somewhere inside of me, a switch is flipped.

She smells like home.

I'd forgotten what it felt like.

As we break apart, instinct overcomes me. I'm not sure how I end up cupping her cheek, my thumb tracing over the freckles that stain her skin. Her eyes are giant saucers, uncertain of the magnetic force wrapped around us both.

"I should go," I rasp.

"So should I."

But neither of us moves. We're still entwined—two autumn leaves dancing in the breeze, wrapped around each other for the show. I'm untethered, falling through my carefully constructed reality, but she's there to catch me.

My lips brush against hers in the briefest, most hesitant kiss. Common sense has packed up, cleaned house and moved the hell out of my brain. This is a stupid fucking idea, but it doesn't stop me from kissing her again.

I need us to be closer, connected, our souls suffused together somehow. I can't stand the space left between us. With a sharp intake of breath, she suddenly kisses me back. Heat zips across my skin and floods my entire body with tingles.

Mouths locked, we move together in a perfect, unchoreographed harmony. It feels so right to let her capture my bottom lip between her teeth, gently tugging to deepen the kiss. Hidden by swaying crops, I surrender myself to her.

"Mi," she breaks the kiss to gasp.

"You're so fucking beautiful."

Kissing along her jawline, I suck the delicate flesh of her throat into my mouth. Her tiny, adorable moans for attention have me rock hard in seconds. I want to taste every single inch of her body and mark it as mine.

Hands skating down her arms, I find my way inside her coat to grasp the generous curves of her hips. The inferno scorching inside of me is heightened by her mouth attacking mine again.

I want more.

I need more.

She's bringing me back to life.

A bellow from nearby forces us to jump apart. As quickly as the haze of desire descended, it dissipates and leaves me cold. My dick is almost bursting out of my jeans, aching with the need to be touched.

Fuck, this is embarrassing.

I'm shamefully inexperienced.

Being a mountain recluse doesn't exactly equate to much dating experience, let alone with my own crap on top of that. I have no idea what I'm doing here. Internally freaking out, I put some distance between us.

"Micah?" she questions, her gaze worried.

"I don't... ah, I shouldn't have done that."

Disappointment warps her features. "I'm so sorry. My head is a mess. I wasn't thinking straight."

I avoid her stare. "It's my fault for starting it. Killian and Zach... they both care about you a lot. They would be better friends than me."

"What? Micah, no—"

"I should go."

Willow flushes a dark shade of red as I climb to my feet, feeling like a complete and utter asshole. I never should have done this. I'm not blind. Killian and Zach have grown close to Willow already. They don't treat all new residents like this.

They're better men than me, and far more capable of looking after her. I can't even look after myself on a good day. She deserves far more than that. Opening up to her was a mistake.

"Micah? Please don't go."

"I can't be your friend, Willow. I'm not capable of it."

My heart implodes into spectacular pieces when she begins to cry. All I want is to lay her down in the crops and kiss her again, over and over, only stopping when she's crying out my name.

Fuck, what I wouldn't give to mean something to someone. She's so close, almost within reach, but the chasm between us is impassable. I can't bridge that gap and be the man she needs right now. That's why I have to walk away.

"Just answer me one thing."

I stop, on the verge of bolting.

"Was that your first kiss?" Willow asks tearfully.

Flooded with shame, I have to unlatch my jaw to answer.

"Yeah, it was."

Without looking up to see her reaction, I grab my backpack and run away at full speed. Storm clouds are gathering, but I can't go back to my empty studio. Not after that. My lifeless existence holds absolutely no appeal now that I've tasted her lips.

Taking the path that leads to Mount Helena, I ignore the rising winds and start hiking out of town. Willow doesn't follow me and I'm glad. I can't turn around and see her face again or I won't be able to make myself abandon her.

CHAPTER 15
WILLOW
I WON'T JUMP - MALDITO

THE WIND HOWLS OUTSIDE of the cabin, screaming fury and hatred as it batters Lola's windows with violent hail. I flinch when a thunderclap directly outside almost shoves me back into a pit of sordid memories.

Crack.

I said scream, bitch!

Crack.

Beg on your knees.

Crack.

Say my fucking name.

Breathing through gritted teeth, I stare into the crackling flames in Lola's open fireplace. The power went out a couple of hours ago. Apparently, that's normal in periods of bad weather up here.

The storm rolled in late last night, earlier than expected. It has been raging for hours, plunging the daytime into impenetrable darkness. I've never experienced anything like it. Not even the Mexican sandstorms were this brutal.

"Mummy?" Arianna cries out.

I tighten my arm around her. "It's okay."

"Where's the giant? I'm scared. He's supposed to keep us safe, isn't he?"

"Killian is at home, baby. It isn't safe to go out in the storm. Someone could get hurt. It'll all be over soon, I promise."

"Okay," she whimpers.

I rub circles on her back, trying to comfort her. Lola returns from the kitchen, carrying a tray of thick-crust sandwiches and homemade soup that makes my stomach rumble. She sets it up on the floor so it's like we're eating a little picnic.

"Normally, I wouldn't allow eating in here, but I think I can make an exception today. I had to heat the soup with a camping stove so it's a little cold."

Arianna settles next to her on the woven rug. "Thanks, Grams. I'm hungry."

"Of course, poppet. Come on, eat up."

Lola ruffles her neatly braided hair and turns her attention to me. "You too, Willow. I haven't seen you eat a proper meal in days."

I wince, feeling too queasy to contemplate eating. I've felt off all week and have chalked it up to the constant state of anxiety I've spent the last decade in. Breaking the habit of a lifetime isn't quick work.

"I'm fine, Lola. You go ahead and eat."

"I have a bullshit radar, missus."

I snort in amusement. "Is that so?"

"How do you think I raised so many boisterous children around here?" She tucks a napkin into Arianna's shirt collar. "No one tries it on with me and succeeds."

Too curious for my own good, I can't help but pry.

"What were the guys like as kids?"

"Killian was a little bugger when he was young," she reveals conversationally. "Always getting into trouble and causing havoc. He thought he was smarter than all of us."

"Nothing's changed then."

"Definitely not." Lola scoffs. "The twins were a bit more manageable, but your grandpa was the patient one, not me. He taught them everything they know."

"How old were they when they came here? The twins?"

Pushing a bowl of soup and a sandwich towards me regardless, she settles back with her own food.

"Their father died... gosh, nearly fourteen years ago."

My heart splinters imagining little Zach and Micah, both ten-years-old, losing their dad so young. I can't even contemplate what would happen to Arianna if I wasn't here to keep her safe. One recent near-death experience was enough to scare me.

"Zach was a terror too, causing trouble from day one. Him and Killian were a deadly combination, pranking the other kids and winding everyone up for their own fun."

"And Micah?""

Lola stirs her soup, deep in thought. "Micah was the silent one. He had such bad night terrors and panic attacks as a child. Zach was the only one who calmed him down."

Unable to stop myself, I think of Micah's hopelessly sad smile. His impromptu kiss has been on my mind ever since it happened. I didn't see it coming, but a dark, sinful part of me wants to do it all over again, regardless of what my brain thinks.

"What happened?"

"Killian didn't tell you?" Lola asks in surprise.

"Not the specifics. I've spent some time with Micah, though. He's... erm, different."

"He was always a good boy, albeit troubled. Their father battled prostate cancer for several years. When he passed on, the police didn't find his body until three days later."

"Wait, what?"

Lola checks that Arianna's absorbed in her meal before lowering her voice to a hushed whisper. "Micah was locked in a room with his father's corpse for all that time."

I have to hold back a wave of nausea. "Oh my God."

"Zach shouted and begged from the other side of the locked door, but Micah didn't respond until the police knocked the bathroom door down to free him."

"And no one was there to help?"

Lola shakes her head. "They lived far away from here. By the time we found out what had happened, it was too late. Killian's parents adopted Micah and Zach, but things were never the same again."

My heart aches at the thought of Micah as a terrified little boy, locked in a room with his father's body for all of that time. He must have been so scared, unable to move enough to even unlock the door. It's an unimaginable cruelty.

"When he was older, Micah started going into town, drinking alone," Lola explains. "Your grandpa staged an intervention when he was eighteen and told him to find another way to cope. That's when they built the studio. Killian's idea."

"Was he always artistic?"

"Oh, yes. They thought it would help him to cope, but we lost him to a whole new vice. At least when he was drinking, we still saw him. Now, nobody does. He's too withdrawn."

I think about the countless priceless sculptures and paintings that litter Micah's studio, each more exquisite than the last. A love story to the richness of the world around him—a world that he's too scared to see with his own eyes for fear of it being ripped away.

It must feel more manageable for him to reduce it down to the safety of a lump of clay, the flick of a brush, something under his control which can't hurt him. People die. Art lives forever. It's the perfect, silent companion.

"Grams?"

The front door slams shut so loud, we both startle in shock and launch to our feet. I order Arianna to stay hidden and follow Lola out into the hallway, where frantic voices are yelling over the sound of hailstones.

"What are you two doing out in this storm?" Lola exclaims.

Killian and Zach are shaking rain from their wet hair, both looking wild with desperation as they stand just inside the entrance. They're soaked through and still wearing their mud-streaked work clothes.

"It's Micah." Killian wrings water from his long locks. "He didn't come back from his hike yesterday. We just checked the studio for flooding and realised."

"When did he leave?" Lola asks urgently.

"Yesterday afternoon, around four o'clock." I earn myself three very surprised looks. "I... uh, saw him on his way out."

"Was he upset? Did something happen?" Killian barks.

I flinch. "We may have... you know, he was—"

"Just spit it out, Willow."

"Kill," Zach warns. "You need to calm down."

"He could be seriously hurt!" Killian shouts at him. "I need to know what happened."

Hugging my midsection, I blink away tears. "I guess he might've been upset."

Killian pins his cousin with an *I told you so* look that only makes me feel worse. I had no idea that Micah didn't come back after he stormed away from me.

"Why was he upset?" Zach questions calmly.

"We... spoke. He stormed off."

Killian's gaze crackles across my skin, charring flesh and bone, until I'm retreating from him in fear. He's forgone his human façade entirely today, opting for cold fury instead. I can't stop myself from replaying his words from last week.

I didn't mean to get someone hurt. Especially not Micah. I care about him too. Killian curses and marches back out into the storm before Lola can grab his arm.

"Where do you think you're going?" she shouts after him.

"To find my stupid fucking cousin!" Killian yells over his shoulder. "He could get killed in this weather. I won't leave him out there alone."

"I'm coming," Zach chimes in.

In a split second, I've made my decision. Grabbing the bright-purple raincoat that I picked up in town, I throw it over my clothes and grab my leather boots.

"Me too. Let's go and find him."

"I hardly think so." Lola fists a handful of my coat to prevent me from leaving. "You're not going out in that storm. Leave this to the boys."

"It's my fault he's out there in the first place!"

"Nonsense. Micah isn't your responsibility." She looks at Zach, her face stern. "Go with Killian and report back within an hour or I'm calling mountain rescue. Got that?"

"Yes, Grams."

I watch him dash back out into the rain, his frame swallowed by the darkness. The crash of Lola slamming the front door shut feels like a right hook in the stomach.

She heads back into Arianna, leaving me to strip off my raincoat. Overcome by anger, I scrunch it in my hands. This is all my fault.

I shouldn't have kissed him or said any of those things. I was feeling vulnerable and lost. He didn't need me to take my own insecurities out on him.

If he's hurt, I'll never forgive myself.

———

Staring at the grandfather clock, I watch the minute hand strike twelve for what feels like the millionth time. Lola has taken Arianna up to bed.

The storm is still raging, and the wind rattles the entire contents of the cabin. Despite its high-tech, sturdy construction, window panes judder and the screaming wind whistles down the chimney breast, threatening to extinguish the fire.

The painful wait has run my nerves ragged. I'm too distracted to keep my mind in check. My nails dig into my palms, unnerved by the whispered words in my head.

All your fault, Mrs Sanchez.

No more fighting back.

You'll never escape here.

This isn't the first time people have gotten hurt because of me. Nobody understands why I keep my secrets locked up deep inside. It's more than the disjointed sense of being different that Micah described.

The threat against myself and Arianna still stands, no matter the ocean between us and our old home. If the man I'm married to can brutalise others for his own pleasure, he can find a way to win back his precious treasure.

That's real power.

He has no limits.

Staring deep into the embers of the fireplace, I'm too deep in thought to hear the creaking floorboards behind me. I startle when a hand brushes my shoulder.

"I'm back, babe."

Hunched over, Zach is soaked to the bone and shaking. Water drips on Lola's living room floor, creating a puddle around him. His usually tanned skin is tinted a shade of freezing cold blue.

"Zach!" I shout.

He easily catches me when I throw myself into his arms. I don't care that he's soaking my sweater and leggings with rainwater. Seeing him safe and sound is the miracle I was waiting for.

"It's okay, Willow. Everything is fine. I came to let Lola know."

"Where was he? What happened?"

Peeling my arms from his neck, Zach guides me back to the sofa. "Micah got caught in the overpass. The route was blocked by flooding. He managed to go the long way around, but he got lost and had to camp overnight."

"Is h-he okay?" I stammer fearfully.

"Mild case of hypothermia, dehydrated and feeling like a fool, but he's fine. Killian already chewed him out for being a moron. They had a huge fight."

"Thank God. I was so worried."

Zach winces as he shakes out his hands, the skin turning a bright shade of red as he warms up. I leap back onto my feet, beginning to panic again. He's sodden and shivering from head to toe.

"You're freezing. Take off your clothes."

"Excuse me?" he says through chattering teeth.

"It's the quickest way to warm up. You don't want to get sick."

"I'm okay, really."

"Use the fire to warm up before you catch hypothermia too. I promise, I won't look."

His gaze trails over me. "Maybe I won't mind if you do look."

With an eye roll, I turn my back on him. "Just strip."

"You don't have to ask me twice."

Grabbing another log of wood from the basket, I add it to the flames and give it a poke, getting the fire roaring again. The sound of a zipper and wet denim being shimmied off sets my heart racing.

"If you wanted me to take my clothes off sooner, you only had to ask," Zach says huskily. "I've got nothing to hide from you."

The pad of his bare feet joins me in front of the fire. Zach sits down, stretching his bare legs and hands outwards to capture the heat. I can't stop myself from taking a peak out of the corner of my eye.

My mouth goes dry.

Holy fuck.

I knew that Zach was muscular like his cousin and brother. Life up here doesn't allow for laziness. But the hard lines that carve his defined abdominals stacked in neat rows across his torso are something else. He's literally ripped.

Zach's strong legs have been honed by hours of work outside, and his skin-tight boxers leave nothing to the imagination. His package is huge. Intimidatingly so. I don't have a whole lot of experience, but even I can see he's well-endowed.

I clear my throat. "Well then."

"Fuck, I'm freezing."

"Want me to make you some tea?"

A wicked smile stretches his lips. "Why don't you come sit here with me while I warm up? Promise I'll keep my hands to myself. Scout's honour."

"You were in the Scouts?"

"Well, Pops' version anyway. It mostly entailed me and Killian sneaking into his cabin to steal his beer. We also practised shooting the empty bottles until we got caught."

With a deep breath, I sit down in front of the fire, tucking my legs up to my chest. Zach's broad shoulder brushes mine for a brief, heart-stopping second. He's staring at me, the smile wiped from his face. It's weird to see him looking serious.

"What did you and Micah argue about?"

I feel my cheeks flush. "Nothing."

"Then why are you turning into an admittedly adorable tomato right now?" He barks a laugh. "Come on, you can tell me. I'm great at keeping secrets."

"Not happening."

"Here's one for you then. Did you know that Killian shaved all his hair off once when he was drunk? Ryder dared him to do it."

"You're joking?" I splutter.

"Nope. His mum nearly killed him for doing it. He looked like a fucking convict and it took months to grow back as well. So, come on. Tell me what happened."

"You've just proven that you can't keep a secret."

Zach draws a cross over his heart. "My lips are sealed, I swear."

I look back into the depths of the fire. "It was stupid. I've never felt comfortable or at ease around people, especially men. But Micah's easy to talk to and he gets me."

Zach's eyebrows shoot up. "He kissed you, didn't he?"

"What? How do you know that?"

"It's written all over your face. He may not know the first thing about women, but no one else has been allowed inside his studio, let alone given something to take home."

"So what? He likes Arianna."

"Micah doesn't let anyone get close to him. He's a lot like you in that respect. I knew he liked you the moment he showed you his art."

I hate what he's insinuating. Truthfully, I want to let people in. I want to belong to someone. My past is the only thing stopping me from giving myself to another person. That's all anyone wants—to love and be loved.

"You're doing a Killian," he prods.

"A Killian?"

"Silence and lots of glaring. It's his signature move."

"I am not glaring," I respond hotly.

His shoulder bumps mine again. Zach's palm snakes closer, until he takes my hand and tangles our fingers together. I don't have the heart to pull away from him. His touch feels so good.

"It's okay that you kissed my brother, babe."

"How is that okay?" I gape at him.

"Because I love Micah. I want him to be happy."

"Clearly, he's not happy. He ran away from me and got himself hurt."

Zach's thumb strokes my inner wrist. "The world works differently here. We don't keep people in little boxes just because it's convenient. If you want to kiss him, you should."

"He kissed me."

"Right, but you kissed him back."

"Does it matter who started it?" I snap at him. "Jesus, Zach. Nobody should be kissing anyone. It was a mistake."

"Kissing is allowed. In fact, if you want to kiss me, I would highly encourage it."

My belly explodes with nervous butterflies. I'd be lying if I said that I hadn't thought about it with all three of them. They're gorgeous. But more than that, Killian, Zach and even Micah have made me feel at home in their own ways.

I smack his shoulder. "You're not helping."

"Keep thinking so hard and steam will come out of your ears." He dares to run a finger along my jaw. "Something to think about. I need to get back and check on Micah."

Grabbing his soaking wet clothes, Zach stretches to his full height, showing off far too many muscles that have heat heading straight down south. There's a dark, intricate tattoo on his bicep that I hadn't noticed before.

Before he can leave me to wallow in my guilt again, I launch to my feet and croak his name. Zach freezes, his eyes zipping over his shoulder to find me. The smile tugging at his lips is so hopeful, I think he was secretly praying I'd stop him from leaving.

"You could stay," I blurt.

He arches a brow. "Here?"

"Everyone else is asleep."

Satisfied with my confession, he drops the bundle of clothes tucked under his arm. His powerful legs eat up the distance between us until every inch of his skin is within my reach. I battle the urge to trace my fingers over his defined collarbones.

"Tell me what you really want, Willow."

"I... don't know."

"That's a lie. You know."

His voice is a silky, confident rasp that makes my thighs clench together. I can't say it. Not out loud. I'm too afraid to acknowledge the desires bubbling up within me for the first time.

"Nothing?" Zach moves closer. "Perhaps you want me to kiss that gorgeous mouth of yours." His hand dances down my shoulder. "Or do you only want my twin brother?"

Breath catching, I'm caught in the sheer magnetism of his gaze. It's impossible not to see Micah in his features, but the person heating my blood in this moment is Zach. Only him. They are two separate entities in my head, and I want them both.

Cupping my jaw, he tilts my head up. "Perhaps you want me to trace every single inch of your body with my tongue, or for me to taste how wet your pussy is in this moment."

"Zach," I gasp, embarrassed.

"What?" he counters. "Don't deny it. I can see your legs pressing together. Does it hurt, beautiful girl? Is your cunt soaking wet and begging for me to touch it?"

Every filthy, shocking word that escapes his mouth turns me on even more. I'm practically sagging against him, my legs trembling with each throb of pleasure demanding to be relieved. I've never felt this intense need before.

"Now she blushes," Zach teases before growing stern. "I don't want to trigger you again like I did in the shop. That's why I've tried to keep my distance."

"I… I don't want you to keep your distance."

"Then you have to communicate. If you want me to touch you, I need to know. I won't lay a finger on you without your consent."

I feel the remains of my uncertainty melt into pathetic mush. Those words are all I needed to hear. He's offering me the one thing I was never afforded. Control. A choice. This is all on my terms, not his.

Leaning into his touch, I breathe out a sigh. "Please, Zach."

"More specific," he demands.

My heart judders in my chest, on the verge of breaking free.

"Please kiss me. Touch me. Make me feel whole again."

"There's a good girl. That's what I wanted to hear."

A hand meets the small of my back, trapping me against the hard planes of his chest. Despite being clothed in nothing but boxers, his skin feels like a furnace. He's warmed up in no time and his electric touch burns into me.

"I want to bury my face between your thighs," he purrs. "And I want you to come all over my mouth so I can taste how sweet you are. Reckon you can do that, babe?"

I couldn't answer him even if I wanted to. I'm dizzy with lust. Years' worth of pent up frustration and pain have led me to this desperate place. But still, I trust him. I know that Zach would never hurt me.

Tugging the hem of my oversized sweater, he guides it over my head, exposing my plain bra. A shiver overtakes me as Zach eases the leggings over my hips next, planting open-mouthed kisses against my stomach while pulling them off.

His mouth moves lower still, and he plants a kiss against the scrap of white cotton holding him back from my core. I can feel how damp the material is. I'm soaked through just from listening to his dirty mouth.

"Such a perfect angel," Zach praises, sliding off my panties to expose my bareness to him. "You're dripping already and I haven't even touched you."

He kneels before me, his quads bulging with muscles that set my pulse alight. I feel oddly powerful, standing over him while he lavishes every inch of my flushed skin.

I'm desperate for the relief of his touch. Nothing else matters, not even the fact we're both near-naked in Lola's living room where anyone could walk in. Zach sits back on the rug and lays down, tugging my wrist to pull me on top of him.

I straddle his waist, holding back a moan as the promising steel of his length brushes against my core. It's an excruciating tease. That sense of pressure has never given me such a thrill before.

"Look at you." He smirks up at me. "Being on top suits you."

"I've n-never done this before."

"What? Been on top?"

I bat aside the brush of bad memories. "Yeah."

"Well, that simply won't do. I'm dying to watch you fall apart with my tongue buried inside you. Come and ride my face."

"You want me to do what?"

Zach snickers. "There's that blush again. Come on, babe. Bring your cunt to me."

Wracked by uncertainty, I let him guide my hips upwards. With a leg spread either side of his head, he pulls my core closer to his face until I'm splayed out over his head.

The moment his mouth meets my folds, I forget my insecurities. Strange new sensations wash over me with each stroke of his tongue, sparking nerves I had no idea existed until now. This is the first time a man has ever pleasured me.

He hungrily laps at my core like he's tucking into a five-star meal. With his hands still engulfing my waist, he encourages me to move, shifting back and forth in a slow undulation. Each shift of my hips rocks me against his mouth.

A sense of pressure begins to unfurl inside of me. It begins as a slow burn like the first wisps of curling smoke rising from a bonfire. When his thumb moves to circle the tight bundle of nerves I've only ever touched myself, the feeling triples.

"You taste like fucking heaven." He comes up for air. "More, babe. I want you to fuck yourself against my face. You can do it."

Releasing my hip, he lets me take the reins. I copy the movements he showed me, lifting my hips and rocking backwards to spear his tongue deeper into my slit.

"Oh, God," I moan.

His thumb keeps circling, toying with my nub and building the pressure deep inside me until it feels like I'm going to explode. I never thought it was possible to get so much pleasure from someone else's tongue.

Head thrown back, I cry out his name when the feeling reaches its pinnacle. Zach's still lavishing my core, the graze of his teeth on my clit pushing me over the edge.

"Perfect. That's it, Willow."

Fireworks explode beneath my skin, over and over again. With a final flick of his tongue, Zach ceases his slow torture and watches me ride out the waves of bliss. This is the first time a man has made me orgasm.

I wonder what he'd think if he knew.

Something tells me Zach would love that.

Floating on a cloud, I come back down to earth as he repositions me so I'm straddling his waist again. He sits up, with glistening moisture scored across his mouth. The son of a bitch looks far too pleased with himself.

"That was a hell of a sight," he says gruffly.

Panting hard, I watch his tongue dart out to clean my come from his lips. He licks up every last drop with enthusiasm, the evil glint in his eye betraying his satisfaction.

"Now I'm back in the lead."

"What?" I groan.

His chest vibrates with a chuckle. "Micah isn't the best twin after all. I'll happily beat him again by making you come all fucking day long."

"Zach! This isn't a competition."

"Of course, it is. One that I intend to win."

CHAPTER 16
WILLOW

SAD DAYS - PRESENCE

SURVEYING THE WINDSWEPT TOWN, tears prick my eyes. Several of the huge, hand-carved wooden cabins have broken windows or damaged roofs. It's the same story across the whole of Briar Valley after three days of bad weather.

Gardens are trashed, picnic benches upturned, and trees have been uprooted. That's just the superficial stuff. Yet nobody looks sad or has dared to shed a tear. They're helping each other clean up and figure out what needs to be done.

"This is terrible."

Standing next to me with his hands on his hips, Killian surveys the damage. "We've had worse storms. This isn't too bad."

"How could it be worse than this?"

He huffs. "Well, at least they're still standing."

"I never took you for a glass half-full kind of person."

To my amazement, he flashes me a toothy smile.

"People can surprise you."

His grin disappears as quickly as it arrived, leaving me to wonder if I hallucinated the whole thing. Killian was the first one at the front door this morning, demanding to see if we were okay and inviting me to help him search around town.

I hid from the storm with Lola and Arianna in the cabin. Albie and Ryder joined us on the second day, braving the howling winds. We passed the time playing card games in front of the fire, drinking Lola's homemade sloe gin and trading stories.

"Speaking of surprises, did you know that Lola and Albie are a couple?"

"No, they're not," Killian blusters.

"I'm not joking. Ryder told me last night. He caught them kissing a couple of months ago. Apparently, they're been dating for a while."

He full-body shudders. "That is the most disgusting thought ever."

Ryder is full of charming one-liners and a crazy amount of gossip. His light-hearted conversations have kept me going for these past few days. He's got the beadiest eyes in the whole town and seems to know everyone's business.

"How's Micah?" I dare to ask.

His jaw clenches into an unyielding line. "Fine."

"No injuries?"

"Nope. The idiot had a close call."

"That's for sure."

Grabbing a huge fallen tree branch, Killian snaps it in half in one easy move. I stare as he flexes his trunk-like arms. When he catches me looking at him, I quickly look away.

"You just gonna stand there gawping?"

"I'm not gawping," I defend.

"Sure you're not."

He really is infuriatingly hot and cold. This whole untouchable grump act is beginning to wear thin. I've seen the gentle giant that lives within him. He doesn't need to pretend for my sake.

"Go knock on the Jacobsons' door and make sure they're okay. I'll finish up here."

I take advantage of the excuse to escape. He's been in a confusing mood all morning, sulking and sparing me odd looks. I'm too scared to ask if Micah told him about what happened between us, and downright terrified to think about Zach either.

Denial is healthy, right?

Who the hell am I kidding.

This is a mess. I've fooled around with both twins, and I have no idea what I was thinking. After Zach slipped out to return to his cabin, all I could think about was the burning path of his lips kissing my body.

Traipsing up the hill, I catch sight of the newest addition to the town. It's a generous cabin made from golden shades of tan-coloured wood, the perfect size for a growing family. The swing set in the garden is half-collapsed from the high winds.

Stuffing my shyness down, I head up the porch steps and knock on the front door. There's a sound of a crying infant inside and it's several seconds before the door swings open, revealing a short, haggard woman.

"Hello?" she says in a thick accent.

"Um, hi. I'm Willow. Killian sent me to check on you."

Running a hand over her brown ponytail, the woman's olive-skinned face brightens into a grateful smile. She looks to be a similar age to me with deep, almond-shaped eyes the colour of unfiltered sunlight and full, pillowy lips.

"Thank you for coming. I'm Aalia."

"It's nice to meet you. Are you all okay?"

"We're fine, but the children... they..." Pausing in her broken English, she huffs. "How do you say? This... noise?"

"Crying?" I suggest.

She clicks her tongue. "Yes, crying. All day long."

"Want me to give you a hand?"

Quickly ushering me inside, she speaks fast in a beautiful, vibrant language. A small boy appears from another room, cradling a tiny, wailing baby to his chest.

He has his mother's dark hair, but with curious, aquamarine eyes that contrast the rich tone of his skin. I'd say he's around Arianna's age. The baby can't be older than a few months, her cheeks stained red from screaming so loudly.

"Mama!"

"Johan, no shouting," Aalia exclaims.

Chastised, he falls silent, still cuddling the baby close. I kneel in front of him, sticking out my hand for him to shake. With a blossoming grin, he balances the baby and shakes.

"What's your name?"

"Johan," he answers shyly.

"Hi, Johan. Are you happy the rain stopped?"

Nodding back, he adjusts the weight of the baby in his arms. I hold out my hands, reassuring him with a smile. There's a cheeky wink in his eyes, despite his shyness.

"Want me to try?"

"Yes, please," he whispers. "She's so loud."

"Babies cry a lot, but when she gets older, you'll have someone to play with. Doesn't that sound good?"

Johan summons a tiny smile. "I'd like that."

"You know, my daughter is new in town as well. She would love someone to play with too, if you fancied it."

"A girl?" He wrinkles his nose.

"I'm guessing girls are yucky, huh?"

"Yeah. They are."

"Well, have a think about it."

Nodding to himself, he surrenders the baby to me. I take her into my arms, cradling the tiny bundle. Johan watches closely for a moment as if assessing whether to trust me with his sister or not.

I must pass the test because he turns away and races back the way he came. Repositioning the baby to get her comfortable, I stand back up and find Aalia watching with a bright, grateful smile.

"He's a good boy, but not when he's cooped up inside."

"Trust me, I know. My six-year-old has been a nightmare during the storm as well. What's this little one's name?"

She strokes a hand over her daughter's head. "This is Amie, my youngest. She cries too much."

I hold her to my chest and begin to rock back and forth. She's so beautiful, already sporting a headful of dark hair and stunning eyes that perfectly match her brother's orbs.

"Hey, pretty girl. You causing trouble for your mama?"

Cooing and rocking the baby, it takes a few minutes for her to drop off. Aalia lets out an exhausted sigh, heading into the kitchen to brew a pot of tea. I perch against the dining table, keeping Amie safe in my arms.

"Did you have any more damage from the storm?" I watch as she adds a mixture of fresh herbs to boiling water. "I saw your garden and swing set."

"That was all. Nothing else."

"Good. I'll tell Killian to get them fixed up for you."

"You are too kind." She sets two teacups down on the table, adding saucers and spoons. "In my country, we drink this tea with friends. It is a custom."

"Where are you from? I hope that's not rude to ask."

"Not at all." She returns with the tea pot and gestures for me to sit. "We're from Egypt, but we have been everywhere. Many different countries, looking for a home."

Aalia pours the steaming tea into my cup. I breathe in the floral scent and take a sip. Exotic flavours burst across my tongue, exploding with hints of cardamon and rich spices. I can't help but groan.

"This is amazing. Thank you."

She smiles at me. "It's a pleasure."

"Your English is great. How long have you been here?"

"We've been in temporary accommodation for a few months. I learned this language in my country, but Johan speaks more than me."

Right on cue, the star of the show returns, his shyness now completely forgotten. He demands my attention and recites the whole alphabet, grinning from ear to ear when I clap. He gives me a little bow, earning a kiss on the cheek from his mother.

"The people here saved our lives." Aalia watches Johan disappear into the bedroom again. "Lola is a good woman. I do not know how to thank her."

"How did you learn about this place?"

"She took us from a friend of hers. No questions."

"That's really good." I take another sip of the delicious tea. "Lola helped us too. I'm here with my daughter, Arianna. We arrived a month or so ago."

"That's a beautiful name," Aalia compliments.

"I'll have to introduce her to Johan. She could use another friend to play with. Rachel and Miranda's kids are a bit older."

"Yes, he needs someone."

"Even a yucky girl?" I laugh.

She shakes her head in amusement. "Even a girl. I am too tired to play with him. Two children is… how do you say, uh… hard. Lots of work."

"I bet. Does your husband help?"

The light that seems to emanate from her extinguishes, and her face shuts down. It's like looking into an awful mirror, seeing the slight tremble of her hands, and the way she studies the circle of light skin around her ring finger.

"He is not a good man."

"I'm sorry," I rush to apologise. "We don't have to talk about him."

"No, it's fine. When he was not happy, he liked to hit. I took my children, and I ran."

Taking my hand in hers, I gently squeeze. "I understand."

Her golden eyes shine with tears. "I hope I did the right thing."

"You did. Don't ever doubt yourself for keeping your babies safe."

Wiping her tears away, Aalia looks from Amie asleep in my arms to my wedding band still in place. She arches a perfectly plucked eyebrow.

"And your husband? He is here?"

"Um, no. We aren't together either."

"I'm sorry, Willow. But you're still wearing the ring?"

"I'm not ready to take it off yet."

"It won't make you bad or, you know, not strong." She struggles over her words. "I was scared to run and to be alone. But we deserve to be happy."

I let out a weak laugh. "You think?"

"I do," she affirms. "Here, I am happy."

"I'd like to be. One day."

"You will. When you're ready to take the ring off, come for some tea and we'll take it off together."

Chest warm with appreciation, I blow out a long-held breath. "Thank you, Aalia. That means a lot to me."

"Us single mothers need to stick together. We can help each other, we don't need these…" She lowers her voice. "*Shitheads.*"

I choke on a mouthful of tea and Aalia has to hammer me on the back. The baby begins to stir in my arms, shaken by the sudden movement. I hush her, trying hard not to laugh and wake her up.

"Where on earth did you learn that word?"

Aalia winks. "Killian called my husband this name."

"Huh. Why am I not surprised?"

Both giggling, we finish our tea. Aalia takes the baby from my arms to breastfeed her and while she's preoccupied, I wash up the cups and saucers. She still needs a few essentials, so I begin a mental list, intent on helping her out.

The sound of crashing from outside alerts me to Killian's presence. He begins to clear the fallen branches from Aalia's garden and when I peer out between her curtains, he's giving the destroyed swing set the stink-eye.

Beginning to dismantle the wooden poles, he smashes them into smaller logs to be burned with the help of a shining axe. Fury fuels his every move. It's clear that something is eating away at him, even I can see that.

"You like him?"

Startled, I find Aalia by my side. "Killian?"

"He is… handsome?"

"No, no. I mean, he is. But no, we're just… friends, I guess? Lola is my grandmother. I came here to find her."

"You have her eyes." Aalia winks at me. "I like her a lot."

"You think?"

"Oh, yes. And all this hair, it's so long. Beautiful."

I run a self-conscious hand over my curly, rain-mussed hair. "I hate the length. My husband never let me cut it. He said it wasn't allowed."

"You want me to?" Aalia mimes a snipping motion with her fingers.

Just like with the thought of removing my wedding ring, an uncontrollable shudder overtakes me. The one time Mr Sanchez caught me trimming my hair, he broke my wrist.

I was always careful after that, snipping off bits here and there, but nothing noticeable. It was the same with Arianna. We had to follow his rules, including for our appearances.

"Another time. I need to build myself up to it."

"I understand," she offers with a smile. "I'm here."

"Thank you. I'll let you know when I'm ready."

After a quick hug, I call goodbye to Johan and step outside. Killian's still loading up the truck with broken wood. We have a bunch more cabins to check out, and I need to start planning for Arianna's birthday party next week.

"If you need a hand with the kids or someone to talk to... you know where to find me."

Standing inside the open doorway, Aalia blows me a kiss. "Me too. Come back and see us soon. I'll cut your hair and make tea. Okay?"

"Okay," I agree. "See you around."

With a final wave, I return to the truck. Killian is all done. He's piled up the salvageable parts of the swing set on the lawn, assessing what remains with his blonde brows furrowed.

I climb into the passenger seat, waiting for him to join me. The whole truck shakes with the force of him climbing inside and slamming the door shut behind him.

"You meet Aalia? Is she alright?"

"Yeah, she's fine. No other damage."

"That's good. We've been in contact with her for a while. Zach and I worked nights for almost a week to get the cabin done early. She was living in a shit hotel."

"I didn't realise she was here all alone. I would've come and said hello sooner."

Killian shrugs. "Lola has a friend who works for the local council. Every now and then, a new family comes here to get away. Some stay and others move on to different places."

"This place is like a rehab centre or something."

"Except most people never leave," he comments. "Briar Valley was half the size it is now when I was a kid."

"You never wanted to leave?"

"No. Never."

"Why?"

Driving away from Aalia's cabin, he focuses on the cobbled road, his lips sealed. I hate that his barriers are slamming back down, pushing me out again. It's like I get so far into understanding him before he shuts me out.

My question hangs in the air between us as we drive through trees stripped of their leaves by the storm. Even the distant mountains look extra snow swept, the peaks peppered with a fresh sprinkle of white powder.

"Lola's always struck me as a private person." I fish for a topic to break the silence. "Even in Highbridge, she wasn't well known. I can't imagine her having many friends."

"She's known Katie for a long time."

My stomach twists. "Katie?"

"She came to stay here once upon a time. Hell, it must've been about twenty odd years ago. I was a kid myself at the time."

He's getting comfortable again, forgetting his bad mood as we drive onwards.

"Does Katie still live here?"

Killian shakes his head. "She left a long time ago. Poor woman had the crap beaten out of her when she first turned up, and this big fucking scar down her left cheek."

My heart explodes out of control.

"Lola took her in," he continues. "They've been friends ever since."

Staring at the side of Killian's head, his long hair pulled back into a bun at the nape of his neck, my nails dig deep into my palms. It has to be a coincidence.

"A scar? On her face?"

He looks at me strangely. "Uh, yeah. It was huge and fresh. Why does it matter?"

"Shit! Stop the car. I'm going to be sick."

"Right now?" he bellows.

"Yes, now!"

He abruptly brakes, causing the tyres to spin. Once we've halted, I fall out of the truck, landing on my knees in the grass with a pained grunt. A hot burst of vomit surges up my throat and I violently retch.

The driver's door slams shut and for the second time, Killian rubs my back as he holds my hair out of the way. This is officially exceeding the amount of times I wanted him to watch me throw my guts up.

"Willow? Talk to me, baby," he pleads.

Exhausted, I lean into his solid weight at my side. He's holding me close and refusing to let go, despite how gross this is. I take a moment to catch my breath, still feeling sick.

"The w-woman… Katie? You said Katie?"

"Yes. What's going on?"

Wiping my mouth with the back of my hand, I make myself meet his alarmed eyes. Fear stares back at me in shades of molten brown, breaking free from his cool control.

"Katie is my mother."

CHAPTER 17
KILLIAN

WILDFIRE (ALTERNATE VERSION) - SYML

CURSING MY ABSOLUTE FUCKING STUPIDITY, I raise my fist to knock on the bedroom door. Lola gave me a very strange look when I refused to disclose why I needed to speak to Willow, but she ordered me to find out what the hell is going on with her.

Sure.

Like it's that easy.

Willow has locked herself away in the cabin over the weekend, pretending to be busy with party preparations for Arianna's upcoming seventh birthday next week, and nursing a supposed migraine. It's bullshit. Her lies aren't even believable.

I wish I could break through her shields long enough to get her to trust me. We've been dancing around each other for weeks and fighting at every turn. All I want is to protect and cherish her, even if it terrifies me to admit it.

"Willow? You in there?"

Silence.

"It's Killian. I just want to talk."

There's a thud of footsteps and the door handle rattles before it swings open, unveiling a very sleepy, bleary-eyed Arianna in polka dot pyjamas. She squints up at me, that stupid butterfly sculpture still pooled in her arms.

"Giant? What are you doing here?"

"Hey, peanut. Where's your mama?"

"She's not here."

"What do you mean… not here?"

Arianna shrugs, padding back over to their unmade bed in her semi-asleep state. She curls up under the covers and the sound of quiet snoring restarts. It gives me a stupid sense of satisfaction to see how much the kid trusts me.

Creeping into the room as quietly as possible, I search around, finding no signs that Willow was packing or intending to leave. She must be in the valley somewhere.

Nearly tripping over a duffel bag peeking out from under the bed, I pause to unzip it, finding a few valuables hidden inside. There's a wooden baby box full of trinkets and pictures of an infant Arianna playing in what looks like a desert.

Beneath that, I find two British passports. I flip them open and stare at the names. My earlier relief at finding her belongings in their rightful place vanishes.

Melody Tanner.

Adele Tanner.

Both Willow and Arianna's pictures are recent, beneath the false names. The birthdates have also been tweaked too. What the fuck? These can't be genuine. They're damn good fakes though, probably worth a small fortune.

The memory of their burned fingerprints comes racing back to me from the mental box I've locked it away in, too angry to even imagine someone hurting them in such a way. Arianna's fingers are healing nicely, the skin now pink and shiny.

I've been patient. Willow needed time to heal and get comfortable, I know that. Trust is earned, regardless of any blood relation between her and Lola. But I've wanted to pin her gorgeous body down and demand answers so many times now.

Somehow, I've restrained myself.

Fuck that.

I want the truth.

Finding Willow and making sure she's okay is my priority, then I can interrogate her until I find out who I need to skin alive and bury in my fucking vegetable patch. Either way, someone's going to pay for hurting her.

Ignoring Lola calling my name, I thump downstairs and run out into the dark night. There's no one around. Zach went into Highbridge a few hours ago to have drinks with Ryder and his boyfriend who's in town.

I know Micah's back in the studio, hiding from the world. He's been even more off than usual since his little incident in the overpass before the storm hit. No one needs to tell me that something went down with Willow. It's fucking obvious.

Racing back to my cabin atop the steep hill overlooking the valley, I'm intent on grabbing a flashlight to search the woods in case Willow has gone for a walk and gotten lost. It happens easily enough around here.

My steps are halted by a trembling figure curled up on our hand-built porch furniture. She's shaking all over, being hammered by the rain pouring down from the dark sky.

Her long black hair looks like spilled ink against her soaking wet skin, tinged bright-red from the cold. She's only dressed in a vest top, oversized linen shirt and sodden blue jeans.

"Willow?" I shout out.

Her head barely lifts at the sharp bite of my voice.

"Willow! You with me?"

Thumping up the steps, I'm at her side in a flash. Sinking into the wet chair next to her, I run a hand down her arm. Willow flinches but doesn't move, staring out into the darkness.

"Willow? Say something, baby."

"My mother abandoned me," she utters.

My anxiety explodes at the lifeless sound of her voice. She always speaks with such quiet but unshakeable hope. It's one of my favourite things about her—that indisputable sense of determination that's kept her going.

"She upped and left without a word when I was Arianna's age. I never saw her again, and she left me alone with a neglectful drug addict."

Fucking-fuckity-fuck.

"If I had any idea, I wouldn't have told you." I scrape a worried hand over my beard. "We didn't know you existed, let alone that you were anything to do with Lola or Katie."

"Lola lied to you, Kill. She's been lying to us all."

Tilting her head up, two bloodshot hazel eyes scour over me. She looks so desperately alone, it's killing me to see it. Reaching out with healing fingertips, Willow briefly strokes my tangled beard before her hand falls back down.

"Please," I beg her. "Come inside. I'm worried about you."

"I thought you didn't have emotions."

"I fucking don't."

"Then why are you so mad right now?"

Pinching the bridge of my nose, I fight to keep my anger in check. She's frustrating and fascinating in equal measure. All I want is to claim her as my own, every goddamn inch, but I don't want to break her.

Willow deserves more than my worthless ass can give her. I've treated her with all the disdain and mistrust I could muster to conceal the truth—that I want her, as much as the other two do, even if they're pretending otherwise.

"Kill?" she repeats.

"Just stop, Willow."

"You can't even answer me, can you?" she laughs bitterly.

"It's not that."

"Then just be honest with me for once!"

"I'm fucking angry because I care about you, alright? Because I actually like you. A lot. And I don't want to see you in pain anymore, but I can't seem to protect you from it."

Locked in the icy constraints of the falling rain, neither of us makes a move. We're trapped in the moment with no hope of rescue. It's too late to turn back now. I've already dived off the cliff's edge to my imminent death.

"What are you doing out here?" I quickly change the topic.

"I needed some space," she admits, still looking shell-shocked at my words. "Arianna has questions, and I have no answers right now. I'm more confused than ever."

Holding out a hand, calloused palm up in invitation, I wait for this beautiful creature to put her trust in me. Even if I should turf her back out on the street and crush these stupid feelings to keep my family safe from harm.

I know something happened with Micah. Zach too. He's been bouncing on cloud fucking nine for days and I'm not blind. They've both been acting weird since she came barrelling into our lives.

That's saying a lot, considering Micah is another species altogether on his good days and Zach has the energy of a puppy in need of constant attention. Willow is bad news for all of us.

But it doesn't stop me from wanting to devour her with every fibre of my being. I've thought of nothing else ever since the day she agreed to stay in town, daring to smile and accept our offer of a real family and home.

That night sparked something inside me that I didn't know existed and can't turn off again. I've never had a real relationship. Women have come and gone out of my life without giving a flying fuck, and I was more than happy with that.

"Please come inside."

"We don't have to talk?" she asks.

"I'm not your damn therapist. You want a wet blanket to cry on, then you're looking at the wrong man. Need me to shoot a motherfucker, or skin a dead deer, I'm all over it."

I try to keep my voice cold to conceal my desperation for answers, but I know it's futile at this point. The breathtaking smile that blossoms across her lips nearly destroys my self-control. She sees me. Fuck, it feels too good.

"Noted. No crying or talking."

"Good." I gesture for her to take my hand. "Let's go find the liquor."

Willow finally accepts. "I'll take a double."

Pinning her shivering body against my side, I guide her into the unlit cabin. It's pitch black inside. I deposit Willow on the sofa and flick a couple of lights on.

"Sit down. I'll find towels."

I slip into the bathroom and take a second to glance in the mirror. My long hair is wet and windswept, framing a mouth pinched with frustration. This is what she does to me—drives me absolutely fucking insane with need.

Walking back out into the open-plan living room, I find the lights turned back off. The glow of freshly lit flames from the open fireplace illuminates the room instead. Willow is crouched in front of it, adding kindling to the fire.

"Here." I toss her the towel. "Dry off."

She catches and wraps it around her shoulders. "Thanks."

"What's your poison?"

"Whatever you have."

Filling two glasses with one of my favourite bottles of whiskey, I sink down next to her on the soft fur of the rug, stretching my long legs out. Willow swigs a mouthful, coughing as the liquor slips down.

"I really hate this stuff."

"It's good for the soul."

She winces. "Not my soul."

Placing the glass down on the tiled fireplace, Willow begins to unbutton the wet linen shirt stuck to her body. I choke on a mouthful of whiskey and quickly avert my eyes.

"I have a vest underneath," she mutters.

Unable to stop myself, I watch her wring out her wet locks, the swell of her breasts stretching the thin material of the vest top covering her chest. I don't think she realises how fucking beautiful she is the most natural way possible.

My fingers spasm with the need to reach out and stroke her soft skin, despite everything telling me not to. One glimpse of her naked wasn't enough. I want to worship her body at every available angle.

"How's Micah?"

"Hiding from us," I answer with annoyance.

"Still?"

"He goes through phases of seeming to get better, then it's like the brakes slam on, and we have to watch him fade away all over again when another depressive episode hits."

"These things take time, Kill."

"I'm supposed to look after him and I'm failing."

Her eyes dart up to mine. "It's not that simple."

"I tried to convince him to go back to therapy the other morning," I find myself saying. "He told me to get lost and slammed the door in my face. Hasn't spoken to me since."

"I think you're being too hard on yourself."

I swallow another mouthful. No matter what she thinks, I can't afford the luxury of letting Micah's behaviour hurt my feelings. Someone has to watch over him, even when he'd rather I let him self-destruct.

Willow stares into the fire. "It was my fault he went hiking in a bad mindset. I tried to apologise a few days ago. He wouldn't even answer the door for me."

Driven by an overwhelming desire that's too intense for me to quench, I slide a fingertip beneath her chin to tilt her eyes up to meet mine. Willow freezes, her lips parted.

"Why is it your fault, baby?" I drag a thumb over her bottom lip, briefly dipping inside her mouth for a second. "Did you two do something?"

"No," she breathes.

"Don't fucking lie to me, Willow."

Her eyes fill with pain. "We talked."

"What else?" I stroke over her cheek, coaxing her compliance. "Tell me the truth."

"I was upset, and he tried to comfort me. Then, it's so stupid... but we kissed."

Unsurprised, I stroke the pad of my thumb beneath her eye, taking care to study every part of her. The sprinkling of dimples over her cheeks. The blueish veins of her eyelids. Thick lashes framing irises perfectly blending brown and green.

"You kissed him?"

"He kissed me, but I didn't stop it."

"And why did you kiss him back?"

She lets out a stunted breath. "To feel something."

Letting my knuckles brush along her jawline next, I cup her cheek in my giant paw. Without a single breath between us, the air is laden with thick, palpable tension.

Yet she doesn't look afraid, even as I explore every inch of her so freely. She won't admit it, but she does trust me. That gives me a ridiculous amount of pleasure.

"Tell me about Zach."

"Kill," she whines. "You don't have to do this."

"Two of the most important people in my life have had their hands all over the third. Behind my back. If I want to know the details, I'll get them."

Her teeth grind together. "Something did happen."

"Have you slept together?"

"No," she rushes out. "Not quite."

"So, you like both of them."

Willow hesitates before nodding shyly.

"What if I said that I've wanted to kiss you since the moment I laid eyes on you? That every single time we speak, all I can think about is dragging you to my bed and making you scream out my name for the whole valley to hear?"

I savour the way her breathing halts.

"What would you say then?" I challenge.

"Kill, trust me. You don't want me. I'm broken."

"Don't say shit like that. You're perfectly whole, even if you don't see it."

I'm too weak to stop the inevitable car crash ahead of us, letting my lips glide against her velvet cheek before meeting her earlobe. She shivers, but this time, it's from pleasure.

"I've wanted to touch you so fucking badly for weeks now," I whisper in her ear. "But once I do, I know that I won't be able to stop. You should leave."

"No," she whispers.

"What the hell do you mean, no?"

"I'm not leaving, Kill." Her hands wrap around my forearms. "Because no matter how every instinct is telling me to run far away from Briar Valley, I want to belong here."

"You do?" I feel my eyebrows draw together.

"More than anything. I'd forgotten what it meant to feel happy until I came here." She flushes, her skin tinged an innocent shade of pink. "You all reminded me."

Slipping my fingers into her long tresses, I massage her scalp, surveying every lump and bump of her skull. I want to memorise it all. Every inch. She is the only woman that has ever meant a damn thing to me.

A contented sigh escapes her full pink lips. Willow unconsciously leans into my touch, her hand stroking up and down my arm, pulling me even closer. She can't fight against it.

"I want you too," she reveals. "That's the truth."

My entire world ends with those words. Reality breaks. My lungs seize. The cabin narrows into a snapshot, until it's just the two of us and nothing else even exists. Despite our fractious relationship—she does want me.

Willow eases the wet towel from around her shoulders, letting the crackle of flames light her bare skin. She sweeps her hair aside, exposing the wet vest top clinging to her curves and leaving everything on display.

I can see her nipples through it, pebbled into sharp points. Sweet Lord. She's so fucking perfect, and the best part is, she doesn't realise it. Willow isn't like those women who try too hard. Her otherworldly beauty is effortless.

"I need to touch you."

"Please," she says softly. "I trust you."

"Good."

Her lips are glistening and begging to be demolished. I slide an arm around her curvaceous waist, tugging her forwards until she lands in my lap. Straddling my body, she looks like a damn queen taking exactly what she wants.

I hold her to my chest, her generous tits swelling against my pectorals. The tantalising promise of body heat and sweet strawberry scent is mesmerising. If I wasn't hard before, I sure as fuck am now.

Shifting on my lap, her eyes widen as she feels just how ready I am to be buried deep inside of her pussy. Lips parted with anticipation, Willow lets her eyes slide shut as she slants her mouth against mine.

The briefest ghost of a kiss is like a lightning bolt hitting me straight in the chest and defibrillating my dying heart. It crumbles the restraints containing the animal within me. My tongue pushes past her lips, demanding more of her obedience.

She begins to grind against me without realising. Hell, she tastes incredible. I palm the back of her head, deepening the kiss until our tongues are fighting a violent battle.

Every time she shifts against me, following a silent rhythm, my cock pulsates with need. I've stroked my length countless times while imagining the golden slopes of her body, but the real thing is infinitely better.

Peppering kisses down the slope of her throat, I slide my fingers under the hem of her vest top, stroking the soft swell of her belly. She gasps when I bring my lips back to hers, stealing another blistering kiss as I lift her from my lap.

"On your back," I command.

Showing her nerves, Willow bites her lip but obeys my order, laying down in front of the fire. I grab a handful of my own rain-soaked t-shirt and rip it over my head.

Her eyes race over my chest, taking in the curls of light blonde hair and chiselled lines. I keep in good shape, more through the demands of work than on purpose. Her smile is full of anticipation and a brief glimmer of fear.

"You don't need to be afraid of me. I would never dream of hurting you."

"I know that," she replies.

Nudging her jean-clad legs open, she lets me kneel between them. I loom over her body, all splayed out and breathless, kissing her lips again to reassure her.

Whatever she's been through, it's left her afraid. Regardless of what happened between her and Zach on the night of the storm, I still have to tread carefully. I've seen her get triggered and it's a harrowing ordeal.

Slowly peeling the vest top off her, I kiss the slightly rounded slope of her stomach and every inch of skin that's revealed. She isn't wearing a bra. Her nipples are hardened into perfect rosy buds.

Massaging her generous mounds, I take a stiffened peak between my fingertips. Pinching lightly to taunt her, Willow squirms on the rug, silently pleading with me for more. She's so receptive to my touch.

When I take her pink nipple into my mouth and suck, her legs squeeze on either side of me. A fine tremble is running over her with each flick of my tongue.

"God, Willow. I can't wait to fuck you raw."

In an instant, everything changes. She bolts upright, almost knocking me off her. Chest rising and falling in a panicked beat, a fine tremble runs over her frame.

"What is it?" I falter.

"I'm… shit. I'm sorry, it's fine."

"No, it's not. What happened? Is it what I said?"

Willow tries to move and cover her breasts, but I grab her wrists before she can, causing her eyes to flare with anxiety. She battles against my grip, and I quickly release her again.

"I just haven't done this before."

"Done what?"

"You know… sex," she mutters.

"I don't understand. You have a kid."

"Look, forget it. Pretend I didn't say anything."

"No, Willow. Tell me what you meant by that. You're married, for Christ's sake."

"So, what? You think every marriage is happy?"

"You're twenty-six. How is this all new? You must've been with men other than the scumbag you're hiding from?"

Her expression shuts down. "Leave it, Kill."

"What aren't you telling me?"

The look on her face is one I recognise from Micah. I've pushed too hard.

Now, her defences are slamming down, leaving me trailing behind her with more questions than answers.

She grabs her vest top to cover her chest, already standing up. I'm seized by an unwelcome rush of panic. It invades my cells and causes my brain to misfire. If she walks away now, I won't get another chance.

"Willow, wait—"

"No, forget it. We're done here."

"Don't run away from me," I plead, unnerved by the emotion cracking my own voice. "Not like Micah does. Let me fix this."

Willow hesitates, sparing me a tear-filled glance, like she's assessing whether I'm worthy of another second of her time. I'm still on my knees but peering up at her instead.

"You're safe with me. I would never hurt you or Arianna. Fuck, Willow. All I want is to make you both happy. Whatever this is… you can tell me, and it won't change anything."

"Yes, it will," she deadpans. "You don't know me as well as you think."

"I know you well enough," I almost shout in her face. "I've spent every day watching you since I pulled you from that ravine. You're the first person I think of in the morning, and the last thing on my mind every night."

Her face pales, but she doesn't speak.

"Your eyes light up when you watch a fading sunset because it reminds you of your home in Mexico. I heard you say that you loved the sunsets there more than anything."

"I did," she chokes out.

"But your favourite time of day is dusk when the darkness falls, and fireflies light up the woods. You drink your coffee black, and tea with milk, but God help anyone who dares to put sugar in it."

"Kill—"

"You think no one notices that you barely eat and wake up half the town screaming with nightmares," I cut her off. "Your daughter is a fucking spitfire just like her mama."

More tears spill down her cheeks.

"You're strong enough to drag yourself up that mountain and nearly die in the process to give your daughter the chance of a better life. I'm in awe of you."

Knee-walking closer, I take both of her hands in mine. This time, she doesn't back away. I'm on my literal knees for the one woman in the world that I'd be vulnerable for.

"You're fucking beautiful," I whisper in a gruff voice.

"Enough, Kill."

"No, it's not. You deserve to be happy. I'm the last person who should be here with you, pouring my heart out, but I'm tired of fighting this. Don't run, baby. Not from me."

It feels like an eternity before she surrenders and collapses into my arms. I catch her before she falls, cradling her in my lap and savouring the sound of her shallow breathing.

I'm terrified that if I close my eyes, this will have been one of those lucid dreams that you wish were reality instead. She will be gone again, back out of reach.

"Come to bed, Willow. You need to sleep."

"Bed?" she squeaks.

I force her to look at me. "Not like that. Let me hold you. When you wake up screaming, I'll be there. I'll fight your demons for as long as you need me to."

"Do you promise?" Willow whimpers.

"I swear on my fucking life. No one will ever hurt you again."

CHAPTER 18
WILLOW

CRAZY IN LOVE - EDEN PROJECT

THE SOUND of chirping birds rouses me from a deep, dreamless sleep. I'm surrounded by stifling heat, and the press of muscles has me panicking before I remember where I am.

Killian's bedroom.

In his freaking bed.

Crap!

His breathing changes as his arms tighten around me, trapping me in place. I can't move an inch. Peeking out through my lowered lids, I take a moment to study his bedroom. It's purely masculine and entirely Killian.

The walls are made of raw, unvarnished wood, and each piece of furniture has been carved from honey-coloured oak. There's an entire wall made of built-in shelves, packed with books on construction and gardening.

His king-sized bed is big enough to fit his giant frame, covered in red plaid sheets made from brushed cotton. While it's tidy and comfortable, everything is practical rather than luxurious.

I'm wearing nothing but panties, and I have a naked leg slung across Killian's huge waist. We fell asleep snuggled closely together after retreating into bed. When I shift, my thigh brushes against something hard and pleased to see me.

Double crap!

"You should go back to sleep," he grumbles in a low voice. "It's still early."

"Sorry. I didn't mean to wake you."

Rolling over with a half-awake groan, he repositions me so we're laying nose-to-nose. Sleepy eyes scrape over me, framed by wild hair that's splayed across his pillow in a blonde bush.

He looks like a grizzly bear that's been awoken from hibernation. Even his chest is vibrating with a purr, causing delicious heat to pool between my thighs. I never imagined I'd wake up to this sight.

"No nightmares," he observes.

"I can't remember the last time that happened."

"Maybe you should sleep on me more often."

"I'm sure you want the bed back to yourself."

His index finger traces the slope of my nose, a little crooked after years of being broken and reset by hand. There's darkness swirling in his eyes, silent and deadly. A wild animal is begging to be set free.

"Hardly," he rebukes. "I've never let anyone else sleep in this bed before."

"What? Not even another woman?"

"Do I look like I'm the relationship type?"

I stifle a laugh. "I have no idea. You did a good job of being a hopeless romantic last night. I think there's a smooth talker in there somewhere."

"Are you teasing me, Willow?"

"Maybe I am."

His chuckle is throaty. "I've kept my hands to myself, but don't expect me to be a gentleman if you're gonna be all cute and shit while naked in my bed."

"Cute and shit?" I repeat.

"You heard me. I'm struggling to find a reason why I shouldn't take advantage of this situation."

Electricity zips down my spine, setting my body alight with anticipation. I should be terrified of being this close to another man, but after last night, I feel like I know Killian. He finally allowed himself to open up.

Tangling my fingers in his hair, I stroke the coarse strands. "Well, for starters, both of your cousins will hear us."

"Maybe that's a good thing," he growls possessively. "I can't stop thinking about your sweet, gorgeous body. I want another taste."

His fingertips dance down my bare spine, leaving goosebumps in their wake. My leg is still hooked over him, adding to the tantalising pressure that's building in my core. He rocks his erection into me again.

"Feel that?" he rasps. "That's how much I want you."

"I want you too."

He searches my face. "I don't want to even attempt to touch you again if you're not ready. Especially after last night. This is all on your terms, not mine."

I bite my lip. "I'm sorry that I freaked out."

"Stop it. No apologies are allowed. It's my fault for being an insensitive jackass."

"You? Insensitive?"

"Ha bloody ha." Killian smirks. "I'd only admit that to you."

"Well, in that case, I'm honoured."

"You should be. I don't give a fuck about anyone else's feelings."

Snuggling closer to his chest, I kiss the carved lines of his collarbones, trailing my lips over his beard to reach his mouth. Killian captures me in a kiss, offering a taste of what my body is screaming out for.

He might not know the truth about my past, but last night was progress. The flash of sheer vulnerability on his face when I tried to leave was exactly what I wanted to see. His human side, beneath the bravado and defence mechanisms.

I can trust him now.

I've seen his true colours.

"Please," I murmur against his lips.

"I meant what I said, Willow. I'm not doing this for the wrong reasons."

"Kill. Shut up and kiss me."

He grabs my face and slams his lips against mine without another whisper of protest. Soft at first, he coaxes me in, his teeth nipping my bottom lip before his tongue slips inside my mouth to increase the tempo.

Mr Sanchez never kissed me. That would've been too intimate for him. He certainly never touched me with gentle, loving reverence.

Blocking his memory out, I stick him in a mental prison and lose myself to the sweetness of Killian's kiss. His palm slides up my thigh, still slung across his body. Every stroke of his fingers is setting me on fire.

Gripping my hips tight, in one sudden move he manages to pull me on top of him. His cock presses up against the heat dampening my panties. I rock into him, desperately seeking more friction to satisfy the building ache.

"You like that?" he rumbles.

"Yes," I admit, writhing on his lap. "It feels... good."

"What else do you like?"

Arching my back as his hands find the swell of my breasts, I release a moan. He rolls my nipples between his fingertips, tugging on the stiffening peaks. My chest feels so sensitive, tingling with the slightest of touches.

"Words," he reminds.

"Fuck," I moan. "I like it when you bite my nipples."

"That's it, baby."

His lips secure themselves to my left breast, lightly nipping and sucking to leave a mark on my skin. Teeth capturing my nipple, he lightly bites down, fulfilling my plea.

"What else?" Killian encourages.

Still grinding against his hard length, I long to remove the fabric barrier keeping us apart. My fear has evaporated. Gone. Right now, I am in control. This formidable beast of a man is begging for the chance to worship me.

"Kiss me," I beg him. "And… pull my hair a bit."

"Damn, Willow. Are you feeling brave?"

"Maybe."

"I think I like this side of you."

Curling a handful of my long hair around his fist, Killian tugs on it to drag my mouth back to his. I land on his chest, my mouth seeking his out with an embarrassing mewl.

He pulls again, harder this time, and the pain blends perfectly with the fire racing over my skin. I love watching his gentleness fade, and hints of his dominance shine through.

"Anything else?"

"I want to forget him," I admit.

Killian hesitates. "Your husband?"

"Help me to forget what he did to me. I need you to replace all that pain with new memories. Good ones."

He curses colourfully. "I am going to break that bastard's fucking skull. I don't even need to know what he did to you. He's already signed his death warrant."

"Come back to me, Kill."

Blinking the haze of anger from his eyes, he blows out a breath. "Keep your eyes on me at all times. You're not allowed to think about anything else. Am I clear?"

There it is again—that hot dominance. I love it.

"Say it. Out loud."

"You're clear," I recite.

Grinning darkly, he flips us over in one deft move. My back meets his mattress, and Killian hangs over me instead. I gasp as his lips secure to my neck, sucking my skin deep into his mouth before releasing.

I can feel the blood rushing to the site of his love bite, searing with a delicious brand of agony. It isn't pain in the sense I'm used to. This hurting is welcome and oh-so hot.

"Mine," he growls out. "You understand?"

"I understand."

Dragging his hot, expert tongue between my breasts, he kisses the slope of my belly until my entire body is trembling with need. My legs part without complaint and he ducks down, taking a sniff of my soaking wet panties.

I feel myself flush with embarrassment. I'm not sure if it's normal to be so wet. Zach marvelled in it too. After enduring so much brutalisation, I think my body is making up for lost time and overcompensating.

"I can smell how wet you are. Is that all for me?"

"Yes," I say in a breathy whisper.

His beard scratches the over-sensitised skin of my slick inner thighs. Sliding his finger beneath the elastic, he teasingly drags the panties to one side, exposing my pussy to him.

I fight to keep still as his thumb rubs over my over-sensitised clit, sending even more heat flooding deep into my core. My legs almost close around his head before he pins them back open.

"Let's get these panties out of the way."

The sound of ripping fabric fills the bedroom. I gape as Killian tosses my ruined panties over his shoulder. There's mischief burning in his eyes. Perhaps, Zach is rubbing off on him after all this time.

Killian secures his mouth to my cunt, skipping past all formalities. I clamp a hand over my mouth as his tongue parts my folds. It feels like he's trying to consume every part of me, demanding all that I have to give.

Holding my moan back is impossible when his finger circles my tight entrance, spreading the moisture before slowly pushing inside me. It's uncomfortable at first and I tense up, threatened by a pit of sinister memories.

He pauses to look up at me. "Just me, Willow. You good?"

I nod back, not trusting myself to speak.

"No one else. Keep those eyes on me."

Clamping down on the flow of memories, I make myself focus only on him. His touch. His tongue. His breath. Killian works his finger in and out of me a few times and each stroke has me begging for more.

It feels incredible, being touched when I actually want it. I had no idea it could feel so good. All the humiliation and self-hatred I'm used to drowning in is refused entry into my mind. Killian leaves room for none of it.

When his tongue returns to my pussy, working in perfect timing with his finger, the heat in my core begins to build. Killian pushes a second finger inside of me, his teeth grazing against my clit at the perfect time.

I moan again, unable to stop the tsunami that drowns me in too many sensations to count. This release hits me all at once, even stronger than the orgasm that Zach teased from me with his tongue.

"Come, Willow," he orders.

Quickening his thrusting fingers, Killian works me into a gasping puddle of need. My vision darkens as the approaching wave of pleasure steals all rational thought straight out of my head.

I can't run. Can't hide. Can't stop this fearless warrior from pushing me over the edge. And I don't want to. He's making me whole again, one piece at a time. All that exists is his touch, his murmured words, the ghost of his warm breath between my thighs.

Crying out his name, my orgasm hits, sweeping all of my inhibitions out to shore. Killian's mouth refuses to lift from my heat, his fingers curled deep inside of me. He's savouring every second of sweet torture.

When I manage to peel my eyes open, he's sat up between my legs, his hand cupping the hardness of his erection through his boxers. Still, he seems reluctant to go further.

"You aren't ready," he answers my unspoken question.

"I think I am."

"No. You're not."

Reaching out, I seize the waistband of his boxers. "Please. All my memories are of pain and fear. I want to remember this moment with you instead."

"Dammit, Willow. I can't think straight when you say shit like that."

Slowly, I nudge his boxers down. "Then don't think at all."

Teeth gritted to suppress a groan, Killian watches me drag the material over the toned swell of his ass. He said it himself. This is all on my terms. I'm choosing to trust him with the most broken, fragile part of myself.

Any final protests die on his tongue when I wrap my hand around the base of his dick that pops free from his boxers. He's intimidatingly large. His cock is thick and long, striped with prominent veins.

"Off," I command.

His eyebrows spike upwards. "Demanding much?"

"Yes. Take them off."

Licking my lips, I shuffle to sit upright while Killian removes his boxers and tosses them aside. The intensity of his heated gaze sets my skin alight.

"Willow," he warns thickly. "This is your last chance to walk away. You're playing with fire."

I pat the bed with a grin. "Maybe I want to get burnt."

He retakes his place, stretching his legs out either side of me, offering full access to every inch of him. I swallow my anxiety and stroke my hand up and down his impressive length.

There's a patch of light hair around the base, dusting upwards towards his packed abdominals. Leaning close, I press a soft kiss on the head of his dick before taking it into my mouth.

"Dammit," Killian hisses.

Cupping a handful of his balls, I suck up and down his length. I can't fit his whole girth in my mouth, the head is already nudging the back of my throat, leaving half untouched.

Turning my head, I lick around the swell of his tip. With each stroke of my tongue, his hips begin to move, thrusting upwards to gently fuck my mouth. I feel his hands fist in my hair.

"Fucking hell, Willow. That feels so good."

The sense of power is heady. This man could snap my spine with a mere flick of his fingers, yet he's the one beneath me now, begging for more of my attention.

I've never been afforded the chance to control a man like this. He might be riding my mouth right now, but I'm the one allowing him to. This is my performance. Under my control. He's nothing more than a puppet to my will.

Gripping the hard planes of his thighs, I feel the sear of moisture escaping the corners of my eyes. He's hitting the back of my throat with each upwards shift of his hips.

Before I can take more of his length, Killian pushes my shoulders, forcing me to release his cock. He's wild-eyed and huffing each breath, glowing embers of animal lust lighting his irises.

"Hang on," he says hoarsely.

Watching him reach into the nearby bedside table, he flourishes a foil packet. My heart hammers violently against my ribcage. Tearing it open, Killian pauses, still uncertain.

"I want this," I assure him. "I'm ready."

"Are you sure, Willow?"

"I trust you. Isn't that enough?"

He considers me, nodding to himself. "Yeah, it is. I just don't want to do anything to fuck this up. You mean too much to me."

My insides turn to pathetic mush. "Come here."

Lips smashing together, his kiss seals any remaining cracks of doubt in my mind. I can feel his need to love and protect in the unspoken ferocity of his lips devouring mine.

Killian would never hurt me.

The safest place in the world is right here.

Breaking the kiss, I watch him roll the condom over his length. When he touches me again, his roughened hands on my skin don't bring pain, but blistering waves of pleasure. I let him lay me down on the bed, his knee pushing my legs open.

I'm still soaked from one mind-blowing orgasm, and his thumb stroking against my clit reignites the heavenly warmth running through my veins with each tiny touch. My legs squeeze his waist, beckoning him in.

Killian peppers kisses along my jawline. "You belong to me now. I'm the only man you're allowed to think of when I'm buried in your cunt."

"I'm here with you. I promise."

His cock nudges my entrance, not quite breaching me. "What do you want, baby?" He slowly pushes inside. "You want me to fuck your sweet pussy?"

"Yes," I gasp. "Fuck, yes."

"Beg me, Willow. I want to hear it."

It should be humiliating, but his gruff demands only turn me on even more. There's no malicious greed behind his words, just lust and passion that beckons me closer.

"Please, Kill. I'm begging you."

"Begging me for what?" he pushes.

I want to scream in frustration. He's inching inside my slit but holding back the final move that will offer me much-needed relief.

"I'm begging for you to fuck me," I mewl, cheeks flushed with embarrassment.

His soft expression melts away like wallpaper peeling from decaying walls. Animal desire is left behind. The man beneath the mask unveils himself—an impatient beast who threatens death to anyone that dares to challenge his control.

Killian snaps.

Actually, finally snaps.

Mouth slanting against mine, he swallows my loud groan as he surges inside of me in one slick move. The agony I've come to expect never arrives. Instead, ecstasy engulfs my senses, blotting out everything else.

Killian slides out of me and shifts his hips, pushing back in to stretch my walls. His strokes are long and confident, filling me to the brim each time, encouraging me to take the extra inches.

"So fucking tight," he hisses.

I can't even garble a response. My brain is short-circuiting. His pumps drag endless moans from my mouth, each louder than the last. I'm panting and begging him for more with every passing second.

Holding my waist, he moves a little faster, finding his rhythm with ease. Each time he enters me, fireworks explode beneath my skin. I want more. Need more. He's making me feel alive, and I'll do anything to hold on to this feeling.

"Willow." He rocks into me. "You." His tongue drags up my throat. "Are." He captures my lips in a kiss. "Perfect."

When I'm about to scream his name, he quickly pulls out and leaves me on the cusp of falling apart. I yell in frustration, writhing and fisting handfuls of his bedsheets. The sudden loss is so acute.

Killian shifts backwards on the bed, dragging me with him. His long legs stretch across the mattress, and he lifts me in the air then drops me on his lap with a grunt. My mind spins with the abrupt role-reversal.

"I want to watch you bounce on my cock with your perfect tits in my face," he explains with a filthy wink.

Manoeuvring my hips to find the perfect position, he lines his length up with my soaked entrance again. I grip his shoulders, circling his waist with my legs until we're flush against each other.

On top of him, I choose the exact moment to sink down on his cock. In this position, he reaches an even deeper angle. I throw my head back and moan his name, relishing the feeling of fullness.

"Kill," I hum.

"Move, baby." He palms my breasts, squeezing gently. "You look like a motherfucking goddess on top of me right now."

It takes a few attempts to find the right movement. Arms wound around his neck, I rise and fall on his length, swivelling my hips to find the perfect angle to relieve the ache deep inside of my core.

He sinks his face between my breasts, his thumbs mercilessly toying with my rock-hard nipples. When he twists one, the sharp stab of pain heightens my rampant desire. The two blend into an inferno that sears my insides.

"Fuck, Kill. I need to come."

His teeth graze across my left nipple. "Are you close, beautiful girl?"

"Y-Yes. So close."

His fingers slide through my hair, and he roughly tugs a handful, causing me to hiss out a curse. I move faster—chasing my release, needing the wave inside of me to crest.

With one hand in my hair and the other moving to hold my hip, Killian's patience expires. He thrusts upwards beneath me, pushing deep into my pussy as I slam down on him. His timing is excruciatingly perfect.

Our shared strokes allow my release to build, my walls clenching tight around his dick. We fit snugly together like lock and key. He's so big, I can barely fit all of him inside me.

Nails cutting into his shoulder blades, I crash down on his cock one more time and feel myself finally reach that unattainable peak. I can't hold it in for a second longer.

"That's it," he directs. "Cover me in your sweet juices."

"Killian," I cry out.

His thrusts remain steady, squeezing every last drop of my release. I cling to him, letting him fuck me senseless, despite my orgasm stealing the breath from my lungs. His strokes don't relent, demanding even more from me.

"So fucking beautiful."

My limbs turn to jelly, and Killian quickly lifts me from his lap, laying me face down on the bed. I grip handfuls of his bedsheets again, still quivering like a leaf.

I've barely sucked in a breath when he lifts my ass into the air and uses the upright position to push back into my slit from behind. The vulnerability of the position almost catches me out, but his murmured praise keeps me locked in the present.

"More," I beg him.

My gasping moans echo around the room as he pounds into me. I doubt there's anyone in the house who can't hear the chaos we're causing. I need him to fuck me to death and leave no space for the demons of my past.

"Take it," he grunts.

Killian's palm cracks against my ass cheek, but the blow doesn't trigger me. I relish the welcome sting of pain, extending my release into a series of explosive aftershocks. His fast pumps rattle the bed frame, testing its construction.

He doesn't hold back, tossing aside his reservations and fucking me into a sweaty tangle on his bed. Each spank accompanies a thrust, his coordinated attack on my body forcing me to ride the waves of my orgasm over and over again.

It doesn't stop. I'm being annihilated, but for the first time, it's entirely my choice. This is a destructive collision of my choosing, and it feels entirely too good to be the one in control of my sexuality again.

"Fuck!" Killian roars.

With a final slam, he stills and booms a guttural curse. Even through the condom, I can feel the surge of heat inside me from his seed. It sends me spiralling again, unable to hold the frayed edges of my mind together.

I'm falling.

Falling.

Falling.

But he's here to catch me.

Killian twists his body to land sideways on the bed instead of crushing me beneath his weight. I'm numb and speechless, floating on a cloud of contentment.

He drags me into his arms and imprisons me against the rapid rise and fall of his chest. All I can hear is the thunderous pounding of his heart, as if it's trying to break free to crawl inside me and find a new home.

"Are you okay?" he gasps.

"Uh-huh." I summon the energy to respond.

The look on his face as he studies my exhausted state is priceless. I'd imagine it's the same look a hunter wears when he's caught his kill. I've been well and truly captured.

"I didn't mean to get so carried away. Did I hurt you?"

"No, I'm okay. Just… need a minute."

"That good, huh?"

I swat his chest. "Careful. You won't fit that ego through the door."

"Hah. I don't fucking care. I have zero desire to ever leave this bed again."

Wrapped up in each other, we rest in silence and catch our breath. My eyes drift shut, too heavy to hold open, despite the morning birds singing outside his window. All I want is to stay here, trapped in the safety of his arms forever.

"Willow," he whispers. "We should get showered before everyone wakes up."

"Mmmm."

"Shower. Now."

"Stop being so bossy. I can't move yet."

Barking a laugh, Killian unpeels himself from me and clambers to his feet. "Shake a leg. I'll even wash your back for you. I'm nothing if not a gentleman."

"That isn't a word I'd use to describe you after what we just did."

"Wow." He snorts. "You might have a point there."

Heading into the bathroom, his chuckling is silenced by the shower turning on. I remain curled up on his bed, unable to move a muscle. It's going to take a while for my brain to catch up on what just happened.

"Killian! You up?"

Shouting echoes from outside the bedroom door. Squeaking in panic, I'm too late to cover my naked body up. The door flies open, revealing a half-awake Zach stumbling in his boxer shorts and an oversized t-shirt.

"Ki—oh, shit. You're not Killian."

"Nope," I exclaim.

Rubbing his eyes, he blinks several times like he's witnessing a mirage. Looking from my bird's nest hair and naked, still-trembling body to the tangle of sheets on Killian's bed, it doesn't take a genius to put two and two together.

"My, oh my. What have I walked into?"

"Zach! Please go away."

"No can do." He crouches down and scoops my ripped panties off Killian's floor. "I guess you didn't want this pair anymore, huh?"

"Ground swallow me up. Please."

Zach props his shoulder against the door frame. "I can practically smell you in the air. I was hoping you'd end up in my bed first, not this caveman's. I'm a team player though."

"Huh?" I stare at him.

"You heard me, babe."

Flushing red, I grab the pillow beneath me and toss it straight at him. Zach easily bats it aside and I throw another, assaulting him with feathers and fabric.

"What the hell is that noise?"

Killian steps out of the bathroom, stark-bollock naked. Rather than rushing to cover his bare ass up, he looks between me and Zach, his lips twisting into a proud smirk.

"Mind giving us some privacy?" he asks in a light-hearted voice. "I'd like to hear Willow scream my name again in the shower before I cook your damn breakfast."

"By all means, go ahead." Zach invites him with a hand wave. "You don't mind if I watch this time, do ya, cuz?"

"I do!" I squeal.

"You're embarrassing her, Kill."

"Me?" Killian drones.

"Maybe I should take over." Zach sends a sultry wink my way. "You can cook breakfast while Willow screams my name instead. Sound good?"

"You'll get your turn, kid. Go on, fuck off."

Still naked, Killian marches over to the door and slams it in his expectant face. I can hear Zach groaning with disappointment from the other side. Killian turns to face me with an exasperated eye roll.

"You better get showered before I climb back into that bed and give Zach something to complain about."

"Z-Zach?"

He scoffs. "You can bet he'll be listening to us now. He's the jealous type. Plus, we have a birthday party to prepare for. Or did you forget?"

Groaning in annoyance, I make my jelly legs stand and try my best not to faceplant. Killian laughs at every reluctant step I take towards the shower. All I want is to burrow beneath his duvet and sleep for another ten hours.

"Shift it, we have work to do." His hand slaps against my ass on my way past. "Princess parties don't plan themselves around here."

CHAPTER 19
WILLOW

WILLOWS - HANS WILLIAMS

WITH MY HANDS clasped over Arianna's eyes, I guide her outside into the warm spring sunshine. The entire town has gathered in Lola's sprawling back garden, a huge green space filled with every decoration imaginable.

There are fairy lights, streamers, balloons and even a bouncy castle. It's everything I've ever wanted for Arianna. She can finally celebrate like a real little girl, surrounded by family and loved ones instead of pain and death.

"Ready, baby?" I croon.

"Yes, Mummy! Show me, show me!"

Steering her into the middle of the massive group, I remove my hands. Arianna squeals loudly, bouncing up and down as she takes in the organised chaos all around us. Everyone is shouting and clapping, setting off party poppers and engulfing her in a torrent of love.

I watch with happy tears pricking my eyes. It's a beautiful sight, seeing her run towards the bouncy castle, surrounded by other kids to play with. She's made friends while being home-schooled by Rachel in the last couple of weeks.

I'm even happier to see Johan running to join in with the fun, leaving Aalia to chat with a small cluster of women fawning over Amie, who's fast asleep in her pram. She's been out and about in town more, socialising with the others.

Miranda appears and traps me in a bear hug. "This is amazing, Willow! You'll have to be our resident party planner from now on."

"It wasn't me." I gesture towards the corner where Killian is nursing a beer and glaring at anyone that dares to approach. "Killian did most of it, and Lola too."

"You've got yourself a good one there."

She winks, squeezing my arm before returning to Doc's side. I watch as she presses a kiss to his lips, despite his arms being casually slung around Rachel's waist. The three of them snuggle together, sharing a conversation.

Their relationship is endlessly fascinating to me. I've never heard of people sharing like they do. I know it isn't the norm, but nothing in Briar Valley is. This place defies every rule and expectation set by the outside world.

But more so, their dynamic intrigues me for selfish reasons. Killian's staked his claim on me for everyone to see, sticking to me like glue and taking his over-protectiveness into overdrive. But that hasn't stopped Zach from flirting and touching me at every opportunity.

And there's still Micah to consider in this stupidly complicated mess that I've somehow engineered for myself. I'm so bloody confused. Is that what they want too? Could I even think about sharing? It seems like an alien concept.

"Mummy! Look!"

On the bouncy castle, Arianna is jumping like a maniac, fighting to get the highest among the other kids. I wave and blow her a kiss, loving the smile on her face.

"Wow, Ari! Be careful," I call back.

Wading through the crowd of people, everyone greets me and offers bright smiles, but I long to escape the onslaught of attention. My stomach has been somersaulting all morning, cramping up so hard, I feel sick.

"Willow," Ryder shouts. "Over here."

He's yelling from the huge gazebo that sits off to one side of Lola's neatly pruned garden. Beckoning me over with a crooked finger, he plants a big wet kiss on my cheek before offering me a beer.

"You look frazzled."

"Is it that obvious?" I sigh.

"Not at all, but I know your frazzled face by now."

Collapsing onto a rattan sofa, I press the cold beer to my forehead. "This is all a bit crazy. I've never seen the whole town together in one place before."

He takes a swig of his drink. "Yeah, it can get a bit loud. Lola likes big parties. We usually have several throughout the year. She loves to play host to everyone."

At the mention of her name, white-hot anger pools inside of my gut. I can't stop myself from searching for her silvery hair in the crowd. She's standing next to Albie as he grills a pile of burgers and hot dogs.

Avoiding her has been difficult. I don't know how to confront her about

Katie. Frankly, I'm not sure I'm ready for what she has to say. I doubt it's going to be a happy story, and my current state of mind is fragile at best.

"Ethan is coming in a couple of weeks." Ryder grins as he always does when discussing his partner. "You'll finally get to meet him."

I force a smile. "I can't wait."

"He's been busy working on this big investigation at work. I miss him so much when he isn't here, but I can't imagine leaving Briar Valley to live with him."

"You'll figure it out." I poke him in the ribs. "You never know, maybe he'll move up here. I'm sure we'd find a use for his detective skills."

Ryder snorts. "Yeah, right."

"I'm serious!"

"He could figure out who keeps taking all the eggs from the chicken coop," he muses.

"It's a legitimate concern. Killian has sworn lethal vengeance on the infamous egg stealer. Ethan could help avoid a very messy, public execution."

"I wouldn't mind seeing Killian take on Ethan. Hot damn." Ryder snickers at my shocked look. "Oh, shut it. Even though he's like family, I can appreciate a good view."

"I'm gonna pretend I didn't hear that."

"Yeah, yeah, whatever you say. Speaking of the asshole himself, did I see you sneaking out of their cabin the other morning?"

I avert my eyes. "Erm, don't think so."

Ryder studies me closely. "You have a terrible poker face."

"I do not."

"And you're a terrible liar too."

"Jesus, Ry. Anything else?"

"Nope. That's all."

Pressing a hand to my aching stomach, I breathe through another wave of pain. To make matters worse, two familiar pairs of short, stocky legs are approaching the gazebo. Seeing the twins side by side is a huge shock to the system.

"Hey guys," Zach greets. "What did we miss?"

I gesture towards the bouncy castle. "The big reveal."

"Sorry, babe. I was dragging this one out of his antisocial cave."

Micah narrows his eyes on his twin. "It's a studio. Not a cave."

"Smells like a cave to me," Zach comments.

Helping himself to a beer, he deliberately doesn't offer one to Micah who looks beyond desperate for a drink. Standing next to each other, their similarities are stark, but so are their differences.

"What were you two chinwagging about?" Zach uncaps his beer and takes a long pull.

Ryder laughs. "Wouldn't you like to know, Zachariah. Can I ask if there's any particular reason why you're walking around in a princess's tiara?"

He adjusts the plastic tiara buried in his caramel hair. "What? I'm embracing the theme. It was this or a zebra mask."

"It's quite the look."

"I figured I'd make a sexier princess," he replies smugly. "Willow?"

"You'd make a beautiful little princess."

"Little?" Zach frowns.

We burst out laughing at the look of indignation on his face. Taking a seat next to his brother, Micah spares me a nod that kills my short-lived good mood. He's avoided me like the plague, and he won't even meet my eyes.

Thinking my luck can't get any worse, I nearly combust into flames when Killian leaves his isolated perch in the corner of the garden and collapses into one of the empty chairs instead. He makes a point of resting a possessive hand on my thigh.

"Sooo," Zach singsongs. "Should we play a game or something? Is truth or dare still a thing at parties? Anyone got a juicy secret to tell?"

"No," Killian and I blurt at the same time.

Zach nearly falls off his chair, he's laughing so hard. Ryder smothers a grin as he polishes off his drink. Amidst the laughing dickheads, Micah sits in stony, awkward silence.

I can only assume that Zach spilled the beans to him about finding me in Killian's bed, very much naked and thoroughly fucked for the world to see. I'll add it to the list of things I need to apologise for.

"I'm gonna get some food," Killian announces.

Zach bats his lashes. "Get me some, cuz."

"Piss off, kid. You've got legs, haven't you?"

Ryder stands, sparing me a wink. "I'll come too, Kill. Back in a mo. Don't do anything I wouldn't do."

"Traitor," I mouth at him.

I'm left alone with the twins both facing me from their rattan sofa. Zach stares at me like I'm a meal he wants to devour, while Micah cracks open a bottle of water, looking longingly at the cooler full of alcohol in the corner.

"How are you doing, Mi?"

He shrugs. "Fine. Got my supplies."

"That's good then."

"I guess."

Zach watches our stunted conversation. "Jesus, Mi. I need to give you some fucking education on talking to women. How are we even related?"

Micah glares at him. "Please shut up."

"Charming. Love you too, brother."

Sweat beads across my forehead while they exchange heated barbs. I fight a fresh wave of dizziness and grab another cold beer to hold against my head. I'm flitting between hot and cold which is worsening my nausea.

As Zach opens his mouth to question me, Aalia arrives with Amie propped on her hip. She's wearing a beautiful, flowing dress, the bright yellow and blue flowers perfectly matching her olive-toned skin and glossy hair.

"Hey!" I blurt, grateful for the distraction.

She offers me a bright smile. "Hi, Willow."

"You made it. Thanks for coming."

"Thank you for the delivery. You're spoiling us."

After visiting her cabin, I wrote down my mental list and handed it to Miranda for this month's supply run. Albie delivered the several boxes full of kitchen equipment and basics.

"If you want anything else, let me know."

"You're too kind."

Amie squeals, demanding her mum's attention. While Aalia digs around in her bag, Zach takes the baby and makes crazy facial expressions to quieten her screams for food.

"Cute kid," he grumbles. "I think I want one."

Micah chokes on a laugh. "You can't look after a fucking potted plant."

"Hey, language! She might hear you, dickhead."

"Babies don't understand shit."

The sight of Zach with an infant in his broad arms nearly causes me to choke on thin air. I wouldn't have thought such a sight would make me feel so many strange things. He looks far too comfortable bouncing Amie in his arms.

Returning with several platefuls piled high with food, Killian unceremoniously dumps one in front of me. His glare is already in place, issuing a silent demand. Carrying his own food, Ryder's trying his best not to laugh.

"Food. Eat," Killian orders.

"Um, thanks?"

Leaning against the side of the gazebo, he ploughs into enough food to feed a family of four. It all disappears into his mouth, one bite after another. It's no wonder he's the size of a house, even if it is all muscle.

"How come she gets fed and I don't?" Zach whines.

"Get your own food, kid."

I study my plate of food, but it makes me feel even more ill. Eating is the last thing I want to think about right now. There's so much food on offer around here with zero strings attached.

You can eat when you learn some obedience.

No more crying, bitch.

Open your goddamn legs.

Eating was the first line of punishment in the mansion. I'd often be refused food by the staff who were under orders from Mr Sanchez and keen to avoid his wrath.

Even though Pedro's father ran the kitchen, he couldn't risk helping me. The last thing I wanted was to get them in trouble either. Only when I got on my knees and begged Mr Sanchez for relief would I be awarded something to eat.

"Willow? You with us?" Killian waves a hand.

I find everyone staring at me and realise I must've zoned out. When Ryder attempts to lay a hand on my shoulder, I flinch back, causing him to halt. Looking into his eyes, all I can see is a pair of cruel blue sapphires staring back at me.

It's so hard to separate these guys from the man that dominated my life, even though I know they're nothing like him. Past and present are difficult to compartmentalise at times, constantly bleeding into one another.

"You don't look so good," Zach worries.

Killian tilts his head. "And you're too pale."

Everyone is watching me like hawks. It causes my anxiety to spiral. My neck is wet with sweat, and I feel like I'm going to throw up the cup of herbal tea I managed for breakfast. I need to get out of the spotlight right now so I can fall apart in peace.

"Be right back," I rush out.

Picking my way back through the madness to check that Arianna is still safe in the bouncy castle with her friends, everything blurs around me and my dizziness increases. Awful, gut-wrenching pain is twisting my insides into knots.

This doesn't feel like anxiety or even a normal stomach bug. The pain is steadily increasing like it's building towards a peak. I'm struggling to even breathe through it.

"Willow!" Lola beckons me over.

Ignoring her shouts, I lean against a tall plant pot to hold myself upright. The world is spinning around me, but I can hear Lola approaching and stopping next to me.

"Come sit with us. Leave those boys to fend for themselves for a while."

"I c-can't right now."

Lola scans over me. "Are you okay?"

"I just need some air."

"Let me come with you." She takes hold of my arm, resting a hand against my forehead to check my temperature. "You look white as a ghost, poppet."

"I'm fine. Please let go of me."

Her worried frown deepens. "What is it?"

Peeling her fingers from my arm, I'm unable to contain my anger any longer. It rises out of me in an uncontrolled volcanic eruption. I don't care that we're surrounded by people, celebrating what should be a happy day.

"Just leave me alone, Lola!"

The group around us falls silent at my raised voice. Lola's face slackens in surprise, and she takes a measured step back, reaching out for Albie. He moves to her side, a pair of barbecue tongs still in hand.

"Willow?" he prompts. "You good?"

The guys are all rushing to join us, abandoning their food and drinks in the gazebo. This is so not the right time to lose my shit. We worked so hard to make this day special for Arianna.

"Poppet?" Lola reaches for me again.

"Don't touch me. I want you to stay back."

"Let's take this inside," she suggests.

"No, I'm not going anywhere with you."

She blanches. "What has gotten into you, Willow?"

Shoving away the hand that Zach tries to grab me with, I hug my throbbing midsection. I'm trembling all over from the exertion of remaining upright, and internally freaking the hell out.

I need to be alone to figure out what's happening to me, but I can't hide until Lola moves out of the way. Hysteria crawls up my throat, forcing me to take drastic action to get out of this situation.

"How long have you known?" I blurt.

Lola stares at me. "Known what?"

"Willow, stop." Killian steps between us, his hands raised. "Maybe now isn't the best time to get into this. Let's get you inside."

"No!" I shout back, swaying on my feet. "Lola has lied to me since my first day here. I'm done pretending that she's some kind of saint."

"What are you talking about?" she demands.

"My mother abandoned me!" I explode, uncaring of our growing audience. "Why did you give her a home? You took her in."

With all the strength swept out of her in an instant, Lola leans on Albie, looking like one strong breeze would blow her over. Rather than answer, her mouth clicks open and shut. She clearly wasn't expecting me to know the truth.

Zach attempts to grab me again. "Let's go inside and get Doc to look you over."

I inch away from them all, feeling like a cornered animal. "No! Stop... everyone stop. I can't... I can't breathe..."

There are too many voices around me, blurring into a confusing storm. It's too much. Too loud. Too overwhelming. All I want is to find a quiet corner to curl up in. I let out a strangled sound as I'm overcome by a wave of blistering pain.

"Willow?"

"Zach, move!"

"Someone grab her!"

Their panicked voices disappear. Everything grows fuzzy, but the sudden rush of warmth between my legs sparks dread deep in my heart. Knees knocking together, the world moves in slow motion as I look down at my once-white sundress.

That isn't right. Bright, accusing red is blossoming across the linen fabric. It takes my mind a moment to catch up. I'm bleeding down there, between my thighs. The swirls of colour are spreading by the second.

It's blood.

And lots of it.

The flow of bright-red pours out of me at an alarming rate and drips onto Lola's freshly cleaned patio. It takes a moment for everyone to stop shouting over each other in the chaos and realise what I'm staring down at.

All I can feel is the gushing crimson river spilling out of me. My body chooses that exact moment to pull the plug. I almost collapse to my knees, before a strong pair of arms catches me. I'm pulled into an awaiting lap.

"I've got you, baby," Killian comforts. "You're okay."

"The blood."

"Don't worry about that." His crooning voice rises, spiked with concern. "Someone get help, right now."

His blue jeans are quickly soaked through and stained beneath me. He holds me against his chest, stopping me from wriggling to escape. I go limp in his embrace, suddenly exhausted and struggling to keep my eyes open.

"Doc!"

"We need to get her to the hospital!"

"No hospitals," I whisper.

Killian stares down at me, his face filled with a look of horror. "Eyes on me, Willow. We're going to get you some help."

"I'm so t-tired…"

"Don't shut your eyes. That's an order."

My eyes drift shut regardless.

"Willow! Don't you dare do this to me. Wake up."

I can hear Arianna screaming my name over his words, but she sounds far away. Everything is spinning, twisting, fraying at the edges. Killian grabs my chin and shakes, but I don't have the strength to reopen my eyes.

"Mummy!" Arianna shouts again.

I want to reply, but I feel like I'm trapped behind a sheet of glass, unable to utter a single word. The approaching darkness swallows me before I can respond to her, and at last, the pain fades into nothingness.

CHAPTER 20
ZACH

WHERE DO I EVEN START - MORGAN TAYLOR REID

STARING through the frosted glass at Willow curled up in a cramped hospital bed, my hands curl into fists. Killian is deathly silent at my side, his entire frame trembling with barely contained rage.

He looks like he wants to smash the entire hospital to pieces and burn whatever rubble remains when he's done. I have no idea how he's maintaining a shoestring of control. It's like someone's taken a melon baller to his heart and brutally scooped it out.

Micah is crouched on the lemon-scented linoleum floor with his back to the wall. He stares at his hands with streaks of oil paint still smeared over each digit. None of us have spoken since the doctor left over an hour ago.

We've just stood here since then, stunned and confused, unable to utter a single word. I'm not sure what we were expecting. When I saw that blood gushing out of her, I knew things were bad, but this situation is far more fucked-up than even I realised.

Did you know she was pregnant?

Which one of you is the father?

I'm sorry for your loss.

Killian grunts in fury before his fist sails into the wall. "Fuck!"

Cracking the white plaster, he leaves a smear of fresh blood behind as his knuckles split upon impact. The pain doesn't even register. The brown-haired nurse in the nearby booth startles, but she quickly looks away when I shoot her an apologetic look.

Cradling his bleeding hand, Killian lets his head drop in complete defeat.

Even the usually confident stance of his shoulders is slumped, unable to bear the anguish of the mess we've found ourselves in.

"Kill," I warn him.

"Don't start," he hisses.

"Keep your cool. We don't want to get thrown out."

"How the fuck did this even happen? When?"

My mind filters back over the past several weeks. I can hardly remember a time when Willow wasn't with us in Briar Valley. She grabbed my attention from the very first time I laid eyes on her broken smile and sad but hopeful hazel eyes.

I've been borderline obsessed with doing everything in my power to inspire that smile ever since. She's on my mind twenty-four hours a day. It goes beyond being attracted to her stunning looks. I love her personality too, along with everything else about her.

"She's been with us for what? Six weeks?"

"So, she was still with him seven or so weeks ago," he finishes, looking nauseated. "The timing checks out."

Then the awful truth is undeniable. Willow was pregnant with her husband's child when she arrived in town, beaten within an inch of her life. I've seen enough to know that he must have been a piece of shit, else she wouldn't be here.

The doctor advised that miscarriages in the first trimester are common. Some people don't even realise they're pregnant until it's too late. It happens more often than we realise, especially under stressful circumstances.

She's been under a lot of stress in general, between the arduous journey to find us to the messy process of navigating a brand new country and life. Killian told us about Lola's little secret too. That must've been the icing on the cake.

"I didn't get the impression they were…"

"What?" Micah finally speaks.

"Happily married, let alone trying for another kid." I shrug, trying hard not to let my jealousy take over. "She said they were getting divorced, for fuck's sake."

"From what she's told me, I'm starting to think a lot of what happened in their marriage wasn't consensual," Killian utters in a terrifying voice. "Like, at all."

Rising to his feet, Micah casts a solemn look into Willow's room before stalking away without another word. I watch him slide a pack of cigarettes from his pocket as he disappears outside to get away from this conversation.

He hasn't smoked in years, but I don't have the heart to stop him. Everything about this is royally messed up. We're facing something far darker than any of us realised, and I fucking hate myself right now for not realising it sooner.

"Bastard," Killian curses. "Dammit!"

"Cool it. The nurse is looking at us again."

"How am I supposed to cool it? This asshole could have been assaulting Willow. God knows for how long. I bet she didn't even know she was pregnant."

"I know, alright?" I snarl at him. "But we need to be calm."

"You be fucking calm!" His voice cracks, breaking his bubble of rage. "I promised her that I'd keep her safe. I *swore* nothing would hurt her, Zach. And this still happened."

"You couldn't have known this would happen."

"I don't give a shit. I've still failed her."

"We all did." I gulp down the lump in my throat. "We should've known the story about the car accident was complete bullshit. That didn't stop us from swallowing it though."

"I thought that giving her time was the right thing to do," he says reproachfully. "I was trying to respect her privacy, but we should've been straight up with her from the start."

"And said what? Did your husband beat you up?"

"I don't know," he snaps. "Maybe."

"You know that would have scared her away in a heartbeat."

Before Killian can bark at me again, we're interrupted by my phone pinging with a text message from Lola. She's been stuck in the downstairs waiting area with Albie ever since we arrived several hours ago.

"Crap. She's messaged again."

Killian shrugs. "Let her wait."

"We should update her."

"Lola is the last thing on my damn mind right now. She's been lying through her teeth to all of us and hiding Willow's mother from her. She can fucking wait."

Reaching into his coat pocket, Killian pulls out the two British passports we passed around a little while ago. He showed us the names that don't match the people we know. It's another question mark on the list of concerns we've ignored.

Willow was serious about disappearing before she arrived in Briar Valley. Enough to pay for high quality false identities. After seeing them, I'm fairly confident she was the one who burned off their fingerprints. It's all beginning to add up.

What kind of monster is she running from?

Why didn't she tell us the truth in the first place?

We had enough sense to use the false name on Willow's passport to check in at the hospital, rather than foil her carefully laid plans. The dawning realisation that we're dealing with something far more sinister than we realised has us all floundering.

"She told Lola that she was married at sixteen." Killian stares at the passports. "I think that was true. We're dealing with a predator here, not some disgruntled ex-husband."

"What makes you think that?"

"She's fucking traumatised, Zach. Isn't it obvious?"

It is—blindingly so. Even when I touched her and made her come on my tongue, she almost didn't seem to know what to do with herself. The inexperience is so obvious. No one has ever made her feel like that.

"That could be for a lot of reasons," I argue.

"You didn't see the way she reacted to me."

"I saw enough the other week when we… you know, hooked up. You're not the only one she's interested in, even if she did end up in your bed first."

"You mean when you were trying to fuck her after she'd kissed your bloody twin brother?" he argues back. "Not sure that's something to be proud of, kid."

"You're a fine one to talk after what I walked into the other morning."

Killian hesitates, replacing his next bitter retort with a sigh. "We've really screwed this up with her, haven't we?"

His humourless laugh knocks the fight out of me. We're sizing ourselves up against each other like that even matters anymore. It's irrelevant. When Willow wakes up, she's going to need all of us to get through this.

Admittedly, this isn't the first time I've thought about our current predicament. I grew up in Briar Valley. That opens your mind to so many things, and the prospect of sharing Willow doesn't sound all that crazy to me.

I clap him on the shoulder. "Look, I think we can agree this is bigger than we thought. I'm willing to bet that her shitty ex is the reason Willow arrived in such a state."

He nods. "I'm certain of it."

"What else do we know about him?"

"Lola caught her googling some jumped-up realtor from the States a few weeks ago." Killian's face contorts with anger. "Willow got shifty and wouldn't answer any questions."

"Nothing at all?"

"She clammed right up. It's like she's protecting that scumbag. I think this goes beyond some messy divorce. She's running for her life and I'm willing to bet he's the reason why."

Leaning against the wall, I sag under the pressing weight of exhaustion. Adrenaline and the crappy hospital coffee we drained earlier have both worn off, leaving me tired and fucking terrified of the moment Willow's eyes will open.

"One of us should go and update Lola."

"Hard pass," he declines.

"Please, Kill. I don't know what to say to her."

Killian sighs again. "Stay with her."

"Yeah, I will."

He reluctantly shuffles down the corridor, disappearing from sight. I gather myself and slip back into Willow's hospital room. They've set her up for a transfusion, and various wires are poking out of her lifeless body.

I sit at her bedside, taking her hand in mine. There's so much I want to say, but none of it feels like enough. I've lost so much in my life, and I know the pain she's going to face.

"Hi, babe." I brush hair from her face. "I know we're a bunch of idiots. None of us realised the truth sooner... but regardless, all three of us care about you so damn much."

The drip of fluids and antibiotics being fed into her IV port punctuates my whispered words. Her heart rate monitor ticks away in the background, but she doesn't stir.

"Whatever it is you're not telling us, it's okay," I offer softly. "All I want is to see that beautiful smile again. We can get through this together. I promise, it will be alright."

Squeezing her hand, my forehead meets the bedsheets as my eyes fall shut. Her breathing is a steady, reassuring meditation that almost lulls me to sleep. It's been hours of non-stop panic and worry since we arrived at Highbridge's small hospital.

Killian was drenched in her blood by then, despite the towels we sandwiched between Willow's legs for the car ride. He didn't complain once. I'm not sure I could have sat there, covered in her blood, without losing my shit a little bit.

The door to the room creaks open. I look up, expecting to see Killian return. My twin brother's devastated eyes find me instead. He takes the empty seat on the opposite side of the bed, seizing Willow's other hand.

"The doctor said she'll be awake soon," he says in a small voice. "They want to keep her in overnight for observations, but she can go home tomorrow if everything's okay."

"Where's Kill?"

"Convincing Lola not to march in here."

I shake my head. "That's the last thing we want Willow to see when she does wake up. This is going to be hard enough to explain as it is."

"Listen, do you think we should move her?" Micah worries his heavily-chewed bottom lip. "Out of Lola's cabin? She'll need peace and quiet to recover."

I'm surprised to hear such a thoughtful idea come from his lips. It's been a long time since Micah appeared to care about anything but his lifeless hunks of clay and oil paint. The emotion buried in his eyes is too intense to hide.

We've always been in tune with each other's feelings, even as kids. Our father always called it a twin thing. It's like I knew when Micah needed me or if he was hurt.

When Dad died and he shut down, we lost that precious connection. But right now, surrounded by the sick and dying, I can feel it flaring to life again.

Micah has spent his whole adult life hurting and I can finally see a way out of that onslaught of pain. Willow is his antidote. She's bringing him back to us.

"You really do like her, don't you?"

He glances away. "What if I do?"

"She likes you too, Mi."

"I'm not the only one though, am I?"

We've made such a mess of this by ignoring the impending problem for weeks. I was happy to joke with Willow about being a team player, but now we're at that crossroads, I'm not willing to walk away without her.

"We need to sit down and talk as a family."

Micah sighs. "That should be a fun chat."

I look at the sickly pallor of Willow's bird-like features. "She can't stay at Lola's like this. We need her close, where we can keep an eye and help her if she needs it."

"The other cabin is still empty," he suggests.

"You really think Killian will go for that?"

Micah shrugs. "Why not?"

"He hasn't looked inside it for years, not since we moved across the street after the funeral. It probably needs a tonne of work and renovations."

"We have a spare room until it's ready."

Considering, I nod. "I'll talk to Kill."

"And what about... everything else?"

Our eyes meet over Willow's still form. The vivid green depths of our irises perfectly match each other, but we're so drastically different. I didn't just lose my father all those years ago. On top of that, I lost my twin too.

He's right here, but the shy kid I used to play on dirt bikes with outside our childhood home is long gone. We haven't been real brothers for years. Yet since Willow turned up, there have been glimpses of the person he used to be.

Small flashes of the person I once knew—the odd smile, a hint of life gleaming in his eyes again, socialising and agreeing to eat dinner with us some nights. Willow has snuck into our lives and shaken everything up without meaning to.

"I'm not going to back off, Mi. I like Willow a lot."

"I don't want you to."

"We live in Briar Valley. Things work differently." I straighten the wire flowing into her arm. "Maybe we can make this thing work between the four of us. It's something I've thought about."

"You mean like… Doc, Rachel and Miranda?"

"Maybe. We could give it a try."

"I don't know, Zach," he worries.

"All I care about is seeing her happy again."

Micah grips Willow's hand. "I want that too."

"Then we figure this shit out before she wakes up. We can move both of them into the cabin and figure out what the fuck has happened to Willow. Together."

"You know, it's weird seeing you take charge instead of Killian."

I'm never one to put myself in control or call the shots. Killian's been our protector and caregiver since he was eighteen-years-old, but right now, he's as broken as anyone about what happened to Willow.

Someone else has to make this decision. I refuse to waste another second pretending like we don't all want the same thing. Her. Regardless of what it will cost us.

"You've got shit to sort out too if this is going to work."

He falls silent. "I know."

"I mean it, Mi. You need to get help. We can't live like this forever. I love you, brother, and I'm tired of watching you throw your life away."

I half expect him to bolt from the room and run all the way back to Briar Valley to hide out in his studio. But Micah stays put, nodding to himself.

"I will, Zach."

"I mean it. You need to go back to that therapist and actually try this time."

Holding firm, I make him look into my eyes as he nods again. This is nonnegotiable. If we're going to be there for Willow in the weeks to come, he needs to lead by example and accept the fact that he needs help.

"Alright, it's a deal. Let's get Killian in here and plan what we do next."

CHAPTER 21
WILLOW

SILHOUETTE - AQUILO

HUDDLED in the backseat of Killian's truck, I re-enter Briar Valley much like I arrived. Broken and defeated. My life has changed so much, but somehow, I'm still trapped in the world's loneliest bubble.

Zach and Killian were there when I was discharged earlier this morning, carrying fresh clothes and a bagged sandwich. I took the comfortable sweats and oversized t-shirt that smelled suspiciously like Killian, leaving the food without a word.

I haven't spoken since.

I'm not sure how I'm feeling.

Or if I'm even feeling at all.

My entire body is numb. Detached. Caught in a state of disbelief. I didn't see this cruel twist of fate coming, not for a second. I must be the stupidest person alive because the signs were there all along.

The sickness, fatigue and hormones running wild. Anxiety and headaches. I chalked it up to the trauma of all that's happened. Part of me wonders if I knew all along but simply didn't want to believe it.

That final night in the mansion was one of the worst in my entire life. Mr Sanchez didn't use protection as he dragged me from my bedroom, kicking and screaming, all the way down to his playroom.

He was so angry and driven by bloodthirst. I'd dared to talk back over dinner, my patience for his taunts wearing thin. In that moment, he wanted to break me back down into the scared little girl he found in that strip club ten years ago.

That's when I knew I had to run before it was too late. Any longer and he would've succeeded in turning me into that person, and I couldn't allow that. Old Willow wouldn't have the strength to run, and I needed to do that more than anything.

"Willow?" Zach peers back at me.

I barely lift my head. "Yeah?"

"We're nearly home, babe."

Pulling his denim jacket closer around me, I breathe in his fruity, tropical scent, letting it transport me to a distant land of white-sand beaches and clear skies. All I want to do right now is run away from them all.

I'm too afraid to look the guys in the eye. I can feel Killian's possessive stare in the rear-view mirror, but I'm ignoring him. Their voices fade away, overtaken by the sympathetic lilt of the doctor's voice as he explained what happened.

Pregnant.

Miscarriage.

Haemorrhaging.

Scarred womb.

Years of abuse and Arianna's traumatic birth have made me into a ticking time bomb ready to explode. He doubts that I'll ever conceive again. Part of me thinks I should be happy about that, but a larger, more complex part of me is distraught.

I lost my baby.

Not his. Mine.

It was a brand new life, barely just beginning inside of me. Now, it's gone. I didn't even know about this baby, but I'm still mourning the loss. I can't explain it. My grief defies reason, no matter the logical arguments I try to talk myself into believing.

How could anyone possibly understand how it feels to grieve something that you didn't know was happening inside of you? I'm sure they're all thinking the same thing. It's good that I lost this baby. I don't have to birth another piece of Mr Sanchez.

But I'm still mourning.

Pain doesn't always make sense.

Sometimes, it just… is.

Driving through the quiet afternoon, Killian cruises straight past Lola's cabin and carries on up the steep hill. He parks outside their cabin, climbing out and reappearing at my door to help me climb out.

"You're staying with us," he says with a thin smile. "The last thing you need right now is more fighting. You can see Lola again when you're ready."

"Ari?"

"She's inside. Missed her mama, too. We'll set the spare room up for you two."

Killian eases me out of the car, an arm curled around me for support. I limp up the steps, ducking through the door that Zach holds open for me, carrying my hospital bag slung over his shoulder. Even his smile seems forced.

The moment I've stepped over the threshold, a blur of white-haired energy races across the cabin. A pair of arms latches around my legs and nearly knocks me off balance with the ferocity of her relief. My beautiful girl.

"Mummy! Mummy!"

"Ari," I gasp.

Tears immediately start to pour, escaping from my eyes in a thick river of agony. When she peers up at me, the look on her face shatters my broken heart into even smaller pieces. It seems like she didn't believe I was coming back.

"Hey, baby."

"I missed you," she keens. "Cuddle?"

"Sure. Let me sit down first."

Unable to lift her, I let Killian guide me over to the sofa. It's occupied by an even more surprising sight. Micah sits up from his slouching position, offering me a tiny smile. I was not expecting to see him out of his studio.

He's clearly been babysitting while the guys came to fetch me from the hospital. There's an animated movie playing in the background and his usual painting clothes are nowhere in sight.

"Hey," he offers.

All I can do is nod.

Arianna snuggles up to me as soon as I sit down, her headful of long hair pooled in my lap. I soothe myself by stroking the pearlescent strands. Waking up in the hospital without her was terrifying. All I wanted was to hold my little girl close.

"Are you feeling better, Mummy?"

"Yeah," I croak, stroking her cheek. "Everything's going to be okay."

"I wanted to come and see you, but Zach wouldn't let me."

Casting him a grateful smile, I tuck a curl behind her ear. "Hospitals aren't nice places, Ari. Zach was just looking after you for me while I was feeling poorly."

"But I missed you," she argues.

"I know, baby. I'm back now. You don't need to worry anymore."

"I'll sort the bedroom," Killian announces.

He disappears deeper into the cabin, carrying my hospital bag. Crouching down to check the fire, Zach adds another log before slumping on the sofa next to Micah. His eyes are barely managing to stay open.

"Was the drive okay?" Micah asks quietly.

"Long. I don't want to see Highbridge again for a while."

My eyes are drooping, the warmth of the fire coaxing me to sleep. I didn't sleep a wink in the hospital after waking up part way through the blood transfusion. I was too worried about the door being broken down and Mr Sanchez storming in.

I snap wide awake with a gasp when Arianna's weight vanishes from my lap. Zach's lifted her into his arms and cradles her snoring body against his chest.

"Easy," he whispers. "I've got her."

"Thank you."

"I'll tuck her in. You get some rest."

I sink back into the sofa cushions. Micah is tending to the flames in the fireplace, casting me the occasional loaded look over his shoulder. I can hear Killian and Zach murmuring in the other room, but neither returns.

"You're here," I say sleepily.

He tosses another log on the fire. "I didn't want to paint."

"Why not?"

"Because Arianna needed me, and I wanted to be with you. That's more important to me than some stupid paint pallets."

Despite all the pain and turmoil, his words pierce the suffocating loneliness that has curled around my bones. There's something about Micah. The others don't see what I do inside of him.

He has the kind of reassuring presence that can only be honed by experiencing trauma. Even his voice is a comfort to me—soft and soothing, barely an octave above a whisper. His entire presence is a soothing balm against my fried nerves.

"Thank you for looking after her for me."

"Of course," he hushes. "She's a good kid."

"Do you mind if I have a bath? I smell like a hospital."

"Yeah, no problem. I can show you where it is, if you want?"

His hand is outstretched for me to take. I hesitate before tangling our fingers together. He tentatively puts an arm around my shoulders, helping me to stand. My body is still incredibly sore and aching despite the painkillers.

This is the closest we've been since the moment we shared among the crops. Ever since then, Micah has kept his distance, remaining closed-off and unapproachable. That person is a stark comparison to the man holding me close now.

"Go slow," he advises.

"I'm okay."

"I don't want you to hurt yourself. I could carry you?"

"Mi," I reassure him. "You don't need to carry me. I'm okay."

Guided through the sprawling cabin, I follow Micah into a darkened bedroom on the left hand side. We pass the spare room where I can hear Zach reading a bedtime story to Arianna in a ridiculous, high-pitched princess voice.

"It's in my bedroom," Micah explains as he opens the door. "Excuse the mess. I don't sleep in here often."

Letting me into the dark space, I glance around while he flips the lights on and ducks inside the en-suite bathroom. Unlike Killian's room, this is decorated in calming shades of blue. The ocean washes against the walls, blending different hues into a calming cocoon.

His double bed has been lacquered a glossy shade of black, contrasting the deep-blue sheets and navy blanket. While his walls are bare, the bedroom floor is cluttered with art books, colour swatches and the odd discarded paintbrush.

"I like your room."

He chuckles from the bathroom. "It's a mess."

On the bedside table, a single framed photograph rests. I can't help but be nosy. Inside the frame is a middle-aged man who looks just like the twins, down to their similar shorter height, thick caramel-brown hair and malachite eyes.

Smiling ear to ear, there's a younger version of both twins hooked under each of the man's arms. They all look so happy. It hurts to see Micah's wide, childish smile. I've never seen him display happiness so easily.

The photograph is positioned at such a specific angle, I imagine that if Micah were to turn over in bed, it would be like his dad is laying there with him, rocking him back to sleep. My heart breaks all over again.

Micah leaves the bathroom and stops beside me. "That's my dad."

"You both look like him."

"He raised us after our mum left. Dad used to take us camping and backpacking all the time. We even came to Briar Valley once for a trip. He was very outdoorsy."

"You don't talk about him much."

He seems to shake himself out of it. "No, I don't."

"Do you miss him?"

His throat bobs with emotion. "More than anything. He was my best friend. We were so close growing up—me, Zach and Dad. It was the three of us against the world."

"I'm so sorry, Mi."

"Yeah," he deadpans.

Turning his back on the photograph, Micah leads the way into the bathroom. It's light and airy, the slate tiles contrasting the panelled walls. The centrepiece is a huge clawfoot tub, full of jasmine-scented water.

"Zach has fancy bubble bath," Micah explains nervously. "He won't admit it, but he's a complete softie for having a bath. Literally spends hours in there."

"That figures."

"If you don't like it, I can—"

"It's fine," I cut him off.

Micah rubs the back of his neck. "I'll leave you in peace. Shout if you need anything."

Before he can run off, I grab his arm. "Would you mind staying? I don't want to be alone right now. But I understand if it makes you uncomfortable."

"Ah, sure. I can stay."

Averting his eyes, he studies the ceiling while I strip off my sweats and Killian's borrowed t-shirt. Undoing my ratty ponytail, I let my hair trail down my back and climb into the tub, sinking beneath the hot water.

"Okay, I'm in."

Micah clears his throat. "Where do you want me to sit?"

Covered by the carpet of fragrant bubbles, I look up at his awkward smile. "Come closer, if you want. You can talk to me."

"Um, t-talk?" he stammers.

"Or not."

"No, that's fine. We can talk if that's what you want."

Sinking down on the floor next to the bathtub, he bands his arms around his knees. I stare into the steaming water, letting him get comfortable around me. As soon as I let my mind wander, the tears come rushing back.

I feel like I'm being battered by an unrelenting hurricane of pain. Running from it is impossible. Futile. I have to surrender to a force larger than myself and let it roll over me in destructive waves, hoping I make it out the other side.

"Willow? What's wrong?"

"I lost it," I sob, biting my lip. "I lost a baby I didn't even know I was having. Why does it hurt? Why do I feel like my world is ending? I'm being so fucking stupid."

Micah props an arm on the edge of the bath to move closer. "I don't think you're being stupid. You're allowed to grieve even if you didn't know what was growing inside of you."

With a scream inching up my throat, I vocalise the darkest thought that's entered my head since I woke up in hospital.

"This… this baby was a part of him."

"Your husband?"

"Yes. So, am I supposed to be glad it's gone? I wish I didn't feel like my heart has been ripped out of my chest, but I do. It makes no sense."

With his rounded chin resting on the bath's edge, Micah tucks a chunk of wet hair behind my ear. Grabbing his hand before he can retreat, our fingers fit together.

"You're human," he whispers. "Being human doesn't make sense."

"What do you mean?"

"We mourn things that don't exist and chase dreams that will never materialise. We cry when we're happy and laugh when we're sad. Our whole existence is imperfect."

"That makes us sound ridiculous."

The corners of his mouth crinkle into a wry smile. "Basically."

"I never thought about having another kid, but it hurts to know that I still lost something so precious. And now… I might not get another chance."

"Life doesn't make sense to me most days. Losing a baby… I don't know if it will ever make sense to you. But believe me when I tell you that you're allowed to mourn."

Strangled by another sob, I let myself fall apart in front of him. Micah holds my hand through every fallen tear, silently stroking my hair. Words aren't needed. Silence offers more comfort than any reason he could give for this tragedy.

The sound of my crying echoes around us, but the others don't intrude. I cry for the baby I've just lost. For myself. For Arianna and the sibling she'll never meet. For the life it could've had. For the pain that created that spark of light and then cruelly snuffed it out.

Micah's the last person I should be doing this in front of, but I feel comfortable letting him see the most twisted, broken parts of myself that can never be fixed. He knows how it feels to be ripped apart at the seams and have to piece yourself together again.

"It's okay, Willow," he comforts. "You're safe with me."

"N-Nothing about this is okay."

"What can I do to help?"

"Would you h-hold me?"

His lips twist into a tiny smile. "Of course."

Standing up, he pulls his t-shirt over his head and undresses. I'm sobbing too hard to protest as he steps out of his jeans, revealing short but lithe legs and packed abdominals.

He's smaller and slimmer than the others, but still well-toned from hours of sculpting. His constant need to express his feelings through art has kept him in trim shape, bulking out his already generous biceps.

Keeping his boxers in place, he climbs into the huge bathtub with me. Water sloshes over the edges, overflowing from the extra weight. Micah slides in at the opposite end. Instinctively, I reach out for him, needing to feel his arms around me.

He pulls me through the water and positions me between his legs. With his chest to my back, his chin lands on my shoulder, lips briefly kissing the side of my head.

"I've got you," he murmurs.

"Please don't let go."

"Never, angel."

The suffocating darkness begins to abate as we soak in silence, allowing me to draw a stuttered breath. If I imagine that this bathtub makes up my entire world, everything feels less overwhelming. I can face this small feat first.

"Can I wash your hair for you?" Micah asks.

"I'd l-like that."

Shifting behind me, he pushes me forwards slightly and encourages me to lean back. My hair is dunked into the water, and Micah's hands run over my head. It feels amazing to be fawned over and cared for.

Reaching for the shelf of products to the left of the tub, he squirts shampoo into his hands and begins to massage it into my long tresses. My eyes fall shut, the tension leaving my body at the feel of his fingers massaging my scalp.

"Does that feel okay?"

"It feels amazing," I whisper.

He begins to rinse off the shampoo. "Good."

By the time he's finished conditioning my hair, I'm half-asleep in the water. Micah drags me back against his chest, his nose burying in my freshly washed hair before his lips kiss the slope of my exposed neck.

I'm not sure what has changed for him to be comfortable touching me so freely, but I'm glad that something good has come from all this pain. We're equals now. He knows I understand his grief better than most people, and that's earned his trust.

"I'm so sorry for being a mess."

"Stop apologising," Micah murmurs. "We can be messes together."

"You're not a mess."

"Not sure my brother or cousin would agree." He releases a regretful sigh. "I've been in denial for a long time. It was easier to act like it's normal to get so low, you don't even want to be alive."

"Denial is a powerful thing."

"Ain't that the truth."

We stay cuddled together until the water chills. When I can breathe without hiccupping and have no more tears left to shed, Micah places a gentle kiss against my temple. I tilt my head to look at him.

"You're going to get through this," he assures me.

"How do you know? I feel so lost."

"For a long time, it felt like I couldn't survive losing my dad. I felt so alone. Some days, I still feel like my world is ending. No matter how long I spend locked away where I can't inconvenience anyone with my misery."

I stop breathing when his forest-green eyes near, our noses brushing together. His lips push against mine, entwining our hearts into a mournful waltz.

"If I can survive, then so can you. Don't make my mistake. Don't lock people out and spend your life alone. It hurts less, but it isn't living. I don't want to be alone anymore."

"You don't?" I whisper.

"I want to live. I think I always did, otherwise I wouldn't still be here."

"Even if it hurts?"

"Even if it hurts," he confirms.

Drinking in the reassurance, I steal the unfettered light inside of him and take it for my own with each brush of our lips. Micah gives it willingly; his strength, his determination, and every ounce of love he has to offer.

He's far stronger than everyone gives him credit for. The world gave up on him, but Micah kept going. No matter what. He survived the unthinkable. Maybe, I can as well.

"I want to live too. You guys make me want to keep going."

"Then I'll kiss you every day to remind you of that."

"I think... I'd like that."

Micah kisses me again, harder this time, imbued with never-ending ribbons of pain and blossoming wildflowers of hope. It all folds into a pure, untainted moment as we exchange souls.

Maybe, I'm allowed to mourn. It's okay to embrace the pain that brings, as long as I remember to come back to life when the time for grieving is done. I have to live.

For Arianna.
For myself.
For the baby I lost.
For the person I want to be.

CHAPTER 22
WILLOW

TAKE ON THE WORLD - YOU ME
AT SIX

"YOU TRUST ME?" Killian rumbles.

"I'm not entirely sure."

He keeps me pinned against his side so that I don't trip over while I'm blindfolded. I'm not a huge fan of surprises, and I have no idea what he's planning. I haven't left the cabin in a while, so Killian seems determined to get me out.

My foot hits what feels like a rock, and I almost stumble. He catches me mid-fall and instead of guiding me by hand, I'm lifted into his burly arms instead.

"Kill!"

"I've got you, baby."

The note of satisfied possession in his voice sends a shiver down my spine. If I thought he was protective before the miscarriage, the past two weeks have revealed his certified obsession with keeping me safely cocooned within his reach.

"Why do I need to be blindfolded?"

"I told you. It's a surprise."

"You know, I hate surprises."

"You're not gonna hate this one," he says knowingly.

The scent of pine trees and spring blossoms perfuses the warm air around us. I've stayed cooped up in their cabin while recuperating, but it feels good to be outside. The transfusion took its toll, worsened by the trauma of everything that's happened.

For the first few days, I was too exhausted and broken to even move. The guys looked after Arianna, doting on me and bringing the medication I was sent home with. It was nice at first, but I'm ready to be a bit more independent now.

"If you're taking me to see Lola, then don't bother."

Killian sighs. "You can't avoid her forever."

"Sure I can."

"She's dropped by every day to try and see you."

"I said no. I'm not talking to her."

His arms tighten around me. "She's hurting right now. I know you're angry with her, but she deserves a chance to explain herself at least."

My heart twinges. "Would you give her a chance?"

"Yeah. I would."

I haven't had the strength to face Lola and learn the truth about my mother. If I start to pull at that thread, I don't know if I'll be able to hold everything together for Arianna's sake. I'm already struggling to be a parent as it is.

"Nearly there," he reveals.

"We've barely walked anywhere. Are we at Ryder's cabin?"

"Nope. Keep your eyes closed."

Setting me back down on my feet, Killian slowly removes the blindfold, and I keep my eyes squeezed shut. He takes my hand, leading me two more steps before halting.

"Okay. Open them."

I peel my eyes open and blink hard. We've walked across the cobbled road. I'm staring at the abandoned cabin the guys grew up in, but something has changed. I can actually see through the previously grimy windows now.

Glancing around, I realise the overgrown jungle of a garden has been tamed, chopping down huge tufts of weeds and wildflowers that previously made the path impassable. The outside is different too. It looks almost brand new.

The wooden panels of the cabin have been stripped down, sanded and stained a flawless brown colour, highlighting the natural lines of the cherry wood. There's a massive red velvet bow wrapped around the garden gate.

"What is this?"

"Your home," Killian says simply.

"I don't understand. This is your home."

"We want you and Arianna to live here."

I gape up at him. "What?"

Ducking down to my height, Killian cups my cheeks in his palms. "It's yours, Willow. We changed the deeds and everything. This is your cabin now."

"You... did that? For me?"

"I would do fucking anything for you. We all thought that you should have a space you can call your own. I know living with us three can't be easy."

I'm too shocked to form a coherent thought. Killian grins at me, placing another kiss on the tip of my nose. His lips meet mine next and his kiss sets alight fiery butterflies in my belly. He's giving me a home. My own slice of Briar Valley.

An excited hoot breaks our kiss.

"Babe!" Zach bellows.

Killian takes a step back. "Incoming."

Jogging over to us in his usual tight blue jeans and plain t-shirt, Zach throws his arms in the air in a dramatic *ta dah* motion.

"So, what do you think?"

All I can do is stare at them both.

"Say something," Killian urges.

Zach studies my face. "I think she checked out."

"We've officially broken her brain."

"You're the one that ordered the fucking bow!" Zach accuses.

"It was *your* idea," he hits back. "I warned you it was too much."

Tuning their usual bickering out, I stare up at the cabin in awe. It feels like the ground has given out beneath me. I've never owned a house before, or even lived alone.

A grumbling engine pulls up on the grass verge. Ryder waves at me from behind the wheel of the restored VW beetle he's been working relentlessly on.

"The party has arrived," he shouts.

Arianna leaps out of the passenger seat in a blur of hyperactive energy, but she still obediently waits for Ryder to take her hand, so they walk over together. She's attached herself to him in particular, loving his playful energy.

"Mummy! Mummy!"

I catch her easily, propping her on my hip. "Hey, baby."

"Micah said there's a present here for me."

Right on time, the door to the studio over the road slams shut. Micah appears, jogging across the grass. He's back in his messy clothes, and his light brown hair is sticking up in all directions with streaks of dried clay flaked on his cheeks.

When he spots us outside the cabin, a smile spreads across his lips, causing his pierced nose to curl up in a satisfied grin. Smiling transforms his entire appearance, brightening his usually sullen aura.

"Am I too late?" he greets, tucking an arm around my waist. "Sorry, angel. Time ran away with me after my phone appointment with Doctor Holmes."

"You're right on time."

"Oh, good. I was worried."

Micah pecks a gentle kiss against my cheek. Between all of the touching, I'm feeling hot and bothered. After coming out of the hospital, it was clear that something had changed. They're all touchy-feely now, even in front of each other.

It freaked me out at first, but when it became clear that all they wanted was to make me feel at home in their cabin, I soon got used to being the centre of their attention. Just don't ask me what this all means. That I don't know.

"Are we all here now?" Zach squeals. "I'm so fucking excited."

"Language," Killian scolds him. "There are little ears present."

Reaching into the pocket of his jeans, he pulls out a set of keys on another neatly tied velvet bow. Killian hands them to me with a pleased smirk contorting his lips.

"Here you go."

Arianna watches me take them. "What's that?"

Taking her from me, Killian lifts her up into the air before swinging her around until she's squealing. "You like living here, peanut? In Briar Valley?"

"Of course!" She smiles wanly.

"Would you like a princess's castle all for yourself?"

Her mouth falls open and her brilliant blue eyes widen with even more excitement. The way that Killian beams down at her takes my breath away. His inner grumpy asshole is nowhere in sight around my little girl.

"This is your new home, Ari."

Following his pointed finger, she looks up at the cabin and lets out an ear-shattering scream that can probably be heard from across the valley. Arianna takes off at full speed, running towards the repaired porch steps.

Killian snorts. "I'll take that as she's pleased."

Zach tucks me into his side, while Micah bravely takes my other hand. With both of them touching me, my skin begins to tingle. They've been doing this a lot. I quite like being sandwiched between the twins and their built chests.

"Ready to go inside?" Zach asks excitedly.

"As I'll ever be."

Micah squeezes my fingers. "Let's go in."

With the front door unlocked, we all filter inside the empty cabin. The small kitchen and living room are lit by bare bulbs hanging from the high, gabled ceiling. It needs a good clean and a fresh lick of paint, but the space is spacious and airy.

It's big enough to fit our whole group comfortably, the entire room lined with floor-to-ceiling windows that let the natural light in. I twirl on the spot, lost for words.

"I want to see my bedroom!" Arianna yells.

Running towards the back of the cabin, she shouts for me to follow. Still holding Micah's hand for support, I duck inside the three decent sized bedrooms that lead off a carpeted hallway.

They're all empty and lined with original wooden floors, gleaming with fresh varnish that highlights all of the stunning imperfections. It's a complete blank canvas.

"I'll give you a moment," Micah offers.

Pressing a kiss to my knuckles that leaves me blushing, he releases me and returns to the kitchen where Zach and Ryder are talking about replacing the admittedly dated cabinets.

I step into the master bedroom at the very back of the cabin, noting the wet white paint covering the walls. The thud of heavy footsteps soon joins me.

"I wanted to get it all painted in time, but we can do the rest together." Killian's firm pectorals meet my back. "We also need to go furniture shopping."

"You're not spending money on us again."

His breath stirs my hair. "Don't fight me on this, baby. We give all newcomers the same treatment. Arianna will need to choose all her princess crap herself though."

"Don't fancy shopping for pink sheets?"

Turning me in his arms, Killian slides a finger beneath my chin to tilt my lips up to his. His eyes bore into me, full of heat. They've treated me like broken glass, giving me time to rest and heal. Now, he's looking at me like a starved man.

"I'm more interested in choosing your bed and breaking it in." His teeth playfully nip my bottom lip. "I called first dibs."

"First dibs?"

He gives me a crooked smile. "Yep. We need to christen every single room."

"Sounds like a challenge."

"I think that I'm up to the task."

Feeling brave, I decide to take a risk.

"What does this all mean, Kill? The four of us?"

"Well, the twins are enamoured with you, and I've made my feelings very clear. We're all done hiding the way we feel. Life's too short, right?"

"What are you saying?" I breathe unsteadily.

"I'm saying that we want to be with you. All of us. I know it's unconventional, but this is Briar Valley. We don't do normal here. It's fucking overrated."

The look in his fire-lit eyes is almost frenetic. I feel dizzy with the overwhelming urge to throw my arms around him and take this leap into the unknown. I want to be happy, but I can't choose. They're all so special to me.

Killian's brows furrow. "What is it?"

"I don't know how I'm supposed to choose."

"No one is asking you to choose."

"But you will one day, won't you?"

He shakes his head. "No, we won't ever make you choose. We want you and if you want us back... then we're yours. That's it. We'll find a way to make this work."

"Someone might get hurt."

"What's life without risk?" he points out.

Seizing a flicker of courage, I twine my arms around his thick neck and stretch up onto my tiptoes to kiss him. We've barely touched since the miscarriage. I didn't think I ever wanted to be touched again after all the pain and turmoil.

I'm ready to change my mind. Killian's lips seize mine in a fevered dance, his tongue pushing into my mouth as he grabs my hips tight. Going with what feels natural, I draw my legs up and hook them around his waist.

Killian holds me against his huge frame, his hands moving to knead my butt. I can feel every hardened inch of him. His erection is pressing into me, and the emotional hell of the past two weeks dissipates.

"I want to be the first one to fuck you in this room," he whispers. "I'm going to bend you over the bed and bury my cock inside that tight little cunt of yours."

"Better buy a bed then," I moan back.

"It's the first thing on my list."

His mouth slants against mine, our tongues dancing together. Palm smacking against my ass cheek, he keeps me attached to his waist, our bodies flush together. If we were alone, I'd take him right now.

No one would blame me for never wanting to sleep with another man for the rest of my life. But over the months I've been here, my mistrust and fear has been chipped away. They've given me the time and space to embrace my sexuality again.

"Mummy! Come see my bedroom!"

Killian gasps as he breaks the kiss, setting me back on my feet before she catches us in a compromising position.

"She's going to be a cockblock, isn't she?" he groans.

"Oh, for sure. Welcome to life with kids."

"Awesome. I'll end up locking her out of the damn cabin."

"Killian!" I exclaim.

"Only joking."

He takes his time kissing me again, exploring every inch of my mouth in a tender caress. Breathless, I'm dragged from the bedroom when he's done driving me wild.

We step inside Arianna's bedroom a few metres down the hall. She's claimed the second biggest room and lays spreadeagled on the wooden flooring in a star shape.

"Ari! You're far too small for all this space."

She pouts at me as she rolls around. "No, I'm not. It's perfect! I'm a growing girl, you know. I'll be as tall as the giant soon."

Killian snickers. "You tell her, peanut."

I punch his shoulder. "Behave."

Leaving Arianna to explore her new room, we walk back into the kitchen. Zach and Micah are measuring the many windows for new curtains, but they both stop to look back at us, noting our hands tangled together.

Their identical smiles make it almost impossible to tell them apart for a mind-bending second. If it wasn't for their slightly different hair lengths and Micah's nose piercing, I'd be in serious trouble. Even their grins are identical.

"You know, I heard the most delicious noise a moment ago." Zach lifts the tape measure up, acting coy. "Did you hear it too, Mi?"

Micah blushes beet-red. "Well, maybe. Um, no. I don't know."

Laughing hard, Ryder doubles over. "Such a smoothtalker."

Zach is staring at his twin brother like he's an alien stranded on earth. "You're really starting to cramp my style, little brother."

"I'm literally three minutes younger than you."

"And don't you forget it either."

"You ain't so smooth yourself, kid," Killian chips in.

Looking horrified, Zach lays a hand over his heart. "I am far more charming than your uncivilised ass. You have about as much appeal as a grizzly bear."

"Maybe I like grizzly bears," I say with a wink.

Fist-pumping in a very non-Killian manner, he takes the tape measure from Zach's hands and resumes measuring all the windows. They all start arguing about some structural changes that I don't understand.

Their voices fade out as I survey the cabin, feeling light for the first time in weeks. This is it—the fresh start we wanted. I'm not naïve though. I know we have got a long way to go yet.

The guys still want answers about my past. I've begged them to be patient with me, and they've backed off while I took the time to rest and recuperate. But their patience is going to expire sooner rather than later. Lola's too.

Regardless of the trouble ahead, this moment feels like a step in the right direction for the first time. Without planning it, I've ended up with three incredible people by my side.

I'll get through the dark days to come.

I trust them to save me from myself.

CHAPTER 23
MICAH

WICKED - MIKI RATSULA

DIPPING my paintbrush back in the splash of deep-green oil paint on the palette, I swirl it around and wipe off the excess. Arianna's blank bedroom wall faces me, ready to be filled with magic of my making.

I haven't told either of them what I've planned for her mural. This is my contribution to the team effort we've undertaken to get the cabin habitable. I had to wait a few days for Ryder to return from town with the necessary supplies.

Keeping the image at the forefront of my mind, I study the outline I sketched and begin to work. The stroke of the paintbrush allows me to find my happy place with ease. I've been pouring my emotions into art for as long as I can remember.

I'm going to paint a magical forest, teaming with fairies, toadstools, stardust and pixies. In the bottom left corner, I've sketched a princess with blonde hair and blue eyes. The queen stands next to her, a raven-haired beauty.

"Mi? You back there?"

"In here," I reply distractedly.

Zach pops his head in with a beer in hand. "Damn, this is gonna be so fucking epic. You'll be Arianna's new favourite person."

"It's about time Killian had his throne toppled."

"Touché, bro. Dinner in half an hour, alright?"

"Are you cooking? Because if so, I'll pass. I'd rather not die today."

He clicks his tongue with annoyance. "For your information, Willow is cooking, but my sausage surprise remains the universe's best dish."

"You're seriously delusional, brother."

"I've actually been thinking that I should go on a cooking show or something. I need a new career path."

"You'll be the first TV chef to poison everyone."

Flipping me off, he leaves me in peace to work. Revelling in the silence, I zone out and lose myself in the mystical scene spilling from my paintbrush. When I work, I inhabit a whole other universe.

My mind can escape into the flicks of oil paint. Reality becomes whatever I want it to be. In this new plane of existence, I live a normal life. My father is alive. The trajectory of our lives was never altered by his devastating loss.

What feels like hours later, my arm is screaming from being held up for so long. I clean up and rinse off the brushes, leaving them to dry on the newspaper-covered flooring. The sound of voices floats in from the other room.

"There is no way I'm painting the walls pink."

"Arianna would love it," Zach argues.

"No! It's not happening. We already indulge her too much."

"Spoilsport."

I quickly wash the splotches of paint from my sun-blemished face before padding out to find the others. Willow hasn't felt up to going furniture shopping yet, so we set up a nest of pillows and blankets in the living room instead of a sofa.

Killian has installed a brand new log burner in the corner, greedily consuming the dried wood inside. The once-dingy kitchen has been scrubbed within an inch of its life. Willow has got it looking brand new; even the old tiles are sparkling and clean.

The scent of homemade lasagne saturates the air, and my stomach growls loudly. Killian's a decent cook, but this smell reminds me of Aunt Lyra and her home cooking.

"There's a plate in the oven for you," Willow explains.

She's nestled in the tangle of blankets strewn across the floor, her head resting on Zach's chest. They're watching a movie on his old laptop, their faces lit by the glow of flames from the nearby fire.

"Thanks. I didn't realise I missed dinner."

"I did try to come and get you." She smiles up at me. "You were fully engrossed. That was a couple of hours ago."

"Shit. Must've zoned out."

Grabbing the still-warm food, I spoon some salad on my plate and join them in the living room. Killian is still outside, sawing wood like a man possessed. He's been very tight-lipped about what he's building for Arianna next.

Sitting cross-legged on the floor, I dig into the lasagne and groan my appreciation. She's a killer cook. I rarely make it out of my studio for mealtimes, but since she temporarily moved in, the thought of eating alone has held no appeal.

"Good, huh?" Zach mumbles.

"So good."

"I used to cook for my father when I was younger," Willow reveals. "I missed it while I was in Mexico. I wasn't allowed to go into the kitchen, even though I was friends with the head chef's son."

"How come?" I ask without thinking.

Her face darkens. "They weren't allowed to feed me without my husband's permission. I snuck in sometimes just to hang out though. Antonio cooked the best empanadas."

Zach's eyes meet mine. She has never revealed much about her past, and we agreed not to push her, even when Killian wanted to roll out the third degree to get the truth.

"They weren't allowed to feed you?" Zach prods.

"He didn't always let me eat if I was bad or I upset him," she answers vaguely. "It would have been bad for them to disobey his orders."

"Bad, how?" I push her.

Willow stiffens, the spell of honesty breaking. "Enough about me. We don't need to talk about this. What should I buy first for this place?"

"A dog," I mumble around a mouthful.

"No! Not a chance," Zach splutters.

"Am I missing something here?" Willow glances between us.

"Zach's afraid of dogs."

"Mi, shut up. I am not!"

Throwing a piece of garlic bread at his head, Zach grabs it mid-air and stuffs it into his mouth with a mischievous wink. He is incorrigible.

"How can you not like dogs?" She laughs.

Zach mock-shudders. "They're loud, annoying and in need of constant attention. You guys have me for all of that."

I take another bite of food. "Finally, something we can agree on."

Willow gets up to grab more beers, handing one to Zach but hesitating when it comes to me. I shake my head. Killian will only chew me out if he catches me drinking.

It's been years since I last drank but he never forgave me for worrying

Lola so badly when we were teenagers. I went off the rails for several months until she ordered Pops to intervene and sort me out.

"I can't believe Killian is still working."

She glances outside at the asshole himself after returning from the fridge. I can see her biting her lip as she spots him, shirtless and sweating. He's been at it for hours out there, chopping what looks like a whole bloody forest down.

"What exactly is he building?" she wonders.

"Not a clue. He won't tell us."

"Whatever it is, it's big," Zach adds.

"Did you see the blueprints for the playground he was working on for the town centre?" Willow takes my empty plate from me. "That thing is huge."

"Aalia sweet-talked him into it. That woman is dangerously persuasive."

Curling up in her place next to Zach again, Willow's curious gaze lands on me. There's a twinkle in her eyes, gleaming with more confidence than I've ever seen from her. She beckons me closer with a single finger.

"Come here," she whispers huskily.

I don't need to be asked twice. Settling against the cushions, I snuggle my body close to her back. Zach flips over to face Willow instead of the movie, so she's sandwiched between us both.

"Where's Arianna?" I search around the room.

"She went to play in the town square with Johan." Willow whimpers as Zach runs a hand down the generous curve of her body, settling on her hip.

"So, we're all alone," he croons.

"It would seem so."

I watch as he brushes his knuckles against her cheek. Zach presses his lips to hers before sliding his fingers into her curly hair to deepen the kiss further. Just watching them make out in front of me is mesmerising.

It gets a whole lot more interesting when Willow shifts to rub her pert, rounded backside up against my crotch. She's writhing between us both, seeking maximum friction. Each movement teases my hardening cock.

It's enough to send me into a panic. I have no idea what to do. Being a twenty-four year old virgin who lives on a fucking mountain hasn't afforded me much experience with women, especially not in the bedroom department.

"Killian's outside," she murmurs.

Zach strokes her hair from her face. "His loss. He can have you to himself later. You're ours right now."

"You mean we don't, um… have to do this together? I don't know how this whole, you know, sharing thing works."

"There are no rules," he answers. "As long as you're open to exploring with us both. The important question is do you trust us?"

"Of course, I do. I'm just inexperienced."

"Me too," I say shyly. "This is all new to me."

Zach looks surprised for a second, his eyes scouring over me. He's always been a flirt and great at talking to people. I'm his polar opposite, despite our identical looks.

He was always a ladies' man, even when we were teenagers knocking back cheap tequila shots in Highbridge's local bar. We clearly inherited different things.

"Let's just have some fun," Zach suggests.

Biting her lip, Willow nods and leans in to kiss him again. Releasing her swollen lips, he gently turns her over so her eyes land on me. Bright and innocent, the hazel depths are filled with nervous anticipation. She's so fucking beautiful.

Zach kisses her neck from behind, sucking the delicate flesh of Willow's throat between his teeth to leave a mark. When his gaze flicks up to me, asking a silent question, I nod.

"Kiss my brother, Willow."

Obediently following Zach's command, she brushes her mouth against mine in a brief tease. Cupping her jawline, I kiss her back, loving the way her pillowy lips part to grant access to the swipe of my tongue.

Zach's hand manages to sneak between us, easing underneath her loose t-shirt. I can see him kneading her breast through her bra. Feeling impatient, I pull the t-shirt over her head so I can get a better view.

Her bra is pink and lacy, imprisoning the swell of her breasts and stiff, prominent nipples inside. I hesitate, almost losing my nerve. This is further than I've ever gotten before, but I want more.

"Take her bra off," Zach instructs. "I want to see our girl's gorgeous tits."

Grateful for the intervention, I reach around Willow to unclasp her bra and pull the cups aside, freeing her breasts. The soft mounds fit perfectly into my hands, and I bring my mouth down to take her rosy bud between my teeth.

"Mi," she moans.

Fuck, the way she whispers my name like it's a prayer for her salvation is addictive. She arches her back against Zach as he traces a teasing finger along the waistband of her jeans.

Rolling her other nipple between my fingers, I pepper kisses across Willow's chest, lavishing every inch of her and leaving pink splotches everywhere I touch with my tongue.

"Want more?" Zach breathes.

Willow's lips part on a gasp. "Yes... m-more."

"Say please, babe."

When she doesn't immediately answer him, he dips a hand inside her jeans. Her eyes scrunch up, and I can imagine the warmth of her wet cunt welcoming his fingers home.

"Willow," Zach prompts.

"Please. God, Zach. Please, I want more."

"There's my perfect girl. Now you're learning."

Pulling his hand back out and unbuttoning her jeans instead, he pushes them over her hips. Willow lets him strip her, exposing the flowery lace of her matching panties. I shuffle backwards to watch the show.

"I didn't see these when we went shopping," Zach complains.

She bats her lashes. "You should pay more attention."

"Clearly. It would be a shame to ruin them, but I'm dying to rip this scrap of lace off your pussy and bury my face between your thighs."

"You could always buy me more," she suggests.

"What an excellent idea. Then I can ruin those as well."

Zach pulls her back against his chest so his hand can skate over her stomach to dip between her legs. Grabbing a handful of the lace, he pulls hard and tears the panties off her, ripping the delicate fabric into pieces.

Willow pushes her legs open to expose the bareness of her pink folds. It gives me the perfect view as Zach discards the ruined panties and wastes no time circling her clit before he pushes a finger deep inside of her.

"God," she moans.

Zach glances at me. "Watch and learn, brother."

Lifting her hips for more, Willow encourages his finger to slide back into her slick heat. She groans again, and I watch as Zach thrusts a second finger into her pussy, his thumb lavishing a spot that has her gasping for air.

"Taste our girl now, Mi."

"Me?" I repeat.

"Yeah. She's so wet for us. Tell me how sweet she is."

Feeling nervous, I rise to my knees and shuffle forwards so I'm sitting between Willow's legs. She looks so good, spread out and bare, the both of us worshipping her body.

Watching me through hooded lids, she opens her legs wider to beckon me closer. Zach pulls his fingers out and I crawl closer, bringing my lips down to her glistening mound.

She's so wet and receptive. Salty sweetness bursts across my tongue as I drag it over her clit. I love the little gasping moans she makes as my teeth graze that sensitive spot.

"Do you like that, angel?" I ask curiously.

"Yes, Mi. I like it a lot."

I run my index finger through her moisture. "Do you want more?"

"Yes, please."

Pushing my finger inside her entrance, I marvel at the rush of heat that greets me. She feels like a furnace, dripping wet and writhing in pleasure. Her back arches again, pushing her pert breasts into the air.

"Do you like that?" Zach wraps her inky black hair around his fist and pulls to capture her attention. "My twin eating your pretty little cunt?"

"Yes," she groans.

"You're such a dirty girl. Aren't you, babe?"

Her moans grow louder as I push two fingers deep inside of her, working them in and out just as I watched Zach do. The effect is spectacular. She scrunches her eyes shut, whispering my name in a fevered prayer.

Each stroke of my fingers makes her pussy clench tighter, dragging her closer to an inevitable release. Knowing that I'm causing her to moan and plead for more feels better than I ever imagined.

I want to make her feel good. Seeing her like this—vulnerable and drowning in pleasure—gives me a thrill. I've never felt any desire to connect with another human being before, but I'd do anything to make Willow sing my name again.

"I'm going to come," she whimpers.

I press a kiss against her pubic bone. "Show me, angel."

Pushing my fingers in and out of her at a faster pace to drive her right to the edge, I feel her legs tensing around my head. When she cries out, warmth spreads over my hand. Her entire body is quaking all over.

"Perfect," Zach encourages. "Fall apart for my twin."

Easing my fingers out, I maintain eye contact with her and bring them to my lips for a taste. Willow pants for air, still coming down from her high and watching me with rapt attention as I sample the tang of her release.

A caveman-like part of me is pleased to see her spent and satisfied. I brought her to that fragile place and made her cry out in ecstasy. She came on my hand, despite my brother's eyes eagerly watching each development.

"Well, wasn't that a hell of a view." Zach plants a kiss on top of her head. "I have an idea. On your hands and knees, babe. Show me that tight ass of yours."

"Now?" she whispers.

"Did you think we were done? You've been such a good assistant, helping with Micah's first lesson. I think you deserve at least two more orgasms. What do you think, Mi?"

"At least," I echo.

Willow's cheeks flush but she follows his orders, positioning herself on her hands and knees. Hands braced either side of me, her face is in line with my crotch, leaving her cunt exposed to Zach from behind.

"Now, I want you to take Micah's cock out," he instructs. "He's too shy to do it himself, so you're gonna have to help him out."

She grabs hold of my belt and starts to unbuckle it. "Okay."

My dick is almost pulsating as she pushes my jeans over my hips and wraps her hand around my shaft, pulling it free from my plain black boxers. Breath hisses through my clenched teeth and her tight grip turns into a slow, teasing stroke.

Fucking hell.

I've been missing out.

"Good," Zach hums. "You're going to let my twin fuck your mouth while I eat you out from behind, gorgeous girl. I want you to come all over my face."

Willow flushes. "I can do that."

"Show me then."

Her perfect pink lips wrap around the head of my cock, and I almost blow my load straight down her throat. When she takes me deep into her mouth, I grab handfuls of her long hair to help guide her bobbing.

"Jesus," I curse. "That feels incredible."

She bobs up and down, taking my length even deeper with each rotation of her head. Hollowing her cheeks out, I can already feel my balls tightening with the need to explode. The new, overwhelming sensations are all too much.

Zach rises to kneel behind her raised ass, resting his hands on her hips. "Keep going. You're not allowed to stop until you make him come."

Then he lowers his mouth between her legs from behind and digs in like she's a fucking buffet, causing Willow to squeak around a mouthful of my cock. He's attacking her drenched pussy with a storm of teeth and tongue.

This is messed up.

Like hell am I stopping it, though.

My grip on Willow's black hair tightens and I hit against the back of her throat. Each time she pulls me into her mouth, I shudder and pump upwards, needing more of her lips closing around my shaft.

I feel the moment she climaxes again, driven wild by the onslaught of Zach's mouth between her legs. Willow's lips tighten into a vice around my cock, and I can just make out her tortured moan.

Zach halts, his lips coated in glistening moisture. "You taste so fucking sweet, babe."

She can't answer him, still gripping my thighs as I rut into her mouth.

Moving faster, she bobs up and down, steadfast in her determination to tease a release out of me to complete her task.

"Keep going," my twin instructs. "Finish the job."

With a low grunt emanating from her throat, Willow takes a handful of my balls and strokes, adding to the sense of pressure. She's everywhere. Infecting everything. All I can feel is her lips sucking me off, while the scent of her arousal perfuses the air.

I'm enthralled.

Addicted.

Utterly and powerlessly in love.

Still holding her hair in a tight grip, I watch Zach drag two fingers through her folds from behind. He spreads moisture across them and positions his hand at her entrance, pushing the digits deep inside her pussy.

He holds them in such a way, it must feel like she's being fucked from behind while I ride her mouth. With both of us filling her up, Willow's entire body is quivering all over. Her tits bounce with each pump of Zach's fingers.

Every time the pleasure of Zach working her tight hole hits her, Willow inadvertently tightens her mouth around me. I won't be able to hold on much longer, and I can almost see another orgasm surging through her.

The three of us are connected in a reciprocal loop, feeding into one another's desires. Our bodies are in tune, all running to the silent beat of the same song. We're chasing the same climax.

At the last second, I grab Willow's chin, making her halt mid-suck. She surrenders my dick, and her face is in the exact right position without her even realising it.

"I'm gonna finish, angel."

"Okay," she gasps. "Me too."

I bellow a grunt, watching as strands of white come coat her face and cheeks. It pours out of me with more intensity than I've ever experienced from my own hand. Drop after drop, I milk myself dry for her.

Just the sight of her skin dripping in strands of my seed is enough to drag out my climax until I have nothing left to give. Watching me fall apart, her mouth forms an 'O' as Zach drags another orgasm from her at the same time.

He spanks her ass, fingers still buried inside her. "Again. One more time."

"Fuck, Zach!" she moans.

"That's it. Let go."

Gripping her chin as the come soaks into her face, I force her to look at me and let me watch every last second of her finishing all over his fingers. She isn't allowed to look away from me.

Her pupils dilate, blown wide with wave after wave of gratification. We're locked in a stare-off, even as someone else makes her come. The pleasure is still all mine. Watching her surrender is the best fucking sight I've ever seen.

Unable to hold herself up any longer, I grab her before she slumps and gently ease her to the floor. Zach pulls his fingers from her cunt and rests on his haunches, licking his lips like the cat that got the damn cream.

I smooth a hand over Willow's hair. "You okay?"

"More than okay," she murmurs back. "I think I lost count though."

"Three times," Zach supplies happily. "I'm calling that a job well done."

I fight the urge to throw a cushion at his head. "Shut up."

Shrugging, he wipes his mouth off on the back of his hand. "Hope you learned a thing or two. Our girl deserves this treatment on a daily basis."

"Daily?" Willow wheezes.

Ignoring my twin's chuckling, I reach for her discarded t-shirt to clean the mess from her face. Zach's voice halts me.

"No, brother. Leave it."

I furrow my brows in question.

"I want to see your dirty little angel covered in come while I have my turn."

Huh. I don't know why that sounds so hot, but the idea of my mark of possession remaining on her while he fucks her mouth too actually turns me on all over again.

Seizing hold of her waist, he flips Willow onto her back. She squeals in surprise, still appearing dazed. I tug my jeans back up and let her head rest in my lap, her glazed-over eyes staring up at me.

"I want you to hold her wrists while I ride her mouth." Zach looks down at Willow for confirmation. "Is that okay, babe? You can tell me to stop at any time and I will."

Rather than answer, she raises her arms, offering her wrists to me. Zach grins at her, unfastening his own tented jeans to free his dick. He yanks her down so that her arms are pulled high above her head, and I move to grip her wrists tight.

"I've spent the past few months dreaming about the moment I'll get to fuck you," Zach growls as he straddles her chest. "I don't think I can wait much longer."

"Then don't."

"This is a lesson for my twin's benefit." He casts me an amused look. "We don't want to overwhelm him on his first day."

I flip him the bird. "Fuck you, Zachariah."

"I'd rather fuck Willow instead, thanks."

Kneeling over her breasts to keep the weight off her chest, Zach drags his thumb over her bottom lip, encouraging her to open up. Willow obeys without a thought, her face still sticky with my come.

She doesn't seem to mind being caught between the two of us, every inch of her body at our shared mercy. I doubt I could do this with anyone but my twin. He's an extension of myself, and weirdly, this feels right.

"That's it, babe. Take all of my cock."

Feeding his length into her mouth, Zach doesn't hesitate as I did. He buries himself to the hilt between her glistening lips and throws his head back with a groan.

Willow's hazel eyes are peering up at me beneath her lashes, even with a mouthful of my twin's dick. I pin her wrists down, keeping her trapped as he begins to pump his hips.

"So perfect," I praise her.

"Isn't she just?" Zach hums. "Look at that. So beautiful."

Tiny beads of moisture escape from her eyes as he roughly fucks her mouth. Still, Willow doesn't complain. She takes every single thrust. It's an unbelievable sight—her, trapped by my hands, while Zach ruts into her mouth, over and over.

I don't even care that he's the one being pleasured. Watching them is thrilling enough. I can almost feel my twin's pleasure through the quakes of Willow's body every time his movements cause her to shift, straining against my hold on her.

Zach moves hard and fast, running at full speed to reach his own peak. He uses Willow's mouth as thoroughly as he worked her pussy until she fell apart for him. Something tells me I should be taking notes.

"You gonna swallow my come?" Zach growls.

She bats her lashes in agreement.

"Here it comes, pretty girl."

Pumping into her mouth with a final bellow, Zach's eyes slam shut. I watch Willow's face with fascination. Her lips are clamped around his length, but beads of come overflow and slide from the corners of her mouth.

Throat bobbing as she swallows his seed, Willow opens her mouth, releasing his cock. Zach braces himself over her, breathing hard and watching her performance with the same fascination that's held me in place.

"Did I do a good job?" Willow asks obediently.

Leaning down, Zach kisses her lips, still stained with his come. "You did a perfect job. I think we've given Micah a lesson he'll never forget."

Both of their gazes slide over to me.

"Ahem." I clear my throat. "We should… cover up."

"I quite like this sight." Zach snickers. "She's covered in both of us now, brother."

"It's a damn good sight if I do say so myself," another voice adds.

The front door clicks shut as Killian steps inside, still bare-chested and dripping with sweat, a flannel shirt knotted around his waist. His eyes lock on Willow, naked and panting in the middle of our sandwich.

"Looks like I missed out on the party," he mutters.

Zach laughs, climbing off Willow's chest and offering her a hand up. She stretches to her full height, uncaring of her bare curves and fuzz-covered pussy on full display to us all.

She saunters over to Killian in the kitchen, confident and unashamed with a new sway in her hips that makes me want to pin her to the floor all over again.

"Want to come in the shower with me? I'm very dirty," she says slyly.

The shock on his face is priceless.

"Hell yeah, I do."

Taking his hand like the queen she is, Willow leads him back towards the master bedroom, the partition door slamming shut behind them. I look up at Zach, and he shrugs casually, like this is all normal somehow.

"Maybe sharing isn't so hard after all."

CHAPTER 24
WILLOW

IT'LL BE OKAY - SHAWN MENDES

DRAGGING the bag of soil across the cabin's generous garden, I curse under my breath. It's heavy, but I'm determined to do this alone. The whole flowerbed is prepped and ready to go, though it's taken time for me to work up the courage to begin.

Killian got the lily plants I requested from over in the town's main allotment. They've been waiting for me for a couple of weeks now, but if I don't plant them now, they will die soon. I'll never be ready to do this.

Some things in life don't get easier with time.

The wounds scab over, but never fully heal.

With sweat pouring from my forehead in the sunshine, I drag the soil over to the quiet spot in the corner of the cabin's garden. It took me a long time to choose this place. Using my bare hands, I dig several trenches, leaving space for the small plants.

Positioning the lily plants, I pack them with more soil before watering each one. It's slow, methodical work that focuses my mind. I zone out from the world, finishing the whole patch and cleaning up any loose ends.

In a few weeks, the flowers will bloom.

Just in time for summer.

Reaching into the plastic bag that Micah presented me with, I pull the freshly carved sculpture out. It's small, spanning the size of my palm. He spent all night crafting a pair of angel wings with last month's fateful date stamped on the bottom.

Placing the hand-carved wings in the flowers, the memorial is complete.

That's when my resolve breaks. Hot curtains of tears spill down my cheeks, stinging in the air. I glance up at the cloudless sky.

"I'm so sorry, little one."

The light, silent breeze answers me.

"I'm sorry that I couldn't keep you in this world, and you never got the chance to live. I wish we could have met you. We didn't get enough time together."

Wiping my cheeks, I run a finger over the intricate angel's wings. My chest threatens to explode with the sheer weight of pain rolling through me. Despite making progress, focussing on paint samples and furniture brochures, recent events are still so raw.

The pain is indescribable.

But more so, the sense of shame.

I couldn't keep my baby alive inside of me. Without knowing it, I failed my own child, before it was even born. That's a very particular brand of self-loathing that only a mother can understand.

But deep down, I know it wasn't my fault. If the roles were reversed, and someone I loved had been through this ordeal, I'd hate to think of them punishing themselves for something so out of their control.

That doesn't help me now.

Other people's empathy has done nothing to ease my guilt. The guys want to help and keep encouraging me to open up to them, but it's so hard to talk about this. It feels safer to be alone with my grief. They can't understand.

"You've grown your angel wings now." I grant myself a tiny smile. "Say hello to Pedro for me. I hope he's keeping you company up there. We'll see you one day."

Sunshine warms my face, drying the tears on my cheeks. It feels like an invisible ghost is kissing my skin, the warmth whispering a silent message.

"For now, you're our guardian angel."

I stay crouched in the dirt, silently crying, until there's nothing left in me but bitterness and regret. It feels like hours have passed when the crunch of footsteps approaches.

"Willow?"

With a sigh, I force myself to stand and face Lola. She tentatively slides through the freshly painted garden gate. It's the first time I've seen her in weeks. My avoidance has worked until now.

She looks devastated, her clear eyes lined with painfully heavy bags and brimming with tears. Her silvery hair looks haphazard, like she climbed out of bed and didn't have the heart to fix it. Even her yellow floral dress is unusually creased.

"Lola."

"Can we talk?" she requests.

"I guess so."

Gesturing to the handmade wooden bench that Killian appeared with last week, we both take a seat and face the memorial across the mowed lawn. I can't even look at her.

"I'm so sorry, poppet."

My tears pour soundlessly.

Lola wipes her own wet cheeks. "There's no pain quite like losing a child. I know I didn't lose your father until he was a teenager, but I understand what you're feeling."

"Do you?" I utter emotionlessly.

Her shrivelled hand clasps mine. "You're not alone, Willow. I know you don't want to talk to me, but I'm here for you regardless."

"I have nothing to say to you. All you've done is lie to me."

"While that may be the case, I have plenty to say to you."

She won't release my hand when I try to pull it away. All I want is to run, leave her with her excuses and bullshit lies. I'm furious with her, but I know it's not all her fault.

The anger pounding through me is a torrid mix of a decade's suffering. My father's addiction. His death. Debts. Poverty. Abuse. Violence. Leaving our home. Fear, hope and every shade of confusing agony in between.

"Please," Lola begs. "Just give me ten minutes and I'll go. I want to explain myself."

"Go ahead." I sigh in defeat. "Ten minutes."

She studies the memorial in front of us. "I'm sorry for lying to you. Things are complicated. I was conscious of not overwhelming you when you first arrived."

"Spare me the excuses, Lola."

"The truth is, I have known your mother for a long time. She tracked me down fifteen years ago and made her way to Briar Valley."

"Why?"

"She was looking for your father… and for you."

I stare at her without understanding. "What do you mean she was looking for us? Katie abandoned us both. I barely remember her."

"But you remember what your father told you about her, right?" Lola's smile is full of devastation. "That she left and never returned?"

I was barely older than Arianna when she left. One day she was there, and the next, she wasn't. All I had was the word of a drug addict, and I was too young to question him.

"He lied to you, Willow."

"What are you talking about?"

"She never abandoned you."

I shake my head. "This is just more of your lies, isn't it?"

"Your father took you from her. She spent the next decade searching the entire country for you both. That search is what brought Katie into my life."

"No! I don't believe you," I shout at her, drawing to my feet. "You're still lying. Why would he do that to me?"

"He was unstable," Lola insists.

"That doesn't mean he lied to me!"

She implores me with her eyes. "You remember her scar, don't you? He attacked her with a smashed vodka bottle one night when she threatened to leave with you."

I rub my temples as my headache explodes. "I... don't remember how she got it."

"Without you, he wouldn't receive any child support payments from the government," Lola continues. "How else would he pay for the drugs? You were his source of income."

More anguished tears spill down my cheeks. "If this is true, why didn't she look for me? He was a shit dad, and she just left me with him."

"She never once gave up hope of finding you."

"That means nothing to me! Why didn't she come?"

Lola's face crumples. "Your father took you and ran. She searched and searched, but you were gone. That's when she tracked me down, hoping that I knew where he was."

I angrily scrub my tears. "You sat in that cabin on my very first day here and lied to my face when you asked me to trust you. What's your excuse for that?"

Wringing her hands together, Lola focuses on the golden wedding band she still wears on her ring finger. The strength that shined through her wizened appearance from the day we met has gone.

Now, she looks like an old, broken woman, unable to fix the mistakes of a lifetime. Not even the scores of lives she's saved in the years since have redeemed her of this sin.

"I'm sorry that I lied to you. No excuses, Willow."

"Just tell me why. That's all I want to know."

"I didn't know what else to say. I did what I thought was the kindest thing."

"But you knew where I was when my father died. Why didn't Katie come then?" I choke on a sob and fall to my knees. "Why didn't my mum come and save me?"

Leaving her perch on the bench, Lola joins me kneeling in the grass. I don't fight back as she pulls me into her arms. Pressed against her cookie-scented chest, I lose all sense of control. Her gentle whispers fail to keep me together.

"I didn't write that letter," she admits tearfully.

"You d-didn't?"

"Your mother wanted to reach out. She came to look for you when the police called me, but you'd slipped through her fingers again. She wrote that letter in desperation."

"It h-had your name on it."

Lola rubs my back in slow, comforting circles. "She didn't want to scare you after so many years apart. We didn't know what your father had told you. It felt safer to pretend it was me reaching out instead."

Shoving her away with a snarl, I scramble to my feet and back away from her. Lola is staring up at me with such raw agony, it hurts to see the pain festering deep inside of her. There's a bottomless pit reflected in her eyes, threatening to drown me.

"Mummy!"

The door to the cabin has opened, and Arianna now stands on the wraparound porch. I panic, scrubbing my tears out of sight. Zach and Micah bustle her back inside, hanging back on the porch as Killian jumps into action.

I glance back at Lola, needing to know the truth. "You're telling me that all this time, after everything that's happened to me, Katie was alive and well."

Lola simply nods. "Yes."

"When that monster took me to a strange country, stuck a ring on my finger and... and... when he forced me to... she wasn't there!"

Her face crumples. She can't respond.

"I needed someone to save me. Nobody did. Nobody, Lola!"

Vaulting over the porch in a rush to get to us, Killian lands on the lawn with a loud thud. He leaves Zach and Micah behind, both of them stuck together and watching the unfolding disaster with horrified expressions.

When Killian attempts to approach me with his hands outstretched, I back away, warning him off. "Stay right there."

Lola climbs to her feet. "I'm so sorry, Willow. I'll never forgive myself."

"I was a child." My voice cracks. "Dad left me with all these debts. People smashing the door down and demanding money. I was homeless for months."

"Willow, please—"

"I spent my nights stripping at a bar for money to pay them off. Did you know that?"

"I... I d-didn't," Lola admits.

Wrapping an arm around her shaking shoulders, Killian whispers in her ear, encouraging her to back off. It makes me even angrier, seeing him comfort her. Not even Zach or Micah have the guts to intervene.

"That's where he found me, you know," I shout at them all. "In that damned strip club. If it wasn't for my father's debts, I never would've been there."

Pushing an inconsolable Lola behind him, Killian faces me. "Willow. Stop."

"No, Kill!"

"Lola's upset enough right now."

"You've all been waiting to hear about him, right? Do you want to hear about what he did that night to make sure I was a virgin before he bought me?"

He flinches, his face paling. "Let's talk about this inside."

"After that, I was shipped off to Mexico to be his plaything for ten years. He forced me to marry him against my will and trapped me there. That's the truth."

It's all pouring out. Every dirty, disgusting detail. Secrets I never intended to show the light of day. Lola looks like she's going to have a heart attack, but Killian doesn't return to her, his attention solely fixed on me.

"Stay back." I raise my hands to protect myself. "Don't touch me."

"I'm not here to hurt you," he offers in a soothing voice. "Just take a breath before you pass out. You need to calm down."

Clutching my painfully tight chest, I fight to drag in a stuttered breath and fail. I'm so fucking angry. Lola. Mr Sanchez. My parents. The entire goddamn world is out to get me. I've been failed, over and over again, by everyone in my life.

The only reason I'm still alive is me. My own determination to survive. Not even for myself, but for the one blessing my marriage gave me—my little girl. She kept my dead heart beating even as it shattered into irreparable pieces.

"I didn't know I was pregnant when I came here because he hurt me so often," I force out. "That was my baby, not his. I still lost it. I lost my baby, Kill."

"I know," he hushes. "I'm so sorry. It isn't fair."

My knees give out as I curl inwards with grief. "Nothing ever is."

"Please, Willow," Killian begs. "Let me help you."

"I fucking lost my own child. I'm so weak!"

Before he can sink to the ground next to me, the pad of small feet overtakes him. I stare through my relentless tears at Arianna, racing across the lawn with her frostbitten blue eyes.

She looks so much like him, but she will always be my girl. All I see when I look at her is hope. It's the same flickering flame of hope that kept me going when I gave birth to her alone, scared out of my mind and in so much pain.

I begged for death that night, but no one answered. Instead, I was given new life. Her tiny, terrified whimpers and thrashing fists screamed for attention, even as I sobbed in a bathtub of my own blood.

Arianna was always the one to get me off the floor, broken and beaten to a pulp after Mr Sanchez relished in his regular fits of rage. I'm not strong. I'm not brave. All that I am… it's for her.

My little girl.

My guardian angel.

She stops at my side, those damned eyes peering up at me. "Mummy, please don't cry. Daddy can't find us here. The giant and his family will keep us safe."

"Ari… please go back inside."

"No, I won't," she protests. "You don't need to be sad anymore."

I kneel in front of her, my entire world narrowing until it's just the two of us. Like it always has been. Me and my little miracle against the whole fucking world.

She places a tiny palm on my cheek. "Aren't we safe here?"

Pulling the remaining shards of my sanity together for her, I summon the world's worst smile for the world's best daughter. It's all I have left to give her.

"We're safe. I promised, didn't I?"

"And Mummy always keeps her promises," she declares. "That's how I know that everything is going to be okay. Because you promised."

Wrapping her hands around mine, Arianna tugs hard, demanding I stand back up. With her to anchor me in the present, far from that blood-stained mansion, I find my feet again. Only because she needs me to.

"Ari," Zach calls from the porch. "Come inside."

She spares me another glance. "Mummy?"

"It's okay, baby. I need to talk to Killian. Go on up."

Arianna releases my hand and reluctantly returns to the cabin. I watch as Zach leads her inside, though he looks desperate to pull me into his arms. Micah is helping Lola, leading her away to give me some privacy.

My legs are weak, but Killian closes the gap between us in a flash. He lets me collapse into his arms and crushes me against his chest, almost cutting off my blood circulation.

"Fuck, Willow. You should have told me."

"I was scared for you to know the truth," I whisper into his flannel shirt. "It was easier to lie. I didn't want you to look at me any differently if you knew what he did."

Cupping the back of my head, Killian forces me to look up at him. His eyes strip back my skin, layer by layer, until it feels like he's looking straight into the centre of my soul. Every last ugly secret I hold inside me is displayed for him to see.

"Nothing in this entire world could make me see you any differently," he says with fire. "I see a mama bear determined to protect her baby, and the strongest woman I've ever met."

"You're wrong. I'm broken."

"Broken wings can still fly. You are living proof of that."

My throat constricts. "All I can do is fall."

"I've got you, and I'm never letting go. None of us are. We're here to catch you if you fall and help you get back up again. That's what family is for."

Lifting me into his arms despite my protests, he carries me back to the cabin, leaving Lola to be led away. There's nothing I can offer her right now. She's one in a long line of disappointments.

I can't be angry with the whole world for failing me, but I don't know how to forgive those who left me behind. I was a child. Vulnerable and alone. They were all adults and they still let me down.

No matter what happens, I will never do that to my daughter. Nobody will ever lay a finger on her while I'm still breathing. I'll do for her what my parents didn't do for me. She will always be safe, no matter what it costs.

Even if that cost is my heart.

And the three men who now own it.

CHAPTER 25
WILLOW

DON'T HOLD ME - SANDRO CAVAZZA

"READY, SWEETHEART?"

Arianna hoists the miniature, sparkly pink backpack up her shoulders. She's wearing her favourite unicorn dress and new strappy sandals which were a gift from Killian.

He's a complete sucker for Arianna's puppy dog eyes and can't resist indulging her every whim, no matter how much I discourage him from spoiling her. With July bringing hot weather, we've had to switch to lighter clothing.

"I'm ready!"

"Got your packed lunch? Water bottle? Pencil case?"

"Mummy," she drones. "Johan is waiting outside! I need to go."

Fussing over her, I smooth her neat, two-part braids and wipe a spot of toothpaste from the corner of her mouth. It's proving harder than I thought to let go of her. We've barely been apart in seven years.

But today is the day that Arianna joins the other children of Briar Valley. Rachel runs a homeschooling program from the barn behind her cabin.

I've fought against it for weeks, but it's time to let her be a normal kid. Even if I hate it. My little girl is growing up.

"Mummy!" she startles me.

"Okay, okay. Go on then and be good!"

Arianna gifts me a toothy grin. "I'm always good."

"Don't be giving Rachel any sass either."

Bounding down the wide porch steps, Arianna hooks her thumbs into her backpack as she meets Johan at the edge of our cabin site. He waves at me, an excited smile etched across his face at the sight of Arianna. The pair have become inseparable.

"Be careful," I shout at them.

"We will," they reply in unison.

The route is safe enough for them to walk back down into the valley alone. Aalia usually takes Johan, but she's started helping out at the shared allotment behind Lola's cabin that supplies fruit and vegetables for the whole town.

Aalia has a real knack for teasing the life out of parched strawberry plants and drooping crops as we suffer through a July heatwave. Amie is more than content to be swaddled and strapped to her back while she works.

As soon as Arianna disappears from sight, my shoulders slump. In front of her, I can just about plaster on a brave face and pretend like I'm keeping it together. It's the moments I spend alone that allow the soul-sucking hole of grief to return.

"Willow!" Ryder yells from across the street. "I'm towing a car into Highbridge to drop it off. Do you want to come and get some fresh air?"

I cup my hands around my mouth to shout back. "No, thanks."

"Sure? Might be good for you."

"Really, I'm fine."

Plastering on a smile to cover his concern, he hops into the cab of Albie's truck and sets off, towing a freshly repaired estate car behind him to return to its owner.

In his overgrown garden next door, Killian is getting his workout in early this morning as he tackles a monstrous pile of wood that needs to be chopped. Lola's hosting one of her regular bonfires next weekend to celebrate Albie's birthday.

"You should have gone," he calls out, resting on his shining axe to take a breath. "Rachel will call if there's an issue with Arianna at homeschool."

Shaking my head, I wave him off. "I didn't fancy it."

Swinging the axe high above his head, he buries it in a slab of wood and leaves it there. His golden-hued skin practically glows in the morning sunlight, lit with a glistening layer of sweat, while his tangled blonde hair flows over his shoulders.

He crosses the street, wiping off his brow on his green flannel shirt. It's unbuttoned and flaps open to reveal the chiselled lines of muscle that carve his chest. I almost swallow my tongue. It should be illegal to look this hot so early in the morning.

"You've barely left your cabin for days."

I stare down at him. "You're worrying again."

"It's kinda my job to."

"Is it?" I snap back.

Hurt crosses his strong features, twisting his lips into a grimace. Ever since my row with Lola, things have been tense. It feels like we're tiptoeing around each other again.

They've all been gifted a glimpse into the horror of my past, and none of them know what to say to me now. I've shut down any further attempts to talk about what I revealed that day.

"I have work to do." I turn my back on him. "The spare bedroom isn't going to paint itself."

As I head back inside the cabin, Killian's loud footsteps catch up to me. My arm is wrenched backwards, preventing me from escaping. I'm powerless to resist the magnetism of his eyes burning into me, demanding something I'm not able to give.

"Willow," he rumbles. "Please."

I push his chest, trying to wriggle free. "What?"

"You've got to stop pushing us away. We can't do this again. I'm not going back to how things were between us when we first met."

"You didn't have a problem with it then."

"Well I do now, alright?" he thunders. "I care about you too much to watch you self-destruct in private while giving us this bullshit smile in public."

"There's nothing wrong with my smile."

"You think I can't tell? I know every goddamn inch of you, inside and out. You're in pain and it's killing me that you won't let me help you carry the burden."

"This is what I need to do to survive! Can't you respect that?" I shout at him.

Recoiling like I've slapped him, Killian's grip on my arm releases. I take a big step backwards, needing space between us before I melt into his arms.

"Fine," he growls out.

"Fine."

"I guess I'll be going then."

With a final muttered curse, he turns on his heel and marches away. I stand frozen in the doorway of the cabin, watching him return to his woodpile and resume chopping with renewed rage. The logs don't stand a chance.

After throwing on my painting clothes in a torrent of frustration, I return to the spare bedroom and face my task. This room has been left until last to be repainted, while I'm beginning to furniture shop for the others.

We've been sleeping off bare mattresses and eating dinner in our laps since we officially moved in. The guys insisted that we could stay with them for as long as we needed to, but I was all packed up by the next day, needing my own space.

A couple of hours into painting, I've zoned out. The monotonous back and forth of the roller against the wall drowns out all other thoughts. I don't register the slow clapping and someone else entering the room until it's too late.

"This is looking great." Zach stops beside me. "Nice and bright."

"Uh-huh."

"You need a hand? Killian's gone to haul all that wood to the town square for next weekend, so I'm off the hook."

"I've got this."

"I know you've got it," he echoes. "I'm asking if you need help."

With a snarl, I throw the roller down into the paint palette. "Did Killian send you over here? What is it with you three? I told you all that I needed space."

Swiping a hand through his hair, Zach sighs. "There's a difference between needing space and hiding from us. Trust me, I know after living with Micah."

The fight is knocked out of me. Pain radiates in his eyes, and in that moment, all I can see is his brother's anguish filtering through into Zach. The two are indistinguishable to my exhausted mind.

"He's spent most of his life hiding," Zach continues, inching closer. "It wasn't until you came along and showed him what bravery looks like that my brother came back."

"I'm not brave, Zach."

"You're the bravest person I know." He stops an inch in front of me. "I just wish you could see yourself like I do. I wish you'd give yourself the credit you deserve."

Tears sear the backs of my eyes. "Please stop."

Shaking his head, he slides his palm across my cheek and cups the back of my head. My breathing hitches, and his lips near, those damned green eyes freezing me in place.

"I need you to know that I'm falling in love with you."

"Y-You... are?" I stammer.

His nose brushes against mine. "Head over fucking heels, babe. I don't give a shit about whether I have to share you. All I want is the privilege of owning a piece of your heart."

Lips parted on a shocked breath, I lose all sense of control. My arms wind around his neck, drawing us flush together. I'm drowning in the malachite depths of his gaze.

"I'm not worth loving, Zach."

His lips tease mine in a brief whisper. "Then I'll make it my mission to spend the rest of my life convincing you otherwise. I don't care how long it takes."

When his mouth imprisons mine, I know fighting is futile. I can run from them until I have no strength left in my body, but it won't prevent the inevitable recapture of my heart. It doesn't belong to me anymore.

Zach tilts my head up and his lips move against mine in a slow, torturous dance. I push my breasts into his chest, seeking relief from the slow-burning ache of need setting my core alight.

He walks me backwards, his kiss deepening into a ravenous wrestle. I squeak as my back meets the still-wet wall, covering me in paint. He doesn't care. His body aligns with mine, our hips pinned together.

The steady rub of his hardness against my belly reveals his intentions. I'm caught in his web, the sacrificial prey awaiting its doom. Zach is going to consume me, and I'll happily be his long-awaited meal.

"Babe," he gasps into my mouth. "I need to feel you around me."

I hook a leg up on his hip, letting his cock push between my thighs. Every part of me is humming, welcoming the rush of endorphins after weeks spent awash with grief.

"Me too."

His teeth nip my bottom lip, becoming more demanding. I moan loudly when his mouth travels along my jawline to the shell of my ear, and he bites down on the lobe. Each graze of his teeth floods my core with more heat.

"I've spent months dreaming about the feel of your perfect pussy clenched around my cock," he says gruffly. "It's taken all of my self-control not to bend you over and fuck you senseless."

Grabbing the hem of his t-shirt, I pull it up over his head. "Prove it then."

"Prove what?"

I ball up his shirt and toss it aside. "Prove that I'm not some broken doll you like to look at. Prove that you aren't scared to touch me, or kiss me, or take me as your own."

He grabs me by the throat, a delicious darkness in his eyes. "You want me to prove it? I'll fuck your tight little cunt until you scream so loud, all of Briar Valley will hear."

"Then do it."

He strips off my loose t-shirt, disregarding the paint soaking into the material. I clasp his shoulders as he drags my leggings and panties down together, too impatient to begin another slow tease.

My pussy is exposed to him, and I can feel how wet I am already. There's an invisible clock ticking down in my head, creating a sense of urgency. Months of tension have driven us to this primal moment.

"Look at this gorgeous pussy," he purrs, kissing over my pubic pone. "Fuck, Willow. I need to taste your sweetness again."

Grabbing fistfuls of his caramel hair, I throw my head back and bite out a moan of pleasure. His mouth lands on my mound, tongue flicking across my clit. I tug on his hair, silently begging him for more.

When his tongue spears my entrance, I cry out again. Nothing but his touch and tongue can break me free from the prison of my anguish. Zach circles my entrance before pushing a finger inside.

"There you go," he hums. "So wet and tight. My perfect girl."

"Zach," I mewl. "Please."

"You're very impatient today, aren't you?"

He adds a second finger, driving it into me without warning. I feel my walls stretch around him, the warmth tricking through my veins. Bucking against his hand, I savour the swipe of his tongue over my folds as he fingers me.

My bare back slides across the wall. I can feel the paint sticking to my skin and hair, but I don't care. All that matters is the feel of him dominating every last dark corner of my mind and driving the demons out.

Zach pauses, licking the gleaming moisture from his lips. I take the chance to unclasp my bra and toss it aside, until I'm completely bare and at his mercy.

"I need you to fuck me, right now."

His eyebrows lift. "What, no please?"

Dragging him up with a tight handful of his hair, I seize his belt. "No. Stop treating me like some precious wallflower. Prove nothing's changed and you still want me, even now that you know the truth."

Zach lets me shove his jeans to the floor and he steps out of them, peeling his boxers off next. His length stands tall and proud, straining to be touched. I seize a handful and begin to pump.

"Turn around," he orders. "Hands on the wall."

"It's still wet."

"I honestly do not give a flying fuck. Do it."

I turn and face the wall. My hands become slick with paint, ruining my hard work, but that doesn't stop Zach from grabbing my hips to pull my ass against his crotch.

"Shit," he curses. "Hang on."

Zach ducks down to reach for his wallet, tucked into his jeans pocket. He retrieves a condom from inside, a grin blossoming on his face when I laugh at his preparedness.

"Hey, you can never be too careful," he defends.

"I really don't want to know why you're so prepared."

"Only for you, if that's what you're thinking. There's no one else."

"Good."

Shoving a hand into my lower back, he bends me over. I stare at the wall, a fine tremble running over me with the torment of anticipation. Zach caresses my hip, leaving me clueless as to when he's going to enter me.

When his control snaps and he finally thrusts into me, it's in one slick, relentless pump. I scream out his name, overwhelmed by the press of his cock buried deep inside of me.

"Goddammit, Willow. You feel so fucking good."

Drawing out again, he slams back into me, adopting a brutal, punishing rhythm. It isn't like the first time I slept with Killian, and he was afraid of making a single wrong move. Zach's gentleness has dissipated along with his patience.

Keeping my knees slightly bent, I take every inch of steel sliding into my pussy. Each stroke adds to the building pressure that submits to Zach's demands for my submission. His hand circles around me, lifting two fingers to press against my lips.

"Suck."

"Why?"

"Stop asking questions and fucking do it."

I take the digits into my mouth and swirl my tongue around his fingers, covering them in saliva. His thrusts slow for a second as his hand glides down my spine. When he tickles the tight ring of muscle at my rear, I almost see stars.

"I want to feel how tight this asshole is too," he muses.

He eases one finger inside of me, and an agonised gasp slips out of my mouth. It's a burning intrusion at first, but as he begins to finger-fuck my rear, I adjust to the strange sensation. It begins to feel good—really fucking good.

"Such a dirty girl," Zach groans. "Do you like that?"

"Yes," I moan.

His cock begins to pound into me again, working in perfect timing with his finger sliding into my ass. When he's stretched me wide enough, he pushes a second finger in, making me cry out so loud, I'm thankful we're alone on a mountaintop.

"Louder, babe. I want to hear how much you love it when I worship this beautiful body of yours."

"Fuck, Zach! More."

He keeps going, fucking me with his fingers and dick, until the coiled band of tension inside my core snaps in a spectacular fashion. I shout his name again, relinquishing control of my own body and handing it to him on a gold platter.

When Zach abruptly pulls out of both holes, I mourn the sudden loss, feeling my orgasm begin to ebb away. He turns me around and shoves my back into the wall with a low growl, yanking my legs up to wrap around his waist.

"I want to watch you fall apart for me, babe."

In this new position, he surges back inside me. My release comes roaring back to the forefront, even stronger than before. I drag my nails down his broad biceps, drawing blood that smears across his tanned skin.

"Now, Willow," he growls.

I feel like I'm going to fracture into a million irreparable pieces. If I wasn't so wildly turned on, it would hurt to take his length with such careless ferocity. The smog of my climax taking over consumes everything.

Zach watches me shatter, stealing every drop of pleasure he can take. Each pump of his dick inside my slit drags out the waves of bliss until I can hardly lift my head. His hands gripping my ass is the only thing keeping me upright.

"I want you to make yourself come again." He walks backwards, taking me with him as he sinks to the plastic-covered floor. "You're going to fuck me now."

With Zach seated on the floor and his legs spread out, I shift to position myself on his lap. My legs band back around his waist, and I grab a handful of his erection, lining it up with my soaked entrance.

Sinking down on him, it's intoxicating to watch his head throw back and pupils blow wide with satisfaction. I did that. Me. There's a strong, powerful man beneath me, but right now, he only lives to service my every whim.

Lifting myself from his lap, I push back down, filling myself with his dick. It takes a few attempts to get the angle right as my legs tremble, weak from one mind-blowing orgasm. His hands move to my hips to help lift and guide me.

Zach begins to rut upwards, driving into me each time I slam down on his cock. Every rough thrust pours pain and pleasure into the vacant spaces of my soul.

"Come on, beautiful," he murmurs. "Spread those sweet juices all over my cock."

A second orgasm is on the cusp of invading my senses. When his hand circles my neck, gently squeezing to test the waters, I feel the approaching peak appear on the horizon. If it was anyone else, I'd be triggered by them clamping down on my throat.

"More," I wheeze out.

His nails dig into my skin. "You like that?"

"Y-Yes."

Our bodies smack together, working in perfect harmony. I feel like I've been dipped in fuel and set alight. Zach begins to chokes me harder. I should be screaming in fear, but the hint of violence heightens my pleasure.

He's guiding me to the edge of an endless abyss, standing ready to make that final, murderous push that will send me plummeting to my death. I'd happily die here in this room, filled with every inch of him.

"You will come back to us." Zach slams the words home with a harsh pump. "No more hiding. Your ours, Willow. Fucking ours. You have nothing to hide from any of us. Say it."

"Yours," I gasp.

Another orgasm rushes over me. I let out a strangled moan as he manages a final stroke upwards into my pussy. Zach releases my throat and buries his face in my breasts, bellowing through his own climax.

We come together in unison. Zach jerks beneath me, pouring himself into the condom. Part of me longs to tear that scrap of plastic and feel his seed filling me up. I want to be claimed by him—body and soul.

My head falls to his shoulder, too heavy to hold up. Aftershocks race over my skin, extending the ecstasy that's corroding my vision. Everything is blurry. I'm thankful we're alone because I can't move to cover up right now.

"Are you still with me?" he asks breathlessly.

I peel my eyes open long enough to look down at him. "I… I don't think I'm ever going to walk again."

Zach presses a soft kiss to my collarbone. "You chose to play this game with me."

"I'll give you that. You ruined my painting though."

"We can fix it together."

"Or we could climb in the shower and do that again."

"Again?" Zach chortles. "You greedy little slut."

Fuck, I never thought being called his little slut would be a turn on. Turns out, I'd happily toss away my pride and be whatever the hell he wants me to be.

"You don't want to fuck me again?" I ask innocently.

His smile turns dark. "There is nothing in this world that could stop me from fucking you again. I want to ride that tight asshole of yours next. Maybe while you fuck my twin."

I forget how to breathe for a second.

"Your t-twin?"

"Hell yes. I can only imagine how wet you'll be then. Full of both of our cocks."

Even with my aching body, a flicker of arousal threatens to reignite this new, wanton creature inside of me. Being sandwiched between the twins was one thing. The idea of being with them both at the same time is too tempting to ignore.

Weaving my fingers into his long tresses, I push strands of hair off his slick forehead. Before I can lock our lips together, the bark of Killian's voice sounds from the other room.

"If you two are done, I'm very frustrated out here."

"Oh my God." I cover my face with my hands. "Please tell me that didn't just happen. He was supposed to be delivering wood into town."

"No can do." Zach snickers. "Looks like he came back early."

"Shit! I need thicker walls. Like, yesterday."

"Nope." Killian's voice travels through the wall. "No can do."

Zach kisses the tip of my nose. "You're cute when you're embarrassed."

"I'm never going to live this down. I literally just told him to get lost before you walked in here. Please move so I can go drown myself in the shower."

"Take Killian with you," he suggests. "Promise I'll cover my ears."

I won't tell him that I don't want him to cover his ears. What I really want is for him to join us in the walk-in shower and fulfil his dirty promises. In my current frame of mind, I'd let all three of them fuck me.

"Willow?" Zach whispers.

I look into his eyes. "Yeah?"

The corners of his mouth crinkle in a smile. "I love you."

Instead of panic or fear, I'm filled with contentment.

"Zachariah… I love you too."

CHAPTER 26
KILLIAN

PURPLE - WUNDERHORSE

"PASS ME THE SCREWDRIVER."

Ryder slaps the tool into my hand, frowning at the complicated booklet of instructions. "This makes zero sense. Why do they make it so complicated?"

"We don't need the instructions, idiot. I know what I'm doing."

"How does your back not break under the weight of your ego, Kill?"

Crouching down beside us on Willow's living room floor, Zach casts a critical eye over the pile of pine-coloured wood and countless screws yet to be assembled. We've been at it for over an hour already.

"I still remember the bookshelf fiasco." He snorts when I give him the stink eye. "There were more parts left over than in the actual shelf."

"Shut up, little asshole."

Jabbing an elbow into his ribs, Zach groans in pain and flops onto his back. "Ouch, dickhead. Someone doesn't like criticism."

"Not from you I don't. You couldn't assemble a fucking cardboard box."

"He's right," Ryder agrees.

Zach glowers at us both. "How can I apply for a disownment? I want a new family."

"No one would take you, kid."

Busy in the kitchen, Willow is slicing vegetables at the counter and watching the three of us bicker with amusement. She offered to cook dinner in exchange for our help assembling her newly purchased dining table and chairs.

I tried to convince her to let me build the furniture myself, but she's on a roll this week, insisting on being all independent and shit. While I love seeing her slowly come back to herself, my possessive instincts are in overdrive.

A primitive part of me loved it when she was living in our spare room and dependent on us for everything. Food. Warmth. Shelter. We gave her this space so she had her own home but letting her find her own feet is giving me stress-induced hives.

"Is that true?" she asks.

"It's why I chopped up the shelf for firewood and made my own." I shake my head in disgust. "Ikea doesn't know how to build shit. I can do a better job myself."

"Too big-headed to take instructions from a piece of paper?" She wanders over with a glass of wine in hand. "I'd like the table to actually stand. It's not just firewood for you to burn."

Grabbing her by the wrist, she screeches in surprise and nearly dumps her glass of red wine on Zach's head. He plucks it from her hand just in time. Willow lands across my lap, staring up at me with wide eyes.

"We always need more firewood. Sure I can't go fetch my axe?"

"You're impossible, Kill."

"I'll take that as a compliment."

Crushing my lips against hers, I steal her breath before handing her off to Zach for safekeeping. We have a table to finish. She gave me a job and I'll get it done, no matter how tempted I am to smash this stupid thing to pieces.

"Don't distract him." Zach pins her in his arms and kisses her temple. "Quit being all cute and sexy as well, or we'll all be eating on the floor again."

Willow draws a little halo over her head. "Me?"

"Don't act all innocent."

"I am the innocent one here. You're the troublemaker, Zach."

"It didn't sound like that from what I heard the other morning," Ryder mutters, his face buried in instructions. "Innocent isn't the word I'd use for those sounds."

Willow clears her throat. "Um."

"Nothing to say?" Ryder winks at her. "That's a first."

Maintaining a stony expression that gives nothing away, I almost break cover when Zach starts laughing. We all heard him screwing Willow in the shower at the weekend. I'm surprised they didn't wake the whole damn town up.

"Don't act all coy," Ryder throws at me. "I know full well that you joined in too."

Still, I don't let my façade crack. "No idea what you're talking about."

"Might be time to invest in some headphones," Zach adds.

Ryder tosses the instructions over his shoulder with a sigh. "You guys should be happy I have zero interest in the female species. It was like a live porno in my back garden."

Willow flames bright red. "I'm sorry, Ry. We'll be quieter."

"You're lucky it's just us up here. Lola would skin both of you bastards alive if she knew what you were doing to her precious granddaughter on a daily basis."

"I'm going to get on with dinner," Willow interjects in a squeaky voice, retreating back to the safety of the kitchen. "Chop chop. Tables don't build themselves."

Admittedly, we may have gotten carried away recently. She has no idea the effect she has on me. I'm not going to apologise for finally enjoying what's mine. Fuck anyone who doesn't like it.

Catching Zach's distracted gaze, I watch him shamelessly checking out Willow's ass, highlighted by the skinny blue jeans she's wearing with a flowing white blouse. I snap my fingers in front of his face, bringing him back to the present.

"You gonna sit there gawking or actually help us?"

Zach shrugs. "I can't do both?"

"No. Stop eye-fucking Willow and focus already."

"Eye-fucking?" he repeats.

"You know exactly what I mean. I'm surprised you weren't drooling too."

He flips me the bird and crouches down next to Ryder, picking the discarded instructions back up. Between the three of us, we have the table and chairs all constructed after another hour and lots of colourful cursing.

I could have built something better in my sleep, but Willow insisted on buying her own furniture for her first real home. This is the most we've ever seen her smile. It's been a long rough patch since the miscarriage, but she's coming back to us, day by day.

We need to keep her distracted and focused on the future. Those endless weeks of blank faces and silence were fucking agony. I felt powerless as she pushed me even further away. That can never happen again, no matter what we have to do to bring her back.

Handing out a round of cold beers, we gather in the living room, surrounded by paint pots and brushes. Willow changed her mind on the last colour we used and chose a deep turquoise for the walls instead to match the dark wood finishes.

"Interesting colour," I complain.

Ryder rolls his eyes. "Shut up. Willow likes it."

"I'm doubting my skills a bit here," Zach worries.

"Fuck it up and you have to fix it."

"Awesome," he drawls. "Very helpful."

Setting himself up with a fresh roller to go over the last colour, Zach ends up getting more paint on himself than the actual wall. Leaving him to make even more mess, I work on securing several abstract paintings that Micah gifted Willow last week.

"Giant! Giant!"

Bursting through the front door, Arianna toes off her sandals and rushes at me without stopping for a breath. I catch her mid-stride before she knocks over a paint can, twirling her in the air and placing a kiss on her cheek.

"Careful, Ari. There's paint everywhere."

"You're tickling me with your whiskers!" she shouts.

I frown at the little devil. "Whiskers?"

"Like a big jungle cat," she explains cheekily.

Silencing Zach and Ryder's laughter with a threatening glare, I rub my beard against Arianna's cheeks again. She screams and demands to be put down. I deposit her in Zach's outstretched arms instead.

"Zach! Why are you covered in paint?"

"Because I'm shit at painting," he replies with a grin.

"Language!" Willow scolds, stepping into the living room with her hands on her hips. "Ari, doesn't Mummy get a hug anymore?"

Escaping Zach's paint-splattered embrace, Arianna races into her mother's open arms. Willow easily plucks her up, ruffling her blonde pigtails. She laughed her ass off this morning when I did Arianna's hair for homeschool.

The devilish child requested pigtails. What was I supposed to do, deny her? Arianna's got me wrapped around her fucking finger and she knows it too. I'll surrender my pride if it makes her grin up at me like she did this morning.

"Sorry, Mummy."

"Hey, baby," she coos back. "How was school?"

"Rachel gave me three new books to read!" Arianna looks over at Zach. "Will you read them to me before bed? I like it when you do the funny voices."

He winks at her. "Of course I will, princess."

"Yay! What's for dinner? I'm really hungry."

"It will be ready soon." Willow sets her back on her feet. "First, Micah has a surprise for you in the bedroom. Go and have a look."

"He does?" Arianna gasps.

"Go on. Don't keep him waiting."

We all head to the back of the cabin which is almost complete. We went furniture shopping last weekend and got all of the remaining essentials. I took great care to choose an extra-large bed for Willow, purely for selfish purposes.

"I wanna see!" Arianna screams. "Lemme in, Micah!"

Willow knocks on the bedroom door, waiting for Micah's voice to call us all inside. We enter the spacious room, and our eyes immediately lift to the furthest wall where his mural is complete after hours of painstaking work.

"Holy shit," I curse.

I've never given a damn about art, but hell. My cousin has some serious talent. He's been hiding this from us for years. I always knew he was good, but this is next level insane.

"It's finally done." Micah nervously spins the paintbrush in his hands. "I can change it if you don't like it, Ari, or rethink... or..."

Cutting off his anxious rambling, Arianna throws herself into his arms. Micah hesitates at first, but soon circles his arms around her to accept the enthusiastic hug.

"It's amazing," Arianna whispers in awe. "Look, I'm a princess! Wow... and Mummy too. Micah! You're so clever!"

The entire surface is covered in a colourful, floor-to-ceiling scene. I saw the sketches he drew up, but this is something else. Each leaf, stalk and sprinkle of stardust on the wall feels like it's leaping off the plaster.

"Willow?" Micah bites his lip.

She gawks at the wall with her mouth hanging open. "Mi, holy crap! I can't believe you did this all yourself."

"Language," Zach throws her words back at her. "Little ears are present."

Scowling at him, Willow flies across the room. She tosses her arms around Micah and this time, there isn't a second of doubt. He presses their lips together, despite us all watching them embrace. When they part, he's grinning from ear to ear.

"I'm glad you both like it," he offers quietly.

"Like it? Your work should be in a gallery or something."

"Nah. I don't think so."

"Stop being so modest," I scold. "This is crazy good."

Micah rubs the back of his neck. "Thanks, Kill."

Retreating from the room, he mumbles about getting cleaned up. I know he's still struggling to adjust to being around people, but he gets better at it with each passing day. Willow's presence in our lives has broken through his icy lake of solitude.

We leave Arianna to dance around her finished bedroom and return to the kitchen. Zach and Micah lay the newly built table with flower-spotted plates and shining cutlery, allowing me to sneak up behind Willow and band my arms around her waist.

"Whatcha cooking?"

She wiggles her butt against me. "Tamales."

"Mexican, huh? Another dish from home?"

"Yeah. It's all I know how to cook."

"Who taught you? The chef?"

Willow falls silent as she stirs the homemade salsa, staring into its herby depths. I hate it when she zones out like this. It's like I can see her falling over the edge of a cliff.

"Come back, baby."

"Sorry... it's just stuff."

"Talk to me. I'm listening."

Her head lowers in defeat. "My friend... he died back in Mexico. Arianna still asks about him sometimes."

Turning Willow's frame in my arms, I cup her suntanned cheeks. The summer has brought out gorgeous freckles and imperfections that pepper her cheeks, but her hazel eyes are still haunted, brimming with secrets.

"What happened to him?" I ask softly.

Tears pool in her eyes. "It took more than just me to get us out of that place, Kill. He was the only friend I ever had. We wouldn't be here if it wasn't for him."

I stuff the automatic feelings of jealousy down where they can't see the light of day. Willow doesn't need to know how pathetic I am, envious of her relying on another man.

If I'd known where she was, I'd have broken her out myself. It wouldn't have mattered that she was a stranger then. I'm physically incapable of standing by while good people suffer, and only the scum of the earth would abuse a mother and her innocent child.

"How did he die?"

"Shot," she croaks.

"Shit, Willow. I'm so sorry."

"I don't want to talk about this right now." She blinks aside tears, her mask sliding back into place. "He's dead and I can't bring him back, so it doesn't matter anymore."

My thumbs stroke over her blemished skin. "I think it does, but I get it. I know what it's like to lose people. I'm here if you want to talk."

She bites her lip. "I'm trying, Kill. Being vulnerable is hard for me."

"I know, baby. I'm trying too. I'll back off, but I'll be here when you're ready to tell me the whole story. Just know that you won't scare me off, no matter what you say."

"Deal," she replies with a smile.

Lapsing into comfortable silence, we work together to finish dinner. It's been a long time since I cooked with anyone. Feeding the twins was usually an activity reserved for me and my mama growing up.

I feel closest to her while cooking. It's been a long time since my parents passed away, but I still feel their absence in every corner of Briar Valley.

The constant reminders forced me to build my walls impossibly high— until Willow knocked them all down. For that, I'm grateful. She will never realise how she's changed my life.

Getting everything transferred to the dining table, we gather the whole rowdy group. Arianna claims the seat next to Micah, still fawning over the paint-smeared son of a bitch. He looks mighty pleased about that fact, letting us settle around them.

"Wait," Willow blurts. "The food might be a bit spicy."

Zach's eyes light up. "Did you use my homegrown chillies?"

She nods. "They're in the salsa and salad."

"Sweet."

"Am I gonna need a glass of milk with this?" Ryder asks.

"Um, maybe."

Grumbling to himself, he disappears to get his drink from the fridge, leaving the rest of us to dig into the meal. Surrounded by my family, all laughing and sharing food, makes me freeze with the fork halfway up to my mouth.

I want to take a mental snapshot of this moment. For the first time in years, this actually feels like a real family. Not just an empty cabin full of broken people. It's all because of her. She's given us a reason to come together.

Taking Willow's hand under the table, I drop a kiss on her head. She smiles up at me, her lashes framing grateful eyes that haunt my dreams every night. Fuck, this girl.

"Thanks for building the table," she murmurs.

Zach cuts me off. "Um, hello. Me and Ryder worked tirelessly to build this bad boy too. I even got a splinter. Look!"

He sticks out his spotless index finger with an exaggerated sigh. Willow shakes her head at his antics, stabbing a tamale and dipping it in salsa.

"You're such a jackass, Zach. Eat your food."

He shoves a huge forkful into his mouth. "I'll make you pay for that later. I'm a very sensitive creature, you know. You'll need to soothe my bruised ego."

Ryder lets out a long-suffering sigh as he sits down. "Can we please save the sexy talk for when I'm not eating? It's making me feel a bit ill."

"What's sexy talk?" Arianna blurts.

Choking on a mouthful, Willow has to hammer Micah on the back before he chokes. Zach is grinning at Arianna, while Ryder points his fork at the idiot threateningly.

"You're corrupting the child, Zachariah."

Zach raises his hands. "Hey, I'm a good influence."

Ryder tucks a loose strand of hair behind Arianna's ear. "Don't worry, squirt. Uncle Ryder will look after you. Ignore these mannerless twats."

"What's a twat?" she asks instead.

Willow's head thumps against the table. "Jesus, it's like feeding time at the zoo."

I smooth a hand over her hair. "You wanted a family, right?"

She groans in response. "Yes."

"Well, now you've got one. Better get used to this."

CHAPTER 27
WILLOW

NEVER SAY NEVER - THE FRAY

I WATCH the first rays of summer sunshine bloom on the horizon between imposing mountains that carve the panoramic view. The light leaks through in glittering beams, and the warmth soothes my skin. August is officially in full swing.

Sipping my fresh coffee, I glance at the silent cabin across the road. Zach's still asleep, but Killian disappeared in his truck a while ago to run some errands for Lola. Micah's back in his studio, though he emerges for mealtimes.

We've fallen into a familiar routine. Each night, we gather around the dinner table to spend time together. Ryder usually joins us, and sometimes Albie as well. Secretly, I think they both love having someone cook for them.

The guys have been taking it in turns to put Arianna to bed each night. She always blackmails them into reading her a story from the books that Rachel refreshes regularly. While the guys pretend to complain, I know all three of them love it.

I'm not sure when things changed, but in a weird way, it feels like we're a real, albeit fucked-up family now. The rowdy, imperfect kind that threatens one another with death and has childish food fights to gain control of the TV remote.

"Mummy," Arianna yells from inside. "I can't find my polkadot dress. What am I going to wear to school?"

I slip back inside. "Don't worry, sleepyhead. Let's go find it."

After locating the dress under a haphazard stack of teddy bears, Arianna gets dressed and I sit down on her bed to plait her hair. She insists on wearing the yellow ribbon that Killian bought her on his last trip to town.

"I still can't find my baby box," she says tearfully. "I haven't seen it since we stayed with Grams. I think I lost it."

"I'm sure you haven't." I smooth her finished hair, straightening the ribbon into place. "Let's get you to school and I'll go look for it, okay?"

"Promise?"

"I promise, Ari."

"Okay," she submits.

With her bottom lip jutted out, she grabs her backpack and races to the front door. Being homeschooled with the other kids has been endlessly good for her. She's growing up so much and gaining confidence every day.

I tried my best when she was growing up to teach her the basics. It was hard going, but I did everything I could to give her a normal life amidst the despair and destruction. It's great to see her learning now like normal children do.

Waving to Ryder working on a crappy looking motorcycle as we walk past, we begin the short hike down into the valley. The whole town is waking up for the day, with windows being thrown open and washing pegged out to dry.

"Hey, Willow!" Harold greets from his driveway.

"Morning. You heading out?"

He tosses a camouflaged bag into his truck. "We're doing an overnight trip. Hoping to catch a deer or two this time."

"Good luck."

Climbing into the driver's seat, he gives me a salute. "Catcha later."

Once he's out of earshot, Arianna tugs on my hand, her mouth downturned. "Mummy, is he really going to shoot a deer? They're so pretty."

"I know, baby. You don't have to eat it."

"I don't want to. I like Bambi."

Ruffling her hair, I try not to laugh and upset her further. She wasn't saying that when she demolished a venison burger at Albie's birthday bonfire. I'll let her remain oblivious for a little longer before bursting that bubble.

For each cabin we pass, neighbours offer greetings. Nameless faces who once meant nothing to me are now treasured friends. I've learned about their lives and histories, piecing together the patchwork quilt of residents in Briar Valley.

Getting close to people was a luxury I never had before, but I finally feel at home here. We've found our place in the world and I'm not afraid to put down some very tentative roots, bottling my fear of it all being ripped away.

After a short walk, we reach the cabin that Rachel's schoolhouse barn is located behind. The few children of the town are floating inside, and she waves at me from the doorway.

"Okay. Have a good day, Ari. Be good."

"I'm always good!"

I duck down to peck her cheek and release her hand. She quickly sprints off to enter the awaiting barn with the other kids, already laughing and chatting to them. It's stupid, but my chest tightens with emotion just watching her go.

"I love you!" I shout after her.

She waves at me again and vanishes inside. Smiling to myself, I turn around to find Aalia fussing over Johan in a similar, over-protective manner. When he pushes her hands away, she kisses all over his face until he turns red with embarrassment.

"Okay, okay. Go on then."

"Bye," he calls happily.

I'm clearly not the only one feeling emotional this morning as she swipes a subtle finger underneath her golden eyes, laughing when she spots me watching her.

"Morning, Willow. Ignore me, I'm being silly."

"Not at all. How are you?"

"Oh, you know. Bearing up."

Sweeping in to pinch Amie's rosy cheeks from her prop on Aalia's hip, I give her mum a quick squeeze next. We've grown close. I pop around to her cabin regularly for a chat and the obligatory pot of tea.

"You want to come and walk with us?" she offers.

"Thanks, but I need to go and look for something at Lola's cabin. I'll catch you later?"

"No fighting with her," she says sternly. "You are still... ah, getting better? Recovering! If I hear shouting, I'll have to come and save you."

"No need." I brush off her concern. "Things aren't the same between me and Lola, but I'm working on forgiving her. We've been keeping our distance until it's easier."

"Family is important, Willow."

"Yeah, I know."

"Come and find me for a cuppa later."

Kissing her cheek, I inch backwards. "I will."

Walking back along the cobbled path that bisects the thick woodland leading to Lola's cabin, I steel myself to see her. The front garden has been thoroughly pruned to welcome the summer, now full of yellow and pink wildflowers.

Taking a breath for courage, I step inside without bothering to knock.

Nobody does around here. It's a bit of a free for all, especially where Lola's cabin is concerned. She has an open door policy for the whole town.

"Lola? You in?" I call out.

Voices from inside the kitchen suddenly fall silent. The door cracks open for Lola to peek out. She blanches when she sees me, her eyes dancing from side to side.

"Poppet, now isn't a good time. Can you come back later?"

Kicking off my shoes, I point upstairs. "I'll only be a second."

"But—"

"It's kinda important. I won't disturb you further."

Cutting off her protests, I race upstairs and let myself into the spare bedroom. It's been cleaned and set back to normal since our abrupt exit. Crouching down to look under the bed, I find the box kicked into the corner.

The guys must've missed it when they packed up our stuff after my trip to the hospital. Laying down to reach for the box, my ear presses against the floorboards and I can hear Lola's familiar voice carrying through the ceiling.

"I don't have room for anyone else," she says emphatically.

"I wouldn't ask if it wasn't urgent."

"We've already taken a case from you this quarter."

"Please, Lola."

Someone is pleading with her, a female voice.

"This family has lost everything and Briar Valley is the best place for them right now."

"You always play on my heartstrings," Lola berates.

"I know. I'm sorry."

Lola's response is too muffled to hear. I climb back onto my feet, cursing my curiosity, and flee back downstairs to get out of here without having to speak to Lola.

I'm halted at the bottom of the staircase by Albie stepping through the front door with armfuls of files and paperwork. His silvery head of hair lifts, two eyes landing on me with shock.

"Willow. Surprised to see you here."

"Hey, Albie. Just picking something up."

"You tell that man of yours his supply delivery from Highbridge is here." He pulls off work gloves and sticks them in his denim jacket. "The boxes are in my truck outside."

"Um, man of mine?"

The twinkle in his eye makes my cheeks flame.

"You're thinking which one, right?" he jokes. "Don't worry, there's no judgement here. I'll let you tell your Grams though. She's darn protective and will flip her shit."

"I have no idea what you're talking about," I splutter.

Albie scoffs. "I'm your neighbour, chuck. Not an idiot."

Unable to offer a single excuse, I remain silent. The last thing I want right now is for Lola to stick her nose in my private business, especially where my complicated relationship with the guys is concerned.

"It's alright. Your secret is safe with me. You coming in?"

"I have to go," I lie.

"I don't think so." He harrumphs. "Come and see your grandma."

Albie thumps towards the kitchen in his mud-caked boots. I follow, internally panicking that he'll spill the beans if I don't. The last thing I want is for him to blab to Lola that I'm… whatever the hell I am, with all three men across the street.

When I step into the kitchen, Lola's eyes widen with sheer panic. Sitting opposite her tiny frame, nursing a mug of coffee, is a middle-aged woman that looks a little too familiar for my nerves to take.

Glossy, raven-coloured hair twisted into a neat plait on her head frames her flawless, moss-coloured eyes that seem to shimmer like the surface of a lake. She's dressed in a smart shirt and jeans with a sparkling engagement ring resting on her finger.

"Oh," I hum.

The woman looks up at me. Her automatic smile of greeting causes the twisted, pink scar splitting her face to pull taut. I have to swallow the bubble of terror that inches up my throat.

"I found this troublemaker lurking in the hallway."

Albie jabs his finger at me, but his smile drops when he spots the woman sat opposite Lola, conversing over cups of coffee and homemade breakfast cookies.

"Oh, erm. Hi, Katie. Nice to see ya."

She waves at him. "Morning, Albie. How are you?"

"Good, good. I'll leave you ladies to talk. I just need Lola to sign off on these contracts."

Startling her out of a daze, Lola quickly gathers herself. "Sure."

After getting her scribbled signature, Albie makes a hasty retreat from the kitchen. His light squeeze of my arm on his way past does little to reassure me. I've been abandoned in the world's stickiest situation.

"Did you find what you were looking for?" Lola asks tightly.

I clear the lump in my throat. "I uh… yeah."

"What was it?"

"I left Arianna's baby box here. Got it now though."

Katie's eyes lift to mine. "I don't think we've met before."

She's smiling politely, but a small frown creases her brows as she studies me. All I can do is stare at that scar, disfiguring her wrinkle-lined features. Lola looks unnerved, but she soon smooths her impenetrable leadership mask back into place.

"Katie… this is, well, she's Briar Valley's newest resident."

"Pleasure to meet you," Katie begins.

"Melody." I finish for her. "And likewise."

"I hope you're settling in well, Melody."

Lola tries to offer me a calming smile, but I feel like the whole world has fallen out from beneath my feet, leaving me to free fall. In an anxious trap, I lose grip of the baby box tucked under my arm. It hits the floor with a crash and everything spills out.

"Oh, shoot. I'm so sorry."

Dropping to my knees, I quickly shove everything back inside and slam the lid a little harder than necessary. I hope Katie doesn't notice the violent tremble of my hands.

"You want a coffee?" Lola offers.

My first instinct is to say no, but as I stare at Katie's friendly face marred by such a devastating scar, I'm overwhelmed by the need to look at her forever in case she suddenly disappears again. I find myself nodding back.

"I could stay for a drink."

Moving on autopilot, I end up sitting in the chair opposite her. Lola fixes my drink and hands it over, retaking her own seat at the table. Taking a gulp to distract myself, I nearly gasp as the hot liquid burns my throat.

"Careful," Lola warns.

Katie sips her own drink, somehow oblivious. She clearly hasn't been told that I'm here. Am I supposed to come out and say it? Do I even want her to know who I am? I've done everything in my power to not think about her for months.

"Katie has another family looking to move to town."

"Oh?" I grind out.

Katie spares Lola a brief smile. "We have a recently bereaved father with two children. I was hoping this would be the place for him to start fresh. He has no other family."

"Our last spare cabin has already been earmarked." Lola frowns to herself. "Unless I can move some things around, make a few adjustments."

"Aalia has a spare room," I interject.

Lola shakes her head. "I'm not sure she will be happy to accept a strange man and his children into her home. Given her circumstances."

"It's worth asking her. It sounds like this man needs your help."

Katie beams at me, full of relief. I can't smile back. I'm caught between falling at her feet in a sobbing mess and punching her in the face.

"I'll speak to Aalia," Lola concedes. "No promises though."

"Thank you so much for trying." Katie reaches across the table to squeeze her clasped hands. "As always, I'm indebted to you."

"You know I'll always try to help."

I watch their exchange with my breath held. It's clear to see the mutual love and respect that exists between them. Lola had years to get to know Katie and build a relationship with her. Years that I didn't have.

Katie looks at me, her eyes trailing over my long black hair. "Have you been here for long, Melody?"

"About six months or so. My daughter and I came here looking for a fresh start. Lola has been kind enough to take us in."

"She's good at that. How do you two know each other? I know just how much Lola likes her privacy. If I wasn't an ex-resident of Briar Valley, I doubt I'd be sitting here."

"She's… a family friend," Lola rushes to explain. "Distant family."

"Is that so?" Katie replies.

"You know me, I've always had a soft spot for strays."

"Oh, I know. Better than most."

Standing abruptly, my chair bangs into the kitchen cupboard with a loud smack. They both look at me with surprise. I grab Arianna's baby box and force a smile that physically pains me.

"I've got to go. It was nice meeting you."

"And you." Katie sticks a hand out for me to shake. "I'm sure I'll see you soon."

It takes all of my remaining courage to take her hand in mine and shake. Her grip is warm and dry. I can feel the cold press of her engagement ring against my palm, the shining diamond capturing my eye again.

"Sure, maybe. Good luck with your work."

"Thank you," she answers.

I race from the kitchen as fast as my feet will carry me. With the front door slammed shut behind me, I stumble down the porch steps and run at full speed into the thick woodland.

When I can't walk any further, my knees slam into the ground. I drop the box and hide my streaming tears in my hands. She looked exactly how I remember her in my hazy childhood memories.

That was my mother.

If I had even a lick of sense, I'd run back in there and demand answers to my endless list of questions. But I'm imprisoned by fear and can't move a muscle.

I'm not scared that I'll hear something I don't want to hear. No. I'm terrified that I'll realise she was just like me—a mother, desperate and afraid, doing the best she could to survive.

I couldn't hate her then.

And I'm petrified of needing her love.

CHAPTER 28
WILLOW

TREAD ON ME - MATT MAESON

THE BLARE of a hand slamming down on a car horn marks Killian's impatience. I pull my long hair up into a ponytail, smoothing my sunflower-spotted blue dress. It's another sweltering day outside. The cabin is stuffy with heat.

"Willow!" Killian barks.

He's hanging out of the truck, glaring at his cousin lounging in the passenger seat. Zach's smoking a cigarette and blowing it straight into Killian's face. I grab my handbag and lock the cabin door, racing over to the truck to climb in the back.

"Morning, grumpy."

I lean between the seats to peck Killian's bearded cheek.

"I'm not grumpy," he defends.

"Tell your face that."

"This moron has been blowing smoke in my face for ten fucking minutes. What took you so long to get ready?"

"I couldn't find a hair tie. Arianna keeps stealing them all."

Moving to kiss Zach's cheek next, I wrinkle my nose and decide to skip him. His mouth turns down in a dramatic pout. He quickly tosses the cigarette aside and drags me closer for a lip-smacking kiss that ignites my core.

"Mornin' babe," he whispers.

"Good morning, Zachariah. What have I told you about smoking?"

His pout intensifies. "I'm down to three cigarettes a day. That's an improvement. Where's my gold star?"

"Arianna probably stole it." I snort.

"Little tyke. I'll get my revenge later."

"Yeah, good luck with that."

Killian throws the truck into gear and takes off in a peel of rubber. We're heading into the city to pick up the curtains we ordered last month. They had to be custom made to fit the massive glass windows that span the entire cabin.

After winding out of Briar Valley and down the steep, wildflower-lined slopes of Mount Helena, we begin to enter back into civilisation. Zach cranks up the radio and rolls the windows down, letting the warm breeze flood into the car.

"You think it's warm enough to swim in the lake?"

"Oh yeah," Zach hums. "Best time for it."

"Arianna's been bugging me about it. She wants lessons."

Killian meets my eyes in the rear-view mirror. "I can teach the sassy little shit, but she has to stop making me play dress up with her."

"Got a problem?" I tease him.

"I spent an hour trying to remove nail polish from my toes the other day."

"You're the one who let her paint them."

"I've got to defend my reputation as the favourite somehow."

His fire-lit eyes narrow on me in the mirror, and I fail to hold back a giggle. We all know he's the biggest softie for Arianna in the whole damn town. No one else can coax Killian's allegiance like she does.

"I'm her favourite," Zach pipes up.

"Like hell you are."

"You're both as bad as the other," I accuse.

They both give me matching innocent looks. I hate it when they gang up on me. It's worse when Zach and Micah decide to tag-team. I can hardly tell the pair apart when they round on me with identical smiles.

"Don't look at me like that. I had to put Arianna in the naughty corner the other day. You're all turning her into a wild child. I caught her swearing again."

Turning onto the main road, Killian laughs under his breath. "That's probably my fault. I called Albie a miserable fuckhead in front of her by accident the other day."

"Kill!"

"Sorry, sorry," he replies. "It just slipped out."

"Don't even get me started on Ryder." I scowl at them. "She's seven years old. I caught him teaching her how to service a car engine. Like, how is that safe?"

"We should teach her to drive next," Killian muses.

I feel the blood drain from my face.

"Only joking," he adds.

"I think she's just enjoying having all this male company in her life." Zach blows me a kiss over his shoulder. "Calm down, hot mama."

"Hot mama?"

"Hell yeah, you are."

"Zach… politely, fuck off."

"What was that? Fuck me? Because I totally would."

"Try to touch me right now and I'll break your wrist."

"She can do it," Killian tells him. "I taught her last week."

"Why the hell would you do that?" Zach laughs.

"Self-defence. It's a good skill."

"Just shut up and drive, the pair of you." I pull my shopping list from my handbag. "We need to pick up supplies for the housewarming in a couple of weeks."

I figured having everyone who helped us settle in over for a celebration would be a good way to say thank you for their months of good will. My life has completely changed since I set foot in this tiny town.

It's all because of them. I've made more friends than I ever thought possible, and I'm actually excited to be the host for once. Especially now that the cabin is finished. A proud part of me wants to show off my new home to them all.

"Remind me to chop more wood for the bonfire," Killian mutters. "Once I've finished the swing set. And the sandpit. Oh, and the wood store."

"Anything else?" Zach scoffs.

"Not all of us are lazy like you, kid."

"Does that mean you'll be topless and sweaty again?" I interrupt.

The look Killian shoots me is full of promising heat. "You like that, baby?"

I squirm in my seat. "I'm saying nothing."

"See? *Baby* gets her all hot and bothered," Zach complains, glaring at the countryside houses appearing around us. "You're stealing all of the attention."

Killian shakes his head. "Call her hot mama again. See where it gets you."

Zach turns in his seat to grin at me. "Well?"

I narrow my eyes on him. "I can still punch you, Zachariah. Don't push your luck. Hot mama is firmly off the table."

"For fuck's sake," he curses. "I'm going to kill Ryder. That name is banned. I've been Zach since I was a goddamn toddler. Only he calls me that name to wind me up."

"What? I like your full name," I say sweetly.

He slumps and shuts his eyes. "Wake me up when we get there."

It's another two hours of farmer's fields, quaint villages and expanding roads before we pull into the bustling chaos of the nearest city. I haven't been here before. We managed to source the rest of the cabin's furniture in Highbridge.

With my nose pressed against the window, I take in the busy city streets, packed full of countless cars, bikes and buses streaming past us. The ebb and flow of traffic is hard to comprehend. I quickly realise why Killian hates this place so much.

"Welcome to hell," he grumbles.

We circle the main streets of the city centre several times before snagging a parking spot on the side of the road. Killian only just manages to squeeze the mud-streaked truck into the tight space, cursing like a madman the whole time.

"Have you thought about downsizing?" I look from the truck to the gleaming cars parked all around us. "Just a thought."

"Leave my truck alone. She's my pride and joy." He opens my door for me. "These crap cars won't get you anywhere near Briar Valley. I drive a real man's car."

"A real man?" I repeat incredulously. "How's that toxic masculinity taste?"

"Great, thanks."

"It's the twenty-first century, you caveman." Zach dares to elbow Killian in the ribs after climbing out. "I wouldn't mind driving a cute little convertible."

"It would have to be pink, otherwise Arianna would chew you out," I say with a giggle. "You'd pull it off though."

Zach bats his lashes. "Well, obviously it has to be pink. Reckon that'll be enough to make me her favourite? This bastard has been the reigning champion for far too long."

Killian grabs Zach in a headlock. "You're driving me insane. Come on, the store's this way."

"Yes, sergeant," he quips back.

"We need breakfast too. I'm fucking starving."

"You're always fucking starving," I mutter.

Trailing behind them, I study my surroundings with ravenous interest. Mexico was beautiful in a raw, rugged kind of way, but I rarely left the mansion to explore. I settled for watching the swirls of sand in the air from my balcony.

On the odd occasion that Mr Sanchez took me to an event or fundraiser for the sake of appearances, I was always far too worried about obeying his rules to take it in. This feels like I'm seeing the world for the first time, and damn, it's pretty bloody beautiful.

Stopping by the family-owned embroidery shop sandwiched between a cocktail bar and a fancy restaurant, we collect my new curtains, and Killian pays the designer before I can.

"Nope," he deadpans. "I've got it."

"You promised not to do this again."

"I promised no such thing. Put your money away."

I reluctantly tuck it back into my handbag. After much pleading and daily knocking on my front door, Lola has loaned me some money to cover buying clothes for the approaching seasons and final finishing touches for the cabin.

With the curtains deposited back in the truck, we decide to grab some breakfast. Zach finds his way around the city on instinct, and he knows all of the back streets to avoid the flow of people, along with a suspicious number of local bars.

"There's a great place up here," he explains as we walk. "They do awesome French toast and these huge omelettes too."

I link our fingers together. "You've been there often?"

"Once or twice."

"How many women have you taken there for a hangover cure the morning after?"

Zach glances at me. "Ah."

"You've clearly spent a lot of time here."

Enjoying his panicked squirming, I let him splutter for a few seconds before pecking his lips.

"Relax, Zach. It doesn't matter how many women you've taken there, or anywhere, for that matter. I'm messing with you."

"I wasn't a man whore if that's what you're thinking."

"Would it be so wrong if you were?" I challenge him. "Why does it matter? Your sex life is your business. I don't understand people who feel it's their place to judge others."

"Really?" He gapes at me. "Why?"

"Because they should just mind their own business. We're all adults and have our own pasts. That shouldn't dictate our relationships in the future."

Halting outside the small, brightly lit restaurant, Zach tells Killian to head inside and grab a table. Once we're alone, he steps into my personal space and grips my chin to tilt my head up. My lips are seized in a fast and hard kiss.

When we break apart, I'm seriously considering skipping breakfast. His hair hangs over his face in the sunlight, framing dimples unveiled by his lazy grin.

Hell, I'm screwed.

"You're incredible, Willow. You know that?"

"Hardly," I whisper back.

Zach kisses me again. "No, you are. You've got so much to give to the world even when you don't see it. I'm so glad I met you."

My heart melts into a pathetic puddle.

"I'm thankful to have you in my life too, Zach. Even when you're being a pain in my ass and corrupting my daughter."

"Told you we didn't need a dog, huh?" He winks at me. "Come on, let's eat before Killian gets even hangrier and eats the waiter or something."

Heading inside the restaurant, we find Killian hunched over a menu in a dark-red leather corner booth. He barely lifts his head as we sit down. He's too engrossed by the prospect of food.

Zach slides me a menu. "Choose whatever you want."

"Thanks. What do you recommend?"

"I usually go for a cheese and tomato omelette. Plus, French toast. Maybe some pancakes too. Oh, I forgot about the pastries. They're homemade."

"Zach," I interrupt. "Slow down."

He flashes me a toothy smile. "What? I'm starving."

"I might just order it all," Killian agrees, placing his menu down. "Sounds good."

Nauseated by their huge appetites, I request a simple omelette and coffee. Killian bellows for the waiter, who definitely doesn't appreciate his lack of manners, then we're left alone with hot drinks and wrapped cutlery.

Zach turns his attention to me. "Have you made up with Lola then?"

I fight the urge to groan. "Stop fishing, Zach. It's more complicated than that and you know it. I took the money because she wouldn't leave me alone until I did."

"Did you talk to her about your mum?"

"No."

"Katie really had no idea who you are?" Killian asks next.

"I don't think so." I sigh. "She kept staring at me, but I think I just threw her off. Lola came over to apologise a couple of days ago. She hasn't revealed my identity to Katie."

His thick brows draw together. "Why?"

"She's giving Willow the chance to do it," Zach guesses. "Lola cares about you, enough to lie to one of her closest friends. She's buying you more time to figure stuff out."

Despite my behaviour in recent weeks, Lola is still doing her best to look out for me. That must count for something. Many people would've simply given up on ever having a relationship with me and let the resentment grow.

"I've never had real parents or grandparents." I stare into my milky coffee. "No one ever looked out for me. I'm not sure I know how to recognise or appreciate it."

"Willow... she loves you," Zach points out. "A hell of a lot. She's made some serious mistakes, but that doesn't change the fact that she refuses to abandon you."

"Shit. You're right. I should really apologise to her."

"She did lie to you," Killian supplies. "Maybe don't go that far."

Zach cuts him a warning look. "She lied for the right reasons. Lola is one of the most kind-hearted people I know. Everything she does is for the good of Briar Valley."

At that, Killian backs off. "True. Her and Pops saved all of us."

"I'll talk to her," I concede. "But what about Katie?"

"Do you want a relationship with her?" Zach prods.

"I don't know the answer to that question."

Killian snatches my hand from across the table. "Then we figure out the answer together. There's no rush. She doesn't need to know that you're here."

"Really?"

"Of course. You can take some time to figure out how you feel."

Nodding, I squeeze his huge paw tight. "Thank you both for being here. I realise I'm a hot mess at the best of times. You've stuck by me through a lot of shit."

"Emphasis on the hot," Zach adds.

Killian smacks him upside the head. "Zip it, Romeo."

Our food arrives, offering a needed reprieve from the emotions twisting my gut. A stack of plates encircles them both and they dig in, shoving huge forkfuls of eggs and bacon into their mouths. I tackle the omelette with less enthusiasm.

"Maybe hot mess could be your new nickname," Zach wonders, gulping his coffee down around a mouthful. "I'm willing to trade out the mama part."

I brush my lips against his ear. "Call me that again, and I swear, I'll murder you in your sleep. Killian already explained how to dismember your body in great detail."

"Was this before or after he taught you how to break my wrist?"

"After," the brute in question answers. "I'll even throw in a free body disposal service to say thank you for getting rid of him. My fucking pleasure."

Zach rolls his eyes. "You both love me far too much to murder me. Who would keep you entertained?"

"It'd be a hell of a lot quieter," Killian grunts.

After a beat of silence, we all burst into laughter. Loud enough to startle the customers in the booth behind us, and the unnerved waiter who gives us a weird look.

Clearly, my time in the wilderness has made me as uncivilised as the guys. I couldn't care less about how insane we are. I've got the family I always wanted right here.

CHAPTER 29
ZACH

LIE TO ME - THE DANGEROUS SUMMER

WEIGHED down by several packed bags of clothing, I groan in exhaustion. "Arianna doesn't need any more dresses. The little monster has enough."

Tucking her new bank card away, Willow grins at me. "You're here to be the muscle, aren't you? Why else would I bring you along?"

"Not much muscle to speak of," Killian chips in.

"I'm the hottest member of the family, and we all know it. See this body? Pure muscle. Take that."

"I reckon Killian could rival you in the muscle department." Willow drops another bag on top of the pile in my arms. "You guys should wrestle and find out."

"You'd enjoy that, wouldn't you?" Killian laughs.

"Well, obviously."

We exit the clothing store and return to the packed city streets. The day is drawing to a close, and we've stayed far longer than we intended to. Showing Willow around and watching her face light up has been fucking breathtaking.

She was so excited when we took her to a popular milkshake shop where you can choose any chocolate bar and have it made into a shake. I snapped a selfie of the three of us sipping away and pinged it over to Micah to make him jealous.

"Should we head back to the truck?" Willow looks longingly at the shops in the distance. "I need to get home for Arianna. We'll have to come back another day to see the rest."

Killian drops a kiss on her head. "Whatever you want, baby."

"Micah texted. He's got Arianna fed and happy." I show her my phone and the photograph he sent. "She's trying to sculpt a vase with him and trashing his clay."

Willow winces. "He shouldn't take her into the studio."

"She loves it."

"Trust me, it's a high honour to be allowed in there," Killian adds.

"I feel bad. She's ruining his workspace."

"He'll cope. Don't worry about him."

Wading back through the crowds, we head through the main plaza, packed with popular restaurants and bustling bars. The office crowd is beginning to arrive for evening drinks and food, congesting the pavements with their smart businesswear.

Killian ploughs into an unsuspecting woman, and I swear Willow looks ready to slap-a-bitch when she bats her lashes and touches his bicep. I manoeuvre her in front of me and hold on tight so she can't attack.

"Calm down, hot mama," I instruct.

"Tell her to stop touching Killian and I will."

Untangling himself from the over-friendly woman, Killian brushes her off and marches away as fast as his legs will allow. He looks less than impressed by the encounter and more concerned by Willow's obvious annoyance.

"See? The city sucks," he complains.

"Let's get out of here before Killian's head explodes."

"Fine by me," Willow mumbles.

Walking in tandem to survive the crush of people, we're almost through the madness when a deep, booming voice calls out. Willow freezes on the spot, almost pulling me off balance in the process.

"Mrs Sanchez! Mrs Sanchez!"

"No," Willow gasps in utter horror.

Every drop of colour has drained from her face, leaving her deathly pale and visibly shaken. She begins to tremble like electricity is burning through her, and the blossoming strength that's steeled her spine vanishes before my eyes.

"My name," she whines. "He knows me."

"Who is it?" Killian demands.

"I don't know. We have to run."

"We can't run. It'll tip them off."

Exchanging a lightning fast conversation with Killian, we attempt to hide Willow between us. Even if we could weave through the crowd, running isn't a good idea if we want to avoid suspicion.

"No, no," she panics.

"Easy, baby." Killian holds her in a tight grip. "You're okay."

"We need to get out of here right now."

"Just breathe. We've got you."

Three broad-shouldered men duck through the crowd of people, blending into office workers with their expensive charcoal suits and unbuttoned shirt collars. The tallest steps closer, wearing a leering smile beneath slicked-back blonde hair and sharp grey eyes.

Willow holds my hand hard enough to grind bones. Even her posture has changed. The person I know isn't here anymore, and I don't recognise the woman standing next to me.

"Mrs Sanchez," the man coos. "What a pleasant surprise. I thought it was you."

She plasters on a strained smile. "Mason."

"Pleasure to see you, my darling."

Killian has to hold back a snarl as the slimy scumbag takes Willow's hand and plants a kiss on her knuckles, his eyes shining with mirth. I'd love to rip his goddamn spine out.

"What on earth are you doing in England? Where is Dimitri?"

"He's not with me at the moment," Willow rushes to explain. "I'm here on holiday... visiting family. How have you been?"

Her voice is all wrong. Weak and obedient in an alien-like way. She's sliding back into the shell of the battered creature we found in the mountains. Killian looks ready to publicly decapitate all three men.

"Busy as usual." Mason flashes a shark-like smile. "I'm visiting England on business. I've invested in a property development nearby."

"Here? In England?" Willow's voice rises.

"There are lots of opportunities for growth. I'll be spending a lot more time here." His smile takes a dangerous edge. "When did I last see you? Was it that fundraiser last year?"

"Oh, I believe so."

"And how is that beautiful daughter of yours?"

I warn Killian with my eyes, silently pleading with him to hold his cool. The mention of Arianna from this snake's mouth has caused the vein in his neck to throb so hard, it looks ready to tear free from his skin.

"She's fine," Willow bites out.

"I'm glad. Listen, I've been meaning to book a meeting with your husband."

"He's working as usual," she squeaks. "You know how... driven he is."

"Of course. Please tell him to drop me an email. We'll get something pencilled in."

Willow sways on her feet. "Sure... will do. I should get back to my hotel. He'll be waiting for me to call. Time zones, eh? It was nice seeing you."

The creepy asshole frowns at how close me and Killian are to Willow. Just when I think he's going to say something and earn himself an early death, one of his men calls his name.

"Coming," he shouts back.

I take the opportunity to shove Willow behind me, even further away from him. With any luck, they'll think we're her security detail. I get the feeling her sleazebag ex could afford it and would want to keep his wife under lock and key.

He offers Willow a stomach-churning smile. "It's been a pleasure, as always."

"Likewise. Travel safe."

"You too, Mrs Sanchez."

The men disappear inside a fancy, over-priced bar catering to the snootier brand of lawyers and managers looking to drink their stress away. Mason makes sure to cast her a final look before vanishing from sight.

Willow sags between us the moment he disappears, almost falling flat on her face. Her legs knock together too hard to hold her upright without our arms around her.

"Who was that?" Killian quizzes.

"Move," she whispers brokenly. "We need to get as far away from this city as possible. If he's contacting Dimitri right now, my entire cover is blown."

"Dimitri is your husband?" I guess.

Willow nods. "They're business partners."

"Fuck. We need to haul ass."

Killian slings an arm around her waist and half-carries her into the crowd. We practically run through the plaza, ducking and weaving to avoid being seen. Suddenly, every pair of eyes on us feels like a threat.

"Go, go, go," I urge him forwards.

"Keep up, Zach!"

By the time we reach the truck, sweating and panting hard, Willow is white as a sheet. I toss the bags into the back and throw the door open, boosting Willow inside as Killian fires the engine.

I've barely slid into the passenger seat before he slams his foot down and we take off. Lurching forwards, I slam the door shut.

"Hold on," he warns.

"Shit, Kill. Don't get us killed."

"You wanted fast. Hold the fuck on."

Cutting in front of a dawdling motorist, he manoeuvres through several tight turns, slicing into the traffic leading out of the city. Blaring car horns follow us and Killian undercuts several more cars to get ahead.

In the back of the truck, Willow is hunched over in a shaking ball. She whispers under her breath as she falls apart, head shaking from side to side like a puppet on a string.

"He's going to find me."

"Breathe, babe."

"No... he knows where I am. We're in danger."

"We're sixty miles from home," I reason. "There's no way that weirdo can link you back to Briar Valley."

"Not safe... not safe," she sobs. "I can't go back. I won't go back."

"Get us somewhere private!" I snap at Killian.

"We need to get home."

"She is going to pass out if she doesn't breathe. Pull over."

I slide my body through the gap and fall unceremoniously into the back seat next to Willow. She cowers away from me, and I have to drag her into my arms by force, clamping down on her forearms to hold her still.

"Get off me," she screams.

"It's me, babe. Zach. You're safe with us."

She thrashes and writhes like she's trying to escape from an invisible attacker. I trap her against my chest and hold on with all my strength. We're losing her fast. I've never seen her fall apart like this. It's scaring me.

"Arianna," she suddenly shouts. "We need to get her. She isn't safe!"

"Willow, calm down. Arianna is fine. Briar Valley is the safest place for her."

"No... not safe... nowhere's safe."

"You need to focus on your breathing."

"I need to protect my daughter!"

Killian breaks every speed limit known to man to get us out of the city as fast as possible. Murmuring reassurances to Willow, I stroke her hair, counting under my breath so she can focus on her breathing.

After half an hour of hyperventilating, she finally crashes. Her body becomes a dead weight in my arms, two tear-logged eyes peering up at me through swollen slits.

"You okay?" I ask softly.

Willow shakes her head. "No."

"Stay with me. We're getting out of here."

"What are the odds that I'd bump into that sicko?"

"What's his deal? Is he dangerous?"

She physically shudders. "Mason is an investment banker, but he dabbles in property among… other things. That's how he came to meet Mr Sanchez."

"Other things?"

"Prostitution, mostly," she says flatly. "His work often takes him to the States even though we lived in Mexico. I met Mason at a fundraiser a year or so ago."

If Dimitri's business partner is dabbling in shady shit like prostitution, Lord knows what the asshole ex himself is involved in. We're in serious fucking trouble.

"Why were you at a fundraiser with Dimitri?" Killian snarls.

"Mr Sanchez had to maintain appearances for his public campaigns," she emphasises. "He's too well known to keep me a secret. I was expected to play the doting wife."

Killian's white knuckles damn near break the steering wheel. He's struggling to keep his temper in check. I'm surprised we got out of that mess without him killing someone.

Willow begins to rock, tears still soaking her cheeks. I don't try to touch her again until we've pulled off the main road. Killian parks in an abandoned car park, surrounded by a thick camouflage of trees to hide us from sight.

"Who is he, Willow?" he near-shouts.

"I told you—"

"Not that jumped up little shit back there. If he comes looking for us, I'll break his fancy fucking legs and stick my rifle down his throat. I want to know who Dimitri is."

"No, Kill. We're not doing this now."

"We've been patient, but I want the truth," he orders.

"He's a monster. I told you what he did to me."

"You've drip-fed us crap for months now," Killian growls at her. "This goes beyond domestic abuse. What scared you so badly you had to flee halfway across the world?"

"You promised to give me more time."

"If that piece of shit back there is a threat to your safety, I need to know," he seethes. "You are my priority, whether you like it or not. Why did you run?"

"I had to run because if I stayed there, I would be dead right now." Willow glares through her tears. "If he killed me, Arianna would have been left alone in the world."

"He threatened to kill you?" I spit out.

"Mr Sanchez didn't give two shits about beating me close to death or making me watch as he brutalised a revolving door of women supplied by Mason and his associates."

Killian punches the steering wheel. "Fuck!"

"He threatened to kill Arianna just to make me behave. All I cared about was protecting her and taking the beatings myself, but he was so unpredictable."

"He hit the kid?" he utters.

Willow gulps hard. "Once or twice."

Arianna is everything that's good and pure in the world. What kind of twisted bastard lays a hand on a child? His daughter, no less. I had no idea things had gone that far.

"Just tell us what really happened, once and for all." Killian's voice is resigned. "Did he try to kill you the night you ran? Was that the final straw?"

Willow twists the ring around her finger. "He was angrier than usual about some business issue. I called him weak and pathetic. That's when he pulled out the baseball bat."

"Jesus," I curse. "He used a bat?"

She nods. "I couldn't move afterwards, and he held a gun to my head while he... he..."

"You don't need to go on, babe."

Willow draws in a ragged breath. "When it was all over, he told me that if I kept this up, he would kill Arianna. I knew then it was time to take the risk and run."

"Your friend helped you?" Killian supplies.

"Pedro got us out and we ran as fast as we could, sticking to the plan."

"Why didn't you go to the police?" I interject.

"Because that wouldn't stop him. He has friends who wouldn't hesitate to silence me if I went public with this."

"Bullshit!" I hiss back.

"Nobody is above the law," Killian agrees stonily. "Let's report this son of a bitch."

"Seconded."

"Stop, both of you!" Willow begins to hyperventilate again. "I can't... I can't..."

"Breathe, babe. Come on. Nice deep breaths."

She frantically tries to suck in air that continues to escape her. Killian climbs out of the truck to clear his head, the door slamming shut behind him. I watch him shout into the sky and fist his long hair.

Willow peels her eyes open, staring at me with bone-deep terror.

"Everything I've done has been to keep Arianna safe. I can't risk her falling back into her father's clutches."

"You think we'd let that happen?"

"I think that if push came to shove, none of us would have a choice. In the eyes of the law, I've kidnapped Arianna and taken her from her father."

Rage wraps around my throat. "That is such crap!"

"It's how the system works. If we were caught, or if I stepped into the limelight to accuse him of anything, we'd be running the risk of her being taken away from me."

Before I can argue against her shitty logic, the back door is wrenched open. Killian grabs hold of Willow and yanks her out. He quickly puts her back on her feet and I follow them outside.

"Goddammit, Willow," he bellows.

"Don't touch me like that!"

"I'm angry, for fuck's sake."

She shoves him away. "Do that again and I'll be breaking your wrist instead."

"Every time we've tried to get close, you've been protecting this scumbag, after he spent the last decade beating the hell out of you and threatening his own fucking daughter."

"I was protecting Arianna, not him."

"That makes no damn sense."

Reaching out with a trembling hand, Willow cups his cheek, despite the fire and brimstone burning in his eyes. I wouldn't get within a metre of Killian when he's like this, but she has no fear. He isn't the monster she's running from.

"Arianna is my whole life. I can't risk anything ever happening to her. I'm her mother, and it's my job to protect her, no matter what. That's why I ran and kept these secrets."

"And what about us?" he yells.

"If Mr Sanchez comes looking for me and Arianna, he'll take down anyone who stands in his way. I can't run the risk of that happening because… because…"

"Because?"

"Because I love you, alright?" She loses her patience. "All three of you. I'd do anything to keep you safe, even if it means tearing myself apart every time I lie and pretend like I don't love you all to death."

We both freeze.

Killian blinks, silenced.

"You've belonged to us since the moment we met." He licks his lips. "You don't need to lie to us anymore. Let us help. Let us keep you safe. You're our family."

The terror begins to clear from her face, replaced by something else. Her entire posture changes—softening, leaning towards his embrace, needing to be held.

"I've never had anyone to rely on."

"That ends now," he says firmly.

Killian captures her lips in a passionate kiss, and I step forwards to trap her from behind. Securing my lips to her neck, I suckle on the soft skin, leaving a satisfying purple mark. Just feeling her in my arms gives me the relief I need.

Breaking their kiss, Willow turns her head slightly to the side so her lips can seek mine out next. I grip her jaw and kiss her back, frantic and hungry, needing answers to all the chaos threatening to tear us apart.

But I don't need answers. Not really. I don't need anything but her presence in my life. She makes our broken family whole again in ways I never thought were possible.

"Zach," she moans.

"I know, baby. I'm here."

"I was so fucking scared."

"Shhh." I peck her plump lips. "He will never hurt you again."

Killian runs his hands down her body to grip her hips. She tugs at my t-shirt, kissing me so hard, it feels like she's bruising her love into my skin. We're connected in a breathless tangle, our bodies entwined and writhing.

"We're next to a main road," she gasps.

Killian's teeth tug on her earlobe. "No one can see us."

"What if someone comes?"

"You'll be the only one coming," I grunt back.

Gaze burning with defiant fire, Willow grabs my belt and undoes it, sliding her hand into my jeans to palm my erection. I buck against her, desperate to feel her heat hugging my cock.

At the same time, Killian's hands sneak underneath the hem of her cute blue sundress. He crouches down to peel the panties down her thighs, tucking them into his jeans pocket for safekeeping.

His hand moves under her dress, circling around her front. She moans, still facing me with her hand wrapped around my length. I can see his hand dipping between her legs.

"Is she wet?" I ask him.

Killian nods. "Fucking soaked."

"She always is." I snicker. "We barely have to touch her."

Willow bites down on her lip. "I… can't help it."

Pushing my jeans and boxers down to my ankles, she bends over, pushing her naked ass against Killian's crotch. I almost swallow my tongue when her mouth bobs on the head of my cock. The open air around us intensifies the sweet torture.

We're in the middle of nowhere, but the road behind the trees hiding our tryst still roars with traffic. At any moment, someone could appear, but it doesn't stop Willow from taking me deep into her throat.

I'm trapped between the truck and her enthusiastic sucking, one hand moving beneath my cock to take a handful of my balls. When she gently squeezes, I almost blow my load. Her confidence is so hot right now.

"Goddammit, Willow."

Licking a bead of moisture from the tip of my dick, she takes it back into her mouth. I grab a handful of her loose curls, pushing into her mouth as her lips tighten around my shaft. She feels fucking heavenly.

Behind her, Killian lifts her dress up to her waist, exposing the bareness of her cunt to the summer air. Willow groans around my shaft as he slips a hand between her legs again.

"You want me to fuck you while my cousin watches, angel?"

Willow hums around a mouthful of my cock. He pushes a second finger into her slit, rubbing the heel of his palm against her clit. She pushes back into him, causing her teeth to lightly graze my shaft.

I tighten my grip on her hair. "Fuck, babe."

Killian works her into a frenzy, forcing her to ride his hand while she tortures me with her tongue and teeth. He stops right before she can finish, and a low growl of annoyance emanates from her throat.

"You got a rubber?" he asks me.

"There are some in my wallet."

Avoiding Willow's bobbing head, he reaches into the pocket of my lowered jeans to grab my wallet. Killian straightens, unbuckling his belt to free his own dick. He rolls the condom over his length while Willow stares up at me with excited eyes.

Seeing her looking at me like that—her mouth full of my dick while her inner-thighs shine with juices—is indescribable. It's her trust in us that's the biggest turn on. Her willingness to be vulnerable and offer a part of herself that others have abused.

Releasing her mouth from my cock, she lets Killian drag her ass up high with a tight grip on her hips, so she's folded in the perfect doggy position. Her dress is so bunched up, I can see her perfect tits begging to spill from the neckline.

"Eyes on Zach, baby," he instructs. "Don't you dare look away."

I lean back against the truck, fisting my dick. "I'll make sure she doesn't."

He plants his feet, ready to surge inside of her. The pleasured moan Willow releases as Killian pushes into her pussy is like a siren's call. I watch them, a hand wrapped around myself. She's bent over and gasping with each rough thrust.

I never thought I'd be into sharing a woman. I've slept with my fair share of them, but this is so much more than the meaningless one-night stands that have defined my sex life. I never wanted to be committed or cared about making someone happy then.

Willow's different.

She's it for me.

The beginning and the end. I live and die with every breath swirling in her lungs. My life starts right here with her and the gift she's given us. I'll sacrifice everything to protect the family we've forged against all odds.

"Kill," she gasps.

"You're so tight, baby. I can feel your walls clenched around my cock."

When her eyes dare to dip, I reach out to grip her chin. Her head is forced back up, and her gaze returns to my face. Willow cries out when I grab her bouncing tit next and squeeze in punishment.

"Eyes up."

"I'm sorry, Zach."

"Do it again and Killian won't let you come. Isn't that right, cuz?"

"Damn fucking straight," he rasps.

She's enjoying being watched, I can tell. It's a thrill, knowing I'm standing here while my cousin fucks her tight pussy. The risk of getting caught makes this even hotter. I'm struggling not to bring myself to the edge.

Gripping her hips, Killian begins to move quicker, his teeth gritted from exertion. Fast and frenzied, he doesn't draw their collision out for the sake of it. This is about survival.

We're dragging Willow out of her own personal darkness, kicking and screaming the whole time. She isn't allowed to give up. We're the only ones permitted to bruise and break her heart before putting it back together again.

"Come for me," Killian orders. "Show Zach how much you love my cock inside you."

Her knees almost crumple as she succumbs to her orgasm. Stroking deep into her, Killian's grip on her hips must be bruising. He's fucking her with an almost animal-like sense of possession, ensuring the entire world can see and hear that she belongs to him.

"Fuck!" he shouts through his release.

I move aside, letting the pair slump against the truck, both gasping for air as they finish together in unison. I'm still stroking my erection, desperate to slide into the warm prison of Willow's cunt. It's killing me to stand here.

"Can you hear that?" she exclaims.

At that exact second, there's a crunch of tires on gravel, bisecting the narrow road that winds into our hiding spot in the trees.

"Someone's coming," I shout.

"Ah, hell," Killian hisses.

Pulling out of her, he quickly discards the condom and yanks his clothing back into place. Willow's dress is shoved back down to cover her nakedness and Killian throws open the passenger door for her to jump inside.

I climb into the back before I'm caught with my literal dick in my hand. It wouldn't be the first time, but I'd like to avoid a complete stranger seeing my bare ass. Killian hops in the front seat to gun the engine.

We peel back onto the road in record time. Killian is breathing hard as he fastens his belt with one hand, the other holding the steering wheel tight. We pass the other car on the way out, but keep our gazes averted.

"That was close," Killian breathes. "Jesus Christ."

Willow grabs my arm. "Zach."

"Yeah?"

Her eyes are pleading. "I still need you. Please."

"Right now?"

"Yes, now," she snaps impatiently.

Willow shimmies through the gap in the seats and throws herself into the back of the truck, landing next to me. Her dress is riding high on her thighs, flashing a glimpse of her bare pussy. It's all I need to get on board.

"Come here, beautiful."

I pull her into my lap, a bare leg on either side of my waist. All I can think about is pushing inside her slit. It's like a red haze of need has descended over me.

Behind the wheel, Killian's watching us while attempting to suppress laughter. Willow balances her hands on my shoulders, her teeth grazing along my jawline.

"I want to ride your cock," she murmurs.

"Take it. I'm all yours."

Tugging my length back out of my boxers, I fist the base, holding myself ready for her. She sinks down on my length and throws her head back. Her pussy is already so wet from her first orgasm.

"Dammit, Willow." I cup the swell of her breast through her dress, rubbing a thumb over her protruding nipple. "We should not be doing this in a moving car."

"Shut up, Zach. I'm in charge here."

Working herself up and down on my lap, her eyes are almost shut. I'm happy to let her take control and explore what makes her feel good. It's incredible to see her finding her own pleasure.

"That's it, babe."

"No talking, Zachariah."

She follows up her order with a passionate kiss that silences my talking. Her teeth nip at my lips, angry and demanding. All I can do is hold on tight to her waist and let her tits bounce in my face while she rides me.

Moving my hands to her ass, I knead the rounded cheeks, encouraging her thrusts to lengthen. She takes my full length inside with each movement, pushing it deep into her pussy and moaning in gratification.

Killian drives as slow as he can, keeping the bumpy ride back into the mountains to a minimum. The closer we get to home, the more frenetic Willow becomes. She moves faster, harder, driving herself to the edge with sheer will alone.

"Are you close?" she whispers.

"Yeah. You feel so good, babe."

Her grin is infectious. "I've wanted to do this for a while."

"Get laid in a car?"

"Maybe," she admits.

Cupping her cheek, I stroke my thumb over her lips. "What else do you want to do? I'd very much like to fulfil all of your dirtiest fantasies."

"I want to play with you and Micah together."

She captures my wrist and moves my hand to her neck, encouraging me to choke her. I'm not one to deny a woman. I clasp her throat, digging my nails in and savouring the stuttering of her breath.

"That could be arranged," I purr.

"I want you both inside me at the same time."

"Such a filthy little whore, aren't you? So desperate to fuck two twins."

Pupils blown wide, she doesn't even look remorseful. It isn't the first time a woman's requested this—we used to get very similar propositions when we were younger, drinking in Highbridge, before Micah retreated into himself.

It never happened.

I'd be very willing to try though.

Her moves grow ragged, and I know she's close to falling apart on top of me. Lifting my hips, I meet her stroke for stroke, until her gorgeous voice is crying out for relief. With her pussy clenching around me, I can't hold on.

My release washes through me in a piping hot haze. The sight of her crying out in bliss finishes me off. Still clasping her throat, I slam our mouths back together, swallowing the syllables of her climax that spill free.

She lumps against my chest in a boneless puddle. I bury my face in her hair, breathing in the familiarity of her scent, curled around the strands of her black hair. What I wouldn't give to stay in this moment forever.

"You alright?" I murmur.

"I am now."

It takes several minutes for her to find the energy to slide off me. She yanks her dress down to cover her lack of panties and wriggles off my lap to sit next to me.

With our desperate fuck-fest over, Killian lays back on the accelerator. The truck lurches forwards, sending us hurtling past fields of corn cast in rays of brilliant sunshine. He gives us both an amused look in the mirror.

"You know, I was hoping to christen that back seat myself."

I snort. "Too late."

Willow covers her face. "I have no idea what came over me."

Killian's eyes refocus on the road. "Neither of us are complaining. Who's ready for round two when we get home?"

CHAPTER 30
WILLOW

I WON'T GIVE UP - CHANCE PEÑA

SITTING cross-legged by the side of the lake, I stare down at the piece of paper clasped in my hands. Sweat drips down my neck from the relentless sun that's baked the mountains and woodland until even the wildflowers have wilted.

I've tried to start this letter a million times in the past few weeks and I've given up just as many times. Pen poised, I bring ink to paper again and beg the words to come.

Something. Anything. Again, nothing happens. How the hell do I even approach this? No matter what I write, this is going to turn into a mess the moment Katie realises who I really am. Words can't fix what's been broken.

Hey, I'm the kid that you lost fifteen years ago. I'm back. Surprise! Want to be my mum again?

Yeah, I don't think so.

Behind me, the sound of Killian's axe splitting wood fills the peaceful silence. Zach and Micah are working together to cover the exterior of my cabin in bright lantern lights. Since our close call in the city, they've all been extra attentive.

For the first few days, we awaited the inevitable fallout. I was convinced my location was blown, and it took a miracle for me not to run again. When Killian threatened to tie me to his bed, I stopped packing my suitcase.

But nothing awful has happened. Mason was simply a close call. He has no idea where I'm staying, and even if he's spoken to Mr Sanchez, they have no way of tracking us back to Briar Valley.

We're safe. I have to keep telling myself that. Safe. Safe. Safe. I just wish that I believed it.

"Mummy! I'm home!"

With a squeal, Arianna leaps onto my back. We both end up tumbling through the long grass. When I get her underneath me, I mercilessly tickle her ribcage until she's screaming for relief, her yellow sundress bunching up her legs.

"You scared me, Ari."

"I can't breathe!" she screams.

Relenting, I release her. We've rolled down the slope I was perched on in front of the decent-sized lake behind the cabins, the still surface feeding water back down into the valley beneath us.

"Can we go swimming?" she pleads.

"I don't know, Ari."

"Please, please, please!"

The summer sunshine has been beating down on the water for weeks. It's clear too, beyond the odd reed and floating lilypad. The guys have been telling us stories about summer nights spent in the water.

"I don't want you to be scared."

"The giant said he would teach me to swim," she reasons. "I'm not afraid."

Her pout grows even bigger.

"Killian's busy right now, Ari."

"Pretty please? With sprinkles and cherries on top? I want to swim!"

Swinging her back onto her feet, I gesture towards Killian in the distance behind his cabin, studying his huge pile of chopped wood. We're having another bonfire for the housewarming and he's in full preparation mode.

"Go and see if the giant is free. If he says yes, then I suppose it's okay."

"Yay!" She squeals.

Clapping her little hands together, Arianna races off in a blur of over-excited energy. I try to resume the letter but end up tucking the paper and pen back into the pocket of my discarded denim jacket, a thousand words still unwritten.

Somehow, a letter doesn't feel quite right. It's so impersonal for such a life-changing revelation. I don't even know Katie, but I feel like I owe her more than that. Even strangers deserve our compassion, and I'm tired of hating the world.

"Willow!"

Zach and Micah walk in step with each other, their floppy hair and easy smiles blurring their identities into one. The lantern lights are all done, and they're both carrying towels. My mouth dries up at the sight of Zach's bare chest.

He's wearing black swim shorts that hang low on his hips, highlighting the delicious 'V' that makes my thighs clench. Micah wears a blue pair with a white t-shirt, and while he's slimmer, his legs are lined with packed muscles.

Hello, twins!

"What's up?" I smile at them.

"The little terror has announced that we're swimming in the lake." Zach drops his striped towel beside me. "I figured we ought to keep our promise."

"Killian took her inside to get changed," Micah explains.

He crouches down to press his parted lips to mine. The way his hand caresses my jawline sends sparks of static electricity bolting up my spine. Micah's kisses melt my insides like nothing else. His gentleness is strangely exhilarating.

"You look beautiful," he whispers into my lips.

"Thanks, Mi. Not painting today?"

"Fuck the paintings. I needed to hear your voice."

I run a hand over his windswept hair. "You should ditch work more often."

He kisses me again, lingering for a tender moment. "Keep talking like that and I will."

When he finally releases me, Zach takes his twin's place and steals a lip-smacking kiss. "You coming in as well, babe? It'll be nice and warm."

"I might do."

"You should," Micah adds. "I know you bought a bikini."

"How do you know that?"

He jabs a finger at his brother.

"It wasn't me," Zach defends. "I told no one."

When I narrow my eyes on Micah, he shrugs. "Twin thing."

Zach topples to the grass, his headful of messy hair landing in my lap. "I told you he has that weird mind reading thing going on. We should perform an exorcism."

"I am not fucking possessed," Micah snaps at him.

"Could've fooled me, little brother."

Huffing under his breath, Micah drops his towel and tugs the t-shirt over his head. The words on my tongue dry up at the sight of his carved chest and defined biceps that are unveiled as he strips off in front of me.

"You're blushing again," Zach singsongs.

"Your brother is stripping. I'm not sure where to look."

He chuckles. "Bit late to start getting shy now. You weren't so worried when you were fucking me in the back of Killian's truck last week."

Micah splutters. "Excuse me?"

Peeking an eye open, I find him staring at me, but there's no judgement on his handsome face. It's something darker, more primitive. A cloud of lust and raw need. The tension between us is at an all-time high.

I'm tired of kisses and stolen whispers. Coaxing Micah out of the depths of his depression has taken months of patience, but the person standing in front of me isn't the silent, tormented man I once met.

We've both undergone our own metamorphosis. In the safety of pine trees and jagged mountains, our souls have emerged from their individual fires. We've pulled each other out of the burning pits to rise anew.

"That was a one-time thing," I try to explain.

Zach looks at me pointedly. "I can't wait to find out what other kinks you have besides getting laid in the back of a moving car."

"Zach! Christ, do you ever shut up?"

"Famously, no. I do not."

Shoving his head off my lap, I climb to my feet and wander over to the lake to dip my toes in. Several billowing willow trees frame the water, along with purple flowers that float on the surface.

The lake runs clear because of a huge, cascading waterfall in the uppermost corner, ensuring a steady stream that flows from the nearby mountain peak. It supplies water to the whole town, fresher than any bottle you'd find on sale.

"Come on, giant. Hurry up!" Arianna yells.

"Alright, peanut. Go jump on Zach for a minute."

I track the nearby voices to the back of the cabin where Arianna waits with a pink towel hanging over her swimming costume. Killian lets her run ahead. He's too busy blowing up a pair of orange rubber armbands.

When he meets my eyes, his mouth is pulled into a crooked smile. They're determined to kill me, I swear. Wearing a pair of red swimming shorts, every inch of his heavily muscled chest and abdominals are on display.

He looks like a sexy Viking warrior with his blonde hair pulled back in a bun, highlighting the sharp lines of his features, covered in the scruff of his beard.

Catching me gawking, he tosses his towel down next to the others and runs to join me at the lakeside. I scream in surprise as I'm swooped into his arms. Killian throws me over his shoulder, his hand cracking against my butt cheek.

"Let me down, Kill!"

"You're looking far too beautiful to be standing there drooling." He lowers his voice. "I want to see you wet and dripping... in lake water."

I batter my fists against his back. "That's not the kind of wet I was thinking. Let me down! Throw me in that lake, and I swear, it'll be the last thing you do."

"Throw her!" Zach shouts.

Lifting my head from hanging upside down over Killian's shoulder, I spot Arianna sitting on Zach's shoulders for a good view of the fiasco. She's even clapping him on.

"Do it, do it!"

"Killian, don't you dare!" I scream.

His arms tighten around the backs of my thighs and for a moment, I think I'm safe. In the next breath, Killian's grip on my skin is gone. There's nothing but empty air as I hurtle towards the water.

Bracing myself, the lake swallows me whole, and I sink beneath the warm water. It's like diving into a massive bathtub. When I break the surface, spluttering and wiping my eyes, everyone is cackling.

Killian looks mighty proud of himself. "Nice dive!"

"You just lost bedroom privileges for a month," I shout back while my dress floats around me. "I warned you!"

His laughter dries up. "You wouldn't dare."

"Try me. Do you know how long I spent doing my hair this morning?"

Zach claps him on the back. "Sucks to be you, cuz. Don't worry, Micah and I will keep Willow warm at night while you're in the doghouse."

Killian grabs hold of Zach's arm, and in one smooth move, tosses him headfirst into the lake. Zach bellows before hitting the water. He nearly drowns me with a tidal wave that rushes in my direction, emerging seconds later to curse his cousin.

"Language!" Arianna chastises. "That's a bad word, Zach."

He coughs up water. "She's your daughter, alright."

I splash him back. "You owe money to the swear jar."

"Fuck the swear jar!"

"That's another pound. You're digging yourself a hole here."

"I can see through your dress, smartass. Nice bra. Very girly."

I look down to find my white sundress completely transparent as water laps at my chest. My yellow bra is glaring through the wet fabric, barely containing the pebbles of my nipples. *Shit.* This is all Killian's fault.

Swimming over to where Zach is bobbing in the water, I wrap my legs around his waist, freeing up my hands to wrench the dress over my head. He holds my thighs as I toss it aside, the material landing on the slope in a sopping wet ball.

"Better?" I sass him.

His finger traces the cup of my soaked lace bra. "It's a shame the kid is here, otherwise I'd show you how much I like this bra and panties set. Especially wet."

"Feel free to show me later."

"Oh, I intend to. Maybe I'll let Micah watch."

"Only watch?"

"Well, that's his decision. Not mine."

I grind against him in the water. "I'm sure you could persuade him."

"I'm nothing if not persuasive."

"Incoming!" Killian breaks our moment.

We swim out of the way before he hits the water in the exact spot where we were happily floating. The impact causes the entire lake to break out in waves. Killian appears near the edge, throwing his arms open for Arianna to jump into.

"Come on, peanut. No need to be afraid."

Micah helps her to slip the armbands on and double-checks to make sure they're secure. He shoots me a reassuring thumbs up, seeming to sense my anxiety from across the lake. She's never swam before.

"I'm scared, giant. What if I drown?"

Killian smiles up at her. "I'd never let you drown, Ari. You trust me, right?"

She nods shyly.

"Then jump, princess. I'll catch you, I promise."

Taking several steps back, Arianna races towards Killian and throws herself off the edge. He plucks her from the air before she even hits the water, gently lowering her into it so she can adjust to the temperature.

"It's so cold!" she squeals.

He kisses her nose. "No, it isn't."

Micah slips into the lake much more quietly and swims in our direction. A loud entrance really isn't his style.

"Now, teach me how to swim," Arianna demands.

"Say please, Ari," I correct.

She pins Killian with her best puppy dog eyes. "Pretty please, giant. I want to swim like a fish."

"Too bloody cute for your own good," Killian grumbles under his breath. "Come on then. Let's do this."

We spend the next hour watching Arianna learn how to doggy paddle with Killian holding her at all times. They stick to the shallower end of the lake, and he turns out to be a surprisingly patient teacher, talking her through the strokes.

"Should we play a game?" Zach asks.

"What did you have in mind?"

"Wait here."

Zach fetches a blow-up ball from the cabin and tosses it at his brother's head. We begin to throw it between us, both twins vying to beat the other. With Arianna deposited on the lake's edge and wrapped up in a towel, Killian jumps back in to join our contest.

"If I win, Zach has to do the washing up for a week," I wager. "That includes the roasting pan. We all know you love to stick the soap in and leave it to soak."

Micah chokes on a laugh. "Busted."

"Exactly. That doesn't count, mister."

"It's a valid cleaning strategy," Zach defends hotly.

"For lazy asses, maybe. But you never come back to it."

He shakes his head. "Fine. If I win, then I get to pick what we play at our next games night. And I think it'll be... strip poker."

"For God's sake," Killian chastises.

"Got a problem with that, Willow?"

I kick my legs to stay afloat. "Nope, fine with me. You're going to lose though."

"We'll see about that."

Micah tosses the ball in the air before catching it. "If I win, then I get to take Willow on a camping date."

Both men gape at him. He stares back, an eyebrow lifted in challenge. This newfound confident streak is not helping me to keep my hands to myself around Micah.

"Neither of us has done that yet," Killian says pointedly. "You want to go first?"

Micah shrugs. "That's what I want."

"I guess it's up to Willow," he concedes.

I wink at Micah. "I'd love that."

We've slipped into this weirdly comfortable arrangement without any formalities like dating. That's reserved for the real world. There are no such expectations in Briar Valley, but I realise that I'd like nothing more than to go on a normal first date.

"I want the same thing then," Killian pipes up. "Willow?"

"If that's what you want. Sure."

All shaking hands in agreement, we spread out to separate corners of the lake. The first person to drop the ball gets a strike, and three strikes equals losing. Zach begins to play dirty, hitting the ball far too hard. I'm the first to be knocked out.

"No washing up for me," Zach boasts.

"Then you won't get dinner cooked for you either."

"Hey!"

"Them's the rules, Zachariah."

Micah's beaten next. His brother's quick reflexes and disregard for the rules overpowers him. He quickly ends up with three strikes and joins me on the other side of the lake, out of the firing line.

Beneath the water, his hands slip under my legs to grab me by the ass. I almost scream in surprise. There's a devilish twinkle in his green eyes as he tugs me closer, holding me against the hard planes of his body.

"I'm still taking you on that date. Fuck them."

"You are?" I grin at him.

"If you'll have me."

"Do you even have to ask?"

Mouth slanting against mine, he seals the deal with a sweet kiss. His lips are like velvet, moving in a slow, languorous tango that threatens to crumble my flimsy self-control. I'm always left wanting more with Micah.

Shifting against him, I can feel his length thickening beneath me. It presses up into the wet lace covering my core, hidden from sight by the water. I'm powerless to stop myself from pushing against his cock, loving the firm press of hardness.

"Willow," he grunts.

"Sorry. I'll stop."

When I try to swim away from him, Micah traps me in place. "No, it's not that. There's just something that I haven't told you."

"Oh?"

Still kneading my ass, his length rocks into me. He's shifting slowly so not even the water rippling betrays his movement. Each agonising brush leaves me desperate for more.

"You know I'm... inexperienced."

I nod, not trusting myself to speak.

"Well, it's a bit more than that."

Staring into his uncertain eyes, the penny drops. He's searching for any trace of judgement, seemingly expecting some kind of rejection. I take his face in my hands.

"You're a virgin?" I whisper.

Micah visibly gulps. "Yeah."

"Why didn't you tell me, Mi?"

"I figured it might freak you out." He bobs in the water. "It just never happened for me. Eventually, I stopped trying altogether."

I'm speechless. Here's this stunning, God-like statue of a man with a heart of pure gold beneath his timid exterior, and he's worried about scaring me off. My heart melts.

"It doesn't freak me out."

"Are you sure?" he worries.

"Of course. You shouldn't be ashamed of that."

"Thanks, angel." His smile turns shy. "So, um. About that date."

I peck his lips. "You're on. I've never been camping."

"I'll make it special. I promise."

The violent back and forth of the ball returns us to the present where Killian and Zach are still battling it out. I snuggle against Micah and watch the game unfold.

Killian swears his head off when he drops the ball for a third time, even with Arianna listening. Zach shouts and hollers in victory, far too pleased with himself for winning.

"I win! Game night is mine!"

Rolling my eyes, I disentangle myself from Micah and climb out of the water, grabbing a spare towel to cover my wet bra and panties. Killian has followed me out and pulls Arianna into his lap, her tiny body still wrapped in a towel.

He begins to comb through her hair with his fingers, deftly plaiting the wet blonde strands. Arianna preens under his attention, her eyes floating shut as she relaxes into his embrace. She's always loved getting her hair plaited.

By the time he's finished braiding the long strands, she's a snoring lump in his lap. The water must've tuckered her out. Killian holds her close, a smile playing across his lips.

"Want me to take her, Kill?"

"Nope," he declines. "I'm good here."

I watch him cuddling my little girl like she's his own. It's stupid how emotional the sight makes me, but I have to blink back tears. Killian looks so content, it hurts my soul.

I love him.

Fuck, I love them all.

And that scares me to death.

CHAPTER 31
WILLOW

SOMETHING IN THE ORANGE - ZACH BRYAN

SMOOTHING my hands down my billowing floral dress, I nod decisively at my reflection. My dark hair is braided and twisted to sit on top of my head in an intricate up-do. Aalia smiles at me from over my shoulder, a can of hairspray in hand.

"Perfect. You are so beautiful, Willow."

"I don't know about that. Is it too much?"

"This is your party. Nothing is too much."

I fiddle with the light linen of my dress. "I just wanted everyone to see the person I am now, you know? This town saved my life in so many ways, and the people in it too."

Giving my hair one last inspection, Aalia pecks my cheek. "I'm happy to see this big smile. I think these boys... they make you happy, yes?"

"Boys?" I feign innocence.

She rolls her eyes. "I know you're with them all. Or... dating them all? I'm not sure about the correct word for this arrangement."

I stifle a laugh. "Hell, me neither. I have no idea how to describe our relationship."

"Having no words is sometimes a good thing." She clasps my hand. "And I see that you took your ring off. Perhaps that says enough."

There's a pale band of skin on my finger where the gold wedding ring once laid. I'm not sure when that switch inside of me flicked, but I slid it off on a whim and never put it back on. Now, it hides with our passports and cash.

"I was finally ready," I admit.

"I'm proud of you, Willow."

"Thank you for being such a good friend to me."

She beams. "Always. Come, let's go."

Checking her own appearance in my bedroom mirror, Aalia adjusts her patterned red smock and marches towards the kitchen. I slip my feet into a pair of sandals and follow, my stomach awash with nervous butterflies.

The housewarming party will be kicking off soon. It's taken a while to get everything ready—organising chairs and tables outside, cleaning up the garden, buying enough alcohol and food to feed an army. Briar Valley parties take a lot of work.

Outside, Killian's already tending to a huge bonfire. He insisted on building it high into the sky. Zach has set up the bar with a slightly worrying level of expertise. He's already banned Micah from it.

"Let me go and find the children. I left Zach out there with Amie." Aalia pulls a face at the thought. "Not a good idea."

"He'll have her causing trouble in no time."

Aalia shakes her head, rushing outside to track down the kids. I'm left in the kitchen with Micah. He's quiet, diligently working alone to chop up the world's biggest bowl of salad.

He wanted a task away from people and interacting. Tonight will be a real test of the progress he's made. I'm already proud of him for giving it a go. Sneaking up on him, I wrap my arms around his waist and rest my chin on his shoulder.

"Hey, handsome."

"Hey there." He chuckles, methodically slicing a cucumber. "I was beginning to wonder if you were going to show your face."

"Aalia insisted on doing my hair for me."

Laying down the knife, Micah turns and pins me in his muscular arms. He tucks a loose black strand behind my ear, one of his signature small smiles making my toes curl in a delicious, spine-tingling way.

"You look stunning, Willow."

I bite my lip. "You don't look so bad yourself."

Dressed in distressed blue jeans and a button-down shirt that's rolled up to his elbows, Micah looks good enough to eat. I slant my mouth over his, greedily drinking him in until his tongue is brushing against mine.

Breaking the kiss, I rest my forehead against his with a sigh. "Guests will be here soon."

"To be continued?" Micah suggests.

"Well, I'm free next weekend for that date."

"Next weekend it is," he decides.

"I can't wait to go camping with you."

With his salad finished, we link hands and walk outside together. My garden has been transformed, and as the sun turns golden and fiery on the horizon, the hundreds of little lantern lights strung outside flick on.

They light the whole cabin in a cosy, warm glow. With his bonfire raging, Killian turns his attention to the barbecue next. Zach is sitting down with Aalia at a table, holding Amie in one arm while nursing a beer.

"Where's Arianna?" I worry aloud.

Micah points over towards the lake. "Right there."

She's playing with Johan near the lake's edge with a huge, life-sized Jenga set that Killian built himself. He presented it to the kids with far too much pleasure.

"Jesus. That thing is huge."

"It's Killian sized," Micah jokes.

"So… huge."

"Pretty much."

Seeing everyone happy and smiling makes my throat thicken with emotion. I wish I could take a mental snapshot and treasure this moment forever. This is what I spent so many years longing for—this scene right here.

"Willow!" Ryder's voice calls.

I catch sight of his crop of curly hair as he arrives, dressed casually in jeans and a loose blue t-shirt. His hand is tightly held by another man. I demanded that he invite his mysterious boyfriend to attend.

Tall and lean, the boyfriend's face is set in sharp, angular lines, framing kind blue eyes that are highlighted by the buzzcut on his head. He's handsome but holds himself with an air of authority.

I walk down the steps to intercept them. "Hey! Thanks for coming."

Ryder gestures to his boyfriend. "Willow, this is Ethan."

I immediately pull him in for a hug. "It's lovely to finally meet you."

He offers me a genuine smile that softens his threatening exterior. "Likewise, Willow. I've heard a lot about you."

"Oh God. All bad?"

"Not at all. It's about time there was a female around here to keep these cavemen in check." He gestures towards the guys, all three of them now gathered around the bonfire.

"I'm not sure anyone is capable of that."

"I'm sure if anyone can, it's you." His smile falters for a second before sliding back into place. "How are you settling into life in Briar Valley?"

"I feel at home here." I match Ryder's smile. "If you'll excuse me."

Leaving them to meet the others, I'm bombarded by a rush of people arriving all at once. Doc, Rachel, Miranda and their kids all give me individual hugs. I'm presented with a giant bouquet of flowers, and Aalia rushes to take them inside.

"The place looks amazing!" Miranda gushes.

"Thank you. It's taken some time, but we got there."

Doc casts an eye around. "Hell of a lot better than before. You've really made this place a home. I'm happy for you, Willow."

I take his hand and squeeze it. "I wouldn't be here if you hadn't saved my life."

He waves me off. "It's nothing."

"No. It's not. Thank you, Doc."

"You're welcome."

His eyes growing misty, he mumbles an excuse and disappears to meet the guys at the bonfire. I give his wives another hug and let them carry on greeting the other guests.

Theodore and Marilyn arrive next with a feast of home baking weighing them down, shortly followed by Harold and Andrea bringing fresh meat and some homemade liquors.

"Don't tell the little one." Harold winks.

"No Bambi's on the menu tonight. Got it."

With everyone grabbing drinks and settling in, I wait for my last guests to arrive. Anxiety is twisting my stomach into knots. I have no idea if this was a good plan, but when letter-writing failed, I followed my gut instincts.

Lola and Albie turn up late. I'm swept into my grandma's cookie-scented embrace, her skin brushing against mine.

"It's good to see you smiling again, poppet."

"Hi, Grams. Yeah… it is, I guess."

She smiles wanly as the nickname slips out. Albie wraps me in a hug, then heads over to join the other men gathered around the fire. I'm left with Lola watching me bounce up and down on my feet.

"Is Katie coming?" I dare to ask.

"I believe so."

My anxiety triples. "Okay, good."

"She's bringing Walker along, the widowed chap we were discussing before. It was a good excuse to get her over here. I didn't know what else to say."

I shake out my trembling hands. "Thanks for helping. I felt like I needed to see her again to figure out what to do."

Lola's eyes are crinkled with concern. "Just be careful. The last thing I want is for you to get hurt again. I'm not sure how she will react to the news."

"Yeah, I will. Let's get a drink."

We rejoin the party while awaiting Katie's arrival. The hum of laughter and conversation wraps me in a comforting bubble. Zach thrusts a glass of wine into my hand. Amie is still propped on his hip, looking perfectly at peace.

He shrugs. "Think she likes me."

I kiss his cheek. "You've got the knack for it."

"Everyone's watching us."

"You have a problem with that?" I challenge.

Zach plants a heavy kiss against my lips. "Nope. Not at all."

Leaving him to fuss over the baby, I walk to the bonfire and step into Killian's embrace. His arms automatically tighten around me, and his beard scrapes the top of my head.

"Nice bonfire. Please don't burn down my cabin."

He secures his lips to mine with a growl. "You like my big fire, baby?"

"It's very impressive."

"That's not the only thing that's impressive."

Albie makes a throwing up sound. "Christ. Please, spare us."

We break apart before he actually pukes, both chuckling at his disgust. Killian turns back to the barbecued food, and I glance over the crowd around the bonfire. Ethan is staring at me and frowning a little.

"Everything okay?" I ask nervously.

He shakes himself out of it. "All good."

Ryder shoots him an odd look. "He's tired, Willow. Big case going on."

"Where do you work, Ethan?"

"I'm based in London." His stare is intense, searching. "I work for a company called Sabre Security. We take on criminal investigations and private contracts."

"Oh. Sounds important."

"We do some good work. I'm leading a team of investigators at the moment tracing a human trafficking ring across North America."

A lead weight settles in my gut. The way he's looking at me is making my spine tingle with alarm. It's like he can see past my carefully applied persona to unveil the truth.

"A trafficking ring?" I repeat.

"Nasty business," he confirms. "I can't say much else."

Ryder drops a kiss on his shoulder. "I am so proud of the work you're doing. Think of all the people who will be saved by your team's investigation."

"Willow," Ethan interjects. "I hope you don't mind me asking, but I've been told a little about what brought you to Briar Valley."

"Ry," I gasp in horror.

His smile droops. "I'm sorry, Willow. It just came out. But you can trust Ethan, he's one of the good ones. I thought… maybe he could help you."

I never should have trusted Ryder with my secrets. Killian was the one that filled him in one night after asking for my consent. I had one condition—his sworn secrecy.

"I think we should talk." Ethan redirects the heat off his partner. "We can either do it here or at my team headquarters in London if that's easier for you."

"Why? I know nothing that can help your investigation."

"I think that you do. Please let me help you," he urges. "We can offer you protection. You shouldn't have to live in fear for the rest of your life."

I back away from them. "I don't need your help."

Before I can escape, he pulls a business card from his pocket and slaps it in my hands. I stare down at the lines of text etched across embossed cream card.

Ethan Tarkington.
Sabre Security - Anaconda Team.

"Call me anytime." Ethan smiles reassuringly. "I'm here to listen."

Moving on autopilot, I tuck the business card into my bra. I'm not sure why I don't toss it into the bonfire and run far from this man. But there's a voice in my head, begging me to hold on to that scrap of contact information.

"I should go. Thanks."

Ethan's eyes follow me all the way back to my cabin, lasering into the back of my head. I'm on the verge of a panic attack, but the tinkle of laughing voices approaching the party doesn't allow me even a second to fathom what just happened.

"Katie!" Lola appears at my side.

Crossing the cobbled path, the woman of the hour arrives. Katie's dressed in a pretty lilac dress with her dark hair loose around her shoulders, showing off her scarred but beautiful features and bright smile.

"Hi!" She waves at us. "So sorry we're late."

There are two men standing on either side of her. One is around her age with salt and pepper hair, wearing a crisp, fitted white shirt, smart dark-wash jeans and an easy smile. The other lingers slightly behind.

He's younger than them, appearing closer to Killian's age. His sandy blonde hair is closely cropped to his head in a neat cut, accentuating his strong jawline and smattering of stubble. He's dressed in black jeans and a blue shirt that's open at the collar.

With a breath, I approach them. "Hey."

Katie turns her smile on me. "Thank you for having us, Melody."

"Was your journey okay?"

"Fine, thanks. This is Don, my fiancé."

"Pleasure to meet you." Don offers me and Lola a hand to shake. "I've heard so much about Briar Valley."

The other man surveys the party, his hands stuffed in his pockets to conceal his nerves. He looks deeply uncomfortable, his clear eyes lined with heavy bags. Grief seems to weigh on his shoulders in a visible cloud.

"This is Walker," Katie introduces. "Briar Valley's newest recruit... I hope."

Walker plasters on a smile that doesn't reach his eyes. "Nice to meet you both."

"Welcome to town," Lola offers. "We're happy to have you here."

"I appreciate the welcome. Katie's told me a lot about you." Walker shoots me a quick look. "I haven't made my mind up about moving with the kids yet."

She pats his shoulder. "Let's go and chat. I can answer your questions."

Lola cleverly takes a seat on the same table as Aalia and introduces her to Walker. She really is a bleeding heart, that woman. Aalia shifts closer to join the conversation, gesturing around towards the thick woods that encapsulate the town.

"I really hope he agrees to this."

Katie's voice startles me. She's moved to my side and gently pats my arm. I will my feet to move and put distance between us, but I can't bear to inch away from her. My body is straining to fall into her arms.

"I'm going to say hello to Albie."

"Sure," I force out.

She guides Don over to the table where Albie and Ryder are discussing an upcoming restoration project, leaving me to suck in a panicked breath. This was such a bad idea.

Two hours into the party, we've cleaned dozens of empty plates. Everyone has loosened up after several drinks. I finally get off my feet and collapse into Zach's lap.

His lips brush my ear. "Are you okay?"

"I'm good. Everyone seems to be having a nice time."

"You worry too much. It's a great party."

"You guys made it possible," I point out.

"All I did was string some fucking lights, Willow."

"I appreciate everything you do for me, no matter how small."

Zach's breath glides over my skin. "Can we kick all these people out? I want to spread your ass across this table and bury my face between your thighs."

Treacle oozes down my spine.

"I could get behind that idea."

"I could get behind you," he purrs.

Lola and Katie interrupt his filthy whispers by taking a seat at the table. I automatically reach for my glass of wine and take a gulp for courage. Her eyes are locked on me, scanning over my hair and face, like she can't quite place me.

"You've finished settling in?" Katie asks.

I take another gulp of wine. "I think so. We're happy to be here. Arianna loves being in the countryside more than anything."

"Where did you live before?"

"We were living in Mexico."

Katie whistles under her breath. "This is a big change for you both then."

"That was the plan." I smile tightly.

"Who exactly are you related to?" Katie's smile begins to wane. "I didn't think you had more family hiding in the woodwork, Lola. You sure kept that quiet."

Lola opens her mouth to speak, but nothing comes out. The awkward silence stretches on, and Zach tightens his arms around me, silently urging me to remain calm. My heart feels like it's going to tear itself free from my chest.

"Well." I clear my throat. "Uh…"

Arianna chooses that exact moment to plonk herself in Lola's lap. Katie looks from her blonde hair and back to me. We don't look much alike. I spent years hearing Mr Sanchez's acquaintances tell me as much.

"This is Arianna, my daughter," I squeak.

Arianna smiles shyly. "Hello."

Katie gives her a wave. "Hey there, little one. Are you enjoying the party?"

"Yes… but Johan ate my cupcake."

"I'll get you another one," Lola hushes her.

"Yay! Thanks, Grandma."

Ah, fuck.

I'd forgotten about the shortened nickname. Arianna is completely oblivious. I stare at Katie as her smile drops away, her expression splintering. She looks straight at me and then to Lola.

"Grandma?" Katie repeats incredulously.

I clear my throat. "Zach… can you take Arianna to get a cupcake?"

"Are you sure, babe?"

Nodding, I climb out of his lap. "Yeah."

Zach reluctantly leaves, taking Arianna's outstretched hand. He mouths at me to shout if I need him to come back. I'm left in the fallout zone of a destructive nuclear bomb.

"Everyone calls me Grams," Lola tries to reason.

I hold a hand up to halt her. "It's okay, Lola. I owe Katie the truth."

Eyes meeting mine, a deadly combination of hope and agony floods her irises. Katie looks ready to run straight at me, or perhaps straight for the exit. The feeling's mutual.

"Katie..." I begin.

She hangs on the edge of her seat, gripping the tablecloth tight. The voices and clinking glasses of everyone else drops away until it's just the two of us, caught on a derailed train hurtling towards the unknown.

"My name isn't Melody. I'm Willow."

"Willow," she croaks. "Oh my God."

"I'm your daughter."

CHAPTER 32
WILLOW

ANOTHER LIFE - MOTIONLESS IN WHITE

CLOSING the door to the cabin, I rest my head against the slab of wood. The rest of the guests made a hasty exit after Lola and Katie started screaming at each other. Albie quickly dragged them apart before they actually began fighting too.

I left Arianna outside with the guys to keep her out of earshot. Ryder and Ethan are handling clean-up duty to give us some time to sort through this mess in the privacy of my cabin.

"Willow?" Lola says softly. "Come sit down, poppet."

"Give me a sec," I mutter.

Rummaging in the back of the kitchen cabinet, I find Zach's secret bottle of whiskey. He's been saving it for strip poker. Gathering three glasses, I walk into the living room with my eyes on my feet, unable to look at the two seething women.

"Drink?"

"Please," Lola answers.

Pouring us all a generous measure, I hand out the drinks and lean against the wall in the furthermost corner of the room. I need as much space between us as possible.

"Is it true?" Katie snaps at Lola.

She clears her throat. "Yes, it's true. Willow is my granddaughter."

"This is… it's… what the fuck?" she splutters. "How could you keep this from me? We speak every single week, and you didn't think to mention that you found my daughter?"

"She was protecting me," I interrupt. "I wasn't ready for you to know who I really am. Lola gave me time to come to terms with the truth."

"What truth?" Katie exclaims angrily.

Pain lances through my broken heart.

"Well… I thought you abandoned me."

Tears stream down her cheeks. "You thought I left you behind?"

"Something like that."

She moves to stand up and approach me, but I hold her back with a raised hand. If she tries to hug me, I won't be able to hold my broken pieces together for a second longer.

"That's what Jack told her," Lola explains gently. "He lied and said that you left willingly. She was raised to believe that you wanted nothing to do with her."

"This is ridiculous!" Katie shouts.

My hands ball into fists. "One day you were there, the next you were gone. I was just a kid. What was I supposed to think? I was a scared little girl who missed her mum."

"I never left you. Jack took you from me."

"I didn't know that, Katie. He lied to me."

"Don't call me that," she snaps through her coursing tears. "I'm your mum, for Christ's sake. I've always been your mum."

"You're not," I say sadly.

Her crying increases until she's hiccupping through every breath. Even Lola's sunken cheeks are wet with tears. I want to cry. I want to mourn. The mother I needed was taken away from me, but all I feel is regret.

That damned letter!

If only I'd had the bravery to follow its handwritten words, instead of allowing fear to dictate my future. I was a kid, but I'd lived enough by then to know better. Katie was at the other end of that desperate call into the darkness.

"I'm sorry he took me from you. When dad died, I was so afraid. The world was a scary place and I convinced myself that I was better off alone."

Katie's shoulders shake with heaving sobs. "I looked for you every single day for fifteen years. Every day. I never gave up, and I scoured the entire country in search of you."

"It's true," Lola confirms. "She never stopped."

"When you didn't respond to my letter, I wanted to give up." Katie scrubs the moisture from her face. "But that didn't stop me from searching. You're the reason I rehome families for a living. I thought… it might allow me to track you down."

An invisible string wrapped around my heart is drawing me across the room. Part of me wants to approach her. Get to know her. Throw myself into her awaiting arms and allow myself to be cared for by the one person I always wanted, but never had.

The other part of me can't forget the memories of my dad screaming, letting me starve, and leaving me alone in the world. Vulnerable and at the mercy of men like Mr Sanchez. As much as I want to, I can't separate the two.

"Where did you go?" Katie clutches her chest.

"I left England when I was sixteen."

"Why? With who?"

"It's a complicated story," Lola answers for me.

I send her a grateful nod. "It is."

"Then uncomplicate it." Katie turns her fury on Lola. "You've known about Willow for months now. Christ, you let her sit opposite me and never said a word!"

"I had to. She needed more time."

"My daughter! You hid her from me."

"I did what I thought I had to for her sake," she defends, her tears shining in the warm cabin light. "I was keeping your daughter safe. Surely you can understand that?"

Wrapping my arms around myself, I slam my eyes shut. It's too much. I spent so long alone, now there are too many people around me. I can't breathe. Can't think straight. Can't remain calm. They're sucking all of the oxygen out of the room.

Katie's voice is laced with defeat. "I have a granddaughter who I didn't even know existed. I can't get that time back now. I've missed out on so much."

"And you think I haven't?" Lola shouts back.

"You knew Willow was here and you still lied."

"I was making damned sure that she'd stay!" she defends.

"Please," I whimper.

Neither of them are listening to me, yelling over each other instead. My breathing dissolves into constricted gasping. The raised voices and lash of hatred unleashes a pit of dark memories. I can't back any further into the corner.

"She's my daughter! You had no right to make that decision. No fucking right."

"I had every right!" Lola yells back.

"Says who?"

"Says me! I'm in charge of this town. You ought to remember that."

Katie scoffs in disappointment. "You're a bitter old woman, clutching at excuses. You've betrayed me. I should have been the first to know that Willow had come home."

"Enough! Stop it, both of you!"

I'm hunched over, my hands on my shuddering knees as my vision begins to blacken from lack of air. Lola tries to speak, but I find the strength to cut her off.

"Get out," I hiss. "Now."

"Willow, please—"

"I said get out! Right now!"

Katie looks at me with such raw longing, it nearly knocks me over. I refuse to budge, pointing towards the front door. She shakes her head and leaves.

"Willow," Lola begins.

"No. You too."

"But—"

"Go!" I scream at her.

Appearing shaken, Lola follows in Katie's footsteps. When the door slams shut behind them, I let myself crumble. An awful sob tears at my throat. I know I won't be left alone for much longer.

Run.

I have to run.

Bolting for the bathroom, I slam the door behind me and lock it, searching for a hiding place. I just want to feel safe again. Crawling into the bathtub, I curl up with my knees to my chest, letting the tears finally come.

A never ending river of regret and pain chokes me in the silence. I've never felt so alone. I found my family after all this time, but it's too late. The damage has been done. Katie was right—we can never get those lost years back.

"Willow? Where are you?"

Slamming my hands over my ears, I curl up even tighter. I want to be left in peace. It was easier to survive when it was just Arianna and me. The two of us against the world.

Before I cared too much.

Before I let people get close.

Before I opened myself up to pain.

I've never had control over my life. How do I take it back? How do I make everything stop hurting so much? I'll never belong. Not really. This was all a futile dream.

Next to my bottle of shower gel, I spot the razor I used to shave my legs this morning. A tiny, whispered voice calls out to me in sinister slithers. I haven't heard it for a long time.

Take control, Willow.

I don't know what I'm doing until the razor is in my hands. Smashing the cheap plastic against the side of the tub, it frees the two sharp blades inside. I don't think about what I'm doing. Thinking is bad. Unnecessary.

I need everything to stop. All the pain. All the confusion. All the heartache and indecision about our future. Even if it's only for a moment. Pain used to focus me, strengthen my determination. It paved the way for our escape.

Drawing my thumb along the sharp blade, I watch the blood rise to the surface. It's beautiful, the rush of air that pierces my lungs with each drop that falls. Mr Sanchez isn't hurting me anymore. Now, I'm in charge. I'm hurting myself.

Biting my lip, I dig the blade into my wrist next, slicing it with a strangled cry. I need to breathe. Relief. Anything. Pressing deeper, I dig it into my arm and sob even harder. Crimson splashes on the polished tiles surrounding me.

"Willow!" Killian booms. "Open this door right now."

The blade falls from my trembling hand, hitting the floor of the tub. Hammering on the bathroom door sends me spiralling further. All I can hear is Mr Sanchez's voice promising punishment if I continue to hide and deny him what he wants.

Get out here immediately.

Else I'll beat Arianna black and blue.

"Stand back, I can pick the lock."

The hammering on the door ceases.

"Zach, hurry!"

"I'm trying, dammit."

I ignore the click of the lock being picked. All I can see is the splash of blood flowing from my arm. It's proof of all the twisted feelings that have been choking me for so long. I can finally see them in the flesh.

There's a gasp, followed by a deep growl of fury. I don't want them to see me like this, but I have no strength to hold it in anymore. This is the real me, beneath the smiles and bravado. This is the person they love.

"Get out," I hear Micah order.

"Like hell. Move out of the way."

"I know how to handle this, not you," he argues in a hard voice. "Give us some space and get the first aid kit from across the street. She'll need stitches."

"Come on, Kill," Zach mutters.

With my eyes squeezed shut, I listen to their footsteps moving away from the bathroom. The door clicks shut again, and fingertips gently brush across my forehead. The hair is swiped from my face, revealing two frightened green eyes.

"What have you done to yourself, beautiful?"

"Micah?" I gasp.

"I'm here, Willow."

"The others…"

"It's just me. I sent them away. Reckon you can take a breath for me?"

Micah's kneeling beside the bathtub, the corner of his mouth tilted up in a weak smile that he's plastering on for my benefit. I'm glad it's him. He's the only one that has seen the thread of darkness sliding through my veins before.

Nodding, I grit my teeth and attempt to suck air in. Micah blows it out and mimes sucking in again. With his hand cupping my neck, I breathe a little better.

"I need to take a look at your arm. Keep breathing for me, alright?"

"Okay," I wheeze.

Turning his attention to my blood-slick arm, he grabs a hand towel to hold against the deep slices I inflicted. The pain barely registers in my numb mind. Micah adds pressure, clasping on both sides of my forearm to stem the bleeding.

"You're okay," he repeats under his breath.

"I'm so fucking sorry, Mi."

"Stop, Willow. You don't have to apologise."

"I… I don't know what I was thinking."

"You're hurting right now," he explains simply. "Sometimes the only way to make sense of the pain we feel on the inside is to see it physically on the outside."

I bite my lip. "I needed it all to stop."

"You have nothing to be ashamed of, believe me. I'm going to lift you up now, and I want you to hold on to my neck. Can you do that?"

"I c-can do it."

"Good. Hold on then."

With amazingly gentle hands, he lifts me from the bathtub and places me on the counter next to the sink basin. I nuzzle his neck while cuddling him tight.

Micah presses a soft kiss against my hair. "Breathe, Willow."

"Please don't let go of me."

"I swear to you, angel. I will never let go of you."

We stay wrapped together like twisted vines until there's another knock at the door, lighter this time, and he retreats to answer. Heavy breathing emanates from the hallway.

"Can I help?" Zach asks frantically.

"We're good here. I'll get her cleaned up."

"Mi, please. I want to help."

"If you want to help, then go."

Shutting the door in Zach's heartbroken face, Micah returns to settle between my parted legs. He rummages in the first aid kit, threading a needle ready for stitches.

"Micah? Do you know what you're doing?"

"Yeah, I do. I need to clean your arm first. It might hurt a bit."

"I'm so s-sorry. You shouldn't have to do this."

"Stop beating yourself up." Hesitating, he rolls up the cuff of his shirt, exposing his wrist to me. "I know what you're going through, and I'm not here to judge."

Inspecting his skin, I study the uneven, silvery scars from old self-inflicted cuts. Micah shivers when I trail a shaking finger over a particularly nasty one. He knows. He doesn't hate me. He isn't disgusted. He... is me.

"Hold still now. I'll go as fast as I can."

I barely flinch as he douses the cuts on my arm in bottled antiseptic and presses a cotton ball against the flow of blood. My pain tolerance is scarily high. The burning fades into the background and I focus on nothing but him.

His luminous green eyes. Messy, caramel-streaked hair. The shining ring in his nose. Kindness clinging to his every move. All the tiny details that I've longed to memorise.

"Deep breath," he murmurs.

Micah traps his bottom lip between his teeth as he glides the needle through my skin and begins to stitch up the cuts in neat rows. His eyes continuously flick up to me.

"You good?" he asks.

"Fine."

"Sorry if I'm hurting you."

"You're not."

Snipping the last stitch, he checks over his work. The stitches are perfect. Almost too perfect. The silver streaks of anguish on his skin speak for themselves. Micah knows all about inflicting pain on the outside to reflect within.

Back inside the first aid kit, he retrieves a small roll of cotton bandage. I lift my arm, allowing him to wind it around in a tight spiral to hold everything in place. Even the way he seals the bandage with a scrap of tape is deft.

"All done."

"Thanks, Mi."

He closes the kit. "The others are probably losing their shit out there."

"I just… need a moment. Please."

Stroking his knuckles against my cheek, he nods. "Take all the time you need. They can wait."

Running the tap, Micah holds my hands in his and rinses them off. Every stroke of his fingertips is gentle. He swirls soap into my palms and washes them for me.

"Do you want to talk about it?" he whispers.

I silently shake my head.

"Okay. Mind if I talk?"

Turning off the tap, he rests against the edge of the bathtub. That almost imperceptible second skin of sadness has slipped back over him, obscuring the smiles and confidence I've come to love. Our torment is entangled in this small room.

"The first time I did it, I was eleven." He stares down at the scars on his arm. "I never meant for it to get out of hand. It was only meant to be one time."

"Why did you do it?"

"I missed my dad. It hurt so bad, I needed to get it all out."

I stroke an unsteady hand over his hair. "Did it work?"

"At first," he admits. "But the high didn't last long, and I had to do it again. And again. And again. Each time sooner than the last. I lost control so fast, I couldn't stop it."

Micah looks up, stabbing me with the determination brewing in his eyes. That clinging sense of sadness dissolves like storm clouds sweeping away to douse their next victims.

"Don't fall down this slippery slope, Willow. Don't start something that you won't be able to stop. I need you to promise me that if you feel like this again, you'll tell me."

When I don't immediately answer him, Micah takes my hand in his and rests it against his cheek, forcing me to acknowledge him. Barbed wire is slicing deep into my throat.

"Promise me, Willow."

"It won't happen again. I wasn't thinking straight."

"No." He shakes his head. "I don't care what you were thinking. All I want is your word that you'll talk to me before hurting yourself again. You'll ask for help."

"Mi… I promise."

"Swear to it?" he pushes.

Leaning closer, I rest our foreheads together. "Swear to it."

"I can't fucking lose you. Not like this."

Lips meeting in a frenetic kiss, I let him take the assurance he needs. While the other two demand physical possession of my heart, Micah's content to sneak into the darkest corners of my mind and set up shop in the shadows.

I'll take it.

Whatever he needs of me.

Sliding his arms under my legs, Micah lifts me into his arms and lets me hide my face in the soft fabric of his shirt. He still smells like fresh oil paint, even in normal clothes.

The cabin is weirdly quiet as we pad towards the master bedroom. Everyone has gone home and left us in peace. Nudging the door open, Micah settles me under the tangled blue sheets on my bed.

"Arianna's gone home with Aalia." He sits down next to me. "Figured you could use some space after that fiasco. Killian threw Lola and Katie out."

I nod numbly. "Good."

"You should lay down and get some rest."

"I can't sleep. Not without them."

Right on cue, the door creaks open again and two faces peer into the room. While Zach looks terrified of finding me in a state, Killian looks more afraid of the intensity of his own feelings. They refuse to move from the doorway.

"Can we come in?" Killian pleads.

I reach out a hand. "I need you to hold me."

His mouth hooks up. "That I can do."

Tentatively approaching, they find their own place in the bed. Micah stretches across the end, a hand tightly wrapped around my ankle. Killian climbs in and traps me against his broad chest, above the roar of his heartbeat.

Zach is the last to slip in next to me, burying his face in my stomach. I slide my fingers through his hair, stroking the lumps of his skull. His breathing is shuddered.

"I'm sorry," I say again.

Killian tightens his iron-grip. "I won't hear it."

"You have nothing to be sorry for," Zach adds.

Between all three of them, I feel the weight lifting from my shoulders. The darkness of the room swallows their individual lumps beneath my sheets until I can't tell where they end and I begin.

Micah strokes the inside of my ankle. "Rest, Willow."

"You're not alone," Zach murmurs.

Killian grunts in agreement. "We're here."

I can face the future with them at my side, but I know how this cruel life works. Nothing lasts. Especially not the good things. If I don't self-destruct, then the world will do it for me. Then... all of our hearts will be in the firing line.

CHAPTER 33
MICAH

SOMEONE TO BREAK YOUR HEART - EMMA JENSEN

ZIPPING UP MY BULGING BACKPACK, I strap the two-person tent to the outside and tighten the cords that hold the whole thing together. It weighs a tonne, but I want tonight to be perfect. We've got a lot of gear to haul with us.

I'll drag the damn thing up the mountain without complaint to keep the promise I made to Willow. Not only is this my first date with her, but it's also my first *ever* date. I've never been with a woman, let alone one that I love.

"I don't know about this," Zach frets.

Ignoring his shadow looming over me, I test the backpack's weight. "You need to ease up. She had a wobble. Time to move on."

"A wobble? Seriously?"

"Making a big deal of it won't help her. You're gonna drive her away if you keep suffocating her. Getting Willow away from town for a night will be good."

Killian stares at me from inside the kitchen where he's brewing his lunchtime cafetière of extra strong coffee. He's barely slept in the last few days, too busy watching Willow like a hawk, even when she's asleep. The incident really shook him up.

"You'll keep her safe?" he deadpans.

"Jesus, Kill. I can take care of Willow and I think I've proven that."

"You got stranded on a mountain in February."

"And we had to rescue you," Zach piles on.

I glower at them both. "That was different. We're heading for St David's Pointe. It's a safe route and we'll be there before dark. Back off."

"You know the route off by heart?"

"Yes, Kill. I've done it a thousand times."

"Got your GPS tracker?"

I tap the keyring attached to the backpack's strap. "Right here."

"Veer even an inch off course and I'll be marching up that mountain to drag you back myself," he threatens. "I mean it, Mi."

"Fuck, Kill. Chill the hell out."

Our bickering is cut off by Willow's arrival. She lets herself into our cabin without knocking like usual, then freezes as her gaze darts between all three of us before ducking.

"Um, hey. Everything okay?"

Killian unfolds his arms like he wants to go to her but decides against it. She's been struggling since the party and holding us at arm's length while everything settles. Katie's daily calls demanding more of her time have become a huge problem.

"Fine," Killian grinds out. "Just going over some ground rules."

"Ground rules?" she repeats. "What are we, kids?"

"The mountain is a dangerous place. You both need to be careful."

"Alright, Kill." Zach lands a hand on his shoulder. "Enough."

Killian huffs and storms outside, pausing to plant a kiss on Willow's lips as he whispers goodbye. Shrugging, Zach pulls her into a hug and pecks the top of her head.

"Have fun, babe. Keep my idiot twin out of trouble and bring him home in one piece, preferably. I'm not quite ready for Killian to be my last remaining relative."

I narrow my eyes. "I'm an adult, you know."

Zach sticks his tongue out. "News to me."

"I'll try my best." Willow snickers. "Look after Arianna for me."

"We have a night of Disney princess movies planned. She'll be just fine."

With another lingering kiss, Zach follows Killian outside, and the pair climb into his truck to resume their daily work. We watch them go and Willow sighs in relief.

"I thought Killian might actually lock me in here."

"I'm sure it crossed his mind," I half-joke.

"No doubt about that. Shall we go?"

Wrestling on the backpack, I take her hand in mine. She's dressed in a long-sleeved white top and loose jeans, the cuffs rolled up to fit her worn brown walking boots. Her hair is pulled off her shoulders in a slick, high ponytail.

"I'm ready," she announces.

"Let's move."

Together, we hike into the sunlit woodland behind the cabins that leads out of Briar Valley. There's a secret route concealed by trees that avoids the town square. Neither of us wants to speak to another human being.

"Watch your step. It's uphill from here."

We stop at the base of St David's Pointe after an hour of climbing over smooth rock and huge, jungle-like tree roots. Briar Valley sprawls across the land between us, dotted with tiny ant people going about their business.

Willow's stamina is good. She doesn't complain as she begins to climb, the terrain becoming steeper. Pausing to tighten the red laces on her walking boots, she bends over, displaying her round ass to me.

She catches me staring at her. "What?"

"I'm glad you agreed to come."

Her smile is grateful. "This was a good idea, Mi."

I tug her towards me, bringing her close enough for a kiss. "We can stay for as long as you need. Forever if necessary. In fact, we could become feral and live out our days in peace."

Willow snorts. "That sounds too good to be true."

"I'm just saying. It could be fun."

"If I didn't have Arianna, I'd actually be tempted."

I peck her cheek and boost her over the next rock. "You're just Willow today. Not Mummy or anything else. We're two people, camping out and hiding from the world."

"Damn, Micah. You know me far too well."

"I know that it's what I would need."

"Thank you. I really did need this."

"I've got your back, angel."

We take a quick break during our ascent. The incline is pretty steep, but I'm familiar with the route that takes us towards my favourite camping spot. There's a guideline already in place that I set up last summer.

I've hiked this route a bunch of times over the years when even the remoteness of Briar Valley got too much for me to handle. It's a relatively easy hike compared to the military-style marches my dad used to take us on.

"How many times have you been here?" Willow asks.

"In the summer, I come every month or so."

"And you camp alone? All the way up here?"

I shrug, hoisting the backpack into a more comfortable position. "Being alone up here really doesn't bother me. I love the silence. It feels like the world doesn't exist."

"Sometimes I wish the world really didn't exist."

"Well for the next twenty-four hours, it doesn't for us."

After five sweaty hours with intermittent water breaks, we've arrived in the misty wilderness of St David's Pointe. It's a treasure trove of spindly pine trees, thick shrubs and thriving mountain flowers nestled in the outcroppings of rock.

"Here we are."

"This place is insane," Willow breathes.

"It's beautiful, right?"

Climbing over a boulder, I hoist myself into the spot I've camped at before. There's a flat shelf of rock that hugs the side of the mountain, big enough to fit the tent and a couple of people. I've dreamed about bringing Willow here.

It has an undisturbed, panoramic view of the stunning valley beneath us, lit by the sun sinking on the horizon in the distance. The afternoon has slipped away, succumbing to the clinging embrace of shadows and darkness.

"Want to help me get set up so we can catch the sunset?"

Willow nods. "Sure."

She takes my outstretched hand and I help pull her over the boulder to plant her feet on the rock shelf. Smoothing sticky hair back from her reddened face, she studies the vast, breathtaking expanse of the horizon.

Briar Valley has vanished into the coverage of trees and low-hanging clouds. We're in a whole different slice of reality up here, superimposed over the rest of the mortal world.

"How did you find this place?"

"I hike a lot and came across it by accident." I lower the backpack to the ground and stretch. "I haven't brought anyone else here though. It's kinda my secret spot."

"But you brought me?"

"You can keep a secret, right?" I wink at her.

Her grin blossoms. "Hell yeah, I can."

Spreading out the thick plastic sheeting and metal poles from my backpack, we manage to put the mountaineering tent up in less than half an hour. It's positioned a few strides back from the edge of the cliff, giving an undisturbed viewpoint of the sunset.

"I'll start a fire," I decide. "Want to set up inside?"

Willow nods and rummages inside the backpack for the rest of our gear. I set about getting a campfire lit with odd twigs and leaves we gathered during our ascent.

Rolling out sleeping bags inside the tent and adding the finishing touches, Willow emerges with a contented sigh. I open the hip flask of whiskey I snuck into my coat pocket and pour two measures into our foldable cups.

"Drink?"

"Thanks. This view is so incredible."

I look straight at her. "Yeah, it sure is."

Willow blushes hard, her freckled cheeks dusted pink. "You're not so bad yourself. As first dates go, this is impressive. I have nothing to compare it to though."

"Me neither," I admit.

"Really? Never?"

Taking a sip, I wince when the liquor burns my throat. "I've never had a girlfriend. You're the first person I've ever wanted to... you know, get close to."

"Damn, Micah."

"People aren't exactly my strong suit. Even Killian's more sociable than me."

"You're better at this than you think." Willow gestures to the blazing, multi-coloured sunset. "I'd class this as very romantic. Are you trying to woo me or something?"

"Woo you? What century is this?"

Her blush darkens. "You know what I mean."

Abandoning my drink, I snag her shirt sleeve and pull her closer. Willow climbs into my lap, her jean-clad legs spread either side of my waist so we're flush against each other.

"Should I be wooing you?"

Her lips brush over mine. "Too late."

Straddling my waist, her pert breasts are pressed up against my chest, straining to escape her top. I feel my dick stand to attention. We've fooled around, kissing and exploring, but I haven't taken things further.

Part of me is terrified to in case I mess things up. But as the world falls into insignificance beneath us, I decide to be brave. Willow is pretty much the only good thing in my life right now. She's the welcome relief of rainfall after years of scorching drought.

"What are you thinking?" she questions.

"Since you arrived here... fuck, Willow. Everything has changed for me. You make me so happy, and I'd forgotten what that feels like. Until you."

Her mouth grazes along my jawline. "I'm so thankful to have you in my life, Mi. More than you know. Your family saved my life."

"Kiss me, angel."

I don't have the raw sexual confidence of the other two. This is all so new. Her mouth secures itself to mine and her teeth lightly nip my bottom lip.

Going with what feels natural, my hands travel to her hips. She's grinding against me, each shift causing my dick to push harder into her core. When our lips break apart, her breathing is shallow and laboured.

"I don't want to assume anything," she blurts anxiously. "Maybe you don't want to lose your virginity with me, or even at all, or you—"

"Willow," I cut her off. "There is no one I want to share this with more than you. I'm just... hell, I'm a bit nervous. I don't want to disappoint you."

"Disappoint me? You could never."

"I'm not exactly Zach or Killian."

Her lips crush against mine. "That's a good thing, Mi. I want you for who you are, and I love everything about you."

Chest burning with emotion, I lift her from my lap and set her back on her feet. Willow kicks off her walking boots as I grab one of the sleeping bags from inside the tent and spread it across the smooth rock surface.

Holding eye contact, she begins to peel off her long-sleeved t-shirt. The fading sunlight unveils her golden skin and plain bra that she quickly tosses aside, freeing the generous swell of her breasts.

"You are so fucking beautiful."

She smirks, pushing her jeans down. "Hardly."

"Don't you dare. Every inch of you is gorgeous."

Jeans discarded, she's left exposed in bra and panties, her skin lit by the glittering beams of sunshine disappearing from sight. I grab her hand and pull her closer, dropping a kiss on the slope of her stomach.

She inclines her head, lips parted on a breathy moan as I explore her body. There are faint, silvery stretch marks across her curvy hips, evidencing the birth of her little girl. I take time kissing each of them.

"Fucking beautiful," I repeat.

Willow lets me pull her back into my lap. I find the elastic tie holding her long hair up and ease it out. Inky waves spill over her shoulders, and she moans as I smooth out the waves while massaging her scalp.

"Where should I touch you?"

Her lips part on a gasp. "I don't know."

"Tell me. I want to know."

She groans when I sink my teeth into her earlobe and softly bite down. "I want you to kiss me down there. You made me feel so good last time."

Pushing her backwards across the rock shelf, Willow splays out on the sleeping bag. I wrap a hand around her ankle, slowly kissing my way up her leg until I reach her panties. She wiggles her hips, helping me slide them off.

"Fuck, angel. Look at that wet pussy."

Her back arches as my mouth meets the furnace between her thighs. She's wet, her legs trembling with each flick of my tongue. I circle my fingertip over her bundle of nerves, loving the way she squirms.

"Talk to me, Willow."

"Mi," she groans. "I want your finger inside me."

"Good. Keep going."

Gathering moisture on my index finger, I drag my tongue through her folds, feasting on the sweet wetness of her arousal. I've barely touched her, and she's tensing up already.

When I push my finger into her slit, she arches off the sleeping bag, leaning into my touch. I love how receptive she is. Her body writhes with each thrust of my digit entering her warmth.

"Mi," she whimpers.

"Yeah, beautiful?"

"I need you inside of me so bad."

"Tell me how much."

Adding a second finger, I stretch her wider, grinding the heel of my palm against her clit. I've been watching very carefully. I know what she likes. The build-up is just as important as the moment I'll push inside her cunt.

"So fucking much," she mewls.

Easing my fingers out, I make sure she's watching as I suck them into my mouth. Juices burst across my tongue, sweet and hot. I love the way her pupils blow wide at the sight.

"Finger yourself now, angel. I want to watch."

Quickly undoing my belt, I strip my jeans and boxers off to palm my erection. Willow reaches for her own tight entrance. She sighs, tweaking her clit before her fingers slide through her folds and disappear.

Watching her pleasuring herself is an exhilarating sight. She works her pussy in time with my hand stroking up and down my length. The distance between us feels like miles but seeing her toying with herself adds to the delicious tension.

"Does that feel good, beautiful?"

"Not as good as your cock would feel. Please, Mi."

"Make yourself come first. Show me."

Pumping my erection, I watch every last detail of her finger-fucking herself. She slides the two digits deep into her core, panting and moaning as she puts on a show for me. When she grabs her tit and pinches her nipple, she finally bursts.

"I'm coming," she cries out.

Riding her own hand, Willow falls apart on the sleeping bag. She massages her breast and continues to strum her clit until her orgasm has peaked, leaving her gasping for air.

Feeling a little more confident, I retrieve the condom that I suffered the embarrassment of asking Zach for last night. She watches me roll it over my length, still fighting for breath after bringing herself to a peak.

"Get over here, Mi."

She spreads her legs wide open, giving me the best view as she pulls her fingers from her pussy. I kneel between them, squeezing my covered length. Now the moment has arrived, my nerves roar back to life.

Teasing my lips along her inner thigh, I rest a palm on her sternum to lay her back down. Her entire body is flushed with desire. She's all supple curves and fuzz-covered skin. I've never seen anything more perfect.

When the head of my cock presses up against her entrance, I falter and lose my nerve. I'm going with what feels right, but if I somehow trigger her, I'll never forgive myself.

"What is it?" Willow asks.

"I'm just… ah, I don't know. Nervous."

Willow reaches out her hands to grab mine. Using my weight to pull herself back up, she wraps her arms around my neck and clambers on top of me instead.

"I've got you this time," she explains.

Her hand circles the base of my length, guiding it to the welcoming prison of her heat. Hands splayed across her lower back, I grunt in pure, mind-blowing ecstasy when she finally sinks down on my cock.

Everything grinds to a halt at that moment. Years of wondering if my social isolation was the right decision fall aside. Those long, lonely nights no longer matter. I'm right where I'm supposed to be—here with this beautiful creature.

"Bloody hell," I hiss out.

Her hips rotate, taking me even further into her cunt. She chases the deeper angle until I'm buried in her all the way, and it feels fucking amazing. Her walls are tight, squeezing every inch of my length.

"I'm going to move now," she warns.

Lifting herself up, Willow pushes back down on me. Each stroke feels like fire is being injected into my blood. I can feel the slickness of her pussy even through the condom.

"Yes, angel. That feels amazing."

Her bouncing breasts smash into my face, and I wrap my lips around her stiff nipple, sucking hard. She loves it when we play with her tits. Her rosy buds have hardened into peaks, demanding more attention.

No longer afraid, I start to lift my hips in response, meeting her stroke for stroke. She clenches even tighter around me, moaning as I lightly bite down on her nipples.

"Mi. Oh, God."

Watching her work up and down on my dick is better than any fantasy I've had about my first time. It's empowering to see the pleasure she's taking from me, but with gentleness and consideration. I rut up into her, my balls already tightening.

"Okay?" Willow checks in.

"Yeah. I can't last long."

"That's f-fine," she moans.

Breathing hard, I grip her around the waist and lift her off my lap, laying her down on the sleeping bag to shove her legs back open. I want to make her fall apart one more time before I finish.

"Lost patience?"

I pin her unbandaged arm above her head. "I'm not afraid anymore."

Gliding back inside of her in one fast thrust, her pussy is so tight around me, it's like we were made for each other. She's hugging my cock with an exquisite amount of pressure. Our slow, tentative collision heats up.

Pushing into Willow's core, I find a rhythm that feels natural. My strokes speed up, gaining power and confidence. Her nails are raking into my back with each thrust, adding a bite of pain that sizzles through me.

With the cool mountain air kissing our skin, and nothing but cliffs and trees around us, we can both throw our inhibitions aside. This is a place of truth. No pointless façades. I need to batter my love into her soul and leave an impenetrable brand.

"Are you close?" I grit out.

"Yes," she groans.

"I want to watch you come all over my dick."

"Jesus, Mi. Keep going."

Chasing the coil of tension deep inside of me, we fuck like animals in heat, our gasps lost in the endless mountains. Just as the sun winks out of existence, Willow's walls clench tight.

She screams my name loud enough to disturb a flock of birds that take off into the night sky. Managing a final pump, I bellow loudly as I finish a second later. She's limp and boneless beneath me, her chest heaving with each breath.

Exhaustion washes over me and I slump on her chest, burying my face in the soft slope of her neck. We don't speak, enjoying the residual waves of bliss. A breeze caresses our flushed skin, and I can feel our sweat mingling.

"Sure you were a virgin?"

I burst out laughing. "Zach gave me some pointers."

"Wow, how helpful of him."

"When he was done laughing at me, sure." I trace my lips along her collarbone. "Not sure I'll be planning any more brotherly bonding anytime soon."

"He'll be so disappointed."

I lift my head to peer down at her. The crystallised shards that carve out her irises are awash with lazy satisfaction. Rising moonlight reveals the curl of her lips in a smile.

"Micah."

"Yeah?"

"I'm in love with you," she murmurs. "I fucking love the bones of you."

My heart convulses in my chest. "Me?"

"Yes. I've wanted to say that for a long time."

Seized by hope, I kiss her, overcome by a desperate need to seal this moment and ensure she can't take her love back. I need to feel that it's real, and this isn't some foolish dream I'll wake up from.

"Willow." My nose brushes against her cheek. "I've never felt about anyone the way I feel about you. When we're together, I feel... well, happy. Whole. Alive."

"You deserve to be happy, Mi."

"And that's down to you. I love you, Willow. That scares the shit out of me to admit, but it's the truth. I'm in love with every single part of you."

Pulling out of her, I remove the used condom and bundle Willow's naked body into my arms. She snuggles against my chest as we crawl into the tent together to warm up. I slide us into the same sleeping bag, our bare limbs entangled.

"Comfortable?"

She hums in response.

I stroke the curls from her face. "I love you."

"How many times are you going to say it?"

"I love you. I love you. I love you. Want to hear it again?"

Willow giggles. "I got the message."

Through the open flap of the tent, we have a view of the darkened sky, peppered with emerging stars and the gleam of pearly-white moonlight. This far into the barren countryside, nature is undisturbed by pollution.

"I'm so glad I met you all. I can't imagine my life without you guys in it."

"You don't have to," I whisper back. "We will never let you go."

CHAPTER 34
WILLOW

RUNNING - NF

DIPPING the spoon into a ziplock bag of coffee, I add several heaps to the metal saucepan of boiling water heated on the campfire outside our tent. It didn't take much coaxing to reignite the wood.

A headful of messy, sun-streaked hair pops out of the tent's flap. Micah blinks the sleep from his eyes, dressed in an oversized tee and his faded jeans from yesterday.

"Do I smell coffee?"

"It's almost ready."

He gives me a sleepy smile. "Yum, thank you."

Filling the two folding cups with freshly brewed coffee, I settle inside the tent flap between Micah's strong, outstretched legs. His chin lands on my shoulder, the flyaway strands of his caramel hair tickling my neck.

"Beautiful sunrise."

I take a sip of coffee. "I wanted to see it."

The summer sun is blossoming in brilliant hues of orange and pink. It's a watercolour painting coming to life in real time, awash with vivid, unfiltered colours and wisps of morning mist curling over the mountains that surround us.

It's the most peaceful place I've ever seen. I loved the rugged wilderness of the Mexican desert too, even if that place brought nothing but doom into my life. Nature in its rawest forms is so beautiful to me.

"Did you sleep well?" he whispers.

"Well enough. It's so quiet up here. I don't want to leave."

"We could grab Arianna and retire to the mountains. I was serious about that." He chuckles. "Frankly, I'd be fine without seeing another human for the rest of my life."

"I agree with you on that, but somehow, I doubt your twin brother and grumpy cousin would be okay with us running away. Unless they could also come with us."

"There's plenty of wood up here for Killian to chop like a lunatic." Micah pauses to sip his coffee. "And I'm sure Zach can find some trouble to get into even up here."

"He usually does. It's his best talent."

"We could build a huge log cabin and properly live off the land. Grow old together and watch the sun rise every single day for the rest of our lives."

"That sounds so peaceful."

"Doesn't it?" He sighs.

Letting my eyes shut, the dream-like world he crafts with his words tugs on my heartstrings. I can picture my life so clearly now. That was a luxury I never allowed myself to even consider before.

Killian, Zach and Micah all play their very important roles in that hazy vision of hope. I need our family more than I need air in my lungs to breathe, and the way they've accepted me and Arianna into their lives gives me hope.

"I want that with you guys," I admit softly. "I want a future here in Briar Valley. I want us to be safe and find our forever."

"You have us."

"For now."

"Forever," he corrects.

"I wish I could believe you, but I've come to realise that life is fleeting. Nothing is guaranteed in this world. All we have is this moment."

Micah gently kisses my hair. "That's why you have to hold on, angel. Hold the hell on and never let go of those who matter. We can make it. I know we will."

Biting my lip, I watch the mountains come to life around us. "I hope you're right."

Finishing off our coffees, I get dressed and slowly pack up all of our equipment while Micah dismantles the tent. We're ready to start the long hike back into town by the time the sun has fully risen.

I have to get back home for Arianna. I've never spent so long apart from her before. I love my daughter more than anything, but this break was needed. Sometimes, I need to be just Willow for a few hours.

Descending the steep mountain slopes in contented silence, our hands are tightly entwined to safely traverse the tumbling rocks. At the base of St David's Pointe, we begin the hike back into the valley.

The heat has calmed down a little, leaving comfortable warmth behind. When we emerge from the forest and spot Lola's cabin emerging in the distance, my smile fades.

There's nothing worse than returning to the problems you've been running from. I wish I could bottle the peace we found in the mountains and keep it with me as a reminder.

Micah tugs me to a halt. "Willow."

"What is it?"

His smile is dazzling. "Thanks for last night. It meant a lot to me."

"I should be thanking you. It meant everything to me. I love you."

We fall into another windswept kiss. The feel of Micah's lips consuming mine obliterates all of the dread blooming in my heart. Our kiss ends when the sound of laughter reluctantly forces us apart.

"Hi, lovebirds!"

Albie's truck is parked outside Lola's cabin, and he hops out with a stack of paperwork and mail in hand from his usual trip into Highbridge. His smile is far too fucking wide.

"Says the man canoodling with my grandmother!"

Albie's mouth drops open. "I have no idea what you're talking about."

"Leave it out. We've all seen you holding hands."

He offers me a sheepish smile. "I'm in so much trouble. Who else knows?"

"I think the whole town figured it out months ago," Micah helpfully supplies. "So, enough with the cloak and dagger act. I'm happy for you both."

"Thanks, Mi. I'll just… erm, I need to go speak to Lola."

Albie races up the porch and lets himself into Lola's cabin to escape the conversation. We fall into fits of laughter. She's going to freak out when she realises that we all know about them. I have no idea what she's worried about.

"He's screwed." I scoff.

"Lola deserves to be happy again."

"You know what… I think you're right. She really does."

Before we can begin to wind down the cobbled path heading home, Lola's front door slams open again, violently crashing against the exterior. A wild-eyed Killian stomps out.

"Willow!" he yells.

Terror washes over me as he races across the clearing with long, frantic strides. I'm quickly gathered into his arms, and the force of his grip creaks my bones. Smashed into his chest, I wince at the thought of bruises forming.

"Kill… can't… breathe."

His eyes search me from head to toe. "Inside. Right now."

"Did something happen?"

He scans our surroundings with worry. "We need to talk. Not here though."

Half-carried into Lola's cabin, Killian doesn't let go of me until the door is firmly shut behind us. Micah abandons his backpack at the bottom of the stairs, following us into the kitchen where the hum of worried voices welcomes us home.

Packed around the dining table are Lola, Zach, Ryder and Doc. Albie has propped himself up in the corner, grinding his teeth so hard, his jaw looks like it's threatening to break. All of their expressions are stony.

"What's going on?" I ask nervously.

Everyone looks us up and down with palpable relief. I've barely placed my feet on the floor before Zach tackles me into a tight embrace as his forehead clashes with mine.

"You're back. Fuck, Willow."

"I told you that I would look after her." Micah looks around at their matching looks of horror. "Why is everyone going crazy? We're back right on time."

"It's not that," Lola says tightly.

There's real fear swimming in her eyes for what I think is the very first time. I've never seen her look afraid like this. She's always been the strong, unshakeable one, holding the whole town together.

I scan around the room. "Where's Arianna? Was she hurt or something?"

"She's with the other kids." Doc tries to reassure me. "Why don't you take a seat?"

Shaking my head, I walk into Killian's arms. I have a feeling I'm going to need him to ground me in the present for whatever comes next.

Clearing her throat, Lola spares me an apprehensive glance. "Someone contacted us last night with an offer to purchase Briar Valley. A cash buyer."

"You're selling the town?" I frown at her. "Why didn't I know about this before?"

"I'm not selling the town," Lola quickly corrects me. "This offer was out of the blue and entirely unwelcome."

Killian's arms are clenched around me so tight, it aches. The tense silence adds to the pressure building up inside of me. Everyone looks fucking terrified. My dread instantly reignites.

"Who was it?" I ask shakily.

"A realtor," Killian growls out. "Lola was offered three million pounds for Briar Valley."

"Who, Kill?"

"Sanchez Real Estate," Lola cuts in. "Someone called Mason contacted us to make the sale on behalf of his business partner."

The buzz of voices around me fades into insignificance. Those three words change everything. Months of progress vanish. The same wordless terror that drove me to run halfway across the world sinks back into my bones.

"Willow?"

Sanchez Real Estate.

"Breathe, Willow."

He's coming.

"Come back, beautiful."

My vision whites out as the terror of distant memories takes full control. Their voices vanish. The world fades. My breathing halts. I'm falling back into the past, and I can't stop the vivid flashback from swallowing me whole.

———

"Mummy! You're scaring me," Arianna whimpers.

Bundling her tiny frame in my arms, I pin her against my aching chest. Blistering agony is wracking my body, but I stuff the pain down. I don't have time to hurt.

"I'm sorry, baby."

"What's wrong?" Arianna asks.

"It's time to go on that little adventure I told you about."

"Now?" she says sleepily. "It's dark outside."

"I know, but we have a plane to catch. Are you excited?"

She smiles up at me. "Yes! Is Daddy coming too?"

Overcome by a wet coughing fit, I push her away from me so I can retch to one side. Hot blood rises up from my throat, spraying across the back of my hand. My chest and ribs are on fire.

I knew when Mr Sanchez appeared with a shining baseball bat that I was in serious trouble this time. I can still feel it connecting with my ribs, his laughter drowning out the sound of my screaming.

"Mummy? Mummy!"

I stare at Arianna's terrified face. "I'm here, Ari. Daddy isn't coming this time. It's just me and you."

"Yay! Let's go!"

"Shhh. We have to be quiet."

Bundling her into a light coat, she waits by the door as I slide beneath her bed, searching for the loose floorboard by touch alone. I had to change my hiding place after Mr Sanchez ripped apart my room in a drink-fuelled rage.

He was convinced that I was hiding something and beat me bloody when he couldn't get the truth out of me. It took every last drop of strength I possess to bite my tongue until it bled and keep our precious secret hidden. This is our lifeline. Our last chance.

Wrenching the wooden board up, I reach inside to grab the two fake British passports and our limited stack of remaining cash. Melody and Adele. I begged Pedro to get one too, though it was to no avail.

He's the only real friend I've ever had, but with his entire family in Mr Sanchez's mansion staff, he insisted on staying behind to protect them. Instead, he's going to get us to safety and go on the run, far from this hellish house.

With everything packed up, I throw the small duffel bag over my shoulder and take Arianna's hand. We have to creep through the house on silent feet, dodging the patrol of private security that my husband hires for his own protection.

I don't know why he needs bodyguards. There's a lot about his dark and shadowy life that I don't understand. Any questions are met with brutality and violence, so I learned to stop asking very quickly.

I've memorised where the CCTV cameras sit, recording the sprawling estate. We duck and weave our way to the deserted kitchens. Creeping inside, I nearly scream when someone emerges from the darkness.

Pedro raises his hands. "It's just me, Willow."

"Thank God. Is everything set?"

When he moves me into the faint light by the back door, he sees my face and lets out a curse. I can only imagine what I look like right now. I'm lucky to be alive after that beating.

"What the hell has he done to you?"

I press a hand to my abdomen. "It doesn't matter. He's in there with another woman right now. It should buy us some time to run."

Disgust stains Pedro's tanned features. He was born and raised in Mexico City. His father is the head chef of the household, while Pedro was awarded a role in Mr Sanchez's personal security team.

Over the years, we've become friends in a series of quiet, secretive snippets. Whispered conversations. Exchanged smiles. Silent jokes and glimmers of hope. He's kept me alive so many times.

When he approached me with an escape plan after nearly eight years of watching Mr Sanchez's abuse, I broke down, desperately accepting his help. Anything to escape this perpetual hell, no matter the risk to us all. It's taken so long to get everything into place.

"As soon as we're in the air, you need to get out of town," I tell him. "Hell, get out of Mexico. I won't let your family suffer the fallout of our actions."

Pedro seizes my hands and squeezes. "It's going to be okay. I swore that I'd get you out of here, and I will. Both of you. Don't worry about us."

Tugging me against his broad chest, his lips brush mine in a brief whisper. I'm too surprised to respond, letting him kiss me gently, frozen like a statute until his forehead meets mine.

"I'm sorry… I just had to do that. I don't know if I'll ever see you again."

"It's okay."

Meeting his eyes hidden beneath a shock of curly black hair, I feel nothing but gratitude. He's been the only friendly face in this purgatory. In many ways, we've grown up here together, trapped by our separate roles and shared hatred of Mr Sanchez.

"If things were different, I would… you know." I wince as pain blurs my vision. "But we both have people counting on us."

Pedro gives me a weak smile. "I know. Me too."

"I don't know how I'll ever repay you for helping us."

"You can repay me by living. Both of you. Live the best goddamn life you can possibly imagine. Promise me, Willow. Promise me that you'll live."

I press a chaste kiss to his cheek. "I promise."

"Good. Let's go. You have a plane to catch."

Leaving him to swipe his pass and disable the alarm, I grab Arianna and bounce on my feet, anxious to be gone. Once the door has been unlocked using his personal swipe card, Pedro lifts Arianna into his arms, taking my hand with the other.

Together, we slip out into the stifling hot darkness, pierced by the tick of cicadas and cars driving past on the road circling the mansion. We sneak around the outside, heading for the exit used by staff only.

Running in tandem, I see the towering gates ahead, ready to be unlocked with another swipe of his card. A tiny flicker of hope burns in my heart. We're so close. This could actually work.

"Nearly there. Hold on," Pedro pants.

"I can hear voices!"

"Just keep running. Don't fucking stop."

The Devil himself must be watching over us, pulling invisible strings to better serve his games. One minute we're inches from salvation, the next I'm running through the darkness alone as Pedro's hand is ripped from mine.

BANG.

The blast of a gunshot has me tumbling to my knees in fear. Arianna is screaming like a banshee, hitting the ground several metres behind me. But I haven't been shot. Looking over my shoulder, the terror of reality sinks in.

Pedro is splayed out on the moonlit sand, a halo of blood surrounding him. In the distance, voices bellow and the crunch of thick-soled boots running to catch us echoes through the night. I race back, throwing myself at his feet.

"Willow… please," he begs. "Go."

"Pedro! No!"

Hot sprays of blood are spewing between his fingers, clasped over his midsection. He can't move an inch, groaning in agony as the crimson tsunami continues to pour out of him. I can't even drag him, not with my waning strength and injuries.

"Go… find the truck. Go!"

Thrusting his swipe card and a set of car keys into Arianna's hands, he shoves her towards me with his remaining strength. I steady her, trying to stop her from staring at his bloodied state.

"Pedro!" she screams.

"Run, muchacha. Go w-with your mama."

"Are you hurt?" I run my hands over her, searching for blood.

"N-No, Mummy."

"Go then. I'm right behind you, Ari."

I can barely see through my tears, holding a scream back as I bite down on my clenched fist to silence it. The sound of shouting assails us. Security is swarming and starting to give chase.

Arianna slips her bloody hand into mine instead of running as I told her to. She tugs hard, forcing me to find my feet and leave Pedro sprawled out on the sand.

"I'm so sorry," I sob.

Blood pours out of his mouth. "L-Live, Willow."

Crying too hard to think straight, I let Arianna pull me along, her shouting forcing me to move my feet. We break into an unsteady run, both of us struggling to remain upright. It kills me to leave Pedro alone in the darkness, watching us disappear.

"Hurry, Mummy! Pedro said he's coming."

Arianna's frantic voice pushes me to move despite everything screaming in protest with each bruise and laceration. We run. On and on. Legs pumping. Hearts pounding. Dodging bullets and fury following hot on our heels.

I can't let Pedro's sacrifice be in vain. My only friend died to buy our freedom. He couldn't keep us safe, but he got us as far as he could. I just hope his family will know what to do now he won't be around to protect them from Mr Sanchez.

"Faster, Ari," I shout, my courage rising. "Don't stop."

"Is Pedro okay?" She tries to look behind us.

"He's fine. We have to leave him."

Her bottom lip wobbles. "I'll miss him."

"Look, there's the truck. Last one there is a loser! Run!"

With the innocence and naivety of her age, Arianna speeds off, heading straight for the shrubbery that conceals the truck Pedro stashed for us. We're so close. Salvation is right there.

All we have to do is get out of the city undetected and drive a few hundred miles to the smallest airport Pedro could find. The flight is booked under our new identities with three more connecting flights after that.

It will stealthily take us across the continent and away from the monster chasing us. We can't risk leaving a breadcrumb trail behind. He's far too well-connected and powerful to let us go without a fight.

Making it to the truck, I take the set of keys from Arianna and quickly unlock it. She lets me boost her into the front seat, taking the duffel bag from my hands.

"We're going to be okay, Ari."

I don't know who I'm reassuring more—her or myself. As I fire the engine and peel out of our hiding spot, a bullet clips the back of the truck and ricochets off. Arianna screams at the top of her lungs, and I shove her into the footwell.

"Stay down!"

The bullets keep coming, spraying across the thick steel of the truck and shattering the back window in a spray of glass. Pedro taught me how to drive a few summers ago while Mr Sanchez was away on a business trip.

Careening through the night to join the road leading away from hell, I slam my foot on the accelerator and watch the sand-blasted turrets of Sanchez mansion vanish behind us.

We're finally free.

CHAPTER 35
WILLOW

DARLIN' - GOODBYE JUNE

FISTING MY LONG BLACK HAIR, I choke back the scream swimming up my throat. I'm shoving clothes at random into a suitcase, paying no attention to what I'm packing in a panicked state of autopilot.

All I can think is one thing.

Run.

Run.

Run.

I can barely suck in a breath, let alone think straight. There's no time to stop and consider my options. No time to say our prolonged goodbyes. No time to mourn all that we've lost. When we're on the road, I'll let myself break.

All that matters right now is keeping Arianna safe. I'll rip my own bloodied heart from my chest and shred it into ribbons with my bare hands if that's what it takes. My pain doesn't matter. I won't let her go back to that place.

I'll die first.

He won't hurt her again.

Grabbing the fake passports and my wedding ring from their hidden place in my wardrobe, I locate the cash I withdrew from my bank account. Old habits die hard, and I've been stockpiling some of what Lola loaned me just in case.

"Willow? Where are you?"

Rather than shouting back, I let the exploding force of nature find me on his own. Nothing can hold Killian at bay. My bedroom door smashes against the wall, nearly breaking from his brute force.

Huge shoulders brushing the door frame, his fiery eyes bounce between my state of disarray and the semi-packed suitcase. The look on his face sends shivers down my spine. He looks ready to lock me in the damn wardrobe to keep me here.

"What the fuck are you doing?" he thunders.

"Packing."

"I can see that. Why?"

"We have to get out of here before it's too late. Our cover is blown. It isn't safe."

"You're not going anywhere. Put the bloody clothes down."

"I'm sorry, Kill." I swipe the falling tears from my face. "I don't want to do this, but I have no choice. He knows where we are. Arianna's in danger."

"No. You can't leave us!"

I'm unprepared for him to seize hold of my suitcase and throw it against the wall with unimaginable rage. Clothes explode everywhere, raining down on us. His chest is rising and falling with each furious breath.

Taking a step back from him, Killian looks sickened by the fear on my face. I put even more distance between us, hating the way his anger causes me to recoil from the man I know and love more than anything.

"Willow… please."

"Stay back," I warn him.

"I'm not trying to scare you. Fuck! You're safe here. I swore that I'd protect you and I will never break that vow. Let that bastard make his threats."

He launches across the bedroom and imprisons me in his arms before I can run for my life. With his calloused hand cupping my cheek, my body betrays me. It longs to curl into the protection of his embrace.

"You have to stay here," he begs. "Where you belong."

"I can't stay," I whisper heartbrokenly.

"We can protect you. It's what we do." His voice cracks. "Please don't do this to us."

"None of you know what we're dealing with. You can't stop him."

"Then tell us! Don't just run like a coward!"

Shoving him backwards with a snarl, I manage to break free from his grasp. Killian watches me sweep up the fallen clothes and stuff them back into the suitcase. I bolt from the room before he can capture me again.

"Willow, wait!"

Following me into Arianna's bedroom, his laboured breathing fills the silence as I grab the barest essentials from her wardrobe and create a small pile. We'll have to buy more stuff on the road. I can't carry it all.

"Mr Sanchez isn't h-human," I stutter out. "There's nothing you could do to keep us safe. He knows where we are. It's only a matter of time until he comes for us."

"Give us a chance. The safest place is still here."

"No, Kill. I have to leave. I don't have a choice."

"You always have a choice," a voice interrupts.

Lingering in the doorway behind Killian, Zach's panting hard from running over here. His expression is bleak, with so much pain radiating over him, he looks more like his green-eyed twin than the lovable goof I know.

"I'm so sorry, Zach."

"If you're really sorry, then stay," he pleads. "Don't run from your family and home."

"I don't want to go!" I explode, more tears soaking into my cheeks. "Arianna's safety is all that matters now. This isn't about what I want anymore."

"Bullshit!" Zach fists his hair. "You can't do this."

Brushing past him with the handful of belongings, I return to the bedroom and throw them in the suitcase. There's no time for weakness. No space for stupid emotions or attachments. I was weak once. I let myself care. Pedro died because of it.

His death is on me.

I won't let it happen again.

Mr Sanchez won't blink before he kills every single person that stands between us and him. Innocent or not, they will die protecting us. I couldn't live with myself if that happened.

"Please, Willow," Killian implores.

I look up at him. "Stop making this even harder."

His expression is fractured, falling into ruinous grief that contorts his features into a grimace. It's more emotion than I've ever seen from him, and it fucking kills me to know it's my fault.

"You have a choice here, alright?" He stares into my eyes. "You don't have to live in fear. We can all calm down and make a plan. There has to be a better solution."

"I won't let you pay the price for my mistakes."

"Then we're coming with you," Zach declares. "Fuck it."

"You can't do that… your lives are here," I plead with him. "I'm not tearing you away from your home and family to go on the run with me. That wouldn't be fair."

"It's our decision to make," Killian says with finality.

"No, it's not. You will never be safe for as long as you're with us. I refuse to jeopardise your lives like that. If I go now... Mr Sanchez will leave you unharmed."

"I won't let you throw yourself to the wolves, Willow!"

"This isn't your choice!"

The ringing of a mobile phone in Zach's pocket interrupts our heated exchange. He answers, his eyes widening in alarm. I can hear Micah shouting down the line from here.

The second his emerald eyes meet mine, I know I'm too fucking late. Fate has found us. It crept in through the cracks in our defences and laid its poisonous roots again.

"What is it? Zach?"

"Arianna's missing. She isn't in class."

"What do you mean, missing?" Killian spits out. "This is Briar Valley. People don't go missing here. She's probably wandered off or something."

Feeling sick to my stomach, I abandon the suitcase and race out of the cabin. My feet slap against the ground in a punishing beat. Over and over. Desperation fuels my muscles and gives me the strength of mind to keep going.

"Willow!" Killian shouts after me.

Sprinting over cobblestones and twisty paths, I'm heaving and almost doubled over from a stitch when I make it back down into the valley. Zach and Killian are right behind me.

All I can see is Arianna's sweet smile when I told her that we were going on the run. *Ice cream and swimming, Mummy. It's our adventure.* She was so ready to escape the perpetual hell of her childhood and start a new life.

I don't care.

Mr Sanchez can have me.

As long as he leaves her behind.

In the town square, all hell is breaking loose. Lola stands on her porch, shouting orders to the gathered group of residents who are setting out to scour the woods. Albie and Ryder are among them, both armed in preparation.

Harold has his usual hunting rifle propped on his shoulder, and he gives me a stern nod. "We'll find your girl, Willow."

"Please be careful," I urge them all.

"You just wait here for an update."

The group dissipates and Lola waves for me to come in. I'm barely able to climb the porch steps, my body sagging from wave after wave of adrenaline. She wraps her arm around my shoulders and bundles me inside.

"How long has she been missing? Who called it in?"

"Rachel noticed she wasn't playing outside with Johan a little while ago," she answers grimly. "There's a good chance she heard us arguing earlier and ran off."

Nodding through my tears, I try to seize hold of the courage that drove me out of that mansion. She has to be okay. We've come too damn far to give up hope now.

"Grams!" Killian bursts into the cabin.

"In the kitchen," she orders.

We all gather around the dining table. Killian and Zach remain within touching distance like they don't trust me not to disappear on them. Lola paces the floor, a phone clasped in her hands.

The back door rattles before it flings open, revealing Micah, red-faced and short of breath. He rushes at me, his limbs trembling with anxiety. I'm pulled into his arms.

"I checked our cabin and the studio. No sign of her."

"Shit. Where the hell is she?"

"We'll find her," he soothes.

"She could be anywhere. How did I let this happen?"

Lola drops a hand on my shoulder. "This isn't your fault, poppet. We've got our best people out there searching for Arianna. She can't have gone far."

The sound of a sharp knock causes us all to freeze in place. Nobody moves a muscle, our breaths held. It comes again; harder, more insistent.

"What the hell is that?" Zach snarls.

I swallow hard. "It's the front door."

Lola glances between us. "Nobody knocks on my door in this town. They just walk in."

Suffocation threatens to steal my consciousness. I feel myself gawp as Killian reaches into the waistband of his jeans, pulling out a revolver. I've seen plenty of hunting rifles around town, but this is the real deal.

"Where on earth did you get that?" Lola exclaims.

He double-checks the chamber is loaded. "Not important. I need to be able to protect my family."

Another knock punctuates the air of shock. It comes again. Three times. Repeated and demanding. Staring into Killian's eyes, all I can see is Pedro looking back at me as he took his last breath.

"Everyone stay here," I say weakly.

Killian cocks the gun. "Like hell."

"This is my mess. I'll deal with it."

"Get your ass back here, Willow!"

Dodging past them, I inch through the cabin towards the insistent knocking. Their footsteps follow me. Through the frosted glass of the front door, three shadows are outlined, becoming clearer as I approach.

"No," Killian roars.

Before he can get himself killed, I grab the handle and throw the door open. The world ends in an instant. Safety is an illusion, one that I've spent months force-feeding to myself.

I was wrong.

We were never safe.

Mason is leaning against the door frame while smoking a cigarette. His interested gaze scrapes over me, lips pulled taut in a fake smile. I'm sickened to realise that I'm actually glad to see him and not a pair of frozen blue eyes.

"Mrs Sanchez. So good to see you again."

"What are you doing here?" I demand.

His two associates flank him on both sides. They're packing weapons and staring at us behind their dark sunglasses and blank facial expressions.

"Call it helping out an old friend." Mason flicks his cigarette aside. "How's the holiday? I have a feeling it's about to be cut short."

Reaching into the pocket of his designer suit jacket, he pulls out a smartphone. When he offers it to me, his smile never once faltering, I have to force myself to take it. The weight in my hands feels like a death sentence.

Killian raises his gun next to me, training it on the soulless demons at the door. They simply stare back without a care in the world. Not even a gun frightens them.

"H-Hello?" I whimper.

There's an intake of breath on the end of the phone line followed by deep, sinister chuckling. I nearly throw my guts up on Mason's expensive shoes. That voice has only existed in my nightmares since I left Mexico.

"Darling wife." Mr Sanchez sighs. "Oh, how I've missed the sound of your sweet voice. You've hidden for a long time. I'll give you credit for that."

I bite my lip hard enough to break skin. Blood slips into my mouth, mingling with the burning bubble of vomit sitting inside my throat. I can almost see him in front of me, an evil shade projecting himself across the continent.

"Nothing to say to your husband?" he sneers.

"Leave me and my daughter alone."

"*My* daughter. She's fucking mine, Willow."

Killian tries to grab the phone from me, and Zach holds him back. Even he knows not to intervene in the Devil's game.

"You found me then," I say unsteadily.

His laugh makes my skin crawl. "My my, haven't we gotten brave. Don't worry, we can discuss your insolence later. How is my daughter?"

"Arianna is fine."

"Fine?" He snickers. "She was kidnapped by her mentally unstable mother. Quite shocking behaviour. I'm sure she's anxious to return home to her daddy."

"I did not kidnap her."

"I think law enforcement would disagree."

My grip on the phone tightens. "You're a monster. I saved her from you."

"But who is the world more likely to believe?"

"I'm her mother!" I shout down the line. "That's who the world will believe."

"An unfit mother at best," Mr Sanchez fumes. "Here's how this is going to work, wife. You'll return home and I'll leave your precious family alone. That's the easy option."

Seizing the flicker of courage in my belly, I let out a strangled laugh. "What's the hard option? Because that sure as hell isn't happening."

His voice is low and dangerous. "I've already dealt with your little bit on the side. Pedro begged for mercy before I finally ended his life."

"Pedro's dead," I gasp. "I saw him die."

"It took longer than expected to break him, but he revealed your new identities soon enough. Mason here was following up a lead when you fell right into his lap."

"You're lying!"

"You know, it took several weeks of torture for Pedro to reveal your little plan to me," he boasts proudly. "I was surprised by how well he held up."

My stomach heaves. I can see it so clearly. I've watched my husband beat enough people, staff and hired skins alike, remaining protected by his money and influence.

With a small fortune, you can make any problem disappear. Even dead bodies. Mason is just one of many sources that provide my husband with his vices and make them disappear without a trace.

Mr Sanchez snorts. "His entire family too. I had to hire a whole new team. When I slit their throats one by one, Pedro watched. That's when he finally broke."

Killian is close enough to hear our conversation. His face shifts to frightening calculation. Before I can stop him, he seizes the phone from my grip and hits the loudspeaker button.

"If you dare to step foot in Briar Valley or threaten my girl again, this will be your fate, you son of a fucking bitch. Listen well."

The blast of a shot nearly bursts my eardrums. I scream out, clutching my head. The fired bullet slices through the air and sails straight into Mason's left-hand bodyguard.

It suckers him in the stomach and he falls, tumbling backwards down the porch steps to hit the ground with a thud. His wails reverberate around us, and he tries to stem the bleeding from his torso with two red-stained hands.

"Does that hurt, you bastard?" Killian hisses.

Mason and his one remaining crony take a step back. I don't think either of them expected our defiance. The brute on Mason's right side rests a hand on his weapon.

"Your girl?" Mr Sanchez utters.

"Damn fucking straight, she is. You won't ever touch her again. Show your face in Briar Valley and I'll take great pleasure in killing you myself."

"You think I'm afraid of some stupid British cunt?"

Killian's laugh is hard as nails. "You should be."

"I have the resources to wipe this place off the face of the earth. Don't think that I won't do it. I want my wife and daughter back. Now."

"They don't belong to you anymore," Zach speaks up. "Willow is ours."

"Don't you know who I am?" Mr Sanchez blusters. "No? You will soon enough. I'll burn your pathetic town to the ground to take them back by force if I have to."

Movement in the nearby tree line catches my eye. There's a flash of clothing and dark hair, then long legs racing across the clearing to reach us. Ryder moves fast, closely flanked by his uncle.

They're at the bottom of the porch steps before Mason can register them, both of their hunting rifles raised. The pair slowly advance to bring our intruders into point-blank range.

"Don't move," Albie warns, the barrel of his gun nudging Mason's head. "I'll blow your goddamn brains out and ensure the police never find your body."

"Friends of yours, Mrs Sanchez?" Mason laughs.

Ryder's teeth are bared, his gun in place. "You're both trespassing. Leave our property or say your goodbyes. Choose."

"You folk have real balls," Mason replies, despite the gun at his head. "I think I like it out here. It'll make demolishing your land even more satisfying."

"I'll die before letting you demolish my land." Lola has stepped forward and narrows her eyes on him. "Clear out. Final warning. We are permitted to use force."

I almost sag from a wave of relief when Rachel and Miranda desperately wave at us from across the clearing. Between them, sobbing and wide-eyed, Arianna is sucking her thumb. Harold stands at her side, his rifle tucked away.

He found her.

She's safe.

"Get these sons of bitches off my land," Killian barks. "Show your faces again and I'll put bullets in them. Welcome to Briar fucking Valley."

Ryder and Albie grab their targets and walk them away from the cabin, smashing their rifles into their heads to drive the threat home. Mason doesn't give a fuck. He's still laughing under his breath at the whole thing.

"This isn't over, Willow!" he yells back.

The phone is still clenched in Killian's hand. Mr Sanchez's voice crackles back to life, his amused cackle setting off explosions of pain in my head. It's too much to bear.

"Hell of a show. Pack your things, wife. I'm coming for you."

Silencing his rambling, Killian drops the phone and swiftly crushes it beneath his boot with a loud crunch. I gawk down at the shards of smashed plastic and glass. Mr Sanchez's threat is still ringing in my ears.

"Ryder," Lola shouts. "Get this snivelling weasel off my lawn!"

With Mason escorted back into the passenger seat of his SUV that's parked in Lola's garden and ruining her flowerbeds, Ryder returns for the final asshole. Killian has to assist, the pair of them dragging his semi-conscious hide to the car.

"And don't come back," she bellows.

With his still-standing bodyguard behind the wheel, Mason rolls down the window to stick his head out. The maniacal smile on his lips sets my teeth on edge.

"Always a pleasure, Mrs Sanchez."

We all watch them reverse backwards, knocking over several of Lola's plant pots along the way. The language muttered under her breath would make even Killian blush.

None of us speak again until the car has turned onto the mountain road leading out of the valley. Mason gives us a wave before he vanishes into the forest.

"Willow," Lola keens. "Are you okay?"

I brush her worried hands aside. "Arianna."

Across the clearing, my little girl breaks free from Miranda's grasp. We both run towards the other, meeting in the middle of the flower-strewn grass. I skid to a halt and gather her into my arms with a choked wail.

"Mummy!" she cries.

"Shhh. I'm here, baby."

"I'm sorry." Her body shakes with sobs in my arms. "I saw the car, and I thought it was Daddy. I hid just like you taught me to."

"You did good." I stroke her hair. "I'm proud of you."

"Is Daddy coming?"

"No, Ari."

Keeping her pinned against my chest, I glance up at Rachel and Miranda. They're holding each other tight, looking ready to bolt as far away from us as possible. Even Harold looks unnerved, though he smiles at me.

Behind them, all of the children have snuck out of the barn and gathered in the garden to watch the commotion. Aalia is with them, petrified and crying her eyes out as she holds them back from approaching us.

Shame punches me in the chest. I did this to them. This is my fault. I've brought trouble to their home… to all of their lives. The sleepy town of Briar Valley is in danger because of me. I never should have come here.

"I'm scared," Arianna weeps.

My heart shatters in my chest, breaking into irreparable pieces. "I'll make us safe, I promise. He won't find us again."

EPILOGUE

BLINK TWICE - JOY OLADOKUN

KILLIAN

LETTING the axe hit the demolished block of wood, I swipe hair from my eyes. The darkness has kept me company for several hours along with the torment of my thoughts. Endlessly playing, over and over again, they refuse to abandon me.

Danger.

Danger.

Danger.

Each thud of the axe hammers that word into my brain. It's a sick, taunting mantra, tattooing fear into the fabric of my weary heart. I've never felt fear like the moment Micah called and told us Arianna was gone.

We tucked them both into bed to let them rest. The poor kid was hysterical after the afternoon's events. Still trembling, Willow was hollow-eyed as she whispered goodnight and climbed in with her little girl.

It hurt to see them both like that, returning to the terror that drove them here. Nothing we said could fix it. Not even Lola could get through to her granddaughter.

Taking a long draw from my beer, I glance at the cabin across the road. The lights are still off. Zach and Micah left both girls to sleep a while ago. I know we should give Willow some space, but fuck. That's the last thing I want to do right now.

We almost lost them.

That was a close call.

Dragging myself inside, I grab another beer from the fridge and wrench the cap off with my teeth. I should have put a bullet between those fuckers' eyes when I had the chance, even if it got me arrested.

"Kill? That you?"

"It's me," I grumble back.

Both splayed out on Zach's bed, a half-empty bottle of liquor between them, I find the twins exchanging furtive whispers. Taking another sip of my beer, I prop myself against the doorframe.

"Ran out of wood to chop?" Zach asks, lacking his usual fire.

"I couldn't just sit there after today."

Micah takes another drink from the bottle. "We were talking about what to do." He winces as he swallows. "Zach thinks we should leave Briar Valley with them."

"Seriously?" I frown at him.

Zach nods solemnly. "It isn't safe for them here and I won't let her run alone."

"We're all safer here," Micah disagrees with him. "We can defend ourselves."

His twin cuts him a scathing look. "Nowhere is safe."

I've never once considered leaving Briar Valley. Never. Even when my parents died and left me up shit's creek with two kids to look after, it wasn't an option that crossed my mind. This has always been my home.

It's the last remaining connection to my folks, and the place where I intended to grow old. All that changed when she came along. Willow. The town isn't the centre of my world anymore... she is.

"What do you suggest then?" Micah sighs.

"We leave immediately. Tonight, if we can."

"No," I interrupt. "Micah's right. Running without a plan is risky and stupid. We can protect Willow and Arianna from here. The whole town is behind them."

"And if this nutjob threatens the other people hiding here?" Zach points out.

Violence hums through me in a low current.

"Then we kill him."

Micah flinches. "Kill him?"

My mouth waters at the thought. "I don't need any help in that department."

"This plan doesn't work if you land yourself in prison for first-degree murder."

"I won't get caught then."

"You expect us to help?" Zach scoffs.

Reaching into the pocket of my jeans, I finger the cool item buried inside. "Nope, Dimitri Sanchez is my kill. But there's something else we need to do together."

Palm outstretched, I show the sparkling engagement ring to them. I dug it out of the family safe earlier. It was a crazy fucking idea that formed in my mind after coming so close to losing both Willow and Arianna.

I let the twins study the white-gold band, studded with a gleaming sapphire. It was my mama's ring, left to me in her will. Since the idea hit me, I've become certain it's the right call.

Willow is my whole fucking world. I don't give a shit what it takes, I have to keep her by my side for the rest of our lives. This life means nothing to me if she's not in it.

"Kill?" Zach's eyes are saucer-like.

His twin looks equally unnerved, but neither of them have run away screaming. They're leaning closer, even if it's subconscious. I'm offering them their whole damn futures on a platter with this ring.

"Do you both love her?" I ask bluntly.

Zach bites his lip. "Yeah. I do."

Micah doesn't hesitate, echoing his twin with a nod. "Yes."

Pinching the engagement ring between my fingers, I turn it over in my palms, considering the glistening jewel cut into a perfect teardrop shape. Mama always had good taste. It's a beautiful piece, and one that I never thought I'd use.

"We all want a future with Willow."

"More than anything," Micah agrees.

Zach nods too. "Of course."

"She wants to run away right now. We have to give her a reason to stay." I meet their widened green eyes. "This could be it. We need her to realise that we're her forever."

A nervous smile lights up Zach's face. He manages to tease one from me too, and Micah joins us with an excited grin. All three of us end up chuckling and clasping hands.

"This is a bit insane." Zach barks a laugh. "She might say no."

"It's going to work," I return.

Raising the bottle of whiskey into the air, Micah toasts and takes another large glug. He passes it to Zach next, who has a guzzle for courage before handing it to me last.

"You sure?" I ask them both.

Zach clears his throat. "She makes us a family, Kill. I want that. I want her."

Glancing at Micah, he meets my eyes without fear. "I can't imagine a world without her in it. I want her in our future, whatever it looks like. I'm sure."

"Then we do this right," I say, taking my own gulp of the whiskey to seal our deal. "The three of us will propose. We'll make her see why she has to stay."

"Arianna is going to scream her ass off."

Micah rolls his eyes. "She's going to make us have a princess-themed wedding, isn't she? This is going to be a circus even by Briar Valley's standards."

Zach claps his twin on the shoulder. "At least it gives Killian an excuse to get his toes painted again. We all know how much he loves that."

"I can still break your nose, Romeo."

"We're going to be tied together for life," he continues smugly. "You'll have to put up with me until we're old and grey."

"Or he could kill you before then," Micah suggests. "Willow will get by with the two of us. Plus, more room in the cabin. It's a win-win."

Breaking into laughter, we drink more liquor to celebrate. We have a plan. A future. A fucking reason to be together again. I have my family back, and it's because of Willow. She brought them back to me. That woman changed everything.

I never planned to commit to a long-term relationship in my life, let alone one with Zach and Micah involved. But right now, I want nothing more than to see Willow's finger with our ring on it, tying her to all three of us forever.

That's worth fighting for.

It's a risk I'm willing to take.

We all pass out by the end of the empty whiskey bottle. I'm the first to rise from my drunken stupor when the sun is up in the sky again. Splashing my face in the bathroom, I throw on a fresh pair of jeans and a scruffy flannel shirt.

Stepping outside in the early morning air, the first thing I notice is that Ryder's latest truck refurb is gone. They weren't supposed to be selling it until next week. Unease settles in my heart, and I quickly walk across the road.

I don't feel fear. It's not something I'm acquainted with. Or rather, it wasn't until I had something to lose. But as I approach my deceased parents' cabin, I'm struck by the emotion so intensely, I break into a run.

"Willow?" I scream.

Tearing my way through the kitchen, I fly into the master bedroom where we tucked them in last night. The bed is empty, sheets tangled in a ball. I spin around in a circle. The wardrobe is ajar and cleared out.

"Fuck! Willow!"

Flying into Arianna's bedroom, it's the same story. The wardrobe is bare. Her favourite hair ribbons and dresses are gone. The stupid butterfly sculpture that Micah first gifted her isn't on her bedside table anymore.

Gone.

Gone.

Fucking gone!

The suitcase that had been left discarded on the floor has vanished, along with the few valuables that Willow had in her cabin. It's like she never existed. If I couldn't see the new paint and furniture, I'd doubt anyone ever lived here.

Nobody answers my screams.

I'm utterly alone.

Fisting my long hair, I fight the urge to smash the entire cabin to pieces. If that slimy bastard Sanchez has them, they can't have gotten far. I'll raze the forest to the ground and let Briar Valley crumble if that's what it takes to find them.

"Killian!"

Spinning on the spot, I train my terrified gaze on Lola and Albie, both stepping inside the cabin. They look rumpled and exhausted. Lola's expression is completely distraught, ageing her into a fragile slip of a woman.

"Grams?"

Her lip wobbles. "I'm sorry."

I haven't seen her look like this since her husband died. She could barely stand from the weight of her crushing grief. That same emptiness is buried in her eyes now.

"They're gone." I gesture around me. "We have to look for them. He's got them!"

Lola takes a step towards me, her hands outstretched. "No, he hasn't."

"What the fuck do you mean?"

Albie gulps hard. "She's safe, Kill."

A red haze descends over me. Rage. Blistering, volcanic rage, rising in a pyroclastic cloud that will destroy everything in its wake. I face off against them both, my hands shaking either side of me.

"Where is Willow?" I spell out.

"She's gone," Lola answers.

"Gone... where?"

She wipes her teary eyes with the edge of her cardigan. Albie's arm is tightly wrapped around her, ensuring she doesn't slump into a devastated puddle.

"I couldn't stop her from leaving," Lola weeps. "I tried, Kill. I really did."

Spinning around, I search the cabin again, my desperation rising. All I want is a single clue. A scrap of home. Something to tell me that Lola's wrong. There's nothing left.

"Where is she?" I growl at them.

"Willow left last night." Lola's smile is drenched in anguish. "She stopped to say goodbye around midnight. We gave her some cash and a burner phone."

"No. That can't be true."

"She wouldn't tell me where they were heading. It isn't safe. I'm so sorry, Killian."

I lose all sensation in my body. It drains out of me like a popped balloon. All of last night, we were plotting our future and celebrating what should have been the best day of our lives. Asking Willow for her hand in marriage.

"You're lying. Why are you saying this? Where is she?"

"It's true, Kill," Albie mutters. "Ryder dropped them off in the city several hours ago."

"Ryder? Where is he? I'll fucking kill him!"

His face darkens. "You leave him out of this. He only wanted to help."

"Help? This is suicide!" I yell.

Albie steps in front of Lola as if to protect her from me. "Sanchez knew where she was. This is the only way to throw him off the scent. Willow knows that."

"No! Bullshit!"

Crying freely, Lola pulls a folded piece of paper from her cardigan pocket. She offers it to me—a dagger for me to stab my own heart on. I make myself take it, despite the razor blades scraping down my throat.

"She told me to give that to you."

I unfold the scrap of paper, tracing a finger over the swirls of ink, smudged by the occasional smeared teardrop. Looking up at the ceiling, I take a breath and make myself look back at the letter.

Killian, Zach and Micah.

Growing up, I didn't understand what love meant. All I can remember was feeling alone. The miles I travelled to reach Briar Valley was the loneliest journey of my entire life.

I didn't know if it was real.

Or if I'd ever make it.

You three weren't part of the plan. All I wanted was to give Arianna the chance to live a life that she could be proud of. Hell, one that I could be proud of. It's all I ever thought about. Being a good mum.

My heart wasn't available, but that didn't stop you from stealing it regardless.

Killian, with your gruff smiles and hidden sweetness. Zach with your compassion and dedication to your family. And Micah with your brave soul, wrapped in so much pain. I love every broken piece of you guys.

You gave me a family.

You gave me a future.

You gave me a reason to live again.

Perhaps I'm selfish for asking this of you, but please, don't hate me for making this choice. You can be angry. Be furious. But please, I beg of you... don't hate me.

I have to protect my daughter.

She will always come first.

I'll live in hope that one day, we will meet again. Until then, please keep my heart safe. I'm enclosing it in these pages for safekeeping. I don't need it if you're not here with me.

I love you all.

Know that.

Forever your girl,

Willow.

Something wet and unknown spills down my cheeks. I can't bring myself to brush the moisture aside. Let it pour. She's earned that much. Willow has taken the final icy wall around my heart and punched her fist through it.

"What did it say?" Albie asks.

"She isn't coming back."

Reaching into my pocket, I pull out the engagement ring, holding it in the palm of my hand for them both to see. Lola glances between me and the ring while Albie's eyebrows rise into his hairline.

"You were going to propose?" she asks.

"Yes." I let my eyes fall shut. "We love her. Enough to ask for forever."

"Oh, Kill. I don't know what to say."

My world ends. Drops off a cliff and falls apart at the seams. The tears are unleashed. I can't stop them now. My last scrap of hope dies a slow death in the ink-stained pages of that letter.

"We love her and now... she's gone. We've lost her."

To Be Continued

BONUS SCENE

MICAH

Rain falls in rapid, cleansing sheets. It soaks into the woodland that surrounds Briar Valley—pine and birch trees mostly, their trunks smooth as they stretch high above me to kiss the cloud-laced sky.

Petrichor lays thick in the air as the rain soaks into the ground, releasing the heady fragrance. Even dressed in a black puffer jacket I stole from Zach's wardrobe, the evening dusk brings with it a frigid breeze that dimples my wet skin. I'm soaked to the bone.

It's day three without art supplies. Caught in another depressive episode, I fucked up my timings and didn't re-order quickly enough. Now I'm stuck waiting for my resupply delivery to arrive. Painting and sculpting are my lifeblood. The oxygen my lungs require.

Without my art, I have no way to release the swirling tornado of grief and despair that took root within me when our father died. When I stared at his dead body as a scared little kid, locked in the bathroom with a corpse until the authorities arrived, the first storm swept in.

I've been caught in sorrow's hurricane ever since.

Trudging up the muddy incline, I'm almost back into town. Lola's cabin isn't far from here, in the centre of Briar Valley. The cabin I share with my twin brother, Zach, and our cousin, Killian, is secluded from the rest of the town and sits above the valley.

As the sun dips below the mountains, highlighting the individual raindrops, I follow the glowing warmth that emanates from the cabins through the tree line. I can see Lola's home from here. It's a sprawling monster surrounded by a cherry-red, wraparound porch.

Briar Valley is my home. The mountainous sarcophagus that imprisons my state of perpetual disillusionment. I stopped caring about the rest of the world a long time ago. Not even the comings and goings of Briar Valley's residents holds my attention.

In many ways, I'm dead already.

Caught in the body of that traumatised child.

Dark thoughts swirl around my mind as I lumber on. At least when I'm knee-deep in clay or watercolours, I don't have time to contemplate the sad state of existence I've created for myself. But inevitably, the paints run dry. That's when my regrets bubble up.

I'm about to emerge into the clearing that leads through town when an unfamiliar sight stops me. A figure stands at the edge of Lola's porch, observing the final streaks of fading sunlight that penetrate the storm clouds. But it isn't our town's formidable leader.

It's a woman.

A stunning, bruised angel.

It isn't her coal-black hair, hanging in perfect ringlets, or her curvaceous yet still bird-like frame highlighted by her drenched clothing that catches my attention. My brain filters through those details with vague interest, preoccupied by studying the look of pure contentment on her features.

She stares up at the stormy evening sky, her eyes flitting over the emerging stars peeking through the clouds like glittering diamonds. My feet freeze, rooting me to the spot, as a small smile plays across her lips. I can see her mouth moving, the words inaudible.

I don't know what keeps me paralysed, unable to look away. It's not like I haven't seen a pretty girl before, though I've never had the confidence to approach one, unlike my twin—Briar Valley's resident playboy. Zach is a ladies man, through and through.

The fascination flowing through me goes beyond mere physical attraction, though. As she toes off her shoes and walks barefoot down the porch, following the patter of raindrops still falling, her smile blossoms. And with it, my curiosity grows.

I watch her feet dig into the saturated grass, her eyes closing briefly like she's savouring the feel of earth beneath her soles. My heart thunders painfully when she does the unthinkable. The mysterious stranger fucking *twirls*, dancing in the pouring rain.

Her head is thrown back, pink tongue outstretched to catch the sweet release of each raindrop. She spins in a haphazard spiral, smiling so broadly, it's a wonder her mouth doesn't split open. Dripping ringlets swing out all around her in a halo.

So beautiful.

My fingers are practically aching with the need to paint this ethereal being —to capture her visible relief, her gratitude, the way she radiates with childlike joy at the natural wonder all around her. A simple rainstorm has provoked that heart-stopping smile, and it fascinates me.

I should have more self-control, but before I know what's even happening, my feet are carrying me forwards. I emerge from the woodland, stomping through the hammering rain. Panic lances through me as her head snaps in my direction, but it's already too late to sprint back into the shadows.

Tightening my soaking wet coat, I contemplate whether or not to try it anyway. But she's right in my path to home. I have no choice. My ever-present anxiety is spiralling out of control with each step closer to the woman I've been inadvertently spying on.

"Zach? What are you doing?"

Jaw clenching, my eyes dart around, searching for an escape route. Of course, she thinks I'm him. It isn't often that I feel jealous of Zach—I care much less than I used to—but his ability to act like a functioning human being is something I'd happily steal.

Instead, I avoid eye contact as I reply.

"I'm not Zach." My throat constricts tightly. "Wrong brother."

The woman stares at me amidst the rainfall. Her apprehensive hazel eyes touch every part of me in an oddly intimate perusal that makes my spine tingle. I can practically see her cataloguing the small details that differentiate me from my identical twin brother.

"You're not?" She tilts her head, droplets of water clinging to her thick lashes.

"I'm Micah." I rub the back of my neck, cheeks burning with shame. "We haven't met."

"Micah?"

Her voice is a melodious tinkle, caressing my senses like the tips of a violinist's fingers skating over bare strings. It holds me captive, beneath the piercing weight of her brown and green eyes, despite my embarrassment.

"Twins," I explain hastily.

"I'm so sorry," she rushes to apologise. "I didn't know."

Another hot burst of awkwardness threatens to hold my tongue hostage until I swallow it down.

"And you are?"

Bare feet shuffling, she glances around. Up close, I can see the bruises that mark her exposed skin in more detail. Her face is all shades of purple, green and yellow, swollen from what I assume was a severe beating. Only fists can leave bruises like that.

Who is this woman?

Why is she here?

And... why do I care?

"Uh, I'm Willow. New around here."

In an attempt to suffocate the barrage of questions trying to spill out of me, I squint through the rainfall into the distance towards the valley. I knew I should've stayed home. My studio is a mess—I should be safely cleaning up in my isolated bubble right now.

A minuscule glimpse in my periphery tells me that she's waiting for a response. Like any sane human would easily provide, right? If I were Zach, I could crack a joke, perhaps invite her over for coffee. Make her feel warm and at ease.

But I'm not Zach.

I'm only half a man.

With insecurity screaming through me, I lose what little courage I found to approach her. I can't even say goodbye. My legs carry me through the bustling wind, back into the safety of darkness and shadows. It takes great self-control not to look over my shoulder.

The memory of her twirling in the wet grass follows me home. It's like her ghost is dancing beside me, twisting and turning, soaking up each droplet of rain to savour the sweet thrill. Has she never felt rain before? What evil has she endured to appreciate a simple storm so much?

No, Micah.

Internally scolding myself, I stomp back to the cabin I share with my brother and cousin. I'm itching to escape into the studio to paint a frolicking figure in shades of charcoal, her ringlets spinning all around her, but I need to change out of my sodden clothes first.

I step inside, greeted by the sight of Killian and Zach watching television over a pack of beers. The hollering of football hooligans emanates from the screen as a game plays out. Their attention is fixed solely on me while I struggle to strip off Zach's sopping-wet coat.

"You went hiking?" Zach frowns at me.

I shrug in response.

"In the rain?" Killian clarifies.

"It was dry when I left."

"You're soaked."

"I'm fine," I deadpan.

His blonde, scruff-covered jaw tightening, Killian looks away from me.

He's the mother hen. Which is a polite way of saying he's annoyingly overprotective, to the point of damn near suffocation. The grumpy asshole loves to breathe down my neck.

"When's your delivery coming in?" Zach asks pointedly.

My skin prickles with awareness.

"I dunno."

"This week?"

He doesn't need to stare at me to know what's going on. Call it intuition or a twin thing, but he's always had an uncanny ability to see past the crap I peddle to them when questioned. I wish he would just accept my shit excuses instead.

"Ryder's going to let me know."

"I could run into town," he offers. "Pick up some emergency stuff?"

I shake my head. "It's alright. You know I'm specific about my supplies."

With a sigh, Zach nods. "Yeah."

Turning away from them, I'm heading for a hot shower that's calling my name when the question that's burning my insides breaks free.

"Who's the new girl?"

"Willow?" Killian immediately growls.

I glance over my shoulder. "We... crossed paths. What happened to her?"

His throat bobs, darkness crossing his rugged features. "A car accident, apparently. Load of shit if you ask me."

"Why would she lie?" Zach counters.

"I'd imagine for all kinds of reasons. I don't trust her."

My twin chortles. "You don't trust anybody, Kill."

"Fuck off, kid."

"Just telling the truth."

Zach isn't wrong. Our cousin is the mistrusting type. For all his fierce dedication to his family, he treats strangers with contempt. No one matters to him beyond those he's deemed worthy of his love and attention.

"I'm going to find out why she's here," Killian vows menacingly. "And who the hell put those bruises on her."

"Why do you care if it was an accident or not?" I blurt out.

His burnished-brown eyes flick over to me, full of accusation. "I don't. Why do you?"

"I... I just..."

Trailing off, the heat that I thought I'd extinguished from my cheeks returns. They're both staring at me again now. *Awesome.* Ignoring them completely, I shove through the door leading to the cabin's hallway, letting it slam behind me.

Back in the safety of my room, I slump against the hewed wood. My breathing is heavy, rapid. The emotions I strapped on my hiking boots and headed out of town to escape have all flooded back. I know why I found her soft smile and palpable joy so enthralling.

Because I want to feel that.

I want to feel alive like she was in that moment.

But I know… I never will.

PLAYLIST

LISTEN HERE:
BIT.LY/BRIARVALLEY1

OUTRUN MYSELF - Jack kays & Travis Barker
mars - YUNGBLUD
Broken - Isak Danielson
lonely - Machine Gun Kelly
Euthanasia - Post Malone
Forest Fire - Brighton
Never Feel Alone - The Dangerous Summer
Home - Gabrielle Aplin
To Love Somebody - The Howl & The Hum
Please Don't Be - Hazlett
The Only - Sasha Alex Sloan
Flaws - Bastille
We Were The Same - Matt Maeson
Bury Me - Friday Pilots Club
The View Between Villages - Noah Kahan
I Won't Jump - Maldito
Sad Days - Presence
Wildfire (Alternate Version) - SYML
Crazy In Love - Eden Project
Where Do I Even Start - Morgan Taylor Reid
Silhouette - Aquilo
Take On The World - You Me At Six
Don't Hold Me - Sandro Cavazza
Purple - Wunderhorse

Never Say Never - The Fray
Tread On Me - Matt Maeson
Lie To Me - The Dangerous Summer
I Won't Give Up - Chance Peña
Something In The Orange - Zach Bryan
Another Life - Motionless In White
Someone To Break Your Heart - Emma Jensen
RUNNING - NF
Darlin' - Goodbye June
Blink Twice - Joy Oladokun

WHERE WILD THINGS GROW

BRIAR VALLEY #2

DEDICATION

For all the single parents, fighting for a better future for their children. No matter the cost of starting over, again and again.

I think you're pretty fucking awesome.

TRIGGER WARNING

Where Wild Things Grow is a small town, reverse harem romance, so the main character will have multiple love interests that she will not have to choose between.

This book is dark in places and contains scenes that may be triggering for some readers. This includes human trafficking, forced marriage, domestic abuse, sexual assault, PTSD, bereavement, self-harm and unplanned pregnancy.

If you are triggered by any of this content, please do not read this book.

"We plant the seeds beneath the bruise. It hurts like hell, but then we bloom."

- Kristin Kory

PROLOGUE

IF I COME HOME – SUZI QUATRO & KT TUNSTALL

WILLOW

Rolling over in the warm sheets covering me, I let loose a contented sigh. The heat from three familiar bodies sandwiches me in until I'm bathed in comfort and reassurance.

Home.

Safe.

Protected.

I can feel Killian's heartbeat pounding through his burnished skin that's pushed up against my chest. Zach lazily strokes my hip from behind while Micah kisses his way up my exposed leg.

Between the three of them, the grip of sleep releases me, and I feel the furnace between my thighs roar to life. I'm on fire. Tingling. Aching. Begging for the relief of their touch.

"You boys sure know how to wake a girl up," I groan.

Killian's lips brush my earlobe. "You're ours, baby."

"And we'd do anything to protect you," Zach adds.

Micah's mouth reaches my pubic bone. "Anything."

With my eyes still shut, I smile at their antics. "I love you three so much it scares me. I'm terrified that I'll lose you all."

"You'll never lose us," Killian growls.

"But I can't let Mr Sanchez hurt you," I reason. "I have to keep you safe from him. He'll use you against me."

"Nothing can tear us apart, angel. We're a family and not even you can change that now. Come home and let us prove it to you."

"Home?" I repeat, feeling more awake.

Killian's voice deepens into an angry rasp. "Come home. Stop running. We need you."

Loud, insistent knocking causes my heart to suddenly explode in my chest. I shoot upright in a tangle of sweaty sheets on the cramped, queen-sized bed and wrestle my eyelids open.

Nothing.

Empty.

Alone.

The tears well up in my eyes like they do every morning when I realise the bed next to me is empty. Nothing but my loneliness and regret surround me as another day of torture begins.

It was all a dream.

I'm not home.

I'm still lost.

The sound of knocking comes again, mirroring the beat of my heart. When the door to my bedroom slams open, Arianna bursts in with a scowl on her face, still dressed in pyjamas.

She doesn't smile much anymore. It kills me inside, more with each passing day, to see her fade back into the scared little girl I birthed alone seven long years ago.

"The door, Mummy. Someone's here. It's too early."

Reaching under my pillow, I grab the switchblade that I keep stashed in case of emergencies. Arianna's eyes grow wide with fear. I motion for her to hide under the bed, safely out of sight.

"Mummy?" she whines.

"It's okay, baby. Keep nice and quiet for me now."

"I'm scared."

"You're okay, sweetie."

Once she's hidden, I hold the switchblade tight and pad into the dreary kitchen at the centre of our cheap, dated apartment. The knocking on the front door is constant.

I'm barely dressed in panties and a loose t-shirt, my now-short, raven hair barely brushing my shoulders. The warm, golden tan that I developed in Briar Valley has been replaced with pale, ghost-like skin.

With the switchblade in my hand, I leave the safety chain on the door and open it an inch, peering out into the crisp winter air.

"Seriously?"

A familiar face waits for me, framed by long black locks and a forced smile. Her bangs cover the twisted scar marring her face, but her moss-coloured eyes haven't changed.

"Let me in," Katie pleads. "It's cold out here."

"You're early by several hours. We agreed you'd never do that. Arianna is hiding under the bed!"

"I know, darling. I'm sorry, but we need to talk. Inside."

Sighing heavily, I shut the door then slide off the chain before reopening it on her weary face. Katie lets herself in then slots the deadbolt back on behind her.

Taking in my disgruntled state, she raises an eyebrow at the switchblade still held ready and waiting in the air. I set it down on the kitchen counter and force air into my lungs.

"Planning to stab me, huh?"

I glare at her. "I thought you were here to kill me."

"Not today." Sadness coats her words. "Get dressed while I put the kettle on."

"Did something happen?" A vice clamps around my hammering heart. "I haven't spoken to Lola since last week. Did you hear something? Are the guys okay?"

"I'm not here to talk about Briar Valley." Katie collapses in a chair at the dining table. "Go sort Arianna out. You don't want her to hear this."

Blinking rapidly, I force myself to move, unable to form words. My mouth has turned into the Sahara Desert, my legs trembling beneath me as I return to the darkened bedroom.

Plastering on a fake smile for Arianna's sake, I crouch down to peer at her underneath the bed. She's curled up in the farthest corner, hugging the butterfly sculpture that Micah gifted her to her chest.

"Is it safe to come out?" she whimpers.

"Yeah, Ari. It's safe."

"I'm still scared." Her eyes are squeezed shut with tears spilling over her cheeks. "I don't think I want to come out yet."

My heart twinges at the palpable fear in her voice. This is no life for a little kid. In many ways, it's worse than when we lived in the mansion. I've torn the only home she ever knew away from her.

We're so isolated out here and stuck in this crappy apartment twenty-four hours a day, too scared to even set foot outside for fear of being recognised at any given moment.

It's a nightmare that feels like it will never end, stretching on endlessly, agonisingly, into the bleak unknown. For as long as Mr Sanchez breathes, we will never be safe. Not here. Not anywhere.

"You can stay under there if it makes you feel better." I stretch out my hand. "Or you can take Mummy's hand and sleep in a big girl's bed. How does that sound?"

"Will you sleep with me?" Her eyes peek open.

"I need to talk to Katie for a moment about some stuff. I'll come cuddle with you after, if you want?"

Her eyes narrow in defiance. "I want to cuddle now."

"We can watch the new Frozen movie again later," I try to sweeten the deal. "I'll even let you break open the emergency ice cream. How's that for a deal?"

Arianna manages to nod. "Okay. Katie's here?"

"Yeah, she's here. I'll come wake you up when it's time for breakfast."

Settling Arianna into my vacated bed, I tuck the covers up to her chin. Her blonde hair has grown so long now, it's spilling down to her lower back. She blinks up at me with jewel-like, bottomless blue eyes.

"I like your bed, Mummy. It's nice and big."

"That's because I have a bigger body than you, Ari. Keep eating your greens, and you'll grow up to be big and strong too."

"How big?" she demands sassily.

"Taller than the tower that Rapunzel was trapped in."

Arianna's sadness swims back to the forefront as her eyes glisten with tears again. "We're in a tower too."

I drop a kiss on her forehead. "I know, baby. It isn't forever though, I promise."

"I want to go home."

The sorrow in her voice is like a knife in the heart.

"We can go home soon, and you'll see your friends again."

"You said that last month," she deadpans. "And the one before."

Arianna sucks her thumb into her mouth, rolling over and giving me her back before I can muster up another crappy excuse to appease her. It takes everything in me not to break down.

I stare for a moment, completely gutted by her words and letting the moisture leak down my cheeks. I'm the world's worst parent. She's suffering along with me, and I can't fix this shit.

Pulling on my discarded sweats from the floor, I flee before she can hear me sob. I'm too ashamed to even attempt to console her. There's nothing I can say to make this any better.

Back in the kitchen, Katie has filled two chipped mugs with fresh coffee and sat back down. She lights a cigarette with shaking hands, slowly inhaling before letting the smoke out.

I take the seat opposite her, pulling a steaming mug into my hands. Not even the hit of strong coffee can alleviate the cloud of exhaustion that has infected us for the five months we've spent hidden.

"Since when did you start smoking inside?" I ask tiredly.

"Sorry." She quickly puts it out. "Long night. We had two new families arrive at the centre. I had to get them temporarily set up in a hotel until an apartment becomes available."

Believe it or not, Katie was the one who saved our asses when we fled. She has connections in local councils across the country due to her work resettling families for the government.

She managed to get us in this crummy apartment when we were hopping from one cheap hotel to another, desperate to stay off the radar.

In a weird way, she stepped up when I needed her the most, and I had no one else in the world to turn to. For the first time in my whole life, I had a mother there to save me.

"Katie," I prompt, my grip on the mug tightening. "The news?"

Staring into the depths of her pitch-black coffee, her mouth is pinched tight with tension. My leg begins to bounce underneath the table, expelling the nervous energy eating away at me.

"Since you've dropped off the radar, Dimitri Sanchez has been playing the sympathy card—claiming you had a nervous breakdown and left with Arianna."

"I already know this," I snap.

"He's used your disappearance to his advantage through a slick PR campaign that's removed any and all suspicion from him."

"The news has been full of his face for months," I spit out. "He's been releasing those stupid statements, playing the doting father and husband."

Katie nods. "His campaign to discredit you has been very well-coordinated. The entire world is convinced that you ran away with Arianna and are endangering her life."

Tears prickle my eyes. It hurts to be accused of deliberately harming my daughter, even when it's far from the truth. The world doesn't hear that. Mr Sanchez is the only voice they care about.

"But we're still safe, right? He hasn't had a location on me since Briar Valley. He doesn't know about you either."

"Sanchez hasn't found you, Willow. This location is still secure and safely off-grid for the time being. That's not why I'm here."

"Then why are you here?"

She rakes a hand through her hair. "I know you don't want to talk to him, but Ethan Tarkington has been in touch again."

Shit. Ryder's boyfriend. I've dodged his phone calls and emails for months now, unwilling to assist in his company's investigation.

"What does he want?"

"He works for Sabre Security, who has been investigating a global, multi-million pound human trafficking ring for the last twelve months."

"He mentioned it to me when we were in Briar Valley. That has nothing to do with us or Mr Sanchez, though."

"Willow," Katie whispers bleakly. "Dimitri Sanchez has been named as a person of interest in their case along with several other men. Sabre is asking for victims to come forward."

Her voice is drowned out by the loud ringing in my ears. Ticking. Buzzing. Screaming. Ten long years of tears, pain and anguish drown out everything else as her words sink in.

"A human trafficking ring," I repeat, my mouth feeling like cotton wool. "I don't understand."

"You told me what he did to you, sweetheart. That's textbook human trafficking. You may not be the only person he's hurt."

I stare deep into her worried eyes. Nothing is computing. What he did to me was beyond the realms of evil, but the thought that there could be others like me out there is unhinging my sanity.

"He's a suspect?" I say in a robotic voice.

She nods. "It's early days, but I've seen the file. It's definitely him. From what Ethan has told me, there are many players involved. He's one of the big ones."

A hissed breath escapes my clenched teeth before I drop my mug. It shatters against the worn kitchen floor, spilling coffee and sharp ceramic shards across the room.

"Willow." Katie recoils.

"N-No!"

"Just breathe for me and think this through. Ethan needs your help to bring Dimitri Sanchez down."

"I c-can't do that… He's too powerful. He has friends everywhere, and I won't risk Arianna falling back into his hands."

"Every second that he's allowed to continue living freely poses a risk to you both and other potential victims. He has to be stopped."

I'm under no illusions. I know what he's capable of, and if the world knew how many people he'd hurt, Mr Sanchez would be locked away for the rest of his life.

That doesn't mean I'm strong enough to do anything about it. Going public would mean facing the demons I fled from when I left Mexico and confronting my past head-on.

"I can't do anything to stop him," I repeat shakily.

"We have the chance to prove that you were trafficked and abused by him." She clutches my hand tight. "We could take him down, Willow. Do you understand what I'm saying to you?"

I slowly nod, feeling the tiniest flicker of hope for the first time in five long, agonising months of emotional hell. This is what I've been waiting for all along.

"I could go home to Briar Valley."

CHAPTER 1
WILLOW

RIDICULOUS THOUGHTS – THE CRANBERRIES

TUCKING my short black hair into a worn baseball cap, I slide a big pair of sunglasses on then check my reflection in the rearview mirror. I'm well-disguised.

The pale blue sweater I'm wearing is loose, hiding my slimmed-down body. Eating isn't something I manage much of these days. I'd probably starve if Arianna didn't need to be fed.

Once a week, I brave the trip to the local supermarket, leaving Arianna safely behind. I have no choice but to leave her alone. It's a risk, but so is breathing while Mr Sanchez still roams free.

Shaking out my hands, I switch off the car engine then recheck the handful of notes that Katie passed over yesterday in an envelope. It's enough to get us through this week.

"Just go inside," I whisper under my breath. "He isn't here. Walk in there, and do what you need to do."

Sliding my hand in my pocket, I finger the sharp switchblade. Mr Sanchez has proven that he can still reach me, even here in England, far from the darkness of his mansion.

Nowhere is safe for us.

Not anymore.

The news stories about our disappearance are relentless as he continues his savage campaign to discredit me by any means necessary.

I'm the evil, unstable mother who kidnapped her daughter and left the golden boy of the real estate business high and dry. The entire world hates my guts, and they don't even know me.

Grabbing a shopping trolley, I keep my chin tucked down and walk into the supermarket as casually as possible. My grip on the trolley is white-knuckled.

The security guard spares me a glance, frowning ever so slightly, but he soon turns his attention to the next shopper. I blow out a heavy breath, repeating my inner-mantra.

Breathe, Willow.

In and out.

Get it done.

I keep my baseball cap and sunglasses in place even inside the supermarket, offering me some sense of protection. I'd rather look like a lunatic than risk being spotted.

By halfway through the weekly shop, my palms are slick with nervous sweat, and I'm itching to run at full speed as far away from this place as possible.

Every person who walks past causes me to freeze, then I have to mentally dig myself back out of a hole of panic to keep walking.

When the cheap burner phone in my pocket vibrates, I let out a shuddered breath before answering the phone call. She's never a second late for our scheduled calls.

"Hey, Grams."

"Willow." Lola sighs in relief. "It's so good to hear your voice."

"It's the same voice you spoke to last week and the week before." I grab a bottle of juice. "How is everything? Are you okay?"

"We're all fine," she answers vaguely.

"What's happening in Briar Valley?"

"The first snow fall came a few days ago. Albie is outside gritting the road as we speak. You should have seen the kids, all screaming and running around."

I smile to myself. "Sounds lovely."

"It was. How's the weather there?"

"It's cold here, but no snow. Arianna keeps waiting with her nose pressed against the window. She's determined to see it for the first time, but I don't think we're far enough into the countryside."

Lola sniffles, and I know she's started to cry. She rarely gets through one of our scheduled chats without shedding tears. The last five months have taken a heavy toll on us all.

Tucking the phone against my shoulder, I reach over an older gentleman to grab some fresh bread, stacking it on top of the canned goods that I also picked up.

"I'm sorry," Lola says. "It's just... we miss you both so much. It isn't the same here without you. The town feels so empty."

"You spent two decades without me," I remind her. "I know it's hard. This isn't easy for us either, but you know that I have no other choice. It wasn't safe to stay."

"I know... it just doesn't make it any easier. It's been months, Willow. Surely it's safe for you to come home now?"

"He's still on the news every single night appealing for information," I grit out. "That isn't safe, and you know it. Not while the world believes the lies he's spent months spouting."

Lola clears her throat. "Perhaps one day it will be safe again. I wish we knew when that day will come, though."

Agony lances across my chest as I battle to remain strong for her sake. My tears are only allowed to make an appearance when I'm alone. I have to be a mum first—strong and unwavering.

"How are...?" I hesitate, swallowing hard. "The guys?"

"They're alive, poppet."

"That bad?"

"I won't lie to you and pretend like everything is fine when it isn't. They're hanging by a thread, much like I'm sure you are."

The backs of my eyes burn, and I clamp my hands into fists until my nails dig into my palms. I have to keep my anguish at bay. I can't afford to fall apart here. It isn't safe.

"Micah crashed Killian's truck last week," Lola reveals. "He knocked over a lamppost."

"He crashed the truck? What was he even doing driving it?"

"He was drunk," Lola admits.

My heart seizes, freezing into a lump of solid ice, impenetrable and alone on a mountain of misery. I'm stranded in a barren wasteland, without them to hold me close.

"Micah's drinking again?" I ask in a low, broken voice.

"Forget I said anything."

"Grams—"

"How is Arianna? Do you need anything?"

"Don't do that. I need to know. How bad is it?"

Heading towards the checkout counter, I freeze when someone stops in front of me. I make myself take a breath when panic grips my throat. It's just another shopper. They don't even spare me a glance.

"He's hurting, Willow."

A bubble of anxiety lodges itself in my throat. "What about Killian and Zach? Aren't they helping him?"

"They have their own feelings about your departure to contend with, sweetheart."

"I see."

If not even Zach is capable of staging an intervention for Micah right now, things are worse than I'd feared. I've broken them all.

"I wish I could tell you something better, but the fact is, the longer you're away... the more it breaks them. I'm starting to think they've given up hope of ever seeing you again."

Leaning against the cart, I cover my mouth with my spare hand, grateful for the sunglasses covering my streaming eyes. Not even my public surroundings can hold the tears back now.

"Willow? You still there?"

"I'm here," I choke out.

"I didn't mean to upset you. Let's talk about something else. Do you need more money? I want to help you."

"Katie... Um, she gave us some cash. We're fine. I don't need your help."

"Please," Lola begs. "You don't have to do this on your own."

I let out a strangled laugh. "I am on my own. Just like I always have been."

"You're not. Maybe it's time to come home. These news stories, it's all bullshit. He can't hurt you, and you can't keep running forever. You have to face this monster sometime."

"I can't do that."

"This plan is doing more harm than good now."

"It isn't safe. I can't come back until it is."

"This investigation could take years," Lola argues. "What are you going to do? Hide until it's all over?"

Composing myself, I resume pushing the trolley with one hand. "Katie told you, then. So much for privacy."

"Ethan wants to help you, poppet. He's a good man. The entire team at Sabre Security is very capable. They can help."

"I wasn't trafficked, Lola," I whisper in a fierce voice. "He was my husband and an abusive asshole."

"You're in denial. You have to face this."

"Denial? Seriously? Give me a break."

"Come home," Lola demands. "It's been five months. Dimitri Sanchez has slinked back to his shady corner of the globe and long since stopped checking if you've come back to Briar Valley."

"That doesn't mean he won't check again at any moment and threaten you all to get to me. I can't let that happen, Grams."

"Please… Just come home."

I swallow the scream attempting to claw up my throat. "I'm sorry, but I can't stop running until he's dead or behind bars. I'm not discussing this anymore."

"Willow, wait—"

Hanging up the call and switching off the phone with numb hands, I feel like the floor is caving in beneath me. Those damned words have echoed in my brain since Katie's visit.

Human trafficking.

Lola's right… I'm burying my head in the sand and feeding myself a pack of lies to scrape together whatever shallow comfort I can find. It isn't working, but I'm out of options here.

Checking out on autopilot, I stuff groceries into bags at random. My mind is too busy yelling and going into self-destruct mode.

It's not safe.

You have to run.

Arianna's at risk.

The cashier gives me an odd look when I smack my fist into my forehead and whimper under my breath. I barely manage to hand over a stack of cash, my hands are shaking so badly.

All I can think about is getting back inside the safety of the old, beaten-up car outside that Katie lent us. After randomly throwing bags in the boot, I climb into the driver's seat and slam all the locks on.

Only then do I let myself crumble completely, slumped over the steering wheel as my lungs wheeze and struggle for air. My vision is fuzzy from a lack of oxygen as a panic attack seizes me.

In my mind, a deep, grumpy voice takes over. Previously, Mr Sanchez taunted me, but now another man haunts my darkest moments. His absence delivers the worst pain imaginable.

Picturing Killian's familiar, fire-lit eyes, his mouth curved down in a scowl, I imagine him whispering to me.

Just breathe, princess.

In and out.

I've got you.

"I miss you so fucking much," I cry, my cheeks stinging with tears. "I never should've left. I hate myself for hurting you all."

Searching for the lump of cool steel still resting in my coat pocket, I clutch the switchblade in my trembling hand, choking on endless sobs.

In these moments... Micah always comes to me too. Staring into my eyes with those forest-coloured orbs of pure intelligence, he offers me a tiny smile, just like he did when he found me bleeding all those months ago in the bathtub.

You don't need to hurt yourself anymore.

You're not alone.

"I'm alone, and I deserve to be."

You made a promise.

Please don't do this to yourself.

"This is all I have left, Mi."

Blocking out his imaginary voice, I flick out the blade and roll up the sleeve of my sweater. New, shiny scars mark my skin. Anxiety is a fucking bitch, and I'm a slave to it now more than ever.

This is the only thing that gives me the strength to plaster a smile on in front of Arianna and be the best parent I can be despite all this carnage.

Even though every time I cut myself to cope, I feel like I'm failing Arianna and failing myself too. It's the single source of control I have left as we freefall through our destroyed lives.

Dragging the blade across my arm, I release a long breath, tasting the relief of oxygen at last. Warm blood runs down to my elbow, and I quickly grab a pack of tissues from my handbag.

We're not living, stuck here in limbo. I'm existing for Arianna yet failing her all at once. What if Lola's right? Is this the worst mistake of my entire life? Have I doomed us all?

Shaking my head, I wipe my eyes then roll my sweater down to hide the fresh cuts. I have to go home. One foot in front of the other. That's how I survived before, and it's how I'll do it again.

Finding that awful, empty space that kept me going for ten long years, I'll continue to float there, inches from drowning, until someone comes along and pulls me out again.

CHAPTER 2
ZACH

IT'S ALL FADING TO BLACK –
XXXTENTACION & BLINK-182

PARKING RYDER'S truck outside the bar, I kill the engine and study the hordes of people packed inside through the steamed-up glass. Saturday night is in full swing with all the locals gathering inside and spilling out onto the snow-covered pavement.

The thump of shitty karaoke makes me wince from here. Some inebriated moron is killing cats in there with that awful screech. Checking my phone, I scan Trevor's text again.

> Trevor: You need to take Micah home before I kick his ass out onto the street. He's already punched someone and broken a table.

"Great," I mutter to myself.

Turning up my coat collar, I hop out then slam the door a little harder than necessary. My twin is being a self-destructive dickhead at the moment, and I'm so over it.

Wrestling my way through the sweaty, leering crowd inside, I manage to get to the bar. Trevor's eyes connect with mine from behind the counter, an annoyed scowl plastered on his face.

"Took you long enough to get here."

"I'm here now." I cross my arms. "Where is he?"

"Bathroom, last I checked. This is the third time this week." He fills up a pint then passes it to an awaiting customer. "I'm not his babysitter, Zach. It needs to stop."

"You think I don't know that?"

"He's in here all the damn time, drinking himself into an early grave and pissing everyone off. Next time, I'll toss him out."

"Calm down. I got the message."

Grabbing Lola's credit card from my pocket, I slide it across the bar. Trevor eagerly takes it then rings up the outstanding tab.

"Give yourself a generous tip as well. I'll go scrape Micah's drunk ass off the bathroom floor."

Trevor slides the card back. "Good luck, kid."

Picking my way to the back of the crowded room, I slip into the men's bathroom. Immediately, the bitter stench of vomit, spilled beer and cigarettes assails me.

Jesus fuck.

This is really not how I planned on spending my Saturday night. Truthfully, I'd like to be at the bottom of a bottle too, but I have to save my stupid twin from himself instead.

"Micah!" I shout angrily. "Where the fuck are you?"

Groaning comes from the farthest stall. I duck down to peer underneath the door after finding a familiar pair of paint-splattered Chucks peeking out.

He's passed out on the filthy floor, curled up in a tight, semi-conscious ball next to the toilet bowl. Charming. It's one of the worst states I've found him in of late.

"For fuck's sake." I gingerly nudge his limp foot. "Micah. Wake up. It's time to go home."

"Piss off," he whispers.

"No can do."

Managing to wrestle his eyes open for a second, he takes one drunken look at me and groans. His eyes screw shut again.

"Just be glad it's me picking you up and not Killian," I reason. "He would take you to a quiet corner and shoot you between the eyes with the mood he's in."

Taking a coin from my wallet, I use it to pick the lock on the stall door. Micah hasn't moved an inch. I doubt he's capable of even walking right now, judging by his liquor-fuelled scent.

Ducking inside, I slide my hands underneath his gangly arms then drag him up to rest against the wall. He's lost a lot of weight recently, given his entirely liquid diet.

He promptly slumps against me, unable to hold himself up. His head drops on my shoulder, and I can feel the pain that's still radiating through him. He hasn't drowned it out yet.

"How much have you had to drink?" I demand.

"Leave... alone... Z-Zach."

"That's not going to happen. You can sleep it off on the way back, but you've got to answer to Lola this time. She's mad at you for pulling this shit again."

"I'm allowed... drink if... want to," he slurs.

"You'll be off to rehab in no time if you keep this shit up. Hold onto me, little brother. I've got you."

"Three m-minutes younger."

"Yeah, yeah. I know."

With his arm wrapped around my neck, I drag him out of the bathroom, his head limply lolling forward. Trevor waits outside to help lift Micah so we're sharing his weight between us.

He's a decent guy. Most people in his position would just call the police and have Micah thrown in the drunk tank for being such a disruptive mess, night after night. He calls me instead.

"Thanks, Trev. I appreciate your discretion."

"Get out of my bar, the pair of you. Go on, beat it."

With a final nod of thanks, I wrestle Micah all the way outside and back to Ryder's borrowed truck. It's like trying to fit an octopus into the front seat as he starts to drunkenly fight me.

"Get the fuck off me," he growls.

"Stop it, for God's sake!"

I try to pin his wrists, but when he clocks me in the face with a strong punch, I lose patience. Spitting blood, I slam him against the side of the truck, knocking the air from his lungs.

"Micah! You're a mess. Don't start with me."

"I said let go!"

"No!" I shout back. "You're my brother and my responsibility."

When he tries to punch me again, I duck the blow and slam him even harder against the truck for a second time.

"Get your stupid ass inside before I knock you out. I'm not afraid to do it either. Don't test me, Mi."

Just when I think he's going to relent and climb in, Micah's face hardens. He lunges forward, slamming his forehead against mine hard enough to send me stumbling backwards.

Using the distraction to attempt to run back to Trevor's bar, he stumbles in the direction we just came from. I spit more blood on the ground and grab his dirty denim jacket before he can get far.

"Stop it!"

Using momentum, I throw him to the pavement, and he lands with a hiss of pain, staring up at me with hazy green eyes.

"Did you just headbutt me?" I yell, gaining the attention of several nearby people. "Jesus Christ. I don't even recognise you anymore. Who the hell are you?"

Rather than answer, he lays there pathetically, rubbing his bruised tailbone. One of the customers from outside the bar walks over to us with a sympathetic expression.

"You need a hand with this one?"

"Thanks, man."

"No problem. Looks like he's a handful."

"To say the least," I scoff.

Between us, we get Micah strapped into the truck's passenger seat, then I slam the door in his stupid face. The guy returns to his friends, leaving me to catch my breath.

This is a fucking shit-show.

Micah has been on a downward spiral for months. He managed to hide it at first, but as Christmas approaches, the last few weeks in particular have been pretty messy.

There's only one person who can save him from himself, but unluckily for us, she's disappeared off the face of planet Earth. When Willow left, she took all of our hope with her.

Nothing was left behind but three empty husks of the men we used to be, with none of us functioning or able to get through the day. By saving herself and her child, she ruined us all.

I wish I blamed her.

I wish I hated her.

I can't do either.

Back behind the wheel, I find Micah's passed out again, leaving me in blissful peace. The drive back to Briar Valley passes in silence with only the quiet chatter of the radio in the background.

Getting back up the mountain road in the icy, snowy conditions is a nightmare, even with the treads that Ryder fitted on the wheels last week when the first snowfall hit.

After several near misses and sliding back down an icy patch of rock, I have to call it quits. We're going to get into a nasty accident if I keep pressing on in the steadily falling snow.

"Fucking perfect."

Micah's silence answers me.

Peeling off my coat, I drape it over him then tuck it around his body to keep him warm. I can see my breath in the truck with the engine off, but at least he won't get hypothermia while asleep.

It's a long, miserable night in the freezing cold. Snow settles on the windscreen, and I shiver in the driver's seat, my hands frozen into two lumps of ice. Micah stirs as dawn breaks.

"Oh God," he grunts.

"I hope your head is killing you."

Shifting in his seat, he looks over at me. "Shit. You're shaking."

"I'm cold. We got stranded in the snow."

"Well... double shit."

When he notices my coat piled on top of him to keep him warm, Micah's eyes duck in shame. I wordlessly accept it back and slip it on to warm myself up again.

"What happened?"

"You were drunk," I huff out. "And acting like a cunt again. Thanks for the punch too."

His gaze sweeps over my face where I know at least one dark bruise has formed. My face aches from the punches and headbutt. He's lucky I didn't leave him in the snow to die.

"Fuck, Zach. I'm so sorry."

"Are you? If you were really sorry, we wouldn't be having this conversation at all. I told you to stop drinking after the accident."

"I can't—"

"If you're about to give me some bullshit excuse, spare me," I interrupt. "You made promises then broke them all over again. Now you can apologise to Grams instead."

Lips sealed, he can't even nod. His entire posture is carved with palpable self-hatred. As much as I want to punish him for being a selfish jerk, it hurts to see him in so much pain.

"Where is she?" Micah whispers.

"I don't know, Mi. Not here."

"It's been months. She should've come home by now."

I swallow the lump gathering in my throat. "Willow is never going to come home. Haven't you realised that by now?"

"Don't fucking say that, man."

"It's the truth, whether you want to hear it or not."

The winter sun begins to crest on the horizon, highlighted by impending storm clouds as the next dumping of snow prepares to arrive. We have to move fast to avoid it.

"Buckle up," I order shortly.

Wrestling with his belt, Micah doesn't bother arguing with me again. He's torturing himself by holding out for Willow to return. Giving up that pointless hope will make this easier for all of us.

Sweeping the snow from the window screen, we gingerly take off and continue up the mountain. The snow has settled into a slippery ice rink, so I drive at a snail's pace to remain in control.

It's another hour before we make it into town safely and in one piece. Frigid sunlight sparkles on the compacted snow, and the daylight reveals an awaiting welcoming committee.

Killian sits on Lola's porch, his head in his hands. The sight of him causes my heart to stutter in fear. I quickly park up the truck, narrowly dodging a dangerous bank of snow.

"Kill!" I shout after climbing out.

His head doesn't lift.

Leaving Micah to struggle out of the truck alone, I sink through huge snow drifts and manage to clamber up Lola's porch steps. Still, Killian doesn't respond to my shouts of his name.

"Kill? What happened?"

When he does look up, the sheer intensity of grief burning in his eyes steals my breath. He's been crying. Unshakeable, terrifying Killian, unaffected by the whole world, has sobbed his eyes out.

"What is it?" I repeat.

All he can do is shake his head.

With the fear of God settling in my heart, I abandon him and run inside the cabin. It's deathly quiet. The usually crackling fireplace is empty.

No freshly baked cookies or brewed coffee scents linger in the air. Something's wrong. Lola is always up at the crack of dawn, baking and setting about her town duties for the day.

And Killian hasn't been awake before midday for months, let alone stepped outside to brace the real world. Just seeing him sitting there was a shock to the system.

Following the faint murmur of voices upstairs, I come across the next obstacle on the staircase. It's Ryder. He's staring at the phone clutched in his hands, the screen displaying an unknown number.

"Ry? What the fuck is going on?"

His gaze crashes into me. "Zach. You're too late."

"Too late for what?"

I watch his Adam's apple bob. Ryder's eyes are bloodshot and swollen too. He stands up then leads me down the hallway where he clasps my arm tight.

"It's Lola. Something happened last night."

My throat constricts. "Is she okay?"

Ryder shakes his head. "We think she had a heart attack. It all happened so fast."

Trying to push past him to burst into Lola's bedroom, he holds me back, keeping me pinned against his chest. His voice is an agonised rasp.

"She's gone, Zach. I'm sorry."

No.

This can't be happening.

Not Grams.

"This is some kind of sick joke." I shove him backwards. "Where is she? What do you mean she's gone?"

"Zach," he placates.

"No!"

Pushing past him, I reach her bedroom then race inside. The awaiting scene tramples on the remains of my heart. Albie is crouched next to the bed, holding Lola's limp hand.

On the left, Doc is talking in low whispers with Rachel and Miranda. Everyone looks wrung-out and pale. Exhausted. Tear-streaked. I look between them before facing Lola's body.

"Grams?" I croak.

Albie looks over to me. "Zach. She's… gone."

"No. This isn't real."

Approaching the bed, I fall to my knees as they fail to hold up my weight any longer. The moment I touch Lola's papery, pale skin, I feel just how cold she is. Waxy. She's already left us.

Reality sets in then. Cruel and painful. I'm staring at her dead body, bereft of the warmth that encapsulates every inch of Briar Valley. That light has vanished from sight.

"No," I croak. "Grams… No."

It doesn't bring her back. No amount of sobbing or screaming at an uncaring God will make her eyes lift. I snatch her hand and let my head crash into the bed, hiding my tears from sight.

Dead.

Dead.

Fucking dead!

I remember the moment when I realised my father had passed on. The emergency services removed him from the bathroom beneath a white sheet, leaving a shell-shocked, younger Micah behind.

I'm staring at the same emptiness. Hollowed out and left to rot. With a scream tearing at my aching throat, I shout endlessly, begging Lola's eyes to reopen. Just once. Even a flutter.

There's nothing. Not a single twitch. A breath. A whisper of life. She's dead and gone. I didn't even get to say goodbye.

I saw her a matter of hours ago. She gave me her credit card last night and told me to bail Micah out again. I vowed to bring him over the second we got back so she could give him a talking to.

"Zach," Albie says in a strangled voice. "I'm sorry, son."

"When?" I squeeze out.

"Only a couple of hours ago."

"I wasn't here."

"You couldn't have known." Ryder hovers behind me. "Everything happened so fast. You know she's had high blood pressure for years."

"I doubt recent stress helped matters," Doc comments. "Lola's health had been suffering for a while now, but she didn't want to worry anyone."

Hearing that she's been battling with her health alone triples my pain. Lola's there for everyone, yet she couldn't even tell us she wasn't well. That hurts more than anything.

"Did… Did anyone try to revive her?"

The look in Albie's eyes is haunted. "I tried. It was too late. She was gone before I even had a chance to fight back."

The bubble of vomit in my throat is searing hot and almost spews out. I feel sick to my stomach. While I scooped Micah off the bar's floor and worried about him… Grams was dying.

"That son of a bitch," I snarl.

Albie startles. "Huh?"

"I was out there saving Micah's stupid fucking ass while Lola took her last breath. She needed me. I wasn't here."

"Zach," he attempts. "Don't think like that."

"I wasn't here!"

Before he can stop me, I abandon Lola's bedside vigil and thump back downstairs. Snow is swirling in the early morning air as I launch myself outside to find my worthless twin.

He's slumped against the tailgate of the truck, peering into the thick, dense snow clouds high above us. Killian still hasn't moved, staring through his silent, never-ending tears.

"You!" I shout.

Micah stirs, his still-hazy eyes sliding over to me. "What?"

"This is your fucking fault!"

Marching up to him, I grab his denim jacket and let my fist sail straight into his face. Micah doubles over, clutching his now red-stained nose.

"What the hell, Zach?"

"I was out dealing with your shit last night and Lola was alone. She died alone because of you."

The colour drains from his face.

"D-Died?"

I jab a thumb over my shoulder. "Go and see for yourself. Lola's dead. She had a heart attack last night."

Staying to watch the realisation dawn on his face isn't an option. I can't keep it together for a second longer. Climbing back into the truck, I slam the door to keep everyone else out.

This is going to break us all.

We need Willow.

We need our family back.

CHAPTER 3
WILLOW

HELL – OLIVVER THE KID

DIPPING the sponge back into the bucket of soapy water, I wring it out then resume scrubbing the sparkling kitchen floors for the third time this week.

They're spotless and permanently smell of bleach, but I can't lay in that bed for a moment longer, staring at the ceiling. My hands crack and bleed as I keep scouring at a vicious pace.

Still, the thoughts roll through my mind like tumultuous waves, one after another, never once relenting. I didn't sleep a wink last night. I was too tormented to relax.

Human trafficking ring.

International investigation.

Prime suspect.

Katie sent over the information that Ethan's company provided to her. I read it over a bottle of wine, drinking half before passing out at the kitchen table for a mere half an hour of rest.

The words *Anaconda Team* are watermarked all over the papers. I barely know Ethan, but Ryder loves and trusts him implicitly. That tells me enough. He's the real deal and a good person.

This is happening.

It's real.

The more I turn it over in my mind like an awful, disgusting pancake, the more sense it makes. I was a minor—vulnerable and clueless. He paid for me and took me overseas against my will.

How many other girls did I see getting beaten, raped and tortured in that house? How many lives were taken in front of me? They all blur into one now.

The sound of Arianna watching a movie on the laptop Katie let us borrow crackles from the other room, startling me out of my daze. She screamed at me when I tried to turn it off.

Scrub.

Scrub.

Scrub.

If only I could cleanse my soul the same way I'm washing the living daylights out of these spotless floors. I want to cut the memories from my skin and bleed myself dry of his poison.

They need your help, Willow.

Scrub.

Testify against him.

Scrub.

Free yourself.

Scrub.

When the pain in my hands becomes too much to bear, I sit back on my haunches and toss the ragged sponge aside. The folder of information on the table is screaming at me.

There're pages of evidence inside, all classified yet given to me in an attempt to sway my decision. Mr Sanchez is one person in a pool of suspects, all being investigated for human trafficking.

He's the real deal. The devil. The head of the snake that's rotting from the head and awaiting a single match to burn its carcass. I hold that power in the palms of my hands now.

"Mummy? The phone!"

Startled out of my thoughts, I heave myself off the floor and snag my phone from the bedroom table where it's ringing. Lola's name is flashing on the screen, but it's outside of our usual schedule.

My stomach flips as I suck in a panicked breath. Shaking myself out of it, I return to the kitchen for privacy then press the phone to my ear.

"Lola? Everything okay?"

There's a long stretch of silence, punctuated by an odd rustling sound like someone's walking on the end of the line. I hold a hand over my pumping heart, beginning to freak out.

"Lola?"

The distant sound of gulping ends the silence, followed by a wet, strangled kind of sob that tugs at my trembling heartstrings.

"Hello?" I repeat shakily.

"Baby."

The kitchen floor is damp beneath my knees as I feel my legs sag. One word in that roughened, aged-whiskey voice of his and the last five months melt away like no time has passed.

"Killian."

He breathes heavily down the line. "Hey."

"It's really you."

Clearing my throat, I let my eyes slide shut, picturing those fire-lit eyes that first greeted me so many months ago.

"Why are you calling me?" I ask in a whisper. "Why now? Killian?"

It takes me a moment to realise that he isn't answering me because... he's crying. Quiet, soul-destroying sobs, betrayed only by the odd sharp intake of breath and tiny whimpers.

Big, scary, impenetrable Killian is sobbing down the line, and I have zero clue what to do. Terror is wrapped around my throat.

"You never should have left," he chokes out.

I feel my own cheeks grow wet. "I know, Kill. I'm so fucking sorry. It was my only option. I didn't know what else to do."

"Willow... she... Lola..."

He trails off, and the sound of the phone clattering against the floor causes me to shout down the line, desperately calling Killian's name even as I hear footsteps thumping away.

Arianna sticks her head out of the bedroom, her eyes widening when she finds me losing my mind on the kitchen floor.

"Mummy?"

"It's okay, sweetie." I wave her away.

"Is it Giant?"

"Ari, go! Watch your movie."

She reluctantly disappears. "Fine."

I pull the phone away from my ear to check and find it's still connected. There's a faint shuffle and some far-off whispers before someone else comes on the line.

"Willow? It's Ryder. You still there?"

"I'm here," I reply quickly. "Shit, Ryder. It's good to hear your voice."

"You too, doll. Look... something's happened. We need you to come home."

"What? Is it Micah? Did he get hurt?"

Ryder sighs, muttering something to another person before returning. "No, it's not Micah."

"Then who?"

He hesitates before speaking in a much firmer voice.

"Just pack your bags, and get in the car. You're needed."

"You know I can't do that, Ryder. I left for a reason."

"Your family needs you," he says curtly. "Fuck that scumbag Sanchez, and fuck this plan. It's time to come home."

"Ry—"

"We can't do this without you!" he snaps. "There's so much to sort out, and the funeral... shit..."

My blood freezes in my veins. I curl my hand into a fist then bite down on it as anxiety floods every inch of my body and leaves me freezing cold. I must've misheard him.

"What funeral?"

Ryder curses. "I didn't want to tell you like this."

"What fucking funeral?"

"I'm sorry, Willow. It's Lola. She had a heart attack... and she's gone."

Folding over to hug my midsection, I stay silent for several long seconds. His words echo on an endless loop, on and on without ever sinking in.

This can't be real.

I just found her. She isn't gone. Not like this. Not now. He has to be mistaken. The sound of Killian's devastating crying comes back to me, and I realise why he was so distraught.

"Willow? Are you still there?" Ryder asks weakly.

"When?" I bite out.

"Last night. Doc tried to revive her, but it was too late. I'm so sorry. I don't know what to say to you to make this better."

"What's h-happening now?"

"Everyone's a mess, and we're still figuring things out. You have to come, Willow. The guys need you more than ever."

I try to silence my own desperate tears. Knowing that Arianna is mere metres away, completely oblivious, gives me the sense to break down quietly, at least.

Ryder stays on the line until I can form words again between my ragged breaths and the steady stream of piping-hot tears. It takes a few minutes to scrape myself together.

"I'm coming home," I finally say. "Give me twenty-four hours."

"Where are you? I'll come and get you."

"I can't... I can't say. Not over the phone, it isn't safe. Don't worry about me, I can find my way back to Briar Valley."

"Are you sure?"

"Just… tell the guys… crap," I curse myself. "I have no idea. Tell them I'm going to make this right."

"We'll be here waiting for you."

We whisper our goodbyes. I'm left staring down at the phone, my ears ringing too loud for me to even think. I spoke to Lola only a handful of days ago.

In the bleak nothingness of our exile, she's been the one constant. The voice at the end of the phone. A tangible, real reminder of the family still waiting for us out there.

I'll never speak to her again.

I'll never get to say goodbye.

It's too late now.

"Mummy?" Arianna peeks her head out past the bedroom door again. "Was that Giant? Is he coming to get us?"

Gulping hard, I find my way back to my feet then bundle Arianna's small body into my arms. We curl up together in my bed with her spooned against me.

My face buries in her long, blonde ringlets. I can feel her heart hammering as she realises I'm crying and begins to panic.

"Are we going on an adventure?" she whispers fearfully. "I don't want to run anymore. I'm tired of running. I want to go home."

"It's okay, Ari." I stroke her hair. "We're going to go home now. Back to Briar Valley. We don't have to stay here any longer."

She turns over to face me. "Really? We're going?"

I nod, biting my lip. "All I ever wanted was for you to be safe, baby. That's it. I'm sorry for putting you through all this."

Arianna strokes the tears from my cheek. "I know, Mummy."

"It still isn't safe, but… there's something we've got to do. I need you to be a brave girl for me again, okay?"

Arianna offers me a devastating grin. "Always. You taught me how to be brave."

"I think you did that all on your own, Ari. I had nothing to do with it."

Curling up in my arms, she snuggles into me like she used to do when she was a baby. I breathe deeply, inhaling the scent of her strawberry shampoo, trying to ground myself in the familiarity.

Arianna gives me the strength to keep going. She always has. I'm going to need that strength now. We all are. Once she falls asleep, I dial Katie's number and slip outside to answer.

"Willow?"

"Katie. Did you hear the news?"

There's a pause.

"Albie called half an hour ago. Who told you?"

"Killian called, and I spoke to Ryder. We have to go back to Briar Valley. I'm going to pack up and leave tonight."

"I'll come to help," she offers.

"No, we're fine. Can I take the car?"

"Of course, sweetheart. We'll be there in a couple of days, I just need to wrap up some business in the city. Will you be okay?"

I rub a hand over my sternum, searing with grief. "I don't know the answer to that question right now."

She sniffles, and I breathe deeply, trying to stop my tears from joining hers. I'm holding them back with a razor-thin slice of control. Not here. Not now. I can't let it out yet because I won't survive if I do.

"I'll see you in Briar Valley."

Hanging up the phone call, I slump against the wall and hang my head. The waves begin. Building. Cresting. Crashing over me. Pain comes thick and fast until it feels like I can't breathe.

The buzz of the phone in my hand drags me back for a second, an unknown number flashing. The only person in my contacts is Lola, so I know one of the guys is reaching out.

Unknown Number: Please hurry.

Squeezing the phone, tears drip down my cheeks. The thought of seeing the three shattered pieces of my heart again is equal parts exhilarating and terrifying.

It's time to return to Briar Valley.

Time... to go home.

CHAPTER 4
WILLOW
HEAVY METAL – DIVELINER

"ARE YOU SAFE?" Katie asks through the hands-free.

Stuffing notes back into my purse, I shove it back in my handbag. We stopped again after driving for hours to refuel and get more coffee for the road. I'm barely able to keep my eyes open.

"We took the long route to avoid the main roads. No issues so far. I left the apartment keys under the plant pot for you."

"Good. Be careful."

"We will."

"Willow?"

I indicate to pull away from the petrol station where we just refilled our tank. "Yeah?"

"If you ever need to come back to the apartment... it's yours, alright? I know things haven't been ideal, but I'll always be here if you need me. I mean it."

"Thank you, Katie. For everything."

"I really wish you'd call me Mum."

"Yeah, I know," I reply lamely.

Katie sniffs, presumably stifling her own tears. I don't offer any comfort. I'm too numb, and frankly, I'm all cried out. There's nothing left in me to feel any kind of emotion right now.

I'm running on zero sleep and crappy petrol station coffee in order to get us home as fast as possible. The last twenty-four hours have been a blur of tears, packing and grief.

It took all day to get everything ready for the journey while figuring out the quickest route back up north. I planned it methodically, avoiding all main roads and cameras.

"Let me know when you arrive," she requests.

"I will."

Disconnecting the call, I feel like an asshole for treating her like shit. Our relationship is still new territory for me. She's proved herself in the last few months, but my trust is flimsy.

"I don't like her," Arianna comments, her feet propped up on the messy dashboard. "She's annoying and moans too much."

"That's your grandma, Ari."

"No, Lola is my grandma."

I blink to clear my vision. I've tried my best to explain things, but getting a seven-year-old to understand death is tricky. Even when Pedro died, she still believed that he was out there somewhere.

"Lola's your great-grandma." I keep my eyes on the snowy road. "But she's in heaven now, remember? She won't be there when we get back, baby. I'm sorry."

"I know, but I can still visit her in heaven. Right?"

"Sure, baby. In your dreams, you'll still see her."

"Like Pedro."

"Like Pedro," I confirm. "Go to sleep, Ari. We've still got three hours to go. Shut your eyes."

Grabbing my coat, I use my spare hand to drape it over her, letting her snuggle up in the seat. The radio is tinny in the background as I keep driving through the night.

The farther north we get, the thicker the snow falls. As dawn rises, we approach the mountain summit that leads into Briar Valley. Mount Helena is as majestic as I remember.

Arianna stirs in her sleep but doesn't wake up, too busy sucking on her thumb. With a final breath for courage, I pull onto the rocky terrain and begin the steep ascent.

Within minutes, we've spun out of control and are stuck on a huge patch of ice. This is ridiculous. Eyes burning, I rest my forehead on the steering wheel and take a breath.

All I can see is Lola—her bright, friendly smile and wizened face. Her scent is in my nose. Freshly baked cookies and all things homey, transferred through her warm embrace.

I loved the way she always pinched my cheeks before saying hello. Our pep talks around the dining table were one of my weekly highlights after we resolved our differences.

"Dammit," I hiss, scrubbing my cheeks. "Get it together."

Grabbing my phone, I send a message to the one number I have saved then wait for whoever is sitting on the other end to come and rescue us. It won't be long, I'm sure.

Turning up the heater, I point the vent in Arianna's direction then hug myself, staring at the minutes counting down on the dashboard clock.

Within half an hour, the glow of headlights finds us. Ryder's bright-red truck pulls up a short distance away, but someone else steps out into the rising blizzard.

Inching through the heavy snowfall, a pair of short, muscled legs approaches the car. Glancing at Arianna, I decide to climb out and do this reunion without waking her.

I'm freezing in just a long, thick sweater and tight yoga pants as I slam the door shut and turn to face our rescuer. Dull green eyes meet mine through the white-laced air.

"Zach," I whimper.

His overgrown, nut-coloured brown hair is windswept and long overdue for a trim. The enthusiastic smile that usually curves his soft, boyish features is nowhere to be found.

His light has dulled.

Vanished. Gone.

"Willow?" Zach stares right at me.

I shuffle my feet while being battered by the wind and snow. "Hi."

Before I can react, he rushes at me in a blur of movement. I'm suddenly crushed against his firm chest. Two strong arms wrap around me like steel bands, and the pressure feels amazing.

I fist my hands in his hoodie, breathing in his familiar, fruity scent. It's haunted my dreams for months. I can almost hear the wild beat of his heart tearing free from his chest.

"Willow," he repeats like he can't believe it.

"It's me." I breathe him in.

"You're here."

Holding me at arm's length, he stares at me, his emerald eyes blown wide with disbelief. There are heavy bags marking his exhaustion, and he seems colder, more serious somehow.

I half expect him to crack a joke, but he slams his lips on mine instead with raw, primal need. I kiss him back, unable to resist. His fingertips stroke along my face as his tongue tangles with mine.

All I can feel is him. His touch. His taste. The sweet, playful, shining light inside of Zachariah that made me fall so irrevocably in love with him even when I didn't want to. It's still in there, beneath the grief.

When we break apart, our foreheads rest together in the chaos of the snowstorm as he lets out a bitter laugh.

"I've spent months imagining what I'd do when I saw you again," he admits in a low whisper. "How much I'd scream and shout at you, or tell you to never set foot in our fucking lives again. Even had a whole speech rehearsed."

I brush my nose against his. "You can yell at me. I deserve it. I've hurt you all, and nothing will ever excuse that."

His hand grasps my jaw to trap me in place. "I'm sure you've hurt yourself more than anyone else. Come on, we have to go before we get trapped out here. We can scream at each other later."

"I'll hold you to that," I murmur.

"I doubt I'll be the only one. Where's the kid?"

"In the car. I'll get our stuff."

Between us, we get everything unloaded and transferred into Ryder's truck. After Zach extricates Arianna from the front seat, he tucks my coat tighter around her and presses a kiss to her forehead.

"Hey, trouble. I missed you."

I have to look away when he brushes a loose strand of hair behind her ear, staring at her sleeping face with the same heartbreaking look of disbelief. It severs my heartstrings to watch.

I did that.

His pain is because of me.

"Zach—"

"It's fine," he interrupts. "I just missed her, that's all."

"She missed you too."

He nods. "Let's move."

All loaded up, I slide into the passenger seat of Ryder's truck, fixing my gaze out of the window as Zach climbs in after tucking Arianna into the back. She hasn't stirred once.

He manoeuvres the truck onto the icy road, relief loosening my shoulders when the tyre treads keep it from spinning out of control like we did. We make it halfway up Mount Helena before he speaks again.

"Where've you been all this time?"

I shrug listlessly. "Here and there. Katie relocated us to an apartment complex in Southampton for displaced families."

"Southampton?"

"We've been hiding out there for the past few months. It's hardly been a five-star holiday. More like witness protection."

He scoffs. "Hasn't been a walk in the park for us either."

I pick at a loose thread in my sweater. "You can hate me all you want, I'll take it. But I came back for Lola, not us. That's the truth."

"How thoughtful," he snarks. "I'm not going to fight with you. Not now. Let's get through this and figure our crap out later."

"Fair enough." My throat locks up, making it difficult to swallow. "How is everyone? The town?"

"In a state of shock. Albie is a wreck. He was with her when it happened. Doc doesn't think she suffered or was in any pain, though."

"Should I be grateful for that?" I ask honestly.

Zach shrugs. "I have no clue. Maybe we should be."

"It's something, right?"

"All I know is the place is a mess already. We don't know how to function without her. She was the whole reason Briar Valley exists."

Reaching over on instinct, I take his free hand and curl our fingers together. Zach spares me a glance before refocusing on the road, his Adam's apple bobbing like crazy.

"She would want the town to live on." I blink away my tears. "It's more than just one person. The family is what makes Briar Valley a home."

"Our family is broken. Has been since you left."

"Zach—"

"Forget it."

I let my hand fall away from his and watch the snow build outside. The sun has risen now, lighting the path ahead as we begin to descend into the woodland surrounding the town.

"How's Micah?"

"Don't ask," Zach growls.

Okay, then.

The awkward silence stretches on until the trees clear to reveal the beginning of cobbled streets. I'm slick all over with anxious sweat, and my hands tremble in my lap.

The idea of facing everyone makes me want to curl up in a corner and hide away from prying eyes. Zach's eyes briefly dart towards me, assessing my knees knocking together.

"Your hair's different," he observes.

"I had to cut it."

"Looks nice."

"Thanks. What happens now?"

"Do you want to get some rest before… everything?"

I nod quickly. "That would be good. I've been awake for over thirty hours."

"Jesus, Willow. How are you not dead on your feet?"

"Every time I shut my eyes, I dreamed of you three," I admit. "Sometimes it's less painful to stay awake until the point of exhaustion than face that every night."

Zach flexes his grip on the steering wheel. "The bed felt so fucking empty without you in it. Our entire lives did."

My chest aches. "It hurt me too, Zach."

"I know, babe. I'm just struggling to understand why we've wasted so much time apart. Life is too damn short."

There it is again—the all-consuming pit of pain when I remember that I'm not coming home and walking into my grandmother's arms. Life really is too short.

She would want us to embrace even the tiniest shreds of happiness, however fragile they may seem in the midst of so much grief. We have to live. For Lola. For her memory.

Zach drives straight through the deserted town. Nobody is braving the weather, remaining safely inside, granting us some privacy. Snow is falling thick and fast.

We haven't seen a single soul when we reach the guys' cabin, nestled amongst white-capped trees and shrubs atop the rugged hill overlooking the valley. It looks magical, coated in December snow.

I deliberately ignore our old home across the road. Just thinking about all that we left behind makes my heart hurt more than it already does. Zach turns off the engine and sighs.

"Micah will be passed out in his workshop. He's on lockdown after his recent behaviour."

"Drinking?"

Zach nods. "Daily."

"Jesus. For how long?"

"A couple of months now."

Unable to dive into that, I force an even breath. "What about Killian?"

"I think he's still with Albie in Lola's cabin." He scrapes his hands down his unshaven face. "You should have a few hours of privacy before all hell breaks loose."

We fall back into awkward silence until I break it.

"Will you shout at me if I say I'm sorry again?"

"Most likely." He blows out a leaden breath.

"Then I won't." I unbuckle my belt. "I'll take Arianna inside."

Before I can climb out, Zach grabs me by the wrist. I fight to conceal my reaction to the bite of pain as his fingers grasp the fresh cuts beneath my sweater that I really don't want him to know about.

The look on his face is scary enough as he looks right through me. Past all the bullshit and lies. My attempt at displaying a strong face. He sees deep into the pits of my tormented heart and understands.

"Willow... I'm so fucking angry at you right now, but I'm also glad that you're home," he finally says. "And I love you."

I manage a tight nod. "I love you."

"Maybe that's enough for now. Lola wouldn't want us to fight about this." He shakes his head. "She'd just want me to be relieved."

Tugging my wrist, he pulls me closer until his lips are within reach. We kiss again, but slower this time. Tenderly. Filling the empty spaces in one another that we each left behind.

There's a burning ache deep inside of me. Far deeper than I could even attempt to reach myself. In Zach's presence, it reignites, burning in slow, lazy embers until my whole body is alight.

"Zach," I whine into his lips.

"I know, princess. Let's get the kid inside. We're going to freeze to death out here otherwise."

Grabbing our bags, I let Zach tuck Arianna into his chest to protect her from the snow. We race through the flurries and escape inside the cabin where the guys' familiar scents slap me in the face.

It smells like pine trees and bonfires. Oil paint and whiskey. Roast dinners and home. All my favourite things, bottled into one essence, pure and inarguably *them*.

"Jesus Christ."

Zach glances around the huge mess. "Yeah. May've let things slip a little bit."

The cabin is the same, but it's covered in layers of clutter, discarded clothes and unwashed dishes. Killian always kept things clean and semi-tidy. This is a complete disaster zone.

I notice they don't even have a Christmas tree up. We didn't either. The big day is only a couple of weeks away, yet I had no plans to celebrate beyond a cheap dinner with Arianna.

"Your room isn't made up," Zach says over his shoulder. "I'll put this one in my room for now. Make yourself at home."

Dropping our bags, I bounce on the balls of my feet. It feels wrong to just invite myself back into their space like nothing has changed. I'm frozen in the entrance and unable to move.

That's where Zach finds me when he returns a few minutes later. His eyes scrape over me, incisive and searching, seeing far more than I'd like him to. Our sadness whispers to each other.

"I should get some sleep," I croak. "Before later on."

"You should." Zach clears his raspy throat. "Unless…"

Trailing off, the need written across his face is so obvious, he may as well be screaming out for my arms around him. I feel the same, but I still can't close the distance between us.

"Babe," he hums. "Please… I need to hold you. I just need to feel you in my arms one more time to know you're real."

My feet move of their own accord. We meet somewhere in the middle, the messy cabin falling away as the softness of Zach's t-shirt meets my nose. God, I've missed his smell.

"Fuck." He rhythmically strokes my hair. "Fuck!"

"I'm right here, Zach."

"You don't feel real."

Unpeeling myself from his arms, I take his unshaved face into my hands and force his eyes to meet mine. The round, youthful angles are covered in stubble, framing his hollow eyes.

"I'm real," I whisper fiercely. "I know this has been the hardest time of our lives, but I'm here now. I'm in your arms."

"Why did you leave us?"

I brush my nose against his. "Ari. It's all for her."

"We could've kept you safe."

"No, Zach. You can't. No one can. We won't be safe until this is all over and Mr Sanchez is gone."

His lashes lift, casting shadows over dimpled skin. "Gone?"

"I don't want to talk about him right now. I just want to feel you. Hold you. Touch you."

Lips pecking mine, I can feel his smile. "I can do that."

Zach's hands move to cup my hips and hold me flush against him. I wind my arms around his neck and lose myself to his kiss, bold and insistent, demanding for me to stay at his side forever.

When his hand moves to hook my leg up on his hip, I begin to shift, needing more friction between us. I can already feel the press of his hardness against my core, and it's driving me insane with need.

When his tongue pushes past my lips to tangle with mine, I can't help moaning into his mouth. Our tongues duel, both fighting a losing battle. He wants the only thing I can't give him.

Forever.

A kept promise.

Our future.

Until we're safe and the monster hunting us has been shackled in the depths of hell, I can't give any of them what they deserve. And that's exactly why I had no choice but to run.

"The others," I gasp. "What if they come in?"

Zach moves to grip my ass. "I don't give a shit. Let them watch."

Lifting me so I'm hooked around his waist, he walks me over to the huge, L-shaped sofa in front of the open fireplace and deposits me on it. I let him quickly peel off my yoga pants.

Wrapping a hand around my ankle, he plants a gentle kiss there then begins to trail his lips upwards. Higher. Higher still. Kissing, nipping and licking a burning path to my inner thigh.

"So fucking gorgeous," he grunts.

Kissing my left hip, his mouth traces the seam of my plain white panties. I know I'm soaked through already. I haven't been touched since I slept with Micah on that mountain top.

"Tell me to stop, babe."

"No," I moan as he kisses on top of my mound. "Please… Zach. I need to feel your lips on me."

Hooking his fingers beneath the elastic, he torturously peels my panties off, inch by slow inch. Bare from the waist down, Zach wastes no time burying his face between my open thighs.

When his mouth latches onto my pussy, I grab handfuls of his long hair and cry out. His lips move like a ravenous machine, his tongue delving into my core and parting my folds.

Thumb swiping over my nub and beginning to circle, I moan again, slamming a hand over my mouth to prevent myself from waking Arianna up. His touch feels incredible.

"You're so wet for me," Zach marvels as he flicks my clit. "Did this sweet little pussy miss me?"

Swiping his finger through the flow of moisture, he thrusts it into my slit in one fast pump. I'm already on the cusp of falling apart, the fast thrust of his fingers driving me to the edge.

"Oh God, Zach!"

"That's it, babe. Say my goddamn name. Don't you dare forget it ever again."

Giving me a moment to catch my breath as I lay tangled in a gasping mess, he quickly unbuckles his belt and shoves his jeans down. His moments are clumsy, he's rushing so fast.

Grabbing his arm, I yank him back down so his body covers mine then wrap my legs around his waist. My hand pushes his boxers down to find the hardened steel of his length.

"Willow—"

"I need you inside of me," I groan pathetically. "Right now."

With fire burning bright in his irises, he lines himself up and doesn't give me the benefit of a warning. The sudden pump of his hips feeds his cock deep inside my entrance.

I bite down on his shoulder to silence the moan of pure bliss. My teeth leave a swollen welt, the sight bringing me pleasure. We're marking each other tonight.

"Hold on," Zach warns.

Keeping a tight grip on his neck, I let him pound into me at a relentless, bruising pace that betrays his still white-hot anger. Each thrust is its own individual punishment for leaving.

Over and over, his cock worships me in the most brutal way possible. When he pulls out and quickly flips me over, all I can do is grip the sofa cushions and let him raise my ass high.

Zach re-enters me at an even deeper angle now that I'm bent over at his mercy. The smack of his hand on my butt cheek sends tingles down my spine like hungry fire ants.

"Fuck you for leaving," he hisses while spanking me again. "And fuck you for thinking we could ever survive without you."

"I won't apologise again," I gasp back. "I had to keep her safe."

Slamming into me again, Zach's voice is a guttural bark. "That's our damn job too, and you know it."

"I'm… her mother. I had to—"

His next thrust cuts me off and all I can garble out is a strangled cry for more. This isn't the sweet, dirty Zach that I remember. He's fucking me even more brutally than his cousin once did.

His fingertips feel like they're bruising my hips, but I don't care. I'm thankful that I was able to keep my sweater on, at least. I don't want any of them to see my arms.

Guided to the edge of a plummeting drop, I stare over the cliff and prepare to be shoved. Zach's reaching his own release. I can feel it in the increasingly rough slam of his hips on my rear.

Just when I'm about to fall apart in the most spectacular fashion, the pressure of his dick inside me vanishes. It's cruelly ripped away as he pulls out and takes a huge step back.

"What?" I scream. "Zach!"

A hand wrapped around his shaft, he pumps it one last time and groans through his release. Come shoots all over my ass until I'm covered in his seed and still hanging on the edge of an orgasm.

I scream and rave. Shout and curse. I'm dripping wet and sticky from his release, but Zach remains at a distance, catching his breath. I realise that he isn't going to let me come tonight.

"That's for leaving," he grunts.

Semi-dressed, he turns and vanishes deeper into the cabin before I can utter a single word of frustration. I'm left alone—coated in come and on the verge of a complete meltdown.

"Fuck you, Zach!" I shout in anger.

There's no response.

This is my punishment.

CHAPTER 5
KILLIAN
SILENT LOVE – JAMES BAY

HEAVING ALBIE'S unconscious body into his room, I dump him on the bed. He can't sleep in Lola's bed after she died there. Even if it's empty and available. The undertakers took her body to Highbridge a few hours ago.

Ryder was no help either. He passed out with his head on the dining table after single-handedly polishing off a bottle of rum. I can handle my liquor, but the world is spinning even for me.

We spent the whole day making a list of what needs to be done. Funeral arrangements, property deeds, complicated legal matters that always seem ridiculous when your loved one is dead.

But life is a cruel motherfucking bitch, and this isn't my first rodeo. I had to grow up fast and take over when my folks died too. I'm always the one to pick up the broken pieces.

"Where's Lola?" Albie mumbles drunkenly.

"Sleep it off, Al. You'll feel better in the morning."

"Lo," he whines.

"She isn't here. Sleep."

With a grumble, he passes the hell out again. I leave him to wallow alone and stumble back into the living room in their cabin. Ryder hasn't moved an inch on the table.

Grabbing a cushion from the sofa, I prop it underneath his head then throw a blanket over his shoulders to make him a little more comfortable. We're all going to have sore heads tomorrow.

It's dark outside, but the heavy dousing of snow somehow manages to brighten the world into a weird, twilight state. When I was a kid, I used to get so excited to watch the first snow fall.

It always made me think of fresh starts and so many endless opportunities in the blank, powdery canvas that would settle over town. Tonight is no different.

Months of pain and torment have all come down to this. While inebriated, Ryder let it slip that Willow was on her way home. I told him that I'll believe that when I see it, already steeling myself against the disappointment.

Perhaps this is our fresh start. A second chance. Or maybe I'm a stupid old fool, destined to get my heart crushed. Crunching through the snow, I'm nearly home when I freeze on the spot.

There are footsteps imprinted in the snow around my parked truck. I follow without thinking, the roar of my heartbeat in my ears the only sound that I can hear.

The footsteps lead across the cobblestone road towards the lake behind Willow's still-dark cabin, cloaked in frozen icicles and crisp, cold darkness.

But there's something else.

A person.

Sitting cross-legged at the lake's frozen edge, a figure stares out into the nothingness. I can just make out the curl of dark, raven hair beneath a baseball cap, far shorter than I remember.

A thick lump gathers in my throat as I draw to a halt several metres away. She's shivering beneath the knitted blanket wrapped around her shoulders and familiar, curved body.

"Willow?" I say like a prayer.

Shoulders trembling, her head turns to spare me a brief, tear-logged glance. Our gazes collide, amber on hazel, despair on grief. Love on irretrievable loss.

"Kill," she sobs.

I'm stuck between running for my life and gathering the bundle of bones into my arms. It's her. My light. My love. The breaker and fixer of my long-dead heart.

"Willow," I repeat.

"Please… I can't do this right now. I want to be alone."

"You haven't seen me for months, and that's all you have to say? You don't want to see me?"

Her head drops, hands moving to cover her face as she turns back towards the lake. "I never got to say goodbye."

The pain in her voice crushes my heart. Tentatively approaching her, I ease myself down next to her in the snow. Neither of us touch, keeping a safe distance.

I manage a quick look at her pale face, lit by the blanket of white all around us. Crystalline flakes of snow pepper the surface of the lake and blanket our surroundings in silence.

"Lola loved you," I reply simply. "And she knew that you loved her. That's all that matters."

"I just wish I could've told her," Willow whimpers. "Last time we spoke, I hung up on her. I was so tired of the same old argument."

"What argument?"

"I was tired of running. Tired of fighting her. All I wanted was to shut my eyes and wake up here, surrounded by my family."

Anger shoots through me. "You never should have left."

"You think I don't know that?"

I shrug, the alcohol in my veins loosening my tongue. "I think you didn't care enough to stay. We didn't matter enough."

Willow suddenly stands up, looming over me on shaking legs. She rips the cap from her head, letting her shorn black hair tumble down to her shoulders.

Her furious eyes strip me down to the core with a mere look. Pain. Anguish. Indecision. Grief. Hope. Despair. It's all there in myriad, confusing shades of hazel-tinged chaos.

"If that's what you believe, then you're not the person I thought you were," she utters. "I left to keep my daughter safe, not to spite you or your ego."

"Baby—"

"Don't *baby* me, Kill. I was in love with you. I still fucking am. I've spent every day dreaming of when I could come home."

"So why didn't you?" I ask pointedly.

Rather than answering me, she turns and storms off, away from the lake and her cabin. I hesitate for only a second before chasing after her like a dog following a dangled bone.

"Wait!"

When I grab her arm, she yanks it free from my grasp, her teeth gritted against an angry hiss. I've kicked the hornet's nest now.

"Do not grab me," Willow warns.

I let my hand drop. "Look, I'm sorry. I'm drunk and stupid and... I'm so fucked up. I don't work without you, princess."

"I can't be what you want me to be. I have to protect Arianna. That's why I stayed away. Not to punish you or to be a bitch, but because it wasn't safe to be here."

Inching closer to her, I reach out, driven by desperation alone. She stares at me with such pain, but she still refuses to budge. I close the final distance between us and tug her into my arms instead.

Fuck asking for permission.

She collapses against me in a weightless puddle of exhaustion. Crushing her into my barrel chest, the rage I've felt since she left dissipates into sheer relief.

"I've got you," I whisper into her hair. "You don't have to walk alone anymore. I'm here, baby."

"You're not," she replies.

"Let me be the judge of that. I swear to whatever God is out there, I'm never letting you go again. Even if you want me to."

"I don't want you to."

"Good, because that is not happening. We deal with this as a family from here forward."

"You'd take me back? After everything?" she scoffs.

I brush my lips against her temple, my throat locked up tight. "I never let you go. Not once."

"Me neither, Kill."

Releasing her, I glower at the dark circles beneath her eyes. The unmitigated exhaustion reflected back physically pains me. She looks dead on her feet and barely functioning.

"When was the last time you slept?"

Peeling herself away from me, she takes my hand. "I don't know. We arrived early this morning after travelling through the night."

"Why didn't you sleep?"

"I couldn't rest, knowing you were out there, hurting all alone. Arianna's gone back to bed inside."

"Come to bed, then," I plead shamelessly. "Just let me hold you for tonight. Everything else can wait."

Willow bites her lip and nods. "Okay."

Hand in hand, we walk back up the garden, leaving the empty cabin and all its memories alone. I hold the front door open for her to enter the warmth.

"After you."

She flashes me a brief smile. "Thanks."

Stepping into the dark kitchen, I shake snow from my long mane of dirty blonde hair. The light in Micah's workshop is glowing from the bottom of the garden, but I don't bother to disturb him.

Willow's been through enough for one day without discovering how much of a mess he's become in her absence. I'm sure Zach's only given her a PG-rated version of that disastrous tale.

"I should check on Ari."

"Where is she?"

Willow walks down the hallway. "In Zach's bed, I think."

After pausing to check on Arianna, fast asleep in Zach's arms in his bedroom, Willow lets herself into my room at the end of the hall. I hesitate, taking a peep in at the little monster myself.

Fuck.

An invisible weight lifts off my chest at the sight of the tiny, blonde-haired lump curled up under the bedsheets with my snoring cousin. I've missed that fucking kid and her sharp tongue.

Seeing her asleep and so innocent looking, the impenetrable wall of ice around my heart begins to crack. Only a couple of millimetres, but enough to let a shred of warmth in.

Willow did what she thought was necessary to keep Arianna safe. If I were in her position, I doubt I would have done any differently. I just wish she'd trusted us to protect them both.

The anger is still there. Simmering. Cooking away on a rolling boil, ready to explode. But not tonight. Right now, I'm grateful. She's back and alive. That's enough for me.

"Killian?" Willow sighs.

"Coming."

When I reach my darkened bedroom, I stop dead in the doorway. Willow has removed her wet, snow-stained sweater, and she's slowly peeling her tight yoga pants over her hips.

"Stop staring," she snaps.

"Can't help it, princess."

Studying the scrap of panties left on her body and the swell of her bare breasts, I nearly lose sight of what we're doing here in the first place.

She needs to trust me again. I can't be a caveman, no matter how much I want to bury myself in her right now, bad blood be damned. My primal self wants to devour her whole.

Pulling off my own t-shirt and ditching my jeans, I slowly approach and gather her tiny body into my arms. She's lost so much weight. Even I can tell in the darkness of the room.

"You haven't been eating?" I trace her ribcage.

"Not now, Kill. Please just hold me."

Easily lifting her, I crawl into the unmade bed, draping her across my bare chest. Willow burrows closer, slotting into my side like we were made for each other, lock and key.

"I missed this so much," she murmurs.

"Yeah," I croak. "Me too."

"You have no idea how many times I dreamed that I was right here with you."

"I have a pretty good idea."

Staring up at the ceiling, I clear my thick throat and prepare to lay it all on the line just as footsteps move through the cabin and the light from a phone flashes into the room.

"Willow?" Zach whisper-shouts.

"In here," she responds without moving. "I'm with Killian."

He stares in at us with sheer longing. "Arianna's asleep. Mind if I join you guys?"

"After your stunt earlier?" Willow drones.

Zach remains silent. I don't bother to ask. He's far angrier than he'll ever let on after months of dealing with Micah's self-destruction. I'm sure he gave her a hard time.

"Fine." Willow breaks the silence. "Come in."

I roll my eyes, shifting Willow over so there's space behind her for Zach to slide into my bed. Luckily, it's big enough for all three of us.

"Come on, kid. Before I change my mind."

"You won't break my legs if I climb in?" Zach asks with a low chuckle.

"If you start snoring, then no promises. Keep your fucking mouth shut for once, and we won't have an issue."

Zach rips his t-shirt over his head. "That's a risk I'm willing to take."

Once he's stepped out of his jeans, he approaches the bed, easing in and trapping Willow between us. She recoils, seeming reluctant to let him cuddle her at first, but eventually gives in.

"I'm sorry for earlier," Zach mumbles.

"Guess I deserved it."

"No. You didn't."

"What did you do?" I ask tiredly.

Zach keeps his mouth shut. Not even Willow is willing to tell me what happened. Fluffing my pillow, I reposition myself into a comfier place on the bed.

"Whatever. Don't tell me."

The silent minutes tick by, broken only by the featherlight patter of heavy snow falling outside my window. My eyes are too heavy to hold open, as much as I want to cherish Willow's warmth.

"Can somebody pinch me?" Zach whispers into the darkness. "I'm not entirely convinced this is real."

Willow jabs him in the ribs with her elbow. "Real enough for you? Some of us are trying to sleep here."

"Noted," Zach groans in pain.

"Shut up, the pair of you." I press a kiss against Willow's soft neck. "I'm drunk and tired. Talk in the morning."

"Killian's drunk?"

"Apparently," Willow surmises.

"I always wondered what that would look like."

"Zach," I warn again. "Zip it, loudmouth."

Falling silent, Willow lets out a contented sigh between us. Just feeling her in my arms again, stroking her soft skin, inhaling her familiar, sweet scent… Fuck me.

It almost makes the last five months of pain, anger and regret worth it. *Almost.* But nothing can ever bring that time back to us, and I have no guarantee that she won't do it all over again.

The only thing that will keep her here, safe in my arms, is if I bring her that asshole's head on a stake. Then she'll finally be free to live the life she's always wanted.

Challenge accepted.

I'll cut it off myself.

CHAPTER 6
WILLOW

RIBS – LORDE

SEARCHING THROUGH THE FRIDGE, I start pulling out ingredients at random. Tomatoes. Eggs. Sausages. Even some slightly questionable looking spinach to go in the omelette too.

The guys are still asleep. Neither stirred as I snuck out of bed, unable to lay there for a second longer. I managed a few hours before I woke up in a dog pile of muscles and limbs.

My heart was pounding from another stress-induced nightmare. Mr Sanchez was there, as he always is, ready to lash out at me with his ice-cold blue eyes and razor sharp tongue.

I know where you are, Mrs Sanchez.

I'm coming for you and that little brat.

You will be mine again.

Startling, I realise an egg has hit the floor, smashing after falling from my trembling hands. *Shit.* I make myself take a breath to force the nightmarish whispers aside.

Half an hour later, I've ruined my first three attempts at the omelette, burned my hand on the stove, and dropped a mug of coffee on myself in between the madness.

With a growl, my back meets the cabinet, and I let myself sink to the cabin floor to bury my face in my hands. I'm so tired. Not just physically, but on a bone-deep, irreparable level.

I thought I'd feel better the moment I set foot back in Briar Valley, but it's like all the shit that's built up in the past few months has followed me here.

Letting my fingers glide underneath Killian's stolen flannel shirt I threw on to cover up my arms, I let out a deep breath while stroking the healing cuts across my wrist.

I'm itching to take my switchblade from my suitcase and cut again, over and over, until this nervous energy leaves my body, and I can finally get some rest.

"Are you going to sit on the floor and cry all day?"

Opening my eyes, I find Killian staring down at me with his arms folded across his bare, chiselled chest. My throat immediately seizes up at the sight of so much burnished muscle.

He's wearing only a pair of dark-green sweatpants, hanging low on his defined hips. His hair is still a long, tangled bush of dirty-blonde strands around the strong, defined angles of his face and jaw.

"Well?" He cocks a brow.

Wiping the tears from my cheeks, I try to plaster a smile on my face but fail to summon it. Killian's featured in my dreams for months, but seeing him in front of me still makes my body hum.

"Breakfast is a disaster."

"So I can see," he quips back. "Were you trying to decorate the kitchen with food?"

"I'm trying to cook, and it's all going wrong!"

He crouches down beside me. "Christ, Willow. Did you sleep at all?"

"I don't need to sleep," I snap, ignoring his outstretched hand. "What I need is to get my shit together and figure out what needs to be done. I have no idea where to even start, planning a funeral."

"It's all done. You don't have to worry."

"Wait, what?"

Killian stares at me. "I took care of it all."

"What are you talking about?"

"The funeral home is sorting the arrangements. They're gonna call me back today. Lola's lawyer will be here in a few weeks to go through her affairs."

My mouth clicks open then shut again. "You... sorted it all?"

"This isn't my first family death." Killian scrapes a hand over his sculpted beard. "I figured you would be overwhelmed with it all, so I took care of it."

"I can't believe you've done everything. I thought I'd have to do it all as her last living relative."

"Why are you so shocked?"

"You know why."

Expression softening, he helps me to stand back up, his hand grasping mine tightly. His skin is rough and calloused against mine.

"Because I'm still in love with you. I've loved you since the day we met, for fuck's sake. That's why I wanted to help. Besides, she was my grandmother as well."

"I love you too," I admit. "It killed me to leave."

"Good," he snarls.

My eyebrows draw together. "Why is that good?"

"Because you almost killed my family with this stupid fucking decision, Willow. You need to know how much it hurt us."

"I do!"

"You did this to us. No one else. You can't blame Dimitri Sanchez for your own decisions, even if he was the cause of them. You could've chosen to stay instead."

"And let him take Arianna?" I almost shout.

"He wouldn't have gotten remotely close. We dealt with him once and all the other times his cronies came back again, looking for you. You didn't give us a chance to keep you safe."

I try to push him away, but he grips the edges of the kitchen counter, preventing me from being able to escape. I'm caught against his lines of god-like, carved muscle.

"You took off and broke my damn heart. Zach's been a wreck. Don't even get me started on Micah. That's on you, princess."

Tears burn in my eyes. "Kill, stop."

"I won't stop. Not until you understand and swear that you'll never leave us again. No matter how scary life gets."

"I can't promise that!"

His jaw tightens into a hard, cruel line. "Then you might as well go now."

Moisture spills over and leaks down my cheeks. He wants me to hurt. Killian needs to see my pain for himself to know if we have a future worth fighting for or not.

"You want to know the truth?"

He waits, silent and demanding.

With a flicker of courage, I throw off the oversized flannel shirt that covers my arms, revealing healing cuts and new scars from our time apart. The remaining colour in his still-tanned face drains away.

"There's your truth," I lash out. "You want to know if I regretted my actions? Every goddamn day. But I had no choice."

A single finger trailing its way down from my wrist, Killian traces the violent slash of a healed cut. It's pink and tight, contrasting with the still-raw wounds from a few days ago.

"What the fuck is this?" he demands in a flat, terrifying voice that pricks the hairs up on my skin. "Who did this to you?"

"I did it to myself, Kill."

"Yourself?" he grinds out.

"Yes."

Yanking my arm away, I throw the flannel shirt back on to cover up the vulnerable parts of myself. I didn't want to show him, but I need him to understand. I didn't run for my own pleasure.

Zach was right. For all the awful pain they've suffered, I have endured it along with them—every last stab in the heart with the time that we were kept apart.

"Willow. Please talk to me."

"There's nothing else to say."

"You can't just show me that and walk away. Tell me what to do." His voice shifts to a desperate rasp. "I want to fix this."

"You can hate me if you want, but hate me for the right reasons. I didn't deliberately hurt your family. I was protecting mine."

His mouth hanging open on a response, the patter of light, child-sized feet halts his next words. The door to the kitchen opens, and Arianna appears, rumpled and dazed in her bunny pyjamas.

"Mummy?" she yawns.

"Morning, baby."

The moment her eyes open properly, she spots Killian. Her sleepiness vanishes, replaced by excitement. She whoops and launches herself straight at him.

"Giant! Giant!"

Killian easily catches her. "Hey, peanut."

Lifted into his huge, tree trunk arms, he swings her around the kitchen in a circle. Her squealing cuts through my brain, but I don't mind. It's the happiest I've heard her in months.

"I can't believe you're here!" she screams.

"I didn't go anywhere." Killian spoons her against his chest and strokes her messy bedhead. "Missed you, peanut."

"I missed you more, Giant. Did you get smaller?"

He suppresses a laugh. "I don't think so. You're just getting bigger."

"I must be growing!" she declares triumphantly.

"Alright, Ari. Let the poor man breathe."

Placed back on her feet, Arianna circles her arms around his legs and refuses to let go. I shove them both out of the kitchen so I can clean up and continue with breakfast.

Killian's still watching me closely, our argument hanging in the tension in the air, as he sits down with Arianna on his knee.

"What have you been up to?" he asks conversationally.

Arianna pouts. "Nothing. I missed my friends and school."

"Well, now you can go back to school. Can't you?"

"I can?" she gasps.

Cracking a fresh carton full of eggs into a bowl, I bite my lip. She doesn't need to know this may just be a quick visit for the funeral. In fact, none of them need to know that yet.

"Did you hear that, Mummy?"

"I did," I hum back.

"I can see Johan again. And Aalia, Rachel... Miranda too! I'm so happy to be home."

The look on Killian's face is so smug. I narrow my eyes at him. He can act innocent all he wants, I know what his game plan is here. Emotional warfare. He's going to play dirty.

"Did you miss Briar Valley?" Killian asks innocently.

"So much," she gushes.

"And do you want to stay here now that you're back?"

Arianna's smile freezes. "We aren't going to stay? Mummy?"

"I... don't know, Ari."

Spotting the signs of a meltdown a mile off, I quickly wipe off my hands and give all of my attention to her. Arianna's eyes fill with tears.

"But we just got back! I'm not leaving!"

"Ari, things are complicated—"

"No!" she screams.

Killian looks surprised at her outburst of anger and quickly backtracks. "Peanut, don't worry. We'll figure it all out."

But Arianna's already fallen into one of her now-regular tantrums as her face turns bright-pink, and tears begin to streak down her cheeks in thick rivers.

"I don't want to live in the apartment anymore," she cries hysterically. "I hate feeling scared all of the time."

"Good job, Kill." I cast him a glare.

He scrubs a hand over his face, his smug smirk no longer in sight. Things have changed while we've been gone, the uncertainty taking a heavy toll on Arianna's behaviour. It isn't her fault.

I approach her slowly with raised hands. "Calm down, Ari. We're home. You're safe."

"I'm not leaving!"

"We're going to stay for a while, baby. I have to sort out Grams's things, and you're going to see all of your friends again."

Peering up at me through her lashes, she looks on the verge of calming down before her tears intensify, and her wails ricochet off the walls around us. I kneel down and pull her into my lap.

"Shh, baby. I've got you."

"What the hell is this?" Killian demands.

"This is your fault!" I yell at him.

"I wasn't trying to upset her."

"But you did with your stupid little games."

He falls silent as I attempt to calm Arianna down. She's hiccupping and clinging to the lapels of my flannel shirt when Zach makes a bleary-eyed appearance in the kitchen.

"What happened?" he asks.

"Your cousin happened."

Killian huffs. "It's my fault."

Crouching down next to me in his plaid pyjama bottoms and t-shirt, Zach peels Arianna from my lap and boosts her into the air.

"Hey, monkey. Why the tears?"

Her chest shakes with hiccups. "I d-d-don't want to leave."

Bouncing her on his hip like she's a little toddler again, he dances around the kitchen and goofs off until Arianna is smiling. Her tears are quickly replaced by laughter.

"Zach! Lemme down!"

"Not until we turn that frown upside down," he singsongs. "Let's finish off this breakfast together, shall we? I'm sure I can burn it much better than your mama can."

"Okay," she submits.

"You're in charge then, Ari."

"I am?" She peers up at him with eager eyes.

Zach waggles his eyebrows. "I'm not gonna be the adult here. Now, where do you want me, chef?"

"I want eggs!"

"Then eggs it is."

He takes Arianna into the kitchen to begin whisking eggs, and I glance at Killian's weirdly anxious face. His emotions are at the forefront as he watches Zach entertain my daughter.

I lower my voice. "Ever use my daughter to emotionally manipulate me again and we're going to have a serious fucking problem. I am not kidding around."

With his head hanging in shame, I breeze past him and step outside to clear my head. It's freezing cold, the snow now stopped and settled in thick, white tides of powder.

It's a winter wonderland and the perfect setting for the approaching festive season, but I doubt we'll be here to see it. Mr Sanchez can find us here. We're not safe.

But for the life of me, I can't find the strength inside myself to leave again. The pain I felt last time has already expanded overtime, and I'm being crushed beneath its weight right now.

There's a loud crashing sound from the bottom of the garden where Micah's cabin lies. Lights are glowing from inside. I can't avoid him forever, even if part of me wants to.

Approaching the cabin and knocking on the door, I wait to be let inside. The crashing continues, and no one comes to open up. I have to heave open the lump of hewed wood myself.

"Mi? You in here?"

Bang.

Crash.

Shatter.

"Micah!"

There's chaos inside—unadulterated, destructive chaos. His studio has been trashed, from ripped canvases to smashed sculptures. Tools have been thrown and windows smashed.

"Oh my God."

Collapsing amidst the madness on a bean bag surrounded by empty beer cans, Micah is semi-conscious. There's a half-empty bottle of vodka still clutched in his paint-stained hand.

The sight of him causes my heart to squeeze.

"Mi?"

His caramel-brown hair is pointing up in all directions, his features mirroring his identical twin brother's soft, rounded face, despite his pierced button nose and slightly darker eyes.

"You again," he slurs.

"Me… again?"

"You always haunt my dreams, angel."

"Oh, Mi. I'm not a dream."

His glazed-over emerald eyes meet mine. "Of course, you are. The others told me to let go and forget you, but I just can't do it."

Heart splintering, I pick my way through the rubble and shards of glass.

Micah continues to loll on the beanbag as I finally reach him and crouch down next to it.

"What have you done to yourself?" I whisper, swiping unruly hair aside.

As my fingertips brush his skin, his eyes flutter shut in a brief look of ecstasy. It takes him a moment to realise that the hand touching him is real and not a dream.

"Willow," he breathes.

"I'm here, Mi. I'm real."

"Not... real."

Burying my fingers in his hair that's slick with grease, obviously unwashed, I press the lumps and bumps of his skull. My hand travels around to grasp his chin to make him look at me.

"Come back," I plead. "We need you. I need you. I'm sorry for leaving and making you do this to yourself to cope."

Tentatively reaching out, his hand strokes over my short, curling hair, verifying the inky black strands are indeed real. With his test satisfied, a streak of soberness enters his gaze.

"Holy fuck. You're here."

"I'm here," I repeat.

Looking a lot more awake, his eyes shine with unshed tears that cause thorny spikes to slice into my throat. He still won't move to embrace me as I desperately want him to.

"Why did you leave me?" he croaks.

Fuck. His voice.

"I'm so sorry," I choke out.

"My head... You left me alone in it."

Uncaring of whether he wants me to or not, I throw my arms around Micah's slimmed-down body and hold him close. He curls up against my chest like a tiny baby in need of love.

"I'm here... I'm here," I reassure.

Each time I repeat the words that he needs to hear, I circle his back in slow, comforting strokes. The smell of beer and liquor clings to him like a second skin, along with the stench of cigarettes.

This is the worst I've ever seen him. I've only heard rumours about the darkest depths of his worst depressive episodes, when the drinking escalates, and he stops taking care of himself.

"How long has this episode lasted?" I ask gently. "You don't look like you've showered or slept in weeks."

"Fine," he mumbles.

"You're not, Mi."

His head lifts, and two devastating eyes scour my face. "I can't believe… you're here. It's really you. Am I that drunk?"

"This is real. I'm home for Lola's funeral. We came as soon as we heard about what happened."

At the mention of her death, he pulls away from me. Micah staggers to his feet and takes a swig from the vodka bottle still tucked into his hands.

"She died while I was out drinking," he bites out. "I d-didn't get a chance to say goodbye. Neither did Z-Zach."

"We didn't either, Mi."

"But that wasn't your fault. This was m-mine."

Taking a seat at the chair in front of his crafting area that's miraculously still standing, Micah's head hits the table with a thump. A second later, his snoring begins.

I stare at him for several astonished seconds, unsure of exactly what I've just witnessed. He's passed out. Stone cold asleep.

I did this.

Me.

It's all my fault.

Grabbing his denim jacket from the hook on the wall, I carefully drape it over his shoulders so he's at least warm. There's a fire crackling in the corner of the room, and I add some more logs too.

He needs a shower, hot meal and proper sleep in a warm bed, but that can be tomorrow's task. I'm here now. I will fix what I've broken and look after him in his own personal darkness.

Back inside the cabin, Killian is washing up mixing bowls and utensils while Arianna eats her omelette on the sofa with Zach. I'm too emotionally exhausted to make her move and sit at the table.

"Micah's drunk," I say quietly.

Killian doesn't even look up from his task. "No doubt."

"You don't have a problem with that?"

He slams a wooden spoon down a little harder than necessary. "I have several problems with it. But it isn't something I can fix."

Abandoning the washing up, he mumbles about needing a shower and leaves the kitchen. I'm left standing in the mess of breakfast with my mouth hanging open.

I don't recognise the people I've come home to. The men I remember aren't here and a terrified part of me is worried they'll never return, just like the old Willow won't either.

Maybe, we're all too broken.

And this cannot be fixed.

CHAPTER 7
WILLOW

HOW DO I SAY GOODBYE – DEAN LEWIS

WITHIN THE WEEK, the time to say goodbye to Lola has rolled around, and she's ready to take her final resting place next to my grandfather, Pops.

Finishing off Arianna's braided hair with a glossy black bow that Killian appeared with, I gently pat her shoulder. She's wearing a simple, black skater dress and shiny new brogues.

"You're done, baby."

Her bottom lip wobbles. "Thanks, Mummy."

"What's wrong?"

"I don't want to say goodbye to Grams."

Turning her around, I pull her into a tight cuddle. "This isn't goodbye, Ari. You'll see her again one day. I promise you."

Her icy blue eyes shine with tears. "Swear it?"

"Swear it." I cross a finger over my heart. "Now go and find Killian and Zach. I have to help Micah for a moment."

Once she's gone, I leave the spare room we've slept in for the last few days and move to Micah's bedroom across the hall. I haven't found the courage to return to our abandoned cabin yet.

We've barely stepped outside, only to reunite with Ryder and Albie yesterday. Everyone else has kindly stayed away to give us the space we needed to adjust and rest after our journey home.

Letting myself into Micah's room, I find the curtains drawn and a lump beneath the covers. I heard him come in late last night after ignoring me for the last few days he's spent in his studio.

My plain black shift dress bunches around my thighs as I kneel on his bed and shake him as gently as possible to wake him up.

"Come on, Micah. You need to get showered. The funeral begins in an hour."

"Not going," he groans.

"You sure as hell are."

Refusing to let him wallow, I peel back the covers then pull on his ankle until he's forced to sit up. My breathing halts. Even with the weight he's lost, his body is carved in lean, muscular lines.

And he's naked.

Completely. Freaking. Naked.

"Where are your pyjamas?" I squeak.

He cracks a yawn. "Don't sleep in them."

Squeezing my eyes shut to offer him a semblance of privacy, I keep tugging on his ankle. "Shower. Now."

"Don't like what you see?"

"I didn't say that."

He eventually agrees to shower after a lot of hungover complaining. When he unsteadily stands up, I'm forced to open my eyes and balance him as we stumble into his en suite bathroom.

"How on earth did it come to this?" he asks groggily.

Leaning him against the bathroom sink, I bypass the bathtub that's full of our shared memories and flick on his small shower in the corner.

"I don't know."

I can feel his eyes on me, hot and searing. His gaze burns me down to the bone and leaves me feeling shaken.

"You look different. When did you cut your hair?"

"Shortly after I left Briar Valley." I check the water's temperature then step back. "Alright, get in. Clean yourself up."

Micah hesitates. "Can you stay?"

Trapped by uncertainty, I nod. "Sure."

"Thanks."

He sneaks past me and climbs into the warm spray, his shoulders curved over like he bears the weight of the whole world on his back. Even showering is a monumental task.

Clicking the door shut, I lean against the wall and let Micah wash in silence. He takes regular pauses to rest on the tiles, exhausted by even the smallest of tasks, obviously feeling like shit.

I get it.

Depression is a killer.

I've been in that dark place myself, where everything is too much and what should be the simplest of tasks, like brushing your teeth or eating, feels like climbing Mount Everest instead.

Flicking the water off, he opens the door, and I hand him a towel from the rack. The tiniest smile blooms on his face at the simple gesture.

"You don't need to do this."

"Would you have showered if I didn't?" I challenge.

"Well, no."

"Then I'll stand here and make you shower every single day until you're able to do it alone. I'm not going anywhere."

"For now," he says sadly.

Unable to argue with him, I head for his wardrobe to look for something suitable to wear, the pad of his wet feet following me. His wardrobe is full of t-shirts and ratty pairs of jeans that won't work.

Micah taps a zipped dress bag. "I wore this to my Aunt and Uncle's funeral. It should still fit."

I'm too afraid to unzip the bag for fear of the grief and sadness that may wash out of it in a tidal wave if I do. Instead, I grab a fresh black t-shirt and a pair of semi-tidy jeans.

"Here. You don't need to be fancy."

Leaving him to get dressed in peace, I find the other two sitting with Arianna in the living room. Killian's wearing his usual flannel shirt and jeans, though he's cleaned up his beard and picked a pair without holes.

Zach is the only one wearing all black with a long-sleeved dress shirt tucked into his tight black jeans. He's trimmed his hair and also shaved for the occasion, lightening his shadow-lined face.

"Micah's just coming."

"Did you get him to shower?" Zach frowns.

"He's showered and getting dressed."

He whistles under his breath. "Neither of us have managed that."

"I didn't exactly ask nicely."

Killian snorts in amusement. "Nice work."

We wait until Micah makes an appearance—pale-faced and contrite—but actually resembling a human being. His twin and cousin both stare at him like he's an alien.

"Shit," Zach curses. "He's alive."

Micah flips him the bird. "Fuck off."

"Little ears!" I scold them.

Laughing to herself in Killian's lap, Arianna is thoroughly enjoying their antics. She missed having them all around to fill the silence.

We filter out of the cabin to join Albie and Ryder outside in the snow. The moment Ryder sees me, I'm pulled into his engine grease-scented embrace for a cuddle.

"You holding up okay?"

"Yeah," I reply flatly.

"You don't need to pretend around me, sweetheart. We're going to get through today as a family. All of us."

His headful of dark ringlets tickle my face as he pulls back to pin me with his warm blue eyes and reassuring smile that match his handsome looks. I've missed my friend so much.

"Promise," he adds.

"Thanks, Ry."

Passing me off to Albie, the silver-haired grump pulls me into another hug. His clear eyes are already covered in a sheen of tears. I've never seen him in a suit before. He looks strange.

"I'm so sorry, Al."

"Me too, kid. Never thought I'd see this day come."

"None of us did."

Interrupting our moment, Arianna is squealing at the top of her lungs as she jumps through the fresh tides of snow that fell last night. Killian stops me before I can shush her shouting.

"She's letting her hair down," he explains simply.

I reluctantly back off. "Alright."

Lord knows, she hasn't had the opportunity to do that of late. Not while cooped up in the cramped space of our old apartment, watching the rain hit against the windows.

We begin the slippery walk into town together. Snow covers everything from the branches of pine and fir trees to the slick, cobbled stones that carve the winding path beneath our feet.

I'd forgotten just how beautiful Briar Valley is. Mount Helena hangs high above us in sharp, jagged points that boast an even heavier dousing of snow, while white-dusted shrubs and trees cloak us in a sarcophagus.

Zach catches up to me and takes my hand in his. "You ready for this? The whole town is gonna be there."

"Not really, but I don't have a choice."

"You don't have to stay for long. Just get the service out of the way, and show your face."

"I can't bail on my own grandmother's funeral."

His fingers clench mine. "You do whatever you need to get through this in one piece. Fuck everyone else and what they need from you. That isn't our priority."

I stop in the snow. "What is your priority, Zach?"

Letting the others pass us, he tilts my chin up and exposes my lips to him. Our mouths meet—hesitantly, tender and exploratory, fuelled by the uncertainty our separation has doomed us with.

"You," he murmurs into my mouth. "It's always been you, Willow."

A tingle runs down my spine. "Does this mean you've forgiven me for leaving?"

"It means that I'm tired of hating you, and I want my family back. We've already lost enough. Today, more than ever, we need each other."

"I need you too," I blurt.

He kisses me again, harder this time. "You've got me, babe. I never stopped loving you. It would take the end of this damn world for that to happen, and even then I'd follow you into the beyond."

Somehow, I smile. "Ditto."

"Then we're on the same page."

Curling into his side, I let him guide me down the steep slopes that descend into the town centre. Familiar faces begin to appear around us, staring at me with varying degrees of shock.

"Willow," Harold bellows while walking into town with his wife, Marilyn. "You're back."

I manage a weak wave. "I'm here."

To my surprise, he captures me in a hug when we rejoin the others. His silvery whiskers tickle my face before he releases me, and Marilyn smacks a wet kiss on my cheek.

"We missed you around here," she explains with a tight smile. "Especially this one."

Harold harrumphs at her comment. "Scared the hell out of me, Willow. Where'd you go?"

"Around," I answer vaguely.

"You back for good?"

Before I can come up with some half-assed answer to get him off my back, the scream of another familiar voice interrupts our reunion.

In the town square, Aalia is standing next to Johan and a tall, dark-haired man with two children. She takes one look at me approaching and freaks out.

"Willow!" she yells.

Aalia races towards me as fast as her skidding snow boots beneath an ankle-length, beaded dress will allow. We collide somewhere in the middle in a sobbing, happy tangle.

"Hi, Aalia."

"I can't believe it's you," she weeps.

I stroke her long brown hair, the coarse strands framing olive-toned skin, deep, almond-shaped eyes and pillowy lips. She's stunning and looks spotless, even with two kids to look after.

Looking over her shoulder, I realise that the man standing with her is holding baby Amie on his hip. It's Walker, the gentleman Katie introduced at my party, with his kids.

We join him in the town square where the guys exchange handshakes with him. Walker nods to me, passing a much-bigger Amie back to Aalia before she starts to cry.

"Willow, right?"

I tentatively shake his hand too. "You remembered."

"Hard to forget that party, it ended pretty spectacularly." His gaze saddens. "Your grams made a hell of a scene with Katie, if I'm remembering correctly."

"She sure did."

"Sorry for your loss."

"Thanks."

Aalia touches my arm. "We mean it, Willow. I know this can't be easy for you. We're here if you need anything."

"I appreciate that."

Arianna has bundled Johan in a hug. The pair are clearly glad to see each other. Aalia kisses her next while Zach fawns over Amie, pulling ridiculous expressions to satisfy her almost one-year-old mind.

We pass countless friendly faces and smiles as we head into Lola's cabin to meet the others. Albie trails at the back of our group, requiring Killian to strong-arm him back inside.

In the living room, Doc, Miranda and Rachel are clustered around the lit, open fireplace, awaiting our arrival. They all give me kisses and hugs, whispering their gratitude that I've returned.

Katie has also made an appearance with her fiancé, Don. She moves to embrace me first. I hug her back to the surprise of the entire room watching us interact.

"You good?" she murmurs.

"Bearing up," I force out.

"I'm here if you need to talk, darling."

"Thank you, Katie."

There's a dull ache behind my eyes already. Plastering on a smile and pretending like I won't run again at the drop of a hat is getting challenging. Worse still, I know from Killian's grimace that he sees through my act.

"Willow," Ryder calls from the doorway. "You remember my boyfriend, Ethan."

Ah, shit.

After filtering into the house and brushing snow from his dark blue suit and grey pea coat, Ethan offers me what he must think is an easy smile, but I can see the tension behind it.

"Nice to see you again, Willow."

I swallow the lump in my throat. "You too."

"I've been trying to get in tou——"

"Are we ready to go now?" I interrupt.

Ethan's mouth snaps shut, and understanding filters into his gaze. I offer him the subtlest shake of my head to warn him off from attempting to broach that topic. Not in front of the guys.

"She's in the kitchen," Doc answers. "If you want to say a private goodbye first."

"S-Sure." I glance at Arianna. "Can you guys watch her please?"

Zach nods, an arm wrapped around her shoulders. "We'll wait here."

Before I can escape, Killian steps into the path of the doorway. I'm forced to look up into his bonfire eyes.

"Need me to come with you?" he growls.

"I'll be fine, Kill."

His eyes move lower to my covered up arms. "Sure about that?"

A hot blush creeps across my neck. "Yes."

"Fine. But I'll be right outside."

It feels like an eternity before he eventually moves aside so I can pass him and Ethan by. The burning, hot weight of his gaze follows me all the way into the kitchen where I click the door shut.

My breath seizes.

The coffin has been placed on the kitchen table where nearly a whole year ago, I woke up, penniless and afraid in an unknown place. That was the day I met Lola and discovered the family I always had.

She welcomed me into town with open arms and did absolutely everything in her power to look after me. Even when I pushed her away out of pain and spite, she refused to budge.

I'll never get to thank her for that.

She deserved to know how much she was loved.

Thankfully, the coffin is closed. I take a seat in one of the kitchen chairs and rest a hand atop the smooth mahogany lid, inscribed with her name and the word *Grams*. That's when the tears come flooding back.

"I'm so sorry," I gasp in pain.

The coffin is silent.

"I wasn't here to say goodbye. You begged me to come home, and all I did was ignore you. I'll never be able to forgive myself for that."

Still, she cannot answer me. That sweet, lilting voice, simultaneously filled with the gentlest brand of love and her own personal sense of supreme authority, will never speak to me again.

My hand strokes the coffin's lid. "I need to say thank you for everything you did for me and Arianna. I didn't know what it felt like to be loved or have a real family until I met you."

In my head, I can see her. Twinkle-eyed and acid-tongued. She tuts at me for apologising and pulls me into her cookie-scented embrace for a cuddle that will never be replicated.

"Thank you." I sniff, wiping my tears aside. "Thanks for saving my life and for giving my little girl a home. Thank you for giving us safety and security when we needed it most. Thank you... for being my Grams."

Standing up, I press a kiss on the inscribed metal plaque that's attached to the coffin then force myself to walk away from the woman who saved my life in the absolute darkest of times.

It's the hardest goodbye.

Lola is gone forever.

CHAPTER 8
WILLOW

I STILL LOVE YOU – BISHOP
BRIGGS

LEAVING the drinks reception in Lola's cabin, I abandon the funeral for a breath of fresh air. The service was nice—simple and quiet in the cloak of trees and snow at Briar Valley's graveyard.

Lola's final resting place is beneath a huge cherry blossom tree that will bloom in the spring in a field of wildflowers that will scent the air when summer returns. Pops lies next to her in his grave.

Outside the cabin, I crunch down the wide porch steps then make a beeline around the back of the cabin to find the quiet vegetable patch where I can have a moment's peace.

I don't expect to find someone already there—his head tilted downwards as he rapidly taps out a text message on his phone.

"Willow." Ethan startles, a cigarette clasped in his other hand.

"Oh… I'm sorry." My feet quickly backtrack. "I… should get back inside."

"No, wait. Please just let me have five minutes of your time."

Stuck between a rock and a hard place, I have no choice but to grit out a breath and join him. He offers me a cigarette which I politely decline, the acrid smoke curling in the freezing cold air.

"I'm so sorry about your Grams," he sympathises. "She was a good woman."

"She really was."

"You came back to Briar Valley fast."

I spare him a look. "I didn't have much of a choice."

"I know that Katie passed along our information to you. My team is working night and day to bring this human trafficking ring down."

"I wasn't trafficked, Ethan."

"Listen, love." His voice is filled with infinite patience. "We all know what that bastard did to you. Continuing to live in denial is helping nobody, including yourself."

Mouth snapping shut, I sigh through my nostrils. He's right. Out there somewhere, Mr Sanchez still has the freedom to beat, bruise and kill whomever he pleases. I'm allowing that to happen.

If someone else had been able to wield the power to free me, I would've begged for them to save us. For Arianna. For a single second of peace from the pain and abuse. Now I'm allowing others to endure the same thing.

"I want to help," I say in a tiny voice. "But I'm so fucking scared. You don't know him like I do."

"I've spent the past twelve months investigating that son of a bitch and his associates across the globe," he replies grimly. "I know enough to confidently say he'll rot behind bars for the rest of his life."

My laugh is bitter. "He has power and influence in places you can't even begin to imagine. Prison wouldn't hold someone like him. Trust me."

Crushing the cigarette in the snow, Ethan rests a hand on my shoulder. "Trust us, Willow. Sabre Security is the real deal. Give us a chance to prove ourselves to you."

I look up into his hopeful gaze. "How?"

"Talk to us. Tell us your story, and let us help you. All we want is justice for every last person this trafficking ring has hurt. There're a lot of people out there waiting for that."

Caught in a trap of indecision, my heart feels like it's going to explode out of my ribcage and tear itself into a million anxious pieces. The thought of another Arianna being stuck in a mansion seals the deal for me.

"I'll do it."

Ethan clasps my shoulder. "You will?"

"On the condition that your company offers me and Arianna protection," I decide. "We want round-the-clock surveillance until this is all over and Mr Sanchez is behind bars."

"We can do that. I'll need you to come down to London to testify, though."

"Okay."

"I'll let you know a date to come down," he rushes out excitedly. "Want to tell the guys about this, or should I?"

"I guess it should be me."

"You're doing the right thing, Willow. We're going to catch this motherfucker, and you'll finally be able to put this all behind you."

I rest a hand on top of his. "I really hope so."

With another smile, Ethan leaves me to have a moment of privacy. It doesn't last long. The crunch of footsteps approaching soon ends my solitude, and I know who it is without having to look.

The combined warmth of Killian and Zach sandwiches me in. I press my face into Zach's dress shirt and feel Killian's hands move to hold my hips as he nuzzles the back of my head.

With their strength around me, I let my brave face fall aside. I don't need to pretend in front of them that everything is even remotely okay when it feels like my entire world is ending.

"What was that all about?" Killian rumbles.

"Mr Sanchez," I whisper into Zach's chest. "He's being investigated by Ethan's company, and I've agreed to testify to help bring him down."

Zach pushes my shoulders back so he can see my face. "You're kidding? Why didn't we know about this sooner?"

"I heard a couple of weeks ago from Katie. I wasn't planning to do it until now."

Killian squeezes my hips with his two paws. "Why not?"

"Because he's a powerful son a bitch with the money and influence to wipe Briar Valley off the map. You don't mess with someone like that. Not when they know exactly where you are."

His nose teases the slope of my neck as he inhales my scent. Feeling the brief touch of his lips on my skin has my pulse racing, even as the funeral continues in the cabin behind us.

Killian's been a tough nut to crack ever since I returned home several days ago. His anger still bubbles to the surface when I least expect it. But he's trying hard to be fair and hold it at bay.

"Can we get out of here?" Zach complains. "The kid's playing with Johan and the others inside. Everyone else is going to head home soon too."

"I'll go and get Ari," I offer.

"No." Killian traps me to stop my movements. "Aalia will watch them for a bit. We need to talk first."

"About what?"

"Not here. Let's go home."

He pins me against his hard, muscled side and marches me out of the vegetable patch. Zach follows, and we ascend the steep, snowy slope back up to their shared cabin.

Once inside, Killian flicks on lights and locates a bottle of amber-coloured liquid from the cupboard. He sets us up with three glasses then sits down at the breakfast bar.

"This time nine months ago, we sat in this very spot," he begins thoughtfully. "We asked you to stay in Briar Valley, where we could keep you safe. And you agreed."

I linger in the kitchen, afraid to move any closer. "I did."

Zach remains at my back, his breath stirring my curls. "We're asking you the same thing again now. You need to stay now that the funeral's over. This is your home."

"I don't have a home," I answer sadly.

Killian knocks back a mouthful of liquor. "Now that's not true, is it?"

Pushing me forwards with a hand on my lower back, Zach moves me closer to his cousin until I'm again caught between them. But this time, I'm looking up at Killian's impassive expression.

The strong curvatures and razor-sharp angles of his face all could slice deep into my skin and rip me apart, limb from limb. I wouldn't even mind right now. I'm turning into putty beneath his intense gaze.

"Is it?" he demands.

"I... don't know, Kill."

"Yeah. You do."

Grasping my legs, he lifts me up and encourages my legs to wrap around his broad waist. My body can't help reacting on instinct, trained by mere touch alone to react to his strength and domination.

"We can't do this right now," I gasp.

"Right now is exactly when we should be doing this," he counters. "We need to feel alive and appreciate what we've got, baby, because it's fucking special. That has to be protected."

I close my legs around his waist. "I think what we have is special too."

"Good."

Then his mouth is on mine, hot and demanding, as his hands cup my butt. Zach's hard chest meets my back again, and his two hands land on my hips to hold me against his cousin's hardening cock.

Zach's lips graze against the shell of my ear. "That's more like it. My left hand just ain't cutting it anymore."

"Charming." I pepper kisses down Killian's beard-covered neck. "So there haven't been... you know, any other women?"

Abruptly, Killian freezes, his tone turning hard and angry. "Are you kidding me with that shit? You really think we would do that to you?"

"Well, I don't know."

Zach's fingers painfully dig into my hips. "There's been no one. You really think any other woman would match up to you?"

Trailing a hand down Killian's chest, I unfasten his jeans and slip a hand inside his boxers to cup his cock. His eyes darken as I find his length and stroke teasingly.

"Nobody?" I double-check.

He leans in to bite my lip hard enough to draw blood. "Hell no, baby. I couldn't stop thinking about you, even when I hated the living daylights out of you for leaving."

"Seconded," Zach hums in a playful voice.

"Should we take this to the bedroom?"

Killian smirks. "Why? I quite like the idea of seeing you naked and begging in my kitchen."

His hands disappear, leaving me to slide down his body. Killian spins me around so I'm facing Zach again before reaching beneath my dress to rip my panties down in one swift move.

I'm left bare and wet beneath the dress, my pussy contracting with the waves of need that blur my vision. My brief, interrupted session with Zach the other day has done nothing to sate my desires.

"Is our girl wet for us?" Zach wonders.

Killian's hand sneaks between my legs to find my dripping core. "Soaked as always."

Mouth capturing mine, I gasp into Zach's lips as his cousin's fingers slide through my folds, gathering moisture before pushing inside me. His thumb swipes over my clit, causing me to moan.

"So wet and tight," Killian murmurs.

Zach breaks the kiss. "I want a taste."

"Wait your fucking turn, kid. She's mine right now."

"Spoilsport," he mutters.

Spinning me back around before dropping to his knees in front of me, Killian lifts the hem of my dress to expose my bare cunt to him.

His lips graze over my heat, tongue flicking across my sensitive bundle of nerves. I cover my mouth with my hand to silence my moaning.

Each touch feels like the first time I've ever been pleasured by a man. It's been so long, my body is working on overdrive, with every sense dialled to ten.

Killian pushes his finger back inside me, securing his mouth to my clit at the same time. I whimper, the sound filling the cabin as Zach prises my hand away from my mouth.

"Let me hear you," he growls. "I want to know how much you love my cousin eating your pretty little cunt out."

"Fuck," I moan as Killian adds a second finger.

He's stretching me wide, using his digits to work me into a frenzy of need. Zach's erection rubs into my ass while he softly kisses my neck and shoulder. I need to feel them. Touch them. Taste them.

"Please. I'm ready."

"Not yet," Zach purrs. "You have to wait."

"I want you to fuck me, Zachariah."

"Do you now?"

He slaps my backside hard enough to sting. My ass cheek tingles, but it only adds to the cresting wave of pleasure that's on the horizon, rapidly moving closer. It's going to swallow me whole.

"Come all over Killian's face," Zach whispers into my ear. "Then we'll fuck you raw, baby girl."

Tweaking my clit again, Killian moves his fingers even faster. In and out. Circling, swirling, curling deep inside of me to reach that tender spot that forces me to explode.

"Now," he commands.

I cry out as my release hits, spreading come across his face that's still buried between my thighs. He thrusts his thick fingers into me until I have nothing left to give.

Coming up for air, there's stickiness scored across his mouth and lips. He licks up every last drop, making sure not to waste a single bit. The sight of him cleaning his lips makes me wet all over again.

"Is it my turn yet?" Zach whines, still standing behind me.

"Not yet, kid." Killian's eyes blaze with carnal fire as he looks up at me. "Ready for me, princess?"

"Yes," I breathe.

He sits back on his haunches, pulling his massive, bulging cock out of his jeans. "Come and ride me then, baby."

Too excited to think of anything but filling myself with him, I slide free from Zach's grip and position myself in Killian's lap. Zach takes the opportunity to sink down to the floor, pouting in disappointment.

"I'll just watch then," he complains.

I glance over my shoulder at him. "Be with you soon, Zachariah."

"Fucking better be."

"Eyes on me," Killian snaps, regaining my attention.

Holding the base of his dick, he feeds the long, hard length deep into my entrance. The moment he's inside of me, I throw my head back and mewl in ecstasy.

"Fuck," he hisses. "That's it, beautiful. Ride my cock."

I lift myself then slam back down on him with the fuel of desperation behind me. Killian's dick sheathes even deeper inside my cunt, and the pressure is almost unbearable, I feel so exquisitely full.

With each thrust of his hips rising to meet my movements, we collide in a spectacular fashion, both battling for ownership of the other. I want to brand myself back into the meaty flesh of his heart.

An insecure part of me couldn't help but wonder if there had been anyone else. I wouldn't have blamed them if there was. I was gone for a long time. But an even bigger part of me is satisfied that there wasn't.

They're mine.

All. Fucking. Mine.

Breathing hard, I look back over my shoulder at Zach. He's freed his cock and strokes it, his eyes locked on us fucking mere metres away. When I wink at him, his eyes sparkle with devilish promise.

"Hurry up," he mouths.

Spanking my ass, Killian forces me to look back at him. He ruts into me with fast, frenzied strokes, battering his possession into my soul with the same ferocity that I'm reclaiming his. We're back. Alive. This is where we belong—together.

Without warning, Killian roars through an orgasm, and I feel the hot spurt of his come filling me up. The sensation causes me to fall apart again, stronger this time, crying out my own incandescent relief.

Warmth spreads between us, and the feeling is so exquisite. I'm full of him, coated and claimed. Killian hides his face in my chest as he battles to catch his breath.

"Shit." He swipes his forehead with the back of his arm. "I wasn't expecting to finish so fast."

I kiss the top of his dark-blonde hair. "It's okay. I came too."

"What about me?" a voice drones. "I've waited very patiently."

Standing behind us, Zach's naked from the waist down now and fisting his proud length. I watch as he pumps his cock, the heat burning bright in his emerald eyes.

"Princess," he rasps. "I need you too."

I take his offered hand and clamber off Killian's lap. Zach seizes the zip on the back of my dress then quickly shoves it down. Thankfully, he's too preoccupied with removing my bra to notice my arms.

With the bra discarded, his mouth secures to the hardened point of my left nipple. His teeth graze against the peak, causing desire to flood my veins again. I want him inside of me too.

"Table," Zach grunts.

Walking me backwards, my tailbone connects with the solid lump of wood. I hop up and let him shift me backwards so he can settle between my legs and return his mouth to my chest.

Killian sits on the floor, watching us both as Zach presses up against the slick heat of my entrance. I'm even wetter after my first two orgasms and still dripping with Killian's seed, but Zach doesn't seem to mind.

"I love seeing you soaked in my family's come." He flashes me a wolfish grin.

"Zach," I groan.

"Don't worry, princess. I'm gonna make you feel good."

"Please. Now."

Suddenly, he surges inside of me, burying himself deep and letting out a guttural sound. The table shakes each time he pushes back into my cunt, slam after slam, pump after pump.

His strokes set my soul on fire and leave me to burn into handfuls of ashes. I can't breathe. Think. Feel. Exist. All that I am is contingent on him, and him alone, for these breathless moments.

"So fucking perfect," he praises while hammering into me.

I grip the edges of the table and hold on for dear life. The salt and pepper shakers go flying and smash against the floor, but no one pays any attention. Not even Killian who watches us fuck with interest.

We cause chaos as we slap against each other in a heat-fuelled tangle. Zach moves to clasp my throat. I was hoping he'd pull out his signature move.

There's no other man in the world I'd allow to hold such power over me again, but when Zach does it, I don't mind surrendering to him. In return, he gives me the safety of knowing he'll allow me to breathe again.

His nails dig into my neck as he roughly fucks me into the table, causing pain to slice through me. I relish in it—every satisfying drop of agony that makes me feel alive for the first time in months.

"I couldn't breathe when you left us behind," Zach says gruffly. "You made me feel like this, beautiful girl. Like I was slowly dying with no way out of the darkness."

His grip intensifies. I don't tap out. Not yet. I need to be punished. To feel the pain that I inflicted upon them. To hurt. To suffer. To be reborn in ashes and rise again into the person I previously became here.

"I fucking loved you with everything I had to give," he adds. "And you threw my heart away like it meant nothing to you. How can I forgive that?"

Hand loosening enough for me to answer, I choke out a response. "You can't."

Zach shakes his head. "You're wrong. I fucking can, and I fucking will."

When he releases my neck, the rush of oxygen into my lungs is excruciating. Pain bursts in my chest and my vision swims from the sheer intensity of relief that the end of his torture brings. I could cry.

I'm being forgiven.

Reborn.

Reclaimed.

Slamming his lips against mine, Zach swallows my scream of pleasure as he climaxes at the same time. Our bodies press together in a slick ocean of sweat, blending us into one unidentifiable person.

He pours himself into me, and I'm filled with his hot come. I can feel it spilling over my thighs as he lifts his head to look up at me.

"Jesus Christ."

"You okay?" I laugh breathlessly.

"That wasn't what I had planned on doing today."

"Are you complaining?"

"Not in the slightest."

Killian grabs a sheet of kitchen tissue and tosses it over Zach's shoulder. He looks sheepish as he moves it between my thighs after pulling out, cleaning up the mess he's made all over my legs.

My mind is a puddle of numbness. No other thoughts dare to creep in. All I care about is the treacle-like warmth pumping through my veins, bringing molten happiness and satisfaction.

"Willow?" Zach asks uncertainly.

"Hmm," I reply back.

"We meant what we said before. You have to stay. There's no other option on the table anymore."

My pleasure fades as I reopen my eyes to look at them both. They're wearing identical expressions of desperate, borderline obsessive hope. I fear for my life if I utter anything other than *yes* right now.

"What if he comes for us?" I vocalise my fears.

"Let the bastard fucking try," Killian growls darkly. "I'd enjoy seeing him face to face. Though he won't have much of a face left by the time I'm done."

"Kill," I gasp.

"Exactly."

Fighting the urge to faceplant, I push Zach's shoulder to make space for my feet to land back on the floor. After cleaning myself up, I ditch the tissue in the rubbish bin and face them both with defeat.

"It's not like I want to run."

"Then stay," Zach demands.

Killian bobs his head in agreement. "Forever."

Between the weight of their combined gazes and the pressure that's reaching a breaking point, I have no choice but to nod. It takes all of my courage to summon that one gesture.

"Fine. But we're moving back into our cabin."

I'm almost knocked off my feet by the pair rugby-tackling me. Sandwiched between them, there's no space to breathe, let alone change my mind. Our fates have been sealed.

We're home.

For good.

CHAPTER 9
MICAH

GONE – NF & JULIA MICHAELS

CHRISTMAS IS NEVER a happy time for me.

It's when my grief hits the hardest.

This year is no different. I wake up to the steady fall of snow the week after Lola's funeral. Things have been quiet around here. The town feels lifeless and empty without her in it.

Working on my latest project—a full-sized watercolour print of St David's Pointe in all its rugged beauty—I ignore the creak of the door opening.

Willow has taken to walking in rather than knocking when I've ignored her. She's determined to pull me out of the depression that's drowning me and has made it her mission to force me to eat.

"Mi?"

Shit. Zach.

Ignoring him, I focus on the snow-capped peaks and white-dusted fir trees that line the mountain pass on my canvas. I had planned to gift this to Lola for Christmas. She loved the mountains so much.

Now I'm going to finish this piece of art and destroy it. Just like every other sculpture and painting I've created since her death and left in ruins around me. None of them are good enough anymore.

"Micah. You need to come inside."

"Go away," I say absently.

"Not a chance." Zach stops next to me. "It's Christmas Day, and Willow's struggling enough without Lola here. Get your ass inside before I kick it."

Pain bites into my chest. Fuck. Of course, she's finding today difficult.

Lola's barely been dead for two weeks, and already we're all expected to move on with our lives. It's unfair.

"She doesn't need me in there, making everyone even more miserable."

"For fuck's sake," he grumbles. "You're really starting to piss me off, little brother."

"Still just three fucking minutes."

"And you have exactly three seconds to get inside before I lose my shit. Your family needs you. Willow needs you. Stop being such a selfish prick."

My hand stilling against the canvas, I let the brush drop. Shame floods my cheeks. It's easier to hide out in here rather than face the concern that still blooms in their eyes at the sight of me.

Things have been rough.

My recent depressive episodes have taken everything out of me, especially since Lola's death. Today is the first day I've made it to sit at my easel, rather than wallowing or drinking.

"Mi," he urges. "Please. I'm begging you."

I feel my resolve crack. "Alright."

"You'll come inside?"

"If you promise to get the hell off my case already."

"Pinkie swear," he vows.

Putting my tools down, I wipe my paint-slick hands off on a rag and follow Zach out of the cabin. Each step adds to the pressure on my chest. I can't believe I'm letting him talk me into this.

I've never celebrated Christmas. Not even last year when Lola cooked a huge family dinner for us all in her cabin and invited the whole town for carol singing.

I always hide in my studio until it's all over and the memories of my father slink back into their badly sealed box. It's easier that way. Simpler. Safer. I don't bother anyone else with my grief.

The moment Zach opens the cabin door, warmth hits me in the face. The fire has been lit, and Killian is bent over the oven, basting a huge turkey surrounded by roughly cut roast potatoes.

"Jesus," I curse.

Killian glances at me. "Well, I'll be damned. Look who decided to show his face."

He's wearing a flowery apron over his red flannel shirt and blue jeans. Willow's trying hard not to laugh as she watches him cook with a glass of red wine in hand.

Her head immediately turns on a swivel to face me, and she smiles broadly with a look of relief that steals my breath. Fuck. I've missed that stunning, ear to ear smile so much.

"Micah," she breathes.

I offer an awkward wave. "Hi."

"You joining us to eat?" Killian asks.

"He is," Zach answers for me.

Giving me a hard shove, I fall farther into the room. It smells amazing in here. Killian is far better in the kitchen when under Willow's supervision than left alone to his own devices.

"Micah!" Arianna shouts.

In the living room, she's curled up in front of the fireplace with… a fucking puppy. The ball of midnight-black fur is asleep in her arms as she strokes its little belly and ears.

"Who got her a puppy?"

Zach chuckles. "Who do you think?"

We all turn to face Killian, the tips of his ears slowly turning bright-red. "What?"

"A puppy? For real?"

"She needs something to protect her."

"But… a puppy?" I repeat.

"Yes! It's a damn puppy!"

He glowers at us all until we're forced to look away before he whips us with a wooden spoon. It wouldn't be the first time. That stony-faced asshole is a complete softie for Arianna.

"Her name is Demon," Arianna states matter-of-factly.

"Demon?"

"Yes." Her smile is wan. "Because nobody will hurt us if we have a demon by our side. Right?"

"Right, baby." Willow ruffles her hair.

Zach snorts. "Just another normal day in Briar Valley, right?"

Snagging a beer, I quickly put it down again when I catch the look on Willow's face. Her momentary happiness has vanished, and she looks gutted at the thought of me drinking alcohol in front of her.

Instead, I approach her and offer a hand for her to take. She hesitantly puts hers into mine, and I curl our fingers together to pull her closer. My lips brush against her mouth in a tentative whisper.

"Merry Christmas, angel."

It takes a moment for her to kiss me back, her hand lifting to bury in my messy crop of hair. "Happy Christmas, Mi."

"Eww!" Arianna squeals. "Stop kissing my mummy."

"Sorry, squirt."

Pecking Willow's mouth again, I leave her and attack the little monkey instead. She screams and wriggles as I tickle her ribs relentlessly, disturbing the cute ball of fur in her lap.

The puppy is an adorable little thing—she looks like a tiny black Labrador Retriever. Her tongue is lurid pink against her pitch-black fur as she attacks me in a storm of teeth and tongue.

"Alright!" I shout. "Ari, call your attack dog off."

"Here, Demon." She claps her hands together.

The dog finally relents and returns to her owner's lap for more cuddles. I'm left covered in hair and slobber, much to Zach's amusement.

"Well played," he mouths.

I glower at him. "Could've helped."

"I didn't tell you to go to war with a puppy."

Killian steps into the room in his flowery apron. "Grub's up."

I'm not sure I can remove the image of him in an apron from my brain without the assistance of industrial-strength bleach. But Arianna and Willow are clearly loving it based on their bright, happy grins.

Having them here feels weirdly good. I was dreading coming inside and had no intention of eating with them, but with their presence here, the cabin doesn't feel so empty anymore.

Arianna rises to wash her hands, stopping in front of me to grab my wrist. "Come with me, Micah."

I'm dragged over to the kitchen sink to wash my hands, her strength surprising for a tiny seven-year-old. She squirts soap onto my paint-splattered skin then traps my hands between hers to lather them up.

"You're always dirty," she scolds.

"Sorry, kiddo."

"Where have you been? I wanted to practice my finger-painting with you, but Mummy told me to leave you alone."

I swallow the lump in my throat. "I'm sorry. I've been feeling poorly."

"Poorly?" She frowns up at me. "I think you mean sad. I don't know why. You need to be happy, Mi."

Drying off my hands, I boost her up into a hug then settle her on my hip. "I'll help you with finger-painting tonight. Is that a deal?"

Arianna grins at me. "Deal!"

"Alright then, monkey."

Carrying Arianna over to the table, I sit her down next to Willow. Ryder appears through the front door a moment later, a Christmas hat covering his curls.

He spots me and does a dramatic double take that makes me roll my eyes. Here we go. He's already prepping some stupid remark.

"Holy fuck. He's alive."

"Language," I snap.

Willow jabs a finger at him. "Micah's right. Language."

Scolded, Ryder spreads his hands in surrender and takes a seat at the table. "You rejoining the land of the living, Mi?"

"For now."

"Aren't we blessed."

"You should be."

"Shut up, you rowdy lot." Killian stands over the table with the turkey in hand. "Time to play happy fuckin' families."

"Kill!" Willow shrills in exasperation. "How many times do I have to tell you guys off for your language?"

With a smirk on his face, he places the turkey down on the table amongst veggies, pigs in blankets, cauliflower cheese and a giant jug of gravy that could wash all of Briar Valley away.

"Happy Birthday, Jesus," he declares triumphantly. "Everyone dig in."

Zach doesn't have to be told twice. He's already shovelling a pile of potatoes on his plate as Killian carves up the bird. There's a ridiculous amount of food on the table.

Ryder watches Killian carve with sadness in his eyes, and I know he's thinking of Lola. Her Sunday night roast dinners are a staple of the town's history and part of what makes us one big rowdy family.

"Wait," Ryder blurts.

Everyone freezes.

"We should... you know, raise a toast. To Lola."

Placing the carving knife down, Killian's expression turns solemn. "Yeah. We should."

Everyone lifts their drinks as I pour myself a glass of water from the jug on the table. Willow's gaze shines with appreciation.

"To Lola," Ryder toasts, his beer raised. "Grams, hope you're having a hell of a time celebrating Christmas up there with Pops."

Clinking our glasses together, no one says anything else as we all silently swallow. Words won't cover it. Lola was far beyond them. In fact, words haven't been enough since she left us.

"Mummy?" Arianna whispers.

Sniffling, Willow wipes underneath her eyes. "I'm fine, baby girl. Eat up."

Zach waves a Christmas cracker in my face. "Come on then, Mi. Pull one."

"What are we, five years old?"

"Pull the damn cracker before I hit you with it."

I do as told just to appease him and snort when he loses. Pulling the miniature dice set and paper hat free from the ruined remains, I read out the joke.

"What do you call a boomerang that doesn't come back?"

Zach shrugs. "No idea."

"A stick."

Bursting into hysterical laughter, Arianna doubles over as she giggles maniacally. "A stick! That's so funny."

"That was terrible." Zach wrinkles his nose in disgust. "Alright, let me try one."

Ripping open another cracker, he pulls his own paper hat on before reading the joke inside. His present was a crappy nail file.

"Okay. Who hides in a bakery at Christmas?"

"Who?" Arianna asks excitedly.

"A mince spy."

She stares without understanding. "I don't get it."

"A mince pie." Willow nudges her in the ribs. "Like the dessert?"

Her eyebrows crease in confusion. I guess she didn't have them in Mexico. Part of me wonders what they were both doing this time last year while still living under that bastard's roof.

"Lola made the best homemade mince pies," Killian muses, his eyes filled with sadness. "Even made the pastry herself too."

"With the little stars on top," Ryder chimes in.

"She spiked the cream on the side with whiskey as well." Zach laughs to himself. "That stuff was seriously dangerous."

"I always wanted to see what one of Lola's famous Christmas dinners would be like," Willow adds to their reminiscing. "Now I never will."

"You'll always have a place at this table," Killian says gruffly. "Regardless of where life takes us."

"Thank you, Kill."

Placing her hand on top of his, the pair share a loaded look. Hope sparks deep in my mind. Since agreeing to stick around, Willow's been different.

Part of me wants it to be true, but I'm struggling to believe she'll stay. She's made promises before, yet that didn't stop her from leaving us at the earliest opportunity.

When Ryder's phone chirps, he mutters something about a video call with Ethan and dips outside to answer. Willow's demeanour immediately changes, locking back up and becoming defensive.

"I'm finished!" Arianna licks her plate clean. "Can I go and play with Demon now please?"

"Sure, baby," Willow murmurs.

Arianna vanishes to roll around in the living room with her new best friend, leaving us to finish up in peace. Killian follows Willow's gaze out of the window to where Ryder's taking his call.

"When does Ethan want you to travel down to London?" he asks abruptly.

"Couple of weeks," she sighs.

When I heard about the plan, I was sceptical. Rehashing the past isn't fun for anyone. It's going to be hard on Willow, and she'll be re-traumatised by dragging it all back up.

"What's he gonna do, then?" Zach jumps in.

"I guess I'll testify on record, and they'll use my story as part of their investigation. Mr Sanchez is just one of several big players being looked into by Sabre Security."

"So there's a real chance to bring this motherfucker down?" he asks.

"Not in the way I want to," Killian grumbles back. "He needs a bullet between his eyes, not a prison cell."

"I'm not visiting you in a prison cell," Willow snaps at him. "That's final."

"How are they going to take him down?" I interrupt. "He's in Mexico, right?"

Willow shrugs. "Extradition, I suppose. It's an international investigation, so they have a lot of resources."

The whole thing sounds precarious. I have a lot of respect for Ethan and his work, but from what we know, Dimitri Sanchez is the real deal.

It's going to take a lot to bring that son of a bitch to justice. Perhaps more than Ethan's company can manage. More than any of us can.

"We're going to be here every single step of the way." Zach grasps her hand.

I can feel his trepidation from here. Our twin bond has always been a two-way street, but in recent years, I've struggled to connect with Zach. That changed when Willow came on the scene.

"So what happens now?" I drag them back.

Her eyes flick up to mine. "I'm staying, if that's what you mean."

"For how long?"

"Forever, Mi," Killian drawls.

"I don't believe it."

Pain flares in her eyes. "You don't believe me?"

Scraping my chair back, I stand up. "You made a promise before. I can't fall for that again."

All of their stunned faces watch me leave the cabin, slamming the door behind me. Anxiety is pushing a hot burst of vomit up my throat, aided by last night's vodka binge, but I hold it back.

"Mi!" Ryder shouts.

I don't stop running until I'm safely back in the confines of my studio, away from the pressure of socialising and plastering on a fake smile like the rest of them. As much as I want to trust Willow, I can't do that.

I won't survive her breaking my heart again.

This is for my own self-preservation.

CHAPTER 10
WILLOW
NEED IT – HALF MOON RUN

IT TAKES until New Year's Eve for me to work up the emotional strength to return to our cabin. We've been living out of the guys' spare room since arriving home before Christmas.

While Arianna plays with the other children out in the snow, I begin to move our bags across the road. The cabin door squeaks in protest as I heave it open and step inside.

Thick dust surges up my nose, and the scent of stale air greets me home. The cabin is exactly as we left it—clean dishes next to the sink, paint swatches scattered about.

It's like we never left.

Yet everything is different now.

Closing the door, I make a beeline for the open fireplace and start stacking logs and kindling to light a fire. I can see my breath fogging up the air, it's so cold. Mountain winters are no joke.

With the fire beginning to crackle, I stand up to survey the space. Everything needs a good clean, but it's still the warm, cosy slice of home that I spent months making perfect for our family.

I missed this place.

The apartment never felt like home, it was merely a temporary solution to our overnight homelessness. I dreamed about coming back to this cabin every night for months on end.

When my dreams turned into nightmares, I stopped wishing for the unthinkable, instead resorting to telling myself that letting go was safer. Easier. Less heartache. I was wrong about that too.

After depositing Arianna's suitcase in her pink bedroom, complete with the fairytale-themed mural that Micah painted what feels like a lifetime ago, I move to the master room.

The room causes my heart to twinge. It's dark-wood flooring and deep turquoise walls match the rest of the colour theme—calming and homey. This place is full of so many happy memories.

"Food for thought?" a voice rumbles.

Heart leaping into my throat, I clutch my chest and spin to face Killian behind me. "Where did you come from so quietly?"

He lifts a burly shoulder in a shrug. "Outside."

"I've never heard you move so silently."

Killian inches closer—creeping, stealthier than a coiled snake, into my personal space. The smell of freshly chopped wood and the surrounding forest clings to his green flannel shirt and mud-splattered jeans.

"What are you thinking about?"

My throat catches. "The past."

He cocks an eyebrow. "Our past?"

"All of ours."

Sliding a calloused finger beneath my chin, he ever so gently strokes along the curved length of my jawbone.

"I've been thinking about that too," he admits roughly. "We've lost a lot of time. I don't want to go into next year without knowing we're going to be okay."

Unable to resist the magnetic pull of his raw power, crackling over me like rapidly spreading flames that sear through my bone and muscle, I surrender.

To him. To us.

To whatever the fuck he needs right now.

"New Year's Eve got you feeling all emotional, Kill?"

He scoffs. "Me? Emotional?"

"Let's skip pretending like you're not capable of it. We both know the truth. For all of your anger, I know that you still love me. I have to believe that."

His breathing halts for a long, painful second. "I do. That's true."

"Then what do you want next year to look like?"

Stroking the backs of his knuckles against my cheek, he slides a hand into my hair and kneads my head. His touch adds to the acute sense of pressure that his fire-lit gaze is causing to build inside of me.

"You, me and the kid," he answers.

"What about the twins?"

"If Micah gets his shit together and I can avoid killing Zach, then sure. But I need us first. If we're broken, I can't look after this family anymore."

"Don't say that, Kill."

"It's the truth," he admits, stroking his hand through my short hair. "I can't look after them if I don't have you here to keep me sane. I'm done living this life alone. I can't do it."

Heart squeezing, I reach onto my tiptoes to wrap my arms around his neck. Killian's hand moves to the small of my back and holds me against his huge, muscled frame.

"You never have to walk alone again," I whisper into his scruff-covered face. "Arianna and I will have protection soon. That means we can stay."

"Am I not enough protection for you, baby?"

I peck his lips, soft and coaxing. "You know that's not what this is about. We need professional security, capable of handling the threat that Mr Sanchez poses."

"My rifle and I looked after you well enough before," he reasons.

"And I know that you always will. This is me trying to look after you as well. That future won't happen for either of us if you're dead."

Killian smirks against my mouth. "That's cute. This motherfucker won't have a head left to talk bullshit with if he comes anywhere near us."

"Alright, big, scary man. That's enough decapitation talk. We should be celebrating the new year."

His smile cracks and fades. I watch the grief filter back into his eyes—infecting the iris and causing his pupil to contract as he retreats from my grasp. It feels like being punched in the chest.

"She should be here," Killian croaks.

I bury my face in his soft shirt. "I know."

"It wasn't her time, Willow. I don't fucking understand this world."

"No one does. All we can hope for is the strength to hold on to each other for as long as we can. Lola would want us to live for that."

"She would, I suppose."

"You know she would."

Tangling our fingers together, I drag his mountainous body back through the cabin and into the living room. It's warming up as the fire roars, spewing heat and the wonderful smell of crackling wood.

Killian lets me deposit him on the rug, and I grab the half-empty bottle of whiskey from the kitchen. It's still there from our last drinking session earlier in the year. We don't bother with glasses and pass it between us instead.

He stares into the flames, warm orange light dappling across his strong, rugged features and lips which are pressed tightly together. I wish I could fathom what goes on in his mind, if only for a second.

"Do you think she's watching us?" he randomly asks. "Up there?"

"In heaven?"

"If that's what you believe in."

"You don't?" I frown at him.

Killian takes a swig and shrugs. "I'm not sure what I believe. Sometimes, it hurts more to think they're watching us and can't let us know they're okay... wherever they are."

I know he's talking about his parents. Killian was barely eighteen when his parents died, and he took the twins under his care not long after, as their father had passed on years before.

"I like to think there's a heaven." I take the bottle from him and sip. "Pedro would be there too, watching over us. And my... my baby. I have to believe they're safe somewhere."

"Shit," Killian curses. "I'm sorry, Willow. I didn't think."

"No, you're fine." I bump our shoulders together. "You've lost people too. Even more than I have. We can talk about this stuff."

Clearing his throat, he stares deep into the fire. "I just... I miss them. Every goddamn day. We never got the chance to say goodbye, now Lola's gone too."

Resting my head on his shoulder, I snuggle closer to try to offer him some comfort. Even if there's nothing I can ever do to fix the cruelness of grief and sudden loss.

"They're here," I murmur through my clogged throat. "Even when we can't see them, they're here. You've never been alone."

"Even when I feel like it?"

"Especially when you feel like it, Kill."

Resting his head on top of mine, I hear him drag in a ragged breath. I don't want to move an inch or cause him to run away. Not now. His shields are down for the first time since I returned.

We sit in silence for what feels like hours, the only sound our breathing and the crackle of flames. The bottle is empty by the time Killian finally shifts and speaks again.

"I'm so fucking glad you're home."

"Yeah," I rasp. "Me too."

"Promise me you'll never leave again?"

"You know I won't make a promise that I can't keep. I will always do what's necessary to protect my daughter. But I have no intention of leaving after I've spoken to Ethan's team."

Killian moans in displeasure. "Fuck, I'd forgotten about that. I can't believe we're going to the biggest damn city in the entire country... voluntarily."

"Stop your grumbling. It isn't a field trip."

"Feels like it," he complains.

"I can go with Zach and Ryder. You don't have to come."

"Like hell. I'm coming."

The creak of footsteps approaching ends our solitude. There's a second's warning before the door to the cabin slams open, and Arianna comes flying in. Her face is a mask of excitement.

"We're home!" she yells.

Aalia follows her in, wearing a blazing smile. "Sorry, Willow. She was missing you."

I throw my arms open. "Come here, baby."

Running towards me, Arianna leaps into my arms. I fall backwards from the weight of her growing body and end up landing across Killian's lap. He peers down at us both in amusement.

"You're getting too big, peanut."

"No, I'm not," Arianna protests. "I need to be as big as you, Giant!"

"Good luck with that," he snorts.

Untangling myself, I dump Arianna in Killian's lap then stand up to hug Aalia. She declines the offer of a drink, too busy fussing over me and pinching my still-gaunt cheeks.

"It's New Year's Eve," she declares grandly.

"So?"

"You need to come and celebrate with us."

"I don't kn—"

"I insist," she cuts me off. "You can't just sit here and drink alone. Come for dinner in a couple of hours. I'm sure Walker would like to get to know you. He and the girls are living in our spare two bedrooms."

"How's that going?"

Her smile broadens. "Very well."

Snickering behind me, Killian seems to be in on the joke. It takes me a moment to catch on to the light dusting of pink across Aalia's olive-toned skin. Oh. It's like *that*, apparently.

"You're... enjoying his company?" I laugh.

She splutters. "I never kiss and tell."

"Sure, sure. Looks like I missed all the drama while I was away."

"Something like that." Aalia winks. "Dinner! Two hours!"

Breezing out of the cabin, she leaves us laughing to ourselves. Walker seemed very nervous when we first met, so I'm glad he's come out of his shell and that Aalia has found someone.

"How long has that been going on for?" I spin around.

"Few weeks now," Killian answers while tickling Arianna's ribcage. "It wasn't overnight. Walker's still pretty mistrusting of us all after all he's been through. Widowed, I hear."

"Poor guy. Recently?"

"Couple of years."

Briar Valley has a way of collecting the lost and broken people in life. It sounds like Walker and his two daughters are no different. I hope they can find some peace here.

"You up for dinner?"

"Got no other plans," Killian replies. "Zach's helping Ryder in the garage, and Micah's in the studio. Doubt he'll come."

The mention of Micah's name causes my heart to thud against my ribcage. He hasn't spoken to me since storming out on Christmas Day, no matter what assurances I give.

"Stop," he interjects.

"Huh?"

"You're worrying about him again. I can tell by the look on your face. Micah will come around eventually."

"How long until he forgives me?"

Placing Arianna down on the rug, Killian approaches and pulls me into a bear hug. "That I can't answer. I'm sorry."

"Not your fault."

He chuckles. "For a change."

With his bearded chin resting on my head, I let out a long sigh. He and Zach have come around, slowly but surely. I never expected Micah to be the one to hold a grudge for the longest.

But in many ways, I've hurt him even more than them. I took his trust and ground it into pathetic pieces after he dared to open himself up. That can't be forgotten overnight.

"Where's Demon?" I pull out of his hug.

"Eating dinner across the road," Arianna answers as she rolls around on the floor. "She was hungry after playing all afternoon."

"Let's go and find her, yeah?"

"Okay!"

Arianna leaps up and zips from the cabin in a blur of energy. Even after running around with the other children, she's still borderline hyperactive, and has been ever since we returned.

With her gone, Killian sneaks up behind me and bands his arms around my waist. His hand finds my wrist and tugs on the long sleeve, a single fingertip skating underneath the fabric.

"When are we gonna talk about this?"

I suppress a shudder as he gently strokes over the rigid lump of a new scar. "We don't need to discuss it."

"I disagree very fucking strongly with that."

"And I'm allowed to have some privacy," I argue. "We all coped in our own ways the last few months."

"So you're not going to do it again?"

"Just leave it alone."

"I can't do that," he retorts.

"You don't have a choice."

Pulling his arms from my body, I step out of his embrace and follow in Arianna's footsteps. I don't have an answer for him right now, and I refuse to lie anymore.

I wish I could say that I'm done with it, but the urge is still there in the background. It flows with each breath that I take, and it's only a matter of time before that overtakes everything again.

CHAPTER 11
WILLOW

JUST LIKE YOU – NF

SLICK SWEAT COVERS my palms as I clench and unclench them in my lap. The hum of Killian's truck cuts through the blare of horns and humming traffic all around us.

"Motherfuckers," Killian snarls.

"Take a breath, cuz." Zach laughs at him. "This is London. Traffic is pretty much guaranteed."

"It's everywhere!"

"Your point being?"

"Shut the fuck up, kid. You're not helping."

"Kill," I hum anxiously. "Please calm down. I'm struggling to keep it together as it is."

Glancing into the rearview mirror, he takes one look at my pale, clammy face and shuts up. We made the tough call to leave Arianna in Briar Valley while we left Wales and travelled into England's capital city.

I didn't want to risk anyone spotting her and raising the alarm. We've already seen that Mr Sanchez has allies in this country—the incident with Mason several months ago proved that.

"Sorry," Killian mutters. "Where is this place anyway?"

"Ethan said we'll know it when we see it," Zach replies, the window open as he lights a cigarette. "Sabre HQ is huge."

Crawling through the huge line of traffic, he's finished his cigarette by the time we arrive in an intimidating business district. Massive skyscrapers kiss the clouds all around us.

The buildings are made of sleek panels of glass and polished steel, forming monstrosities that carve the city's landscape. Killian's grip on the wheel tightens. He really hates this place.

All around us, men and women run all over the place in their smart business wear and sleek high heels. No one walks at a casual pace. We're far from the slow living of Briar Valley.

"That's the place." Zach whistles. "I recognise the logo from the news."

The biggest building of them all lies up ahead in huge, tinted proportions. It stretches up so high, I can't see the top floor, surrounded by low-hanging London clouds.

A logo is proudly displayed above the sprawling entrance steps, lined with dark-clothed security agents in black sunglasses. It's an intricate thumb print, the text below pronouncing the words *Sabre Security*.

"We're here," Killian declares.

"Fuck me," Zach exclaims. "It's even bigger than I imagined."

Following the signs into the parking garage, we're screened by security and given a thorough checking over before we're allowed through. Ethan has our names on a visitor's list in preparation.

Killian curses constantly while attempting to park the truck between two slick sports cars, both worth more money than we'll ever see in our lifetimes. It takes him three attempts.

"Bastard thing," he hisses. "Let's get this over and done with. I want to get home before the next snowstorm blows in."

Zach claps him on the shoulder. "We need to worry about one thing at a time. Ethan's booked us a hotel for the night."

Cursing again, Killian climbs out in a storm of annoyance. He really is a grumpy son of a bitch today. I wish I could blame him.

"Willow!"

Walking through a rear entrance door, Ethan waves us over. He's whispering into the comms slotted in his ear when we reach him.

"Yeah, they're here. Alright, Hud. We can handle the interview if you need to head off early to be with Brooklyn."

Finishing up his conversation, Ethan offers us a round of handshakes. Killian's silently sizing him up with a scowl on his face.

"Sorry for that," Ethan apologises. "You've caught us on a busy day. A friend of ours has gone into labour."

"Bad timing?" I laugh nervously.

"Not at all. Thank you for coming in, Willow. We're glad you're here. Let's go inside."

He waves us in and scans his security pass to let us inside. That's where my jaw drops. Led through a service corridor, the reception we step into is breathtaking.

A seemingly endless ceiling stretches into the heavens, while sleek floors and glass walls brighten the space. Much like outside, people buzz around in all corners.

Some talk on phones while others talk to one another, exchanging whispers and heated conversations. There's an intense hum of energy from everyone amidst the hustle and bustle.

"We're going to head upstairs and meet the rest of my team first," Ethan advises. "Then we'll have a chat about the investigation and your role moving forward."

Without thinking, I take both Zach's and Killian's hands. I need them to hold on to me right now so I don't run out of here screaming.

The elevator ride is full of tense silence until we arrive on a high level, the floor-to-ceiling windows offering a panoramic view of London's impressive skyline.

Holding the door open for us, we're ushered into a big, plush office, complete with a dark-wood conference table, coffee trolley and several people whose heads turn in our direction.

"Everyone, this is Willow Sanchez." Ethan gestures towards me. "And Killian." He waves again. "Along with his cousin, Zach."

We all smile tightly, feeling the tension and pressure. There are two men and one woman sitting inside, all in their mid to late thirties and wearing the same all-black clothing as everyone else.

"Warner." Ethan points at the salt and pepper haired man. "This is Hyland." He includes the huge, boulder-like man in his wave. "And this is Tara. We're the Anaconda team."

The woman offers me a wave. Her long, light-brown hair is tied up in a no-nonsense ponytail that shows off her young face and cool, professional smile.

"Sit down, guys. Help yourselves to a refreshment."

After introductions, we take our seats and a round of coffees. Ethan sets himself up at the head of the table to preside over us all.

"There are several teams at Sabre Security operating under different divisions," he explains. "We're one of the investigating teams. It's a big operation."

"Looks like it," I croak.

"Our team has been investigating this human trafficking ring for over a year now, stretching from here to the United States, Mexico and Brazil. We're looking at a massive international gang."

My throat thickens with the surge of sickness threatening to rise up. I swallow hard, washing it down with a swig of coffee. Their eyes are all on me, even subtly when they think I'm not looking.

"How many victims have you tracked down?" Killian asks in a hard, angry voice.

"Officially? Over forty-five," Warner replies. "Along with another thirty who refuse to go on record about what happened."

"We suspect the real number to be in the tens of hundreds," Tara adds with a shudder. "There are more people out there."

Sliding my hand beneath my sweater sleeve, I stroke my fingertips across the fresh cut I slashed into my wrist this morning. I had to hide my face in a towel as I sobbed so Arianna didn't hear.

Those women out there are me. We're the same person, our blueprints reproduced and reprinted across the globe, over and over, for other people's sick pleasure.

No matter what I say or do here, I can't take back the pain and bloodshed I know they've suffered. Intimately. The memories are still raw in my mind despite a year passing since I escaped.

"Willow?" Hyland prompts.

I look up at him. "Yes?"

"We understand that you've requested protection. Our team will be returning to Briar Valley with you to ensure your security."

"All of you?"

"Myself and Hyland," Tara supplies.

"I'll remain here with Ethan and the other teams to continue the investigation," Warner finishes. "We'll get the job done."

"I... feel bad," I admit in a low voice.

Killian rubs my shoulder. "Why, baby?"

"I'm taking them from their jobs and the investigation."

"Our number one priority is to keep you safe," Ethan offers. "That matters above all else, including the case."

Absently rubbing my chest, I nod and force a breath. "I'll tell you everything I remember about Mr Sanchez and his men. He had a lot of people working for him, and other business associates."

"Any information you can give us will help." Warner nods encouragingly. "We want to identify these people to ensure everyone involved is brought to justice."

All drawing out laptops and notepads, the entire room's focus is on me as they start a voice recorder. Sipping more coffee, I dive into a description of Mr Sanchez's Mexico mansion and all its staff.

I get halfway through before it becomes too much. Just describing the marble floors and dark, brocade wallpaper brings up a plethora of awful memories, dipped in blood and tears.

"We understand that Dimitri Sanchez has a personal security team." Ethan slides a file across the table to me. "Tell me, do you recognise this individual as one of them?"

Opening the file with shaking hands, I almost throw up at the photograph inside. Pedro's face is staring back at me in printed pixels, displaying every last smile line and twinkle in his eyes.

"P-P-Pedro," I gasp.

"He's been missing for over a year," Ethan says sadly. "We've also heard from Mexican authorities that his family disappeared at the same time he did."

Buddum.

Buddum.

Buddum.

All I can hear is my heartbeat roaring in my ears, drowning out the rest of his words. I stare down into his familiar, love-filled eyes. A gaze that soothed me in the darkest of times.

He died alone. In agony. Knowing that his actions had cost him, and his family, their lives. I walked away from that mansion, but none of them did. I have to live with that.

"I... excuse me," I blurt, my chair scraping back. "I'll be right back."

Zach tries to snag my sleeve as I pass, but I flash him a warning look and burst out of the room alone. I need a moment to take a breath without all of their eyes weighing me down.

Scanning the corridor, I spot the sign for a bathroom then run at full speed to escape. The stall door doesn't even shut behind me before I'm on my knees and retching into the toilet bowl.

Over and over, acid spews up from my stomach and splatters against the pristine ceramic as I sob my eyes out. I can't even stop when the bathroom door creaks open.

"Are you okay in there?" a female voice asks.

Uncaring of how gross it is, I rest my sweaty head on the toilet lid and suck in a breath. "Not really."

"Breathe in through your mouth, so you can't smell it," she advises kindly. "Want me to get you some water?"

"I'm f-fine."

"You don't look it."

The sound of a tap running precedes her reappearance at the stall doorway. A wet paper towel is pressed against my forehead as she cleans the sweat from my face.

"That's it, deep breaths."

She sucks in a loud breath then blows it out for me to copy. Following her lead, I make myself recreate her exaggerated breathing to free up my lungs. The shadows at the edges of my vision begin to fade as each intake relieves some of the pressure.

"Give me your hand, I'll help you up."

"Th-Thanks."

Putting my faith in the complete stranger, I let her drag me to my feet and flush the toilet. Turning to face her, I realise she's a similar age to me, at least in her mid-twenties.

Her mousy brown hair is long, almost brushing her lower back, framing flawless blue eyes that compliment her porcelain skin and slightly crooked nose.

Something about her makes me pause. Maybe it's the haunted look in her crystal-clear eyes. Or maybe it's the darkness wrapped around her features that seems to call out to my soul.

"I'm so sorry you had to witness that," I choke out.

She shrugs. "I've seen worse. You looked like you needed a friend. I'm Harlow."

"Willow."

"Our names are kinda similar, huh?"

I move to the sink to wash up. "I guess so."

"That means we were meant to meet each other in here," she jokes.

"I guess so."

"You're not Willow Sanchez, are you?"

"You know me?" I look up at her.

Harlow smiles reassuringly. "Nothing bad, I swear. Ethan told me you were coming in today. I was hoping to catch you at some point."

"Do you work here or something?"

"Not really," she says mysteriously. "It's complicated. I wanted to say hi and see how you're getting on with the team, but it seems my question has been answered already."

"It's going okay, I just freaked out a bit," I admit with a short laugh. "It's intense, going on the record in front of strangers."

"I've been there." She holds my gaze. "It's the hardest thing you'll ever do, but I promise, this is the right thing for everyone."

Her voice tells me that she understands, perhaps more than anyone has ever been able to before. I can see it in her eyes, the familiar pain and heartache mixed in with that darkness.

She's been where I am. I can't fathom how or why I know, but that kind of trauma reveals itself to fellow survivors. We can see each other's pain for what it is as clear as day.

"How did you do this?" I ask honestly.

Harlow offers me a hand. "Not alone."

Even though she's a stranger who I barely know, I trust her. The shadows in her eyes are so familiar, I can almost taste them, but there's light too. It clings to every part of her—the glimmers of hope.

With a deep breath, I take her hand. "Thank you."

She winks. "Don't mention it."

Chest still tight, we exit the bathroom together and head back down the corridor. Harlow refuses to release my hand, holding on tight so I don't fall over in my dizziness.

"You do this on your terms, though." She squeezes my hand. "Don't let them push you to your breaking point. Take another break if you need it."

"You're suspiciously well-versed in how all this works."

"Personal experience," she admits.

"As part of this investigation?"

"No, not this one. My case wrapped up around six months ago."

"Then why are you still here?"

Her lips twist in a rueful smile. "The owners of the company keep me around. For now."

I have a feeling this is an inside joke that I'm not privy to. I've yet to meet Ethan's bosses, but if they're anything like this place, they must be intimidating.

Outside the door, I almost freak out again. Harlow stops in her steps before the panic attack can fully take hold and places her hands on my shoulders so she can encourage me to breathe again.

Dragging in deep gulps of air, I make myself remain calm. It's just a room full of people. I've faced far worse and survived. Blood. Pain. Death. Torture. I can tell my story and live through it again.

"Remember, you've survived 100 percent of your worst days," she says with a knowing wink. "You sure as hell can survive this."

"Shit." I laugh shortly. "Maybe we *were* meant to meet each other today, Harlow."

Her hand squeezes my shoulder. "I don't believe in maybes anymore. Only fate."

"Is that so?"

"Doesn't everything happen for a reason?" she challenges. "We're here right now because we're supposed to be."

"I'm not sure that I believe in fate."

Harlow shrugs. "Then believe in yourself. It's the same thing. Believe in the fact that you'll get through this because you have to."

Blinking away tears, I rest my hand on top of hers. "Thank you, Harlow. I'm glad we bumped into each other."

She smiles. "Me too. Ready to do this?"

"As I'll ever be."

CHAPTER 12
ZACH

MAN OR A MONSTER – SAM TINNESZ & ZAYDE WOLF

I DON'T KNOW who is more traumatised by the day's events—Willow, Killian or myself. Hearing every last horrific, blood-slick detail of her kidnapping, trafficking and abuse has left me gutted.

But not just gutted.

That word can't adequately describe how I'm feeling right now. I am incandescent with rage unlike anything I've ever felt before. Fury. Hellfire. Righteous anger that'll consume us all if I'm not careful.

That son of a bitch, Dimitri Sanchez, targeted Willow as a vulnerable teenager, trafficked her across the globe then stuck a ring on her finger to make it all seem legal to the public eye.

He locked her in a mansion and spent a decade raping, beating and emotionally and physically abusing the living daylights out of her. And he got her pregnant. Young. Before abusing his kid too.

Son of a fucking bitch!

"I need a drink," I grumble.

Ethan claps me on the shoulder as we walk on the hotel's plush carpet. "You've got the suite for the night. After today, you certainly deserve to rest up, and take full advantage of the room service."

"You can bet your ass we intend to."

He chuckles under his breath. "I'll send a car tomorrow morning. We want to ask a few more questions before discussing Willow's protection moving forward."

"Sounds good. Willow needs a break."

"Make sure she gets some rest, Zach."

Both of us are studying her slumped shoulders and lowered head in front of us. Willow is exhausted after almost four hours of cross-examination and evidence documentation.

After her breakdown, she knuckled down and got through it like a motherfucking trooper. An incredible goddamn warrior princess far more capable than I've ever given her credit for.

Now Killian is carrying her in his arms back to our hotel room. I think it makes him feel better to hold her close like a child, offering the only shred of comfort and protection he can after hearing all she's endured.

"Alright, this is yours." Ethan hands me the key card outside our hotel room. "See you first thing. Thanks again for today, Willow."

She lifts her head to spare him a glance. "No problem."

"Your testimony is truly invaluable. We can't thank you enough."

"I just want to see him brought down," she says tiredly. "That's all."

"We're going to do our very best to do exactly that." Ethan offers her a reassuring smile. "Sleep. We'll talk more tomorrow."

With a final friendly wave, he disappears back down the corridor and into the elevator. We unlock the hotel room door then step inside the fanciest room I've ever seen.

Fuck.

Is this how the other half live?

Thick, silver-speckled grey carpets span the massive floorspace, split into sections that organise the suite. There's a sprawling king-sized bed covered in gold-laced sheets and a fully-stocked bar.

Several over-stuffed sofas surround a glass coffee table topped with perfect red roses, and a quick peek in the bathroom reveals a clawfoot tub big enough to fit a whole family.

"Fucking fancy shit," Killian mutters as he sets Willow down. "I miss home."

"It's been twelve hours," she points out.

"Twelve hours too long."

I roll my eyes. "Caveman here can't be without his axe for too long. The world will implode if he is."

Killian flips me the bird. "Shut up, kid."

"Love you too, cuz."

"Love isn't the word I'd use to describe how I feel about your annoying backside."

"Ever the charmer, Kill."

Shaking her head at us both, Willow mumbles about using the bathroom and vanishes. The sound of the shower flicking on follows, then her quiet sobbing in the falling water.

"Should we go in there?"

Killian shrugs. "She needs time. That was rough going."

"I hate the thought of her going through this shit alone," I grit out. "She survived that hell on her own. That doesn't mean she has to now."

"You want to go in there and figure out what the fuck to say after what we just heard?"

Defensive, I square up against him. "Maybe I do."

"Then be my guest. I don't have any words right now."

As much as I feel like a deer caught in the headlights, and words are failing me too, I won't sit out here while Willow suffers. She deserves better than that from us, regardless of the past.

Mind churning with ideas, I snap my fingers. "What about the ring? We still need to ask her."

All he does is stare at me—a thick, blonde eyebrow raised in an incredulous look. Fine. It may not be my brightest or most romantic idea, but at least I'm trying.

Killian lowers his voice. "Right now? You really want this to be her memory of that moment?"

"I'm just fishing here. I want to make her feel better."

"The thought of spending the rest of her life with a shit-for-brains twat like you isn't going to improve her day."

"Hey, I don't have shit for brains."

"Could've fooled me."

"I just have no brain at all, apparently."

He breaks out into quiet, rumbling laughter. "That I don't disagree with. Terrible idea, Zach."

"Alright, back off. It was just a thought."

When the sound of Willow's hiccupping sobs intensifies, Killian's blank façade breaks. He scrubs a hand over his beard and snarls under his breath with the same fury that's eating me up.

"She's in pain, and I can't fucking fix it. Again."

Gingerly approaching, I rest a hand on his shoulder. "This isn't on you. We always knew that testifying for Ethan was going to be messy."

"Still," he harrumphs. "I can never bloody fix it, can I? Whenever she's hurting, I can't do a goddamn thing."

"None of us can, Kill."

"That really doesn't make me feel better."

Unable to give him a single crumb of comfort, I pat his arm and decide to hell with it. He can sit here and feel sorry for himself all he likes. I'll step up and be whatever the hell Willow needs right now.

She's back in the trenches of her past, and I won't let her wallow in the darkness alone. Someone has to reach on down there and yank her up before she drowns herself.

Letting myself into the steam-filled bathroom, I can see the soft, rounded slopes of her curves through the moisture-flecked glass. She's still crying in the shower but quieter now.

"Willow?" I call out.

Her sniffling stops. "Zach?"

"I'm coming in. Make some space."

Quickly peeling off my tight blue jeans and long-sleeved tee, I step into the walk-in shower and pull her straight into my arms. She feels like a tiny, trembling wreck against my bare chest.

"I'm here," I whisper into her wet hair. "Right here, babe. You aren't alone."

Her face buries in my pectorals, hidden from sight. I hate to admit that I know the sight of her swollen eyes and devastated smile a little too well now. We've been through hell together over the last year.

And something tells me that hellish ride to the depths of Lucifer's fires is only just beginning. What Willow did today will change everything—for the better or worse, I can't yet decide.

The race is on.

We're coming for Sanchez.

Rocking Willow beneath the warm spray of water, I stroke a hand up and down the length of her spine. She's managed to put some weight on since returning, but not enough to make up for what she's lost.

Studying her small curves, my eyes catch on a bright-red slash that causes an invisible hand to squeeze my windpipe. Taking a closer look, I realise what I'm looking at.

"Uh, babe?"

Willow hums tiredly in response.

"Mind telling me what the fuck this is all about?"

I'm holding her wrist in my hand, gently rotating it to show the fresh, jagged slash across her milky skin. It's layered on top of scars—thin, silvery scars that weren't previously there.

I've seen these marks before. Only once. My brother bears the same scars on his skin. The alcohol wasn't always his worst coping mechanism, and the fear I once felt for him is rushing through me now.

"It's n-nothing," Willow protests.

"Nothing? Doesn't look like *nothing* to me," I spit back.

She tries to pull her wrist from my grip, but I tighten my hold and hold it in plain view. My eyes won't tear from those damned silver spikes of pain and self-inflicted fury that blemish her skin like lightning strikes.

"How long has this been going on for?"

Her throat bobs. "A... A few months. I wanted to tell you—"

"But you didn't," I interrupt.

"I promised Killian that I'd stop." Tears well in her eyes again. "He's going to kill me."

"Killian fucking knows?"

Anger pulsates through my veins. I'm not an angry person. My cousin holds enough hatred for the world for the both of us. But this shit... This is too much. He should've told me.

"I'll kill him!"

"Zach," Willow protests, grabbing my bicep. "Just take a breath. It's one tiny little cut. I needed something this morning, and it's nothing serious."

"Nothing serious? You're cutting yourself, babe! You've been doing it for months."

The tears are now coursing down her cheeks in shimmering rivers of shame. Making myself stop and breathe through my fury, I bring a hand up to cup her cheek.

My thumb tenderly brushes over her skin, smoothing the tears aside. "I'm sorry, gorgeous girl. I just can't deal with the thought of you doing this to yourself."

"It was only a few times, Zach."

"I can see for myself that isn't true."

"But... I had stopped." She gnaws on her bottom lip. "I wanted to. For Ari and for myself. Today just got the better of me. It was a one-off thing."

I stroke my thumb down to her lips, caressing the soft, pillowy swells. "Promise?"

She lets me probe her mouth with my finger, the tip of her tongue swiping over my thumb. With her wide, hazel eyes staring up at me like bottomless pools of freshly brewed coffee, I can't stay mad.

Even though I want to scream.

Smash. Rave. Shout.

Willow doesn't need rage right now. Killian's or mine. She needs compassion and understanding. If anyone knows how to love someone on the verge of self-destructing, it's me. I'm a self-taught expert.

"Promise," she murmurs around my thumb.

Moving my hand to her hair, I ease my fingers into the wet strands to massage her scalp. She leans into my touch, her mouth parted on a low, needy whine. My other hand moves to squeeze her hip.

Despite everything, the feel of her slick, wet body turns me on. I can't help it. I'm magnetised to her like a moth to a flame, unable to resist the tempting glow of light.

"Willow," I say throatily.

Her chest pushes into mine, the hardened points of her nipples teasing my skin. "Yes?"

"I need you right now, babe. I'm sorry, but I can't think straight."

Her leg hitches up to catch on my hip. "I need you too. Make me feel good again."

"Are you sure? After today?"

"Please."

Dammit. That word on her tongue has always been my downfall. Powerless against her siren's call, I bring my hand between her legs then skate upwards. Her pussy is already soaking wet.

"Fuck, babe. You're so wet already."

"I'm sorry."

My grip on her tightens. "Don't you dare fucking apologise to me for that. I'm going to make you feel good, okay?"

Nodding obediently, she lets me seize her mouth in a firm kiss. Her lips are like molten caramel against mine—sweet and velvety soft. God, she's perfect. So fucking incredible, I can hardly take it.

We continue to kiss in the steam-filled shower, our bodies slick and sliding against each other. With her leg hooked up on my hip, I have the space to explore her cunt, teasing her clit before sliding a finger deep inside of her.

Willow gasps in pleasure as I curl it slightly to stroke against her sensitive nerve endings. Her warmth beckons me in, so I add a second finger to stretch her tight cunt wider.

"That's it," I encourage, fucking her with my hand. "Let me stretch this tight little pussy nice and wide before I fuck you."

"Jesus, Zach. You have the filthiest mouth."

"You love it."

Willow's blush is evident, even in the hot shower. "I do."

Working her into a frenzy, I pull my hand away before she can finish and bring my fingers to her lips. Willow opens her mouth, willingly sucking them in to taste her own tang on my skin.

"Perfect," I praise, letting my fingers glide against her tongue. "Now a little deeper, babe."

Relaxing, she lets me slide the fingers farther into her mouth. I want to see how much she can take. She needs a distraction right now, and I'm more than willing to give it.

Pushing my fingers towards her throat, she takes them all the way in before gagging a little. When I pull them out, they're coated in strings of saliva that stretch from her gorgeous mouth.

"Such a good princess, aren't you?" I whisper, smearing her saliva across my thumb pad. "What if I pushed my cock deep into that perfect throat of yours now?"

Rather than answering, Willow sinks to her knees. She takes my cock with both hands then sucks it into her mouth, causing me to throw my head back as I'm hit by a wave of bliss.

"Shit, babe. You take it so fucking good for me."

Bobbing on my length, she hollows out her cheeks to increase the pressure. Each suck causes my balls to tighten. Her mouth is a warm, heavenly prison wrapped around my cock.

Gathering her short hair into my left hand, I hold it tight and guide her movements until I'm roughly fucking her mouth. I want to fuck the despair from her mind and leave no space for it to return.

Each thrust into her mouth feels blissful. She's an absolute pro. Her mouth tightens and loosens at the perfect moments with tiny little rotations.

Cupping the back of her head, I push deeper into her mouth, feeling the tip of my cock press against her throat. She struggles a little but doesn't make a move to push me away, continuing to suck instead.

"That's it, gorgeous girl. Keep going."

I want to bury myself in her cunt and fuck her until she cries out my name for the whole hotel to hear. This is how wild she makes me. Fucking reckless. Out of my mind with lust.

My heart beats in a rapid staccato as my balls tighten, ready to burst. She's driving me right to the edge. My legs are trembling, and I fight to control myself, overcome by tingles zipping up and down my spine.

Around her, I can never think straight, let alone when she's on her knees in front of me, those stunning hazel eyes looking up at me through thick, luscious black lashes.

Seconds before I shoot my load down her pretty throat, I still her movements and slide out. She licks her glistening lips and peers up at me with an innocent look.

"Are you going to fuck me now?"

"Yes, babe. Stand up, and bend over for me like the good little slut you are."

"Yes, Zachariah."

"There's a good girl."

Eyes flaring with desire, she follows my orders and presses her hands to the shower wall. Her pert, perfect ass is pushed out as her spine curves, giving me full access to her pussy.

Pumping my cock, I line myself up with her then slam into her. I just need to feel her clenched around me. Willow cries out, louder than the shower can possibly drown out.

I pull out and surge back into her again, over and over, letting her know that she can't expect sweet and gentle. Not after today. I'm too fucking angry to look after her right now.

But we need this.

Both of us.

The rough, painful collision of two angry people fucking out their frustrations at the world. Her brokenness is only enraging me more, and I can't do a damn thing to fix it but this.

My palm tingles as it smacks against her ass, roughly spanking her skin. She moans again, losing herself to the storm of sensations as her cunt squeezes around my cock buried inside her.

"Zach," she keens.

"Yeah? Are you okay?"

"M-More. I need more. Please... choke me like you used to."

Hesitation sets in. "You want that?"

"I can't fucking breathe, knowing that asshole is out there, hurting other people. I need you to help me breathe."

Sneaking my hand around her torso, I bring it up to the smooth slope of her neck. I can feel how fast her heart is beating as I clench her throat.

"You want to breathe, baby girl?" I whisper in her ear. "Well, you're not allowed to. Not until I say so."

Pushing backwards against me, she encourages me to resume slamming into her. I keep her throat clamped tight in my hand and resume a battering pace, worshipping her cunt into oblivion.

Water cascades around us, the entire hotel ceasing to exist. Nothing else matters. Not Sabre. Not Sanchez. Not even the investigation. It's just us—safe in each other's anger and passion.

Sensing her struggling for air, I release her throat and grant her a brief second of salvation. "Breathe, babe."

She follows my orders, gulping down air into her stuttering lungs. When my generosity expires, I resume my tightening grip and cut off her air supply again.

It goes on... clamping, releasing, squeezing and breathing. Each time she comes close to an orgasm, I still my movements and offer her a sliver of air to keep her on that painful cliff, without allowing her to fall off.

"Zach," she whimpers during a breath.

Hearing the pain in her voice, I quickly drop my hand. "What is it? Too much?"

Certain I've gone too far, dread rips through me. Her head falls, shoulders slumping and tears flowing. Quickly pulling out, I spin her around so I can tilt her chin up and see her face.

"Talk to me," I beg her.

Willow's tears are flowing. "Why me? Why did he do this to me?"

"I... don't know, babe."

The knife buried deep in my heart twists at the misery in her voice.

"Anyone in th-the whole entire fucking world, and he chose m-me. Why?"

After pressing kisses to the flushed skin on her throat, I secure my lips to hers. "There isn't an answer to that question, my love. You can't drive yourself crazy asking it."

"But I need to know. I *have* to know what I did to deserve this pain."

Wishing I could take it all away, I wipe her tears instead. "Nothing. You did absolutely nothing. You're all that's good and pure in this world."

Sniffling, she swats away her tears, her pupils dilating. When she reaches for my still-hard cock, I know we're going to finish what I started, regardless of how fucked this moment is.

I grab her ass cheeks and lift her, walking forward until her back meets the tiled shower wall. Her mouth seeks mine out, hot and heavy as I slide back into her cunt at a new angle.

With her pussy walls hugging my length, I can't hold on for long. It's too much to handle. Plunging in and out in rapid succession, I chase my release to the finish line, thrusting at a hard and fast pace.

Burying my face in her chest, I roar through a climax so intense, it blurs my vision. I can feel her falling apart too—quivering and moaning as I hold her up. The emotional storm caught in this shower with us heightens the moment, leaving us both winded.

Once her aftershocks have stopped, I let Willow slide down my body. "Are you okay?"

She nods, red-faced and breathless. "Better now, thanks."

I crook a finger under her chin then stroke a stray tear from her cheek. "I love you so fucking much, Willow. I'd do anything for you. Anything at all."

"I know, Zach. I feel the same way."

"You don't need to hide shit from me." My eyes stray down to the cut on her wrist. "Just talk to me. Please. There's nothing we can't figure out together."

She gulps hard. "I'll try."

"Good enough for me."

Before our mouths can gravitate back together, there's a loud bang on the bathroom door and Killian's voice echoes through the wood.

"You two done in there? Some of us have to pee."

Willow's forehead crashes against my sternum. "Charming."

CHAPTER 13
WILLOW

HEAVY IN YOUR ARMS – FLORENCE & THE MACHINE

CLUTCHING Harlow's hand tight beneath the table, I take a sip of water to moisten my dry throat. We're on the third hour of questioning as we wrap up our final session in London.

Having exchanged numbers the day before, Harlow offered to sit in on the session with Ethan and the Anaconda team for moral support. I didn't hesitate before accepting her kind offer.

Having the guys here makes me feel more comfortable, but it's harder to be honest in front of them. I don't feel the same pressure with Harlow—she can clearly handle herself and isn't shocked by my story.

"If I'm understanding correctly." Ethan taps a pen against his lips, "Mason Stevenson is Dimitri's supplier, yes?"

"He's a fixer," I reply with a sigh.

"How so?"

"Supplying is only half of his role. Whatever mess Mr Sanchez makes, Mason cleans up. Including the dead prostitutes."

"I see. He's more of a right-hand man, then."

"You could say that."

Keyboards tap and pens scribble. Brows are furrowed in concentration. Faces are pale. The deeper down Alice's rabbit hole we fall, the grimmer their expressions become.

Mason is the tip of the iceberg. There are suppliers, fixers, security detail, dealers and so much more that props up Mr Sanchez's legal real estate business' foundation of evil and sin.

The version of him that exists for the outside world isn't real. His slick smiles, designer finery and eloquent speeches at charity fundraisers are all part of that carefully constructed image.

Harlow's grip on my hand tightens. "You okay?"

"Yeah," I whisper back.

"We can take a break if you need to."

"I'm okay to continue."

She offers me a smile of encouragement. Refocusing on Ethan and Warner, both leading today's questioning, I blow out my held breath.

"Mason is the man who tracked us down several months ago. He later travelled to Briar Valley to threaten my daughter's life if we didn't return to Mr Sanchez."

"That won't happen again," Tara interjects. "We'll be providing you with round-the-clock security from now on."

"Mason's the real deal." I lean forward, taking the time to look intently at each team member. "Don't underestimate him. If Mr Sanchez has tasked him with bringing us back, he won't rest until that's done."

"Don't underestimate us," Hyland grumbles.

Tall, well-muscled and broad-shouldered, he's an even burlier version of Killian, something I didn't think was possible. My Viking lumberjack has some muscular competition in this guy.

Despite the heavy scarring across his knuckles and continuous lack of a smile gracing his lips, Hyland is solid. I can see the goodness behind his grumpy disposition and gruff kindness.

"Threats aside," Ethan intervenes with a frown, "Mason Stevenson could be our way in. He can lead us straight to Sanchez's black market operations."

"He also owns a successful real estate business and dabbles in investment banking, so he often travels across Europe." I take another sip of water. "It won't be hard to find him. Capturing him will be the issue."

"How so?"

"Mason travels nowhere without his personal security detail and months of preparation. He's careful. Conscientious. You won't find a single shred of evidence to pin on him."

"We'll see about that," Ethan quips. "I'm going to need a list of his known associates."

Nodding, I take the pen and notebook he offers. I was invisible to all of Mr Sanchez's men which allowed me to hide in plain sight, listening and observing their every move.

I know a damn sight more about their businesses, both legal and not, than any of those monsters would ever give me credit for. I just never had a reason to use the information until now.

Sliding the list of names back over to him, I bite my bottom lip. "There are more, but I can't remember all of it. Most probably used false identities too."

"Something is better than nothing," Warner remarks as he flips through his notes. "What about Pedro? Was he involved in the darker sides of Sanchez's business?"

A shiver runs down my spine, but I hold it together. My voice comes out raspy and forced.

"No. Only personal protection."

"You're sure about that?" he challenges.

"I have no reason to protect a dead man."

Blanching, Warner ducks his gaze. "Right you are."

The urge to snap at him again burns through me. I have to bite my tongue to hold a sarcastic retort in. I've made it clear that Pedro is off limits.

I won't have his name dragged through the dirt, regardless of what his job was. Yes, he protected the animal who made my life a living hell. That doesn't mean he's to blame for Mr Sanchez's depravity.

"I think we have everything that we need for now." Ethan clicks his laptop shut. "You'll be needed for further questioning should anything new come up, Willow."

"I understand."

"Thank you again for your cooperation. We'll keep you updated on the case's progress and ensure this information is put to good use."

"What about our protection?"

"We'll be following you back to Briar Valley," Tara supplies. "Hyland and I will take it in shifts to ensure your security until the case is through."

Killian's deep, growing voice speaks for the first time. "We'll arrange suitable accommodation for you in town."

"That would be appreciated," Hyland replies.

"I expect hourly updates," Ethan instructs his team members. "Nothing gets past you. Understood? Willow and Arianna's safety are my sole concern at this point."

Tara dips her head in submission. "We've got this."

"Alright, then. You're all free to leave."

With a deep sigh of relief, Zach shoots to his feet. He's practically itching with nervous energy and starts bouncing on the balls of his feet.

Killian's warm hand grips my shoulder. "Come on, baby. Let's get the fuck out of here."

"Yes please. I need to see Arianna."

Letting him pull me to my feet, I summon what feels like a pathetic excuse of a smile for the Anaconda team. All offer their thanks while Hyland and Tara climb to their feet to follow us.

"Mind if I walk you out?" Harlow asks.

"Not at all."

"My ride's waiting downstairs for me anyway."

Bringing up the rear, she tails us to the elevator, then we ride down in exhausted silence. Killian's still holding my shoulder, drawing tiny circles into my skin with his thumb.

On the ground floor, Harlow skips ahead to meet the three shadows leaning on the reception desk. They're talking amongst themselves, but two stop talking when Harlow approaches them.

"Hunter," she chirps happily.

Tall, dark-haired and sporting a shiny metal disk that's implanted into the side of his head above a scarred ear, the man throws his arms open to embrace her.

Hunter's classically handsome and well-dressed in what are clearly expensive jeans. He moves with an air of authority, even in the almost-empty reception area. Everyone seems to gravitate around him.

His partner in crime is an intimidating boulder of a man who causes prickles of fear to stab into my scalp. He's huge—bigger than Killian and Hyland—as though his body is literally carved from muscle.

"Where's my kiss?" he growls.

Harlow pecks Hunter's cheek. "Sorry, Enz. You're still in the doghouse for messing up my takeout order last night."

"I forgot one bloody dish!"

"The steamed broccoli is her favourite part of the meal," Hunter snarks.

"Too right." Harlow straightens and waves us over. "Willow, this is Hunter and Enzo. They used to run Sabre Security."

"Before we handed it over to this lump of meat." Enzo smacks the shoulder of the third man.

With raven-coloured hair, several shiny facial piercings and a body full of dark, intricate tattoos, he's no less intimidating than his friends, though his blue eyes are warm with recognition.

"Willow," he greets. "I'm Hudson Knight. My brother and I run the company. Heard a lot about you."

I subconsciously curl into Killian's side. "Nice to meet you all."

"How's the Anaconda team treating you?" Hunter asks.

Trying not to stare at his strange head implant, I shrug off his question. "They've been great."

"You're in good hands, Willow. They'll take care of you."

He smiles at Tara and Hyland, who both seem to blossom under Hunter's praise. Despite not running the company anymore, it's clear he's still the true source of authority around here.

Hudson's palpable authority is a little different, more entrenched in silent threat than overt power. He looks terrifying, but there's also a strange softness about him that sets me at ease.

"Where's Leighton?" Harlow pouts. "He promised me bubble tea."

"At the hospital with the others and Brooklyn," Hudson answers. "Want to head there now?"

"Yes! I am dying for baby snuggles."

Turning back to me, Harlow pulls me into a tight, fast hug. Her lips touch my ear so she can whisper.

"You've got my number. Call anytime, night or day. I'll be a non-judgemental listening ear."

"Thank you. That means a lot."

"You're not alone, Willow. Even when it feels like it."

Reluctantly releasing me, she pecks my cheek and gives me a final stern look. All four of them gift us with handshakes and goodbyes before disappearing towards the parking garage.

"Shall we get this show on the road?" Hyland suggests. "It's a long drive back to Wales."

Killian cracks his neck. "Let's get out of this damned city."

"Not a fan?" Tara laughs.

"You could say that," Zach answers for his cousin. "Killian's allergic to people and traffic. You'll see once you arrive in Briar Valley."

Both nod, seemingly prepared for what will undoubtedly be a shock to the system. Our tiny, quiet town is the polar opposite of this people-infested sweatbox, even in the dead of winter.

After loading up into Killian's truck with the other's blacked-out SUV parked nearby, we peel out of the parking garage with a squeal of tyres. Killian is clearly desperate to escape.

"You alright?" Zach asks quietly.

I snuggle closer to him in the backseat where we're both sitting. "Tired and I miss Arianna. But I feel good about doing that."

"You were amazing, babe."

"I hardly think so. All I did was tell the truth."

"Zach's right," Killian chimes in. "You did so well. That questioning was rough to listen to, let alone face."

Chest warm with appreciation, I lean between the seats to kiss Killian's beard-covered cheek before cuddling close to Zach again.

"Thanks, guys. I'm glad you were both here. I know it can't have been easy."

Neither answers me. The truth is heavy in the air between us. They both knew what happened to me in Mexico, but hearing about the abuse first-hand has confirmed their suspicions.

I'm broken.

Perhaps irreparably so.

But around them, I want to be whole again. I'm desperate to stitch my shattered pieces together and live the life I always dreamed of while stuck in that soulless mansion.

I deserve that chance at happiness. We all do—especially Arianna. Now's the time to put the past aside and fight like hell for it, even if it's the hardest thing I've ever done in my life.

Winding through the afternoon traffic, Killian curses and swerves his way out to the motorway heading west. Hyland and Tara follow behind in their SUV.

"How do we feel about those two?" Killian asks.

"They're helping us," I point out.

"I know, just don't love the idea of inviting two strangers into Briar Valley. How do we know they're trustworthy?"

"Because Ethan trusts them," Zach answers. "We have to respect his judgement. He assigned them to this job for a reason."

"I still don't like it. Strangers don't belong in Briar Valley."

"If you want me and Arianna there, then you'll accept them too," I snap at him. "That's final."

Jaw setting in a tight line, Killian nods once. "Fine."

He swerves past a slow-moving lorry, and my stomach lurches. I've been nauseous, awash with anxiety, the entire time we've been in London. His sour mood isn't helping.

An hour into our journey, Killian lays down on the accelerator. I watch our speed creep up, frowning at the back of his head. We're on a quiet country road, heading through rural England.

"Kill?"

He doesn't acknowledge me.

Tara and Hyland are a couple of cars behind us, maintaining a safe distance since our last stop for coffee and fuel. Between us, the other two cars are nondescript and unassuming.

"Killian? You okay?"

Still nothing.

When he abruptly brakes before speeding up again, Zach seems to catch on to something. He glances over his shoulder to look through the rear window, his brows furrowed together.

"Take the left here," he orders.

At the last second, Killian indicates and quickly turns with a squeal. The blacked-out SUV follows along with one other car—a dark-red, new model with tinted windows.

"They're following us," Killian clips out.

"How do you know?" I glance between them.

"They've been tailing us since we left London," he responds grimly. "Watch this."

Laying down on the accelerator once more, he takes another turn then speeds ahead, leaving the other two to catch up. The red car follows, battling to regain the distance between us.

Right on cue, Zach's phone rings. He answers with a barked grunt.

"Yeah?"

On the other end, I can hear Hyland's raspy growl.

"We thought so too. What should we do?"

As he speaks, an invisible demon wraps its claws around my windpipe and begins to twist. Wrenching. Strangling. Clenching. Air ceases to fill my lungs as panic sets in.

"Who is it?" I squeeze out.

"Could be nothing." Zach takes my hand into his. "Breathe, babe. We have security with us."

"What if it's him?"

"There's a gun in the glove compartment," Killian reveals, sending a swarm of hornets through my belly. "Just not a legal one. Zach, grab it."

"You have an illegal gun?" he barks. "Jesus, Kill!"

"I'm not fucking apologising. I got it for exactly this reason. Now take the damn thing, and be ready."

Swearing under his breath, Zach ducks between the seats to take the gun out. It's a small, compact model, different from Killian's usual hunting rifle. I feel the colour drain from my face.

This is real.

It's happening.

Cutting in front of a slow car, our tail quickly approaches. Also undercutting the dawdling driver, Tara and Hyland are hot on their heels, sandwiching the suspicious vehicle between us.

When it drops back slightly, the vice around my lungs eases enough for me to drag in a stuttered breath. My relief is short-lived, though. The red car quickly surges forward. I scream as it rams into us from behind.

We lurch to the side, and Killian fights to keep his truck on the road. The car doesn't hesitate before slamming into us again—harder this time, causing metal to groan in protest.

"Fuck!" he roars.

With another ram, he loses control of the steering wheel, and we careen off the road. We fly over a grassy slope, heading straight for a wooden fence.

"Killian!" I scream.

But it's too late.

There's no time to move out of the path of danger. At the last second, Zach throws himself on top of me to shield my body, an almighty bang of airbags exploding as we make impact.

Crunch.

Smash.

Shatter.

Pain explodes through my body as we're jerked forwards, the truck falling onto its side and beginning to tumble. The warmth of blood seeps across my head, and I can hear Killian's yelling, but it sounds far away.

Please, I whisper internally.

I can't die like this.

When the truck eventually crashes to a stop, I'm somehow still conscious. The weight of Zach's body is crushing me, still slumped over my curled-up form. Killian has fallen silent.

The stench of smoke invades the vehicle. All I can hear is my own roaring heartbeat which slams against my ribcage in a painful beat. Agony is pulsating through my extremities.

"Willow!" I hear someone shout.

My eyes feel heavy, almost too heavy to hold open. With the last wisps of my strength, I heave Zach's weight aside and manage to lift my head. The awaiting sight cuts off my hammering heartbeat.

Zach.

No.

Bright-red blood pours from a huge gash in his forehead, slashed wide open by a jagged shard of glass. He's unconscious. Slumped over. Rapidly paling and bleeding profusely.

I scream. Beg. Plead and wail. His eyes don't lift. Killian remains silent. Voices and shouts surround me before the blast of a gunshot pierces the ringing in my ears. Then silence.

The last thing I see before I black out is Zach's slack face.

Empty and lifeless.

CHAPTER 14
MICAH

STAY WITH ME – YOU ME AT SIX

I HATE HOSPITALS.

The noise is overwhelming after so many months of silence in the quiet bliss of my studio. If I close my eyes, I can almost imagine the wet clay sliding between my fingers as I find my happy place.

The wail of a baby crying interrupts my daydream. After waiting for hours on end in the rural, countryside hospital near the crash site, my mind can't help but wander.

"Mi?" Ryder waves a hand in front of my face.

My eyes snap up to meet his. "Yeah?"

"Need a coffee or something?"

"Have you got anything stronger?"

"I wish," he snorts.

We're sitting in the clinical, white-washed waiting area of the emergency care unit. Opposite me, Killian has his elbows braced on his knees and his head in his hands.

By some miracle, he escaped the accident with only superficial cuts and a sprained shoulder, despite being in the driver's seat. The truck hit the fence and rolled, according to authorities.

"You guys doing okay?" Ethan strolls into the waiting area.

Standing up, Ryder walks into his arms so the pair can exchange kisses. He arrived by helicopter not long after Willow, Zach and Killian were all rushed in for urgent care.

We got the call a few hours ago. Some asshole ran them off the road—

paid for by Mr Sanchez, no doubt. The son of a bitches were on a suicide mission to end Willow's life no matter what.

"Peachy," Killian speaks for the first time.

Ethan gives him a sympathetic look. "If it's any consolation, our two perps are dead. Tara and Hyland shot them on sight."

"Jesus," I mutter.

"We'll identify them as soon as possible, but if this is Sanchez, he would've been careful to use people who can't be traced back to him."

"So we're screwed?" Killian deadpans.

Ethan shrugs. "We're doing what we can."

This shit is a far cry from the peaceful life we're supposed to be living. Guns and violence don't belong in our story, but here we are. Living out the plot of a damn action movie.

Taking their seats, Ryder and Ethan's hands remain tightly entwined. Killian finds the energy to lift his head and looks at me beneath the gauze covering his sliced-up face.

"We should be in there," he croaks.

"We will be," I assure him.

"When?"

We're really in shit if Killian's deferring to me for some kind of plan here. With a sigh, I leave my seat and take the creaky plastic chair next to him so our shoulders brush together.

"As soon as the doctors will let us see them, we'll be in there."

"She needs us."

"And we're here, aren't we?"

Here—but that doesn't make up for the weeks I've spent treating Willow like crap and avoiding her. I thought that by keeping my distance, it wouldn't hurt when she left.

But she didn't leave. Not by her own choice. Those assholes almost took my girl from me, and I've wasted all this time keeping her at arm's length, all for nothing.

We could've lost her. Fuck, we still may. Nothing in this life is guaranteed, just the promise that more pain will always come. It's up to me whether I want to face that pain alone or with her by my side.

Killian's hand reaches out and clasps mine tight. "This has to stop, Mi. She needs you."

It's like he can read my mind. Sighing again, I silently wish I had a very strong drink in hand and force myself to nod.

"I know, Kill. It will."

"You swear it?"

"I'll make this right, I promise. Willow deserves that much."

"She never wanted to leave us," he tries to explain. "I know it's hard to accept. Believe me, I do. But she did what she felt that she had to for her daughter's life."

And deep down, beneath the anger and sadness, I know that. Better than anyone. Arianna is her whole life, and being a Mum is what kept Willow alive all the years she spent fighting to survive.

But that didn't stop it from hurting like hell when she took my heart in her hand, ripped it clean out from behind my ribcage and tossed it aside in a blood-slick lump. That pain was unbearable.

"She's my everything," I admit. "I just… I didn't know how to handle her coming back. It hasn't felt real."

"And it's up to us to keep her here, no matter how much she wants to run and hide," he urges. "This is going to be the fight of our lives, Mi. We need each other."

"More than ever," Ryder interjects. "You guys aren't doing this alone. The whole town wants to keep Willow and Arianna safe."

Between them both staring at me, I feel my cheeks flame red. The realisation of exactly how fucking stupid I've been washes over me. That ends today.

If Willow needs me, I'll be there. Regardless of the past. She came back to us, and it's high time I grew up. That blessing can't be ignored any longer in favour of my depression and grief.

The door to a clinical room clicks open, and Willow's two doctors emerge, both dressed in white and carrying clipboards. We all immediately stand, though Killian is stiff and grunts in pain.

"How are they?" Ryder asks.

"Zach has a moderate concussion and has required several stitches," Doctor Putland answer him. "He's doing well and has regained consciousness. We'll be discharging him in the morning."

"And Melody?" Killian demands, being careful to use Willow's false identity.

The second man, Doctor Vale, glances between us all. "Might I ask if any of you are Melody's significant other?"

"I am," we blurt at the same time.

Both doctors stare at us for a moment before quickly hiding their surprise. Doctor Putland waves us over to follow them into the room.

Leaving Ryder and Ethan behind, we're led into a brightly-lit clinical space down the corridor. Behind a blue curtain, Willow is resting upright in a hospital bed.

She's banged up, her arm bandaged from being sliced by glass and face bruised in mottled shades of green and purple down one side. My throat tightens. Shit. They've done this to my girl.

But she's awake and still looking so fucking stunning, it hurts my heart to see her coal-black hair and shining eyes. She bursts into tears when she spots us entering the room.

Shoving me forwards, Killian hangs back so I can approach first. I move without an ounce of hesitation. Willow lets me bury my face in her neck as my own tears well up.

"You're okay." My words sound strangled.

Her hand buries in my overgrown hair. "I'm alright, Mi."

I repeat it again, needing to convince myself. While I locked myself away at home like a petulant fucking child, she was out there, getting hurt. I'll never forgive myself for leaving her again.

"I'm so sorry I wasn't there—"

"Stop," she interrupts, lifting my head so our eyes can meet. "This isn't on you."

"But you needed me."

Willow hesitates. "I did."

"Then this is on me. I swear to you, angel, I won't ever do that to you again. Please forgive me."

Her expression softens. "There's nothing to forgive."

We embrace again, sharing a soft, gentle kiss despite our audience. When one of the doctors clears their throat, I reluctantly release her and take a small step backwards.

"Miss Tanner," Doctor Putland begins.

Willow startles at the false name but quickly smooths a blank expression into place. "Yes?"

"Your injuries are all mild; you've been incredibly lucky to escape unscathed."

"Then why are you still holding her?" Killian asks suspiciously.

Doctor Vale steps forward. "We sent Miss Tanner for a routine scan and some blood tests when she arrived. As you didn't mention it, I think this will come as a surprise to you."

He looks at our girl meaningfully.

"What is it?" Willow breathes.

"Melody, you are pregnant. Congratulations."

You could hear a pin drop in the hospital room. No one says a fucking word. All I can do is stare at the look of complete and utter shock on Willow's face as her mouth opens and shuts several times.

Silence.

Long, suffocating silence.

"P-Pregnant?" she finally speaks.

The doctor nods. "Approximately five weeks. The baby is healthy, no signs of injury following the accident."

My mind rushes to connect the dots. She's been back with us for a while now, since before Christmas. Unless she's seeing someone else, the baby is ours. One of us is having a kid.

Or… all of us.

I really don't know.

"Are you sure?" Willow squeaks.

They both nod back.

"A baby," Killian repeats, dumbfounded.

"But I thought…" Willow trails off. "They told us that I'd never be able to conceive again when I had a miscarriage last year. I have too much scarring."

"Miracles do happen, Miss Tanner. You're going to have a rainbow baby after all."

Oh my God.

An actual child.

Our baby.

Bursting into loud, back-breaking sobs, Willow crumbles between us as we surround her. Killian buries his face in her hair as I hold her against my chest, stroking her back.

It seems neither of us know what to say.

We don't need to ask whose it is.

That doesn't matter right now. Willow's having a kid, and we're going to be fathers. Everyone and everything else pales into insignificance—even the differences that have kept us apart.

"A baby," she hiccups. "We're having a baby."

The doctors file out to give us some privacy, but we don't move. Willow remains trapped between us until her sobs fade into tiny whimpers of what sounds a lot like fear.

I tilt her chin up with a crooked finger, forcing her tear-logged eyes to lock on me. "Talk to us, angel."

"I never th-thought I'd get another chance," she whispers.

Killian smooths her hair. "You heard them. It's a miracle."

"But… there's so much going on." She shakes her head. "How can I possibly bring a baby into this mess? We're not safe yet. I can't have another child."

I grip her chin tight. "Whatever you want to do, we'll support you. But don't throw away this chance because of that bastard. He's taken enough from you."

"Micah's right," Killian agrees. "Do you want this baby?"

Willow bites her lip and nods. "More than anything."

"Then I guess we're having a kid."

Hearing him say it out loud feels like an electric shock to the system. For the first time in months, I can feel my body. It's humming. Trembling. Shaking with anticipation.

I'm alive.

The numbness leaves me.

I don't have time to waste, wallowing in the pits of my loneliness when Willow's here, pregnant and hurt. Pregnant with *our* child.

She shakes her head. "We haven't used protection. Jesus Christ."

Killian strokes a single finger down the slope of her crooked nose. "Fuck. I completely forgot about that."

Both of them glance up at me.

"What?" I frown back.

I can see the worry dancing in her eyes. We all know the baby isn't mine. It sounds like Killian and Zach are both in the running.

They're waiting for me to be upset. While part of me feels like I'm intruding on their moment, I sure as hell am not walking away. Not now. I've done more than enough of that.

"Do we want to know?" I ask honestly.

Killian shrugs. "I don't think it matters whose it is. If we're doing this, then we're going to do it together as a family."

Relief floods me at his words. The assumption I made is correct. We've never discussed this, it didn't seem like it would ever be a possibility. But I'm glad we're on the same page.

There's a knock on the door before it creaks open, emitting a limping, bandaged Zach. He shrugs off the nurse's grip on his arm and steps into the room.

"Willow!"

"It's okay," she rushes out. "I'm fine."

Slowing down, Zach wobbles on his feet for a moment, and I'm forced to grab him so he doesn't fall. He steadies himself on my arm.

"Someone drove a damn car into me," he complains moodily. "Is that why I have such a bad headache? Or did I drink too much?"

I quickly pull him into a back-slapping hug. "Good to see you awake, brother."

"Jesus. Who are you, and what have you done with Micah?"

"Hilarious. Want me to hit you with another car?"

"Try it," he challenges. "I survived one hit, I can take another."

"No!" Willow shrieks. "Christ, guys."

Rolling my eyes, I release him. That's when he spots our faces, all misty-eyed and flushed, realising that something is going on.

"What's wrong?" Zach quickly asks.

Willow wipes her tear-stained face. "We... uh, have some news."

"News," he repeats. "Are you okay? Did the doctors say something? I tried to shield you as best as I could from the crash."

"I really am okay, Zach." She flashes him a wobbly smile. "Better than okay."

Looking between us all, grinning like fucking idiots who don't have clue what rollercoaster lies ahead, Zach doesn't catch on.

"Mind filling me in, babe?"

Willow's tears begin to flow again. "You're going to be a dad."

Frozen on the spot, his mouth falls open. "Come again?"

I squeeze his shoulder. "She's pregnant."

Still, Zach doesn't unfreeze. "With...?"

"Our baby," Killian finishes.

Hearing those words, the most magnificent, over-enthusiastic smile blooms on his lips. Zach crosses the room in a limping blur to gather Willow into his arms, bruised skin and all.

"Holy motherfuck!" he yells so loud, I'm sure the whole hospital can hear us.

"Zach," she scolds him, mortified. "Language!"

We all burst into laughter. Despite the pain and turmoil of the past few hours, it feels good to hear that tinkling, excited sound fall from Willow's lips. Shit. We're really doing this.

Zach's eyebrows raise. "Ah, hell. Last month?"

Flushed pink, Willow shrugs. "I guess so."

"I totally forgot."

"We both did." Killian laughs.

All huddling together, we hug in a breathless tangle. None of us have the right words. Maybe there aren't any. Just happiness and pure fucking bliss for a single, solitary moment of our lives.

This is it.

Our forever.

It's on the horizon.

Once Willow's tears have dried up, she shoos us out of the room to speak to the doctors in private. We catch the words *high-risk pregnancy* before the door to her room clicks shut.

We look at one another, silently communicating before we slip outside to talk in private, away from Ethan and his team. The moment the cool, winter air slaps my face outside, reality settles in.

Willow isn't safe.

That sick piece of shit tried to have her killed. There's no doubt that the two idiots in the car were paid for by his dime, even if we don't have evidence to prove it yet. That wasn't an accident.

"What now?" I ask, urgency surging like a shot of adrenaline through my veins.

Killian faces the overcast clouds as his shoulders slump. "Shit, we're in so much trouble. We can't risk anything making this even harder for Willow than it already will be."

"What do you mean?" Zach questions.

"You heard them in there. The chances of her losing this baby are already higher than average. Do you want her to go through another miscarriage?"

I feel myself blanch. "Fuck no."

Zach shakes his head. "Not a chance."

"There's a possibility it will happen. We need a game plan and fast. I won't let that asshole get another chance to hurt our girl."

"So what do we do?"

His expression hardens. "We go on the attack. I want him taken down in every single way possible."

Zach leans against the wall, clearly exhausted. "How do we do that?"

"Hiding isn't working anymore."

"So what do we do?" I frown.

"Whatever it takes. We need him to stop spreading lies about Willow and her disappearance. Then Sabre Security can find that motherfucker and bury him."

We both nod in agreement. The day that wanker is behind bars—or even better, dead in the ground—will be the day we finally rest. This is a war that we have to win now.

"What about Willow?" Zach glances at me. "And the... you know?"

Killian's jaw tightens. "Yeah. I know."

"Know what?" I look between them.

Neither looks willing to tell me what's going on. Frustrated, I raise my hands in exasperation.

"What are you both talking about?"

"Willow's been cutting," Zach reveals.

For the second time today, I'm caught off guard and speechless. Killian avoids looking at me while Zach won't look away, ensuring I know exactly what's been going on while I've been fucking around with paint and clay.

"She's self-harming?" I ask in an unfamiliar voice. "Again?"

He nods. "For a while now."

Memories of the last time this happened threaten to overwhelm me. Finding Willow in that bathtub, crying and blood-stained, was harrowing. I was the only one equipped to deal with her in that situation.

"How long?"

"Mi—"

"How fucking long?"

"Months," Killian answers, sadness etched into his features.

Bracing my hands on my knees, I let my head fall in shame. "Shit. How bad?"

"Pretty superficial," Zach replies weakly. "She hasn't been doing it much since coming home. Looks like the worst of it was done during her time away."

Right around the time I hated her for leaving and spent every waking moment cursing her existence. Meanwhile, she was out there, hurting herself and unable to cope with her own personal hell.

I'm an asshole.

The world's biggest.

"Fuck!" I shout, kicking the hard brick wall. "I can't believe I didn't realise."

"Mi—" Zach begins.

"No, don't even say it."

"How could you have known she was doing that?"

"I get it," Killian interrupts us, laying a hand on my shoulder. "I felt the same way when I found out. But we know now, and we have to help her."

"You said she'd stopped?"

They exchange a long, hard look.

"Mostly," Zach replies, his lower lip trapped between his teeth.

Fucking *fuck!*

Feeling like the absolute worst person on the planet, I walk away from them to gather myself before I do something stupid like punch the wall and break my hand.

I could've helped her. Hell, I could've stopped her. I did before. Instead, she lived with this alone for months. Just like I did at one time. She swore she'd come to me, but I pushed her away too far.

No more.

That ends today. She's my girl, and I won't rest until I make this right again. For her, for Arianna… and for our baby. Willow will never be alone in this world again for as long as I draw breath.

That's a vow.

CHAPTER 15
WILLOW

SPOTLESS – ZACH BRYAN & THE
LUMINEERS

THE SMELL of toast and frying bacon meets my nostrils. Peeling my eyes
open, I catch sight of Killian walking in, dressed in a pink, flowery apron.
Huh. I'm definitely still asleep.

"Morning sunshine," he coos.

Blinking hard, I wait for the dream to fade and reveal the real world.
Instead of that happening, he places the tray of breakfast down in front of
me, a blazing smile on his usually grumpy face.

"Kill?" I moan groggily.

"Wake up. It's time to eat."

"Are you… real?"

Cursing, he unties the apron and swiftly chucks it on the floor. "Do you
believe I'm real now?"

For extra measure, he moodily stomps on the floral fabric to convince me.
From the sour look on his face, tinted with a hint of humour, I realise this isn't
actually a dream.

"Why are you cooking for me?"

"You're knocked up with my kid," he replies happily. "Therefore, I am
going to stuff you full of food at every opportunity for the next nine months.
Get used to it."

Letting my head hit the pillows, I huff in annoyance. "Great."

Day one of this bullshit and I am already over it. I knew from the moment
I saw their faces that this would send their overprotective instincts into
overdrive.

Around me, the pale walls of my cabin are lit by winter sunshine as Killian opens the curtains. I pull myself up and take a bite of toast.

We arrived home late yesterday afternoon from the hospital. Zach and I were discharged after being kept overnight for observation, both roughed-up and heavily bruised.

"Where's Ari?"

"Eating eggs with Micah." Killian sits down on the bed next to me. "I convinced her not to come screaming in here for attention."

"Thanks. My head is pounding."

"Need some more pain relief?"

Nodding, I wait for him to grab the pills I was discharged with, then I wash the tablets down with coffee. Peering over the rim of the mug, I pin him with a look.

"This is decaf, isn't it?"

Killian plasters on his best innocent expression. "No idea."

"You're such a controlling son of a bitch."

"You're pregnant!"

"Shh." He playfully nips at my fingers when I attempt to cover his mouth. "Don't go yelling about it. I'm not ready for Ari to know just yet."

"When can we tell people?"

Lord, I never thought I'd see the day Killian acts like an excited puppy who's got the bone. All it took was getting knocked up after a protection-less sandwich.

"Not yet! It's way too early. I need to get to at least twelve weeks, when things are more stable."

His face softens. "It's going to be okay, baby."

"You can't promise that."

"But I can promise that we'll do everything in our power to make it okay, no matter what it takes."

Reaching up, I stroke his blonde beard until I'm cupping his cheek. Killian leans into my touch, his fire-lit eyes piercing mine and filled with determination.

"You promise?" I ask huskily.

Passion burns in his gaze. "Swear on my life."

"It isn't just our lives we're gambling with anymore, Kill. This baby is at risk now too."

"Don't say that," he murmurs, his big hand reaching around the tray to cover my belly. "You and our baby are going to be just fine. Arianna too. We're going to fix everything."

"Lola used to say the same thing to me." I put down the toast, which turns to ash in my mouth.

Pain flickers in Killian's eyes. Even he can't believe that we're safe. Not here. Not now. We've fired the first shot, and that convenient little car accident was Mr Sanchez responding.

"She'd be so fucking thrilled right now," he says.

"Yeah... She would."

"Having Arianna around was the highlight of her life... but seeing us have a baby together? Damn, princess. That would've been everything to her."

"If we live long enough to have this baby."

He leans forward, his eyes narrowing. "Don't say that."

"Why not?" I challenge. "It's true. You think he'll stop at a car crash? Mr Sanchez obviously knows we're on to him."

"Tara and Hyland are outside," he reminds me. "Armed to the teeth and looking scary as fuck, I might add."

"That doesn't make me feel better."

"This was your plan!"

"And maybe I was wrong." I shrug. "We can't beat him. Not like this. I won't risk our lives again."

Incensed, he looms over me on the bed, pausing a beat before capturing my lips in a breath-stealing kiss. I let his mouth devour mine for as long as he needs. The crash has shaken us all badly.

Seeing Zach unconscious and covered in blood is something I never intend to repeat. But I won't hide away—that isn't going to stop Mr Sanchez from threatening our lives all over again.

No.

I'm going to flush him out.

Expose every last drop of his depravity and force him to show his true colours to every single person he's poisoned against me with his false narratives. Only then will I let Sabre drag his ass to prison.

We're taking our lives back.

"I need to pee," I mumble against Killian's lips. "Don't get any ideas."

"Damn," he grunts. "This kid is being a cockblock already, huh?"

Pushing his shoulder, I quickly relieve myself and find him gone when I return. His shadow looms in the kitchen where another technicoloured, heavily bruised face greets me.

"Morning," Zach offers.

I have to swallow the bubble of shame that looking at his painful face brings. "Hey. How are you feeling?"

"Like someone rammed a car into me." He laughs it off. "What about you?"

"Pretty much the same."

"What about…?"

Trailing off, he casts a side look at Arianna who is happily stabbing the pile of scrambled eggs on her plate. When his eyes duck down to my midsection, I catch on.

"Fine. Just a little nauseous."

"Sit down." Killian guides me over to the table. "I'll bring your breakfast in."

Before taking the empty seat, I pause to drop a kiss on Arianna's head. She's eagerly shovelling her breakfast down in preparation to return to school with the other children this morning.

"Does your face hurt, Mummy?"

I ghost a finger over the bandage covering a stitched cut on my forehead. "It's fine, baby."

She freaked out and had a meltdown when we arrived home yesterday, all bruised and battered from the crash. It took hours for her to stop crying out of fear.

"Who are those funny people outside?" Arianna wrinkles her nose.

Just outside the window of our cabin, two figures stand at the front door, one on either side. Tara and Hyland are wearing their usual all-black clothing with thick jackets on top to protect against the wind chill.

"They're friends of mine," I quickly lie.

"Friends?"

"To keep us safe, Ari."

"You mean like knights?" she asks excitedly.

"Yes, like knights protecting their princess. That's you, baby."

"Wow! I've never seen real knights before. Can I go and say hello?"

I ruffle her perfect braids, no doubt courtesy of Zach. "Of course. Maybe ask if they want a cup of coffee?"

With a huge smile, she skips off to introduce herself. We all stifle laughter as Hyland crouches down on one knee to reach her height, folding his massive body in half to do so.

"What's your name, sweet pea?"

"Arianna," she replies matter-of-factly.

"My name's Hyland." He sticks out a paw-like hand for her to shake. "You're gonna come to me if anything makes you feel scared around here, alright, kid?"

"Alright. My mummy wanted to know if you'd like coffee."

He chuckles. "I think we're okay, kiddo."

Tara makes a pout at me then mouths, "So cute."

When both of them stiffen, pushing Arianna behind them and reaching for concealed weapons, my heart leaps into my mouth. But the tinkle of Aalia's voice settles me again.

"Morning!" she calls cheerfully.

"Aalia and Johan are here!" Arianna cheers.

She rushes back inside to grab her backpack and coat. I help her pull the pink, sparkly pack on and fuss over her for a few more seconds before eventually dropping a kiss to her cheek.

"Have a good first day back at school, Ari. Be good for Rachel and Miranda."

"I'm always good," she sasses, hands on her hips.

"Yeah, yeah. I mean it."

Arianna rolls her eyes. "I will, Mummy! I promise."

"Good girl." I smooth her plaits.

Stepping outside, Hyland secures himself to her side. I move to the door to watch Aalia size up Arianna's new protection with a visible gulp. He looks even bigger next to my tiny little girl.

"Morning, Willow!"

I wave back at her. "Hi."

"You new here?" Aalia jokes as she peers up at Hyland's monstrous height.

The smile that graces his lips is weirdly gentle and patient.

"Something like that. Shall we go?"

"Lead the way."

"I'll let you do the honours," Hyland jokes.

"What a gentleman."

He laughs and falls to the back of the group, remaining an invisible but ever-looming presence to protect Arianna from harm. They vanish, leaving the three of us in peace, with Tara remaining on guard outside.

We return to breakfast and eat in silence until the front door clicks open again, emitting a shocking sight. Zach's fork clatters loudly against his plate.

Micah is dressed, showered and walking steadily as he enters my kitchen to make his own coffee. There's almost a bounce to his movements after weeks of being hunched-over and downbeat.

"What?" He frowns at us all.

"You feeling okay?" Zach chuckles.

"Fine. Just got some work to do this morning."

"Did you sleep in the studio last night?" I ask.

He shakes his head. "My bed."

When he vanished after we came home from the hospital, we assumed he was too overwhelmed by what happened and would lock himself away again.

"We should talk about sleeping arrangements," Micah declares. "We can't be split across two cabins when the baby gets here. It won't work."

Reaching over to Zach, I gently click his mouth shut from where it's hanging open. "Um, sure. We can talk about that. Bit early, though, isn't it?"

"Never too early to be prepared," Micah quips.

Stuffing a banana into his pocket, he takes his coffee and vanishes back out into the early winter morning to head for his studio. We're left in stunned silence, watching his perky footsteps.

"Did everyone else see that as well?" Zach asks urgently. "Or am I just losing my shit after that head injury?"

"How many fingers am I holding up?" Killian lifts a hand.

"Uh, four."

"Seven." He shakes his head. "You're definitely losing your shit, kid."

"No!" Zach protests. "That was totally four."

"Clinically insane, in my professional opinion. That head injury knocked whatever brains you had left out of you."

Eyes narrowed, Zach grabs an unbuttered slice of toast and launches it at Killian's head. "Fuck you, Kill!"

"The truth hurts!" he chortles.

Needing to escape their antics and loud voices, I take my coffee back to the bedroom and softly shut the door. Stronger waves of nausea crash over me with each footstep I take.

When they subside, a prickle of anxiety remains. This is really happening. I couldn't believe my ears when the doctors revealed that I was pregnant again, after being told it was virtually impossible.

Standing in front of the floor-length mirror in the corner of my bedroom, I rest two hands above my slightly rounded belly. It hasn't been truly flat after having Arianna, and I'm naturally curvy anyway.

"Hey there, little bean," I whisper to myself.

Inside me, there's a new life growing. Expanding. Developing senses, neurons, nerve connections. Thoughts and feelings. Hopes. Dreams. So many endless possibilities lie within my belly.

"I'm going to keep you safe. I promise."

Even to my own ears, the promise doesn't ring true. I can't keep my unborn child safe without throwing myself into the cage to fight to the death. Mr Sanchez can't be beaten from the shadows.

I have to take this into the real world.

I have to speak up for all the victims.

Still cradling my belly, I gently stroke the rounded slope, envisaging the person who will one day stand beside me. Another Arianna, or a younger brother for her to endlessly annoy.

I can picture Micah's tiny, sweet smile on them, or Zach's deep, empathetic green eyes. Killian's strong angles and his gruff, gentle kindness. All the best parts of them.

We're going to have a baby.

A life. A future. A chance.

I can't waste that—not for Mr Sanchez.

"Okay, kiddo." I let my hands drop from my belly. "Let's do this."

CHAPTER 16
WILLOW

WHERE IT STAYS – CHARLOTTE OC

"WOW," Ethan's voice crackles through the speaker.

"Yes. I know it's a bit radical."

"You could say that." He chuckles. "Where'd this idea come from?"

Sitting at the table in Lola's kitchen, I nurse my green tea, almost losing the mug in the stacks of paperwork and bound files. This place is an absolute mess.

On the opposite end of the table, Albie is combing through a box full of receipts for Lola's monthly expenses. He hasn't spoken a word since we got to work a few hours ago.

"Me," I answer honestly.

"Making a public statement against Dimitri Sanchez is a very bold move," Ethan points out. "You'll be making even more of a target of yourself."

"I prefer to look at it as defending myself. He's been speaking about me to the world through the press for months. I deserve the right to offer some kind of defence."

"I'm not disagreeing with you," Ethan replies. "Just concerned for your welfare. This won't be an easy thing to do, but we can help you to do it if that's your wish."

Looking up, I meet Albie's eyes. He's staring at me now, his focus no longer on the receipts. Holding his gaze, we share a silent conversation. I can see his fear and concern. It's all there on his face.

But there's something else.

Something *more*.

It's a look of respect... and pride. Mouth gently curving upwards in a small, encouraging smile, he nods and returns to his task. I blow out the breath I didn't realise I was holding.

"It is," I confirm.

"Alright, then." Ethan clears his throat. "Our PR representative, Lucas, will be in touch to discuss the details. Start to think about what message you want Sanchez to receive with this."

"That he's a sick son of a bitch, and we're coming for him?"

"Maybe not that." He laughs back. "We want to play our cards close to our chest until we're ready to make a move. Clear your name without setting off his suspicions even more."

"Got it. Do we have an update on the car accident?"

"We've been investigating the two perps. Both are ex-inmates who have long rap sheets for paid illegal activities, least of all murder-for-hire."

My blood freezes. "Seriously?"

"He paid them, Willow. Of that we're certain. We may not be able to prove it right now, but we will in time. Someone must've spotted you in London and reported back to him."

"Who on earth would be able to do that?"

Ethan hesitates. "I... don't know."

There's pain in his voice at admitting that. I wish I could give him a hug. He's got the shitty job of steering this crazy train to its final destination.

"That's okay, Ethan. We'll figure it out."

"I really hope so, love. Give Ryder a kiss for me?"

"I will. Be safe."

He ends the call, and I lock my phone, dropping it in between the stacks of files.

"Damn, Willow." Albie smirks. "Hell of a move."

"I have to do something." I knead the back of my neck. "We can't go on like this forever."

"I think you're doing the right thing."

"You do?"

"Hiding from this shit isn't going to make it go away. The last year has proved that much already. It's time to get up and fight the bastard."

My chest warms with appreciation. "Thanks, Al."

"You got it, kid."

Standing up to refill our drinks, I peek outside the kitchen window at the garden and vegetable patch. Hyland is standing outside while Tara takes her break, nursing his coffee and watching the perimeter.

It's been weird, getting used to being followed around everyday. Arianna quickly adjusted to having an escort to school after the first few days, but I'm still finding the whole thing a bit odd.

"Isn't he cold?" I wonder.

"That man's made of fucking steel," Albie answers in a gruff voice. "Never seen such a lump of meat in my life. Doubt he even feels the cold."

"He must."

Tara and Hyland have been welcomed by the town, taking one of the smaller, older cabins at the edge of the property. They don't spend much time in it anyway.

Ethan calls to check in with them every day, along with regular contact from the rest of the team. Having them here does give me a sense of reassurance as we heal from the accident.

"What else is there to do?" I change the subject.

"Most of the necessary arrangements are done." Albie flicks through his papers. "The lawyer will deal with Lola's will, and we'll have to take it from there."

"Okay, good."

Diving back into organising the papers I've got strewn around us, we don't come up for air until the guys arrive with lunch. Killian has made it his mission to feed me at any available opportunity.

He slaps down a thick-crusted ham sandwich in front of me and growls in his low, gravelly voice, sounding more like a wolf feeding its cub than a grown human.

"Eat."

"Yes, sir," I snark back.

"Good girl."

Zach suppresses a laugh as he boosts himself up on the kitchen counter and dives into his sandwich. He and Killian are covered in sawdust after working on a new cabin on the east side of the town.

Micah pauses to kiss my cheek. "Afternoon, angel. How are you feeling?"

"Okay." I beam up at him. "What are you painting?" I swipe a lick of wet paint from his cheek.

"That's a secret."

He winks, causing prickles of desire to sweep through me.

"Even from me?"

"Even from you," Micah replies.

Plopping himself down on the counter next to Zach, Micah's eyes are filled with humour. He's been working on some secret project for the past week, since the accident.

The change in him has been huge in the last few days. He's been coming out of the studio for meals and sleeping in his bed again. Even showering everyday, without my assistance.

He's coming back to us.

Slowly but surely.

"What's with you guys?" Albie watches us suspiciously.

"What do you mean?"

"Something's up." He studies each of our faces, his gaze pinging between us.

"No, it isn't," I lie.

"That's some steaming bullshit right there."

Zach looks like he's ready to burst. When his face begins to turn pink from the force of holding it in, I finally crack.

"Fine." I sigh dramatically. "You can tell him."

"Really?" Zach grins.

"Just no one else."

"If we tell Albie, then we have to tell Ryder too," Killian reasons. "That's only fair."

"Guys! We said we weren't doing this until twelve weeks!"

Connecting the dots, Albie's face lights up. "Oh God."

It's been a long time since I saw him with a genuine smile on his face. Albie abandons his work and scoops me into a huge hug.

"Willow! Are you…?"

"Yes," I breathe into his flannel shirt. "Around six weeks."

"Heck!" he bellows.

Stomach fluttering with excited butterflies, I hug him until he puts me back down in my chair. Albie's smile hasn't faded. It's plastered on and oh-so-bright.

But I spot the moment it hits—the grief. Filtering in like the inevitability of night swallowing day, his features fall as his eyes fill with pain.

"Your Grams… she'd be over the moon."

I grasp his hand tight. "I know, Al."

"I wish she were here to see this day."

"She is. Somewhere."

His throat bobs. "Somewhere."

Releasing my hand, Albie slips out of the room to take a moment to himself. The guys are all wincing and looking a little contrite for setting him off again.

"That went well," Killian rasps.

I scrub my face. "We should've known it would upset him."

"We can't tiptoe around Albie and the others forever," Zach says. "This is our good news to share. We deserve the chance to celebrate it."

"He's right," Micah chimes in.

Sitting back down before the nausea sets in again, I take a big bite of my sandwich, which tastes like dust in my mouth. All of this is so bittersweet.

With lunch finished, the guys hang around, waiting for the lawyer to arrive. Albie makes a reappearance, and we all stand up when the growl of an engine approaches Lola's cabin.

Hyland moves to the front of the house to greet our guest. Stepping outside onto the front porch, I watch the tall, willowy woman from Highbridge get a pat-down search for weaponry.

"Apologies," Hyland tells her.

She appears flustered. "Why is this necessary?"

"That's our business, ma'am. Thanks for your cooperation."

Checking her briefcase for good measure, he declares her clean before she's allowed to approach the cabin. Her slick brown hair is slightly rumpled from the thorough search over.

"Good afternoon. Are you Killian Clearwater?"

Killian steps forward. "That's me."

"Pauline Arkwright."

"Good to meet you. Come inside."

Ushering our guest into the cabin, we return to the kitchen and quickly clear some space on the table. Micah sets to work making Pauline a hot drink as I take the seat opposite her.

"Mrs Sanchez," she begins, eyeing me. "I understand you have some concerns about our discretion regarding your identity."

I swallow the lump in my throat. "That's correct."

"Allow me to assure you that any information discussed here is protected by client privilege. I am not at liberty to disclose your identity to anybody. You can be honest with me."

Reassured, I nod back. "Thank you."

"So to confirm, your full name is Willow Sanchez?"

"That's correct."

Her eyes sparkle with recognition. "Very well."

After we questioned the identification procedure, I had no doubt that her office would investigate me. My name is splashed all over the news, courtesy of Mr Sanchez's PR campaign.

"I was Lola's lawyer for twelve years," she continues, seeming to soften. "I'm sorry for your loss. She was an incredible woman."

My throat tightens. "That she was."

"Lola has a significant number of assets that we need to discuss, most of all being Briar Valley."

Snapping open her briefcase, Pauline pulls out a glossy manilla folder then slides it over to me. I gingerly accept it, my heart slamming against my ribcage.

Inside, the lines of text and complicated legal jargon blur across the page. I'm too overwhelmed to understand any of it. This is the final confirmation I didn't want.

Lola's gone.

Dead.

Never to return.

I thought it had hit me at the funeral, but sitting here, confronted by the monumental task of settling her affairs, the realisation deepens.

She isn't going to walk through those doors at any moment. This is it now, all we're left with is paperwork and happy memories. It feels wrong for such a huge presence in our lives to amount to so little.

"Lola recently changed her will," Pauline reveals. "A little under twelve months ago. She has made you the sole beneficiary of her entire estate."

"M-Me?" I gasp.

She nods. "You will be inheriting the deeds for Briar Valley, her cabin, and a significant lump sum of assets and cash amounting to two hundred thousand pounds."

"Fuck me," Zach mutters.

Wiping off my sweaty palms, I fight to keep my voice even. "I... d-don't understand. Why so much?"

"Lola has been resettling families for the government for decades and reaping the rewards of that arrangement. She invested in a wide portfolio of stocks during that time."

Holy. Freaking. Shit.

"This is too much!" I protest. "I don't want the town. I don't even want her money."

"It's yours now," she explains kindly. "Lola has gifted her estate to you. She must have loved you very much and wanted you to have it."

Feeling dizzy, I take a moment to breathe. Briar Valley. It's mine. She wanted me to take the town in the event of her death and continue the work she started here.

The town that saved my life.

The town I love, more than anything.

"Oh my God," I say to myself. "I c-can't do this alone."

The warmth of a hand circles between my shoulder blades, offering silent support. I can smell Killian's musky, pine tree scent behind me as he ducks low to whisper in my ear.

"You're not alone, baby. We can help you figure this out."

"I'm here to help too," Albie speaks up.

I glance at him. "You knew about this, didn't you?"

He shrugs. "Might've."

Zach and Micah crowd me so I have the warmth of three bodies pressing into me. Their touch grounds me before I lose my mind over what's happening right now.

"I need you to sign some paperwork for me." Pauline taps the folder. "Property deeds will be transferred into your name by the end of the week."

This can't be happening. I've barely come to terms with last week's surprise… Now this? It's all too much. Abruptly standing up, I make my apologies and bolt outside.

"Willow?" Hyland calls as I rush past him.

Halting, I clutch my tight chest. "I'm fine. Just need a moment."

He moves to stand next to me. "Take a deep breath. In through your nose, out through your mouth. Let's do it together."

Clasping my shoulders, he mimics the breathing pattern and encourages me to follow. I take several deep breaths, forcing air into my panicking lungs.

"That's it," he whispers reassuringly. "You're doing good."

We stand like that for several long moments. I can practically feel the pressure of the guys' gazes through the kitchen window, giving me a moment of privacy.

When the rush of fear has begun to abate, I breathe clearly and murmur my thanks. Hyland releases my shoulders after a final squeeze.

"My kid brother has OCD," he informs me without me asking. "He's suffered with panic attacks for years. Used to scare the hell out of me when we were younger."

"You're good at calming people down."

Hyland offers me a toothy grin that doesn't match his rough exterior. "It's my job to look after you."

"Thanks." I force a wobbly smile.

"Go back inside. Those men of yours are about to lose their shit, if their faces are anything to go by."

Snorting to myself, I slip back inside. Everyone's where I left them—drinking and chatting. Thankfully, no one says anything about my outburst and lets me quietly sit down again.

Retaking my seat, I pick up the pen that Pauline left and flip to the last page. It's a legal contract, allowing me to officially accept the contents of Lola's will. This is it.

"Where am I signing?" I ask, itching to escape again.

Pauline points towards a dotted line. "Right here."

Hand shaking, I manage to scrawl my signature across the line before placing the pen back down. Seeing it there, spelled out in ink, ignites a sudden rush of determination that overtakes everything.

I can do this.

For Lola. For us.

I have to continue her legacy.

CHAPTER 17
KILLIAN

THE OTHER SIDE OF LOVE – JACK SAVORETTI

HURTLING the axe into the woodblock, I split it into two perfect halves. My shoulders ache from several hours of aggressive chopping to release my anxiety.

Willow's inside puking her guts up. I hate seeing her suffering, even if it is for a good reason. Hell, a fucking amazing reason. We're having a kid. Us. Together.

I've been a wreck on the inside ever since finding out. This pregnancy isn't going to be easy, none of us are under any illusions about that. But we've been given something so precious.

We can't ignore that.

This could be our last shot.

Lining up the next log, I falter at the last second and almost hack into the ground next to the cabin instead. Ryder's truck is careening up the steep slope at full speed.

"Killian!" he yells out the window.

I drop the axe. "What is it?"

"You need to see this."

Slamming on the brakes, he comes to a halt with a spray of mud. I quickly wipe my hands off on my ratty blue jeans and climb into his truck. He's panting hard, like he ran to his truck then drove straight here.

"Did someone get hurt?"

All he can do is wordlessly shake his head.

"Show me, then."

Instructing Hyland to stay back and watch Willow while we're gone, I climb into the truck, and Ryder takes off with a hissed curse.

Driving back into town quickly, we bump over rocks and uneven bends in the makeshift road. It's a quiet Friday, and everyone's preparing for the weekend ahead.

As we make it back into the town centre, I can immediately tell that something is off. I spot the swarm of black vehicles haphazardly parked around the town square from far off.

All are marked with a logo.

SANCHEZ REAL ESTATE.

My entire body freezes up with an icy stab of rage. There are at least a dozen vehicles—cars, trucks and vans—parked near workers in matching uniforms.

At the head of the group, two men wearing hardhats are deep in discussion over a clipboard and measuring tape.

"What the fuck is this?" I growl.

Ryder quickly parks up. "No idea. We should go back for Tara and Hyland."

"Hyland's covering Willow, and Tara's off duty. Come on, we can handle this."

Climbing out of the truck, I approach the two developers who appear to be surveying the land around them, exchanging ideas under their breaths. Both watch me coming towards them with matching, smug smiles.

"What are you doing on our land? This is private property."

"Mr Clearwater, I assume," the first greets. "We've been instructed to begin prepping for the upcoming development."

"What fucking development? Briar Valley is not for sale!"

He flashes a shark-like smile. "Everything is for sale for the right price. We can make you a very significant offer."

"Even if this was my land to sell, I'd rather see Briar Valley burn to ash than end up in your fucking hands."

The second developer laughs. "That can be arranged. We'll be needing a fresh start for our modern apartment blocks to be built."

I'll die before seeing Lola's legacy be demolished to make way for some shitty apartments sold at half a million pounds apiece. That isn't happening while I'm alive.

"Get out of here!" I snarl, shaking all over.

"It isn't illegal to look around. We're simply sizing up the land and having a little exploration of your delightful town."

Ryder hisses from beside me. "Trespassing is illegal!"

"Go before I put a goddamn bullet between your eyes," I add menacingly. "This is my town. You're not fucking welcome."

After smirking to one other, they pack up their belongings and instruct their workers to load up. At the last moment, the first developer presses an envelope into my hands.

I don't open it until their taillights are heading out of town and climbing back up the unforgiving slopes of Mount Helena. My insides are searing with anger at the intrusion.

That motherfucking animal!

If Dimitri Sanchez thinks he can intimidate us with these psychological games, he's got another thing coming. We're not so easily scared off, and this is our property to defend.

"What does it say?" Ryder asks, panic clear in his tone.

Taking his arm, we walk over to Lola's porch and sit down on the wide steps. I tear into the letter then scan over the neat, pretentious writing that turns my stomach.

If you think that my wife belongs to you, then you're sincerely mistaken. Willow Sanchez will always be mine.

I'll burn down this pathetic town of yours unless you return my property. It will be my sincere pleasure to see it destroyed.

Don't test me.

Dimitri Sanchez

"Son of a bitch."

Ryder reads over my shoulder. "He's a twisted fuck, isn't he?"

"This bastard is really starting to piss me off. Someone needs to end him."

"Just say the word. I'll do it with pleasure."

Scanning around the town square, my scalp prickles with alarm. If those dickheads can just drive in here like they own the place, then we're not secure enough to keep Willow safe.

"We need to step things up around here." I scrunch the letter up into a ball. "I want people on the town's perimeter."

"To do what?" Ryder scoffs.

"We at least need to know if some asshole is gonna turn up in town and start making threats. We have the right to defend our land."

Looking thoughtful, he nods. "We could have some of our best hunters out there keeping an eye. Not our fault if someone accidentally gets shot while crossing our land."

After sharing a laugh, we fall back into silence. I'm fucking shaken up. Nothing much used to faze me, but worry and fear are quickly becoming new constants.

We have so much to lose. Willow. Arianna. Our future. The stakes are higher than ever, and so much of this is out of my control. I can't just sit here and split logs all day. I have to do something.

"She needs to make that public statement," I decide. "Sooner rather than later. This bastard needs putting in his place."

"Did she tell you what she's gonna say?"

"Not yet."

Ryder bites his lip. "I think she's planning to announce that she's filing for divorce. Willow wants to kick him where it hurts."

"Fucking good."

The amount of pleasure that gives me almost makes me dizzy. I hate the fact that that man can still call her his wife. We're the only ones who deserve the right to one day call her that. Not him.

"I hope she kicks him in the teeth, and he looks like a wanker in front of the whole world," I spit. "He deserves nothing more."

Ryder stands up and offers me a hand. "Let's go speak to Harold. He can arrange a team of people to maintain the perimeter."

I take his hand and let him heave me up. Never thought I'd see the day we'd have to turn the quiet bliss of Briar Valley into a damn battleground, but nothing in our lives makes sense anymore.

This madness won't last forever.

We'll find a way to beat him.

———

With evening shadows cloaking the cabin in darkness, I leave Micah and Zach to entertain the little terror in the living room.

Willow's in bed nursing a headache after spending the afternoon on the phone to Lucas, Sabre's PR rep. She doesn't protest as I begin to run her a steaming hot bath.

"Come on, princess." I scoop her up into my arms. "Let's get you relaxed and comfortable."

"My head hurts," she whimpers.

"I know. The painkillers will start working soon."

Sitting her down on the edge of the huge clawfoot bathtub, I tip in an extra large scoop of jasmine bubble bath then check the temperature. I don't want it too hot for her.

Willow's head lolls, resting on my shoulder as we wait for the tub to fill up. She's wrung-out and exhausted. Morning sickness has well and truly arrived in the past few days.

"When are we releasing the statement?"

"At the end of the week," she replies sleepily.

"And you're happy with that?"

"It's just a written statement, I don't have to show my face or anything. Pauline has draw up divorce papers."

Relief pierces my chest. Despite the emotional turmoil, I'm still glad that she's taking this step. It's another inch in the right direction after a year of letting that man continue to oppress her.

"I'm proud of you, baby."

"You are?" she hums.

"Hell yeah, I am. This is you fighting back against Sanchez. I'm so fucking proud of how strong you're being right now."

Turning her head, she kisses my shoulder. "Thanks, Kill."

"Always."

Easing myself from her embrace, I flick off the taps then beckon for her to stand. Willow lets me undress her, peeling off comfortable sweats and one of my t-shirts that's swamping her body.

I duck low then brush my lips down—over her ribcage, hips, pubic bone —until I can press a tender kiss to her belly. My voice chokes up as I picture the little baby growing inside.

"We've got you, sweetheart," I whisper into her warm skin. "Just keep cooking in there, and let us take care of the mess out here."

Willow's hands slip into my hair, releasing it from the hair tie keeping it in a loose bun so it slips over my shoulders. When I stand up, she tugs on the hem of my flannel shirt and tee.

"Come in with me?"

I raise an eyebrow.

"Not like that," she quickly adds. "I just need you to hold me tonight. I don't want to be alone with my thoughts."

"I'm here, Willow. You're never alone when it's us. I made you a promise before, and I'll never break it."

"They were here," she whispers brokenly. "His men were in our town. I still can't believe it."

"I shouldn't have told all of you."

"How can you keep your promise when the devil is already knocking on our front door?"

After lifting her into the steaming hot water, I kick off my jeans and boxers to follow her into the bath. We settle together in the water, her small body cradled against my chest, between my legs.

"He's playing games with us." I stroke her hair, soaking the short black strands. "We're not going to rise to it."

"Rise to it?" she laughs. "He's threatening to bury the whole damn town unless I return to him."

"And that isn't going to happen."

Willow remains silent.

"Is it?" I demand, grabbing her chin and twisting so she looks up at me. "Your place is right here. This is your land now."

"What if I don't want it? What if all I want is to live a quiet, peaceful life, away from all of this madness?"

Pressing our foreheads together, I softly kiss her parted lips. "It's coming, baby. You just need to hold on a little longer."

Moving my hand around her body beneath the water, I bring it to the slope of her belly and rest it there. Her eyes fill with tears as she peers up at me beneath thick lashes.

"This is our future," I murmur.

"Yeah?"

"The baby, Arianna and the twins. We're a family, and I won't let anything take that away from us. Not even you."

"I don't want to take it away," she sniffles.

"Then trust me. Trust us. Trust that we will see this through… together. As a fucking family."

When the tears spill over, I slowly kiss them away, tasting the salty tang of her sadness. My hand strokes over her stomach before moving lower to dip between her thighs.

"Let me make you feel good, baby girl."

"Mmm." She pushes her ass against my cock.

Teasing her inner thighs with gentle strokes, I move lower, easing my hand down to her core. She's slick in the bath water, her legs parting to grant me access to her wet folds.

Rubbing my thumb over her clit, I love the little moans that slip from her mouth. Her back arches against my chest, pushing her legs farther open so I have more access to her cunt.

"Is my girl's perfect pussy wet for me?"

"Yes," she whines.

"Tell me what you want."

"P-Please… touch me."

"Where?" I bite down on her ear lobe.

Willow sighs, her thighs clenching around my hand. "I need to feel your fingers inside of me."

"You're such a good girl, aren't you?"

Rewarding her, I dip a digit into her molten core. She's wet—receptive and sensitive to even the slightest of touches from me. Easing my finger out, I push it back in deeper.

"Kill," she moans.

"Yes, princess?"

"More."

Chuckling, I kiss around her ear and down to her neck, letting my teeth nip the soft expanse of skin there. I want her to be covered in my marks and touch. She's mine. Every goddamn inch of her.

Pushing a second finger into her slit, I stretch her wider. Willow's moans grow in pitch with each thrust, her body writhing in the steam and scented bubbles.

I begin to move faster, picking up the pace and teasing each moan past her lips with a feeling of total satisfaction. Only we can take every ounce of control from her in such an intimate way.

"Are you going to come all over my hand?"

"Yes," she mewls.

"Show me. I want to feel your juices running all over me."

Flicking her bud again, I slam my two fingers deeper into her cunt and watch as her mouth parts in a perfect, pink O. She cries out in pleasure, her walls clenching tight around me.

"Killian!"

"That's it, baby. Say my fucking name."

With a final cry of ecstasy, she falls apart. Her sexy body quivers with each wave of bliss, and her warmth coats my fingers in stickiness.

Slumping against my chest, her eyes slide shut. I slip my fingers from between her legs and wash them off in the water before banding my arms around her from behind.

"Perfect." I kiss the side of her head. "You okay?"

"Yeah," she breathes out.

"Can I wash your hair for you?"

"Okay."

Lifting her head so I can access the short strands, she allows me to soak her hair in water. I grab a bottle of shampoo then begin to lather, working in methodical silence.

"Kill?"

I pause while massaging her scalp. "Yeah?"

"I need you to know that no matter what happens, I love you so much. I want to have this baby and future with all of you. I want our family."

Rinsing off the shampoo, I grab the conditioner next. "I know. Me too. We're going to be okay."

"Swear on it?"

"I swear, Willow."

Her eyes flutter shut as I massage conditioner into her scalp, swallowing a bubble of shame. I just hope that what I'm saying is true and not just a fantasy.

CHAPTER 18
WILLOW

I FEEL LIKE I'M DROWNING –
TWO FEET

PEERING OUT of the cabin window, I stare at Micah's studio. He's been locked in there for the past few days, and I'm worried that he's slipping back into old patterns. I've barely seen him.

Zach and Killian are out doing road maintenance after the recent snowstorms washed out some of the tracks. With Arianna at school and Tara posted outside, I hate being alone.

It reminds me of the endless days spent locked in the apartment in Southampton. When I'm alone, the dark thoughts begin to swirl and expand like curling cigarette smoke in the crevices of my brain.

This is ridiculous.

Just go over there, Willow.

With a sigh, I step outside into the February air. Tara immediately perks up when she spots me, looking up from the phone clasped in her hands.

"Willow? Everything okay?"

"All good, I'm just heading over to see Micah."

Her eyes twinkle. "He's an interesting one, isn't he?"

"You could say that."

"I'll give you two some privacy. Shout if you need me."

Leaving her posted outside the cabin, I crunch over frost-bitten grass as I approach the cabin. The weather is still frigid, even with March quickly approaching.

It's as cold as the day we arrived in Briar Valley this time last year. It's almost like nothing has changed, when in reality, our lives are completely different now.

"Micah?"

Knocking on the studio door, there's no answer at first.

"Mi? It's me. Can I come in?"

When I knock again, Micah's panicked voice calls back.

"Go away!"

Gut twisting, I open the door and step inside without permission. "That's not happening. What's going on?"

The scene I was expecting to find is nowhere to be found. There's no rubbish strewn across the floors or empty liquor bottles. No scent of vodka or cigarettes. Instead, Micah's old chaos awaits.

Paint is covering every surface along with a fine dusting of sawdust and wood chippings. At the centre of the room lies a massive baby cot, under which Micah is laying with a paintbrush in hand.

"Mi?" I squeak.

He moves to sit up so fast, he smacks his head on the cot. "Shit, Willow. I told you not to come in. It was supposed to be a surprise."

"I thought you were drinking in here!"

Rubbing his head, he sits up properly. "Just working. You don't need to worry."

Inching closer, I take in the breathtakingly beautiful cot. It's been carved with painstaking detail, from tiny wooden roses cut into the glossy mahogany to intricate brocade designs in the walls.

"Wow, Mi. It's so freaking incredible."

A blush tinges his cheeks. "It's not done. You weren't supposed to see it yet."

I trail my fingers over the exquisitely carved handlebars, loving the smooth wooden surface. "It's perfect."

"Consider it an apology for being such a dick to you when you returned."

"You had every right to be angry with me, Mi."

He shakes his head. "Avoiding you and drowning my sorrows wasn't the answer, though."

Taking a seat on the floor next to him, I grab a paintbrush and dip it in the pot. We work together, painting the slopes of the cot and each joint in the frame individually.

"I'm sorry," he adds.

"You can stop apologising."

"Not yet."

Sighing, I dab paint on one of the carved roses. "I'm sorry too. We haven't treated each other right. I'd like to fix that."

"Me too, angel."

"So… where do we go from here?"

Micah gnaws on his bottom lip. "Do you still want to be with me?"

"Of course, I do."

"I really wouldn't blame you if you didn't want to."

Annoyed, I dab him with the paintbrush, smearing his arm with the light cream colour. "We're not discussing this."

"Yes, we are. We're adults."

"I don't want to be an adult today. I'm over it."

Smirking to himself, Micah lifts his brush and taps the tip of my nose with it. I can feel the thick paint on my skin, dripping down until it's smeared across my chin.

"Got you back," he teases.

I hit him again—on the cheek this time, covering him in paint.

"If you want a war, I can bring it."

Micah lifts an eyebrow. "Is that a threat?"

"You bet your ass it is."

Dabbing me again with another smear of paint, he takes my wrist and yanks me closer so our mouths smack together. The moment his lips are on mine, everything changes.

The gentle playfulness melts into something else, something hotter. A roaring bonfire ignites between my thighs as his tongue slips into my mouth to tangle with mine.

Mouths duelling and hands exploring each other, the pace quickly picks up. Months of nothing but building tension erupts to an explosion between us. I want to crawl inside the shell of his skin.

"Fuck," he gasps into my mouth.

"I need you, Mi."

"I need you too, angel." He grabs a handful of my ass and squeezes. "But should we… you know, in your state?"

"State?" I repeat with a laugh. "I'm pregnant. Not out of action. Stop being cute, and fuck me already."

Grinning so wide it reveals the soft dimples that mark his cheeks, he uses the tip of his finger to gather the paint on my face, wiping it onto his other hand. Micah slowly massages his way down my shoulder and arm.

Once the paint is smeared over the marks on my arms, covering them from sight, he hesitantly clicks his mouth open to speak again.

"You should've told me."

My eyes laser in on his sad face. "You should've too."

"With what?"

"The drinking, Mi."

"You weren't here."

"Neither were you."

Sighing, his lips ghost over mine. "I guess that's fair."

Grabbing his chin, I kiss him more firmly, staking my claim across his mouth with a lash of teeth and tongue. We've treated each other like shit, but that doesn't matter now. Nothing else does.

It's just us.

As it should be.

With the slickness of fresh paint still between us, Micah pulls the short-sleeved t-shirt from my body and quickly unclasps my bra to free my breasts.

He palms them, spreading paint over my stiff nipples with his fingertips. The sensation of the cool liquid causes me to gasp into his mouth, loving the strange feeling.

"I missed these gorgeous tits," he marvels. "Did they get bigger?"

"Everything's going to get bigger."

"Damn. That's awesome."

"You're so adorable."

Cocking an eyebrow, he leans in again to bite down on my bottom lip so hard, pain zips down my spine.

"Adorable?" His palm smacks against my ass. "I'll show you adorable."

The quiet, shy virgin I met a year ago vanishes as lust blazes in his eyes. It's been too long. Too hard. Too much distance.

With a hand against my sternum, he pushes me backwards so I'm laying down on the paint-splattered sheet covering his studio floor. Micah unfastens my jeans then begins to pull them off.

The sides of his hands brush against my thighs and hips, adding to the tantalising sense of pressure that's blurring my vision. I want him. Us. Everything and anything in between.

"I want to bury my face between your thighs, angel," he purrs, peeling off my white panties. "And I want to make you come all over my tongue."

"Jesus, Mi."

Pushing my legs open, he kneels before settling between them to gain full access to my core. The moment his mouth meets my pussy, I arch off the sheet and cry out.

"Fuck!"

He's hesitant for a moment, but he soon forgets his nervousness and buries his tongue in my cunt. Adding his thumb to my clit and swirling it, I'm soon seeing stars behind my eyes.

"That's it, baby girl," he coos.

Gripping handfuls of the sheet, I buck and writhe, melting under his increasingly confident attention. Once he sees my reaction, Micah goes to town as he dives into his meal with enthusiasm.

Sliding his finger through my folds, he spreads come and saliva to moisten it before pushing inside my entrance. I slam a hand over my mouth to swallow my scream of pleasure.

"No," he scolds, prising my hand away. "I want to hear you. I've thought about this moment for months."

Working his finger in and out of my tight hole, he begins to thrust, his eyes locked on me. I can't run away from his gaze. I'm pinned and at the mercy of his tongue lavishing me.

"Come for me," Micah orders, flicking my bundle of nerves. "Let me taste those sweet juices in my mouth."

His filthy words leave me with no choice but to give in. The waves are approaching—building, expanding, growing more intense. I'm swallowed whole and shoved off into the deep end.

When Micah looks up from between my thighs, his mouth is scored with shiny moisture. He takes his time licking his lips, slowly but surely showing me how much he enjoys the taste of my release.

"You're so perfect, angel. That was incredible to watch."

Sitting up on my elbows, I grab the scruff of his stained t-shirt. "We're not done yet. Come here and finish what you've started."

Eyes on fire with need, he strips off his paint-covered clothing, leaving him standing in his tight black boxer shorts. My throat tightens as every sculpted inch of lean, compact muscle in his short frame is unveiled.

The bulge in his boxers offers a silent promise. He's as gorgeous as the day we first slept together on the mountaintop amidst wildflowers and evening mist.

"Like what you see?" Micah asks, sounding far too much like his cocky brother.

"Maybe."

"I missed you so fucking much, angel."

I crook a finger, beckoning him closer. "Come and show me how much you really missed me."

He approaches then covers his body with mine. We're still on the floor, disregarding the paint pots and mess of brushes causing chaos around us.

Micah retakes his place between my legs then secures his mouth to my nipple, gently biting down. I wriggle beneath him, desperate to feel his touch. His throbbing cock is so close to my centre.

"Do we need protection?" he murmurs.

"I can't get more pregnant, can I?"

Micah chuckles. "I have no idea. But if you're fine going without..."

I'm unprepared for him to pin my left leg to the floor and slam inside me in one slick pump. The sudden impact causes me to scream out so loud, I worry that Tara will come running at any moment.

He buries himself to the hilt inside me, his eyes rolling back in his head. Shifting my hips, I encourage him to move and slam back into me. I'm practically shaking with need.

"We should slow down," Micah worries, his movements stilling. "I don't want to hurt you while you're like this."

"I'm fine, Mi. Stop worrying so much."

"Are you sure? It doesn't hurt, does it?"

"No," I answer, cupping his dimpled cheek. "Please. I want you so bad. Make me forget all the months we've wasted."

With a wicked gleam entering his eyes, he kisses me fully on the mouth. The lines between him and his twin are blurring so much. If I didn't know better, I'd struggle to tell the difference.

He's changed.

I've changed.

We're in the unknown now.

Pulling out, Micah repositions himself then pumps back into my pussy. The thrust is punishing, slamming his length deep inside me and igniting my core. I rake my nails over his paint-slick skin.

"Oh God," I groan.

Each jerk of his hips sends me spiralling, deeper and deeper into a bottomless pit of desire. I'm falling. Tumbling. Losing myself and all the anxiety that's plagued me for months.

All that exists is us—our bodies, breath, minds—entwined and moving together in a tantalising dance. Nothing else matters when we're together.

"Willow," Micah moans, pumping into me in fast, frenzied strokes. "You feel so good, angel. So good."

Before I can come again, he abruptly pulls out and halts his movements. I scream at the loss of pressure, feeling suddenly empty.

"Come and ride me," he gasps, sitting back on his haunches. "I don't want to come yet. You're so tight and wet."

Letting him pull me up, I clamber onto his lap then position my legs on either side of his waist. Micah hisses when I take his length and push it against my entrance.

Sinking down on him, we both moan loudly, locked in a breathless, sweaty tangle. At this angle, he reaches an even deeper place, brushing that illusive spot that drives me wild.

I lift myself on his lap then push back down, feeding his length back into me at a steady pace. Each pump drives me back to the edge of falling apart.

"You're so fucking gorgeous," he praises, cupping my bouncing tits. "Like a damn goddess, riding my cock."

Fuck, has this dirty-mouthed devil been inside of Micah all along? He's forgotten how to be shy, and his compliments feel so good.

Grabbing a nearby paint pot, he winks at me with that damn wicked gleam in his eyes again. I watch him lather his hands in paint and move them back to the swell of my breasts.

"I want to paint you, Willow. Every luscious inch of you. Will you let me do that one day?"

"Yes," I mewl.

"Naked?"

Working myself on his shaft, I can't protest. "Yes."

"That's my perfect, little angel. Let me see these incredible tits covered in paint now."

Smearing the paint over my chest, the bite of cold liquid heightens my pleasure. He massages it into my skin, holding the heaviness of my breasts in each of his palms.

"Does it feel good, baby?"

"God, yes," I bite out.

"Imagine this body laid out on my canvas in paint and ink," he muses, mostly to himself. "It'll be a masterpiece."

Thumbs swirling and fingers spreading, he covers me in paint then tweaks my rock-hard nipples again. As the paint warms up, my skin flushes with sweat, and I'm overtaken by trembles.

"I'm close," I cry out.

Micah begins to thrust upwards, lifting his hips to meet me halfway. "Me too."

We're both moving and grinding, chasing our own highs with nothing but mess and madness around us. If anyone else were to walk in, there'd be no explaining this scenario.

Just before I can fall apart, Micah captures my lips in a final kiss that swallows my moans. I gasp into his mouth, feeling the swipe of his tongue against mine as our orgasms hit.

We come at the same time, and Micah growls through his release, our lips remaining locked together.

I can feel his hot come pouring into me and slipping between us. The warmth causes fireworks to explode beneath my skin—popping, bursting, crackling with flames and almighty bursts of ecstasy. I slump against his chest, my arms wound around his neck.

"Christ." Micah holds me close, our skin practically glued together. "I love you so much, angel. It scares me to death."

"You won't lose me again."

"Now we have even more to lose. I want this family with you so badly, but I'm terrified of what it means for us."

Lifting my head, I look into his dark, forest green eyes. So much uncertainty stares back at me. Fear. Grief. Anxiety. Excitement. There are too many emotions for me to begin to untangle.

"I promise you, Micah, that we will make this work. Our family will survive. We always do."

He nods with a scared, slightly crooked smile. "We always do."

"No matter what."

After holding me against his chest for a few moments, he heaves me up and spoons me in his arms like a small child. Micah grabs a clean sheet from his shelf then throws it around us to cover our naked bodies.

"Let's clean up," he decides. "I want to take care of you."

"Okay." I smile at him, brushing a sweaty tendril of hair off his forehead.

We leave the studio and make a beeline for the guys' cabin. Across the street, Tara is still standing in place outside of my cabin, taking a phone call. She blanches when she sees us.

Grimacing in shame, all I can do is give her a little wave. She tries really hard not to laugh while she waves back and continues her phone call.

"New friend of yours?" Micah asks quietly.

"She's nice actually."

"I still don't love having strangers here."

"They're keeping us safe," I remind him. "That's the condition of us staying. We have to be safe from any threats."

"I know, angel."

Carrying me into the cabin, Micah heads for his bedroom and into the bathroom. He places me down on the floor and flicks the shower on before spinning to face me.

"Can I... No, never mind," he trails off.

"What is it?"

Rubbing the back of his neck, he peeks up at me shyly. "I just wondered if I could touch the baby for a second."

My heart melts. "You don't have to ask, Mi."

"Yeah, I do. I'm not just going to touch you without your permission. That's totally weird."

"It's your baby too!"

"Whatever, I still want consent."

Laughing hard, I drop the sheet and stand naked in front of him. "Okay, then you have my consent."

Smiling to himself, Micah kneels down in front of me. I have the tiniest, almost imperceptible baby bump, accentuated by my already round belly and wide hips.

"What do I do?" he wonders anxiously.

Rolling my eyes, I take his hands and lift them to my belly. With his palms cupping me, I hold his wrists to keep them there. His thumbs stroke over my skin in wonderment.

"Hey," he whispers in a tiny, amazed voice. "Hi, little one."

Tears well up in my eyes. The paint smeared all over me is drying and flaking off, but it doesn't conceal the life that's blossoming between us.

Our life. Our future.

It's right there for the taking.

"I'm going to look after your mama, alright? We love you so much already. So much."

I have to blink tears aside before they roll down my cheeks.

"Be good," Micah instructs, placing a gentle kiss right above my belly button. "We'll see each other soon, little one."

With his lips on my belly, I feel content for the first time since returning. I'm whole again in this moment. Nothing else matters, and the miles still to climb fall into insignificance.

CHAPTER 19
WILLOW

FALLING APART – MICHAEL SCHULTE

"ALRIGHT, THEN." Lucas's voice rumbles down the phone line. "We're preparing to release your public statement on the hour. Any last minute changes?"

I clear my dry throat. "I don't think so."

"Good. We can expect a barrage of media attention. Probably nothing national, but the sleazy gossip mags and celebrity news pages will be all over this shit as Sanchez is involved."

Scratching Demon's ears, I focus on the feeling of her coarse black fur. "I understand."

We're sitting in Lola's living room, surrounded by half-filled boxes and packing tape. Killian and Zach are working on boxing up her possessions while Albie continues to sort paperwork in the kitchen.

"You're doing a brave thing, Willow," Lucas offers. "We'll do our best to manage any fallout and Dimitri Sanchez's response if any."

"Thank you, Lucas. You've been a huge help."

"Well, that's my job. It's been a pleasure. Take care of yourself."

"You too."

Tossing Zach's phone aside, I rub my aching temples. This isn't a day I thought I'd ever see—I'm getting a divorce. Officially.

Lola's lawyer has arranged the paperwork. It's been delivered to Mr Sanchez's real estate offices by courier, and now the real war will begin.

"Babe? You good?"

Zach stands behind the sofa, leaning over to massage my shoulders.

Releasing my temples, I blow out a tense breath. That phone call was tougher than I'd anticipated.

"The statement will be released on the hour," I answer shakily. "Lucas and his team will monitor the response and keep us posted."

"And what's in the final statement?" Killian asks, his head in a box. "Did you make any changes?"

"That Mr Sanchez was abusive throughout our marriage and engaged in illegal activity. I've fled from his violence, filed for a divorce and will be taking full custody of our child."

Nodding to himself, Killian seals the box in his hands. "Good. Short and simple."

"I don't like it," Zach gripes.

"Why not?"

"Abusive?" He stops massaging, his lips wrinkled with disgust. "That doesn't even begin to cover what he did to you and others. The world needs to know what a piece of shit he is."

"And it will when the time is right. Ethan instructed me to protect the ongoing investigation."

He huffs in frustration. "This is bullshit. He's out there strutting around and running his mouth. I want to fucking end him."

Reaching up from my seated position, I clasp his firm bicep. "We will, Zach. Be patient. His time will come."

"We don't have time to be patient."

"We have plenty!"

"Nine months." He throws his hands in the air, his eyes darkening. "Two of which have already gone. I want him behind bars by the time our baby is here."

"Who's talking bullshit now?" Killian glowers at him. "He should've been behind bars years ago. Willow and Arianna matter just as much as our baby does."

Slumping, Zach looks contrite. "Yeah, of course. It's just—"

"No, kid. Just nothing. That's final."

Falling silent, Zach looks like a kicked puppy. I hate that look on his face.

"I really didn't mean it like that," he mutters.

"I know. It's okay, we're all stressed."

"No excuse to be an asshole," Killian comments.

"Hey," Zach snaps at him. "Is this coming from you, oh mighty one? King of the assholes on his throne?"

"If I'm king of the assholes, you're my lackey. And I say get back to work, packing bitch. We have shit to do."

"Not your packing bitch," Zach murmurs under his breath in a derisive tone as he resumes bubble wrapping delicate trinkets.

We're finally beginning the mountainous task of clearing up Lola's stuff. It won't be thrown away but put into storage, safe and sound. Having it around is just a constant reminder of her absence.

Returning to the stacks of TV magazines next to the sofa, I laugh to myself at the folded down corners and circled programs that she wanted to watch. She loved her gardening shows.

"Nice," Zach snorts as he glances over my shoulder. "If it involved a rake or soil, you can bet Grams would watch it."

"I don't know how she found the time alongside running the town. There's so much to do around here."

"We're doing alright," Killian chimes in. "The place hasn't burned down yet, so that's something."

Lifting my notepad from next to me on the sofa, I flash it at him. "Have you seen my to-do list?"

"You're making an actual list?"

"Summer will be here soon! There's so much to do!"

Zach snatches the notepad from my hands and begins reading before I can steal it back. He dances away from me in the process.

"Plant summer crops, weed vegetable patches, organise hunting schedule, clear out cold storage, catch up on taxes…"

His huge, dramatic yawn causes me to glower at him.

"Boring," he singsongs.

I manage to snatch the notepad back. "She left me in charge. I have to take that responsibility seriously, or this won't work."

The easy smile falls from his lips. "I know, babe. I'm just kidding around with you."

"Well, don't. Not about this. Lola trusted me to do her job. I can't let her down."

Standing up, I stack the magazines in the overflowing rubbish bag then leave the living room to find Albie. My eyes catch on the ticking grandfather clock in the hallway as I pass.

It's time.

The statement just dropped.

The panic and fear I was expecting to rush over me doesn't come. Instead, determination filters into my bones. I'm taking control of my life and finally standing up to that monster.

Now we wait. He will fire back, there's no doubt about that. Letting me or

Arianna go without a fight isn't in his nature. But we're in the limelight now, and the public will protect us. At least, I hope so.

He can't hurt us if the entire world is watching, or he'll risk tearing apart his only defence against the oncoming storm—his picture-perfect public image. That gives us an advantage.

"Albie?" I step into the kitchen.

He looks up from his perch at the kitchen table, and the moment our eyes lock, I feel a rush of stickiness between my legs. It takes a moment for the penny to drop and terror to set in.

Warmth.

Blood.

Bracing my hand against the doorframe, I bring my hand to my stomach and breathe through my gritted teeth.

"No," I whine. "Please, no."

"Willow?" Albie immediately shoots to his feet. "What is it? Are you okay?"

"Not again. Please!"

He rushes over, gripping my shoulders and taking my weight against his body. The warm sensation has settled, but I can feel it soaking through my panties and plain black leggings.

"Is it the baby?" he asks urgently.

All I can do is nod.

"Guys!" Albie shouts. "Kitchen, now!"

The thud of a box being dropped echoes through the house followed by thumping feet. When Killian appears next to me, he takes one look at my face and goes white.

"What is it?"

"I'm b-bleeding," I choke out.

He looks down between my legs. "A lot?"

Nodding, I let Albie transfer me into his arms. Zach is fisting his hair and freaking out behind Killian.

"Call Doc," Killian snaps at him before turning to Albie. "Go and find Micah."

Both step aside to follow his orders as Killian tows me towards the downstairs bathroom. Once inside, he squats down in front of me and grabs the waistband of my leggings.

"Can I?"

"Y-Yes."

Pulling them down, he takes a look at the sodden fabric and somehow manages to turn an even paler shade of white.

"Fuck, Willow."

"Kill," I begin to sob. "What if…?"

"No, don't say it. Let Doc come and take a look at you, okay?"

Shaking my head, I'm hardly able to see him through my falling tears. I brace my hands on his shoulders and let him pull me onto his lap, not caring about the blood smeared over my thighs.

We cling to each other, terrified and desperate, until Zach returns with Doc in tow. He stands back to let him into the room.

"Willow?" Doc asks in a gentle voice. "Can I come in and have a look at you please?"

"Yes, D-Doc."

"Zach's filled me in on the situation. You should've told me about the baby. I need to know so I can look after you properly."

"We're sorry," Killian cuts in. "We wanted to wait until after the first trimester before telling anyone, given it's high-risk."

"That shouldn't include her physician."

"No," he admits shamefully. "I guess not."

Crouching down next to us, Doc takes a look at the wet leggings and blood smeared across my legs. It's not much compared to the tsunami that poured out of me last time.

"We need to bring her over to ours," Doc decides. "I have sonogram equipment in my home office. It'll be quicker than travelling to Highbridge."

"Am I having a m-miscarriage?" I hiccup through my tears.

"I don't think so, Willow. Some bleeding can be expected, especially as you're having a high-risk pregnancy. But let's make sure, okay?"

His words are a tiny pinprick to the balloon of fear sitting on my chest. I draw in an unsteady breath and nod. Killian wraps a towel around my lower half as I'm boosted into his arms.

I bury my face in his flannel shirt to hide from anyone milling around outside. It's the middle of the day, so most people are busy working on allotments or housework while the kids are at school.

Racing across the town square with Hyland following hot on our heels, we get to Doc's cabin. He leads us down a dark, wood-lined corridor to his home office, leaving my bodyguard outside to stand sentry.

It's a huge room, filled with bookshelves and medical equipment. After rolling a piece of blue protective paper over the examination table, he gestures for Killian to set me down.

"Just here please."

Removing the towel, I'm laid down in my panties and shirt. When Killian tries to move away, I cry out, snatching his hand into mine.

"Please d-don't leave me!"

He ducks his head to kiss my knuckles. "Never, princess."

Killian perches himself on the end of the table to let Doc wheel the sonogram machine closer. I lift my shirt so he can squirt gel across my raised belly and bring the wand to my skin.

"Let's take a look, then," he hums, his eyes on the black and white screen. "How many weeks are you?"

"Nine," Killian answers for me.

Before Doc can respond, the door to his office slams open. Zach, Micah and Albie arrive, all puffing from running fast. Micah's face is a picture of terror as he looks between me and the machine.

"What happened?"

"Just a little blood." Doc frowns at the screen as he moves the wand around. "We're doing some tests to assess the baby."

"Blood?" Micah repeats.

Pulling his twin into a side-hug, Zach holds him close. "Didn't the doctors say this could happen? Like spotting or something?"

"It can happen," Doc replies. "Willow has a scarred womb and significant internal trauma from Arianna's birth, so some blood would not be entirely surprising."

Breathing evenly through my nose, I fight to remain calm by latching on to his words. Just the sight of red between my legs caused me to spiral into a pit of panic after what happened.

"Okay, here we go." Doc turns the screen so we can all see as he points to a speck of grey. "There's your little one."

It feels like everyone is holding their breath—terrified and silent.

"And there's the heartbeat. A very strong one too, for this stage of the pregnancy. Would you like to hear?"

"Yes," Micah rushes out.

Fiddling with the machine, he flicks a few switches and moves the wand again. The sound of a rapidly fluttering heartbeat fills the room. My tears intensify, and I'm quickly sobbing again.

"It's okay," I weep, still clutching Killian's hand. "I didn't lose it again."

Head lowered, he kisses my hand. "You're okay."

The twins crowd around us, both misty-eyed and sagging with relief. We all cling together in a tangle, their hands rubbing my back and smoothing hair from my tear-soaked face.

"I'll give you guys a moment." Doc retreats, smiling to himself as Albie follows him out.

"Thank you, Doc."

"It's a pleasure, Willow."

Once we're alone, Micah lifts my chin and presses a kiss to my forehead. "Breathe, angel. Our little one is okay. You're okay."

"I w-was so scared, Mi."

Standing next to his brother, Zach kisses the top of my head and smooths my hair. "Everything is going to be alright now."

"Zach," Killian warns.

I know what he's thinking. That's a promise Zach can't keep. We may be here again another week's time, having the same conversation but with a different ending.

The sound of a phone ringing breaks the moment, and Zach fishes it from his pocket. He takes one look at the caller ID and frowns.

"It's Lucas."

"Don't answer it," Killian snarls.

Before he can hit the red button, I shout. "No, we need to know what's been going on since the statement was released."

"After what just happened?" Killian pins me with a glare. "You need to rest. No more stress."

"Back off, Kill. I've been working towards this day for weeks. Give me the damn phone."

Caught between us, Zach relents and passes the phone over. I accept the call and hold it to my ear, pulling the towel back over me to hide my bloodstained legs.

"Lucas?"

"Willow. I'm just calling with an update for you. The statement dropped half an hour ago, and we're getting a positive reaction so far."

"Positive?"

"The media is taking your claims very seriously." Despite the good news, his voice sounds strained. "But that's not the reason why I'm calling."

I look around the room, meeting the eyes of each guy surrounding me. My family. My loves. I can face anything with them at my sides, holding me steady in the comfort of their love.

"It's Dimitri Sanchez," he continues grimly. "He's responded."

CHAPTER 20
ZACH

WHERE THE WILD THINGS ARE –
LABRINTH

SPREAD ACROSS OUR KITCHEN TABLE, the newspapers are all open to yesterday's leading story in the trashy gossip section. Ryder brought them back from a trip into town for supplies.

A photograph of Dimitri Sanchez at his most recent charity ball is splashed for the world to see.

Sanchez: I'm not an abuser.
Real estate tycoon at centre of divorce battle.
Missing mother speaks up.

Nursing her morning coffee, Willow stares at the newspaper with a blank look on her face. I close the nearest one, hiding Sanchez's ugly mug from sight. I really hate that motherfucker.

He's released his own statement, disputing all of Willow's claims and labelling her as a psychotic, unhinged mother on the run with his precious angel. It's a steaming pile of crap, obviously.

But that didn't stop it from triggering Willow and sending her spiralling over the news last night. She went to bed a sobbing wreck, needing all three of us to hold her until she eventually dropped off.

"Enough," I scold her. "Stop reading them."

"I need to know what's going on, Zach."

"You've been staring at them all morning. Let's get out and do something to take your mind off it."

"Like what?"

I snap my fingers. "We could carry on clearing Lola's cabin. I'm not moving in there if it's full of those creepy stuffed animals and fine china—"

"We're not moving into her cabin, period," she cuts me off. "We've discussed this already."

"No, we suggested it last week, and you shot us down. That isn't a discussion in my books."

Sighing, Willow swallows another mouthful of coffee. "Why would we want to live in her cabin? We have two perfect homes."

"You've answered your own question. Two homes. That isn't going to work once the baby arrives."

She tugs at her bottom lip, seeming to consider my words, before moving to the sink to wash her empty cup. "Maybe you're right."

I almost fall over. "Wait, what?"

"I said maybe you're right."

"Just like that?"

"What is with you?" she laughs. "I hadn't thought of it like that. I just didn't like the idea of washing the memory of Lola away."

"Jesus, we're in trouble if you're gonna start agreeing with me all the time. I'm a bit freaked out right now."

Willow flips me the bird. "Screw you, Zach."

"Love you too, babe."

"Yeah, whatever."

"So what are we doing today?" I flip all of the newspapers shut. "Not reading these, that's for sure."

Willow creases her brows, deep in thought. "What about shopping? Arianna needs some lighter stuff for the spring."

Her eyes stray back to the newspapers, full of that asshole's vicious lies. Willow is the most dedicated, incredible mother to Arianna, making all of this even more difficult to swallow.

"Let's go shopping."

"Not a chance." Killian speaks from his perch on the sofa, nursing a headache. "My head is killing me."

"You weren't invited, oaf." I narrow my eyes on him. "It's just me and Willow. We'll take the cheerful twins for protection."

"Cheerful?" she chuckles.

"He's talking about Tara and Hyland." Killian snorts to himself. "They hate Zach so fucking much."

"I don't know why." I sigh dramatically. "All I tried to do was tell some jokes to break the ice."

"What kind of jokes?"

"Dad jokes," Killian replies for me.

"There's nothing wrong with my dad jokes!" I defend. "They're the best kind. The cheerful twins just have no sense of humour."

"Or your sense of humour sucks."

I lay a hand over my heart. "You wound me!"

Killian rolls his eyes. "And you give me a headache. Shut your big mouth, and go shopping already."

Willow moves outside to let Tara and Hyland know about our plan. The moment she's gone, I get hit with a typical Killian lecture about safety. Like I'm not capable of looking after our girl.

By the time she returns, he's chewed my ear off, and I'm ready to run at full speed out of Briar Valley for some peace and quiet. We grab our jackets and Willow kisses Killian goodbye.

"Be safe," he commands sternly.

She pecks his cheek. "Yes, boss."

"I mean it, princess. Don't make me regret letting the pair of you out. Stick with the security, and watch each other's backs."

"We'll be fine, Kill."

All piling into Hyland's huge, blacked-out SUV, I rattle off the instructions to Highbridge. The pair are as stony-faced as usual and on high alert after the public statement was released.

"I don't like this," Hyland complains.

"I still need some freedom," Willow combats, refusing to be intimidated. "I can't hide away up here forever."

Harrumphing, he tightens his grip on the steering wheel and focuses straight ahead. Tara gifts us both a tight smile in the rearview mirror. She's a little friendlier than her counterpart.

The drive into Highbridge is tense, but we make it in good time. Now that it's almost spring and the snow has thawed, the drive down Mount Helena is smoother.

People mill about the quiet town, the day in full swing. Shops are open, letting in the first whispers of almost-warm air while customers drink hot beverages outside cafes.

Hyland parks up in a tight space and lets us climb out before locking the SUV. Both he and Tara look out of place in their smart black clothing and concealed holsters that only we can spot.

"Go and get a coffee." Willow points towards a shop across the road. "We'll be in there."

"Not a chance," Tara snips.

Hyland crosses his arms. "Seconded."

With a sigh, Willow takes my hand. "Come on. Let's just pretend we're alone."

After fighting so hard for protection, it seems she's as exasperated as the rest of us are by the constant shadows following us. It's been exhausting since the novelty wore off.

Inside the small clothing store, I'm hit by a wave of déjà vu. It's the same store that we shopped in when they first arrived in Briar Valley, over one tumultuous year ago.

"Let's do this." I pick up a sparkly pink dress and hold it to my body. "How does this look? Reckon I can pull it off?"

Willow giggles. "You look handsome."

"Pink is definitely my colour, right?"

"Sure, princess."

I blow her a kiss. "Thanks, babe."

Placing the dress back on the rack, I opt for a knitted, flower-spotted cardigan next, eliciting another laugh when I struggle to fit my wrist inside. Even Tara manages a small smile.

Willow shakes her head at my antics. "You're insane."

"The best kind of insane." I drop a kiss on her cheek. "Insanely in love."

"Christ. How long have you been working on that line?"

"Only the past three hours. Did I do good?"

"Terrible."

"Ouch, babe. That hurts."

Bypassing my grabby hands, Willow stops to select some short-sleeved t-shirts and lighter dresses. Once spring hits, the heat in the mountains will quickly follow.

It's my favourite time of year, when the snow thaws and everything comes back to life. Wildflowers bloom throughout the valley in every shade imaginable.

"Arianna's been a lot better since we came home." Willow adds the clothes to the basket in my hands. "I think she really missed Briar Valley and her routine."

"She's a good kid. Living in that apartment for twenty-four hours a day must've been hard on her."

"Temper tantrums had never been an issue before then," Willow admits. "But she hasn't had one in a while. I think Demon helps her keep her calm and manage her anxiety."

"Don't tell Killian. He's already gunning for the boyfriend of the year award, and we don't want to give him anymore ammo."

Grabbing some striped white and pink tights, Willow rolls her eyes. "You guys are the worst."

"I'm taking that as a compliment."

"You really shouldn't."

Moving to the back of the store with our silent guards in tow, Willow searches through a pile of glitter-covered sandals as I survey the store. The hair on the back of my neck is standing on end.

It's just being out in public again. We've been keeping ourselves even more secluded than usual since the accident. It scared the shit out of us all. Apparently, even I wasn't ready for the outside world so soon.

But maybe the threat is always there. Hidden. Ticking away in the background. I have no way of mitigating something I can't even see. That's Sanchez's real power over us.

"Zach?" Willow holds up a pair of shoes. "What do you think?"

"Not really my style, babe."

"Jackass," she mutters. "For Arianna, obviously."

"Doesn't she have enough shoes? And clothes, for that matter?"

Willow shrugs. "I like spoiling my little girl."

"Lord. We're gonna have the world's most pampered kid, aren't we?"

Glancing around, she checks that neither Hyland nor Tara can hear us and gives me a sweet smile.

"You bet we are. This baby's going to have everything they'll ever need, living in Briar Valley."

"The whole town is going to freak out and spoil our kid when they find out you're pregnant. Rachel and Miranda will lose their shit."

"Aalia too," Willow chimes in.

Metal hangers clang against the railing as she roots through the clothing, searching for her next find. Tara and Hyland chat in low murmurs nearby.

"When are we going to tell them?"

"Soon," she says vaguely.

"We agreed twelve weeks. That isn't far away now."

"Maybe we should have a party or something. That'll be a good excuse. But we need to tell Arianna first."

"Yeah, of course. Do you think she'll be happy?"

Willow hesitates over a pair of denim dungarees. "I don't know. I thought so, but I'm worried she'll feel threatened by the idea of another child around."

"It's normal for kids to feel that way. She'll be fine once the baby is here, though."

"You think?"

Wrapping my arm around her shoulders, I peck her cheek. "Definitely. Don't worry about Ari, we'll make sure she's okay with everything."

"Do you know how much I appreciate you guys treating her like she's your own?" Willow beams up at me. "I just realised that I never told you that."

Ignoring the store around us, we share a tender kiss. I stroke her lips with mine, needing her to know that the pleasure is all mine. Arianna has brightened all of our lives.

Willow finishes the kiss with a final peck. "I love you, Zachariah."

"Ditto, babe."

Stealing the dungarees from her hands, I chuck them in the basket. There's plenty in there, but we keep shopping for another hour, buying too much and goofing around.

"God, this feels good." Willow sighs happily as we check out. "I didn't realise how stir-crazy I was starting to feel in town."

"We needed to get out for sure."

"I just wish we could do it without looking over our shoulders the whole time."

Before she can pay, I snatch the purse from her hands and tuck it under my arm where she can't steal it back. The cashier takes my bank card instead.

"Hey!" Willow protests, adorable with her scrunched nose and pout.

"No arguments. This is my treat."

"Zach, you can't just do that."

"Why the hell not? You're mine. I can treat you and Arianna any damn time I please, and I will."

Clutching my arm, she manages to wrestle the purse back. "You don't need to pay for us all the time."

"I want to. End of discussion."

Willow snorts in derision. "Who isn't open to discussion now, huh?"

Tucking loose black hair behind her ear, I bop her nose for good measure. "Touché, baby girl."

With the clothes paid for, I chuck them at Hyland to carry. He looks less than impressed but doesn't complain as he takes the bags.

"Asshole," he whispers just loud enough for me to hear.

"Careful," I warn with a sweet smile. "Your boss is fucking my best friend. I'd hate to put in a bad word against you."

That immediately causes his back to stiffen as he plasters on a false smile. "Shall we head out?"

Trying hard not to laugh, Willow and Tara take the lead as we exit the shop. We've just stepped onto the pavement outside when our peaceful morning trip shatters spectacularly.

The flash of cameras almost blinds me from the small team of reporters clustered outside the store. They swarm us until we're surrounded on all sides with no way of escaping.

"Willow Sanchez! Over here!"

"Zach," she gasps in horror.

Stepping in front of Willow, I attempt to shield her from the hum of reporters with their cameras. Tara is yelling at Hyland to bring the car around as she takes Willow's other side for protection.

"Is it true that you kidnapped your daughter?"

"Why would you lie about Dimitri Sanchez and the abuse?"

"Did he rape you?"

"Enough," I scream at them. "Back the fuck up before we have a problem. I have zero qualms about breaking your goddamn faces."

One asshole snaps a photo up close of me. I grab the camera from his hands and smash it so hard against the pavement, shards of glass go flying into the air.

"Hey!" he barks. "I'll sue you for that."

"Go ahead. I ain't worth shit, mate."

"Asshole!"

Grinding the remaining pieces beneath my shoe to piss him off even more, I let Willow curl into my side to hide from them. She's trembling all over, a hand pressed protectively over her belly.

"Babe," I grind out in warning. "Careful."

It takes her a moment to realise what she's doing. The last thing we want is for her piece of shit ex to realise she's pregnant with our baby.

Quickly dropping her hand, Willow squares her shoulders and faces the cameras. "I'm telling the truth. Dimitri Sanchez is an abuser."

The camera flashes intensify.

"Is that why you fled?" a female reporter asks, somewhat more kindly. "To escape the violence and abuse?"

"I left Mexico to protect my daughter. I didn't want to see her get hurt anymore."

"Are you saying he abused his daughter too?"

"I'm saying he isn't the person the world thinks he is. You should be asking him these questions, not me."

With a roaring engine, Hyland jumps the curb and brings the car to a halt. Tara yells at the top of her lungs for the reporters to move aside as she bundles us through the madness unscathed.

We fall into the back of the car, and I quickly buckle Willow in before

Hyland can floor it and send her flying. At the last moment, she rolls her window down to shout out a final comment.

"Watch yourself, Dimitri," she warns in a cold, hard voice. "The past is going to catch up to you, sooner rather than later."

Closing her window, Willow instructs Hyland to get us out of here. We take off with another throaty purr and merge back into traffic, leaving the chaos behind us.

"How the hell did they find us?" Tara asks.

"They must've traced me back to Briar Valley, and they've been camping out here in case we showed up," Willow answers grimly.

Grabbing Willow's hand, I tune Tara's cursing out. "Babe... do you realise what you just did?"

She blinks up at me in confusion. "What?"

"Jesus, Willow. You named him. Publicly. I've never heard you call him Dimitri before."

Pink rushes to Willow's cheeks as she realises the incredible feat she's just achieved. Naming her monster, in front of the country's cameras, no less. It was spectacular to watch.

"I did." She seems shocked, her mouth opening and closing.

"You said his fucking name, baby. I am so proud of you right now. He needed to hear that warning."

My heart feels like it's going to burst. The son of a bitch can watch that footage and panic his sick little heart out at the thought of all the dirt Willow has on him.

"I meant it," Willow adds, steeling her spine. "He's going to pay. I'm done hiding. His days as a free man are numbered."

"Promise?"

Willow's forehead presses against mine as she breathes me in. "Promise."

CHAPTER 21
WILLOW

HOME – EDITH WHISKERS

THE WEEKS PASS FAST LEADING up to the party. We invited the whole town but kept the reason why under wraps. I'm still wary after the spotting incident and more on edge than ever about the pregnancy.

We stopped buying newspapers after the first couple of days, instead opting to block out Mr Sanchez's lies. His crusade against me has gone rather quiet, almost suspiciously so.

He's still out there.

Plotting.

Biding his time.

Choosing a loose linen dress that covers my slightly raised midsection, I leave my short hair loose and curly, opting for no makeup. I'm too worn out to make much of an effort.

"Hey," Micah murmurs as he enters the bedroom and stops behind me. "You doing okay?"

"Just tired."

"We don't have to do this if you don't want to."

"I know, but I don't want to let everyone down. Besides, we can't keep this a secret for much longer."

He skates his knuckles against my cheek then drops a kiss on my lips. "Then let's face the music, blow it off early and curl up with a movie. Sound good?"

I lean into his warmth. "So bloody good."

"Problem solved. If it gets to be too much, just tell us, and we'll send everyone home. You know people are going to be freaking out."

My eyes flutter shut. "Oh God. I'm not ready for this."

"Yes, gorgeous. You are."

He runs his hands over my hair to smooth the curls, peppering my jawline with kisses before dropping a final one right between my eyebrows. I'd rather lock us both in here for the day.

"Mi," I whine.

"We can't right now, angel."

"Then don't tease me!"

He raises an eyebrow, trying hard not to laugh at me. "Is this a pregnancy thing? One kiss and you're good to go?"

I squirm uncomfortably on the spot. "Pretty much."

"Let's see what we can do about that then, shall we?" He hums to himself as he fondles my overly sensitive breasts. "You gotta be quick, though."

Heat floods my core. "I can do quick."

Walking me backwards, my legs hit the bed, making me slump on the mattress. Micah kisses his way down to my collarbones as he raises the hem of my dress, pushing it up over my thighs.

"Be quiet," he orders, kissing his way up my inner-leg. "I don't want the others to interrupt us."

Pulling my panties off, his mouth secures itself to my mound, and I swallow a moan. Micah's lips are so sweet and attentive, he knows how to apply just the right amount of pressure.

With his tongue gliding through my folds, his thumb circles over my clit, sending sparks flying. I moan again, unable to hold it in. That's when the footsteps begin to approach.

"Dammit," Micah grumbles. "That didn't take long."

Without bothering to knock, Zach prowls in with a smirk on his face. He has a knack for appearing at the worst possible moments.

But as I note the tent at the front of his plain black jeans, evidence of his arousal at overhearing a single moan, I reconsider. Perhaps this is exactly the right moment to appear.

"I thought I heard something." He grins at us both. "Maybe I was mistaken. Did I hear anything?"

Leaving the decision up to us, I spread my legs wider, giving him a flash of my bareness. "You did."

Micah shakes his head with a grin. "I can never escape this asshole, can I?"

"Nope," Zach answers for me.

Inching closer, he settles on the bed behind me, leaving Micah to resume his task. "You're in charge, little brother. Don't mind me watching over here."

My lips are claimed by Zach in a hard, fast kiss as Micah's wet tongue returns to my pussy. With Zach's tongue in my mouth while his twin lavishes my core, I'm set alight with both of them pleasuring me at once.

Caught between them both, all I can feel is the steadily increasing embers of desire crisping my insides. I need a release, an end to the constant onslaught of fear and worry.

Their touch leaves no space for the bad thoughts to sneak in. Rather than Zach bossing Micah around, this time, the shyer twin is taking charge and torturing me instead.

"Are you going to come all over my twin's face?" Zach whispers in my ear before biting down on the lobe.

"Zach," I gasp.

"Yes, babe?"

His hand has snuck down my body to cup my breast through my dress. I need more. Want more. My nipples have stiffened into peaks and are begging to feel his lips wrapped around them.

"What is it, babe?" he teases. "Do you want more?"

"Yes."

"Too bad we have guests arriving in ten minutes then, isn't it?"

Plunging a finger deep into my entrance, Micah pauses to look up. "She's going to come at least twice before then. That's a promise."

"He sounds confident, doesn't he?" Zach laughs.

"I am," Micah snips back.

Curling his finger deep inside of me, I fall apart within seconds. Having both of them watching me is so damn hot, the feel of their skin on mine pushing me over the edge.

"Mi," I moan, my eyes squeezing shut.

"That's it, angel. Let go."

He doesn't stop fucking me with his hand, the heel of his palm grinding up against my sensitive clit. It milks every last drop of my release from me until I'm spent and trembling all over.

"Pretty good," Zach critiques. "But I think I can do better."

Micah narrows his eyes. "You're welcome to try."

"Turn around, babe. Show me that gorgeous ass of yours."

Taking the hand that Micah offers, I eagerly spin around on the bed so that my rear is facing Zach in a doggy position. I feel so naked and exposed like this, every inch of me on display to him from behind.

"Look at that glistening cunt," he preens happily. "So fucking perfect. Reckon we have time for you to take my cock?"

My insides quiver at the thought. "Please."

"Please what, Willow?"

Micah watches his twin tease me, a hand snaking into his own jeans.

"Please give me your cock," I whisper through my embarrassment.

"That's my perfect girl," Zach praises. "You only had to ask."

Pain crackles down my spine as his hand connects with my ass cheek in a playful spank. The spikes of heat cause wetness to flood my core all over again as I prepare to be filled by him.

These endless seconds of anticipation are torturous. I'm staring up into Micah's interested eyes, a hand fisting his shaft as Zach unzips his jeans to free his length behind me.

Knowing his twin is watching every moment is gasoline on the inferno between my legs. I feel the tip of his dick press up against my slit, the pressure intense. I'm so oversensitive these days, the slightest touches are mind-blowing.

"Fuck," Zach hisses as he slowly slides in. "This gorgeous little cunt is so fucking tight, babe."

Gripping the bed sheets, my eyes don't drop from Micah's as he begins to pump his dick in long, measured strokes. At the exact same time, his twin moves and thrusts into me from behind.

"So hot," Micah whispers in awe.

A hand gripping my hip, Zach spanks me again. "Isn't she just?"

I want to scream and shatter into a thousand spectacular pieces. Their attention is too much. Too acute. There's nowhere to hide beneath the weight of their combined eyes locked on me as I'm thoroughly fucked.

Each slam of Zach's hips adds to the strength of the second orgasm that's rising up inside of me. The time pressure only makes this hotter. At any moment, guests could arrive and interrupt us.

When Micah kneels on the bed and kisses my lips, I lose myself to the soft, gentle sweetness of his mouth. I can still taste the salty tang of my come on his tongue.

"I want to fuck this pretty mouth of yours," he murmurs. "Is that okay, angel?"

The fact that he still asks melts me inside. Nodding, I open my mouth and greedily accept his length. His cock is long and hard as it slides against my tongue like velvet.

He takes a handful of my hair and grips it tight as he begins fucking my mouth. The twins must have some kind of psychic ability because they move in perfect synchronicity without uttering a single word to each other.

With both holes filled by them, my orgasm is inches away from falling into my lap. So close. I'm a moaning, writhing mess between them as my core tightens and heart explodes.

"Come all over my cock." Zach pushes into me. "Show me how good we make you feel, babe."

"We want to see you fall apart," Micah adds.

Fisting the sheets even tighter, I let the rush of heat consume me. Blistering. Overwhelming. I'm on fire and falling in a tight, dizzying spiral into the deepest depths of pleasure.

With another hard spank, I let myself implode. Zach shudders behind me and roars through his own release, triggered by my pussy clenching tight around his length. We climax together in a breathless tangle.

Still rutting into my mouth, Micah watches us both in fascination, chasing his own orgasm until the very end. I'm relishing the delicious pang of aftershocks when his hot, salty come fills my mouth.

Pouring himself into me, he cups my jaw and strokes a thumb over my cheek, silently praising me. I blink in recognition, sucking on his length to steal every last drop before I obediently swallow his seed.

"Fuck me, angel," he whispers with wonderment in his eyes. "How are you so bloody perfect for us?"

Wiping off my mouth, I collapse on the bed. "I'm really not perfect."

Zach carefully rolls me over so the pressure is off my belly. "You damn well are."

Climbing off the bed, Micah disappears into my ensuite then reappears with a wet washcloth. He passes it off to his brother who brings it between my legs to clean the mess from my inner thighs.

They're so thoughtful and attentive—even more so now than ever. But they still aren't afraid to touch me and give me the pleasure I need to survive each day without losing my mind. I love that about them.

"You... uh, may need to fix your hair." Micah points at my head, looking sheepish.

I glance up at the full-length mirror in the corner of the room, finding a bird's nest of black curls. "Awesome. Good job, guys."

Zach soothes my sore, spanked ass with a gentle stroke as he pulls my dress back down. "You're totally welcome."

With a sigh, I sit back up. "I suppose we should go out there and face the music."

"Together." Micah takes my hand.

"Together," Zach echoes, taking the other.

With both of them by my side, I blow out a breath and prepare to tell the world our secret. I can do this. With them to keep me safe, there's nothing we can't face... together.

———

The party is in full swing in my back garden. Dozens of tables are dotted about with glasses and dishes. Everyone is in attendance—the whole town turning up for hog roast and red wine in the cool sunshine.

After scarfing down food and a few too many drinks, the mood is relaxed. Killian's cleaning up the food as he shoots me a knowing wink from across the grass. It's almost time.

"Shit." I shake out my sweaty hands. "I don't think I can do this."

Standing on the wraparound porch, Aalia's arm slips around my waist. "Of course, you can. This is your family. They're all going to be so happy for you."

She was ecstatic when we told her a few days ago. I needed a woman to talk to, someone I could trust. Aalia was thrilled to be one of the very first to know.

But the one person who should be here today, the one person I actually *want* to tell, is nowhere to be found. I hope that somewhere, Lola's watching down on us and smiling at the madness.

Leaving her fiancé to continue chatting with Albie and Ryder, Katie walks over to us and bundles me into a hug. She smells like floral perfume, and red wine clings to her lips, but I hug her back.

"You okay, sweetheart?"

"I'm good, Katie."

"Are you going to get this mysterious announcement over and done with so we can finally talk about this?"

Blinking, I stare up at her grin. "I'm sorry?"

She rubs my arms. "I'm your mother, Willow. A mother always knows."

Mouth opening and closing, I can't even deny it. Her smile is too wide. With tears pricking my eyes, all I can do is nod in confirmation.

"You are?" She's practically bouncing on her toes.

"Twelve weeks."

"Holy shit, sweetheart! What did Arianna say?"

"She was so excited." I smile at the memory of her squealing and grinning when we told her last night. "She wants a little sister to play with."

"I bet she does."

We embrace again, Aalia watching on with tears in her eyes. It feels better than I expected to tell them, like we don't have to be alone in this wild, crazy journey anymore.

With both of them boxing me in, all three guys meet me at the bottom of the porch steps, and we call everyone to attention. Everyone's eyes are on us at the head of the garden.

"What's the big stink?" Ryder jokes, knowing full well what's going on since the guys told him.

I wave him off, feeling nervous. "We wanted to get the whole town together for a party. This is the first time we've been together since Lola passed."

The mood sobers. Everyone knows that Lola left me Briar Valley in her will—news travels fast around here. Yet no one has raised the issue. We're all still mourning the loss of our leader.

"I know she's here in spirit today with us all because we have some exciting news to share."

Clinging tight to Micah's hand for courage, I drop a palm to my belly. My eyes are locked on the pine trees at the back of the garden so I don't run away from the sudden roar of applause.

"Oh my God!"

"Congratulations!"

The first people to reach us are Harold and Marilyn, offering their personal congratulations. One by one, we're bombarded by people, all hugging and squeezing each one of us.

Killian saves Arianna from the crowd by boosting her onto his shoulders, so she doesn't get squished. She's beaming, obviously enjoying all the extra fuss over her as everyone asks if she's excited.

"I'm going to be a big sister," she tells everyone animatedly. "How cool is that?"

Killian bounces her on his shoulders. "Very cool, peanut."

"Higher, Giant. Higher!" she yells.

I'm bundled into another lung-squeezing, tight hug from Ryder. He pecks my cheek too then steps aside to shake each of the guys' hands.

"Willow." Ethan nods, his expression grim. "I'm really sorry to do this right now, but can we talk? Something has come up."

"What is it?"

"Not here."

Waving the guys off before they can follow us, I take Katie's arm instead. She looks surprised by my decision but lets me drag her back into the cabin with Ethan in tow behind us.

Closing the door against the party that's kicking up a notch, I turn to face Ethan. "Do you want a drink or something?"

"No, I'm fine. I have to drive back to London tonight."

"Has something happened?"

He gestures for me to sit down. "You could say that."

Taking a seat at the dining table, I clutch Katie's hand tight. She looks as anxious as I feel.

"What is it?"

Ethan begins to pace the kitchen. "We've been monitoring Sanchez's official residence since your divorce announcement. Now that we have more evidence, we're preparing to make a move on him."

My heart leaps into my mouth. "You are?"

"We've been gathering witnesses and evidence for months to get to this point. Monitoring his location was part of our information gathering phase."

"I don't understand," Katie interjects. "You've known where he is this entire time? Why not just go in there and arrest him?"

Ethan shakes his head. "Not that simple. This is a very complex investigation, and we needed to wait for the perfect moment to make our move. We've been preparing for that to come."

"So... it's time?" I ask hopefully.

He looks crestfallen. "He's gone, Willow."

The floor falls out from beneath my feet, my stomach dropping with it. "What do you mean, gone?"

"Our surveillance team performed their daily check-in and found the place deserted. Nothing left. Not even a single piece of furniture or speck of dust."

Gobsmacked, I have no words. Not a single one. That mansion was an impenetrable fortress, the pinnacle of Sanchez's empire, but a trace on his location at least.

Gone.

Gone.

Gone.

The word echoes on a loop in my mind, taunting me over and over again. I should've known his silence was too good to be true.

"Where could he have gone?" Katie asks urgently.

"Anywhere in the world. He has the money and resources to run faraway from anywhere we can find him. We think he may have been spooked."

"By me," I finish.

Ethan says nothing. I don't need him to. The day I threatened Mr Sanchez to those cameras, I sealed this moment's inevitability.

"We'll find him," Ethan reassures. "His assets and wealth are still traceable. He can't hide from us for long."

But he hid his true self all this time, my inner-voice whispers. Long enough to take me and keep his illegal operations under wraps while presenting a lie to the outside world. A whole decade, if not longer.

Fingers itching with the urge to find my switchblade and a quiet corner to cut in, I make myself take a deep breath. I can't do that anymore. I don't want to. No matter what my demons say.

"What happens now?" I gulp down the lump in my throat.

"We work on picking up his trail. My team is already on it. Tara and Hyland will remain here for your protection."

"Do you think Mr Sanchez will come for us now?"

Ethan wrings his hands together. "There's a possibility."

With terror spiking through my veins, I let Katie pull me into a side-hug. It's as much for her comfort as it is for mine.

While I'm grateful for our miracle, this is seriously bad timing.

I can't let him find us.

Not now.

Not ever.

"Should she run?"

"Running won't help anyone," Ethan replies with a head shake. "He can find you anywhere, Willow. Stay here where my team and your family can keep you safe. The limelight will protect you."

"There's enough of that on me at the moment." I squeeze the bridge of my nose.

"Exactly. Sanchez can't try anything while the world is watching. He wouldn't take that risk. Use that to your advantage."

"I'm not going anywhere. This is my home. I have to protect it, as much as it protects me. Lola would want that."

Smiling, Ethan nods. "I think she would."

"I don't think it's safe," Katie worries, clenching my hand tight. "You should come back with me. The apartment is still there."

"No. I'm not leaving."

"Willow—"

"My decision is final."

Hearing the conviction in my voice, she doesn't press the issue. "If that's your decision, then I'll respect it."

"There's something else." Ethan glances at me, uncertain. "We've found another victim, but she's refusing to go on the record."

"Of Mr Sanchez?"

He nods grimly. "We're trying to convince her to aid the investigation, but we've been unsuccessful so far."

"So what does this have to do with me?"

"We want your help to convince her to go on record and help us nail this motherfucker."

Stumped, I gnaw on my bottom lip. I have no desire to look in the eyes of another woman who was in my position. Facing my own darkness is hard enough without being confronted by others.

But the more evidence and testimony we have against him, the safer my children will be from that monster. He needs to be put away, and for a long time. This will help to achieve that.

"What do you say?" he asks hopefully.

Looking up at Katie for confirmation, I force myself to nod.

"I'll do it."

CHAPTER 22
WILLOW

THE STAGES OF GRIEF – AWAKEN
I AM

FLICKING THROUGH THE CASE FILES, I fight to stave off an impending headache. There are hundreds of pages of witness testimony in here along with other case evidence and logs of information.

Ethan left the file with me when he returned to London a few days ago, asking me to read over the other women's evidence to prepare myself to speak to the new victim that has been found.

It's hard reading.

One woman, named only as Caroline, describes meeting Mr Sanchez in a bar in Norwich almost fourteen years ago. He offered to buy her a drink, but it must have been drugged.

Next thing she knew, England was a distant memory, and she'd been shipped across the world under a false identity, drugged up and compliant. Just reading it triggered a memory that I'd long since buried.

There's a noxious, bitter taste in my mouth. Head spinning, I stumble and almost trip up the aeroplane steps until a man with an earpiece catches me. He's tall and dark-haired with cruel, terrifying eyes.

"Careful, bitch," he growls.

"Bring her," another voice commands.

I'm lifted over the man's shoulder, and the world flips on its head. Pain radiates through my jaw from the swift punch he delivered when I tried to run away earlier.

Blood is thick on my tongue, mixing with the taste of whatever they've forced into me. It's been nothing but pain and blood since we left the club under the cover of night.

"Get on the fucking plane." He takes a handful of my hair and yanks hard. "You've got a long flight ahead of you, whore."

Flight?

Plane?

I want to scream. I want to beg for my life, run and leave these scary people far behind. What happened in the club… I can't even think about it. The blood. The pleading. Mr Sanchez didn't stop violating me even as I begged for my life.

Snapping out of the horrid memory, I feel a shudder wrack my body. I try not to think about those early days. What I can remember of that journey was hard enough to tell Ethan's team.

It's the same story.

Vulnerable women, targeted and drugged, taken from their homes to be exploited and abused at the hands of a monster. All different ages and circumstances but bound by their suffering.

There are countless other stories just like Caroline's in this file. Heidi. Paula. Erika. I have no doubt these aren't their real names, needing protection from someone like Mr Sanchez and his associates.

There's a whole ring of them—powerful businessmen, hiding behind their confident smirks and blazing personalities to conceal the real source of their wealth and power.

"Shit," I curse to myself.

Flipping to the section on the identified players in the human trafficking ring, I recognise several of the men who have been photographed with long-range lenses.

They're his friends. Associates.

Bastards.

Mason's in there, grinning widely as he drinks champagne with his wife, Georgina, outside a fancy cocktail bar. I recognise the dusty streets of the Mexican capital. I have no idea when this was taken.

When a hand lands on my shoulder, I startle from fear. Killian spreads his hands in surrender, a worried smile on his face.

"Only me. What's all this?"

"Information." I blow out a breath. "I'm preparing to speak to that woman Ethan told me about."

"Sure you're up for that?"

"No, not in the slightest. But I have to try."

Nodding, he drains the last of his coffee then fills the kettle to boil another. He and Zach have been working all morning on the new cabin while Micah is back in the studio, finishing up his latest project.

Life has been normal. Too normal, almost. I can't relax or feel safe while knowing that Mr Sanchez could be anywhere in the world right now, even England. He's prowling ever closer.

"He needs to find the fucking bastard before worrying about more damn evidence," Killian grumbles. "I'm sick of watching you torture yourself over this man."

"Ethan will find Mr Sanchez. I trust him."

"It's Sanchez I don't trust, not Ethan."

"Are you still running patrols on the perimeter?"

Killian smooths his long hair, tied back in a messy ponytail. "Every night. The hunters are having a hell of a time catching deer while out there all night."

"I bet Harold's loving it."

"To his bones."

After kissing the top of my head, he brews a fresh coffee. I resume looking at the case files, nausea twisting in my stomach. Their faces are still staring back at me, those smiles burned onto my brain.

"You eaten today?"

I hum noncommittally.

"You have to eat, Willow. And rest. I don't like you sitting there for hours, reading this shit over and over again."

"Kill," I warn.

"It's true. At least go and sit on the sofa where it's comfier. You need to rest after what happened with the bleeding."

"I am resting. Right here. Go back to work."

"Fine." With a curse, Killian heads back outside.

He's been even more overbearing than usual recently, and I'm over it. While I appreciate everyone's concern, it isn't needed. I know how to take care of myself, and I have work to do.

Another lengthy case file later, Demon nips at my feet, demanding attention. I scratch her ears to satisfy her.

"You're such a little attention hog when Arianna isn't here."

The cute as hell dog licks my hand in response then begins to bark. She's getting antsy after being inside all morning.

"Come on, then. Let's go for a walk."

Closing the files up, I stick my head outside to look for the guys, finding them nowhere in sight. Only Tara is standing guard on the porch steps with her phone in hand, no sign of Hyland.

"Everything okay?" she asks.

"Good. Just getting ready for a walk."

"Sure thing."

Snatching my phone from the kitchen counter, I write a quick note for the guys on the pad stuck to the fridge then lace up my walking boots. I need to clear my head after reading those files.

Demon follows me outside when I whistle, letting me attach her lead so we can go for a walk in the dreary afternoon drizzle. I don't mind the rain. It's soothing to me.

Tara straightens as I step outside, her eyes flicking over me.

"Where are we off to?"

"Walking this troublemaker." I waggle the dog lead.

She smiles brightly. "Let's go."

We leave the cabin and head into the woods together, enjoying the plush greenery and moss-covered trees. Everything smells wet and earthy. Wildflowers are beginning to bloom as spring arrives.

"I'd forgotten how lovely the town is in the spring."

Tara nods, walking slightly ahead of me. "It's definitely a lot different than London."

"I bet. I'm sorry you're stuck here with me."

"You don't have to apologise. It's my job."

"I just feel bad for pulling you both off the investigation."

"I've been working for Sabre for a long time. Investigations come and go." She hesitates, sparing me a glance over her shoulder. "It's the people who matter most."

"Even when they drive you insane?" I laugh. "Zach has a tendency to fill silence with humour."

"Doesn't he just," she jokes before sobering. "This place has been a welcome break. Working for Sabre isn't exactly easy or allows for much time in the quiet countryside."

"Well, you're welcome anytime. I mean it."

"Thank you, Willow."

Deeper into the woodland, we pass Harold and Theodore out hunting. Both stop for a quick chat and to rub Demon's belly. She loves all the fuss and attention that people give her.

Leaving them to continue hunting, I decide to push on, loving the fresh air and sense of freedom. The guys wouldn't like me walking so far, but their over-protectiveness is stifling at times.

"There's an outcrop up here." I point ahead into the trees. "You can see the whole t—"

A sudden, fiery burst of pain explodes through the back of my head. My hands and knees hit the earth, agony blurring my vision until the forest is a green blur around me.

Slumped over, I can just make out the bloodstained rock that's clasped in

Tara's left hand. It hits the ground with a thud. My pain-filled mind is spinning at the sight of her looming over me.

"I'm so sorry, Willow," she keens. "I have no choice."

"Ch-Choice?" I slur.

"The threats he made… Look, I have a family too. I need to protect them. This is life or death."

He.

Mr Sanchez.

Trying to push myself upright, I crumple when her boot connects with my lower back, shoving me back down. I'm too weak to fight back as warm blood trickles down my neck.

"Shit," Tara curses in a panic. "Shit, shit, shit."

"Please. You d-don't have to do this."

"He's going to kill everyone I love," she sobs. "Unless I deliver you to him. That's what he said when he tracked me down."

"How long h-have you been working for him?"

Rather than answering me, she just looks sick. At herself. The world. Everything. The Tara I thought I knew was a lie all along. That's when the missing puzzle piece clicks into place in my foggy brain.

"The accident… They followed us," the words stumble out. "That was you, wasn't it? You told them where to f-find us."

"I'm sorry," she repeats, reaching for her gun. "Now you're going to come with me. We need to get out of here without being seen."

"This will never work!"

"Get up and walk."

Unable to stand up alone, she's forced to drag me to my feet. More pain bursts behind my eyes as the blood continues to flow from my head. I'm woozy and dizzy, so much that I can only stagger.

"I'm sorry, Willow. I didn't want any of this to happen."

"Then s-stop this."

"I can't do that."

"What h-happened to this job being about the p-people?"

I can feel the gun pressing into my back. One shot and that'll be it. Over. She'll send me and the baby hurtling into the arms of death with a single, split-second decision.

I can't let that happen.

Not now. Not like this.

Focusing on the sound of Demon chasing after us and barking like crazy, I ignore Tara's cursing and try to formulate a plan. She's clearly acting impulsively after seeing an opening to snatch me.

That's my advantage. Her panic. If I can find the right opening, I have to make a run for it. I'll die on my feet fighting to be alive before letting her shoot me in the middle of a forest.

"There's a mountain road out of Briar Valley up ahead," Tara instructs, the gun still painfully pressing into me. "Take a right, and keep walking."

"What's your plan from there?"

"God knows," she mutters. "Staying alive."

"When did he contact you? How?"

"Enough talking! Just walk."

Ducking beneath a fruit tree, I spot several cabins in the distance, through the underbrush. Briar Valley is far below us. As far as anyone is concerned, I'm safe with Tara. No one is coming for me.

I have to do this myself.

Alone.

With a breath, I deliberately trip over a rock and fall to my knees again with a dramatic cry. Pain slices through my legs, but it's overshadowed by the violent hammering of my heart.

"Get up," Tara hisses.

"I can't."

"I don't have time for this!"

Ducking down to slide her hands beneath my arms, she's momentarily distracted. This is my opening. Murmuring a silent prayer, I dig my heel in and prepare to strike.

Rising above her as fast as my unsteady body will allow, I move quickly and snap out my balled-up hand. It collides with her left cheek harder than I was expecting, and she falls backwards.

Something in my brain clicks. I shift into a strange, focused state where all I can see is the bead of blood on her cheek from my punch. Keeping up the momentum, I hit her again.

THWACK.

Tara falls flat on her ass, grunting in pain. I take the chance to bolt away from her into the nearby trees. The forest passes in a terrifying blur around me as Demon chases, hot on my heels.

"Willow!" Tara shouts.

Screaming as loud as my lungs will allow, I race back in the direction we came, hoping to come across somebody. The woods are unrecognisable in my state of complete and utter panic.

"Willow! Stop!"

"Leave me alone!" I scream back.

Dodging through fir trees and wild berry bushes, I don't notice the tree root until it's too late. Hurtling through thin air, I fall again, scraping my hands on a thorny bush in the process.

Face-planting in a muddy puddle, I scramble and try to find my feet again, but it's too late. Demon whines as Tara approaches, a trail of blood staining her face.

"There you are." She grimaces. "You have a hell of a right hook."

"Get away from me!"

"I can't do that, Willow. Come quietly, or this will get messy for both of you."

Tara nods at the swell of my small bump. I protectively cover it, feeling a surge of fury. She'll have to go through me to touch my baby. I'll rip her fucking face off with my bare hands.

"Touch me again, and you'll live to regret it," I spit at her.

Lifting the gun, she trains it on my midsection. My heart stops dead in my chest, and the tears almost threaten to fall, but I hold them back, refusing to show her even the smallest shred of weakness.

"Move," she snarls.

"Please, Tara. Don't do this."

"I have no choice."

Before I can stand up again, there's a distinct, metallic click. Footsteps crunch over fallen twigs, and a figure emerges through the thick tree line with a hunting rifle raised high.

"Hands up," Harold barks, holding the gun steady.

Tara switches her aim to him. "Back off, old man. This doesn't concern you."

"Well, you're pointing a fuckin' gun at my girl here, so I think that it does."

Shuffling backwards, I grab Demon and hold her close to keep her safe. She's snarling her head off and far too ready to throw herself into the fight despite still only being a tiny puppy.

"Final warning." Tara cocks the gun threateningly. "I'm leaving with Willow, one way or another."

Harold refuses to back down, inching closer to the gun instead. I want to grab him and scream at him to run away. She's unhinged and more than ready to shoot him.

Everything happens so fast, it's a petrifying blur. Tara lunges at the same time Harold moves to squeeze the trigger on his rifle. The pair smash into each other, then there's an almighty bang.

Ears buzzing, I desperately crawl through the mud to reach Harold. He's fallen backwards, winded and pale-faced. I search his body for injuries, but find nothing.

Opposite him, Tara is gasping in pain. She's curled up tight and clutching her stomach where blood gushes out, encircling her in a crimson puddle that soaks into the moss.

"Gotcha," Harold wheezes. "Are you okay, Willow?"

"N-No."

"It's alright, kid. I'm here. You're safe now."

After struggling to lift himself, he pulls me into a side-hug. I peel his hands away to crawl closer to Tara. She's still conscious and trying to cover the gushing wound in her midsection.

"We can't let her die!"

"She deserves it," Harold spits. "Self-defence."

"Help me!"

Muttering to himself, he pushes Tara's hands away and uses his own to apply pressure to the wound. I just watch. I'm barely able to hold myself upright, let alone tend to her. Blood is still trickling from the back of my head.

Reaching for my phone, I blink through my dizziness to find Zach's number. He always has his phone on him. The ringing sounds far away as I sway, battling to remain kneeling upright.

"Hello, hot stuff," he answers. "To what do I owe the pleasure of hearing your heavenly voice?"

"Zach," I sob.

His tone immediately changes.

"Willow? What is it?"

"T-Tara... she... H-Harold shot... Help. Need help."

"Woah, slow down. Take a breath, babe. Where are you?"

"N-Near St David's Pointe, below the outcrop you sh-showed me."

"Hold on, babe. We'll be there soon."

Clutching the phone in my bloody hand, sobs begin to rattle my frame. Over and over. Violent, chest-aching sobs that I can't control. We came so close to losing everything.

"Willow," Tara chokes out. "I'm s-s-sorry. He didn't g-give me a choice."

Blood is trickling from the corners of her mouth as Harold struggles to keep her conscious. She's ghostly white and staring at me with so much pain in her widened eyes.

"You always have a choice," I reply shakily. "Always."

Another wave of dizziness taking over, I lay down on the moss-covered ground, and my eyes slide shut. I can hear Harold repeating my name, but it's easier to curl inwards to protect my belly and let the darkness take over.

It feels like hours have passed before approaching voices and shouting startles me back to reality. Tara's unconscious a few metres away while Harold shakes her, over and over again to no avail.

"Willow!" Killian's voice echoes through the woods.

Harold shouts back, directing them over to our blood-slick tangle amidst the trees. When the first pair of hands reach for me, I yelp and battle against them, terrified of being touched.

"Baby," Killian pleads, his voice low and broken. "It's me. You're safe."

"K-Killian!"

I'm lifted onto his lap, and Zach leans over us both to cup my cheeks. He searches my face and eyes, wearing a look of total panic that sends my own anxiety spiralling again.

"What happened?" he asks urgently.

All I can do is point at Tara, unconscious and bloodied.

"Who shot her? Is Sanchez here?"

"Tara t-tried to take me," I weep, still cuddling my bump. "She's w-working for him."

Zach swears colourfully, glancing over the scene as he tries to process the madness around us. Killian is also cursing beneath me as his hands find the source of the blood covering my mud-stained clothing.

"Fuck," he says to himself.

"She... hit me with... a r-rock."

Gently probing my head with soft fingers, I hiss when he hits a sore spot. Killian kisses my hair and apologises, holding me so tight in his arms, I almost can't breathe properly.

"She was supposed to be protecting you!" he growls in a deadly tone. "I'm going to fucking kill her myself. She doesn't deserve our help."

"No," I gasp.

"Willow——"

"Get D-Doc. Help her."

Curling my arms around his neck, I snuggle into his flannel shirt, needing the comfort of familiarity. The pain in my head reaches its peak, and my vision darkens again, swallowing me whole.

Fading.

Fading.

Gone.

CHAPTER 23
MICAH

DAWNS – ZACH BRYAN & MAGGIE
ROGERS

"I DO NOT GIVE A FLYING fuck about your excuses, Ethan!"

Killian screams down the phone as he paces the length of the living room. His hair is standing up in all directions as he tugs at it, on the verge of pulling the whole damn lot out.

"No, it's not good enough. She was supposed to be protecting Willow, not trying to fucking kidnap her! She has a bloody concussion and five stitches because of that woman!"

"We should intervene," I suggest.

Sitting next to me at the dining table with a beer, Zach shakes his head. "It won't help. He's been like this since finding Willow yesterday, no matter what we say to him."

"Can you blame him?"

His expression hardens as rage filters back in. "Not in the slightest."

I can taste his anger on the tip of my tongue. I'm feeling it too. Seeing Willow, trembling and bloodstained in Killian's arms, was a fucking harrowing sight. Doc had to stitch up the nasty gash in her head.

After another scan, he confirmed that the baby is fine. No damage from what happened. Despite that, I can't help but feel like our luck is bound to run out eventually.

"I want the other one gone too," Killian hisses into the phone. "I don't trust the lot of you. My family will take care of what's ours. Focus on finding that motherfucker so we can move on with our lives."

"Shit. We need Hyland." I rub my throbbing temples.

"Do we?" Zach combats, staring at the beer clasped in his hands. "The guy could be on Sanchez's payroll too for all we know."

"I highly doubt it. He's as angry as Killian, if not more."

His expression turns sour. "I don't need your fucking doubt, Mi. I want our girl to be safe from assholes looking to hurt her. Is that too much to ask?"

Apparently, it is.

The very people we were supposed to trust with Willow's safety are now in doubt and everything has been turned upside down. Willow's traumatised by what happened, and frankly, so are we.

"Sort your shit out," Killian snaps. "Then we'll talk."

Ending the call, he tosses the phone aside and fists his hair again. His pacing doesn't stop—back and forth, up and down, beating the floor into submission. He'll wear footprints into it at this rate.

"Kill, enough," I try to placate.

"No. This is bullshit. Ethan has nothing but excuses for why one of his own was blackmailed by that sicko. Apparently, Tara featured in a press conference and her name was given."

"That's all he needed?" Zach scoffs. "A name?"

"He has the resources to track people down if he wants to."

"Son of a bitch." I rub my eyes.

Killian nods, his face a mask of fear and anger. "No one is safe. We can't trust anyone."

All of our eyes sweep over to the front door where Hyland is stationed outside and beating the hell out of himself too. Deep down, I know he had no idea. But that doesn't mean the mistrust isn't there.

"What do we do?"

Shrugging at my question, Killian resumes marching up and down. "Ethan's hauling the whole team in for questioning. The entire investigation is up in the air until they find out if any information has been compromised."

"What about Tara?" Zach asks.

"Still in the hospital, under arrest."

Digesting that, we all fall silent. This is a huge mess. Not only has it derailed our one shot at peace—Sabre's investigation into Sanchez—it's shaken us all to our very cores. Someone got to Willow. On our land.

If Briar Valley isn't safe, then nowhere is. We can't protect her, no matter where she runs or hides. There will always be that threat in the background, regardless of what we do otherwise.

"Is she still asleep?" Killian glances towards the back of the cabin. "Arianna left for school hours ago."

"I'll go and check," I offer.

Leaving them to continue fretting, I head through the partition door that leads into the back of the cabin. Willow didn't want to go home after what happened and being checked over by Doc.

She opted to sleep in Killian's bed and we all piled in together, needing our own reassurance that she was still with us.

Softly knocking on his bedroom door, I peer inside. The bed is empty, sheets rumpled and unmade. Checking the bathroom next, I follow the quiet sound of crying that's becoming louder.

"Willow?' I knock on the door.

The sound suddenly stops.

"It's Micah. Can I come in?"

"Mi," she cries. "I… think I need to be alone."

"I understand, angel, but I don't think I can give you that right now. Please let me in."

It's several long, painful seconds before the door clicks open. Willow stands on the other side in her comfortable clothes for a day of bedrest—stretchy yoga pants and one of Zach's oversized tees.

"You doing okay in here?"

Her face is red from crying. "Not really."

"Want to talk about it? No pressure, I promise. Just me and you."

Eyes darting from side to side, Willow swallows hard. "Come in."

I enter the bathroom and look around, finding everything in place. She was clearly hiding in here for a reason, though. She's shaking all over and refusing to even make eye contact with me.

"How are you feeling?" I stroke a hand over her arm.

"Bit dizzy still, but okay," she hiccups, wiping moisture from her face. "I'm just a bit overwhelmed with everything. I heard Killian on the phone and freaked out."

"He's just upset, angel. Ethan's team was supposed to be trustworthy."

"It isn't Ethan's fault."

"Killian needs someone to blame right now. He's angry."

"Being angry won't help anyone." Her tear-logged eyes finally flick up to me. "When will it all end, Mi? I don't think I can do this anymore."

Cupping her cheeks, I stroke her tears aside. "Soon, baby. It'll all be over soon."

"You can't promise that."

The pain emanating from her is a knife to my heart.

"But I can promise that we're here, no matter what happens. You can always trust us."

"Just no one else," she finishes.

Moving down to her mouth, I run my finger over her bottom lip. "Well, no. Not right now. We can't risk trusting anyone else with your safety after what happened."

"It just makes no sense. I thought Tara was a good person."

"Good people can still make mistakes. Sanchez found her pressure point and threatened it. Fear must've taken over."

Willow nods. "That's what he does."

"She's been placed under arrest in the hospital. Sabre's investigating the entire team to weed out anyone else who's been compromised."

"Shit, Mi. This is such a huge mess. How did we get here?"

Pulling her into my arms, I hold her close. "I don't know. But we're here, and you're not alone right now. You don't have to hide away in here from us."

"I wasn't hiding, I....."

Mouth snapping shut, she shakes her head. I dip a finger beneath her chin to raise her eyes back up to mine.

"Then what?"

Tears fill her eyes again. "I wasn't going to do it, I promise."

"Do what, Willow?" I press.

With a sigh, she reaches into her bra and pulls out a small, metal switchblade. My stomach flips. I stare at her in disbelief, trying hard not to appear judgemental.

"What were you doing with it?"

She bites her lip. "I was just trying to figure out how to get rid of it. I don't need the temptation just laying around. Not when I feel like this."

Taking a deep breath, I hold out a hand, and she drops the blade into it. I turn the cool metal weight over, hating the mental image it conjures. All I can imagine is her making those scars on her skin.

"You want to use it?"

Hesitant, she nods. "I'm scared. It's triggering me."

"You don't need to be ashamed of that, angel. I said before that you can tell me anything. I won't ever judge you for feeling triggered."

Tucking the switchblade into my jeans pocket, I take her hand. She lets me guide her from the bathroom, and I pull her into my side so we can slip past the other two.

"Where are we going?" Willow whispers.

"To a safe space. You need to feel that again."

In the living room, Killian halts his pacing. "Where are you two off to?"

"We'll be in the studio if you need us."

Before he can protest, I steer Willow outside and wave off Hyland. The last thing we need is that lump of meat following us around. That'll only trigger Willow even more.

At the bottom of the garden, we enter my quiet, dimly lit studio where comfortable silence and the smell of oil paint envelopes us.

When I feel overwhelmed, I come to my safe place to escape. Perhaps she can do the same. Firmly closing the door behind her, I gesture around the warm space.

"Make yourself at home. We can hide out in here for as long as you need. I promise, it's safe."

Willow manages a small, sad smile. "Thank you, Mi."

"Don't mention it."

Walking over to the shelf housing canvases and supplies, I use the step to reach the very top shelf where a small, carved box is hidden at the back. Fetching it down, I twist the padlock to open it.

"What's that?" Willow looks over my shoulder.

"This is a fail-safe, for when I don't think I can control myself. I lock everything away and put it out of reach."

Opening the box, inside is stashed my own blade—a black-handled knife, antibacterial wipes and bandages. The self-harmers holy grail. I can hear how loud she gulps from just behind me.

"But you can still reach it," she points out. "And you know the code to unlock the padlock."

"That's the whole point."

"I don't understand."

"The power not to cut will always be mine. This is just a way of proving that to myself. Plus, out of sight, out of mind."

Putting her switchblade inside, I lock the box and put it back up on the shelf before moving the step away so it's unreachable. Immediately, Willow seems to deflate a little, her shoulders slumping.

"Does that feel a bit better?"

Surprisingly, she nods. "Actually, it does."

"Tricking the mind sometimes works."

"Sometimes?" She laughs weakly.

"I'm not perfect. Nobody is. I just take it a day at a time."

Turning to face her, she snuggles into my chest, her lips brushing against my pulse point. We stand and cuddle for several silent seconds, just feeling each other's breath. We're here. Alive. Safe.

Those blades won't win—not while we have each other. I'll pull her out of the depths of hell for as long as this stunning, perfect angel needs me to, whether she'll admit it to herself or not.

And in return, the breath entering and leaving her lungs will keep me alive. She doesn't even have to do anything. Her existence in this world is enough to keep blood pumping through my veins.

"What should we do now?" Her breath catches. "I don't want to go back in there and face this mess yet."

"Then we don't have to."

"Are we just going to hide in here?"

"What if we did some painting instead?" I hesitate, my eyes trailing over her. "Or... I could paint you, if you wanted."

"Right now?"

"Just sit for me, that's all. It could be relaxing. Shit... don't worry, it's a stupid idea."

"No, Mi. It's not." She smiles shyly. "I'd like to sit for you. Can I keep my clothes on, though?"

"Yes, of course."

"Cool. Let's do it."

Grabbing one of the bean bags on the floor, I fluff it up then add a couple of cushions to make a comfortable place for her. Willow smooths her t-shirt and hair, appearing self-conscious.

"Is what I'm wearing alright?"

"You could be wearing a bin bag, and you'd still be the most gorgeous woman on the entire fucking planet."

She bites the inside of her cheek, her eyes ducked. "You always say the sweetest things."

"Just the truth, that's all."

Taking a seat on the bean bag, she gets comfortable in the nest of cushions. I set up my easel and stool a few metres away before turning my attention to the paints. I have to get this just right.

Oil paints are too harsh to capture her beauty, so I opt for watercolours instead. I want it to be subtle and striking at the same time, built with layers of shadow and perfectly blended hues.

With the colours set up, I light a couple of candles and fiddle with the lighting in the room until it reflects off her perfect features at just the right intensity. Willow watches me the whole time—her gaze curious as she nervously wrings her hands.

"I like how you move around your space." She laughs ruefully. "Is that a weird thing to say?"

"This is my safe place. It's where I feel most at home, and I can be myself."

"I can tell. You're different in here."

"Different in a bad way?" I take my seat.

Willow shakes her head. "No, it's a good thing."

"You can relax. No one will bother us in here."

Releasing a sigh, Willow relaxes further into the bean bag and stares off into space. I begin sketching the outline of her rounded features, slightly crooked nose and full, plump lips.

Every inch of her is incredible. She's so beautiful, but in an effortless way. It's completely natural, from her makeup-free skin to every blemish and freckle on her face.

We sit in comfortable, relaxed silence, the only sound my pencil scratching against the canvas as I complete the outline. Candlelight flickers against her features, softening each curved line.

"When did you start painting?"

Wetting my paintbrush, I dip it into the palette. "A few years after my dad died. It was Pops's idea, actually. He bought my first easel."

"Really?" she asks.

"I was a bit of a wild child as a teenager. I'd get into trouble for drinking and causing trouble. Pops thought I needed an outlet to deal with stuff."

"But why art? What about it allows you to cope?"

Focusing on the shape of her hips, I lean closer to paint the edges of her body. "The world feels safer when it's being painted by my hand. I can make reality whatever I want it to be."

Her expression is wistful. "That sounds peaceful."

"It can be, until the thoughts creep back in. I couldn't find much solace in my art while you were gone. It didn't work anymore."

She continues twisting her hands together, mouth opening and closing with hesitation. "I understand that. It's how I felt when I started... you know... while I was away."

"How did it happen?"

"By accident at first." Willow shrugs.

"Tell me about it."

"I was feeling so overwhelmed and like I couldn't cope. I wasn't able to look after myself, let alone be a mother to Arianna. It happened in a desperate moment."

"And you never regretted it?"

"Every single time."

I continue painting, slowly pulling her secrets free with each stroke of the brush. "Why?"

"I felt like I was letting Arianna down by doing it, but cutting was the only thing that gave me clarity during all those months. I had no other choice but to take that risk."

"I get it. Whatever lets you cope, right?"

"Right." She smiles weakly. "But things are different now. I'm home, and I have you guys again. I don't need to listen to that voice anymore."

"That doesn't mean it isn't still there," I point out. "That's why you need to keep your promise and come to me when it gets too loud. We'll figure it out together."

"Thanks, Mi. I'm lucky to have you in my life."

"Meeting you was the best thing that ever happened to me." I spare her a quick glance. "You've changed everything. For all of us. We're not whole without you, angel."

"Me neither. Let's hope we never have to separate again."

Gloom slips over her, the shadows entering her eyes again.

"Let's hope."

Because that's all we have left now.

Hope.

Pointless, flimsy fucking hope.

CHAPTER 24
WILLOW

FORGED IN THE FIRE – CAYLEE HAMMACK

A KNOCK on the cabin door startles me from brushing Arianna's hair. We both freeze, and my hands quake a little, even though I know I'm being ridiculous.

If someone were here to kidnap me, they wouldn't knock. But after everything that happened with Tara, I'm feeling more on-edge than ever and unable to relax.

"Mummy?" Arianna whimpers.

"It's okay, baby. Carry on brushing your hair for me."

Handing her the brush, I peck her cheek then move to answer the door. I've been on bedrest since the incident, letting my concussion heal and the events settle in my mind.

But this morning, I was determined to get up and return to our cabin. The guys are stiflingly protective enough without me laying in their bed all day, being waited on hand and foot.

Swinging the door open, I find Ryder waiting on the other side. "Since when did you start knocking?"

With a sheepish expression, he steps aside to reveal Ethan standing behind him. I immediately go on high alert, taking a step back and preparing to slam the door shut.

"Wait," Ryder rushes out. "Just let him speak."

"Why? I want nothing else to do with his team."

"Willow," Ethan attempts. "Please, hear me out. I know you're shaken. We all are. This isn't us, and I want to make it up to you."

"Make it up to me? Your employee tried to kill me!" I lower my voice before Arianna follows me out here. "She pointed a fucking gun at my unborn child, Ethan. How can you fix that?"

"We've arrested Mario Luciano."

Feeling like the floor has been swept out from beneath my feet, I almost stumble. Both men wait on the other side of the door, silently pleading for me to let them in.

Mario.

The man who sold me to Sanchez.

It's been years since I thought of him. The slimy bastard was my first employer for the few shifts I worked at his seedy nightclub, giving lap dances and wearing ridiculously skimpy clothing.

"Fine," I say stiffly. "Come in."

Before they pass me, I stop Ryder in his tracks. He instructs Ethan to go ahead and sit in the living room with Arianna.

"I know you love this man, Ry. But do you trust him?"

"With my life." He nods solemnly. "This isn't Ethan's fault. He's trying his best to fix things and see this case through."

"You better be right. We can't handle anything else."

"I know, sweetheart. If you can't trust Ethan, then trust me."

I let him wrap his arm around my shoulders. "I do trust you."

"Then hear him out."

Ryder takes me into the living room where Arianna is telling Ethan all about her homework assignment for Miranda's class. Micah has been helping her sculpt a miniature model of Briar Valley.

"Ari," I call out. "Time to get going, missus."

Hopping down from the sofa, she rushes to grab her schoolbag and lace up her boots. I can see Aalia and Johan walking up the snaking path to the cabins through the window, ready to pick her up.

"Bye, Demon." She scratches her dog's ears lovingly. "Look after my mummy today."

My heart squeezes. "Come on, baby. Say goodbye to Uncle Ryder."

"Bye, Ryder!"

With her passed off to Aalia, I return inside to find Ethan and Ryder sitting on the sofa together. Both decline the offer of coffee, so I sit down in the armchair next to the fireplace.

"Willow," Ethan begins. "Look, I know that nothing I can say will ever make what happened better. We're all in shock, as much as you are. I've worked with Tara for the last eight years."

"Yet she still managed to pull the wool over your eyes?" I snap at him.

"Truthfully, yes. We've been blindsided by this. No one anticipated Sanchez to target the team in an attempt to get to you."

"The team? There are others?"

He winces a little. "Two of our support staff were also threatened. That's how he knew that she was placed on your personal security detail."

Hands balling into fists, I fight the urge to toss him out of the cabin. Anger is far from my default setting, but my baby's life was threatened. I have to protect the life growing inside of me at all costs.

"How can I trust any of you again?"

He raises his hands in a placating way. "Because we're the good guys here. This was a huge slip-up, but it won't happen again. Please give us a chance to prove that to you."

I lean forward in the armchair. "Tell me about Mario."

Ethan sighs. "After hearing your testimony, we worked on tracking him down. The nightclub you worked in was shut down several years ago by the police, so tracing him was a little difficult."

"But you found him?"

"We did—running in a club in Soho under a new identity. Thought he'd slipped off the radar. He was arrested late last night and brought in to custody."

Despite everything, I feel a surge of victory. It feels good to know that he didn't slip through our fingers after what he did to me as a child. If it wasn't for Mario, Mr Sanchez never would've found me.

"What happens now?" I ask in anticipation.

"He's being questioned by Hudson and Kade as we speak. Mario is facing charges of human trafficking and more. We've got our first player behind bars, Willow."

My heart is trying to break through my rib cage, but for the first time in what feels like forever, it's for a good reason.

"Oh my God."

I wish the guys were listening to this instead of working. Even though his team is responsible for the recent mess, I could kiss Ethan right now. Mario is facing the rest of his life in prison, and it feels incredible.

"He will be formally charged and face trial for his crimes," Ethan continues. "But we're also going to use him to gain more information on the ring as a whole."

"You're not offering him a plea deal, are you?"

"No. He may negotiate for a reduced sentence if he provides helpful intel, but his crimes are too severe to be dismissed. You're not the first woman he's sold into sexual slavery."

Flinching at those words, I wrap my hands around my belly as if I can protect the life inside me from all this evil. I don't want my child to ever know the pain and suffering that I have.

"This leads us back to why I'm here." Ethan leans forward, his eyes pinned on me. "We still need your help with the other victim. I want you to meet her and convince her to testify for the case."

"Seriously?" I scoff. "You want me to involve another innocent person in this after what happened to me? You can't keep her safe. Hell, you can't keep any of us safe."

"The sooner we end this, the safer you will all be," he contends. "Her information may give us a new lead. Sanchez is gone, and we need to find him as fast as possible."

"Please, Willow," Ryder begs. "We're all here to support you. This is the right thing to do."

"Don't lecture me on what the right thing to do is," I bark at them. "Where were you when I was bleeding on the ground and inches from death, huh?"

Pain lances across his features. "That isn't fair. We had no idea."

"Exactly my point! You had no idea. Nowhere is safe anymore, and I can't risk my life or my baby's life again. Please… just go."

When Ethan opens his mouth to speak again, I raise a hand to halt him. His shoulders sink as disappointment visibly slips over him.

"I'm sorry," he offers sincerely.

"I know you are. But it isn't enough. I just want my life back."

"You won't get it on your own." He stares at me, hardened determination in his gaze. "You have to fight for it."

Standing up, Ethan casts me a final look and shows himself out. Ryder pauses on the threshold, looking back over his shoulder at me with furrowed brows.

"He's right, sweetheart."

"Just go, Ry."

He shakes his head. "You have to fight for it."

Leaving me in silence, I stare down at my trembling hands. Their words still echo in my head, even as the front door slams shut so I'm alone again.

All I've ever done is fight. I'm tired. No, I'm exhausted. The constant fighting to survive has taken everything from me, and now that I finally have another chance to live, I'm being pulled in two different directions.

Demon jumps up on my lap and burrows into my body, seeking attention. I stroke her coarse black fur and fight back a wave of tears.

"What do I do?"

Too bad she can't answer me.

"I'm so fucking scared of losing this chance... of losing my family," I admit, my cheeks wet. "But if I don't do this, he won't ever stop. My family will never, ever be safe. I have no choice."

Licking the back of my hand, Demon blinks at me with wide puppy eyes. I can see my own reflection in her glossy black irises—tear-stained and rumpled. I look beyond done with the world.

But the world isn't done with me. Not yet. I still have one more fight left to win, and it's the biggest fight of them all. I said it myself... There's no choice but to keep going and bring Mr Sanchez down.

The door creaks, and Killian sticks his head full of tousled, dark-blonde hair in. He sees me curled up with Demon, and his expression softens.

"You alright?"

"I'm okay."

"I just passed Ethan and Ryder outside." He steps into the room, his usual jeans mud-stained and messy. "Can't believe that guy had the nerve to show his face around here."

"He's still Ryder's boyfriend, Kill."

"But that's not what he came for, is it?"

I shake my head. "He still wants me to speak to the victim they've found. I told him to get lost, but now I'm not so sure it was the right thing to do."

Moving closer, Killian crouches down in front of me, his huge hands landing on my legs. Conflict burns in his bonfire eyes, twisting and writhing, reflecting back my own inner turmoil.

"Part of me wants to tell Sabre to fuck off to kingdom come," he admits roughly. "But I don't know how else we're going to fix the mess we're in without them."

"Yeah," I say flatly. "I feel the same."

"As much as I want to make this decision for you... baby, I can't do that. This is your call to make."

Staring at him incredulously, I realise he's serious. Protective, overbearing Killian who forces me to eat meals and makes sure I get eight hours sleep every single night is letting me make this decision.

"Since when?" I laugh.

He shrugs. "Some battles I can't fight for you, as much as I want to. I've realised that hiding you away and pretending this isn't happening is not going to keep you safe from harm."

"Jesus. Who are you, and what have you done with Killian?"

"People change, princess."

"Clearly."

"After all the shit we've been through, I trust you more than anyone else in this fiasco. You'll make the right decision for everyone. We need to end this."

Too stunned to speak, I let Killian drop a kiss on my forehead and stand back up to return outside. I'm left staring after him, gobsmacked at the person who's just given me free rein to make this call.

Shit.

This is exactly what Mr Sanchez wants.

He wants to break my spirit and force me to give up. He wants me to be alone, afraid and too weak to continue. Then I'll give in. He'll get what he wants—my submission.

No matter how hard things get, I cannot give that to him. He spent a decade breaking me down into the weak, damaged person he needed me to be, and I refuse to be his broken toy any longer.

"No more," I whisper to myself.

Quickly chasing after Killian, I stop him on the porch steps and grab his shirt sleeve. He's wearing this weird, knowing smile, like he knew all along that all I needed was a push.

"Go and get them to come back. Please."

Killian's smile broadens.

"That's my girl."

CHAPTER 25
WILLOW
ANGEL ON FIRE – HALSEY

I NEVER THOUGHT I'd be back in London.

Sitting in the backseat of Killian's truck, we park up outside a small, closed café on the outskirts of Hammersmith. It's empty aside from the three men who wait outside wearing hardened expressions, surrounded by their armed guards.

I recognise Hudson and Ethan, both in matching all-black clothing and gun holsters. The third man has slicked-back, pearly-blonde hair and wears a blue suit that sets him apart.

Releasing the steering wheel, Killian shuts off the engine. "Looks like this is the place. Who's the new guy?"

"Not a clue," Zach replies from the seat next to me. "Some welcoming committee. They look like fucking stormtroopers or something."

"This isn't Star Wars, Zachariah," Micah chuffs.

"As Grams would say, they've got a face like a slapped ass."

I choke on a laugh. "She'd say that?"

"It was one of her favourite lines."

"Classic Lola," Killian concurs.

Heart twinging in my chest, I rub a hand over the phantom pain. Her absence shows itself in the strangest of moments. I wish she was here now to hug me and tell me that everything's going to be okay.

No one dares to walk near the three men, seeming to sense the threat that radiates off their packed shoulders and muscular frames.

They've shut the café for this meeting and set up surveillance. Every precaution under the sun has been taken to keep us safe now that we're exposed in the capital city again. Mr Sanchez would have to be a miracle worker to make it through their layers of security.

I blow out a breath. "Let's get this over and done with."

"Wait." Killian pins me with a fearsome look. "Just say the word, and we'll get you out of there. No questions asked."

"I'll be okay, Kill."

"He's right." Micah grabs my hand. "If it gets too much, you need to tell us. This isn't worth risking your health for."

"I'll let you guys know, okay?"

Zach gives me a charming smile. "Okay, babe."

"Come on. We shouldn't keep them waiting."

Micah climbs out of the car, then moves to open my door for me, wearing one of his usual reassuring smiles. It immediately sets me more at ease. I'm glad to have all three of them here this time around.

With the guys trapping me between them, we approach the others. Ethan smiles tightly, wearing a mask of tension, while Hudson offers me a hand to shake before introducing the third man.

"This is my brother, Kade."

A welcoming smile tilts Kade's lips. "It's a pleasure, Willow."

"Nice to meet you."

His hazel eyes are friendly as they search my face, giving the impression that he can see past all my layers of defences. But I don't feel threatened—he has a warm, reassuring presence.

"We're expecting Elaine to arrive shortly," Hudson informs us. "Let's all move inside."

Guiding us into the café, we all take seats around a small table. The atmosphere is heavy with anticipation, and the guys glower at everyone but me, all on high-alert.

"So," Kade breaks the silence. "We need to put a wire on you to record the meeting."

"You're not fucking touching her," Killian thunders. "Hands off or lose them."

Kade laughs. "Willow can attach it herself."

Lips sealed in a tight line, Killian still doesn't look happy as Ethan hands me the wire and voice recorder. I feed it beneath my t-shirt then tape the wire onto my breastbone.

The small black box is tucked into the waistband of my jeans to pick up the conversation with Elaine. I've memorised the brief and questions Ethan sent me beforehand.

"When is she arriving?" Killian fires off, obviously still grumpy. "We have places to be."

"Any moment. We're only here for security, given recent events," Hudson answers. "We'll move to guard the entrances and exits while you talk to Elaine."

Ethan shifts forward to look at me. "Willow, it's really important that we get her testimony. We need a lead on Sanchez, and she may know someone or something that could help track him down."

"After all this time?" I frown at him.

"We've checked all of his registered properties and everywhere mentioned by other victims." Hudson's words are clipped, sounding frustrated. "This victim is older, from before your time. She may have new intel."

"He's holed up somewhere," Zach surmises.

"Exactly. Someone is helping him."

"Who?" I ask.

"Well, we've got Mason and his other associates in Mexico and the States under surveillance too. They aren't involved."

Crap. Mr Sanchez could be anywhere, plotting anything, and we have no idea. If this woman can help us, then I have to try.

"What about Mario? Did he give you anything?"

"Not a damn thing." Kade scowls. "He's clammed up and is refusing to speak."

"Yet," Hudson adds ominously.

Cracking his knuckles, the sense of danger is so palpable, I have to force myself not to flinch away from him. I mentally remind myself he's one of the good ones. Even if my brain can't see past his intimidating exterior.

"How did you find this woman in the first place?"

"Her name was given up by another victim," Ethan answers. "But she's unwilling to speak to us directly. It took weeks to convince her to meet with you."

"What is she so afraid of?"

"The same thing you are." His eyes duck low. "Dimitri Sanchez and the power he wields. She has too much to lose."

A lump forms in my throat.

Here I am, risking it all.

Am I doing the right thing?

The sound of voices from outside interrupts our murmurings. The layer of armed guards maintaining the perimeter have stopped a short, thin woman with greying-brown hair from entering the café.

"That's her." Hudson stands up. "We'll be right outside, Willow."

"Okay, thanks."

The others follow suit, waiting for my guys to copy them and stand up. Zach and Micah both stop to kiss my hands.

"Be careful," Zach whispers.

"I will."

"Shout if you need us," Micah adds.

Letting them both pass him, Killian hesitates, staring at me for several seconds as if attempting to burrow deep into my brain.

"I'll be fine," I whisper to him. "Go."

"Are you sure about this?"

"What happened to trusting me, Kill?"

"I trust you," he insists. "It's this fucking world that I don't trust. It seems determined to take you away from me."

I hold his gaze, reaching up to smooth the wrinkle between his brows. "I won't let it."

He nods once then kisses me firmly on the lips. I watch the three of them leave, passing Elaine in the doorway as she timidly enters the café.

Standing up, I wait for her to approach. Her narrow hips are cloaked in an ill-fitting pair of jeans with a cream sweater.

"Willow?" she croaks.

"Hi. Elaine, I'm guessing?"

Nodding, Elaine takes the seat opposite me. "Hello."

"Is that your real name, can I ask?"

"What do you think?" she snaps back.

"Fair enough."

"I'm not staying for long." She sighs wearily. "I just wanted to tell these people to leave me alone. I don't want to speak to anyone about the past. That's final."

"I understand. I thought we could just talk—"

"No," she interrupts.

"Please, Elaine."

"There's nothing else to discuss. Instruct your associates to leave me alone. I have a life and a family. I don't want them knowing about this."

"Look, you're scared. I get it. I'm terrified too, all of the time. But that's no way to live, and it won't end unless we bring Mr Sanchez down."

Elaine flinches. "He made you call him that too?"

"Yes. We're not so different."

"I hardly think so."

"We went through something similar at the hands of that monster. You can talk to me about what happened to you. All we want is the truth so we can bring him to justice for what he's done."

Air hisses out of her nostrils. "I just want peace."

"So do I. Help me to get it for all of us."

Visibly wilting, Elaine looks down at her entwined fingers, twisting together. I can tell that I'm getting through to her. She just needs a push.

"He hurt me every day," I reveal, my chest tight with pain. "It was relentless. My daughter suffered too."

"You have a daughter? With him?" she asks in shock.

"Yes, Arianna is his. He beat her as well."

She looks stunned to learn this, her features twisting with anger at the thought of Mr Sanchez hurting an innocent child. I decide to keep going.

"Some nights I just laid there and let him do it. That was easier than fighting back. But other times, I would kick and scream until he beat me into submission."

She hesitates, paling further. "I never fought back."

"That isn't something to be ashamed of."

"Isn't it?"

"No," I insist fiercely. "What he did to us was evil. It's his fault, not yours. That's why he has to be punished."

Elaine looks contemplative as she chews her lip. "He deserves to rot in prison for everything he's done to you. To all of us."

"Then help me put him there. Please."

Softening, she moves to the edge of her seat. "I'm so scared."

"That's why we do this together. Not alone."

"And if I do this, will I be left alone?"

"Yes. All we need is your testimony."

She nods tersely. "What do you want to know, then?"

"When did you last see him?" I quickly ask before she changes her mind.

Her eyes go faraway, misted-over by the past. "Twelve years ago. I managed to run during a business trip in London."

"You were married?"

"No," she says quietly. "Nothing so formal. When we met, Dimitri was very charming. I was enamoured immediately. I had no idea who he really was until it was too late."

"So you were in a relationship?" I poke further.

"Yes, a very passionate one at that."

I want to delve into what she means, but I force myself to stick to the list of questions that Ethan drilled into me.

"And how did he take you?"

"I agreed to go on holiday with him to Florida. That was the last time I saw England until we returned to London, almost a year later."

"Did you ever think about going to the police?"

"I was too scared to speak up after I escaped him. You know how powerful he is."

I've never heard of Mr Sanchez having a relationship like this. There were women involved in our life together—women he'd rape, beat and abuse, provided by Mason's supply lines.

But the way Elaine describes her time with him is different. He didn't traffic her using violence and threats like the rest of us. This version of him took his time to groom her before making his move.

"What happened then?"

"It felt like a honeymoon. We were so in love with each other, I thought I was the luckiest girl in the world." Her eyes well up. "I still remember when everything changed and the first time he hit me."

Her words take me back. I remember it too. Strapped into a seat in the aeroplane, groggy and drugged up to my eyeballs, Mr Sanchez struck me for sobbing and ruining his peace.

Elaine wipes underneath her eyes. "It got bad fast. He'd become so angry, furious even, and take it all out on me. The beatings worsened, and I was so terrified, all I wanted was to go home. But he wouldn't let me."

"He kept you there?"

"Not in America. After the holiday, we returned to Mexico. He was living in Tijuana at the time. The trip there was so awful... He wouldn't stop hurting me, even when I begged for relief from the constant pain."

Reaching across the table, I take her hand into mine. Instead of pulling away as I was expecting, Elaine squeezes my fingers and gives me a wobbly smile. We've both been through the same living hell.

"These locations in Florida and Tijuana... do you have any addresses?"

Her eyes scurry around the café. "One, maybe."

"What about a description for the other? Rough location?"

"I may... Maybe I can write a description or something. It's been a long time, and a lot of the memories are a blur."

Excitement pulsates through me. "Anything can help."

"I don't want my new name attached to any of this information," she hurries to say. "I have a new life now, and my husband knows nothing about what happened to me. That's why I didn't want to come forward."

"We can keep the information anonymous."

Nodding, she pulls a pen from her handbag then scribbles down some information on a napkin. I eagerly take it, feeling like I'm holding the Holy Grail. This could be something we can use to track him down.

"When are you due?" She nods towards the hand rubbing my small bump.

"I'm about sixteen weeks along, so another five months or so."

"An autumn baby. How wonderful."

I rub a hand over my belly. "We haven't found out the gender, we want it to be a surprise."

"We did the same with my first two." Elaine smiles wistfully. "It makes things even more exciting."

"You have kids?"

"Four altogether."

"Wow, busy house."

"You don't know the half of it." She laughs a little before sobering again. "I have to keep them safe, Willow. They can never know about any of this. It would kill them."

Unable to stop myself, I lean closer, softening towards her. "You never wanted to tell your husband?"

"Of course, but he wouldn't understand. I don't want anyone to look at me differently. They would if they knew what Dimitri Sanchez did to me all those years ago."

"I thought the same thing for a long time." My chest burns at the thought of the guys. "But people will always surprise you, and I should've given the men I love more credit than that."

"Men?" she repeats.

"Uh, it's a little complicated."

Her eyes twinkle as she becomes more comfortable. "As long as they make you happy, it doesn't matter how complicated things get. You hold on to those men, and never let them go."

"I have no intention of ever doing that."

"Then you're one of the lucky ones."

Releasing her hand, I swallow to clear the lump growing in my throat. Old Willow never would've believed I'd be here now, facing my fears and doing it regardless of how terrified I am.

She didn't have the strength to run headfirst into the war we're currently facing. I'm not entirely sure I have that strength now, but it isn't going to stop me from proving Mr Sanchez wrong in his quest to break me.

"I think your husband may surprise you too," I offer honestly.

She snorts. "I really don't think so."

"He deserves to know, Elaine. If he loves you as much as it sounds like he does, he'll stand by you regardless of your past. That's what love is, right? Accepting each other unconditionally."

She looks down at the scarred Formica table, seeming to think about that. I glance outside where the others are standing guard, surely trying hard not to watch the meeting unfold behind them.

If I'd trusted the guys long before I did and told them the truth, things may have ended differently. They begged for it so many times, but I couldn't give it to them until I had no other choice.

But they loved me anyway.

I'm so lucky to have that.

"That's why I'm going to fight this until the end," I continue, feeling my determination harden. "For that unconditional love and the people who gave it to me. They deserve my fight."

Elaine watches me, the corners of her mouth curling upwards a little. "Not all of us are as strong as you, Willow. But I suppose…" She waves her hand as if to wipe away the rest of her unspoken thought. "I'm glad we have someone to fight for all of us."

"I'm not strong." I shrug her off. "A few days ago, I kicked the team out of my house and swore I'd never meet you. I was afraid of putting myself back in the firing line again."

She nods in understanding.

"But here I am." I gesture around the empty café. "Because no matter how afraid or tired of this world I am, I want to be a good person, not the broken little girl Mr Sanchez made me into."

This time, she reaches across the table to initiate, taking my hand into hers again and gripping tightly.

"Thank you. From all of us."

I squeeze her hand back. "You don't have to thank me."

"I do. I'm just praying this will be enough to bring that monster down… for all of our sakes."

"Me too."

Letting me go, she stands up and grabs her handbag. I panic, desperately trying to remember the list of questions. My mind has gone blank, filled with emotion instead.

"It was nice to meet you," she offers sincerely. "And I hope you find whatever it is you're looking for in life. I hope… you can find peace. That we can all find peace."

I stand up too, following in her footsteps. "Let me give you my phone number. Please call me if you need to talk to someone."

Quickly scribbling it down on a napkin, I hand the number over to her. She hesitantly takes it then nods in thanks.

"See you around, Willow."

Watching her go, I feel a twinge of pity for the small, frightened woman. I can see strength in her, beneath the battle scars and pain. She survived Sanchez. That takes a strength most could never dream of.

Elaine walks out with her head held high, straight past Ethan, Hudson and Kade. She doesn't stop to speak to them, even as they call her name. This trip wasn't for them. It was for her... And me.

Striding back in, Killian rushes to my side first, pulling me into a hug like we've been separated for years rather than minutes. The other two aren't far behind with the team.

"Are you okay?" Killian fusses over me. "Did she upset you? I'll go drag her back here by her hair if need be."

"Cool it, Kill." I chuckle. "We're good."

"Sure?" he worries, his gaze and hands roaming over me.

"Alright, caveman." Zach claps him on the shoulder. "Let's turn the testosterone down a notch, shall we? You're gonna drown poor Willow in it."

"Fuck off, kid," he growls.

Wading through them, I step into Micah's arms, needing his quiet assurance. "She was fine. We talked for a bit, and I got the information we needed."

Picking up the napkin from the table, Ethan scans over it. "She gave these to you?"

"Yes. Two properties from her time with Mr Sanchez twelve years ago. One in Florida and another in Tijuana. She didn't remember much else."

"What else did she say?" Hudson presses.

"That he didn't traffic her initially. They had a consensual relationship that turned bad before he forced her back to Mexico and held her there for a year. He was abusive—physically and sexually."

"Shit," Kade mutters.

"Precisely," Ethan echoes. "This just got a hell of a lot more complicated."

"Did I do something wrong?"

"No, sweetheart." Ethan smiles appreciatively. "You did good. This is information we can use. I just wasn't expecting to hear another side to the story. That may not work in our favour in Elaine's case."

"We have to protect her. She wants to remain anonymous."

"And she will. This is just information to give us a new lead on Sanchez's location."

Moving into Zach's arms last, I stifle a laugh when he blows a raspberry on my cheek. His grin widens as he spots the smile on my face. Only he can make me feel better in tense situations like this.

"Well done, Willow," Kade compliments.

"Thanks. I don't know how you guys do this for a living."

Hudson shrugs. "You get used to it."

Pulling the wire from my chest, I hand it and the voice recorder to Ethan. "Got everything you need?"

"We'll see if it's enough to give us a lead. Thank you for coming back. We're going to try and end this now, I promise you."

"Better keep your word."

"He will." Killian wears his best hunter's smile. "Else he won't have any fucking legs while running around after criminals."

"That a threat?" Ethan chuckles.

"Consider it a promise. Ryder can always find a new boyfriend."

"Alright." I grab Killian's arm to steer him away. "That's our cue to leave. I want to go home."

"Amen to that," Zach hums.

CHAPTER 26
KILLIAN

DEAD MAN'S ARMS – BISHOP BRIGGS

"FUCKING TRAFFIC," I snarl.

Staring at the line of vehicles blocking the motorway leading back into Wales, I lay my hand down on the horn, blaring the queue of red lights. Fucking assholes. I knew this trip was a shitty idea.

"We're going to be late." Zach stares ahead at the queue.

"Call Aalia, and let her know. Arianna will be waiting up for us."

"Phone's dead."

"Mine's at home," Willow adds from the backseat.

Her head is resting in Micah's lap. She spent much of the trip back from London napping after her eventful morning. He leans down to nuzzle her hair and kiss her forehead.

"We'll be home soon. I'm sure they're all fine."

"I hope so." Willow sounds worried.

"Arianna's safe with Aalia and the others," Zach chimes in. "We'll be home in a couple of hours. Go back to sleep."

I watch Willow curl her hands into her chest in the rearview mirror. She falls back asleep as we crawl through the traffic. The miles pass by at a snail's pace, stretching the journey on for twice as long as it usually takes.

"What did you think about that woman?" Zach asks quietly.

I focus on the traffic ahead. "She struck me as pretty shady, but Willow seemed to trust her. We'll see if her intel pans out."

"I don't love that we're putting all our bets on some random woman's information from twelve years ago."

"And you think that I do?" I cut past a dawdling motorist to move ahead. "She's our last resort."

"I hope you're right. I'm not sure how much more of this Willow can take."

"She's stronger than you think," Micah counters from behind me. "Look at what she did today. Sabre would have nothing if Willow hadn't gone in and spoken to Elaine for them. She did amazing."

"Micah's right," I agree. "Willow did that, not them."

"I know she's strong," Zach claps back. "I just wish she didn't have to be quite so strong. Isn't that supposed to be our jobs? Being strong for her?"

"No," I correct. "It's not anymore."

"Huh?"

"Coddling Willow has never done us any good. She's a strong, independent woman, and that's why we love her. We have to let her do this how she sees fit. Today proved that much."

"Jesus, Kill. Did you have a fucking personality transplant?"

"Shut it, kid. I'm just telling it how it is."

"Well, you're freaking me out with all this mature, non-egotistical talk. Anyone would think you'd been hit around the head."

"Feel free to walk back to Briar Valley," I growl at him.

"That's more like it."

Lapsing back into silence, we crawl through the traffic inch by painful inch. Willow doesn't stir again, lightly snoring from her balled-up position in the backseat with Micah.

By the time we arrive in the rural, rugged mountains that house Briar Valley, hours have passed, and we're all desperately tired. Zach and Willow's eyes fling open when I slam on the breaks at the sight ahead of us.

"What in the living fuck is that?"

All of us strain to look out of the window as awful, shocked silence reigns throughout the truck. Rising high above the forest of fir and pine trees is a billowing, black cloud of smoke.

"A campfire?" Micah says hopefully.

"That's no campfire." I rev the engine and take off. "It's an actual fire."

Racing up the mountain road at breakneck speed, I guide us over bumps and rocks, moving far faster than safety would usually allow for. Willow goes white as a sheet when she spots the smoke.

"What is that?" she asks in a rush of panic.

Micah holds her to his chest. "We're not sure."

"Shit! Arianna's up there!"

"Everyone is," I state grimly. "If that smoke's coming from town, we're in serious trouble."

Turning onto the mountain pass, we begin the descent into Briar Valley. Immediately, the air becomes thick with black smoke so dense, it's like tar is seeping through the car's vents. Soon we're all coughing.

The woods are hazy and speckled with black ash, choking all remaining wisps of light from the early evening shadows. We're still moving fast but having to navigate the poor visibility and woodland.

"Motherfuck," I blurt out as we hit a rock.

It scrapes along the bottom of the truck, eliciting an awful, metallic screeching sound. Bouncing to the next bump, we move from obstacle to obstacle, dodging trees and smoke in all directions.

By some miracle, we reach Briar Valley relatively unscathed. The visibility reaches an all-time low as billowing black smoke infiltrates the air, choking everything in its path. No leaf or petal escapes untouched.

I manage to guide us through the smoke, and as the trees thin out, the source of the chaos becomes clear. Wild, rampant flames stretch so high into the sky, they must kiss the heavens.

Fire is burning bright ahead of us, as if the devil himself has deigned to visit us and reign down hellfire. Wood, furniture and carpet are being consumed in a greedy roar of pure evil.

Lola's cabin.

Up in flames.

"No," I utter in horror.

Everyone stares ahead—gobsmacked and horrified. Her cabin is unrecognisable through the destruction, the structure being eaten alive by fire. I can just make out the shadows of people in the clearing around us.

Slamming my door open, I immediately double over at the rush of heat and ash that greets me. It sears my lungs—crisping, infecting and metastasising into a red-hot cancer.

"Stay inside," I yell at the others.

Zach completely ignores me and hops out. "Not a chance!"

"Kid!"

"Move," he shouts.

We run around the truck together, trying to fumble our way through hazy, smoke-filled air that wraps around our throats like burning-hot barbed wire.

"Killian!" someone yells.

At the edge of the property, Ryder and Albie are attempting to fight the flames. We're too remote for fire trucks to get up here, so we have some equipment for ourselves.

Fire extinguishers and powdered foam are no match for the hellish beast that's invaded Lola's home, set up shop and decided to burn the entire damn thing to nothing but ash. We're powerless.

Willow appears from the car, a hand clenched over her mouth. "Where's Ari?"

Ryder points towards Rachel and Miranda's cabin. "The schoolhouse with the other kids."

Taking off, she runs at full speed to find her daughter. I'm glad to see her away from the flames, and I wave for Micah to follow after her to keep her safe. Willow shouldn't have to see this.

Picking up a fire extinguisher, I can't even get close enough to use it. The heat is sweltering, a tidal wave of fire and ash sweeping over us all, spitting and writhing in all its God-like fury.

"What the fuck happened?" I scream.

Albie wipes his sweaty forehead. "Doc raised the alarm a couple of hours ago. Place has been burning ever since."

"How did it get so out of control?"

"By the time we got here, it was too late," he shouts back. "It was already out of control. Someone must've laid the place with gasoline."

"Someone?" Zach bellows.

With a grim expression, Albie points towards the corner of the property where a wooden sign has been hammered into the ground. It's a real estate sign, embossed with a company name.

SANCHEZ REAL ESTATE.

That wasn't there this morning when we left. I have to fight the urge to smash someone's fucking face, and right now, I couldn't care less whose it is. That motherfucking bastard did this.

Sanchez.

We all watch the flames crawl closer, consuming the sign until it crumbles like the rest of Lola's cabin. Sanchez's name curls up and vanishes in a puff of smoke.

"How? We have patrols!" I bark at them.

Ryder jumps back when flames spit out at him. "Whoever did this was in and out fast. They must've left their vehicle in the woods and come in on foot to dodge the patrols."

Vision hazing over with red, I stare up at Lola's legacy... burning. Nothing left to show for the woman but handfuls of hot ash and treasured possessions turned to a fine powder.

She's truly gone now.

"He knew this cabin belonged to Willow's grandmother," I spit out. "He fucking *knew* this was all she had left. And he burned it anyway. I'm going to peel the fucking skin from his face!"

That damned letter.

He warned me to stay away. Fuck, he warned us that Briar Valley would burn. But that didn't stop us from poking the devil regardless and stupidly expecting there to be no consequences.

This is it.

The consequences of our actions.

———

Morning light reveals the extent of the damage, unfiltered and unapologetic. While birds chirp and the sun rises, Briar Valley mourns the loss of its heart, cruelly torn out at the root.

Lola's cabin is gone.

I suppose we should be thanking some God or another that Mr fucking Psycho didn't decide to go on a burning spree all over town or manage to get to Arianna.

He went for the jugular. The heart of all our lives, the soul of our memories. This place represents the entire family, and he's shredded us all down to our cores, leaving everyone behind to pick up the pieces.

It's gone.

Kicking a pile of ash that I think used to be a dining chair, I continue picking through the rubble that's still burning in places. Rainfall came early, knocking out the last of the flames before they spread.

A smouldering wreckage is left now. Unrecognisable as the building it once was, Lola's ghost no longer has a home to haunt but a disaster zone instead.

"Jesus fucking Christ," Albie swears as he stares across the smoking wreck. "It's like something off the TV."

"Doesn't feel real, does it?"

Shaking his head, he continues picking through the rubble. "I can't believe it's gone. This cabin was the first thing to be built in this town."

"And the first to go."

"Don't say shit like that, Kill." He cuts me a glare. "We ain't losing anything else around here."

I gesture towards the smoky remains. "Didn't think we'd lose Lola's cabin either, did we? But here we are. Fuck, Al. Open your goddamn eyes."

"My eyes are open well enough, son. And I'm telling you that we ain't losing anything else."

Scoffing at him, I turn away only to find Willow standing in the town square, her hands over her mouth. She stares at the place where Lola's cabin once stood.

Pulling off my gloves, I slowly approach her, trying hard not to set her off. She looks dead on her feet, and her eyes are puffy from crying the night away as we watched the cabin continue to burn.

There was nothing any of us could do but let the fire burn out once the rain began. Saving the remains was impossible without heavy machinery which simply can't handle the drive into town.

"Baby." I pull her into my arms. "Go home. You don't need to see this."

"It's gone. Everything. All of it."

"Please, Willow."

"All those memories." She hugs her midsection. "Just gone."

Sighing, I kiss the side of her head. "I know, princess. There's nothing any of us could have done. It was already too late."

Rather than sobbing her eyes out for another second, her expression hardens into cold, righteous fury. "He did this. After everything... all the threats... he actually did this."

"He's a sick bastard, Willow. We knew that."

"But to send his men to do this? To burn our home?" Willow grits her teeth. "That fucking *reptile*. I'm going to see that he rots behind bars until he begs for death to come and relieve him."

Stomping away in a cloud of anger, she catches up to Micah outside of the schoolhouse. People are gathered inside for breakfast and coffee, needing the moral support of the whole community.

Ryder exits and trails over, his phone in hand. "Ethan and his team are on their way up to investigate. I told him there isn't much evidence left."

"That fucking sign," I snap, my hands tightening into fists. "I know what I saw. His men were here, and they did this."

"We know, Kill. This has Sanchez written all over it."

"Fuck! That asshole was here!"

"We don't know that," Ryder tries to placate. "He most likely sent his lackeys to do it. They were here before, pissing on our land and throwing their weight around. I doubt he's even in the country."

Despite knowing he's probably right, I can't help imagining Sanchez waltzing onto our property and setting the cabin alight with a big ass fucking smile on his face.

He would've taken so much pleasure in doing it, but I know there's no chance he would've left without taking Arianna with him. That's why he can't have possibly done this himself.

Peeling his face off won't be enough retribution. I want to nail his fucking hide to my wall like a hunting trophy and spit roast the rest of him. That son of a bitch won't get away with this.

Ryder drops a hand on my shoulder. "We should go inside and wait."

"No, Ry. I need to clean this shit up."

"There's nothing else to be done right now. You're mourning. Come and join your family."

"I don't need my fucking family!"

"Yes, you do," he shouts back. "Because that is what they're here for, you hard-headed asshole! Now march yourself inside, and be with the town. We need you right now. Willow needs you."

Taken aback, I stare into his pain-filled eyes. He stares right back, letting me see just how deep this cut has wounded us all. We've lost the last remains of our leader, and nothing will ever bring them back.

"Fine," I grumble.

Letting him guide me away from the ruins, I take one last look over my shoulder at what remains of Lola's legacy. Albie refuses to budge, still staring at the ash, his tears silently falling.

Mark my words...

This will be the last thing Sanchez ever does. I'm done letting him hurt my family and get away with it. Fuck Sabre. Fuck the investigation. Fuck all of it.

I'll kill him with my bare hands.

He'll never hurt my family again.

CHAPTER 27
WILLOW

ALWAYS COME BACK (ACOUSTIC)
– MARTIN KERR

STARING AT THE WRECKAGE, my tears don't fall. I have none left. The depression I experienced after the fire has been set alight and transformed into an anger that burns so hot, I hardly know how to contain it.

They were here.

His men.

Because of me, the entire town has been threatened, and Lola's cabin is gone. I've brought danger back to their door. Again. Like I didn't learn my lesson the last time we ended up in this situation.

Ethan and Warner pick over the rubble and sift through the ashes, searching for any evidence. They arrived several hours ago after hearing the news and rushing up from London.

"Willow?" Aalia stops at my side.

"There's nothing left."

"I know." She pats my arm with a sympathetic smile. "Stop blaming yourself, this isn't your fault."

"Yeah, it is."

Turning me to face her, she holds me tight. "This is on him. Mr Sanchez and his men did this, not you. Remember that."

We embrace tightly, but still the tears don't come. I'm not capable of them right now. All that's left after sobbing my heart out all night long is rage. Lonely, bitter rage.

"I'm supposed to be the one protecting this town," I grind out. "Instead, it's burning because of me."

"Willow, he did this to you. He hurt you. He trafficked you. He threatened you." Aalia loses her temper. "He burned the cabin down! Stop blaming yourself for Mr Sanchez's... his..."

"His?" I find the strength to laugh.

"Asshole... behaviour," she finishes, breaking down into inappropriate laughter. "You've done nothing wrong. We need you as our leader more than ever right now."

Finally, the tears well up. "Thank you, Aalia. I'm glad that I have you in my life."

She squeezes my waist. "I've got your back."

"And I've got yours."

"Let's go inside and rejoin the others."

Taking my hand, she tows me back towards the schoolhouse. Rachel and Miranda have called off classes for the day, letting everyone gather to eat, drink and be together while Ethan's team conducts their investigation.

Being together is how Briar Valley copes with trauma. The town looks after its own, and dealing with grief isn't something that's done alone. Seeing the cabin burn has brought it all back up after Lola's death.

Inside the schoolhouse, several long tables have been set up. Rachel is buzzing around with one of her kids helping, doling out sandwiches and steaming cups of tea to the masses of people crowded inside.

Miranda sits at another table with Doc. They're talking to Harold, Marilyn, Andrea and Theodore in low murmurs. It feels like walking into another funeral, everyone's attention turning to me as I head inside.

"What's the latest?" Theodore speaks up.

"The investigation is still ongoing," I address the room. "But it's looking like arson. They've found evidence of fuel canisters near the burn site."

Whispers sweep over the other residents, gathered to listen for updates. We all knew this was deliberate, especially given the sign that Killian saw last night. But hearing the proof is another thing.

"What happens now?" Walker asks.

He's sitting with his two kids at a table with Johan and Amie. His eyes are darting around the room nervously, like he expects it to burst into flames at any moment.

"Sabre will continue their investigation for now."

"But are we safe?" he presses.

Feeling the burden of responsibility, I glance around the room, feeling the collective weight of their gazes on me.

"No," I admit. "Briar Valley isn't safe right now, but nowhere in the world is. I'm sorry that I've brought this trouble into your lives, and you're welcome to leave if that would make you feel safer."

Standing up, Harold's expression is severe. "We're not going anywhere, Willow. This is our home and yours. We won't be forced out by some punk with an attitude problem."

Marilyn takes his hand and nods. "We will stand by you."

Theodore and his wife, Andrea, both nod in agreement. Slowly but surely, everyone around the room joins in—nodding, muttering their agreement, smiling up at me in an attempt at comfort.

My chest tightens with emotion. "You'd all do that? For me?"

"You're our family," Miranda says simply.

Doc kisses the side of his wife's head. "And we protect our family in Briar Valley."

Rachel takes Doc's other hand and gifts me a small smile. "We'll stand by you until the end of the line, Willow. This fight isn't just yours now. It belongs to all of us."

Everyone hums in agreement, still filtering through the stages of shock and grief at the violence we've all witnessed. Their land burned last night too. It doesn't just belong to me.

I have to wipe my cheeks and plaster my strong, Lola-like expression of unflappable leadership back into place.

"Thank you all for being our family. For looking after me and my children. I never expected to find this when I came to Briar Valley, but I have no regrets. It was the best decision I ever made."

They all smile back—accepting and full of love.

"So thank you," I repeat, my voice thick.

Walking to the back of the room, the three pieces of my heart seal the moment. Killian beams up at me while the twins both watch on with matching looks of adoration.

I turn back to Walker. "As for what happens now... we do what we've always done in our lives. We rebuild."

Hugging his children tight, he nods back. "We rebuild."

Harold kisses his wife's cheek. "It wouldn't be the first time."

She chuckles. "Or even the second."

Stepping from the front of the room, everyone turns back to their food or begins to disperse. I find a quiet corner to move to, and the guys meet me there so we can press together.

"Good job, princess." Killian firmly kisses me on the lips. "They needed to hear that."

"I just told the truth."

"And not everyone would have the strength to do that," Micah says, sliding his fingers into mine. "But you do."

"Lying to them won't help."

Walking into the schoolhouse with his shoulders hunched, Ethan is followed closely by Hyland and Warner. The remaining members of the Anaconda team are all here to respond to last night's events.

Ryder flashes across the room to fuss over him, but Ethan brushes him aside, his eyes laser focused on us. We gather in the quietest corner of the room, away from listening ears.

"Willow," he greets.

"What's the latest?"

He hesitates, a hand raking through his hair. "Perhaps we should discuss this alone."

Before Killian can snarl at him in his usual animal-like way, I hold up a hand to stop him. "They're as involved as I am now. Whatever you have to say, we all need to hear it."

Ethan nods. "We're going to make a move on Sanchez."

"Wait, what?"

"We think that we've located the properties in Florida and Tijuana using Elaine's intel. If he's hiding out there, we will arrest him and take him into custody."

Anticipation floods my system. I knew they were searching for the houses, but it seemed like such a long shot.

"Do you really think he'll be there?"

"I can't make any promises, Willow. But we're going to try."

"When?"

"We're splitting up and flying out tonight," Warner answers solemnly. "I'll be taking Florida."

"And I'm heading to Mexico," Ethan says. "If he's there, he'll be arrested for his crimes and extradited back to England. We'll get him, Willow."

"What about Hyland?"

Ethan's eyes stray over to his man, stationed by the door with a gun strapped to his hip. He watches everyone like a hawk.

"He's clean," he confirms.

"How can you be sure?"

"We were thorough."

Tentatively, I nod. "I'm trusting you, Ethan."

"I know. We'll be leaving him here for your protection. You can trust him, despite everything that's happened. He's a good man."

I swallow the need to point out that we thought the same about Tara. Any protection is better than none. Last night's events have proven how exposed we are.

"We're going to make this right," Ethan vows. "I promise to earn your trust in us, Willow. We're not all like Tara."

"I appreciate that."

Killian looks less than impressed with the offer of protection, glowering at him so fiercely, I'm surprised the skin doesn't melt from his bones.

"We have to go back to London to prepare." Ethan briefly touches my arm. "We're going to send some extra muscle to help man the perimeter for you too. Will you be okay?"

"We don't need your help." Killian doesn't let me respond.

Ethan gestures outside at the smoking wreckage. "Clearly, you do. These men and women are highly trained. Put them to use."

With a final squeeze, Ethan backs away to speak to Ryder, who looks like he's freaking out about the Mexico trip. I watch the pair begin to argue for a moment before looking away.

"I hate that guy," Killian rumbles.

Zach rolls his eyes. "You hate everyone."

"Not true."

"Isn't it? You've been telling me that you hate me since we were eight years old. Ethan's a good guy, Kill. He's trying to help."

"We have to let him do his job," Micah chimes in.

"I don't have to fucking like it, though." Killian harrumphs. "Like, at all."

Stomping off, he leaves me with the twins. Zach moves to my back and bands his arms around me from behind, his chin resting on top of my head as he strokes my belly.

"You know… it's our birthday next weekend."

"Wait, it is?" I gasp.

"Yep." He pops the P dramatically.

"Why didn't I know that? We didn't celebrate last year."

"We don't tend to celebrate." Micah shrugs, toying with my fingers. "Birthdays just remind us of Dad."

Zach nods, his eyes filled with sadness. I hate seeing their pain. This day should be a happy occasion for them both, not filled with grief.

"We should celebrate!" I declare.

Neither looks convinced. Pinning them both with my best stern glare, I put my hands on my hips.

"We're celebrating."

"What kind of celebration?" Micah wrinkles his nose.

"There's nothing I want more than to be here with you," Zach protests.

"Like every other day? Not a chance. How old are you guys going to be?"

"Twenty-seven years young." Micah pulls me into his chest. "If we're going to celebrate, I don't want to do it here. This place is full of bad memories."

"Then where?"

"We could get a hotel in Highbridge," he suggests.

Zach frowns. "Is it safe?"

"We can take the last remaining cheerful twin with us."

Bursting into laughter, we all look out the window at Hyland, currently getting his ear chewed off by Killian outside. He looks far from cheerful, being yelled at again.

"I don't know if this is such a good idea." Zach worries his lip.

I stroke a hand over his bicep. "Leave Killian to me, I'll win him over. A break will be good for us."

"Even after what happened last night?"

"Because of what happened last night," Micah intervenes. "We've lost so much already. I just want one normal night for once."

I rub where there's a pang in my chest. "I don't want to leave Arianna again, though. Not after everything."

"Bring her, then. I'm sure Aalia would be happy to babysit for a night in a fancy hotel." Zach winks at me, getting on board with the plan. "We don't want her to overhear anything."

Feeling myself flush, I turn to hide in Micah's chest. "Tell your twin he's making a hell of an assumption that there will be anything to hear, especially in my current state."

Micah's chest vibrates with a chuckle. "You're not getting lucky, Zach. Sorry, man."

"Dammit." He snaps his fingers. "So close. Shouldn't have knocked her up."

"Zachariah!" I splutter.

His eyes twinkle with mirth. "Only joking."

"Don't make me set Hyland on you."

Zach bursts into laughter. "I'm so scared."

"He's clearly very eager to get back in my good books. I'm sure he'd happily dole out a beating."

"Sounds kinky."

"It really won't be."

Kissing the tip of my nose, he playfully ruffles my hair. "That's what you think."

CHAPTER 28
WILLOW
A LITTLE BIT HAPPY – TALK

STANDING IN THE APRIL SUNSHINE, I watch Killian and Zach as they clear the concrete foundation where Lola's cabin once stood. Their shovels scrape against it, filling the warm air with noise.

They've almost cleared the whole site after working for the past several days to dig through the rubble. Anything salvageable has been set aside on the edge of the property.

We need to clear the property so plans can be made to rebuild. I'm not going to sit and mourn like the rest of the town. Lola would want me to move on and build anew.

So that's what we're going to do.

In her memory.

"You just gonna stand and gawp?" Zach yells.

Propping a hand over my eyes to shield the sun, I smile back. "Basically, yeah."

Both of them are working with their shirts off and jeans slung low, displaying rippling muscles that carve their chests and abdominals like beams of delicious steel.

Their tans are already glowing, despite it only being Spring, and a layer of sweat covers their gorgeous bodies. My core floods with heat just watching them working.

Down, girl.

Not the time.

Ignoring the ache between my thighs that seems ever-present since I got pregnant, I refocus on the clipboard in my hand. I have a list of tasks and urgent sign-offs needed for the town today.

The town is hard at work preparing for the season's transition. Summer crops are being planted while the winter vegetables are being harvested and prepared for cold storage.

Materials need to be ordered for the new cabin build, and plans have to be authorised before construction can begin. Albie is working on the paperwork and permits.

"Willow!" Aalia walks over to me from the town square. "There's a leak in the schoolhouse. Water everywhere."

"Great," I groan. "Kill!"

Placing his shovel down, he jogs to us, his fuzz-covered pectorals bouncing with each step and making my throat tighten again. Aalia watches my reaction with a low chuckle.

"Stop drooling," she whispers.

"I am not."

"You could have fooled me."

"Just checking out what's mine."

"So you should," she jokes.

"Yeah?" Killian stops in front of us.

I quickly wipe the grin from my face. "There's a leak in the schoolhouse. Can you get someone to take a look?"

Nodding, he yells over his shoulder for Zach. "Kid, go take a look at this leak."

Zach pouts. "Why is that my job?"

"Because I fucking said so, alright?"

"Dickhead," he cusses.

Complaining under his breath, Zach ditches his shovel and throws his t-shirt back on. Now it's my turn to pout. He disappears with Aalia to head over to the schoolhouse.

Killian slings an arm around my waist. "How are you feeling?"

I stretch onto my tiptoes to kiss him. "Fine."

"Tired? Sore? You should go and rest."

"I'm okay, Kill. You need to start taking my word for it."

"Never." He kisses me again, lingering for a moment. "Shall we talk about what you want this new cabin to look like?"

"Are we planning to live in it?"

He shrugs. "We need more space. This would be a good opportunity to build it exactly how we want it."

Holding my hand tight, he leads me onto the concrete. We walk through the ash piles together, trying to imagine the invisible walls and floors where Lola's home once was.

"I'd like an open plan kitchen and living room this time." I point towards the back where it used to be. "We could have a big, open space. Nice and airy."

Killian nods thoughtfully. "Should be easy enough to do. We'll need room for people to come over too."

"What about the sleeping arrangements?"

He hesitates. "Do you mean whether we should have separate rooms or not?"

"Yes. What's the plan there?"

Walking around the space, he looks up, his eyes moving as he imagines the beams of wood and steel that will build the new, modern cabin.

"I think separate bedrooms is a good idea. We still need our own personal space sometimes. But we could build one big room for nights when we all want to be together."

Glancing around, I envision the layout and nod. "That could work."

"The baby's room will go here." Killian's hand waves through the air. "And another here."

Shock floods my system.

"What? Another?" I splutter.

He shoots me a smirk. "You think I won't stick another one in your belly at the first opportunity? You're lucky I'm not trying to do it right now."

Stunned, I can't formulate a response beyond semi-hysterical laughter. "Kill! I haven't even had this baby yet!"

Sauntering over to me, he holds my hips and traps me against his bare barrel chest. Sweat clings to his muscles.

"But you look so fucking sexy like this. I can't help but feel sad, knowing it's going to be over in a few months. I love knowing that my baby is growing inside of you."

Delicious warmth pulses through me again, hot and heady. His caveman-like behaviour is both ridiculous and a huge turn on.

"Okay, then. Another baby room... apparently."

"Don't sound so surprised," he snickers. "The others are totally on board."

"Wait, you guys have *talked* about this? Since when?"

Tapping his nose with a quirked eyebrow, he releases me and resumes striding around the space. I have to take a moment to cool off before I actually jump his bones in public.

"I want a bigger garden this time." He waves towards the green space around us. "The little ones will need room to play and run around."

"We could extend in that direction, where the vegetable patch used to be."

Killian studies the strip of scorched earth, blackened and dead. He nods to himself.

"That should be big enough."

We spend another half an hour walking around, discussing and brainstorming ideas. By the time Albie interrupts us with some more papers for me to sign, we've mapped out the whole house.

"Got things figured out?" he asks.

"I think so."

"Your Grams would be happy to know you guys will live here and make some new memories." He nods towards the blackened concrete. "Especially after what happened."

"We need some new, good memories to move on from all this."

"Exactly." He smiles for what feels like the first time in weeks.

After taking back the signed paperwork, Albie climbs in his truck to return home. I don't know what I would've done without him in recent weeks, taking care of business and showing me the ropes.

Inheriting the town has been a huge learning curve, but the responsibility feels weirdly good. This is my home, and knowing that everyone stands behind me gives me strength to run it right.

"Why haven't we heard from Ethan yet?" Killian wonders.

"I don't know, Kill."

"What's taking them so long?"

"Ethan arrived in Mexico and Warner in the States yesterday, so we should hear anytime. I think Ethan was preparing to make a move today."

"He better fucking call."

"And he will. We're trusting him, remember?"

"Right," Killian echoes in an unhappy bark.

Circling his wrist, I pull him back into my embrace. He almost has to fold himself in half so that I can hug him as I run a hand over his messy ponytail, smoothing the flyaways.

"This is the closest we've gotten in months, Kill. I'm trying really hard to have a little faith here. I need you to do the same."

"Faith?" he laughs bitterly.

I smack his chest. "What else do we have?"

Expression growing serious, he sighs. "You're right. I'm just sick and tired of constantly worrying."

"You're going to be a father soon. Better get used to constantly worrying."

He chuckles again, this time with a real smile. "I still can't believe I'm lucky enough to be having this kid with you."

Kissing him in an attempt to communicate all the words I can't get into his thick skull, I let my lips part, our tongues dancing together. It doesn't matter who sees us. I need him to taste my certainty.

"We will always have each other."

"Come hell or high water," he murmurs into my mouth.

"Exactly. I love you, Kill."

"Fuck, baby." He rests his forehead against mine. "I love you so much it hurts. I never thought I was capable of it until you came bursting into our lives, and it all went to hell."

"Hell in a good way?" I giggle.

He pecks my nose. "The best kind of hell."

"Good."

Separating before someone wolf-whistles at us, we hold hands among ashes and lost memories, both determined to create something new. Something wonderful. Our future… together.

"I should check on that leak." He groans in annoyance. "Zach will only fuck up the repair job if I'm not there to supervise."

"Lost faith already?"

"Fuck faith," he answers drily.

Stifling a laugh, I let him lead me over to the schoolhouse. Arianna is playing outside with the others on her lunch break, giving me a wave as we pass.

Inside, Zach is on his hands and knees beneath a table, inspecting a giant puddle. His head lifts and smacks into the table when he hears us approaching.

"Shit." He rubs his head.

Killian barks a laugh. "Any luck, kid?"

"I don't have a bloody clue. Something's leaking."

"Thanks for the evaluation, Einstein."

"You're so welcome. I put a lot of thought into that."

Killian rolls his eyes. "Clearly. Move out of the way."

Joining him on the floor, Killian sets to work, and I trail off to join Rachel at the front of the room. She's sorting through dried artwork and munching on her sandwich at the same time.

"Do that pair have half a brain between them?" she asks with a short laugh.

"I wouldn't hold out much hope. They're staring at a puddle of water right now."

Giggling to ourselves, she pulls out a giant sheet of paper and hands it to me. On it is a painting of a butterfly, perfectly matching the sculpture that Micah carved for Arianna last year.

"This is Ari's painting," Rachel announces happily. "She's got a real knack for it."

"Wow. This is good. Micah's been doing lots of art with her recently. She finds it calming, and it's helped with her temper tantrums a lot. She hasn't had one for weeks."

"Well, keep it up." Rachel smiles at me.

"Mind if I take this?"

"Go ahead."

Tucking the painting under my arm, panic flares in my chest when I feel my phone ringing. I make my excuses and back out of the room to answer, leaving before the guys can catch up.

"Hello?"

"Willow," Ethan greets.

Fuck. My heart hammers erratically as I step outside.

"What is it? Are you okay?"

"We're all fine," he assures me. "The raid went down a couple of hours ago. I'm sorry, but it was unsuccessful."

Disappointment punches me in the face.

"Nothing?"

"The properties were completely empty. Not even a single piece of furniture. Sanchez wasn't there. I'm sorry, sweetheart."

Gulping hard, I force a breath. "It's okay. It was a long shot."

"That isn't all. We've decided that we have enough evidence, and it's time to make a move on Mason Stevenson. We got intel saying he's currently in Miami. Warner is joining the FBI to arrest him."

"Oh my God."

The net is closing in on Mr Sanchez and his associates. Just the thought of Mason being trapped behind bars gives me an exciting thrill. He's a disgusting snake who deserves to be there.

"He'll be extradited and put on trial in England. You'll be given the opportunity to testify against him and Mario Luciano."

"T-Testify?"

Ethan's breath rattles down the line. "It's important that we don't lose these convictions."

"How would we lose them?"

"We're dealing with very powerful men who've spent decades warping the law to suit them. I want everyone to take the stand so they are locked up for the maximum sentence."

Imagining myself facing either of them makes me feel sick to my stomach. I don't want to stand in front of the world and reveal anything about my past. I'll only be judged.

"I don't know, Ethan."

"Think about it. We're asking everyone who's been interviewed by Sabre to testify. He'll be in custody by tonight."

"Okay… I'll think it over."

"Good. I have to go, but I'll call when it's done. Be safe."

The line clicks as the call ends, leaving me standing here with my heart hammering. Everything has tilted on its axis at the thought of publicly testifying against these monsters.

Elaine was right about one thing… Not everyone understands. We can't count on the world not to judge us, the victims, for our actions too. Humans always see the worst in each other.

"Willow?"

With his loose jeans and black t-shirt covered in flecks of dried paint, Micah approaches from the winding path that leads into town, carrying Killian's toolbox.

"Mi."

"You alright? What happened?"

"He wasn't there. The raid was a bust."

"Shit. I'm so sorry."

Chewing my lip, I twist my fingers together anxiously. "That isn't all. Warner and the FBI are arresting Mason tonight. He's being brought back here to be put on trial."

"Tonight?" Micah repeats, sounding as shocked as I am.

"I guess they can't risk anyone getting wind of the investigation and running now that we've raided Mr Sanchez's properties. Ethan's going to call me when it's done."

Placing the toolbox down, he pulls me into a tight hug. "Fuck, angel. That's great news."

"He's going to get what he deserves… at last."

Gripping my jawline with his hand, Micah softly kisses my lips. "It's better than nothing."

"Ethan wants me to testify against Mason and Mario during the trial."

His excitement fades. "He said that?"

"Apparently, we'll all be asked to take the stand. All the women."

Nodding, Micah runs his hands up and down my arms. I suddenly feel chilled, despite the warm weather. Talking to Sabre was terrifying enough, but getting up in front of a courtroom...

"What are you going to do?" he asks.

"I don't know. I'm scared."

"You won't be alone."

"You guys can't exactly do it for me."

"No, but all the other women will be there to support you… And us too." He sticks out his pinkie finger. "Swear on it."

Somehow managing a laugh, I take his little finger and squeeze. "You better be."

"This is your chance to confront them after all these years. You can see to it that justice is served for all the fucked up shit they've done to you all."

"I know, Mi. It's just intimidating, the thought of facing them."

"It will be, but you're a fucking badass. I know you can do it."

"A badass?" I snicker.

"You know it."

Snuggling into him, I breathe in his familiar oil-paint and sawdust scent. He smells like the studio. Our safe place. Our silence. It settles me and allows my heart rate to slow down.

"Do you realise what this means?"

"What?" I burrow into him.

"It's only a matter of time before Sanchez is caught. All of his associates are being hauled in. He's bound to be panicking, and he'll get sloppy. This is it."

Micah releases me so our eyes can meet. The certainty there astounds me. He's usually the most nervous, uncertain one of us all. But right now, he looks powerful and sure.

"This is the end of the road," he declares confidently. "We're almost there."

"And if it's not? If we can't find him?"

"Then we keep looking. None of us are going anywhere. Our future is right here in Briar Valley, regardless of Sanchez and his threats. Nothing will ever change that. We're forever."

"Forever?"

His nose nudges mine as we share a kiss.

"Forever, angel."

CHAPTER 29
WILLOW

I FOUND – AMBER RUN

"I'M NOT SURE ABOUT THIS."

Aalia clicks her tongue, standing behind me in the luxurious hotel room. She scans over my outfit with admiration in her almond eyes.

"You look perfect!"

Arianna stands on my other side, smiling widely. "You look so pretty, Mummy."

Running my hands over the loose, black material, I move to cup my swollen belly. Nothing fits anymore, and I felt underdressed in the two maternity dresses that I brought to wear.

"Why do I need to get all glammed up? It's just dinner."

Aalia laughs like she's privy to some joke that I don't get. "Sure."

"What's that supposed to mean?"

"Nothing, nothing."

We're camped out in one of Highbridge's two hotels—the nicer, more expensive one. It's the twins' birthday, and Aalia agreed to look after Arianna while we get dinner in town to celebrate.

Hyland is stationed outside with three extra men, ensuring we're as safe as can be. Despite that, I'm still nervous to go out, and the debate over my outfit hasn't helped my anxiety.

"Hair up or down?"

"Definitely down," Aalia decides. "It goes with the dress."

We settled on a black number, the light, chiffon fabric accentuating my curves. It has capped sleeves and lace detailing, matching the low pair of heels I borrowed from Miranda for the occasion.

Fluffing my loose curls, I add a swipe of pale pink lipstick and call it quits. I've gotten far too used to wearing oversized tees stolen from the guys and stretchy yoga pants.

"Okay, I think I'm ready."

Arianna pouts, flopping on the giant hotel bed in her pyjamas. "It's not fair. I want to come."

"I'm sorry, Ari. Not this time. Mummy's going out to celebrate the twins' birthday."

"But I want to celebrate as well!"

"I know, kiddo."

Pulling her into a cuddle, I smooth her hair. Leaving her behind after the fire wasn't an option. Two of Hyland's men are staying behind to guard the hotel room.

"Be good, baby." I kiss the top of her head. "You can order whatever you want to eat with Aalia, okay?"

That causes her to finally smile.

"Anything?"

I pass her the room service menu. "Go for it."

"Even ice cream?"

"Especially ice cream!"

She dives into the menu with an excited cry, flipping straight to the dessert section. Aalia smothers a laugh.

"She'll be no trouble, Willow. Stop worrying."

After pulling Aalia into a hug, I blow them both kisses and grab my handbag. There's a knock at the door, signalling the guys' arrival. Aalia opens it to reveal the three most gorgeous humans on the whole planet.

"Damn," I comment breathlessly.

Micah's hand lowers from the door. "Hi."

He's cleaned up, slicking his hair back to reveal his defined cheekbones and nose ring. His usual paint-splattered clothes are gone, replaced with plain black jeans and a polo shirt.

Next to him, Zach looks almost identical, aside from his sky-blue dress shirt hanging untucked from his jeans and lack of nose ring. He's also cleaned up, shaving and trimming his hair a little from hanging over his vibrant green eyes.

But Killian is the biggest difference. I'm used to seeing him in hole-filled clothing that's streaked in dirt, but with his hair down, dressed in a fresh pair of blue jeans and a tight black t-shirt that reveals his biceps, he looks good enough to eat.

"Drooling again." Zach smirks.

I click my mouth shut. "Sorry. Little hard not to."

"Like what you see?" Killian chuckles.

"You guys clean up well."

Micah holds out a hand for me. "You look so incredible, Willow."

"Thanks, Mi."

Giving him a little twirl to show off the flowing fabric, I take his hand, a shiver rolling down my spine as he kisses my knuckles. Zach and Killian kiss a cheek each, and it feels like I'm on fire beneath all their touches.

"Ready to go?" Killian rumbles in a low voice.

"Can't we blow off dinner and go to your room instead?"

He runs a finger over my bottom lip. "As tempting as that sounds, we have a reservation. Let's go."

"Buzzkill," I mutter.

Leaving the hotel with Hyland's men following in a tight, armed formation, we walk across the street. The evening air is pleasantly warm, and I'm toasty tucked between the twins' walls of muscle.

Stopping outside a small bistro lit by candlelight that leaks through the framed windows, Killian gestures for me to go ahead. I keep hold of the twins and head inside the quiet space.

It's the most perfect restaurant. The place only has a few tables, and it's completely empty apart from us. We're led to a circular table in the middle surrounded by candles and fresh flowers.

"This is so romantic."

Zach pulls out my chair for me. "Only the best for you, babe."

"It's your birthday we're celebrating. Not mine."

Killian takes his seat. "We haven't exactly had much opportunity to take you on dates before, so we're making the most of it."

Stomach alight with butterflies, I sit down between the twins and directly opposite Killian. The waitress comes to bring us a bottle of water and menus before leaving us alone again.

"Did you guys book the entire restaurant?"

Micah jerks a finger outside. "They insisted."

Hyland and his men are stationed at the restaurant's entrance, giving us some privacy.

"So what's with the fancy spread?" I gesture around.

"What? We can't spoil our girl?" Killian laughs.

"Something's going on. You're acting strange and... happy."

"Being happy is strange now?"

Now it's my turn to laugh.

"What do we have to be happy about right now?"

Zach takes my hand on top of the table. "Everything."

Micah nods in agreement. "We're making the most of the good and ignoring the bad tonight. That's the deal."

When the waitress returns to offer us a wine list, the guys all refuse.

"You can drink if you want. I don't mind."

"Not without you," Killian declines.

After pouring us all water instead, he braces his elbows on the table then stares intently at me. I shiver beneath his attention. There's something in his eyes tonight—an excited, burning passion.

"So," I begin. "Shall we toast?"

All lifting our water glasses, we clink them together.

"Happy Birthday." Killian lifts his glass toward the twins.

Both shrug him off.

"Happy Birthday," I echo.

Obviously, neither are comfortable with celebrating the day. Knowing the absence they must feel at their father's loss, I can empathise. Celebrating without Lola here feels hollow now.

Anticipation fills the air as we order food. Something's up. The twins are both jittery and seem on-edge, while Killian's got the smouldering stare nailed tonight.

"So what do you guys want for your birthday? I haven't gotten you anything."

"I know what I want." Zach winks at me.

"Me too," Micah adds.

"And what's that?"

Reaching across the table to take my folded hands into his, Killian brushes my knuckles with his thumbs. "Willow, there's a reason we asked you here tonight."

"I figured as much. What's going on?"

"It's nothing bad," Zach rushes to assure me, reading my trepidation. "But first, we should tell you the whole story."

"The whole story?"

Micah rests a hand on my leg beneath the table. "Before you left Briar Valley, we made a decision."

"A big one." Zach fiddles with his napkin. "We decided that we wanted our family, regardless of whatever life throws at us. Regardless of whether it meant we had to share you."

My chest constricts. "Guys, you're kinda freaking me out right now."

"No!" Killian intervenes. "Look, before you left we talked and realised that we all wanted forever with you, and we were willing to do whatever to make that happen."

My heart stops dead in my chest. I glance between them all, too terrified to ask if they're going where I think they are with this.

"We know that we're not perfect." Zach laughs nervously. "And things haven't been easy for us, but this right here is all that matters. Us. Together."

"And we don't want anything to jeopardise that ever again," Micah says with a small, shy smile. "We need to know that it will always be us at the end of every single day."

"And it will be."

"We know." Killian waggles his eyebrows. "We're going to make sure of it."

All standing up, Zach pulls my chair out so they can crowd around me. I forget how to breathe as one by one, they drop down on one knee, the candlelight flickering off their matching excited expressions.

"Oh my God," I squeak.

"Babe, I've loved you since the moment we met," Zach confesses. "You were all bruised and terrified, but I still thought you were the most beautiful, incredible woman I'd ever seen in my life."

"And I was too scared to even speak to you." Micah laughs at himself. "You thought I was Zach, but I didn't care. I wanted to see you again from that very first time. I was fascinated."

"And when you lied to me about your name, I was secretly impressed." Killian reaches into the pocket of his jeans. "You had the brains and courage to protect yourself, no matter what I said."

Pulling out a small, red, velvet ring box, he holds it in his huge hands and pops the lid. Inside is the most stunning diamond ring with an oval stone, surrounded by sparkling circles of jade on a white gold band.

Everything narrows to a snapshot. The restaurant falls away. The staff watching. Our security posted outside. Danger and violence following us at every turn. None of it matters as I stare at the ring.

"This belonged to my mother," Killian explains. "I took it out of the safe the day you left. We made a pact to propose to you, but then you were gone. I get it now, though. I know why it had to happen."

"We needed to see life without you in it." Micah looks sad for a brief moment. "That pain was necessary to make us see the truth, because we wouldn't have had the strength then to survive this."

"We had to lose you," Zach finishes. "To fight for our fucking lives to get you back, over and over, every time the world takes you away from us. And we'll spend the rest of our lives doing that."

My cheeks are soaked with hot, salty tears that stream over my skin. I have no idea what to say. That festering wound is still there—the guilt for what I did to them.

Hearing their confessions has brought it all back. I hurt them. Us. Our family and all that I hold dear in this life. We lost so much time because of my own fear.

But somehow, despite all the odds, we've managed to hold it together. Throughout fires, threats, violence and pain, it's still us. And it always will be. No matter what happens, nothing will ever tear us apart again.

"So, Willow..." Killian pinches the ring between his thick fingers. "Will you marry us?"

Mouth flopping open, I cover it with my hands to hold back a choked sob. All I can do is nod my head and look between all three of them in utter disbelief.

"You're sure?"

Zach scoffs. "You really think we'd do this if we weren't sure?"

"But... my divorce isn't even final yet..."

"We don't care about that." Micah grips my knee. "All we care about is you. Nothing else matters right now."

With a balloon of hope exploding behind my ribcage, I fight back a squeal. "Then... yes!"

Killian slides the ring onto my left hand, and I stare at the huge, twinkling diamond in shock. It's the most stunning thing I've ever seen, completely unique and delicate.

I'm crushed into Killian's chest first as he seals his mouth on mine, hot and demanding. We kiss like there's no audience, both dancing with the other in a self-destructive battle of passion.

When someone clears their throat, the twins manage to peel him away from me and launch their own attack. Mouths meet and fingers entwine as I'm trapped between them, their lips trailing over my throat and lips.

"How long have you been sitting on that ring?" I choke out.

Killian shrugs. "Since you left. We just needed to find the right time to tell you how we felt."

"I'm so sorry," I rush out. "I can't imagine how much it hurt to find me gone after you'd decided to do this."

"No apologies." Zach kisses me again. "We don't need them anymore. All we need is you."

"You've got me, Zachariah."

"Good." He nips at my chin.

"And you've got us," Micah says assuredly.

With all three of them sandwiching me in, I believe it. I've got them forever, no matter what Mr Sanchez does to us. It doesn't matter. Let him burn our whole lives down if that's what it takes.

We'll still have each other.

He can't take that away.

———

Zach slams my back into the hotel door, his mouth devouring mine. I can barely breathe through the intense attack as his lips consume mine in a frenzy.

Watching us both with matching lust-filled expressions, Killian and Micah patiently wait their turn. I'm at their collective mercy tonight after blowing off dinner early to return to the hotel.

"Fuck, babe," Zach growls into my lips. "I want you so bad."

"Open the door," I command.

"Yes, ma'am."

Scanning the key card, he walks me backwards into the low-lit room. There are two huge king-sized beds in the room, sat amidst opulence and thick, dark blue carpets that warm the space.

Still steering me with his hands on my hips, Zach's mouth lands back on mine, hot and heavy. His tongue pushes past my lips to meet mine in an unapologetic tangle.

The backs of my thighs hit the mattress, and I fall back onto the closest bed. Zach covers my body with his, twisting to the side to avoid squishing my midsection in the process.

With his hard muscles pressing up against me, rivulets of desire coil through me, leaving me wet and breathless. Even the slightest of touches is a huge turn on.

"I want to fuck you until you beg me to stop because you can't possibly come anymore," he says into my lips. "How does that sound?"

"Like an empty promise until you prove it."

"Oh, I'll prove it, babe."

"You better."

Lips moving to skate along my jawline, he kisses the slope of my throat, his teeth nipping my over-sensitised skin. Each nibble causes my heart to explode behind my rib cage as lust takes over.

Zach's head moves lower, dipping over my sternum as he cups my breast through my dress. My nipples are already rock-hard with anticipation. I want his mouth wrapped around one.

"This is a sexy little dress you're wearing," he hums, ignoring the other two taking seats nearby. "I'm fighting the urge to rip it off."

"It's Aalia's, so I wouldn't if I were you."

"Dammit."

He tugs me up to pull the zipper at the back of my neck. When he can't undo it, Micah leans over from his perch nearby to help his twin unzip me.

"Thanks, little brother."

"Hurry up," Micah complains. "Some of us are impatiently waiting for our turn too."

"Nothing could convince me to rush this."

"Son of a bitch," Killian curses.

Ignoring him, Zach eases the dress off my shoulders, pulling the top half down to unveil my bra. He makes short work of tearing it off to reveal my bigger, heavier breasts. His eyes are wide with satisfaction.

"You're so fucking gorgeous, babe."

"Zach," I whine. "Please touch me."

Taking a mound in each hand, he secures his mouth to my nipple, biting and torturing the rosy bud. I arch my back, pushing my chest farther into his face as I seek more friction.

Feeling the bed dip with someone moving, I open my eyes to watch Micah circle the pair of us. He moves to stand at the edge of the mattress where he pulls off my heels, pushing my bare legs apart.

"I can't wait." He flashes a dirty smirk. "I want to taste this pretty little cunt of mine."

"Yours?" I gasp.

"You're going to be my wife, aren't you?"

Kneeling on the hotel carpet, he leaves Zach to his ministrations as he pushes my dress farther up my legs. I writhe on the bed as Micah slowly peels my panties off, exposing my soaked core.

With his twin still lavishing my nipple and peppering kisses across my chest, Micah's head moves between my thighs. The moment his mouth meets my pussy, I cry out in pleasure.

"That's it, baby," Killian praises, standing over us to watch the show. "We're all going to fuck your sweet pussy tonight."

Micah's mouth is a teasing, hot presence against my clit as his tongue flicks through my folds. When his finger meets my bundle of nerves and circles, I can't suppress moaning loudly again.

Zach's hand moves to grip my chin tight. "Do you like that, babe? My twin eating your wet cunt while I play with your gorgeous tits?"

"Yes," I groan.

"How much?"

Pinching my nipple, he lightly twists, sending a burst of deliciously sweet pain through my nervous system.

"I like it a lot." I try to writhe to relieve the pressure, but Micah's head between my legs keeps me trapped.

"God, angel," Micah hums from beneath my bunched-up dress. "You're so sweet, gorgeous girl. Such a perfect, pretty pussy."

His hot, dirty mouth only turns me on even more. I moan as he dives back in for more, lapping at my core with long, enthusiastic licks. Killian unzips his jeans above us and frees his cock.

He watches me closely while beginning to stroke his length, a dark, dangerous fire burning in low embers in the depths of his irises. His cock strains in his hand, long and painfully hard.

"Jesus," he groans. "I cannot wait to bury myself inside of you, princess. Even with these two knuckleheads watching us fuck."

Throwing my head back, I hold his eye contact as bliss washes over me. The beginning sparks of an orgasm are burning in my veins, intensified by his attention on me.

Micah slides a finger through my folds to moisten it then pushes it deep into my slit. The pressure is exquisite, stretching my walls and adding to the acute sense of impending implosion.

He begins to move, fucking me with his hand and only stopping to swipe his thumb over my clit. Zach's mouth lands back on mine, swallowing every moan escaping my lips.

"Make her come," Killian orders them. "She's on the verge."

"Such a bossy bastard," Zach whispers, his teeth nipping my bottom lip. "Come on, babe. Give it up for us."

Sliding a second finger deep into me, Micah follows his brother's words with several fast pumps, pushing me right over the edge. I scream out his name, my legs tightening around his head.

It hits me in long, slow peaks of burning bliss. My body is full of heat, tingling and filling my extremities. As I come down from the high, I find Micah sitting up from between my legs.

"That was so hot." He licks his lips.

Zach glances down at his twin. "Seconded."

"Alright." Killian kicks off his jeans, patience spent. "Come here, baby. I'm done watching this shit. I want you to sit on my cock."

"Hey," Zach protests.

"Shut up, kid. She was mine first. Get in line."

Moving out of the way to let his cousin step in, Micah sits down on the bed next to Zach. I let Killian pull me up, wrapping my legs around his waist as I'm lifted into his arms.

He ditches his boxers and walks me across the room to sit down on the other bed, so I'm planted on his lap. His length is brushing right up against my slit, an inch from heaven.

"You okay on top?" he checks. "I don't want to hurt you."

"I'm good, Kill."

Pulling my dress over my head, I'm naked and trembling all over with need. Killian rests back, his hands braced on the bed, letting me take full control of the moment while the other two watch on.

I reach between us to fist his length, stroking it in the palm of my hand. His eyes roll back in his head as I line it up with my entrance and waste no time sinking down until he's filling me to the absolute brim.

"Goddammit," he hisses.

Lifting myself, I sink back down so he fills me again, loving the overwhelming pressure of his cock stretching me wide.

"Do you like it when I ride you?" I tease.

His hands grip my hips tight. "Fuck yeah, baby. You look so powerful on top of me like the queen you are."

Using the momentum his hands provide, I begin to move a little faster, his hips shifting upward to push his shaft deeper inside of me. The twins both watch with rapt attention, both breathing hard.

Killian moves us at a slow, steady pace, rutting into me while letting me control our movements. I shift and writhe on his lap, seeking the perfect angle to make my body sing.

When his cock brushes the hidden, sweet spot buried deep inside of me, I throw my head back and cry out. He props himself up then buries his face in my chest to lavish my tits with his tongue, moving from one breast to the other.

"Are you going to coat my cock in your sweet juices, baby?"

"Yes," I keen.

"Show me, gorgeous."

Steadily increasing his pace, he thrusts up into me until we're colliding in a hard, fast tangle of sweat and gasping. I can see Micah pulling his length from his jeans out of the corner of my eye as he begins to stroke himself.

Just seeing him pleasuring himself at the sight of us fucking is enough to finish me off. I cry through another climax, my vision dimming with the cloud of ecstasy that invades my extremities.

"Killian!"

He roars through his own release, the warmth of his come filling me up and spilling over. I slump down onto him, both of us fighting to catch our breath.

His chest vibrates with a chuckle. "Think you're done? I don't think so, dirty girl."

A pair of hands land on my hips and easily lift me. I fly through the air, ending up spooned in Zach's arms in a fireman's hold. He plants a kiss on my forehead while walking me back over to the other bed.

"We waited our turn," he quips. "Now you're ours."

Placing me down on the bed on my hands and knees, he settles behind me, his hand cracking against my ass in the perfect, spine-tingling spank.

Sliding off his clothes while I watch over my shoulder, he strokes his huge cock. I need it inside me. I want to be filled to the brim with his length. Zach obliges my frantic panting by sliding deep into my cunt.

"God!" I cry out.

"I'll take it," he jokes. "You want me to be your god, baby girl? It's a done deal."

Moving to stand in front of me, Micah's fisting his length at the perfect height to press it against my closed lips. I eagerly open up, taking his length deep into my mouth and bobbing on it.

With Zach fucking me from behind and Micah's dick deep in my mouth, I'm overwhelmed. My pussy quivers as yet another orgasm threatens. They've barely touched me, and I'm already done for.

Killian watches the entire thing, propped up on his elbow and studying our tangle with contentment. No matter what he says, he loves sharing me like this with his family.

"She's so wet now," Zach marvels. "I love fucking this sweet cunt after my cousin's loosened you up, pretty girl. Is that fucked up of me?"

I can't answer around a mouthful of his twin's dick. All of this is a little bit fucked up, but none of us are complaining. This is just how we work, regardless of what the outside world may think of this arrangement.

Cupping a handful of Micah's balls, I gently squeeze, sucking him deeper into my throat through hollowed-out cheeks. He groans, gripping my hair so tight it's almost painful.

Zach spanks me again, still moving at a relentless pace. From this position, there's no pressure on my belly, so we're free to play as rough as we like.

I know he loves seeing me like this—pregnant and full of his cock. They all do. Their mark of possession is growing inside of me, and nothing can ever take that away.

"Such a perfect princess," Zach praises, spanking me again.

Reaching around my waist, he finds my clit and tweaks it, sending another jolt up my spine. My teeth graze against Micah's shaft, and he grunts, fisting my hair tighter.

"Think my twin's getting close," Zach whispers into my ear from behind. "Shall we give him a turn?"

Pulling himself out of my mouth, Micah fists his length and pumps it. "Yes. You should."

Snickering to himself, Zach stills his movements before sliding out of my pussy. The sudden loss is painful, so I whine, needing to be filled again. He wastes no time flipping me over on the bed.

My feet land back on the thick hotel carpet so I'm facing Zach this time, bent over with my ass raised high.

"Mi," I whine.

"I'm here, angel."

Soothing my sore ass cheek with a stroke, I feel his warmth at my back. My hands are on Zach's thighs as he shifts down, giving me access to the glistening length of his cock.

"You going to let me ride your mouth?" He grins down at me.

"Maybe," I sass.

"Maybe?"

"You heard me."

Winking at him, I take his dick in my hand and begin to work it up and down. He lays down, dropping his head to the mattress, enjoying the pressure of my hand gripping his erection.

At the same time, Micah pushes the tip of his cock into my entrance, moving teasingly slow. I push back against him to fill myself up, unable to wait a second longer to feel him inside me.

"Shit," he hisses. "You're so tight, angel."

Kissing around Zach's length, I drag my tongue up the side of his shaft. "Your twin likes my pussy."

Zach bursts into laughter. "Obviously, babe."

"That doesn't make you jealous?"

"If you don't suck my cock in a moment like the dirty little slut I know you are, I may just get jealous."

Searing with need, I lick my way up to the tip of his dick then take it into my mouth. His growl of pleasure gives me so much satisfaction. I feel so powerful when I'm pleasuring them.

"That's it," Micah encourages as he begins to move. "You're going to be a hell of a wife if you keep this up, Willow."

Wife.

I never thought that word would make me feel so warm and loved. I'm going to be a wife and a mother. I've gotten everything I ever wanted.

To be loved.

To belong.

To be someone's whole world.

Surrounded by the men I love, I lose myself to the moment, revelling in explosions of blissful agony. Micah's moving fast behind me, chasing his own climax.

With yet another orgasm about to take over again, I move faster on Zach's dick, determined to taste the salty tang of his come on my tongue. His erection jerks in my mouth before he explodes.

"Fuck, babe!"

Hot come pours down my throat in a long spurt. I obediently swallow before releasing his cock and licking my lips so he can watch.

"You're incredible." He cups my cheek in awe.

Micah's fingers dig into my hips. "I'm gonna come."

His climax hits at the same time as mine. We collide—falling apart together, both shattering into spectacular pieces with perfect synchronicity, his seed adding to the warmth filling me.

I grip the bed sheets as I'm wracked by so much pleasure, it makes my legs weak. After several orgasms, I'm suddenly too exhausted to hold myself up.

Micah catches me before I drop. "I've got you, angel."

I'm lifted up, and I curl up into Zach's side, feeling the warmth of Micah's body settling behind me. Killian joins us on the bed, adding to the dog pile, his boxers now replaced.

"That was an interesting show," he comments.

"Shut up," Zach claps back.

"I'll die a happy man if I never have to see your pasty backside again for the rest of my life, kid."

"No promises."

"I can't believe I'm marrying you idiots." I laugh to myself. "What the hell am I thinking? Two divorces?"

Killian snorts. "It's hilarious that you think we'd let you divorce us."

Micah chuckles. "Hysterical, actually."

"You're all morons." I let my eyes slide shut. "But… you're my morons. Forever."

Killian kisses the top of my head. "You damn well know it."

CHAPTER 30
ZACH

FOREVER – MUMFORD & SONS

"CONGRATULATIONS!"

Clinking our champagne glasses together, we all knock back the gross, bubbly liquid, aside from Willow and Micah. Rachel and Miranda are drinking with Doc, Ryder, Albie and the rest of us.

Willow's cabin is packed to the rafters with our family, all gathered to celebrate the big news. Arianna has been bouncing off the ceiling all day since we told her about the engagement.

"This is so exciting," Ryder exclaims. "I'm going to be a best man!"

"Bit of a bold assumption," I joke.

He cuts me a glare. "Like you'd ask anyone else. Unless you want me to be a bridesmaid, Willow? I look killer in a dress."

Giggling, she sips her orange juice. "I think we have that front covered, thanks, Ry. At this rate, half of Briar Valley will be arguing over who's doing what in our wedding."

"When's the big day?" Albie takes a seat on the sofa.

"Not for a while." Willow rubs a hand over her protruding belly. "We need this one to come along first, and there's still the divorce to finalise."

"Your Grams would be so proud," Doc says wistfully. "She always loved an occasion to celebrate."

The room quietens as we feel her absence, but Willow's smile doesn't falter. She knows that Lola is still here with us, especially in these moments. All of us can feel her here, celebrating with us.

"You should set a date!" Aalia insists.

"No, no." Willow shuts her down. "Not until all of this is over."

Moving to the living room, we all take seats as Killian remains in the kitchen, cooking up a storm. He offered to cover Sunday dinner for everyone, taking over Grams's old post.

There's a knock at the door before Walker pokes his head in. "Mind if I join you? The kids are playing with Johan outside."

"I want to go!" Arianna squeals.

She races off to join the others, rushing past Walker as he slips inside to join us. He plants a kiss on Aalia's lips before accepting the beer that Albie offers him.

"Congrats, guys," he says to all of us.

Willow gives him a bright smile. "Thanks, Walker."

"Anything else you want to spring on us while you're here? Another baby? Extra puppy?"

We all share a laugh.

"I guess we're doing life a bit fast at the minute," Micah worries.

I clap him on the shoulder. "Making up for lost time."

He nods. "Exactly."

Willow watches us both with a grin. I know she loves it when we're getting along and not driving each other insane. After last night, I can't imagine ever being unhappy again.

She's ours. Forever. Part of me is still shocked that she said yes. There was still a hint of doubt, despite Killian's self-assuredness that this was the right time to take that leap, given recent events.

"I heard you're rebuilding the cabin," Walker says conversationally. "I was wondering if you needed any help?"

Killian halts with a saucepan in hand. "Yeah?"

"I've done my fair share of tiling and plastering over the years if you need an extra pair of hands. I'd like to be useful."

Aalia kisses his cheek. "He's been wanting a job to do ever since arriving in Briar Valley."

Nodding, Killian sets the saucepan under the tap and fills it with water. "You can start Monday. We need all the help we can get."

The smile that fills Walker's face is radiant. He's a good guy. None of us know him well as he keeps his cards close to his chest, but he's looked after Aalia well enough and treats her right.

"What about me?" I pout.

Killian narrows his eyes. "Didn't I fire you already?"

"Like ten million times over the years. I don't tend to pay attention. Where do you want me, boss?"

"As far away as possible," he says under his breath before ducking to look in the oven and check the roast chicken.

I flip off the back of his head. He'll only break my finger if he catches me. Pouring more champagne for everyone, Micah refills his glass with orange juice then fixes Willow's next. She gives him an appreciative kiss on the lips.

"Not drinking?" Albie asks him.

Micah shakes his head. "Not anymore. I've been dry for almost eight weeks now."

Everyone congratulates him, and Micah turns bright-pink. I elbow my twin in the ribs. I'm secretly so relieved, it barrels me over. He's been like a new man recently.

"Going back to the house," I redirect. "We only have a few more months before the little spud arrives. Will it be done in time?"

"Little spud?" Willow repeats, her brows furrowed. "Are you comparing our baby to a potato?"

"Uh… maybe?"

It's her turn to flip me off.

"That's you out of this confusing, co-parenting quadrilateral."

Killian barks out a laugh from the kitchen. "Zach doesn't even know what a quadrilateral is. Right, kid?"

"Asshole. I know what it is."

Halting his cooking, he cocks an eyebrow. "Humour me, then."

"It's a… um, fuck," I stumble, my brows knitting together. "An equation? Or is it a fraction? Some maths bullshit, I think. No, it's a shape. Shit. That can't be right."

Everyone bursts into raucous laughter. I fight the urge to soak them all in shitty, over-priced champagne. Even if Willow would kill me.

"Hey! I have brains!"

"Of course, you do," Willow coos as she blows me a kiss. "We're only kidding, Zachariah."

"For the record, it's a four-sided shape," Micah whispers. "Or a confusing as fuck parenting square."

I snap my fingers. "Totally knew that."

"How does that actually work?" Aalia wonders. "The parenting, I mean. All of you."

We shake our heads.

"I guess we'll figure it out as we go along." Willow worries her bottom lip. "We can't screw it up that badly, surely?"

Micah squeezes her thigh from next to her on the sofa. "Of course, we won't. This kid's gonna be just fine."

"And you've got the whole town to help fuck them up even more." Ryder chortles.

"Like we need any more help," Killian rumbles.

Sliding a hand beneath her belly to manoeuvre herself up, Willow joins him in the kitchen to help with dinner. We all drink and chat until the food is ready, and Killian calls us to the table.

Gathering around the cramped space, we all manage to sit down. Willow rolls her eyes when Killian takes the heavier dishes from her and gives her a light bowl of veggies to carry instead.

"Sit," he orders gruffly.

"Yes, sir," she snarks back.

He swats her on the behind. "I mean it."

With everyone sitting down and the table full of food, we take a moment to toast the one person missing from the table before diving in. I halt, a forkful of food halfway up to my mouth.

I can remember when this table was empty. Not even Killian and I made it to sit down with each other, and Micah was incapable of leaving his studio for even a breath of fresh air.

Our lives have changed so much, and it's all down to her. Willow. Our forever. Our soon-to-be wife. Saying those words, even internally, gives me a little thrill. I love seeing our aunt's ring on her finger.

After dinner, I flip a coin with Micah over who gets the honour of washing up. Losing the bet, it falls to me and Ryder to clear the table while everyone else relaxes in the living room.

We get the table emptied before turning to the washing up. It's a mountainous pile next to the sink. I'm convinced Killian made an extra mess for his own amusement.

"You speak to Ethan?" I ask quietly.

Ryder drops his voice. "He arrived home a couple of days ago. They arrested Mason yesterday, and he's on his way back to England."

"That's what I heard when he called this morning to update us all. Willow seemed to take the news well."

"She's going to have to face him, you know." Ryder fills the sink with soapy water. "Mason is as much a part of her past as that asshole Sanchez is."

"I don't want her within a hundred miles of him, Ry."

"Keeping her locked away from this won't help. If she doesn't face her demons, they'll haunt her forever. He'll go on trial soon, and she'll be called to give evidence against him and that other wanker."

Just the mention of Mario Luciano, the motherfucker who sold my girl to

Sanchez, causes me to drop a plate into the sink so hard, it clatters loudly. Ryder jumps and slops water everywhere.

"Chill out, Zach."

"Chill out?" I hiss.

"Yes!"

"You want us to put our wife in a room with the men who exploited her as a sixteen-year-old child. Excuse me if I'm not feeling too fucking calm about that."

"Not your wife yet, mate."

Grabbing the carving knife, I mime slicing his head off. "Keep going. I dare you."

He stifles a laugh. "I'm just saying."

"Well, don't." I drop the knife into the sink that's now full of bubbles.

"If Willow's on board with testifying publicly, then there isn't much you can do to stop her. Better get your head around that fact."

Turning to slide the next stack of dishes over to him, I gulp down a bubble of fear. Willow's doing good right now, despite all the odds. I'd hate anything to set her progress back.

But if this will ultimately give her the healing that she needs, who am I to deny her that? She deserves the chance of a happy, healthy future, without all this trauma weighing her down.

This may be how she gets that.

We have to let her try.

"I hate this shit so much."

"I know." Ryder bumps me with his shoulder. "If it's any consolation, Ethan's confident that Mason will squeal on Sanchez and reveal something we can use. That slimy fuck is desperate to save his own backside."

"What about the others they arrested?"

"Two other players are being brought in by the FBI as we speak. I reckon they'll all turn on him sooner rather than later. Loyalty doesn't run that deep in people like this."

I nod to myself. Ryder is right. The net has closed in on Sanchez even more, and his entire life is now in jeopardy. Bringing these assholes in was the right decision.

"What happens now?"

Ryder shrugs. "The Anaconda team will interrogate them all and get the information we need."

"And?"

"I don't fucking know, alright? I don't work for Sabre. Ethan can't tell me everything."

"He's your boyfriend."

"Is he?" He laughs bitterly. "I've seen him twice in the last four months. You guys speak to him more than I do. I feel like I'm in a relationship with a ghost."

Placing a clean dish in the cupboard, I rest a hand on his shoulder. "I'm sorry, Ry."

"It's not your fault."

"Have you spoken to Ethan about this?"

"What do you think?"

Scrubbing the roasting pan a little too enthusiastically, his jaw is clenched tight with tension. I feel like a complete asshole. We've been shitty friends to him, focused on our own chaos going on while Ryder's suffered for it.

"I'm thinking of leaving Briar Valley," Ryder blurts out.

"What? You're kidding?"

He shakes his head. "Long distance just isn't working anymore, and I don't want to lose Ethan. Perhaps if I move to London, we can make things work."

"You belong here with your family."

"You all have your own lives." He shakes his head. "I have nothing without Ethan. Can't you understand that?"

Making myself take a breath, I nod. "Yeah. I can."

"Then you understand why I have to do this. Albie's on board with it, and he's promised to support whatever decision I make. I have to do this for my relationship."

"Shit. This is really happening."

"I don't know when," he rushes out. "But yeah, it's happening soon. I haven't told Willow yet. I'm scared too."

"She will support you no matter what."

"I know… I just can't help but feel like I'm abandoning you all."

Ditching the dishes, I yank him into a hug. Ryder hugs me back, and I hold him there as his shoulders shake with the emotion rolling over him.

"We will support you no matter what," I whisper in his ear. "You're our brother, and all I want is for you to be happy. That's all."

"But—"

"No buts, Ry."

A breath whooshing out of his lungs, he releases me and nods. "When did you get so damn mature?"

"Can't be a kid forever, right?"

"I guess not… kid."

Hands clasped, we share a laugh then resume washing the dishes as footsteps approach. I feel Willow's arms wrap around my waist from behind, her sweet, floral scent betraying her presence.

"You look cute covered in soap suds," she murmurs.

"I always look cute, babe."

"Full of yourself much?"

"Always. You know me."

"A little too well, unfortunately."

Letting my waist go, she drops a kiss on Ryder's cheek before moving to the fridge to retrieve the orange juice. I pin him with a glare then pointedly move my eyes over to Willow.

"You've got this, right, man?"

Ryder panics, his eyes bugging out. "Uh."

"I'll leave you to finish up. Keep him company, babe."

Willow frowns at me, and I wink at her. She moves to lean against the counter, and before I leave the room, I hear Ryder splutter as he tries to figure out how to tell her the news.

Back in the living room, Killian has broken out a pack of cards and sits playing poker with Albie and Doc. I pause to scratch Demon's ears from her curled-up perch on the floor.

"What are we betting?"

Killian inspects his cards. "Who has to make the next supply run into Highbridge."

"Sweet. Deal me in."

Shuffling the cards, he hands me a stack and gestures for me to take a seat. I sit down, swallowing the rest of my abandoned champagne before inspecting my cards.

It's a couple of rounds before Willow and Ryder join us, both of their eyes red-rimmed. She gives me a small smile.

"Everything okay?" Killian asks worriedly.

"We're fine," she replies.

"Sure?"

"Go back to your game, Kill."

Grumbling, he resumes staring at his cards. Retaking her seat next to Micah on the sofa, Willow snuggles close to him. Ryder nods at me, indicating that everything is alright.

I'm happy for him, even if the thought of losing him hurts. His relationship has to take priority. This long-distance bullshit can't be easy, and Ethan's practically family at this point.

Before long, Willow has fallen asleep in Micah's lap. His eyes slide shut soon after, and I can practically feel the contentment oozing off him. He doesn't need to drink or hide anymore. His girl is all he needs.

She's all any of us need.

This right here is what we're fighting for. This crazy, imperfect life, surrounded by family and friends.

Willow gave us that.

She made us whole again.

CHAPTER 31
WILLOW

HAPPY NEVER AFTER – VIOLA

AFTER SQUIRTING the gel onto my belly, Doc lifts the wand to my skin and begins to move it around.

I lay back on the examination table and try not to feel nervous. It's just a six-month checkup. Nothing to worry about.

"How have the past few weeks been?" he asks.

"Good. My back's a little sore, but I'm mostly tired."

"That's to be expected at this stage."

"I felt the same with Arianna around six months pregnant."

Doc studies the sonogram equipment. "And what about your stress levels? I know that the recent arrests have been difficult for you. It's important that you're trying to rest and keep healthy."

"I'm doing okay, Doc. Really."

He summons a smile. "Good."

The past few weeks have passed in a blur with Arianna's recent eighth birthday and the case moving at a million miles an hour. We needed some time to decompress.

Almost half a dozen players in Sanchez's trafficking ring have been arrested and charged. I've never heard Ethan sound so happy, now that he finally has results for all their hard work.

With the investigation in full swing and arrests being made, my role has been smaller, aside from regular updates and continued security protection.

It's given me some time to rest and catch up with all the changes in our lives. Things have changed so drastically, I've needed a moment just to catch my breath and exist.

"Here we are, then."

Turning my attention to the black and white screen, my eyes prickle with tears. The baby is less of an amorphous blob on the screen and now a small, miniature human, nestled in grey matter.

"Is it healthy?"

"All looking perfect," Doc confirms. "Sure you don't want to know the gender?"

"No, we still want it to be a surprise."

He grins at me. "Oh, it will be. I'll give you a moment."

Flooded with excitement, I lift a hand to stroke my fingers over the greyscale image. "Hey, baby. We're so excited to meet you soon."

After leaving me alone with the baby for a few seconds, Doc wipes the gel from my belly then gently pulls my loose t-shirt down. I wipe under my eyes to clear the few tears that escaped.

"Have you thought much about the birth?"

"Hmm?"

He gives me a pointed look. "It's only a few months away, Willow. We should discuss what arrangements you'd like to be made. I've facilitated several home births in Briar Valley before."

"Oh. I'm not so sure."

"That's understandable after Arianna's birth, but you won't be alone this time. We'll be here to support you throughout the whole thing. But if you'd prefer to go to Highbridge, we should plan in advance."

"I don't want to go to the hospital."

"You're sure?" he checks.

"Yes, I'm sure."

"Alright, then. I'll make the arrangements for a home birth."

Sitting up, I adjust my clothing. "Thank you, Doc. You've been amazing in supporting me through all of this."

"It's my job, love."

"But you've gone above and beyond. I can't thank you enough for making me feel so comfortable and at ease."

He beams at me. "It's a pleasure."

Putting my shoes back on, I give him a quick hug before leaving the clinic room. Miranda waves at me from the kitchen where she's baking as I exit their house, intent on checking on the cabin build.

The moment I've stepped outside, my phone begins to buzz in my pocket. I check the caller ID and answer when I see that it's Ethan. He's been calling almost every day with news.

"Ethan."

"Willow," he rushes to say.

"What is it? Are you okay?"

"I have news. We've been given a trial date for Mario Luciano."

My feet halt. "We have? When?"

"Given the nature of the case, the high court has moved the timeline forward. His trial will take place next month, three weeks before Mason Stevenson's will begin."

"They've both been given dates?"

"I know it's a bit of a shock."

Rubbing my chest, I battle a wave of confusing emotions. Anticipation is humming through me at the thought of getting this whole thing over and done with, along with a heavy dose of terror.

"What does this mean for me?"

"We'd like you to testify against them at both trials. You'll need to take the stand and give your version of events relating to the charges of human trafficking and sexual slavery."

"Christ, Ethan. I don't know if I can do it."

"I believe in you, sweetheart. None of this would've been possible if not for your help. You can do this."

Hesitating, I clutch the phone tight. Killian, Zach and Walker are putting up stud walls on the cabin site, loudly bickering amongst themselves in the process. I can see them from across the town square.

I have to do this for them. The guys. The town. My family. Putting these monsters behind bars is the right thing to do.

"Okay, I'll be there."

"You will?" Ethan's relief is audible.

"Of course."

"Thank you, Willow. You've been amazing. I can't thank you enough for all of your help throughout this case."

"It's the least I can do. We're family. Speaking of... When's Ryder moving? Did you set a date?"

"In a couple of weeks."

"How're you feeling about that?"

His sigh rattles through the receiver. "I'm excited to have him around more, this is a big step in our relationship. I'm just sad it means taking him from his family."

"We'll still be here for him. For both of you."

"I know, sweetheart. It's just crappy."

"When isn't life crappy? We have to live for the small moments, not the 99 percent of shit we face the rest of the time."

"Right you are," he chuckles. "Give him a kiss for me."

"I will. Be safe."

We end the call, and I begin the short walk over towards the guys. My phone rings again, and I answer with a short laugh.

"Ethan—"

"Mrs Sanchez," a deep voice booms.

Dread spikes through my veins, ice cold and sharp. Ribbons of pain slice into me, phantom sensations of a time long passed, marked by agony and misery.

"Nothing to say, darling wife?" Mr Sanchez laughs.

"Dimitri," I whisper.

"Oh, ho. Look who's getting brave. When did I give you permission to call me that, you little whore?"

"What do you want? Why are you calling me?"

"I thought we could have a chat."

Fumbling with the phone, I try to locate a setting to allow me to record the call but find nothing. Instead, I scurry over to the cabin site so there are witnesses to the phone call.

Killian raises an eyebrow as I approach, and I mouth *SANCHEZ* as clearly as possible. He immediately stiffens, his face reddening with rage as he storms over to me.

I hold a hand up and mouth *NO*.

"Willow," Mr Sanchez snarls. "Are you listening to me?"

Flicking the phone to loudspeaker, I swallow my nausea. "I'm listening."

"You've been evading me for over a year now. I think I've been patient enough, don't you?"

"Patient?" I scoff. "You burned our property, crashed our car, tried to have me killed! You think that you've been patient?"

"More than enough," he snips.

"You're delusional."

"My patience is running extremely low. It's time to come home, dearest wife. I'll forgive this divorce nonsense if you bring my daughter back to me."

"Not a damn chance in hell."

"Language, bitch!"

Zach has to restrain Killian to stop him from smashing the phone into pieces. He punches Zach in the stomach, and the pair tussle, forcing me to walk away to escape the noise.

"You don't get to call me that anymore," I snap back. "I'm not your wife. I'm not your anything. Don't contact me again."

"I'll kill her."

His words stop me on the verge of hanging up. My chest is so tight, the pain is almost too much to bear.

"W-What are you saying?"

"Arianna," he replies simply.

"You will not touch my daughter."

"When I get her back... I will slowly and painfully kill her while I make you watch for daring to fucking disobey me. How does that sound now, wife?"

Now I want to smash the phone just to bleach his disgusting voice from my brain.

"Fuck you," I spit into the phone. "She was never your daughter to begin with. You're going to get exactly what you deserve, I'll see to it."

"Ah, that brings me to the reason for my call," he singsongs, sounding even more unhinged than usual. "I've heard my friends are going to be on trial soon."

"How the hell do you know that?"

"My lawyer hears things, Willow."

Fucking lawyer. That must be where he got my number from too. He should stick his client privilege up his ass, and tell us where this son of a bitch is hiding.

"If you dare to testify against Mason or Mario, there will be the severest of consequences for your disobedience. Do you understand what I'm saying?"

"You can't stop me from doing the right thing."

"I'm not talking about burning a pathetic pile of wood or crashing a car," he growls threateningly. "I will end the lives of every single person you love before I take your life from you too."

"Death doesn't scare me after living with you for ten years."

"It should, darling. It really, really should."

Shaking all over, I wave off Walker as he tries to approach, the other two still wrestling with each other. Killian is bright-red and shouting his head off about killing Sanchez as Zach holds him back.

"Don't even think about doing it. I've been restrained up until now, but my patience has officially expired. You will bleed for me, wife. I've earned that penance from you, fair and square."

Rather than melting into a terrified puddle, I straighten my spine and let loose my own unhinged laughter. Mr Sanchez is silent on the other end of the phone, hopefully taken aback by my reaction.

"I've bled enough for you, *husband*," I say mockingly. "No more. Enjoy hell, you're going to rot there for an eternity by the time I'm done with you."

Ending the call, I cut off whatever response he was about to delight me with. When Zach sees the call is finished, he finally releases Killian, who shoves him away with a frustrated howl.

"You little shit! She needed me!"

"She needed no one but herself," I correct him.

Killian looks over at me. "What the hell happened?"

"More threats. Nothing I couldn't handle."

"Willow." He reaches for me.

"No, Kill. He threatened my child, and I told him exactly where to stick his bullshit. I don't need you or any man to tell me how to be a mother."

Tucking my phone away, I turn my back and storm away from him. I'm shaking like a leaf, but deep down, I feel empowered for the first time in a long time.

Mr Sanchez has no power over me anymore.

That time has passed.

Now it's my turn to rule.

CHAPTER 32
WILLOW
DAGGER – BRYCE SAVAGE

SIFTING through the countless sheets of notes I've written, I fist my hair and try not to freak out. I've been running over my statement all morning in preparation for next week's trial.

It has frayed my nerves, and I'm beginning to regret my decision. Burying myself in work and running the town allowed me to escape the impending trial, but now that the weeks have passed, I have to face it.

Mario's trial.

The beginning of the end.

It's been a long time since I allowed myself to think of what he did to me, but there was no avoiding sitting down and writing out what I need that courtroom to hear.

What he did to a vulnerable sixteen year old, alone and afraid in the world in the wake of her father's death. That scared little girl needed someone to look after her, and she was exploited instead.

"Bastard," I whisper to myself.

The papers crunch in my hands as my fists tighten. All of the women who worked in his club deserve to see him behind bars. He victimised us all and allowed so much violence to take place.

He's just one monster.

One of many.

Around me, the early summer breeze is warm and smells of wildflowers. I'm sitting next to the lake, relishing in the peace and quiet while the town runs through its usual Tuesday routine.

"Mummy!" Arianna shouts. "Look at what Demon can do."

She's playing with the not-so-small puppy behind me. Looking over my shoulder, I find her chasing her in a circle. The yappy thing is fighting to regain control of the chew toy.

"Don't wind her up, Ari."

"She likes it!" Arianna insists.

Sitting opposite her and sketching in his notebook, Micah looks innocent when I shoot him a glower.

"What?"

"You're supposed to be watching her, Mi."

He runs a hand through his unruly locks. "I got distracted."

"By what?"

Turning his notebook around, he shows me an amazing drawing of the lake in front of us. I'm sitting at the edge of it, sketched in smoky shades of charcoal.

"You can sketch other things than me."

"Someone's grumpy," he snickers.

"I'm not."

"Can I go for a swim?" Arianna asks excitedly. "I haven't been in the lake since last year."

"I suppose it's warm enough now."

"Yay!" she screams.

She rushes back inside the cabin to get changed, leaving us alone. I fold up the papers in my hand then tuck them inside the pocket of my discarded denim jacket.

Micah abandons his drawing and moves to sit next to me, winding his arm around my shoulders to pull me close.

"Talk to me, angel."

"I'm really not in the mood, Mi."

He taps my denim jacket. "Is it about this? The trial?"

Sighing hard, I fist a handful of grass and pull it up. "I'm just a bit nervous now that it's come around. The past month has gone too fast."

"I know, baby girl. But you're going to do just fine."

"How do you know that? What if he gets away with it? That man is a snake. He can talk his way out of anything."

Micah slides a finger beneath my chin to tilt my head up. "Mario is going down for his crimes, along with every other scumbag who dared to hurt you. I know it."

"Do you promise?"

His expression falls.

"See? You can't know that."

"I can know something," he argues. "You're going to be fine, no matter the outcome. This baby is still going to be safe. We and everyone in this town will make sure of it."

Leaning in, I rest our foreheads together, breathing in his familiar oil paint scent. "I really hope so, Mi. I'm tired of being afraid."

He moves his hand to rub my lower back which is spasming with pain. I'm becoming increasingly uncomfortable as the pregnancy goes on, and the stress is only making it worse.

"You should go in the water too," he suggests. "I read that swimming can help with aches during pregnancy."

"Since when are you reading about pregnancy?"

His eyes drop to the ground. "Since the day we found out."

Feeling my annoyance soften, I softly kiss his lips. "I love you, Micah. Thank you for always taking care of me."

"I love you too, angel. With all of my heart."

Offering me a hand, he helps me up, and I strip off my light summer dress just in time for Arianna to return in her striped, two-piece swimsuit.

I'm wearing a bra and boy shorts which can get wet. Walking all the way inside while I'm this tired and achy doesn't sound particularly appealing.

"Let's go in, then, baby."

"I'm so excited!" she squeals.

Easing myself into the water, I watch Micah strip off before helping Arianna in. He's so stunning, carved from lean lines of muscle and tightly packed abdominals.

"Come on, squirt." Micah holds out his arms. "You can jump."

Screaming her head off, Arianna launches herself into the air and lands in his arms. Micah slowly lowers her into the water so the slight chill isn't a shock.

"It's so cold," Arianna complains.

I float around in the water, finally feeling at peace. "It's lovely and warm. You can go back inside if you don't like it."

Teeth chattering, she bobs around for a moment before squealing about how cold she is again and climbing out. Demon follows as she runs back inside to find her towel and get warm.

"So cute." Micah laughs.

"More like a little devil. It isn't that cold, and she made us get in."

"Give it up, angel. She's fine."

Swimming over to me, his body wraps around mine beneath the water. I let my legs find his waist then entwine them around him so that he's holding me in the water, taking the weight off my body.

"How does that feel?" he asks.

"So much better. My back is killing me."

"You're working too hard. Killian's warned you about getting enough rest this far into the pregnancy. He'd kill us both if he saw you going over that statement again."

"What Killian doesn't know can't hurt him, Mi."

He snorts. "That's true."

"Besides, he's working night and day on the cabin with Zach and Walker. I need something to keep me busy too."

"Yes, but not this."

"I have nothing else."

He leans close to peck my lips. "You have me. Let me be the distraction you need."

"I'll take a distraction."

Sealing our mouths together, I kiss him more passionately, letting my lips part. His tongue meets mine before sliding into my mouth to dance with it.

We sway in the water, our kiss increasing in intensity. Arianna doesn't come back to disturb us, so I tighten my legs around his waist until I feel the pressure of his cock at my heated core.

"Micah…"

"Sorry," he says sheepishly. "Can't help it."

"We can't do this here."

"No one's watching," he whispers, glancing around the empty greenery. "Arianna won't be back out until she's dried off."

My lower belly clenches with need. They've been giving me regular orgasms to help with the discomfort, relieving my tension at every available opportunity. Their touch has kept me sane.

Sliding his hand up my thigh, he moves to cup my breast through the soaked material of my bra. I moan, leaning into his touch. My nipples pebble in the water.

"What do you need, baby girl?"

"You," I plead.

"Where?"

"I need to feel you inside of me, Mi."

He cups the back of my head, his mouth pillaging mine. "You'll need to be quiet."

Humming in agreement, I let his lips devour me, our tongues battling for consumption of the other. The water sloshes around us from the nearby waterfall, silencing our quiet moans.

I undulate against him, his dick pressing up against my boy shorts. Wet fabric is the only thing keeping us apart.

"You feel so good, baby girl."

My lips touch his ear. "I'll feel even better wrapped around your cock when you bury it inside of me."

Micah groans. "You are the worst."

"I'm taking that as a compliment. Now hurry up and fuck me before my daughter comes back."

"Yes, angel."

Hands sinking beneath the water, he grips the waistband of my shorts and pushes them over my hips. The soggy fabric lands on the bank at the side of the lake.

"I'll leave your bra on in case someone comes," he says roughly. "Wrap your legs around my waist again."

Following his command, I pull our bodies flush against each other. He must kick off his boxers beneath the water because next thing I know, they're floating on the surface of the lake.

"Classy."

Micah winks. "You know me."

Tossing the wet material aside to join mine, he grabs hold of my ass to hold me against his body in the water. His length pushes into me, and I shift to guide it to my pussy.

"Oh God. Mi."

Pushing deep into my slit, he moves to pull out before sliding back in at a different angle. Open air kisses my skin, and the slosh of moving water is the only evidence of our secret tryst.

"Work yourself on my cock, baby girl," he encourages.

Wrapping my arms around his neck, I pull myself up and push down on his length, taking him deeper inside myself with each thrust.

"Perfect," Micah compliments.

Our mouths lock again, lips crushing together and teeth clanging. His pumps beneath the water are slow and tender, stroking into me at a gentle pace that eases every last ache in my body.

Keeping an eye on our surroundings, I move with each thrust, seeking a release. I want to fall apart. Scream. Burst into pieces and relieve the pressure eating away at me.

"Mi, I can't hold on for long."

"Come for me, gorgeous."

He slips a hand inside my soaking wet bra to find my nipple. Seeking out the hard bud, Micah pinches, applying just enough pain to send me spiralling.

"Fuck!" I squeal as quietly as possible.

He holds me tight, letting me float on a cloud of happiness in the warm water. Then his hips shift, and he slams back into me—harder this time, touching that sweet spot of ecstasy.

"You look so perfect when you come, angel."

Pulling out of me, Micah swims us both over to the edge of the lake. He spins me around so that I'm pressed against the side, my hands gripping the lake's edge and ass bent out for him.

"Remember, quiet," he whispers.

Holding my waist, he pushes back into me from behind. The new position sets me off again, and I have to swallow a cry of pleasure that would certainly bring people running over.

Micah holds me tight and pushes into me, taking advantage of the position. His mouth is buried in my neck, and I can hear his ragged breathing as he roughly fucks me in the water.

"I'm close," he pants.

"Me too."

"Again?"

"Yes," I breathe.

Picking up the pace, he moves hard and fast, racing towards his own conclusion. His cock is worshipping me in all his gentle brutality, over and over again.

I feel my walls clench tight around him in the water. We climax together, setting one another off until we're both flying. Micah groans through his release as I moan loudly.

Slumping against the lake's bank, I fight to catch my breath. Micah snuggles up against my back and nuzzles my neck from behind, his lips nipping my earlobe.

"You okay?"

"I'm good," I hum. "Better than good."

"That was incredible. You're amazing."

"Mi." My lips stretch into a smile. "You're not so bad yourself."

"I love you, Willow."

My heart hammers hard. "I love you more, Mi."

"Not fucking possible."

I'm pulled into his arms, and he fetches my boy shorts for me to slide back on. I could float in the water forever, naked and satisfied.

Slowly getting dressed, we both climb out onto the bank, sheepish and satisfied. No one saw a thing.

"Hungry?" Micah holds out a hand.

"Starving."

"I could totally go for some mac and cheese right now. You know the dried stuff in the packet that you'd eat as a kid?"

Laughing, I accept his hand. "Come on. We've got some. I'll cook it for you."

"Thanks, angel."

Micah pulls me close and kisses the side of my head. I slide an arm around his narrow waist, hugging his body close to mine.

"Want me to go over your statement with you while we eat? You don't have to do this alone, you know. We're all here to help."

"That would actually be good."

He pecks the top of my head. "No problem."

With his touch keeping me warm, the last, clinging specks of anxiety melt away. I'm safe in Micah's arms. My future husband. The father of my child. My love. Nothing can hurt me here.

Not the world.

Not Mr Sanchez.

Not even myself.

CHAPTER 33
WILLOW
TERESA – YUNGBLUD

THE HIGH COURT IS AN IMPRESSIVE, gothic building in Central London, surrounded by bustling streets, tourists and hailing taxi cabs going about their busy lives.

Its Victorian design is made up of huge arched doorways and spiralling turrets, the slabs of smooth grey stone towering above me in an intimidating way.

Staring out through the window of the SUV, Zach's grip on my hand tightens. There are dozens of camera vans parked up outside, and reporters are swarming everywhere.

"Shit." Bile creeps up my throat.

Security officers hold them back at every opportunity, but they push and shove, desperate to catch a glimpse of the people participating in today's high-profile trial. I'm terrified to step out of the car and into the limelight.

"Babe?" Worry bleeds from Zach's tone.

"There're so many of them."

"I know, fucking vultures. We'll make this bit fast."

Ethan nods in agreement from the front seat. "In and out. No questions, no statements."

Killian sits next to him, his lips pressed together in an unyielding line. This is his idea of hell on earth, and I don't blame him this time around.

We travelled down to London last night, bringing Rachel, Aalia and Arianna with us. Arianna is back at the hotel with Rachel, none the wiser, while Aalia opted to come with us.

"Last chance to change your mind," Killian offers.

I shake my head. "That's not going to happen. I need to do this."

"Just checking. Let's get this show on the road."

"You guys will stay with me?"

"We can't come up on the stand with you." Micah's expression is tortured. "But we will be right there listening, every step of the way. If you get overwhelmed, just look at me."

I squeeze his hand. "Thanks, Mi."

"You've got this, angel."

With a deep breath, I smooth my plain-black shift dress, the material pulled tight over my baby bump. This is the first time I will go public with my pregnancy. It's making the guys extra stabby.

I know Mr Sanchez will be watching. He'll see me and know that his control over me is well and truly done. I'm not sure what his reaction will be, but he made promises during that phone call.

I will bleed for him.

Well, that's what he thinks.

Stepping out of the SUV, a roar of noise barrels over me followed by shouts of my name, cameras flashing and even some applause. The reporters and onlookers are going wild at the sight of me.

"Willow! Willow!"

Killian grabs my shoulder. "Keep moving."

We're quickly surrounded by security and Zach has to stop his cousin from releasing my shoulder to punch a particularly overzealous reporter, determined to get a close-up shot.

"Kill," I beg.

"Fucking reporters," he snarls.

"I know. Just keep walking."

Feeling someone else's hand slip into mine, Aalia gives me a reassuring smile. We're escorted up the grand steps and into the building, far from the baying vampires determined to get a statement.

"You're okay." Aalia squeezes my hand. "We're all here."

Leaving Arianna with Rachel and Ethan's men still leaves me feeling exposed. Even if she's probably safer than where we are.

Inside the building, Killian lets go of my shoulder. We're all searched and put through security machines to scan for weapons. We're then given passes that hang around our necks on bright-yellow lanyards.

"Keep breathing," Zach advises as he kisses my tied-back hair. "You're doing great."

"This place is so huge."

"It's the real deal here, babe. Only the biggest cases are taken to the High

Court to be heard."

"That doesn't help, Zach."

Rubbing a hand over my belly, he pauses to kiss my lips, despite our surroundings. I savour the brush of his mouth on mine, the warmth of his hand a balm to my frazzled nerves.

"That's my girl," he whispers in my ear.

"Always yours," I murmur back.

Killian nods in agreement, picking up on our whispered conversation despite his cold mask of concentration. He looks like a soldier at war, determined to protect me at all costs.

In contrast, Micah's anxiety is palpable. His shining nose ring twitches as he fidgets, nervously glancing around the tightly packed space. Not even our heavy security detail sets him at ease.

Ushered down a towering corridor lined with fine art and gold, gilded frames hang high above us as we're taken to our seats in the courtroom. It's another intimidatingly fine space.

The walls are made of dark wood panelling with sconces built in to light the dim space. The docks stand at the front of the room, facing a room full of red velvet chairs for the audience.

"You're up first, Willow," Ethan informs me.

"Great."

"You'll be called to the stand then asked to give an oath before giving your testimony. Mario's lawyer will have the opportunity to cross-examine you after we've asked our questions."

"That isn't fucking fair," Killian growls.

"I agree, but this is how proceedings work. There's nothing we can do."

"It's fine." I lay my palm on Killian's chest. "I don't mind."

"Willow—"

"This is how it's going to go, Kill. We've got to go along with it."

Chastised, he sits down in his seat with a loud huff. Neither of the twins look particularly happy either, but they have the sense to remain silent, unlike their grumpy cousin.

Sitting down, I cradle my bump while waiting for the room to slowly fill up. Several other women enter, dressed in formal clothing, a couple offering me tiny, shy smiles in greeting.

When one enters wearing inappropriate jeans and a blouse, my heart leaps into my mouth. She never did give a shit. Lia takes one look at me, and her eyes well up, halting several metres away from me.

"Willow?"

I slowly stand up. "Lia. You're here."

The spell breaks, and we run to each other, sobbing and hugging in a tangle. It's been over a decade since I last saw her in the club, showing me the ropes and doing her best to look after me.

"What... How?" I splutter. "I thought..."

Her smile is tight, pulling at the deep lines around her mouth and eyes. "Things changed after you left the club."

She doesn't elaborate. I don't need her to. I can see it in her eyes—the pain and horror. Mario sold her, just like he sold me. Just like he sold us all, in one disgusting way or another.

"You're here to testify?"

She nods. "I want to see that weasel get taken down, once and for all."

Squeezing her arm, I pull her back into another hug. She laughs when she can't get her arms around me properly because of my protruding bump caught in the middle of us.

"Jesus, girl. You were just a kid when I saw you last. Now you're having a baby?"

"I have an eight-year-old at the hotel."

Lia shakes her head, sending strands of bleached blonde hair flying. "Fuck, Willow."

"Things change. It's been a long time."

"That it has."

Kissing my cheek, she hugs me one last time before taking her seat next to another woman. Everyone's eyes are on me. I'm sure they've seen recent news reports or read my story online.

What am I to them?

A martyr? Someone to pity?

Or someone to look up to?

"Who was that?" Zach asks.

Ethan answers before I can, looking down at his phone. "Lia Hartley. She volunteered to testify against Mario when he was arrested. She's worked for him for the past decade, bouncing from club to club."

"I used to work with her," I admit. "She was assigned to show me the ropes, though that meant just offering me drugs to get through the shift in most cases."

If I could, I'd smash my fist into Mario's face over and over again for what he's done. Instead, all I have are my words. I have to use them to take him down and ensure he can't get back up again.

With the room now full, we're all called to attention. The judge enters, dressed in finery and walking with his head held regally high as he takes his seat to preside over us all.

It's the defendant's turn to enter next. Taking both of the twins' hands for comfort, I hold on tight as the side door swings open, and several armed guards enter, trapping someone between them.

This is it.

Dressed in an expensive black suit, Mario Luciano looks the same as he did eleven long years ago, from his silvery hair to his cold, dead eyes, stone-cold and emotionless.

The moment he spots me, a grin blooms on his lips. I have to let Micah go to rest a hand on Killian's arm as Mario winks at me ever so slowly. I don't want him getting arrested too.

Mario is placed behind a thick, glass screen in a box off to the side. His lawyers gather at one of the tables adjacent to Ethan, his bosses—Kade and Hudson—along with their legal counsel.

Seeing movement out of the corner of my eye, I spot Harlow across the room, subtly waving at me. She offers me a reassuring smile that warms my chest. I nod back, thankful she's here.

Ethan's lawyer stands up. "The prosecution calls our first witness, Willow Sanchez."

Heart constricting painfully, I extricate myself from the guys, meeting each of their eyes before slipping down the aisle. My statement is clutched tight in my trembling hands.

After swearing an oath on the Bible, I take the witness stand. I'm situated to the left of the judge, overlooking the entire room and all of its occupants, their eyes all glued on me, making things even more terrifying.

"Mrs Sanchez?"

Ungluing my tongue from the roof of my mouth, I lean closer to the microphone. "Yes?"

"My name is Miss Javier, and I'm going to be asking you some questions today."

"Okay."

"Please, take your time. I appreciate this must be difficult for you." Miss Javier gestures towards Mario in his pod. "Do you recognise the defendant?"

"Yes, I do. That's Mario Luciano."

"And how did you come to know the defendant?"

Smoothing out my statement, I suck in a stuttered breath. "At sixteen years old, I went to work in a strip club in Dagenham. The club was owned by Mario."

"Sixteen is very young to be engaged in such work. Illegal, in fact."

"My father had just passed away, and I was left with significant debt to be paid off. I had no other family that I was aware of and no choice but to work."

Sweat beading on my forehead, I avoid looking at the guys. They know about my past, but it still stings to admit out loud how desperate I was back then. I hate for them to think of me like that.

"And how many shifts did you work for Mr Luciano?"

"Approximately three."

"What did this role involve, exactly?"

I wring my hands together. "I was serving drinks, dancing, speaking to customers and giving lap dances. Other girls did more, though."

"More?" she prompts.

"Sexually. I was still new and wasn't asked to perform any sexual acts at the time, but I saw them going on. Women were sold to customers in exchange for money that went to Mario."

"Interesting." She steeples her fingers in front of her. "You witnessed these acts of prostitution firsthand?"

"Yes, many times."

I try hard not to look at the jury, but I already saw the looks on their faces. My insides burn hot with shame. Their judgement hurts, even years later. Not many of us were there by choice.

"Tell me about the reason why you left the club."

I glance down at my papers. "During my third shift, Mario introduced me to a man called Dimitri Sanchez. He referred to him as a dear friend and asked me to show him a good time."

"And what did that entail?"

"Mr Sanchez took me to a back room that was reserved for sexual acts and locked the door. I was unable to escape."

Miss Javier's stare is sympathetic. "Tell me what happened next."

"Mario had told Mr Sanchez that I was a virgin. Mr Sanchez wanted to check for himself."

"I see. He wanted to check your virginity?"

Feeling sick to my stomach, I nod. "Mario had arranged for me to be sold to Mr Sanchez and assured him of the quality of his product. They had already discussed a pre-agreed price for me."

"Tell me, did he... check?"

I swallow hard. "Thoroughly."

Killian's head is lowered, a muscle twitching in his cheek. Zach is staring at a spot on the wall, his Adam's apple bobbing tellingly.

Only Micah holds my eye contact—strong and unwavering, ensuring I feel his support even from across the room.

"Mr Sanchez beat me and raped me that night. I was later drugged and transported to an aeroplane where he took me overseas, back to his home in Mexico."

Lia's cheeks are soaked with tears as she watches me from across the room. I can see her guilt, but she couldn't protect me from those monsters. No one could.

"I was purchased by Mr Sanchez from Mario for the purpose of becoming his wife. I did not consent to this, nor was I given a choice. Because of Mario, I endured a decade of abuse and sexual violence."

One woman on the jury has the strength to look at me, her face wet with tears. When our eyes meet, she quickly looks away, wiping off her cheeks. I look down at my papers.

"Mario Luciano is a cold-blooded monster, responsible for the sale and enslavement of countless women, underage and not. He doesn't feel emotion, nor does he care about what he's done."

"Is there anything else you want the jury to know, Mrs Sanchez?"

I look over at the jury members, meeting each of their gazes, one by one. "He's guilty as hell."

Miss Javier nods. "Thank you."

Taking her seat next to Ethan, my attention is drawn over to him. Ethan gives me a tiny thumbs up of approval, a poor excuse for a smile tugging at his lips and looking a little sick.

Moving my gaze to the back of the room, I look at Harlow next. She doesn't look sick. Hell, she doesn't even look fazed. Her reassuring smile hasn't faded at all, and I'm glad.

Standing up from their table, Mario's lawyer takes her place in front of the microphone. "Mrs Sanchez, my name is Mrs Teller. I'm going to be cross-examining you today."

"Hello," I say tightly.

Her smile is smug. "Let's begin by asking this—did you or did you not willingly enter Mr Luciano's employment?"

"Well, yes…"

"And did you or did you not willingly enter the room with Mr Sanchez? Were you dragged? Forced?"

"No, but I was scared—"

"Scared?" she laughs. "Or ready to make some money, hmm?"

"That isn't fair!"

"You've already told this jury that you worked for Mario to pay off your father's debts. In that sense, was he not helping you? A scared, young girl in need of a father figure?"

"Father figure?" I scoff bitterly. "He fucking sold me!"

"Language, Mrs Sanchez," the judge scolds.

Settling back in my seat, I take a second to cool off. The lawyer looks far too satisfied with the reaction she got out of me.

"Mr Luciano employed many troubled women in need of support." She looks at the jury, wearing a plastered-on, fake smile. "He performed this vital community service out of the goodness of his heart."

Killian looks ready to explode. When he finally meets my eyes, I stare at him, silently pleading for him to calm down. If he causes a scene, my entire testimony will be thrown into doubt.

"I was sold." I scowl at her.

She rolls her eyes. "You went with Mr Sanchez of your own free will, didn't you... *Mrs Sanchez*. All that money must have been very tempting for someone like you."

"Mrs Teller," the judge snaps. "That is inappropriate."

"My apologies, your honour. I'm finished."

Retaking her seat, she whispers to her colleagues, still wearing that smug-ass smile that I want to wipe from her face.

"You're done, Mrs Sanchez," the judge says in a much gentler tone.

Nodding, I gather my papers and return to my seat. There are low murmurings all around me as the next woman takes the stand, a few years older than me and avoiding all eye contact possible.

Once seated, the weight of the moment crashes over me, and I feel a wave of dizziness. I'm shaking all over from a combination of humiliation and rage. All of the air seems to have left the room.

"Willow?"

Consciously, I know Zach whispered my name, but in the panic of the moment, I can't process whether he said anything else. I can no longer hear his voice. All I can hear are Mario's words as I stood in the club, terrified and trembling in a skimpy outfit in front of two total strangers.

She'll take good care of you, Mr Sanchez. Willow is brand new, like you requested. She's yours for the price we discussed.

"Babe, look at me."

When he tries to touch me, I violently flinch. Zach shrinks back, wearing a horrified look at the sight of me recoiling from him.

Go with Mr Sanchez, Willow. Best behaviour. Don't let me down now.

"Come back, angel."

Micah's hand lands on my shaking leg. I shoot up, unable to tolerate the feel of someone touching me. I'm spiralling down a hole of terror, worsened by the pair of cold, dead eyes still locked on me across the room.

Mario grins.

He fucking *grins*.

"I-I need the bathroom," I blurt.

Aalia stands up with me. "I can take her."

The guys all look crestfallen as Zach nods on behalf of the group. I can't even look at them right now. Not while that monster is staring at me and sending me flying back into the scared skin of a sixteen year old.

Bolting down the aisle, I head for the nearest exit. Aalia follows, her heels tapping against the floor. We burst out into the corridor, and I make a beeline for the nearest bathroom.

"Willow!" Aalia calls.

Slamming the stall door shut, I quickly slide the lock into place and collapse on the closed toilet lid. My head falls into my hands, breath coming out in short, painful rasps.

"I'm here, Willow. Just outside this door. You're not alone."

Clutching my head, I fight to breathe steadily, the air slipping between my fingers. His voice still plays in my head on repeat, blurring with Mr Sanchez's deep, throaty boom of evil.

You will address me as Mr Sanchez. Nothing else. Is that clear?

"You can't let him win," Aalia says emphatically. "Do you hear me, Willow? You did good. He's going to go down for a long time."

Clutching my tight chest, I try to hold on to her words, but it doesn't cut through the haze of panic. Nothing does.

Not even the knowledge that I'm the one out here, enjoying freedom, while Mario will never see the free world again.

The door to the bathroom clicks shut, then I hear Aalia shift.

"Hey, what are you do—"

There's a loud bang before a shadow hits the floor outside of the bathroom stall. Long hair peeks underneath the door as it spills around the black and white tiles.

"Aalia!" I scream.

"Quiet, Willow. Get your ass out here, or she's toast."

My fear triples. Lia. I'd recognise her voice anywhere.

"Lia? What are you doing?"

"My job," she hisses. "Open this door, or the pretty girl gets it. Your choice."

Hands slick with sweat, I quickly unlock the door to unveil Lia looming over Aalia's unconscious body. She's bleeding from a small gash in the corner of her mouth, and blood is smeared over Lia's knuckles.

"What did you do to her?"

She shrugs. "What was necessary. We don't have a lot of time."

"Time for what? You're insane!"

"I fucking have to be," Lia growls. "Do you have any idea what a huge pain in the ass you've been? If you'd just come quietly instead of fucking everything up for us all…"

Awful, sickening reality snaps into sharp focus. Bloodstained and snarling, she isn't the regretful, teary-eyed person she pretended to be in front of everyone.

That was all an act. Just like Tara's façade was.

Lia works for them.

The monsters.

"What have you done?"

She shakes her head. "I'm sorry, Willow. You don't understand. The things they give us… the money…"

"Money? You're threatening me for money?"

"Threatening." She laughs to herself. "That implies there's a negotiation. We will not be negotiating. You've gone a step too far this time."

Pulling out her phone, she flips it around to show me a video on the screen. My heart leaps into my throat as I recognise a long-range shot of the hotel we left Arianna and Rachel in.

"She's in there," Lia says triumphantly.

"You d-don't know that!"

"You just confirmed it for me. So here's what is going to happen. Unless you want your precious daughter to feel a world of pain, you're going to come quietly."

"I know you won't dare touch her!"

"Won't we?"

On the screen, the camera flips down to show a gun held in the gloved-hand of someone watching over the hotel. I gulp down a bubble of nauseous fear. They're so close to my little girl.

I pull at my hair, feeling myself unravel. "Sabre's men are guarding her. You'll never get to her."

Lia laughs again. "Four assholes playing cards and drinking coffee? I hardly think they'll be a problem."

"When did you start working for Mr Sanchez?"

"Someone had to replace you." She shrugs nonchalantly. "Mario thought I'd be a good fit for the job. He keeps me supplied with all the good stuff, and I live a happy fuckin' life. Simple."

"Simple? You're taking his drugs in exchange for hurting people!"

"Like I give a fuck about who gets hurt." Wiping blood off her knuckles, she grabs my arm. "Time to go, else the little one is going to get a rude awakening. Your choice."

"They won't let you take me out of here."

"That's why you're going to walk out yourself." Her grip tightens painfully. "Better make it convincing too, or that gun will get some use. What's it going to be?"

Swaying on my feet, I stare down at Aalia. She's still out cold but breathing. It won't take her long to wake up and raise the alarm. I can't gamble with Arianna's safety.

"Alright," I say reluctantly.

"Good choice, mama bear. Move it."

Still holding my arm under the pretence of supporting me, we leave the bathroom together and exit into a long, carpeted corridor lined with security. I have to plaster on my best fake smile.

"Where's the exit?" Lia asks innocently. "We're in need of some fresh air after that testimony, if you know what I mean."

One of the officers looks sympathetic. "I'll escort you both."

With an armed guard at our backs, I feel a burst of relief. I can make it out of this. If we can just stall long enough, the guys will come looking for us and find Aalia.

The thought of those armed assholes with guns outside Arianna's hotel soon kills my relief. She's in imminent danger. If I have to play this ridiculous game to protect her, then that's what I'll do.

"Over here." The guard points.

"Oh, thank you," Lia gushes.

He leads us off to an alarmed door leading outside. Inputting the code, he opens it to let us out, waving off the additional security officers who jump into action.

Once through, Lia guides me over to the stone wall that marks the outside of the court and props me up. Heart pounding, I feign dizziness, still hoping to buy some time.

"You okay, ma'am?" the guard asks.

I want to scream. Run. Fight and rave. I will not go back. Not now, not ever. Forcing myself to think of Arianna at the end of a gun, I keep my head lowered to hide my terrified tears.

"Just a little dizzy."

"It's intense in there." Lia rubs my arms, doing a great job of playing the concerned friend.

The guard chuckles. "For sure. Let me go get you some water."

No!

Whipping my head up, I'm about to launch myself at him when Lia grabs a discarded brick from a damaged wall nearby and throws her whole weight at the guard.

With a stomach-churning thud, it connects with the back of his head. He lets out a strangled cry and hits the ground, blood gushing from his head to form a crimson pool on the concrete.

Lia chucks the brick aside, breathing hard. She pulls her phone back out from her pocket and dials a number.

"It's me. We're on the east side, third emergency exit."

Hanging up the call, Lia looks over at me. I've inched away from her, hugging my midsection tight to protect myself from her. Gaze softening, she almost looks sad for a moment.

"She'll be safe," she says in a low voice. "All he wants is you, Willow. The kid will be left alone. Do this for her."

"F-Fuck you," I spit back, my words coming out shaky. "He will never leave Arianna alone."

"I'm trying to help you. It was this or watch him kill every single person in that courtroom to stop this trial. Be grateful he opted for the first scenario."

Feeling a sudden, wild burst of courage, I decide to launch myself at her with my fists raised. I get a few inches before her knuckles slam into my jaw, and I hit the ground with a burst of pain.

"Nice try," she snorts. "You're out of practice, bitch."

"Fuck!" I scream. "Someone help me!"

Eyes flaring with alarm, Lia advances towards me, her leg pulled back on a kick. When her foot connects with my side, I beg for her to leave me alone, doing my best to shield myself.

"Next kick's on that fuckin' baby's head," she warns. "Shut the hell up."

Choking on endless sobs, I curl up on the hard ground, begging for an alarm to begin blaring. The guys can't be far behind.

An engine growling, tyres crunch as a car approaches, breaking straight through the gate and past several security guards protecting the outside of the court.

That's when an alarm begins screaming. The car is huge—a massive, muscled SUV with tinted windows not unlike Ethan's giant beast. But the men who climb out of it aren't Sabre operatives.

I recognise two of them.

Sanchez's men.

He's here.

Lyon, one of Sanchez's men, crouches down next to me, his putrid breath intensifying the nausea already curdling in my stomach. "Pleasure to see you again, Mrs Sanchez. It's been a while."

"Leave m-me alone."

"No can do, I'm afraid. The boss has been waiting very patiently for this delivery. Come on, petal. We've got somewhere to be."

I want to throw up at the repulsive pet name. He took great pleasure in calling me that before, usually as I limped out of Mr Sanchez's playroom, covered in blood and bruises.

As he tries to lift me, the alarm still slicing through the air, I fight back. Kicking. Scratching. Yelling. Anything to buy some time. It's no use, though— he's too strong, pinning my arms against my sides with the help of his men.

"Sedate her," Lyon commands.

Another man approaches with a hypodermic needle in hand, pulled from his cargo trousers. He dips it into a tiny glass bottle then draws back the syringe to fill it with clear liquid.

"No!" I wail. "Let me go!"

But my cries for help are completely useless as the needle plunges into my neck regardless, filling me with fiery ice. Still, I continue screaming my head off, desperate for someone to hear me. The reverberating sound of my pleas soon grow quieter and feebler as I lose control of my extremities.

Helplessness floods my paralyzed body. I'm lifted and carried over to the car, where Lyon tosses me in the back next to Lia.

"Stubborn woman," she whispers. "There's no escaping him, Willow. Not for any of us."

That's the last thing I hear before darkness consumes me, and the world vanishes from sight.

CHAPTER 34
MICAH

LOVE WILL TEAR US APART –
ODINA

SABRE HQ IS IN CHAOS.

Pure, uncontrollable chaos.

Several screens play news footage from today's postponed trial while others are set on scathing news reports, ripping the company to shreds for their negligence. It isn't Sabre's fault, though.

It's ours.

We did this.

Because of our pure stupidity and weakness, Willow is gone. Vanished. She's dissolved back into the thin air from which she appeared.

In the corner of the room, Aalia sits sobbing. She's been a wreck since we found her in the bathroom, bloodied and unconscious. The doctors looked her over, and luckily, she only has minor injuries.

"I want fucking answers!" Ethan bellows.

The entire room cowers beneath his authority. Not even Hudson or Kade bat an eye as their employee whips his subordinates into shape. Everyone is working at a million miles an hour.

Zach doesn't look up, his head in his hands. "I can't believe we let this happen."

"I know, Zach."

"She was right fucking there! Right there! We let this happen."

"I know," I repeat angrily.

"Taken from right under our goddamn noses——"

"I said I know!"

Furious, I stand up and storm away from him. I don't need to listen to his running inner-commentary to feel like complete and utter shit about this. And I don't have time to feel guilty. I'm too busy being terrified.

He's got her. That sick, twisted motherfucker has got our girl, and we cannot rest until we get her back. We all know what he'll do to her now that he's gotten her... And there's still the baby to think about.

He'll kill her.

I just know it.

I move to the back of the room where Killian is pacing up and down in a storm of destructive rage. He's preoccupied by searching through printed out screenshots of the surveillance footage.

I'm sure Sanchez threatened Arianna. It's the only reason she would've had to walk out that door and make herself exposed.

"Why would she do this?" Killian hisses.

I take the papers from his hands and touch his shoulder. "They must've threatened her little girl, Kill. You know she'd do anything to protect Arianna."

"Even jeopardise her own life? The life of her unborn child?"

"You know how she is. Her daughter comes first."

"Fuck!" he growls, punching the wall hard enough to split the plaster. "We should've gone with her."

"She didn't want us touching her."

"It doesn't fucking matter! We should've gone!"

Unable to argue against his logic, I remove my hand from his shoulder and let my head slump. The self-loathing is all-consuming.

I can't take a single breath without it crashing over me in tidal waves. We failed. And this time, it may just cost us everything.

"Guys." Ethan stops next to us. "We're going to find her, I promise."

"It's been hours," Killian barks. "Where is she?"

"We've tracked the vehicle all the way out to Twickenham, but they changed into a new truck with fake plates. We're doing our best to track where it went next."

"Your best isn't good enough." Killian glares at him.

Turning on his heel, Killian storms out of the room, taking his rage with him. It feels like a bomb has gone off in his absence. We're all reeling and trying to wrap our heads around what's happened.

"How did we let this happen?" Ethan covers his face with his hands.

"You didn't."

"We had over a dozen agents posted around the court, yet he still got to her. How is that not my fault?"

Unable to offer him any comfort, all I can do is shake my head. We're all asking ourselves the same thing right now.

It feels like there is nothing we could've done to stop Sanchez from finding a way to use his wealth and power to infiltrate the securest courtroom in the country.

"Lia was working for him this whole time," Ethan hisses. "She's been in contact with us for months. How the hell didn't we see this coming?"

"How could you?" I ask tiredly. "She wanted to help prosecute Mario."

His eyes screw shut. "This is my fault."

"No, Ethan. We all did this. All of us have failed Willow."

"I have to make it right," he says determinedly.

Returning to his tables full of operatives all working at computers and pouring over maps, I glance around the packed room. Even Harlow is here, doing her best to help.

Agonising hours pass, full of frustration and dead ends. Sanchez's men were prepared and took all the necessary precautions to avoid being traced.

The trail goes cold again, and Zach snaps, forced to leave the room to take a break. My heart aches as he passes me. I can feel the breadth of his soul-punching pain. It's in me too. The self-hatred.

God, if I could take a blade to my wrist right now, slice it down to the bone and bleed myself dry just to bring her back into our lives, I'd fucking do it. Without hesitation. I'd die for that quick fix.

Leaving the room, I step out into the stairwell for a breather and find Zach smoking on the steps. Sitting down next to him, he puts a cigarette into my outstretched hand and lights it for me.

We sit together in silence, smoking and freaking out. He doesn't need to speak for me to know what he's thinking. It's the same thing that's on repeat in my mind, a silent, frantic prayer up to the heavens.

Dear God, please let her be okay.

Don't let him touch her before we come.

"I love her so much," Zach rasps in a broken tone. "I can't lose her now, Mi."

"You won't. We're going to find her. Both of them."

"What if we're already too late?"

I touch his knee. "Don't say that. We'll find her because we promised that we always would. I'm not going to break that promise any time soon."

"We made so many promises." He smokes his cigarette dejectedly. "And we've broken them one by one, over and over. We couldn't keep her safe."

"We tried our best. All of us. This guy is just too good."

"Too good?" he scoffs. "He's a fucking psychopath. Can you imagine what he's doing to her right now?"

I've been trying my best not to imagine that. We all know what he threatened to do if he ever caught Willow again. She disobeyed him by testifying. He'll be furious beyond words.

"You think he'd hurt a pregnant woman?" I ask in a tiny voice.

Zach crushes his cigarette beneath his shoe. "I think he's spent his entire life exploiting vulnerable people, and he won't hesitate to do the same all over again."

I continue smoking my cigarette, breathing in the noxious fumes. *Don't think about it. Don't think about it.* I have to chant it internally. If I don't entertain the thoughts, I can imagine she's still okay.

She has to be.

Lord, she fucking has to be.

"Guys," a voice calls down the stairwell.

We both look up, finding Ryder looking down at us from the floor above. He moved into the city last week, taking his truck full of belongings with him. It feels like a lifetime ago.

"What are you doing here?" I call back.

"Brought Arianna and Rachel in. They wanted to be here where it's safe."

We join him on the floor above. The room we exited is still a bustling nightmare inside, but now Arianna has joined in the crying chaos.

"I want my mummy," she sobs hysterically.

Aalia's doing her best to calm her down but failing miserably. Passing Zach, I approach Arianna slowly, my hands outstretched to placate her. She only screams even louder.

"I want Giant!"

"Someone go fetch Killian."

Zach vanishes to find him. Accepting a hug from Rachel, she runs a hand over my wild, mussed-up hair and whispers in my ear.

"Willow's a tough cookie, Micah. We'll find her, and she'll be fine."

"I hope so," I croak back.

"She survived ten years with that piece of shit."

"That was before she ran away and began the process of divorcing him. Not to mention got pregnant with another man's child and engaged to us three idiots. He's going to kill her."

Rachel falls silent, her face pale. "We don't know that."

"Don't we?"

The door slams open again, admitting Zach and a red-faced Killian. He takes one look at Arianna, and his expression shatters into a devastating look of pure grief.

"Peanut," he calls.

Arianna's head snaps up. "Giant!"

"Come here."

Rushing over to him, she's swept up into his arms and spun in a small circle. Arianna clings to his neck, her hysteria dying down into quiet, hiccupping sobs that shake her tiny body.

"Where is Mummy?" she demands.

"She'll be back soon, peanut. I promise."

Arianna's tears continue to fall. "She promised to never leave me. Was I bad? Did I do something wrong?"

I run a hand down her back, her words pushing the dagger in my heart even farther in. "You did nothing wrong, Ari. This isn't your fault."

"Micah's right," Killian consoles.

Taking a seat, he pulls her onto his lap and cuddles her close. She looks even smaller compared to his massive frame towering over her, but her sobs are steadily calming down.

"Guys, we have something." Ethan approaches us. "Mind if we talk over there?"

With Arianna looking a lot calmer, Killian reluctantly hands her off to Ryder for a cuddle then joins us to approach the packed table on the other side of the room.

A newcomer has joined the masses of people, sitting without a laptop and anxiously picking her nails. I recognise her from the trial. She's still wearing her formal clothing and low heels.

"This is Meghan." Ethan gestures towards her. "She was supposed to testify today along with Willow and Lia."

Meghan grants us a tiny wave. "Hello."

"So?" Killian growls out.

She wilts even further. "I... I know Lia a little from the outside world. We used to b-be friends when we worked for Mario."

"Tell them what you've just told me," Ethan says calmly.

She blows out a breath. "Eight or nine months ago, Lia vanished. We worked together at his new club in Soho. She disappeared overnight, and I knew that she'd been sold."

"Sold?" Zach repeats.

"To someone," Meghan clarifies. "Everyone knows it happens, but none of us talk about it. We just do our jobs and get paid, hoping that it won't one day happen to us if we're good."

"Who was she sold to?" Killian demands.

Meghan's hands shake in her lap. "Dimitri Sanchez."

Cursing up a storm, Killian throws his head back to look at the ceiling and take a cleansing breath. He's on the verge of smashing this entire office to pieces.

"Wait, hold up." Everyone's attention shifts towards me. "She was sold to Sanchez?"

Ethan nods. "It appears he was in the market for a replacement after losing Willow. She isn't working for him. She *belongs* to him."

We all wear matching expressions of shock and disgust. That sleazy bastard was literally tormenting Willow for months, playing the doting husband and father, while torturing another woman.

"Today was the first time I saw Lia in months," Meghan adds. "I couldn't believe it. She was caught off guard to see me there. I don't think she expected me to testify now that the club's been shut down."

"I don't get what this has to do with finding Willow." Killian loses patience, his hands thrown into the air. "We're wasting time!"

"Kill, slow down." Ethan holds up a hand. "That isn't all. Meghan, carry on."

"Lia came from a well-off family, you see," Meghan continues after clearing her throat. "She didn't work for Mario because she had no other choice. It was all about getting the drugs her family wouldn't fund."

"Shit," I curse.

"Her family's dead now," she rambles nervously. "There was a car accident a few years back. She inherited the family home in Lancashire."

We all freeze, catching on to her words.

"A family home?" Zach repeats. "In England?"

Meghan nods. "Mr Sanchez would need a bolthole, right? Somewhere to take Willow that isn't tied to him?"

"And the scumbag wouldn't stop to consider that we'd dig into Lia," Ethan finishes. "She isn't even a human being to him. Perhaps he's using her for somewhere to stay off the radar."

"What the fuck are we waiting for?" Killian jumps to his feet, looking ready to find that address and jump in the first available vehicle he can find.

Ethan strides over to one of his operatives, sitting behind an array of open laptops. "Find me everything you can on Lia Hartley."

CHAPTER 35
WILLOW

JEALOUS LOVER – ANIMAL FLAG

"HAPPY BIRTHDAY, ARI."

Ruffling her short blonde pigtails, I cuddle her close to my chest, ignoring the pain as her body presses against my bruised torso. On the floor of her bedroom sits a single, tiny cupcake with a candle in it that Pedro brought with him.

"You have to make a wish, baby."

She's too young to have any idea what I'm talking about, but I keep up the pretence anyway, lifting the cupcake and helping her to blow it out. Standing behind me, Pedro quietly claps.

"Good job, Ari," he coos.

Laughing to herself, Arianna claps her hands together joyfully. I peel the cupcake's wrapper then pull off a bite for her to munch on, twisting to look up at Pedro.

He's beaming at both of us, full of happiness. This is the side of Pedro that no one else sees. The side that's reserved just for us and no one else in this Godforsaken mansion.

Arianna curls up in my arms, sucking her thumb into her mouth which is smeared with cupcake icing. Her eyes flutter shut, as Pedro takes a seat next to me on her bedroom floor.

"I wanted to get her a present," he sighs, gently tracing a knuckle down her cheek.

"You would've gotten in trouble."

"I know, but it would have been worth it."

"He'd kill you, then me."

His eyes are sad. "He's killing you regardless, Willow."

Coughing wetly, I try to conceal my wince of pain. "I'm fine."

"No, you're not. He can't keep doing this to you."

"It's been nearly five years, Pedro. Nothing has changed, and nothing ever will."

Reaching out to grasp my hand, he holds on tight. "*It won't unless you get out of here. I could help you. We could leave together.*"

I smack his hand away. "*We would never make it.*"

"*Of course, we would. Together.*"

"*Keep on dreaming. This is my life now. I've made my peace with it, and so should you.*"

A determined fire burns in his eyes.

"*We'll get out of here, Willow. I swear on my life, I will get you out. No matter what it takes, you and Arianna will be free to live out happy, healthy lives, far from this place.*"

I feel a single tear streak down my cheek. "*Don't make promises that you can't keep.*"

Pedro smiles. "*I never do.*"

———

I wake up to the sound of screaming. Shooting upright on a soft, pillowy mattress, I blink to clear the haze from my vision. Where am I? This isn't my cabin. I don't recognise the pale grey walls.

That's when it all comes back to me in a horrifying rush of realisation. The trial. Lia. Being drugged. Raising my hand to my neck, I feel the sore, bruised skin where the needle went in.

My other hand immediately rests on my bump as horror infiltrates my system. I'm groggy and achy, but everything else feels normal. My clothes are still intact.

"Are you okay in there?" I whisper to the baby.

I wish I could crawl in there and check that everything's alright. I've got no idea what drugs they shot me full of, but it feels like I've been out for hours. My entire body is heavy and numb.

Where the hell are we?

Manoeuvring myself up, I manage to get my feet on the floor and look around the plain bedroom. It feels more like a guest room, with a wide, four-poster bed covered in fresh white linens.

I almost jump out of my skin when the sound of screaming comes again —louder this time. It sounds like it's right beneath me.

Heart beating fast, I creep over to the door and press my ear against it. The sound of fists hitting flesh is instantly recognisable to me. Someone's getting the hell beaten out of them nearby.

Crap, I need to get out of here. Is Mr Sanchez watching me right now? I know he's here, wherever we are. It's only a matter of time before he comes for me, and the torture begins.

Searching around the room, I frantically look for some kind of weapon, but there's nothing. Not a single personal possession, almost like this entire room is just a façade rather than a real home.

"Shit!"

Sitting down on the end of the bed, my head falls into my hands. I was so stupid to follow Lia out of that court, but I had no other choice. It was that or risk Arianna's life, so I'd do it all over again.

Even though I know it landed me here, back at square one—trapped, alone and afraid, in an unknown house in the middle of God knows where. But this time, I know what's coming.

I won't survive it.

Neither of us will.

The tears come, hot and overwhelming. Cradling my unborn child, I allow myself a moment of weakness and sob uncontrollably, letting the fear take over before I have to be brave again.

When the screaming stops, I abruptly look up, awash with fear. Are they dead? Whoever was being hurt has been silenced, one way or another. A shiver rolls over me. I've seen it happen enough times.

Enough, Willow.

Time to face the devil.

With a deep breath for courage, I scrub the tears from my face and smooth my dress. The door is unlocked, the handle twisting and clicking open when I walk over to try.

There's an empty hallway on the other side, long and stretching onwards, with thick carpets and framed abstract art on the walls. The house seems old, the ceilings are high and stretch above me.

"H-Hello?"

Movement on the left startles me, and I realise that Lyon is leaning against the wall, his glossy black hair flopping over his eyes. He takes one look at me and sneers.

"Look who's up."

"Lyon," I gasp.

"It's been a long time, petal. You still know how to put up a fight."

My eyes stray to the deep, bloody scratch on the left side of his face. I have a vague memory of lashing out and scratching him as he shoved me into a car. It looks swollen and painful.

"Suits you."

He bares his teeth. "It'll suit you better when I tear your fucking face off with my bare hands."

"I'd like to see you try." I hold my midsection protectively. "Let's get this over and done with. Take me to him."

"Look who's so eager for her punishment." He chuckles maniacally. "Come on then, petal. The boss man is waiting."

Grabbing me by the wrist, he pins my arms behind my back at an awkward angle. I hiss in pain, pulling in an attempt to wrench myself free of his grip, but I'm completely stuck.

"Little bitch," he hisses.

"Ever the charmer, Lyon."

"When did you get such a smart fucking mouth?"

"Since I decided to stop giving a shit about assholes like you."

"Don't worry, we'll soon beat that attitude out of you."

Escorted down the corridor, I take in as much of our surroundings as possible. It seems to be someone's home, but it's empty and bare, almost like the owners vanished, or all of their possessions were sold.

Down a grand staircase, we emerge into an entranceway marked by a circular table with a vase full of long-dead flowers on it. The door leading outside is protected by two of Sanchez's heavily armed thugs.

"What is this place?"

"Somewhere no one will ever find you," Lyon answers confidently. "Those assholes aren't coming for you here."

But he doesn't know the guys like I do. They're not just any assholes. They're *my* assholes, and I know they'll always come for me, regardless of how long it takes. I just have to hold on.

Lead over to a set of carved double doors, Lyon stops outside then knocks once. There's movement on the other side of the door before another armed guard swings it open.

Here we go.

Feeling strangely calm, I lift my head high, determined to face Mr Sanchez with no fear. I'm ready. He's threatened my children for the very last time.

"Bring her in," a throaty voice booms.

Shoved into the low-lit living room lined with rich carpets and spotted with the odd piece of furniture, I come face to face with the devil himself.

"Willow. How nice of you to join us."

Mr Sanchez still looks the same—from his slicked back, salt and pepper hair, perfectly trimmed beard and strong, bearded jawline to his handsome looks and spotless, expensive suit.

He's Satan in disguise.

Evil behind a pretty exterior.

I take a wobbly step into the room. "Dimitri."

His smile slips. "What have I told you about addressing me correctly, bitch?"

"I no longer take orders from you."

Doubling over with crazed laughter, he wipes imaginary tears from his eyes. "Oh, how you've changed, darling wife. I quite like this version of you. She has some backbone."

"No thanks to you."

Shoving me farther into the room, Lyon escorts me over to a plush, green velvet sofa where I'm deposited. Mr Sanchez's icy blue gaze doesn't stray from me, taking in all the little details.

He licks his lips, already salivating over my pain. When he spots the glinting engagement ring on my left hand, his carefully constructed mask begins to fray at the edges.

I keep my head held high.

"Who are they?" he demands, his spit flying. "On what universe are these worthless pieces of shit better than me?"

"They don't beat and rape me, for starters. That should've been an easy guess."

He takes a menacing step closer. "Enough of your smart mouth!"

"No." I jump up from the sofa, refusing to let him talk down to me. "It's not enough. Nothing will ever be enough for what you put me and my child through."

"My child," he snarls, his lip curling as if he smelled something rotten. "I'll get her back, Willow. They can't keep her safe forever. Not from me."

"Touch her, and they'll kill you."

"And what if I touch you?" He cocks an eyebrow mockingly. "You're my fucking property, after all. Bought and paid for like the whore you are."

"I belong to myself! I'm not yours!"

Striding over, he backhands me so hard, I feel my lip split. Pain buzzes through my head as blood dribbles down my chin.

"Silence," he shouts in my face.

"You think I can't take one little slap?"

His dark eyes stray down to the swell of my pregnant stomach. "I know you can, wife, but can that little demon spawn inside of you?"

Covering my stomach, I cower away from him, hunching over to protect myself. Triumph burns in his eyes. I can take his beatings, but I have to think about the baby.

"Speaking of..." Mr Sanchez prowls around the sofa, his eyes locked on my belly. "I was most surprised to see you on the news all knocked up."

My mouth opens, but no words come out.

"How dare you," he spits at me. "I will burn their touch from your skin before I kill them in front of you."

"Leave them alone," I whisper brokenly.

He snorts. "Like they left my property alone? Look at the fucking state of you."

When he reaches down to painfully grab my breast through my dress, I shrink farther into myself. All I want to do is fight back, but I'm powerless to do that in this condition.

"You should be full of my baby, not theirs." His hot breath meets my ear. "But that's no trouble. We'll soon get it out of you and remedy this situation."

"No!" I screech.

Unable to hold it in any longer, I throw my fist out, striking him in the face. Mr Sanchez stumbles backwards, looking stunned.

Before I can advance, Lyon grabs hold of me from behind and pulls me down, pinning my arms to the sofa above my head. I kick out with my legs, screaming my head off.

"Let her go," Mr Sanchez orders. "I like it when she fights back."

Lyon releases me, and I surge to my feet, determined to run. Even if it's back to my room. All I need is to get away from him before he can touch me.

Banking left, I try to flee across the expensive rug, but a foot catches me at the last second. My legs are swept out from underneath me, leaving me sprawled across the floor in a breathless tangle on my back.

Mr Sanchez laughs as he looms over me, a foot on either side of my body. He moves closer to hover over my chest then places a hand low on my belly, right above the baby's swell.

"What am I going to do to you?" he hums.

"Touch my baby, and I'll kill you."

"Hilarious, darling wife." He barks out a sinister chuckle. "I'd like to see you try."

He lowers himself to settle between my legs, pushing them open with a knee. Disgust inundates my system when I see his cock straining against his trousers. No. Not again. He won't get another chance to touch me.

When he leans close to drag his tongue up the side of my face, I snap my knee upwards, slamming it into his crotch. Mr Sanchez's eyes bug out as air whooshes out from between his lips.

"I'll cut it off next time," I warn. "You wanted me to fight back, right?"

Falling onto his side, I shove him off me then hurriedly roll over to climb to my knees. Lyon's there in a flash to restrain me again, but this time, there's a gun in his hands.

"I'll blow your goddamn brain out myself, little bitch!"

I flinch when he presses the cold steel into my temple.

"No," Mr Sanchez groans. "Take her downstairs with the other slut, and ensure she learns how to behave."

Wrestled to my feet, the room sways around me. Lyon's nails dig deep into my wrists as he drags me from the room, leaving Mr Sanchez on the ground, cupping his sore crown jewels.

His sharp, burning gaze on me is the last thing I see before the door swings shut, leaving me alone with his pet psychopath. I struggle to breathe as he drags me by my wrists.

"What is it with you ignorant sluts causing so much damn trouble?" Lyon growls.

I thrash in his grip. "Get the fuck off me."

"You want me to get off? That's what you want?"

Slamming me into a wall hard enough to send stars bursting behind my eyes, he covers my body with his, grinding his hardness into me. I want to throw up on him.

"I'll get off if you say so," he whispers in my ear, his teeth grazing the lobe. "That what you want, pretty little slut?"

Tears course down my cheeks, hot and sticky. When he finally releases me before someone notices him feeling up the boss's property, a relieved breath escapes my mouth.

"Not to worry." Lyon smirks. "We'll pass around what's left of your ass once the boss is done with you."

I don't see the blow coming until it's too late. His fist smashes into the side of my face, crunching bone and sending pain exploding through me. Before I can even open my eyes, he delivers yet another agonising punch.

"Fucking whore," he lashes out.

When his knuckles connect with my nose, I feel it burst. Hot blood runs down my throat and begins to choke me as I scream at the top of my lungs. The pain is indescribable.

Please.

Please let them find me.

"That's more like it." Lyon wraps his hands around my throat and squeezes. "I like you better when you're silent."

The squeezing tightens into a vice-like grip that makes my lungs burn. I scratch at his hands, desperately fighting for breath, but there's no oxygen flowing into my chest.

"It's a shame I can't kill you yet." He sighs dramatically. "But I'm a patient man. I'll wait until Mr Sanchez is finished to have my turn."

Releasing my throat, I double over, feeling like my chest is on fire, spluttering and coughing as air rushes to my lungs.

Grabbing a handful of my hair, he smashes my head into the wall—once, twice, three times. I can feel blood soaking into the back of my head as the wall slices my scalp open.

"Night-night, bitch."

With the final plaster-cracking blow, the world and all of its agony wink out of existence. Only this time, I go into the darkness willingly, desperate for a brief moment of peace.

CHAPTER 36
WILLOW

PROMISE ME – BADFLOWER

"WILLOW. WAKE UP."

Rolling over on a painfully hard surface, I can't peel my eyes open. They're too heavy. Glued shut. Pain and nausea roll over me in great, blurring tidal waves, both warring for supremacy.

"Ari," I groan.

"It's me, dummy. Your girl isn't here."

"Ari…"

"Willow!"

I manage to lift a hand and raise it to my stuffy nose, feeling the tender skin and bruising. The burst of pain at my touch allows me to peel my eyes open.

Everything hurts. My busted nose. My head. I can feel blood crusted around my neck and ears from the blows that knocked me into the arms of unconsciousness.

"Damn, girl. They did a real number on you."

Following the familiar voice across the dank, low-lit room, the floors and ceilings made of damp concrete, I find a shadow propped up against the wall on the opposite side.

Lia's shoulders are slumped as her head hangs low, obscured by the darkness of what looks like a disused basement. She's sitting with her knees pulled up to her chest protectively.

"L-Lia?"

"The one and only."

"What are you doing down here?"

She shrugs, wincing a little. "May have pissed Mr Sanchez off when you were brought in. It didn't exactly go down quietly."

As she leans forward, her face shifts into the weak beam of light leaking through the window at the top of the room. It reveals heavy bruising and swelling, warping her features into a misshapen caricature.

"Jesus," I rasp.

"Not a pretty sight? You should look in the mirror. Not looking so hot yourself there."

I can feel just how *not hot* I'm looking based on the steady hum of agony racing through my veins. Lyon delivered a brutal beating.

"The baby!" I panic and move to cup my stomach, searching for any signs of bruises.

There's nothing, but the wet stickiness between my legs sends my pulse rate skyrocketing. Lia watches with widened eyes as I drop a hand between my legs, and it comes away smeared with red.

No.

Please, God, no.

"I'm bleeding," I state numbly.

"Fuck."

Eyes slamming shut, I feel the tears spill over. "This is all your fault."

"I know." Her voice is a broken rasp, betrayed by her pain.

Grabbing hold of my terror and strangling it, I reopen my eyes to pin her with an accusatory glower.

"You did this to me! What did I ever do to you?"

"It's nothing personal." She waves a hand dismissively. "I had to do as he asked."

"So he'd continue to supply you, right? This has to be about drugs. That's why you're working for him."

"Working." She laughs bitterly. "I was bought and paid for, just like you. There's no quid pro quo situation here. If I'm good, he gives me a bump. Simple as that."

Stunned, I wrestle my aching body upright. "He bought you?"

Lia nods, silent.

"How long?"

"Months, I think. It's hard to tell."

I search for even a shred of sympathy but come up empty.

"I never would've done this to another woman when I was in your position," I hiss at her. "Never."

"But you didn't stop him from killing them, did you? The women he hurt in front of you?"

"How… How do you know about that?"

She shrugs. "He likes to talk about you."

With that disgusting realisation, I'm hit by a wave of pain and nausea. I can still feel myself bleeding down there, worsening the sense of panic that's eating me alive.

I begin to hyperventilate, feeling the pressure of Lyon's hands at my throat again. The baby has to be okay. It has to be. This is just a bit of spotting. Nothing to worry about.

My mantras ring hollow. I'm not even twenty-eight weeks. I can't have this baby right now. That only worsens the terror causing me to fall apart.

"Willow?" Lia asks worriedly.

"Can't… d-do… this…"

"Motherfucker," she huffs. "This was not part of the goddamn deal. Alright, I'm coming over."

Managing to ease herself up, she limps over to me, cursing the entire time. I distantly realise that she must've been the one screaming. She's been beaten as badly as I have, if not even worse.

Lia slumps onto the cold, hard floor next to me then wraps an arm around my shoulders. Even if I hate her guts for landing me in here, I can't help but lean into her, needing some sense of comfort.

"You're okay," she whispers. "It's just a bit of blood. Breathe."

"The b-b-baby…"

"Don't even think that, Willow. The kid's gonna be fine, alright?"

Rubbing circles onto my back, she guides me through breathing until I can suck in a clear breath again. I rest my head on her shoulder, waiting for the sobs to dissipate.

"We good here?" Lia drones.

"What the fuck is your problem?"

"You're my problem!"

"I didn't do anything."

"If you hadn't pulled this shit and ran away… I never would've ended up here. Do you know what he does to me, for fuck's sake?"

"Yeah," I answer flatly. "Trust me, I know."

We sit there, cold and shivering. Even our hatred can't keep us warm in this freezing cold lair.

"How the hell did we end up here?"

"Beats me," Lia murmurs.

"Where are we?"

Her head lowers. "This is my old family home. Mr Sanchez needed somewhere to lay low while in England, and I wanted to avoid getting my ass beat this week."

"So you gave him a place to hide?"

"I have to survive too, dammit. You know how the game works."

Lifting my head, I glance around the basement. "We have to get out of here. There must be a way out."

"There isn't."

"I cannot die down here!"

Pushing off her shoulder, I scramble to my feet, blinking the haze of dizziness away. The basement is seven steps across and nine steps wide. There's nothing in it but us and a tonne of dust.

Trying the door in the corner of the room, it doesn't budge an inch. Locked up tight. Even when I slam my shoulder into it and cause my body to scream in pain.

"Shit!" I throw my hands up.

"Found your magic escape route yet, Mystic Meg?"

"You're really not helping."

Lia curses as she probes her bruised face. "I'm being realistic."

Leaning against the wall, I stare at her and imagine burning a hole through her head. "I really hate the sight of you right now."

"Ditto, sweetie."

My back skids down the wall as I sit back down and bury my face in my hands. I can only imagine what the guys are thinking right now. They'll be losing their minds with worry.

God, I miss them. I miss them so fucking much. All those months I spent alone in that crummy apartment were just wasted time when I could've been with them, living the life of my dreams.

"I never should've left them," I scold myself. "They were right there, and I walked away. God, I'm so stupid."

Lia almost manages to look sympathetic. "He would've gotten to you one way or another. Don't beat yourself up."

"I'm here, aren't I? Why shouldn't I blame myself? If I'd just stayed with the guys instead of pushing them away…"

But in that moment, I couldn't even see them. All I saw was my trauma, staring back at me and taunting. I wasn't able to see the overwhelming love they've given me in the past year.

"Do you love them?" Lia asks.

I swipe aside tears. "With my whole heart."

"Then fight for them, Willow. He's going to try to break you now. Don't fucking let him."

Staring at her through my tears, I somehow find the energy to laugh. "Thanks for the advice."

"One captive to another." She winks.

Falling back into silence, I watch her curl into a tight ball and squeeze her eyes shut. That's when the tears hit me at full force again, too many emotions barrelling into me like a speeding freight train.

I did this.

I left them.

If only I'd screamed or fought back. Or found some way to raise the alarm without jeopardising Arianna. But deep down, I know this isn't my fault. Not really.

Mr Sanchez would've found a way to get me back, whether through violence or subterfuge. It was this or watch the people I love suffer, and I'll always do whatever it takes to avoid that.

Even sacrifice myself.

My unborn child.

My life.

I'll die living with that guilt. The shameful guilt of realising that I've chosen one child over the other, allowing Arianna to live at the expense of my unborn baby. We won't survive this place.

It feels like hours pass in a blur of tears and quiet, desperate sobbing. Lia stays silent, leaving me to fall apart in peace. My entire body shivers and shakes in the freezing cold air.

When the sound of heavy footsteps and voices breaks our solitude, Lia's head snaps up as she quickly finds her feet.

"They're coming."

I let her pull me up. "What do we do?"

"Stay quiet, and don't piss him off even more than you already have. Do you want another beating?"

"No." I recoil, still feeling the sticky mess between my thighs. "I can't take another."

Both backing up, we press ourselves into the ice-cold wall so we're as small as possible. At the last second, Lia takes my hand into hers and clenches it tight.

"We'll be okay," she whispers.

"How do you know?"

"I don't."

The door clanks open, old and groaning on abused hinges. Lyon steps into the room first, followed shortly by Mr Sanchez in a fresh blue suit, his hair slicked back to unveil his impish grin.

"Evenin' ladies. How are we feeling?"

Neither of us responds.

Prowling into the room, Mr Sanchez glances around the space with a sneer. He doesn't even spare Lia a glance, far too fixated on staring at me like he's discovered a hidden treasure.

"No more funny business." He points his index finger at me.

I stare up at him, petrified and unable to hide it any longer.

"My patience has now expired. You're going to do as I say, when I say it, or your baby will pay the price."

A shudder rolls over me. "Yes, sir."

He grins at me. "That's more like it. We're leaving this country by sunrise, but I'm not going anywhere without my daughter."

"You'll never get to her."

"Oh, I know." His grin widens. "That's why you're going to call those bastards and convince them to surrender my girl to me. We're going to be a big, happy family again."

Alarm pierces my chest. "They'll never do that."

Pulling a gun out of the holster around his waist, Lyon points it at me. "They will if they don't want to hear us blow your fucking brains out."

Storming across the room, Mr Sanchez grabs hold of my chin and yanks hard so I'm forced to look up at him. Righteous fury burns in his blue eyes, sending stabs of fear throughout my body.

"Don't test me again, Mrs Sanchez. This is your final warning. Don't forget what you are to me." He inhales deeply. "*Replaceable.*"

I gulp hard, looking between him and the gun. "What do you want me to do?"

"Good girl. You're going to call those men and lay out the terms. I want Arianna delivered, safe and sound. She will be alone." He emphasises the last word. "Else you're going to pay the price."

"Delivered where?"

"I have men waiting near Manchester airport."

My blood chills. "The... airport?"

His eyes sparkle with malice. "This piece of shit country isn't our home, wife. We're returning to Mexico as soon as we have Arianna."

Pulling out a phone, Lyon hands it to me, the gun still aimed at my chest. "Call their number."

With trembling hands, I take the phone, shakily tapping in Zach's number and putting it on speakerphone. All I can see is that gun pointed right at me, a second away from firing and ending everything.

Mr Sanchez doesn't move an inch, still invading my personal space and staring down at me as I let the phone ring. When Zach doesn't answer, he growls out a curse.

"Again."

"It's an unknown num—"

"Again!" He slaps my face, reopening my split lip.

Licking blood from my mouth, I hit redial then wait, my heartbeat roaring in my ears. I'm a second from giving up hope when the line engages, and a familiar voice causes my adrenaline to spike.

"Who is this?" Zach answers wearily.

"Zach," I rush out. "Don't hang up the phone."

"Holy fu… Willow? Is that you?"

"I'm okay, I'm okay," I trip over my words in a panic. "You have to listen to me, Zach. I don't have a lot of time."

The gun inches closer, still trained on me. Coming to an awful, gut-wrenching decision, I crush the remains of my hammering heart, knowing I have no other choice. I won't surrender Arianna.

"No matter what they do to me, do not give her to them! Don't give them Ari!"

Whoosh.

Thud.

Mr Sanchez's fist connects with my stomach, and I fall, crashing to my knees. I can't help but cry out as a hot burst of vomit spews from my throat at the sudden avalanche of pain in my belly.

"Willow!" Zach's voice screams.

I watch through my streaming tears as Mr Sanchez picks up the phone. "I want my daughter back. You're going to bring her to me, or I'll kill your child. The choice is yours."

"Listen here, asshole—"

Drawing back his foot, Mr Sanchez boots me in the rib cage. I shriek in agony, curling inwards to try to protect myself from the blows raining down. It's all I can do.

"Stop it!" Zach howls. "Stop hurting her!"

"The girl," Mr Sanchez hisses. "Manchester airport. Two hours."

Zach hesitates. "We will never surrender Arianna to you."

"Then listen to the sound of your child dying."

As Mr Sanchez lifts his foot to kick me again, Lia flashes across the room. She moves so fast, her bruised body is a blur. I scream as she tackles Mr Sanchez with her remaining strength.

The pair hit the floor and roll, wrestling with each other. Lyon snarls a frustrated curse as he retrains the gun on their tangle of limbs, fighting for a clear shot.

All I can see is Lia. Teeth bared and brows furrowed, battling for her life. For my life. For what's right. Not even Zach's bellows of my name pierce the slow motion bubble that's encapsulated us all.

The bang of a shot being fired slices through the room, silencing everything. Mr Sanchez pushes Lia's limp body off him before rolling up onto his knees, now covered in fresh blood.

"Fucking whore!" he bellows.

"Lia!" I yell.

But it's too late. She stares up with blank, empty eyes, slumped across the floor as blood pools around her from the hole in her chest. Dead. Gone. I can't restrain the hysterical sounds coming from me.

"Wanted to do that for months." Lyon smirks.

"You killed her!" I wail.

He turns the gun back to me. "Silence, little bitch!"

"My child!" Mr Sanchez howls. "I want my fucking daughter!"

Through the chaos, a familiar voice cuts through the haze. The first voice I heard when I woke up in Briar Valley, terrified and alone. My protector. The man who had the courage to start this whole adventure.

"We're here, baby," Killian croons through the phone. "Hold on for me. I'm coming for you."

I look down at the fallen phone as an almighty crashing sound devours his voice. The small windows high above us shatter into thousands of pieces, sending shards slashing through the air.

Gunfire swallows everything. My stuttered breathing. My hammering heartbeat. Mr Sanchez's furious shouting. Flashes break through the darkness, and bodies begin to swing into the room.

Launching himself at me, Mr Sanchez takes me down before the first black-clad agent can collide with him. We hit the ground and roll together, both warring to gain the upper-hand.

"You're mine, Willow!" he shouts at the top of his lungs. "You will always be mine!"

Wrapping my hands around his throat, I dig my nails in and squeeze with all of my strength. It isn't enough to throw him off, but I'm able to flip us over and manoeuvre myself on top.

"I was never yours!" I spit in his face. "Not for a single second of those ten years! Rot in hell!"

His fist connects with my face, throwing me off again and allowing him to climb back on top. With blow after blow raining down on me, I begin to choke on a mouthful of blood.

"They don't get to have you." He punches me in the throat. "No one else gets to have you but me!"

With my eyes falling shut, the pummelling suddenly ceases. So much pain is running through me, I can hardly feel it anymore. My brain has found its familiar numb space and switched off to it.

This is it. My end. In those dark, desperate seconds, all I can see is them. The men who saved my life, time and time again, with their unconditional love. Their acceptance. Them. I've lost that forever.

Until there's a touch.

A whisper.

The brush of softness.

Roughened fingertips stroke over my face, swiping through blood and over bruises to push sweat-stained hair aside.

"Baby," a grief-stricken voice murmurs. "Open your eyes, princess. Come back to me. Please, please come back to me."

But I still can't open my eyes. Not yet. The world is slipping through my fingers like quicksand, and I can't hold on to it.

"I love you," he whispers heart-brokenly, his voice fractured with agony. "God, I fucking love you. Open your eyes for me, baby."

"Kill," I moan groggily.

He sucks in a sharp, relieved breath.

"It's me, Willow. I'm here."

Fighting with my last vestiges of strength, I peel my eyes open and look through the blur of pain and tears up at my saviour. He's here. Real. Looking down at me through his own tears.

Killian.

It's always been Killian.

Sliding an arm underneath me, I'm lifted upright where I manage to curl into his chest. All around us, Sabre's men infiltrate the basement, carrying heavy weaponry and fearsome expressions.

"You're here."

Killian presses the gentlest of kisses to my forehead. "I made a promise, Willow. And I never break my promises."

Lingering over us, Ethan pulls off a thick facial shield and sheaths his gun. He takes one look at me and blanches.

"Jesus, Willow. What have they done to you?"

All I can do is sob, "The o-others?"

"We need medical in here right now," he says into his earpiece. "And bring the other two in. She needs them."

Holding me in his arms, Killian wipes blood from his knuckles. Mr Sanchez has been pinned to the floor by Hyland, and Warner holds a gun at his back.

"Take her for me," Killian demands.

Ethan doesn't move. "You can't kill him."

"You think I need your fucking permission, Tarkington?"

Still refusing to budge, Ethan moves to block the path to Mr Sanchez's pinned body. I raise a shaking, blood-slick hand to grab Killian's lapel and tug.

"Kill," I whisper weakly. "Please... I need you."

His expression breaks—shattering into a look of such intense grief and regret, it physically chokes me. His pain is almost more overwhelming than mine.

"Look at what he's done to you," he says in a pained voice. "You're bleeding, Willow. The baby—"

"He'll be okay."

"He?"

Moving my hand to my belly, I manage a nod. "I think it's a he. Don't you?"

By the grace of God, a smile lights his lips. "Yeah, I do."

"Then trust me. He'll be okay. We're survivors, aren't we?"

A single tear rolls down his cheek. "That you are, Willow Sanchez."

Shouting precedes the arrival of the twins, thumping their way down into the basement at full speed. Zach skids into the room first, wild-eyed with terror and struggling to breathe.

"Willow!" he screeches.

Closely followed by Micah, the pair fall to their knees beside me. Neither knows where to look or what to touch, sitting powerless instead as I steadily bleed onto the concrete floor.

"Angel," Micah whimpers. "What did... he..."

"I'm okay." I cough wetly. "Just a bit banged up."

"Banged up?" Zach repeats.

Killian tries to move again. "That son of a b—"

"Kill!" I cry out.

Freezing still, he holds me tighter, spooned in his arms like I'm a newborn baby unable to look after itself. I suck in a painful breath and look at Micah.

"Don't let him kill Mr Sanchez, Mi."

He shakes his head. "Willow..."

"No! He needs to be punished for what he's done. I want justice, not death. All of the women he hurt deserve more than that."

Zach smooths down my hair. "We've got you, babe. He'll go down for the rest of his life. We'll see to it, I promise you."

Above us, Ethan nods. "Swear on it."

With their promises relieving some of the pressure on my chest, I grasp Micah and Zach's hands, letting myself float on a cloud of numbness until the medical team arrives.

"Sir, please step aside."

"No!" Killian shouts. "I will not!"

"Don't l-leave me," I sob.

He cuddles my broken body close. "Never, baby."

"Never," Zach echoes.

Micah ducks down to kiss my cheek. "Never, angel."

My eyes slide shut, safe in the knowledge that my men have me, and they'll never, ever let me go again.

CHAPTER 37
KILLIAN

SOLID GROUND – VANCE JOY

HOSPITALS HAVE to be my second least favourite place on the earth, right after cities. Nothing good happens in these places. Aside from the reunions. And fuck, this is about to be a big one.

Holding Arianna's tiny hand in mine, I walk her along the long, gleaming white corridor that leads to the hospital ward. Willow's been under observation since she was brought in last night.

"Giant?" Arianna looks up at me. "Will Mummy be okay?"

"She's going to be just fine, Ari."

"Do you promise?" She wrinkles her nose. "My daddy used to promise things, like he'd hurt Mummy if I was bad or naughty."

Kneeling down so I'm at her height, I take both of her hands in mine to squeeze. "This isn't that kind of promise, Ari. I swore that I'd look after you both, and I'm a man of my word."

She finds the courage to smile. "Okay."

"Okay?"

"If you promise."

I kiss her forehead. "I do."

"Then I believe you."

Standing back up, we walk down the rest of the corridor and stop outside Willow's door. There's a small group of people inside—Doc, Aalia, Rachel and Miranda—who all step out to give us some privacy.

Katie's already back at the hotel. She stayed with her daughter all night after she heard the news. The mad woman hasn't left her side for a moment, only succumbing to sleep when we demanded that she get some rest.

"How's she doing?" I ask Doc.

He pats my shoulder. "The doctors here know what they're doing, Kill. She'll be alright."

"I'm not asking them, I'm asking you."

Doc nods, sadness emanating from his eyes. "It's nothing a little time won't fix."

"The baby?"

"Count your lucky stars the baby survived that beating. It was touch and go, but there's no permanent damage. Someone must be looking out for you lot up there after all."

I send a silent prayer up to the heavens to the one person I know is looking down on us with absolute certainty.

Thank you, Grams.

Thank you.

Releasing my shoulder, he heads off down the corridor with the others to give us some privacy. The twins are still inside, sitting at Willow's bedside, keeping her company.

I look down at Arianna. "Listen, Ari. Your mum's a little bit sore right now, so I need you to be gentle. She may look different too."

"Different? How?"

"She has some marks and bruises that look a bit scary, but I promise, she's alright. Everything is going to be fine. Can you be a big, brave girl for me?"

She sucks back in her trembling bottom lip. "I can."

"Then let's go see your mummy."

"Okay, Giant."

Holding the door to the room open for her, my eyes connect with Willow's teary ones. She's connected to several IV lines, feeding her painkillers and antibiotics. A machine is monitoring the baby too.

Her face is a heart-wrenching technicolour painting, not unlike the mess she was in when she first arrived in Briar Valley. Skin blackened and face misshapen, she looks worse for wear but still fucking beautiful.

"Ari?" she whimpers.

Tentatively stepping into the room, Arianna looks her up and down. "Mummy?"

"Come here, baby. It's me."

That's all it takes. Hearing those words, nothing else matters. Arianna runs into the room, and Zach catches her before she can launch herself at Willow and hurt her.

He places Arianna down on the edge of the bed where she takes her mum's hand and lightly cuddles her, beneath the swell of her bump that's hidden underneath the white sheets.

"I was so scared," Arianna cries. "I thought I'd never see you again."

Willow holds her daughter's hand tight and strokes her neatly plaited hair. "I'll always find you, Ari. You know that."

"I know, Mummy."

"You're my little girl. Nothing will ever tear us apart." Willow swallows hard. "Not even your daddy. He isn't going to be a problem anymore."

Arianna looks up, face frozen in fear. "He's… gone?"

Willow nods patiently. "Your daddy did some very bad things, Ari. He's going to be in prison for a long time. I'm sorry, baby."

Chewing on her lip as she thinks, Arianna eventually nods back. "Good. He's where the bad men belong."

"Yes, he is."

Laying back down on her mum's legs, Arianna clings on tight, her tears saturating the hospital sheets. I move to stand at the end of the bed between the twins who are sitting in chairs on either side.

"Have the doctors been around yet?"

Zach looks up at me. "About half an hour ago. They want to keep her in for another day before thinking about a discharge."

"And the baby?"

"The consultant did another scan." Micah strokes Willow's needle-filled arm. "Everything is looking alright for now."

I breathe out a sigh of relief. "Thank God."

Listening to us, Willow looks equally as relieved. We were all fucking terrified and convinced we'd lost the baby when we found her, barely alive and covered in blood.

She'd been bleeding again as a result of all the stress, but as Doc put it, by some miracle, she didn't go into premature labour. We dodged a very badly-timed bullet thanks to the medical team here.

All holding each other, we're left alone until Rachel and Miranda come to take Arianna back to the hotel we've commandeered near the hospital.

"Mummy," Arianna whines.

"I'll be coming home soon, baby," she tries to comfort her. "Come back and see me tomorrow, okay?"

"Okay." Arianna pouts. "But who's going to tuck me in?"

"How about Uncle Ryder?" A voice offers.

Standing in the doorway, Ryder and Ethan are holding hands. Willow smiles up at them when they enter the room together.

"You came."

The skin bunches around Ryder's eyes as he glances over her bruised face. "Couldn't miss seeing my best girl, now could I?"

After exchanging a quick hug, Willow clasps his arm. "You'll take her back and tuck her in for me? She's funny about that."

"Of course." Ryder bends down to scoop Arianna up. "Come on, poppet. Let's go and raid the hotel mini fridge for snacks."

"Okay!" she agrees enthusiastically.

After pausing to drop a kiss on Willow's cheek, Ryder takes her daughter out, and the door clicks shut behind him. Ethan watches his boyfriend go before pulling up a chair at Willow's bedside.

"How are you doing, sweetheart?"

She winces a little. "Sore."

"We're just glad you're okay. You took a hell of a beating or two in that place."

"I had no other choice." She glances between us nervously. "Keeping Arianna safe was my priority. He threatened her."

"We figured as much," Zach concludes.

"I followed along with Lia, but I had no intentions of going with her from the courthouse. By the time the car with Mr Sanchez's men came, it was too late to escape."

Micah squeezes her arm. "No one blames you, angel."

Willow shakes her head. "I blame me. I put myself and my baby in danger."

"To protect your daughter," he points out.

She gives in with a nod. "Yes. It was all for her."

"That's called being a mother." I take a seat next to Ethan. "And we understand. You did what you had to do to keep her safe."

"You forgive me?" Willow's eyes bounce between us.

Zach kisses her knuckles. "There's nothing to forgive."

Blinking tears aside, Willow looks back up to Ethan. "What about Mr Sanchez? Where is he now?"

"Being held at Sabre HQ pending further investigation," he answers. "He'll be transferred to a high-security prison within forty-eight hours and sentenced for his crimes."

"What are we looking at?" I interject.

Ethan smiles. "Life."

Zach whistles. "You think he'll go down?"

"Without a shadow of a doubt. We have countless witnesses and victims ready to testify and all the evidence we need. He's toast."

"And the trials?" Willow croaks.

"Rescheduled, for both Mario Luciano and Mason Stevenson. All of them will see their day in court, Willow. I'm keeping my word."

Hearing that Dimitri Sanchez is locked up in a cell right now, alone and forced to confront the reality of life behind bars, gives me the tiniest sliver of satisfaction. Tiniest. I'd rather he was dead.

But that won't give Willow the closure and peace she needs right now. There's no justice in death, just punishment, and she needs that justice to heal and move on with her life. I can respect that.

"So… it's over?" Willow asks hopefully.

Ethan rests his hand over hers. "It's over. The trafficking ring has been dismantled, and everyone is going down. You did it, Willow."

"I did nothing," she insists.

"No, you did. This investigation is over because of you. We won. The case has officially been closed."

With those words, Willow bursts into tears. Ethan looks surprised for a second before he inches closer.

"Can I… hug you?"

"Please do," she cries.

The pair carefully embrace, dodging wires and tubes. Even Ethan has tears in his eyes when they separate again.

"There's something else." Ethan says hesitantly. "I wanted you to hear it from me. I'm leaving Sabre Security."

"You're doing what?" I frown at him.

"I've worked for this company for over a decade, and I'm tired. This was my last case. Now that it's over, I've decided to go as well."

"But… Ryder just moved to London for you," Micah says.

Ethan looks sheepish as he glances back at Willow. "That's the thing. I was wondering if you had a spare cabin. I figure we'll need our own space if we move back to Briar Valley together."

She breaks out in a massive grin. "I can think of a couple that'll be empty soon. You can take your pick."

"You'd have me?" Ethan asks with a coy smile.

"Any day of the week. You can help solve the mystery of the egg stealer. It's still unsolved, twelve months later."

"Sounds like a job for an expert."

I punch him in the shoulder. "You can be our official, live-in security expert. We have some strange old types around town. Could use the muscle."

"Consider it done."

We all break into laughter. Ethan quickly makes his excuses to leave and give us some privacy, promising to come back with more news soon.

"How are you really feeling?" I narrow my eyes on Willow once it's just the four of us.

Her smile fades. "Like shit."

"What can we do?" Zach asks worriedly.

"Just hold me."

He runs a hand up and down her leg. "We're here, babe. None of us are going anywhere."

We all crowd closer around her, touching whatever bits of her we can access that aren't bruised or taped up. Willow cries until she has no tears left.

"I want to go home," she hiccups.

"Soon, baby." I entwine our fingers and squeeze. "The doctors need to keep you in to monitor the baby. We want you both to be safe and healthy."

"I'm with you." Her hazel eyes flick up to me, full of adoration. "I'm always safe when I'm with you." She looks at the twins. "All of you."

Micah kisses the back of her hand again. "You never have to be scared again, angel. You're safe now. For good."

"I don't know about that," Zach chuckles. "She lives with us three morons. That's plenty of reason to be scared."

"And she's having our kid," I add. "Who wouldn't that terrify? What if it comes out looking like you pair of ugly oafs?"

Zach sticks his tongue out playfully and Micah looks at me with indignation. Willow laughs so hard, she winces and has to take a moment to breathe through the pain.

"Don't make me laugh. It hurts."

Zach glares at me. "Your fault."

"Don't want to get picked on? Don't look like that. Simple."

"I'm the hot twin! Look at me!"

Coughing under his breath, Micah elbows his brother in the ribs to shut him up before Willow hurts herself laughing again. Zach yelps before falling silent with a smirk.

"So… hot twins and their grumpy, oversized cousin." Willow's eyes sparkle with mirth. "What's the plan now?"

We all look at each other before I answer. "Now we go home."

She pauses to squeeze all of our hands, one by one.

"I already am home."

CHAPTER 38
WILLOW

SPIRIT – JUDAH & THE LION

A HAND RESTING on my huge, swollen bump, I stare up at the finished cabin as Killian installs the very last window. After months of painstaking work and a labour of love, our home is finally finished.

Killian screws in the last bolt then climbs down the ladder to stare at his handiwork. He looks gorgeous as always in low-slung jeans and no shirt, despite the autumnal weather.

"Kill!"

He spins on the spot. "What the hell are you doing up?"

Waddling over to him, I walk straight into his arms and kiss him on the mouth. "I'm tired of bed rest."

"Willow, you're five days overdue. Do I have to tie you to the damn bed?"

"Mmm, sounds kinky. Let's go."

He gives me the stink-eye. "It's really not. You're a nightmare patient. Admit it."

Rolling my eyes, I kiss him again until he softens. "I'll admit no such thing. Come on, grumpy. I just wanted to watch you finish off the last bits. It looks incredible."

Arms wrapped around each other, we look up at the cabin. It's a real beauty, carved from dark-stained oak, steel and polished glass. Even bigger than Lola's previous three-story beast.

"Better late than never," Killian grumbles.

"I reckon the baby stayed in there past its due date just to give you time to finish."

He snorts. "In that case, perfect timing."

Holding each other close, it isn't long before the twins join us, both finished up for the day. Zach took Micah into Highbridge to stock up the shop.

It took some convincing to get Micah on board with the idea of selling his artwork in an actual store. His days of ad hoc, online sales and invisibility are over. We're dragging him into the limelight.

Using money from Lola's estate, I purchased the small, corner plot a couple of months ago, located in the quieter end of Highbridge's bustling town centre.

It needed some renovation, but Killian quickly took care of that. Now everything is ready for its first official opening in a few weeks. Micah's art will finally get the appreciation it deserves.

"You get everything moved over?" I ask.

Micah drops a kiss on my lips. "That was the last of the canvases. Just got to take the last few sculptures and finish setting everything up."

"I bet the studio looks empty."

He laughs. "Plenty of space to fill it up with even more art."

Shoving his twin out of the way with a grin, Zach steals me from Killian's arms and lays a dramatic kiss on my cheek.

I push his shoulder, my body protesting at the sudden movement. All my joints are aching something fierce now that I'm overdue.

"How are we doing?" Zach singsongs.

"We? You're not the one pregnant and five days overdue, mister. I'm fucking uncomfortable and miserable. How are *you* doing?"

"Oh, excellent. Very much not pregnant, thanks."

"Micah, please punch your brother for me."

He holds up his hands. "I'm a pacifist."

"I'll do it," Killian volunteers. "Come here, kid. Take it like a man."

"Sexist!" Zach accuses.

Getting him in a headlock, Killian thumps Zach right in the stomach, forcing him to double over with a cough.

I cringe, feeling a little guilty, but then pain hits me in the belly again, and I feel a lot less bad about it.

"Here comes another one."

"Contraction?" Micah worries.

Nodding through the pain, I rest my hands on my knees, folded over as I breathe through the spasming. They've been coming on and off, but my water hasn't broken yet.

"We're close." Killian rests a hand on my lower back. "Bed, Willow. No arguments this time."

"Yes, sir. Can someone give me a ride?"

Micah takes my hand. "We've got the truck."

Climbing into the backseat, I sit down as comfortably as possible, my bump barely fitting inside the space.

I've suddenly ballooned in the last month of my pregnancy, much to the guys' delight. They can hardly keep their hands to themselves.

We arrive home to packed boxes and chaos. Killian decided we needed to move into the cabin as soon as possible, before the baby comes. But with a few delays, the timeline has gotten all messed up.

"I'll get Ryder to help me move the rest of this stuff out of here," Zach says, lifting a box labelled *kitchen*. "We need to move fast if we're going to get this done before the spud arrives."

"Zachariah, I've warned you about the *S* word."

"And how much you love the nickname? Sure."

"Jackass."

"Your jackass, babe. Forever and ever."

With a wink, he props the box on his shoulder then disappears, leaving Micah to manoeuvre me over to the sofa. I slump onto it with a sigh, taking the weight off my swollen feet and ankles.

"You need anything, angel?" he fusses, fluffing the pillow behind me.

"Just you."

Smiling, he sits next to me and begins to massage my shoulders. "You've got me."

"Distract me. How's the shop looking?"

"Chaotic, but it'll come together." He bites his bottom lip. "I can't believe it's actually happening after all this time."

"It's going to be great, Mi. You'll be amazing."

"I'm not a good people person."

"Then we'll hire some front-of-house staff or stick a name tag on Zach." I wince as more pain stabs through my lower belly. "He can chat all the customers to death while you paint."

Micah laughs. "That's actually not a bad idea."

Inhaling sharply, more cramps hit me in a bigger wave this time, taking my breath away. I lean over, moaning through gritted teeth as my lower back twinges in protest.

"Shit." Micah rubs my back. "That was a big one."

"I don't think we have long. You should get the guys."

"What about the cabin?"

"It can wait until after. I need you all here with me."

Micah grabs my phone from the kitchen table to round everyone up. "I'll ask Aalia to pick Arianna up from school and keep her occupied for a bit."

"Thanks, Mi."

Left alone, I place both hands on my tight belly and imagine the life inside. It's been another tumultuous, messy as hell pregnancy, but despite all the odds, we've made it to this moment.

"Hey there, little one." I stroke over my swollen bump. "Thanks for sticking with me, baby. I'm so excited to meet you. We made it."

I have to keep telling myself that, over and over again. We made it. That still doesn't feel real, even if the monsters who tried to break me are all safely locked up behind bars.

Mr Sanchez's trial is set for January, while Mason Stevenson and Mario Luciano, along with other members of the human trafficking ring, have both been sent down for lengthy sentences.

I know I'll have to face him again. There's no avoiding it. But now I get to sit in that courtroom, safe in the knowledge that he will never hurt me or another woman again.

Justice will be served.

That's how I sleep at night.

The contractions continue for hours, over and over, until I'm sweaty and exhausted. When another hits, even stronger than the last, I cry out Micah's name. He's back in a flash to hold my hand, rubbing my back and whispering assurances.

As we're riding the wave of another spasm, warmth gushes from between my legs. I take one look down at the wet patch spreading across the sofa and my breath stalls in my chest.

"Mi!"

"Shit." His eyes are wider than I've ever seen them. "Was that your water breaking?"

"Yes. Call Doc! He needs to come."

"I'm on it, angel."

Briar Valley moves fast in an emergency, so before long, the guys are all back where they belong. Doc arrives soon after with Rachel and Miranda to assist, loaded down by medical bags and fresh towels.

"Alright, then." He crouches down in front of me. "It's go time, Willow. Let's have this baby."

Tears pour down my sweaty face. "I'm scared, Doc."

He places a reassuring hand on my leg. "You're going to be just fine, kid. We've had a lot of experience. Your baby is in safe hands."

With Killian's help, I strip off my drenched lower half then manoeuvre down onto the towel-covered floor. Doc ducks his head between my legs, only to come back up seconds later.

"There's no time to move her to our cabin. She's fully dilated."

"Crap," Zach curses. "This wasn't the plan."

"Plans change." Doc looks up at me. "It's time to push, Willow."

Killian grips my hand tightly. "We're here, baby. You're not alone."

Pain rips through me again—blurring my vision with agony. Sweat drips from my forehead, and my entire body trembles with tiny earthquakes as I scream and push.

The cycle repeats. Scream. Push. Scream some more. Pain. Dizziness. Sweat.

"Push again, Willow. Just keep pushing."

Their words filter into my mind as my body takes over, entering a primitive state. Rachel dabs my forehead with a wet towel while Miranda stays with her husband, monitoring the situation.

The guys take turns holding my hand until one of the others gets impatient for a turn, and they have to swap over.

"How much longer?" Killian growls. "She's hurting!"

"We're close," Doc confirms. "I can see the head."

"I love you." Micah kisses my temple. "And so will this baby, Willow. You're so close now. Keep going."

"Almost there," Zach murmurs.

Killian nudges Micah away and takes my hand. "You've got this, baby."

The pain is blinding. Over and over. Hitting me relentlessly in every last corner of my body, until I can hardly grit out a scream through my clenched teeth. Doc's head is still ducked low.

And then... bliss.

Relief.

I draw in a deep breath.

The sound of a wailing infant fills the half-packed cabin. Everyone falls silent, as if struck by the most magical, awe-inspiring bolt of lightning. Doc's head lifts as he cradles my baby in his arms.

"One healthy baby boy," he pronounces proudly.

"Oh my God," Zach manages through tears.

"Who's cutting the cord?"

Killian claps Zach's shoulder. "You're up, kid."

"Me? Shouldn't it be you?"

"I think you can handle this one."

Zach looks completely freaked out, but more at Killian trusting him with something important than the idea of cutting the cord.

Taking the scissors from Doc, he slices through the umbilical cord, his eyes red with tears and mouth hanging open in shock.

Miranda passes her husband a towel, then Doc cleans and wraps up the screaming bundle before carrying him over to me. My heart explodes in my chest as I hold my son for the very first time.

He's here.

We made it.

Body sagging, I slump into Killian's arms as our baby cries into my chest. He's so small and perfect, his eyes sealed shut and features soft. The love that rushes over me is indescribable.

"Our son," Killian says in wonderment.

I look up and find the big guy sobbing his damn eyes out.

"Oh, Kill."

"Not a word," he snarks.

"We have a son," Micah whispers.

All of them are bawling, and unable to control it, I join in. The entire roomful is crying and smiling, all looking down at the angelic bundle of perfection clasped in my arms.

"We're dads now." Zach shakes his head. "I actually have to be an adult."

"I'll believe it when I see it, kid," Killian mumbles, wiping off his face.

"What should we name him?" Micah drops the gentlest of kisses on our son's bright-red nose. "What about after your father, Willow?"

Confusing emotions wash over me, mingling with my tears, pain and joy. That man brought nothing but misery into my life. I don't need his memory when I have my family and future right here.

"No. Not that." Looking up at the twins, I smile. "What about after your dad?"

"Hayden?" Zach asks, a grin blooming. "I like it."

"Hayden," Micah repeats.

Killian smooths a giant hand over his son's head. "Hell of a name."

"Hayden it is." Doc wipes off his hands. "Congratulations."

Leaving the room to give us a moment to ourselves, we all snuggle and pass the baby around. Seeing the guys holding their son for the very first time is enough to set me off again, the tears stinging my cheeks.

"He's so small," Killian says in awe.

Zach clasps his shoulder. "You're just huge, Kill."

"You calling me fat, asshole?"

"Hey," I snap at them. "Language. Little ears are present."

Both rush to apologise while Micah rolls his eyes at their antics. When there's a soft knock on the cabin door, I hear Doc answer before the sound of Arianna's excited voice travels into the cabin.

"Should we let her in?" Micah asks.

"Yeah, it's fine."

Covering myself with another couple of towels, I take Hayden back into my arms and snuggle him close. His eyes are still sealed tightly shut, but he's fallen silent, his lips popping adorable little spit bubbles.

"Mummy?" a little voice whispers.

Arianna sticks her head into the room, appearing tentative. I nod for her to come in.

"It's okay, Ari. Come and meet your little brother."

"I have a brother?"

"Yes, baby. You're a big sister now."

Creeping closer, she kneels next to me, her eyes blown wide. Micah makes sure she's sitting comfortably before propping a cushion up on her lap to bridge the gap.

"Want to hold him?" I ask her.

"I can?"

"You just have to be nice and gentle, baby. Like this."

Demonstrating for her, I slowly lift Hayden onto her lap and ensure she's holding him correctly. Arianna clutches the towel-wrapped bundle, her mouth hanging open for a moment before her lips stretch in a smile.

"He's so small," she coos. "And... and... ugly."

"Hey!" Zach laughs.

"He's all red and shrivelled up!"

Killian smacks his forehead. "Aren't kids the best?"

But I'm too busy staring at my little girl holding her brother to pay any attention. My entire life is right here, bottled up into two amazing human beings. My world. My love. My everything. This is our family.

That's what I ran for.

That's what I survived for.

This moment and all that's to come.

EPILOGUE
YOU'VE GOT THE LOVE –
FLORENCE & THE MACHINE

WILLOW - TWO YEARS LATER

STARING at myself in the mirror, I bite my gloss-covered lip. "Is it too boring?"

Fussing over me, Katie adjusts my long, white veil. "No, darling. The dress is perfect for a Briar Valley wedding."

My wedding dress is a simple, silk slip with thin spaghetti straps and a low back, exposing just the right amount of skin while maintaining a little mystery.

I wanted something light and cool for our summer wedding. It's the summer solstice today, the longest day of the year, and the whole town is geared up for a hell of a show.

"You look so beautiful." She wells up as she stares at me in the mirror.

"Thanks, Mum."

Her tears only intensify at that name. I started calling her Mum not long after Hayden was born, almost two years ago, but it still makes her teary to hear it after all that we've been through together.

Lifting my hand to rest it on top of hers, we lock eyes. Despite everything that I've suffered, a small part of me can be glad. It brought me my family, my mother, my home.

Without all that pain and suffering, I'd have nothing. No life. No future. No happily ever after. That's the thing about pain—it demands an equal and offers hope in the purest of forms.

Pain gave me life.

Pain made me who I am.

But living? That's a job for the person I am now. The person I became when I saw a world without all that pain and realised that hope is the greatest possible gift this world ever gave me.

"Are you ready?" Katie asks.

"As I'll ever be."

She kisses my cheek. "I'm so proud of you, Willow. You're an incredible woman, and it's an honour to be your mother and friend."

I blink away tears before they ruin my light makeup. "I love you."

"I love you too, my sweet girl. Come on, then. Let's get you married."

Holding her hand, I glance around our huge, master bedroom. It's three times the size of a regular bedroom with two king mattresses pushed together to make a single, mega-sized bed.

Hayden has his own room now, but more often than not, he ends up back in bed with us by midnight. Arianna is far too old for that, or so she claims. She's a mouthy little spitfire at ten years old.

Lifting the hem of my dress, I walk down the stairs to find my bridesmaids —Aalia, Rachel and Miranda—all waiting at the bottom for me in pale shades of buttery yellow.

Standing in front of them, Arianna is dressed in her own yellow dress, perfectly complementing her pearly blonde hair that's neatly plaited with bows. Her mouth falls open when she sees me.

"Mum! You look so pretty!"

I duck down to kiss her cheek. "Thanks, baby."

"Oh, Willow." Aalia covers her mouth. "You look stunning."

"Thank you, Aalia."

Rachel wipes her tears aside. "Just breathtaking."

Miranda pulls her into a side-hug, fighting her own tears. "You're perfect, Willow. So perfect."

"Come on, guys. You're all determined to make me cry."

Laughing it off, they take their places ahead of me, preparing to walk out of the arched front door that Killian carved himself.

With the tinkle of music playing, I clutch my mum's hand tight and take the bouquet of Briar Valley wildflowers, wrapped in a pink ribbon. Nothing else would've done the job.

Arianna takes her place at the head of the convoy as my flower girl. She leads us all, her head held high with pride. The bridesmaids follow until it's time for me to go.

"I'm nervous," I admit quietly.

Katie squeezes my arm. "I won't let you fall over."

"Promise, Mum?"

"Always, Willow."

With her grip holding me tight, we exit the cabin together, and brilliant sunshine blinds me. The sweet, intoxicating scent of summer washes over us, full of blooms and earthy richness.

The entire town has turned out for the wedding. Everyone sits in their Sunday best on white-painted chairs, all facing a wicker archway laden with sunflowers picked from the fields.

When I see the guys for the first time, everything stops. The rest of the wedding melts away until it's just us for the very first time all over again. The years we've been together suddenly vanish.

All three of them wear matching suits in the darkest shade of green, reminiscent of the thick, impenetrable forest around us—the same forest I almost died dragging myself through to get to them.

Micah's smile captures me first. It's as sweet and innocent as the first time I saw it over the dinner table, stunning those around us.

When Killian looks up at me, he doesn't smile. His mouth is too busy hanging open in awe, his eyes stretched wide with such intense adoration, it would scare most people.

Luckily, I'm not most people.

I love his adoration.

Zach's the last to look up—his emerald-green eyes meeting mine. Grinning like the child at heart he is, he winks at me.

Immediately, I'm set at ease. Nothing else matters but the short walk back into their arms. Eating up the distance between us, I stop next to Ryder's chair to kiss my little boy, snuggled up in his arms.

"Go get 'em," Ryder whispers.

I kiss his cheek. "Thanks, Ry."

Ethan gives me a thumb's up from the seat next to him, sitting with Harlow and all four of her plus ones, recently arriving from their new home in Australia just for the day.

Meeting the guys at the front of the town square, I pass my bouquet off to Katie then face them. We have no vicar or officiant, as this isn't a legal wedding, but everyone who matters is here.

Us.

It's always been us.

And it always will be.

"Willow." Killian takes my hands first, ever the commander. "You look so incredible, baby."

"Thank you, Kill."

He holds my hands tight. "I know I'm not a perfect man. Far from it. But you make me a better person, and I want to spend the rest of my life making you smile... just like that."

A grin on my lips, I drop my voice low so no one else can hear. "I love you because you're a grumpy, over-protective bastard."

"Good," he growls in a deeper voice. "Because I am absolutely not about to change. So we're on the same page."

Cupping the back of my head, he captures my lips in a hard, fast kiss that makes the crowd wolf-whistle. When we separate, the tips of his ears are burning pink.

"Will you marry me?"

"Yes. I will."

We kiss again, barely managing to separate when Zach clears his throat and steps up next. I'm passed along, all of us laughing at the ridiculousness of it.

"Willow—" he begins.

"Before you say anything," I interrupt him. "Zachariah, you are the most childish, infuriating person I have ever met, and I love you with my whole heart regardless. Will you marry me?"

His mouth splits into a wide smile. "I do."

We share a kiss, right where Killian's lips left off, and everyone claps again. Katie watches on with tears sparkling in her eyes.

"For the record, I love you too," Zach adds. "Even when you don't get my dad jokes or let Killian call me *kid*."

"Good. You're stuck with me now."

"Forever?" he laughs.

"You're damn right, we're forever."

Kissing again, he reluctantly hands me to Micah. My sad-eyed, quiet boy. The man who took the longest to love me and the most to forgive me. Of course, he's the last to hold me close.

"Willow," he bites his lip nervously. "I had a lot planned out that I wanted to say, but standing here... hell, I've forgotten all of it."

"Maybe we don't need words, Mi. We have each other."

"We do." He nods. "Through the darkest of times, we've always had each other. You've loved me at my absolute worst."

"As have you."

"Then I guess we can love each other at our best for the rest of our lives, right?"

I lean in to peck his lips. "Right."

"Swear on it, angel?"

Even on our wedding day, he's still insecure. Still uncertain. Shaking my head at him, I take the first of the solid gold bands from Arianna's outstretched hand and slide it on his finger.

"I swear to love you on all of your worst days, Micah. And all of your best ones too. Hell, maybe even the days in between as well."

He steals my breath with a final kiss that scatters my thoughts. Only Micah can give me the most extraordinary butterflies, reserved solely for his quiet shyness.

I move back to Zach to slide the next ring on his finger, then Killian last. As the head of the family, he takes the honour of placing the final gold band above his mother's ring.

"Are we married now?" Zach laughs.

"I think so."

Whooping loudly, he grabs my hand and lifts it into the air, entwined for the whole town to see. We're overcome by a raucous wave of applause that must echo throughout the mountains.

As we walk back down the aisle, Killian grabs Arianna and boosts her onto his shoulders. She squeals at the top of her lungs.

The one thing that hasn't changed as she's grown up? He's still her giant, and she's still his precious peanut.

Zach takes Hayden from his Uncle Ryder and holds the little tyke in his arms, now writhing and laughing as he's tickled. That leaves Micah to take my hand and brush a thumb over my knuckles.

"Okay?" he whispers.

I squeeze his hand. "I'll be better than okay forever, Mi."

He smiles again. "Me too. We did it, angel."

"We sure as hell did."

Swooped down low to the ground, my hair brushes against the grass as he dramatically kisses me, stealing some of his twin's moves. As soon as I'm placed back on my feet, the town engulfs us.

Surrounded by my crazy, adoptive Briar Valley family, new and old, my heart is fit to burst. It's perfect. Everything. We fled the darkness to find our home, and boy, did we find it.

I spent a decade living in empty spaces—the place between existing and living. The desolation. The darkness. The unknown.

But that space I mentioned?

Well, that's where wild things grow.

The End

BONUS SCENE

KILLIAN

"Listen up, men! We have a fucking party to organise!"

Staring around the circle, I give Albie, Walker, Ryder and the twins my best stink-eye. No one warns you that having a kid makes you go soft.

Our little bean is turning one in the morning, and even though it's been the best year of my life, I now have a reputation for being a total softie.

That won't do.

This party has to be perfect.

So much of our journey to parenthood was imperfect. We're under no illusions about that. Our family had to fight tooth and nail to find a slice of happiness, and if that ain't worth celebrating, nothing is.

"Kill," Zach groans dramatically. "Hayden won't even remember this party. Chill out, will you?"

"It's our boy's first birthday, kid!"

"The little monster doesn't even know his own name!"

"I don't care. He's getting the biggest party Briar Valley's ever seen."

Standing next to him in the town square, Ryder fights a smile as he nudges Zach's shoulder. "Don't rile him up. You know he's been ordering balloons and decor for months now."

I jab a finger at Ryder. "Shut it."

"You want to tell them about the giant, inflatable bouncy castle, or should I?"

Little shit.

Admittedly, I might have gone slightly overboard. But this is *our* baby boy.

That kid deserves the fucking world, and whether he will remember it or not, I'll damn well make sure he gets it. His sister and mum, too.

"What's the theme?" Micah asks, absently picking dried paint off his fingers.

Walker's eyebrows raise. "There's a theme?"

Bursting into loud guffaws, Ryder doubles over before I can answer. That's it. I really am going to kill him this time. The day he opened the first box of decor and saw what I'd ordered, he had a laughing fit.

"Kill?" Ryder prompts between chuckles.

"Cowboys," I mutter.

"What was that?" Zach asks expectantly.

Cheeks flushing, I cross my arms over my flannel shirt. "I said cowboys."

Right on cue, they all break out in laughter. Even Walker. Man, I wish he was still the shy man who originally rocked up on our doorstep. There was a time when no one dared to even look my way in Briar Valley.

Now they're out here laughing like a pack of hyenas. Oh, spines are gonna fucking crack.

"That's it!" I bellow. "Everyone, grab a goddamn box and move it."

Faces red and still chuckling, they all start to collect the many boxes of decorations we have to set up in the centre of town. I lugged them out of our home, Lola's rebuilt cabin, to gather them next to the clearing.

Thank God we finished rebuilding the three-story monster shortly after Willow gave birth. We needed the space as a family of six, and luckily, I still found room to put the supplies for today's grand event.

Thankfully, Willow had an appointment to go wedding dress shopping with Katie and Aalia this morning. We arranged the party for tonight so we could spend Hayden's actual birthday together as a family.

Leaving Zach and Micah to tackle the various inflatable cacti and cowboy figures, I snag Ryder's elbow and steer him over to the bouncy castle. We eventually get it unpacked, rolling out layers of tacky plastic.

"You know we live in fucking Wales, right?" he huffs.

"I'm aware."

"Then why the hell are we having a cowboy party?"

"I didn't realise there were rules," I snap back. "You don't think it's cute?"

Ryder wrinkles his nose. "Did you just say the word *cute*? Fuck, Kill. You're getting old."

"Shut the hell up already." I locate the air pump. "Before I make you."

Chortling away, he unfolds the last plastic creases then locates the nozzle for me to attach the pump. We get the mechanism working, shooting air into the plastic frame until the bouncy castle is slowly aerating into an elaborate rodeo scene.

I clap my hands together eagerly. "It's perfect."

Ryder snorts. "Does it look like the Pinterest board you created?"

"Actually, yeah."

Reeling back, he casts me a disbelieving look, his mouth hanging open. "Uh, Kill. I was joking. Wait, you have a fucking Pinterest board?"

He ducks out of my way before I can throttle him. Honestly, life was simpler when it was just us three. No one gave me shit. But I wouldn't trade our current life for anything in the world. Until Willow came along, our souls were as empty as my parents' once abandoned cabin.

The dark-haired beauty breathed life back into us, one at a time. I was doomed from the moment we properly met—her splayed out on Lola's kitchen table, beaten within an inch of her life, terrified and shouting for her little girl.

In that moment, something awakened inside of me. A whole other person I didn't know I was capable of being. Soft. Gentle. Loving. But only for her, and the little peanut she brought into our lives as a package deal.

"I had to get the decor right," I justify hotly. "And the colour scheme!"

Ryder's eyes bug out. "Sure. Can't have the colour scheme off, can we?"

"Alright. Enough of the sarcasm."

Before he can utter another word, I clap him around the back of his head. He doubles over, collapsing into another laughing fit, so I leave him to go check on the twins.

The town square is really coming together. Garlands hang from strung lights above the picnic tables, matching the array of inflatable toys, brown and green balloons, and various kids' games. Albie is overseeing the work, gruffly ordering Walker around.

I stop next to Albie. "It's coming along."

"You've gone overboard, Kill."

"No such thing."

Albie scoffs, shaking his head. "I suppose there isn't to a man in love."

Glancing at him from the corner of my eye, I watch his wrinkles pull taut, his face contorted by a grief-stricken frown. Albie has never quite recovered from the loss of Lola.

I clasp his forearm and squeeze. "We all miss her too, Al."

He sucks in a loud breath. "I know. Just wish she was here to celebrate the important stuff with us."

"She is. You know Lola wouldn't miss her great-grandson's birthday for the world." I gesture around us at the unfolding chaos. "We just can't see her is all."

"You reckon she's still with us?"

"I think they all are. Everyone we've lost." My throat thickens, straining my voice. "They never left."

Head lowering, Albie stares down at the grass. "Thanks, Kill."

I squeeze his arm once more before turning away to give him a moment to gather himself. Lola's death continues to affect us all—the entire town misses her. But Albie lost the love of his life, and for that, I don't know if there is a cure.

"Killian! You ready for the food?"

Across the clearing, Miranda stands at the edge of her garden, hanging over the white picket fence. I wave back, gesturing for her to bring the food out. Rachel emerges from the house, a towering stack of platters balanced in her arms.

"Rach!" Miranda protests. "You shouldn't be carrying all that."

"I'm perfectly capable, Mir."

As Rachel approaches, I rush to take the plastic trays of sandwiches, savouries and miniature cakes from her. She's only a few weeks away from giving birth, and their husband, Doc, has been fussier than ever over his wives. You'd think after three kids, the guy would've calmed down.

Yeah, right.

I still remember how afraid I was a year ago when Willow went into labour. Knowing that our lives were going to change forever, I was scared of what that would mean for my family. Our life in Briar Valley. The woman we'd vowed to make our wife.

But I needn't have been so terrified. From the moment I laid eyes on Hayden's chubby little cheeks, I felt a love I'd never experienced before. Unlike anything else in the entire world. A piece of my broken soul snapped into place in that moment, and I finally felt whole.

"Doc will have me shot at dawn if he sees you lugging those platters around," I grumble as she passes.

Rachel flashes me a grin. "I don't need you or any man telling me what I'm comfortable carrying, Killian Clearwater. Now make yourself useful."

Grabbing the stack of tablecloths from the top of her pile, I quickly spread them out on the picnic tables so she can lay the food down. Rachel fusses over the arrangements until she declares the job done.

"They're on their way back." She looks around at the decorated square. "Aalia texted. Should we gather everyone to surprise them?"

"That's the plan. I hope Willow's going to like it."

Miranda stops next to her sister, casting her own eye over the space. "She'll love it, Kill. You know Willow doesn't care for a fuss."

Both dispersing to begin rallying the troops, I gather the guys together then crack open our cooler full of beer. Albie joins us to clink the green glass bottles together, all sharing a silent toast. Even Micah with his water.

We quietly drink as the town begins to gather. The stack of presents on a nearby picnic bench grows, piled with hand-wrapped gifts and even a miniature toddler bike that Harold and Marilyn proudly wheel in.

By the time everyone has arrived, the town square is bustling with life and energy. Briar Valley continues to grow, taking on new families in need as quickly as we can construct cabins for them.

I know that long-term, Willow plans to expand the town farther in her late grandmother's honour. People like Aalia and Walker—desperate individuals, searching for a fresh start—will come to this safe haven just like she once did.

Tuning out the sound of Zach and Micah bickering over whose present is the biggest, I watch the tree line for signs of car lights. Any moment now, they will arrive. My stomach is churning with anticipation. I can't wait to see the smile on Willow's face.

"I can hear an engine!" Doc declares, now sandwiched between his wives.

Everyone's attention turns to the rough pathway that leads into town. Sure enough, a car's engine is grumbling ever closer. The twins shut up in time for Katie's familiar red estate car to emerge from the thick woodland.

It swings to a stop outside our home, the back door immediately flying open with a *thud*. I know who it will be tearing out of the car before her headful of light-blonde hair emerges, framing excited blue eyes and a grin wide enough to surely hurt.

"Giant! Giant!"

Arianna races towards me in a blur of hyperactive energy. She still hasn't grown out of her clinging attachment to me. Frankly, I was terrified she would. I'll happily keep the little demon this innocent age forever.

"Hey, peanut."

Launching herself at me, I catch her mid-air and twirl her around. She squeals at the top of her lungs, writhing in my arms in an attempt to escape so she can drink in all the decorations and party games.

"Is this all for me?" she gasps.

Zach chuckles, reaching over to ruffle her hair. "No, Ari. It's your brother's birthday, remember?"

She juts out her bottom lip. "But I want a party too!"

"We'll do another party for your birthday," Micah suggests, ever the peacekeeper. "How does that sound?"

"But I want princesses and mermaids. Not cowboys!" Arianna protests.

Setting her back down, I struggle to bite back a grin. "Sure, Ari. Princesses it is."

"Yay!"

Seemingly appeased, she bounds off to explore the Wild West scene we've created. Johan, Aalia's eldest, perks up when he sees her approaching to play. The pair are practically joined at the hip.

"Kill? What is this?"

Willow's voice slicks over me like a cool mountain breeze on a summer's day. This woman could bring me to my knees with nothing but her voice alone. Turning around, I lay eyes on my gorgeous, soon-to-be wife.

My reply is drowned out by the sound of the entire town yelling, "*Surprise!*"

Willow startles, her hazel eyes filling with moisture as she takes in the scene around her. Hayden is balanced on her hip, his crop of nutty-brown hair pointing in all directions.

"Oh my." Willow laughs wetly, a few stray tears escaping. "This is so amazing."

I swoop in to plant a kiss on her plush lips. Her tears smear across my skin as her mouth lingers on mine, silky-soft and full of tender affection. We break apart at the sound of Hayden gurgling loudly.

"Hey, bud." I pluck him from Willow's hip and nuzzle his hair. "Happy Birthday."

"You know it isn't until tomorrow." Willow giggles.

"Who says we can't celebrate twice?"

She sighs, shaking her head. "You spoil us, Kill."

"Only the best for *my* family, baby."

Dropping another kiss on my cheek, Willow retreats to accept embraces from Zach and Micah. They trap her between them, showering our girl with kisses and whispered greetings.

Despite the years we've been together, she still looks at us all with such fucking devotion, I could never doubt that Willow is meant to be ours. I think I knew it from the moment we met. It just took a while for me to get that realisation through my stupidly thick skull.

"Whose idea was this?" Willow asks.

Zach points a finger in my direction. "Ask Briar Valley's resident event coordinator."

I shrug, blowing a raspberry on Hayden's chubby cheek until he squeals. Willow's eyes soften as she watches me play with our son. He's a spitting image of the twins, but it doesn't matter who his biological father is. Hayden's our boy.

"Pass me the troublemaker." Micah stretches his arms out.

I hand him off, the little tyke babbling away when he's snuggled into Micah's chest. They're inseparable most days.

Convincing Willow to take maternity leave was a hell of a challenge that didn't last long. While she attends to the day-to-day running of the town, Hayden often stays with Micah in his art studio. Hayden's come home covered in harmless, watercolour paint more than once. But what's invaluable is the way he's brought my cousin to life.

Willow gave us that.

She gave us fucking *everything*.

"You weren't kidding about
the theme," Katie says in greeting. "I was half-expecting a real-life rodeo."

I roll my eyes at her. "Don't you start too."

She smacks me on the shoulder, smiling broadly. "Good job, Kill."

"Thanks."

Joining Willow and Aalia, the three of them blur into the crowd of people. The whole town has turned out to celebrate Hayden's birthday—new residents and all. Willow takes the time to thank everyone individually. She's taken to her role as Briar Valley's matriarch like a fish to water.

Hanging back to avoid the tight crush, I snag another beer then find an empty seat at a picnic bench. I'm content to watch my family talk, joke and laugh. Zach's arm-wrestling Ryder's newly declared fiancé, Ethan, who left his job at Sabre Security to join us.

"Give up, E!" Zach bellows.

"Never." Ethan puffs in exertion. "You better pay up this time. I want my front lawn mowed."

"Not going to happen because I will never lose!"

Watching them incredulously, Ryder whispers something to Albie before the pair start laughing at the ridiculous display. When Ethan prevails, slamming Zach's fist into the table, Ryder sweeps in to kiss him.

"That's my man." He beams proudly.

Ethan smiles up at him. "You want Zach to mow our lawn?"

"Hell yeah. You're up, Zachariah."

"Fuck!" Zach grouses.

I'm so wrapped up in the entertainment of watching Marilyn approach to smack Zach's head for his bad language that I don't feel Willow sneaking up on me. A soft hand studded with a familiar engagement ring clasps over my eyes, blotting out the scene.

"Guess who?"

With a low growl, I twist to seize her waist and drag her onto my lap. She lands with a surprised squeak, her head tilted back to expose her lips to mine. The feel of her soft curves in my hands will never get old.

"You'll never be able to sneak up on me."

"Damn," she says breathlessly. "Thought I'd got you this time."

"Not a chance."

Noses brushing, we share another long, slow kiss. I don't care that our entire family surrounds us. I drink her in, one hand burying in her loose black curls to cup the back of her head. The moan that spills from her throat makes my cock ache with need.

"Kill," she murmurs into my lips.

"Later, I promise."

"Then don't tease."

Pecking her mouth again, I rest our foreheads together. "I just wanted to feel you. I missed you."

"I was gone for three hours."

"That's three hours too long for my liking."

Huffing, she wears an indulgent smile. "Will you drop the overbearing, protective grump act once we're married?"

"You're joking, right?" I frown at her. "Baby, I'm going to be overbearing and protective for the rest of our lives. You're mine."

"I suppose I can live with that." Her voice drops to a sultry whisper. "But only if you promise to prove it in the bedroom tonight."

I stroke my thumb over her cheek, tracing sun-kissed skin. "That sweet little cunt of yours is also mine for the rest of our lives. I have no problem proving that to you tonight or any night, baby."

"And how exactly do you plan to prove it?"

Shifting my hips beneath her, I ensure she can feel just how much her dirty whispers affect me. Even in public. I'm harder than fucking steel at the tempting promise of her weight pressing into me.

My lips touch her ear. "First, I'd throw you down on our bed to strip the clothes from that beautiful body of yours. I want you naked and trembling for my touch."

"Yes," she purrs. "And then?"

"Then I'd push those creamy thighs open to expose your soaked pussy. I want to see what belongs to me before I bury my face in your cunt to taste it. I want you coming all over my tongue."

"Fuck, Kill."

My dick presses against the zipper of my jeans at the sight of her heavy lids, her teeth digging into her plump bottom lip.

"And only when you've cried out my name and spread your juices all over my face will I reward you with my cock, baby. I'll fill your tight pussy up and make you come again... no, three more times."

"Three?" Willow moans quietly.

"My girl deserves no less."

A fine tremble is running all over her. Casting a quick look around, I find the party in full swing. Everyone is busy chatting, eating and watching the kids enjoy the bouncy castle. I can sneak her away for ten minutes.

"Are you wet, baby?"

Willow nods, her lips parted on a sigh. "Yes."

"Then let's make this quick. I'm going to explode if I'm not inside you immediately."

Lifting her into my arms, I hold her cradled against my chest in a bridal carry. Willow laughs as I almost trip over the damn picnic bench in my haste to escape.

"Eager, Kill?"

"You have no idea," I grumble.

"Oh, I think I do." She lifts a hand to cup my beard-covered cheek, her expression sobering. "Thank you for the party. I love you."

Carrying her towards our cabin, I marvel at the fact that I hold the entire centre of my universe in my arms. It all begins and ends with her. Our Willow. The mother of our child. Our future wife. The woman who gave me a reason to live again, a family, a future.

Briar Valley saved her.

But she saved us.

"I love you too, Willow. Forever."

EXTENDED EPILOGUE

WILLOW

Studying the façade of Briar Valley's newest log cabin, I jot rapid notes down on my clipboard. Our latest expansion into a neighbouring farmer's land is proceeding on time.

He sold it to us for a reasonable price after two previous purchases in the last few months. We're growing once more. Lola's vision is coming to life.

Ever since Hayden was born, I've found myself obsessed with the same dream that my grandma once travelled into the valley to achieve. A peaceful world, providing homes to all who need one, where those who've been touched by misfortune can begin anew.

By the time Hayden's second birthday rolled around last year, we'd taken on hundreds of acres of new land. The more we grow, the more demand we face. Briar Valley has become a nationwide sanctuary for the lost and in need.

"Be careful!" I shout up at the rafters.

Zach pauses while hammering a roof tile into place. "You worried about me, babe?"

"I wouldn't want you to fall and harm a hair on your pretty little head, Zachariah."

"Aww." He winks down at me. "I love you too."

"Hey! Pay attention!"

While flirting shamelessly, he almost hammers a nail into his right hand. Zach quickly halts before he can seriously injure himself, shrugging it off with a laugh. He's determined to give me a heart attack one of these days.

"Where is Ryder? He's supposed to be supervising you!"

Zach chortles as he lines up another nail. "I don't need supervision."

"You broke your collarbone falling out of a tree last year, Zach!"

"I was chasing Arianna up there," he scoffs. "It's the little monkey's fault."

Honestly, he isn't wrong about that. The chaos that ensues between Arianna, Zach and Hayden all teaming up is going to send Killian to an early grave.

Micah usually joins me as the voice of reason in our chaotic family. Since he opened his third art store last year, he's taken on several new members of staff, including a general manager. Which means he can be home with us a lot more.

When my phone vibrates in my pocket, I tuck the clipboard under my arm to answer, noting Arianna's name flashing on the screen above a photo of us at her recent twelfth birthday celebration. It's my favourite shot of us together.

"Yes, sweetheart?"

"Mum," she chirps happily. "Can I go into Highbridge with Johan tonight? We want to catch that new movie."

"How are you getting there? Your dads are all working."

"Walker's going to take us. He's driving Aalia and Amie to the airport for their flight to Egypt first."

"Okay well, be safe. And have fun."

"Thanks, Mum!"

Arianna is already chatting away to Johan in the background before she hangs up. They head into town often to eat, shop or go to the movies. The guys usually take turns chaperoning them if Walker is busy.

I've caught Johan giving my little girl heart-shaped eyes for a while now, but Arianna sees him as a brother. They've grown up together in Briar Valley and forged a strong friendship over the years.

"Arianna's off to the cinema," I shout up at Zach.

He pauses, waving his hammer in the air. "With Johan?"

"Yes, Walker is chaperoning."

His lips pressing into a thin line, Zach still looks far from pleased.

I return my attention to my clipboard. The guys are all incredibly protective of Arianna in their own ways, their hijinks only worsening as she's started to grow up. Especially Killian.

He had a meltdown when she came home with pierced ears a year ago after our girls' shopping trip. And let's not even mention when she talked about colouring her natural blonde hair. That got her threatened with all manner of things.

"Aalia and Amie are off tonight too."

"They're heading home?" Zach hammers in another tile.

"Seems so. I'm happy for them."

"I never thought she would go back to her home country."

"It's where she grew up, Zach. She hasn't seen her family in years."

"I know, babe. I just want her to be safe."

"She will be. Aalia knows what she's doing."

After a lengthy court battle, Aalia and her children finally got their citizenship a few months ago. It was a complicated legal battle—we all know how hostile the world can be to refugees, though I'll never understand why—and she can now finally visit her home again.

"I have to find Killian to go over the plans for the south side expansion. Please be careful!"

He absently blows me a kiss. "I will."

"Don't be late for dinner!"

With a final worried glance, I begin the trek back towards town. All around me, freshly painted cabins boast their new residents. Families. Single mums. Immigrants. Widowed husbands.

People from all walks of life, regardless of their differences, have found refuge here. And that fact alone makes all the hard work, investment and sleepless nights worth it. We've built something truly special here.

I just wish Lola were alive to see it.

And I hope that she's proud.

By the time I've made it back to our cabin at the centre of town, a thin sheen of sweat peppers my forehead. The walk took me longer than usual after being stopped by smiling faces along the way to chat. I had to decline at least ten cups of tea.

Killian isn't waiting in the kitchen like he should be. We have a whole box of paperwork to pour over. I'm about to call him when the front door slams open and closed.

"Kill?"

"Mummy!" Hayden bellows.

Throwing the kitchen door open, he barrels inside to wrap his short arms around my legs. Hayden looks more and more like the twins with each passing day. His soft brown locks are haphazardly piled on top of his head, forever pointing up in all directions.

With brilliant green eyes that resemble cut emeralds, he stares up at me with a beaming smile that takes my breath away. My little miracle baby. We didn't realise our family was incomplete until he came along and made us whole.

"Hi, baby."

He yawns dramatically. "Missed you!"

"Missed you too, kiddo. Have you seen Daddy around?"

"Behind," he mumbles.

Right on cue, the door opens and closes again. I can hear Killian puffing for breath from here. He must've chased Hayden all the way home. The kid loves to give his old man a run for his money.

"Hayden Clearwater! How many times do I have to tell you—"

Bursting into the kitchen, Killian's as stunningly rugged and downright handsome as the day we met. Granted, his shoulder-length, blonde hair is sprinkled with silver now, his eternally-tanned skin bearing more wrinkle lines than before.

Not a single day has passed, besides our wedding day, when he isn't wearing a flannel shirt and ripped blue jeans. I've told him off until I'm blue in the face for dragging mud inside on his work boots, but he still traipses through the cabin in them.

"Lost something?" I ask sweetly.

He pulls up short, his heavy frown morphing into a heart-stopping smile just for me. I accept the quick peck to the cheek he offers before he turns his attention to the giggling three-year-old hiding behind me.

"You can't just run off like that, Hay! What if Uncle Ryder was driving one of his trucks through town, huh?"

I place a hand on Killian's firm chest. "Alright, Kill. Ease off."

"I don't want him to get hurt!"

Hayden juts out his bottom lip as he peeks around me. "Sorry."

Sighing, Killian scrubs a hand over his face and beard. "It's... fine. Just listen to me next time, okay?"

Hayden nods then darts around me to hug his father. Killian's eyes close briefly as he cuddles his boy close. He worries far too much. Briar Valley is the safest place on Earth—we haven't seen trouble here in years.

"You still want to go over those plans?" Killian asks. "Sorry I'm late."

"Let's get started on dinner instead. I've stared at enough paperwork for one day."

He chuckles throatily. "Yes, ma'am. Where do you want me?"

"Peeling potatoes, mister." I turn my attention to Hayden. "You want to help Mummy cook?"

He breaks out into a toothy grin. "Yes!"

———

Watching Micah rinse off the final plates, I swirl the red wine in my glass. I'm sitting up on the countertop, legs swinging as we unwind for the day. It's our routine to find a quiet moment just for each other when no one else needs our attention.

"Ivan seems really promising." Micah stacks the dishes in the dishwasher. "We had a supplier issue with our canvas totes, and within the hour, he had it resolved and secured a discount as an apology."

"That's great, Mi. I'm glad he's working out."

"It's just nice to be home more." He sticks a dishwasher tablet in then sets the cycle to commence. "I feel like I missed out on so many bath times and family nights while the business was getting established."

"Hey." I reach out to touch his arm. "You've always been around for the important stuff. Besides, we all know how important selling your art is."

His mouth curves down with obvious regret. "Not as important as family."

With the kitchen taken care of, he dries off his hands then approaches me. I let my thighs part, inviting Micah to step between them, his legs pressed up against the kitchen cabinets. Malachite eyes that were once filled with sadness now stare up at me with peace and contentment.

"Thank you for supporting me while I figured things out, Willow."

Micah rakes his teeth over his lip, somehow still nervous despite all our years together. Putting my wine glass down, I move to stroke his jaw, tracing the defined bone.

"I will always support you, no matter what. You're my husband."

"How did we get so lucky to have a wife like you?" He smiles tenderly.

"I could say the same thing about you three. We've found our happiness, Mi. And for that, I'll always be thankful."

"I think we worked hard enough for it, angel."

Memories of the turmoil and pain we endured to get right here resurfaces, and I let the pain flow through me. I don't have to pretend the bad times didn't happen. Without all that we suffered, I never would've found my home.

I'm thankful for the pain.

The trauma.

The grief.

While I'll never forget what I weathered at the hands of Dimitri Sanchez and his sadistic traffickers, I can now look back on the ordeal with acceptance and a sense of peace. There's no undoing the past. We can only choose to live with it and rebuild.

Yes, the case is still ongoing. I secured my abusers' convictions and laid my past to rest, but even now, there are still women out there seeking justice. Huge, international trafficking rings aren't dismantled overnight.

"We earned our happy ending, huh?" I laugh quietly.

Micah strokes a loose curl back from my face. "I'd say so."

Leaning in, he teases his lips across mine. Featherlight. Coaxing. Micah's always been the gentler twin, and years haven't hardened his soft soul. He's still the tender-hearted man who found me dancing in a rainstorm, kissed me in a cornfield, and gave me his virginity on a mountaintop.

Killian will always be my protector.

Zach makes me laugh every single day.

But Micah… he's my safe place. Now and forever.

Lips parting, I let my tongue dance with his. Exploring my mouth like it's our very first time all over again, he kisses me with such passion and care, it's no wonder I seem to spend my days falling for him all over again.

Arms winding around his neck, I shift to the edge of the countertop, needing to feel his body against mine. My legs wrap around his midsection, pulling us flush together, while his hands move to grip my hips.

Micah groans into my mouth, his tongue sliding against mine. I can taste the richness of red wine still serenading his taste buds. We finished a bottle over dinner, laughing and joking together as a family.

"When's Arianna home?" Micah whispers.

"Walker texted. They're going to be another couple of hours yet."

"Then I'll take advantage of having you all to myself."

"Please do."

Lips securing back on mine, his tongue resumes plundering my mouth. His kiss has intensified, losing its gentle edge. Now he's hungrily sucking on my lower lip, the bite of his teeth sending heat sizzling down my spine.

I quickly reach down to grab the hem of my loose sweater, breaking our kiss to pull it over my head. I want to feel his skin against mine. My husband. The man who held me in my lowest moments and taught me how to put myself back together again.

"Fuck, angel." Micah's eyes sweep over my lace bra. "You're as beautiful as the first time I saw you."

"Shut up and kiss me, husband."

He chuckles. "And as bossy too."

"Well, some things never change."

Lips moving away from mine, he trails kisses along my jawline and down the slope of my neck. His mouth lavishes my throat with attention—kissing, sucking, leaving the lightest of bites that set my blood on fire.

Between our busy schedules, it isn't often that I get Micah all to myself. His twin and cousin demand my attention once the kids have gone to bed, then we pile into bed altogether, the huge mattresses spanning the entire bedroom.

"Shall we go upstairs?"

"Hayden," I gasp.

"He'll be asleep by now."

"And I don't want to wake him up."

Micah reaches behind me to grab my bra clasp. He drops the pile of lace to the kitchen floor, his attention fixed on my breasts. Taking one in each hand, he softly squeezes, his lips securing around a hardened nipple.

The light graze of his teeth causes me to moan. He sucks my bud into his mouth, applying enough pressure to send my desire into overdrive. I want to feel him covering every part of me, leaving no inch of sensitive skin untouched.

Pushing his shoulders, I encourage him to release me and step back. Micah follows the silent command, letting me hop down from the countertop. I quickly unbutton my jeans then push the worn denim down to pool at my ankles.

"Strip," I demand.

"Right here?" He cocks an eyebrow.

"Do you have something better to do?"

"Not at all." He unveils a smirk that suspiciously resembles his twin brother.

Drinking my fill, I watch him strip off his paint-flecked clothing. In the store, he still wears his comfortable clothes, never one to draw attention to himself. But his body is hard and defined beneath his casual attire, lined with muscles I've memorised across nights like these.

"I want to taste you," Micah declares, his gaze searching over me. "Go and lay on the kitchen table, angel."

"The table?" I laugh.

"Yes. Move it."

Feeling giddy, I approach the hand-carved wooden table that Killian spent weeks lovingly crafting. I'm sure he didn't build it for this purpose— surprisingly, this is the first time it has seen any action.

With everything from dinner cleared away, I'm free to climb up on the smooth surface, laying down on my back. Micah pulls a chair out of the way so he's positioned at the end of the table, grabbing my ankles to pull my butt to the edge.

"Perfect," he murmurs before his tongue sneaks out to wet his lips.

Gooseflesh rises on my legs as he pulls the cotton panties from my body, taking his time to torturously slide them over my thighs. I'm already shaking from anticipation. With the panties discarded, he's free to peruse my entire bare body on display.

"My gorgeous wife," Micah says dreamily. "Open wider, Willow."

No longer shy, I spread my legs open, propping a foot on each corner of the table. I'm completely exposed. The vulnerable position sends my heart rate skyrocketing. Years ago, something like this would've triggered me. But not now. I trust Micah with my life and soul.

Knees bending, he brings himself eye-level with my centre. Warmth is already pooling in my core, but the moment his head moves between my thighs and I feel his tongue slick across my folds, I almost jerk off the table.

"Mi!"

"Hold still," he orders, hands clamping down on my hips.

I don't even have any bedsheets to fist as he laps at my core like I'm his dessert. His mouth is hot and attentive on my clit, making my nerves sing. Tongue swiping over my pussy lips, he licks and sucks in a well-rehearsed rhythm.

A breathless moan escapes me as he breaches my entrance with a finger, pressing deep into me. Paired with his tongue lapping at my clit, the sensations become overwhelming, and my back arches off the wooden surface.

"Oh God!"

"Hush, Willow."

Pulsing his finger inside me, he rolls my bundle of nerves beneath his thumb, stroking in time to the thrusts of his wet digit. I can't keep my mewling silent.

The kitchen door opens, causing Micah to startle. He pulls upright, his lips shining with my juices. Zach steps into the kitchen, mouth hanging open at the scene unfolding before him.

"Am I interrupting?" He waggles his eyebrows slyly.

"Little bit," I squeak.

Clapping his twin on the shoulder, Zach takes his time looking over me, not in the slightest bit bothered that we're both naked in the kitchen. It wouldn't be the first time we've been caught like this.

"Join us or get out," Micah mutters. "But I have a job to finish."

"Oh." Zach's eyes sparkle with amusement. "By all means, go right ahead."

Ignoring his brother still lingering behind him, Micah returns his mouth to my cunt. This time, he pushes two fingers inside me, stretching me wide with each pump of his hand. I lock eyes with Zach, writhing and moaning, my entire body lit up with pleasure.

Still grinning, Zach moves around the table, already rushing to unfasten his belt. Anticipation rolls down my spine as he stops on my right side, pushing his jeans down low enough to pull his thick shaft free.

"He *did* invite me," he explains cheekily. "Are you going to take us both, babe?"

"Always," I purr back.

Turning my head to the side, I part my lips and loosen my jaw. He takes the invitation, moving closer until he can push the head of his cock against my mouth. I greedily suck his hard length in.

"That's it, babe."

Zach grunts, a hand moving to fist my loose curls. I try to focus on taking him into my mouth and sucking deep with each movement, but the pressure of Micah's lips on my pussy is frying my brain.

Taking control, Zach begins to pump his hips. I let him set the pace, too overwhelmed by the multitude of sensations to do anything else. He fucks my mouth, thrusting slowly at first, letting me adjust to the feel of his dick filling me up.

Just as Micah scissors his fingers inside me, causing stars to burst behind my eyes, Zach's cock nudges the back of my throat. Between the two of them, I can feel an orgasm coming. It's too overwhelming to hold it back.

"Come for us, Willow," Micah urges.

One more swipe of my clit and I'm gone for. The release comes hard and fast, surging through me. Zach's length in my mouth silences my cries, his erection thickening at the muffled sounds of my climax.

The pressure between my legs vanishes as Micah's head lifts, my clit twitching as I watch him lick his lips, marked with my release. With his hard cock standing proud, he wraps a hand around his shaft, slowly working over the engorged length.

I know what's coming as he manoeuvres, able to position himself perfectly as I'm perched on the edge of the table. Spreading my legs wider, I invite him in, aching to be filled. I want to feel him sheathed inside me.

"You want us both to fuck you?" Micah asks with a raised brow.

With a mouthful of his twin's cock, all I can do is blink and hope he reads my pleading expression. Thankfully, Micah knows me inside out. He can see how desperate I am to take them both right now and wastes no time inching into my pussy.

"Fuck, angel. You take me so well."

Saddled fully inside me, his head throws back as he growls deeply. The slight movement gives me a clear view of the kitchen doorway. Lost in my orgasm, I hadn't seen my third and final husband sneaking into the room.

Leaning against the closed door, Killian watches the show with his corded arms folded over his chest. His breathing is heavy, and the fire burning in his gaze betrays how turned on he is by watching us three.

As Micah pulls back only to slam into me once more, I can't focus on anything but the feeling of complete fullness. Zach's movements are growing frenzied, his cock roughly sliding in and out of my mouth, chasing his own eruption.

Each time he pushes past my lips, his twin brother surges into my pussy. The two of them seem to have synced up without having uttered a word. The coordination is making my brain cells short-circuit as I lose myself to the moment.

"I'm going to come in your perfect mouth, babe," Zach grunts. "And I want you to swallow every last drop. Got that?"

I tighten my lips around his shaft in response, more than ready to fulfil his desires. Micah pistons into me just as Zach manages a final pump, his length pulsing in my mouth with the first spurts of his release.

I let him fill my throat with his hot seed, obediently swallowing every drop just as requested. Zach watches in awe, his green eyes wild and breathing ragged. When he pops out of my mouth, I make a show of licking my lips.

"That's my perfect girl," he praises. "Maybe my twin will make you come again now, hmm?"

"Please," I moan.

"You heard her, Mi." Zach nods to his brother.

Returning his hand to my clit, Micah resumes applying pressure as he picks up the pace. He's hammering into me now, the table starting to groan with each lurch of his hips. I'm surprised Killian hasn't pushed off from the door to yell at us all.

His cock tucked back into his boxers, Zach turns his attention to my chest. He takes my left breast in hand, fondling the soft swell while running his thumb over my right nipple in teasing circles. The extra stimulation hits me right where I need it.

Between the gentle touches he's lavishing on my breast and nipples and Micah's hips undulating with each hard stroke, I'm a mess of over-stimulation. The knowledge that Killian's silently watching and enjoying every last panting gasp sends me hurtling to the edge once more.

"Let go," Zach breathes. "Come all over my twin's cock, Willow."

"Yes!" I shout out.

Clenching tight around Micah, I feel myself detonate. The kitchen fades away with the force of my orgasm, vision blurring and core clenching tight. I'm plummeting through a delicious nirvana, my entire body humming.

"Willow," Micah rumbles.

My climax must send him into his own release because he spasms above me, mustering a final pump before crying out. Warmth rushes into me in a satisfying spill. I pant for breath, sweat-slick and spent as Micah slumps over me.

"Damn." Zach chuckles. "I do love seeing our wife get so thoroughly fucked, she doesn't care where the hell it happens."

"He started it," I say, trying to catch my breath.

Laughing roughly, Micah braces himself over me, his own chest rising and falling in rapid succession. The sly son of a bitch doesn't even deny it. This is the side of Micah that no one but us will ever see.

"As fun as watching is, I'd like my turn with our wife too."

Killian's voice is a low, toe-curling growl. The twins startle, finally noticing him lingering at the back of the kitchen. He steps forward, his blue jeans tented at the crotch.

"If she isn't too sore, that is," he adds.

I eagerly watch him, desperate to lay my hands on his body. "Sit down, Kill."

Grinning devilishly, Killian unfastens his jeans then shoves them all the way off along with his boxers. No one could ever accuse the man of being shy. Naked from the waist down, he takes a seat.

Micah steps out of the way to let me sit up. I don't care that his essence is trailing down my legs. These men belong to me. All of them. Always. I want them to know how proud I am to call them mine.

Hopping down from the table, I saunter over to Killian. I'm rumpled and messy from the twins' ministrations, but it doesn't stop him from greedily running his bonfire-lit gaze all over me.

"You look fucking incredible right now, wife."

Smiling, I hover over him, a leg on either side of his seated body. The long, rock-hard promise of his erection brushes against my entrance, a mere breath from where I want him.

"Did you like watching?"

"You put on a hell of a show," he returns smugly. "Who wouldn't like that?"

"It's rude to spy, you know."

"Not spying when I own this ass." Killian's hand grabs a handful of my backside, roughly squeezing. "They should be grateful I'm letting them touch what's mine."

Moving his hands to grip my hips, he retakes control by pulling me down onto his lap. The sudden movement causes me to impale his cock, the generous length sliding inside me in one fast surge. I cry out, my hands moving to his shoulders to steady myself.

"Fuck! Kill!"

"Perfect," he says gutturally. "That's it, baby. Take all of my cock."

My awareness of Zach and Micah watching us fades away. All I can focus on is Killian—his touch, his breath caressing my skin, every place his skin touches mine, the fiery electricity that hums where we're joined.

I'm overwhelmed by him. I have no choice but to surrender to the lifting of his hips, spearing my pussy with each upwards pump. He's so deep inside me, I can hardly hold my head upright, succumbing to the feverish tempo.

Exhausted and sated, I didn't think I had another orgasm in me. But Killian always has to have the final word. Even in the bedroom, he's no different. He manoeuvres me on his crotch, ensuring each motion touches the spot within me that will send me flying again.

"Please," I whine.

"I know, baby. I want to see that pretty mouth of yours cry my name like you did theirs."

Desperate to come apart around him, I begin to match his strokes. Each time he shifts up into me, I bear down, meeting him pace for pace. We collide spectacularly, spurred into a frenzy by the other.

Killian's mouth returns to mine—swallowing every last satisfied sound he's coaxing out of me. Even my moans belong to him. My soul was stamped as his from the moment we locked eyes and he refused to let me die.

He gave me a home.

A family.

A chance to begin again.

Arms curled around his neck, I plaster myself to his body, riding each wave rolling in. Every fresh burst of ecstasy pushes me closer to that tantalising cliff all over again. He's determined to coax one more out of me.

Killian's head lowers, his face hiding in my chest as his lips skate over my breastbone. I can feel how unsteady his breathing is. We're both close. Trapped in our own little secluded bubble.

"Kill," I mewl. "I... Please..."

"Are you coming for me, baby?"

"Yes! Yes!"

Letting the rapture creep over me, I feel his muscles tense. Clinging to Killian as our climaxes collide, I fall through each iteration of sweet agony. The feeling of him swelling inside me only adds to the riotous explosion consuming my senses.

I go limp against his muscled frame, unable to move an inch. Suddenly exhausted, I'm trembling all over. My body feels strung out, satiated in the most exquisite way from all the pleasure lavished onto it.

"Let's get you cleaned up," Killian murmurs.

"Mm," I mumble unintelligibly.

"I've got you, baby."

Lifted into his arms, I crack open an eye long enough to see Zach and Micah following us. With the three of them doting on me, I don't know how I'll ever be happier than I am at this moment, with my perfect family.

The world tried to tear us apart.

But we didn't let it.

In the end... we won.

———

The shrill sound of a ringtone pulls me from unconsciousness. I'm smothered in warmth. Someone's curled up behind me, their body melded to mine, while I make Micah into the little spoon by hugging his back.

Quiet falls once more, and I tune back in to the sound of heavy breathing. Based on the light snores, it's Zach snuggling me from behind. Killian prefers not to cuddle up with the twins and usually takes the other end of the bed or one of the spare rooms.

Just as I'm about to fall back to sleep, the sound comes again. *Buzz. Buzz. Buzz.* Micah groans in his sleep, but Zach is out like a light. Not even the devil could wake him from his slumber. Cursing under my breath, I peel myself from his arms.

My phone is plugged in on the bedside table. Leaning over Micah, I flip it over, finding the screen lit up with an incoming call. It takes a moment for the name to register. Why on earth is Hyland calling me?

I haven't heard from Ethan's old teammates in the Anaconda team, my former protection detail, in years. Sabre Security has continued to reach new heights ever since, heading up the investigation into the trafficking ring Dimitri Sanchez left behind.

"Hyland?" I whisper in greeting. "Is that you?"

"Willow," his deep voice rushes out.

"What's going on?"

"I'm sorry to be calling you so early."

Worry bubbles up within me. "Are you okay?"

"Ethan isn't picking up the phone. We're in trouble."

Sitting upright, I cover my bare chest with bedsheets. "What kind of trouble?"

"The dangerous kind. We need a place to lay low. I hate to ask, but we've been backed into a corner and—"

"Hey," I interrupt. "You don't have to explain. There's always space for you in Briar Valley."

He blows out a sigh. "Thank God. I'm sorry to do this to you. If I had any other choice, I'd keep you out of our mess."

"You know we're off-grid here. It's safe."

"That's what I was thinking. Listen, we'll be there in a few hours. Is that okay?"

With one hand, I start shaking the guys awake. Micah jolts up first. When he sees me on the phone, he sets to work waking his twin up.

"Of course. We?"

"The whole team," Hyland clarifies. "And... we're bringing someone else with us too."

"A client?"

He clears his throat. "Not exactly."

"Seems like we have some catching up to do," I tease gently. "You at least going to tell me her name?"

Hyland chuckles softly. "It's Ember. She's the one in trouble. We're still working on the trafficking operation in South America... and we've kicked the hornet's nest."

Unease rolls over me, hearing how Sanchez's legacy continues to impact countless victims still suffering the consequences of that bastard and his vast web of associates.

"No trouble will find you here. I'll see you in a few hours, okay?"

"Thanks, Willow. I owe you big time."

The line clicks as it disconnects. I'm left staring at the phone clasped in my hand, trying to make sense of the alarm bells ringing in my mind. Something is trying to resurface—a vague memory of years long past.

Ember.

Why do I know that name?

The Anaconda team's story will begin in Fractured Future - a brand new, dark why choose romance coming in 2025.

PLAYLIST

LISTEN HERE:
BIT.LY/BRIARVALLEY2

If I Come Home – Suzi Quatro & KT Tunstall
Ridiculous Thoughts – The Cranberries
IT'S ALL FADING TO BLACK – XXXTENTACION & blink-182
Hell – Olivver the Kid
heavy metal – diveliner
Silent Love – James Bay
Ribs – Lorde
How Do I Say Goodbye – Dean Lewis
I STILL LOVE YOU – Bishop Briggs
GONE – NF & Julia Michaels
Need It – Half Moon Run
JUST LIKE YOU – NF
Man or a Monster – Sam Tinnesz & Zayde Wolf
Heavy In Your Arms – Florence & The Machine
Stay with Me – You Me At Six
Spotless – Zach Bryan & The Lumineers
Where It Stays – Charlotte OC
The Other Side of Love – Jack Savoretti
I Feel Like I'm Drowning – Two Feet
Falling Apart – Michael Schulte
Where The Wild Things Are – Labrinth
Home – Edith Whiskers
The Stages of Grief – Awaken I Am
Dawns – Zach Bryan & Maggie Rogers

Forged In The Fire – Caylee Hammack
Angel On Fire – Halsey
Dead Man's Arms – Bishop Briggs
Always Come Back (Acoustic) – Martin Kerr
A Little Bit Happy – TALK
I Found – Amber Run
Forever – Mumford & Sons
Happy Never After – VIOLA
Dagger – Bryce Savage
Teresa – YUNGBLUD
Love Will Tear Us Apart – Odina
Jealous Lover – Animal Flag
Promise Me – Badflower
Solid Ground – Vance Joy
Spirit – Judah & The Lion
You've Got The Love – Florence & The Machine

ACKNOWLEDGMENTS

Thank you for reading Willow's story! This duet has been a whirlwind ride into the unknown, and I'm so grateful to all of you for sticking with me.

Writing Briar Valley challenged me in so many ways—pushing me to delve into the mind of a mother, lost and afraid, but determined to find herself again. Willow's courage has taught me so much, and I hope you've found some hope in her tale too.

As usual, I have an army of incredible people to thank for getting me here.

Thank you to my mum, first and foremost. Your strength and determination inspired so much of this story. I love you unconditionally.

To the people who keep me going every single day. Clem. Lilith. Kristen. Eddie. There are too many of you to count, but I appreciate every one of you for keeping me afloat.

Thank you to my amazing editor and proofreader, Kim, for making this book baby shine and dealing with my many emotional breakdowns. You're the best, and I'm so lucky to have you!

I also want to say a massive thanks to the team at Valentine PR for all their help and for being fabulous at what they do.

Finally, thank you to my readers, old and new, for supporting my work and making this dream a reality. You're all the reason why I keep writing and baring my soul. Thank you for reading.

Stay wild,

J Rose xxx

WANT MORE FROM THIS SHARED UNIVERSE?

The timeline of Harrowdean Manor runs parallel to Blackwood Institute. Learn more about Brooklyn, Hudson, Kade, Eli and Phoenix by diving into the dark and twisted world of another experimental psychiatric institute.

mybook.to/TwistedHeathens
mybook.to/SacrificialSinners
mybook.to/DesecratedSaints
bit.ly/BIBoxSet

Set in the same shared universe, the Sabre Security series follows Harlow and the hunt for a violent, bloodthirsty serial killer. Featuring cameos from all your favourite Blackwood Institute characters.

bit.ly/CorpseRoads
bit.ly/SkeletalHearts
bit.ly/HollowVeins
mybook.to/SSBoxSet

Dive into the world of Harrowdean Manor next. This is a dark, why choose enemies-to-lovers romance set in a different psychiatric institute during the same timeline as Blackwood Institute.

mybook.to/SLTD
mybook.to/BLAA

ABOUT THE AUTHOR

J Rose is an independent dark romance author from the United Kingdom. She writes challenging, plot-driven stories packed full of angst, heartbreak and broken characters fighting for their happily ever afters.

She's an introverted bookworm at heart with a caffeine addiction, penchant for cursing and an unhealthy attachment to fictional characters.

Feel free to reach out on social media. J Rose loves talking to her readers!

For exclusive insights, updates and general mayhem, join J Rose's Bleeding Thorns on Facebook.

Business enquiries: j_roseauthor@yahoo.com

Come join the chaos. Stalk J Rose here…
www.jroseauthor.com/socials

NEWSLETTER

Want more madness? Sign up to J Rose's newsletter for monthly announcements, exclusive content, sneak peeks, giveaways and more!

Sign up here:
www.jroseauthor.com/newsletter

ALSO BY J ROSE

Blackwood Institute

Twisted Heathens

Sacrificial Sinners

Desecrated Saints

Sabre Security

Corpse Roads

Skeletal Hearts

Hollow Veins

Briar Valley

Where Broken Wings Fly

Where Wild Things Grow

Harrowdean Manor

Sin Like The Devil

Burn Like An Angel

Standalones

Forever Ago

Drown in You

A Crimson Carol

Writing as Jessalyn Thorn

Departed Whispers

If You Break

When You Fall

Printed in Great Britain
by Amazon

48388008R00403